Samuel Gardner Drake

The New England historical and genealogical register

Samuel Gardner Drake

The New England historical and genealogical register

ISBN/EAN: 9783741164323

Manufactured in Europe, USA, Canada, Australia, Japa

Cover: Foto ©Andreas Hilbeck / pixelio.de

Manufactured and distributed by brebook publishing software
(www.brebook.com)

Samuel Gardner Drake

The New England historical and genealogical register

These are the Lines that shew thy Face; but those
That shew thy Grace and Glory, brighter bee:
Thy Faire-Discoueries and Fowle-Overthrowes
Of Salvages, much Civilized by thee
Best shew thy Spirit; and to it Glory Wyn;
So, thou art Brasse without, but Golde within.
If so; in Brasse (too soft smiths Acts to beare)
I fix thy Fame, to make Brasse steele out weare.

Thine, as thou art Virtues.
John Davies Heref:

THE

NEW ENGLAND

Historical and Genealogical Register,

PUBLISHED QUARTERLY, UNDER THE PATRONAGE OF THE

New England Historical and Genealogical Society.

FOR THE YEAR 1858.

VOLUME XII.

BOSTON:
SAMUEL G. DRAKE, PUBLISHER,
13 BROMFIELD STREET.
1858.

Publishing Arrangement for 1858.

SAMUEL G. DRAKE, EDITOR.

COMMITTEE.

REV. WILLIAM JENKS, D. D.   JOHN WARD DEAN,

HON. FRANCIS BRINLEY,   HON. TIMOTHY FARRAR,

WILLIAM H. WHITMORE.

BOSTON:
H. W. DUTTON AND SON, PRINTERS,
90 Congress Street.

GENERAL INDEX.

NEW ENGLAND

HISTORICAL AND GENEALOGICAL REGISTER.

Vol. XII.   JANUARY, 1858.   No. 1.

NOTES ON THE INDIAN WARS IN NEW ENGLAND.

CHAPTER I.

Causes of Indian Wars.—Land not the Cause.—Other Causes.—Lands not taken from them without their Consent.—Plymouth vindicated by Gov. Winslow.—Plymouth's Care for the Indians.—Voyagers kidnap them.—Hunt, his Apology.—Smith's Encounter with some.—Weymouth's Conduct.—Harlow's.—Exploit of Pecham.—Escape and Exploit of Epenow.—His Attack upon Capt. Dermer.

There is an extensively prevailing opinion that the Indian War of 1675, 1676 and 1677, generally denominated King Philip's War, grew out of the encroachments upon their lands by their white neighbors of New England. It will be seen, in the progress of the narrative now undertaken, that the land of the Indians was not the cause of the war; but that there were other causes, about which very little has ever been said. These causes it is intended to explain, before entering upon the details of the war.

Had every white inhabitant who sat himself down by the side of an Indian been kind and generous, discovered less of avarice, and not taken pains to make himself offensive by his unmistakable haughtiness, few cases of contention would have arisen. What is tolerated, or rather suffered, in civilized society, is not so easily borne where there are no conventional ranks. In civilized society, so called, that part of it possessing the greatest wealth are very apt to carry themselves in a haughty and offensive manner towards the poorer portion. This is quietly submitted to by the latter. Indians could not understand this; for among them all were equal; and insults were never borne, except by those physically unable to revenge them.

At the first, that is, when the white people came first among the Indians, the latter looked upon the former as creatures of different flesh and blood; scarcely animals. But after a time they became enlightened. They saw that men of a different colored skin from their own lived by eating and drinking, the same as they themselves did. They saw also that the white men were as susceptible of wounds and injuries in their persons as others of their own color. Hence, in all apparent physical circumstances, the two races were equal. Now all this being demonstrated by actual experience, the Indian began at length to inquire into the cause of his being treated as an inferior. And it was not until he learned that the white man set a high value on things upon which he set none, or very little; and he saw, too, that when things were in his possession they were of little value, but that as soon as they were transferred to the white man's hands they became of great value. He therefore said to himself, "It is the Indian's property in the white man's hands that gives the white man importance, makes him arrogant and covetous: and he despises the Indian as soon as his ends are answered, and when the Indian has nothing more to part with."

Neighbors thus circumstanced must necessarily fall out; and, being physically equal, personal collisions will ensue. Therefore, that the contentions with the Indians grew out of possession of their lands by the white man without adequate compensation, is not a necessary condition in accounting for Indian wars, and, so far as New England is concerned, is without foundation; for, however small the compensation given for land, it was, as a general thing, all the land was worth at that time; nor would it ever have been worth more in the hands of the Indians. They could make no use of it, or of but a very small part of it. To kill a deer on a hundred or a thousand acres of land once in a year was certainly a very small income for so many acres.

Any one will find, by an examination of all the public records of New England, that in no instance was land taken from the Indians without their consent, and without what was then considered a fair compensation. Cases, indeed, may be found where white men settled upon land not purchased of the Indians; but, so far as is known, they were always compelled to vacate such possession on complaint of the Indians. It should be remembered, too, that the Indians often invited white settlers to come and reside among them, giving them freely as much land as they wanted. This kind of acquirement of land, however, was never acknowledged by the country; and, when the Indians were tired of such settlers, they were, on complaint of intrusion, compelled to remove.

The war with Philip began in the colony of Plymouth; and there were those who charged the people there with bringing on that war by their injuries to the Indians. But the Governor of that colony wrote a letter of vindication to the Rev. Dr. Increase Mather, which the Doctor printed in his little quarto history of the war. The letter of Governor Winslow is dated the first of May, 1676. In that letter there is evidence of great sincerity; and there can be no doubt of its truth in every particular. Indeed, its honest simplicity will ever carry conviction with it, and is good evidence of the entire integrity of its author. Among other things he speaks of the "undeserved aspersions that some ignorant, or worse than uncharitable, persons would lay upon" that colony "respecting the grounds of these troubles," and adds, "we have endeavored to carry it justly and faithfully towards them at all times, and friendly beyond their deserts. I think I can clearly say, that, before these present troubles broke out, *the English did not possess one foot of land in this colony but what was fairly obtained by honest purchase of the Indian proprietors.* Nay, because some of our

people are of a covetous disposition, and the Indians are, in their
straits, easily prevailed with to part with their lands, we first *made a
law that none should purchase, or receive of gift, any land of the
Indians, without the knowledge and allowance of our Court;* and
penalty of a fine, five pound per acre, for all that should be so bought
or obtained." Besides this guard for their security and protection, it
was provided by the same General Court of that colony, "that Mount
Hope, Pocasset, and several other Necks of the best land in the Colony,
(because most suitable and convenient for them,) should never be
bought out of their hands."

Thus the colony of Plymouth took much better care for the Indians
than the Indians did for themselves; and Governor Winslow very
justly remarked, that, if those lands had not been reserved by law,
the Indians would have sold them long before the time he wrote.
"And," continues Mr. Winslow, "our neighbors at Rehoboth and
Swanzy, although they bought their lands fairly of this Philip
and his father and brother, yet, because of their vicinity, that they
might not trespass upon the Indians, did, at their own cost, set up a
very substantial fence quite across that great Neck between the English
and the Indians; and *paid due damage if at any time any unruly horse
or other beasts break in and trespassed.* And, for divers years last past,
(that all occasion of offence, in that respect, might be prevented,) the
English agreed with Philip and his for a certain sum, yearly, to maintain the said fence and secure themselves. And *if at any time they
have brought complaints before us, they have had justice impartial* and
speedily, so that *our own people* have frequently complained that *we
erred on the other hand in showing them over much favor."*

It would be a mistake to suppose that any one act or circumstance on
the side of the English or the Indians was the cause of the bloody war
which broke out in 1675. But it grew out of a combination of causes,
already explained, which commenced almost as soon as the English
traders and settlers came into the country. Even some of the first
voyagers, through their imprudence, incurred the hatred of the Indians
on various parts of the coast. As early as 1614, a Capt. Thomas Hunt,
in imitation of the captains of slavers on the coast of Africa, kidnapped
twenty-seven Indians in the neighborhood of Patuxet, (afterwards
called Plymouth,) carried them to Spain, and sold them into slavery.
Capt. Hunt was under the command of Capt. John Smith; but this act
of Hunt was done without the knowledge of Smith, and was by him
severely censured. He was left in the Massachusetts Bay, by Smith,
with orders to make up his cargo of fish, furs, and oil, and then to
proceed to Malaga; "but this vile act," says Smith, "kept him ever
after from any more employment to those parts."

The only apology which can be offered for Capt. Hunt is, that, in
those days, slavery was nowhere considered morally wrong. All
nations believed it right, and countenanced it under certain circumstances. Hunt was censured, therefore, mainly because he had made
the trade to this coast dangerous, if he had not entirely destroyed it,
by provoking the vengeance of the Indians. The Indians were looked
upon as a degraded, inferior, and faithless race, and no more to be
regarded than the Africans. This, at least, was the general impression.

The twenty-seven Indians carried off by Hunt were, according to the statement of Dr. Increase Mather, "sold for twenty pounds a man, until it was known whence they came; for then the friars in those parts took away the rest of them, that so they might nurture them in the Popish religion." The same author says that twenty of them were taken at Patuxet, and seven from Nauset, since Eastham.

This was one of the most serious difficulties which happened before the Pequot War; but it was by no means the only one, and it was never forgotten, even to the time of the war with Philip.

It is not intended to notice all the difficulties between the English and Indians which occurred before the war of 1675, but only the most important of them; which will be sufficient to show how animosities originated, and how they were from time to time increased and perpetuated, until that war finally burst forth, putting the very existence of the entire English settlements in peril, and ending with the destruction of the Indian power.

Before the Indians had much intercourse with the white people, they appeared to the latter exceedingly simple, and could be easily imposed upon by the selfish, unscrupulous, and crafty. Capt. Smith calls them "silly salvages," and says "they were very kind, but in their furie no lesse valiant; for, vpon a quarrel wee had with one of them, hee, only with three others, crossed the harbor of Quonahassit to certain rocks whereby we must pass, and there let fly their arrows for our shot." This affair was at Cohasset rocks. As Smith proceeded down the bay, " vpon small occasion," another quarrel arose. Forty or fifty Indians attacked the English, who fired upon them, killing one, and wounding another with a shot through the thigh. And yet, as Smith relates, in an hour after they made up and became friends again. These are some of the events of 1614.

Many of the natives were carried away from the coast of New England besides those kidnapped by Capt. Hunt. Some of them may have gone voluntarily, but those stolen or forced away seized the first opportunity to be revenged for such ill usage. Several of these have become historical characters. They feigned contentment in captivity, and laid plans of escape artfully, which, in some instances, they executed successfully. As several of these circumstances and events are of deep interest, and show the progress of the relations between the English and Indians, it may be thought by the reader that some of the most important of them should be given. It is therefore proposed to go a step back, and to take up a few of the leading incidents here hinted at.

To the kidnapping of several Indians from about Pemaquid, in 1605, Sir Ferdinando Gorges imputes the colonization of New England. That barbarous act was committed by Capt. George Weymouth; not, however, to make slaves of them, but, by kindly treating them, to induce them to give his employers a more perfect knowledge of the country than they could otherwise obtain. Yet this is a poor excuse for depriving people of their liberty; for at the bottom of all such acts lies the same cupidity which is the cause of robbery and greater crimes. Gold and other rich mines were supposed to exist in the country, the knowledge of which the English expected to obtain from the Indians.

It was on the 4th of June, 1605, that Weymouth put in execution his plan of seizing the Indians which he carried from the coast of New England, already mentioned. In the account of his voyage, published in London, the same year, is a minute detail of the transaction, which cannot well be given excepting in the language of the writer of that voyage. It therefore follows: "About eight o'clock this day we went on shore, with our boats, to fetch aboard water and wood; our captain leaving word with the gunner in the ship, by discharging a musket, to give notice if they espied any canoe coming, which they did about ten o'clock. He therefore, being careful they should be kindly treated, requested me [James Rosier] to go aboard, intending with dispatch to make what haste after he possibly could. When I came to the ship there were two canoes, and in either of them three savages, of whom two were below at the fire; the others staid in their canoes about the ship, and because we could not entice them aboard, we gave them a can of pease and bread, which they carried to the shore to eat; but one of them brought back our can presently, and staid aboard with the other two; for he being young, of a ready capacity, and one we most desired to bring with us into England, had received exceeding kind usage at our hands, and was therefore much delighted in our company. When our captain was come, we consulted how to catch the other three at shore; which we performed thus: We manned the lighthorseman [boat] with seven or eight men: one standing before carried our box of merchandise, as we were wont when I went to traffic with them, and a platter of pease, which meat they loved: but, before we were landed, one of them (being so suspiciously fearful of his own good) withdrew himself into the wood. The other two met us on the shore-side, to receive the pease, with whom we went up the cliff to their fire, and sat down with them; and, while we were discussing how to catch the third man, who was gone, I opened the box, and shewed them trifles to exchange, thinking thereby to have banished fear from the other, and drawn him to return; but when we could not, we used little delay, but suddenly laid hands upon them; and it was as much as five or six of us could do to get them into the lighthorseman; for they were strong, and so naked as our best hold was by their long hair on their heads; and we would have been very loth to have done them any hurt, which of necessity we had been constrained to have done if we had attempted them in a multitude; which we must and would rather than have wanted them, being a matter of great importance for the full accomplishment of our voyage."

Such was the manner in which Capt. Weymouth possessed himself of five of the natives, whose names were, as given by the writer of the voyage, "Tâhanedo, a sagamore; Amóret, Skicowáros, Manedo, gentlemen; and Saffacomet, a servant."* "And so it pleased our great God," wrote Sir Ferdinando Gorges, that Weymouth, on his return to England, "came into the harbor of Plymouth, where I then commanded. I seized upon the Indians. They were all of one nation, but of several parts, and several families. This accident must be acknowledged the means, under God, of putting on foot and giving

---

* These names are very variously spelt. See *Book of the Indians*, p. 70-71, ed. 1851

life to all our plantations. And, having kept them full three years, I made them able to set me down what great rivers run up into the land, what men of note were seated on them, what power they were of, how allied, and what enemies they had."

The next year, however, 1606, two of these Indians were sent out with Capt. Henry Challons, to aid in trade and discovery in New England; but Challons was taken by the Spaniards, and the Indians with him. Their names were, as then given, Assacumet and Manida. Yet, after a time, one, if not both, of them returned to England. In 1607, another of them, Sketwarroes, was sent with Capt. Raleigh Gilbert, to aid him in his settlement of a colony at the mouth of the Kennebeck.

In 1611, Capt. Edward Harlow made a voyage to the coast. At Monhigon Island he seized three Indians, whose names were Pechmo, Monopet, and Pekeninme; but Pechmo leaped overboard and escaped. He was a bold and daring fellow, and determined to be revenged. Collecting a few men, he seized upon the ship's boat, cut it from her stern, and got off with it, in spite of all the ship's company could do. Nor could they retake it, it was so well guarded upon the shore by the Indians, with their bows and arrows, who had also bedded it in the sand. Seeing that nothing more could be done in the eastern parts, Capt. Harlow proceeded southward. At Capoge he succeeded in kidnapping two others, Conconam and Epenow; and at Nohono, Sakaweston. With these five Indians he returned to England.

Some of these Indians had deceived Sir Ferdinando Gorges by making him believe they knew where gold was to be found in abundance; and he obtained a promise from Epenow to discover it to him. Accordingly, Sir Ferdinando sent over Capt. Hobson, in 1614, very confident he would make a good voyage, and obtain very important information about the riches of the country; but he was doomed to be sadly disappointed. Capt. Hobson had with him three Indians, Epenow, Assacumet, and Wenape. On arriving at Cape Cod, Epenow's friends and acquaintances visited the ship, and with them he planned an escape. They were kindly entertained by the captain, and when they left promised to return in the morning, and to bring some articles for traffic. "But Epenow," says Sir Ferdinando, "privately, as it appeared, had contracted with his friends how he might make his escape without performing what he had undertaken, being, in truth, no more than he had told me he was to do, though with loss of life. For otherwise, if it were found that he had discovered the secrets of his country, he was sure to have his brains knocked out as soon as he came ashore. For that cause, I gave the captain strict charge to endeavor by all means to prevent his escaping from them. And, for the more surely, I gave order to have three gentlemen of my own kindred to be ever at hand with him; clothing him with long garments, fitly to be laid hold on, if occasion should require. Notwithstanding all this, his friends being all come at the time appointed, with twenty canoes, and lying at a certain distance, with their bows ready, the captain calls to them to come aboard; but they not moving, he speaks to Epenow to come unto him where he was, in the forecastle of the ship; he, being then in the waste of the ship, between the two gentlemen that had him in guard, starts suddenly from them, and, coming to the captain, calls to his friends, in English, to come aboard; in the interim, slips himself overboard; and, although he were taken hold of by one of the company, yet, being a strong and heavy man, could not be stayed; and was no sooner in the water, but the Indians sent such a shower of arrows, and came withal desperately so near the ship, that they carried him away in despight of all the musquetteers aboard, who were, for the number, as good as our nation did afford. And thus were my hopes in that particular [voyage] made void and frustrate."

It is clearly seen from the narrative of this succession of injuries, that the white people could, from the first, expect nothing but treachery in return for the fraud and injustice they themselves had continually practised upon the natives of New England.

Five years after the voyage of Capt. Hobson, namely, in 1619, Capt. Thomas Dermer, another of Sir Ferdinando Gorges' men, came to Capoge, the place where Epenow made his escape, and there met with him. The shrewd Indian could speak some English, and he narrated to the captain his adventurous escape from Capt. Hobson, at which account he made himself very merry. He learned from Capt. Dermer that he was in the service of Gorges, and made very particular inquiry about his old friend, and his affairs. Meantime, he suspected Dermer was sent to seize him, and to take him to England. He therefore conspired with other Indians to take the captain prisoner; and they actually fell upon him. "But he, being a braue, stout gentleman," drew his sword, and freed himself from them; though not without fourteen wounds, some of which were of so serious a nature that he was obliged to go to Virginia to have them attended to. He lived to make another voyage to America, and died upon the coast, of fever.

CHAPTER II.

FROM what has been stated it will appear evident that nothing but trouble could be expected to follow between the Europeans and Indians on this coast, whenever and wherever they came together. The voyagers had incurred their vengeance, and therefore, when they could entrap any of them, they took savage satisfaction in treating them only as savages knew how to treat them.

About the year 1616, a French ship was wrecked on some part of Cape Cod. Its crew saved themselves and their goods; but as soon as the Indians discovered them they made them captives, and used them in their cruel manner, giving them only such victuals as they gave their dogs, robbed them of everything, and, in the end, killed them all but one; that one married a native, and had posterity. About the same time there came another French ship into the Massachusetts Bay. This the Indians treacherously captured, and put the whole crew to death; and, after plundering it, they set it on fire, and it was consumed.

Up to this time the Indians were very numerous along the whole coast of New England; and especially so around Massachusetts Bay, the waters of Rhode Island and Connecticut. In 1617, or about that time, there came upon them a deadly pestilence, which prevailed to such an extent that many places were nearly depopulated; especially the tract of country between the Massachusetts and Narragansct Bays. But for this, doubtless, the English could not have obtained a foothold in the country at the time they did. The pestilence was more fatal, probably, in the region of Plymouth than in any other part of the country; and this caused those who came to that place to settle to attribute the destruction of the Indians to an overruling Providence, that they might not be molested by them. Certain it is the Pilgrims met with but few of the natives for some time after their arrival; but when they made their appearance it was in a hostile manner; and it was only owing to their weakness that the English were not driven at once from that icebound and inhospitable shore, upon which, by untoward circumstances, they had been cast.

As there had been no intercourse hitherto between the Europeans and Indians but what had ended in hostilities, none other could be expected now by the latter; and, accordingly, every motion of the Pilgrims was watched. Notwithstanding the pestilence had carried off multitudes of them, there were now several tribes dwelling at and about what is since Warren, Bristol, Eastham, Weymouth, and Braintree. There were, likewise, many seated upon the rivers, far into the land; but of them little was known for a long period. Some time in March, 1621, the Powwows of all the tribes assembled " in a dismal swamp," and there, " for three days together, held their mysterious conjurations " to find out the intentions of the English, that their tribes might know how to meet them. The English, however, were much at a loss to know what that powwowing affair meant, though they did not hesitate to pronounce it something diabolical, and that it had special reference to them in their coming into the country. Meanwhile their fears were considerably abated by the appearance of an Indian among them. This was Samoset. He spoke to them in their own language, and, as he approached their village, uttered, in a firm voice, " Welcome, Englishmen! welcome, Englishmen!" His visit happened about a month after the great meeting of the Powwows, namely, on the 16th of March; and he was the first Indian with whom the English were able to speak since their landing in the previous December. He was naked, "only a leather about his waist, with a fringe about a span long." The weather was very cold, and, says a writer then there present, "we cast a horseman's coat about him. He had been with the English at Monhiggon, and knew by name the most of the captains or masters of vessels who had for many years frequented that and adjacent parts." The Pilgrims questioned him "of many things," and he readily communicated whatever he knew; "said he was not of these parts, but of Monstiggon, and a Sagamore. He had a bow and two arrows; was a tall, straight man; the hair of his head black, long behind, only short before, and none on his face at all." On his asking for beer they gave him "strong water, some biscuit, butter and cheese, and pudding, and a piece of mallard; all which he liked well." He told them that the place where they were settled was called Patuxet, and that about four years before, all the inhabitants died of an extraordinary plague, and that there was neither man, woman, nor child remaining; and, says the writer, "indeed we have found none."

Through the kind agency of Samoset, the Pilgrims, the next day, became acquainted with another Indian, named Squanto, said to have been one of those carried away by Capt. Hunt. Thus, by that misfortune, he escaped the pestilence which swept off every other inhabitant of Patuxet, now Plymouth. He had lived some time in England, and was with Mr. John Slanie, a merchant in Cornhill, London. He, also, could speak some English. Squanto, and likewise Samoset, came from Massasoit, (who, according to Samoset, had in his tribe about sixty men: and of the Nausets he said there were one hundred.) They had been sent by him to learn whether the English were friends or enemies. And finding them friends, Massasoit himself, with many of his men, visited them on the 22d of March, only six days after the first appearance of Samoset, and entered into a formal treaty, consisting of seven articles. Massasoit and his tribe were friends to the English as long as that Chief lived. But a tribe or clan of the Pokanokets, living at Mattapoiset, under a Chief named Caunbitant, were displeased, and caused them frequent alarms. At length an armed force was sent against them, and they were terrified into submission. This was in the month of August, 1621; and on the 13th of September following, Caunbitant and eight other Sachems came to Plymouth and signed a treaty with the English.

In 1622 another settlement of the English was begun at Wessaguscus, since called Weymouth. These settlers were, in general, profligate and unruly, and, by their bad management, soon reduced themselves so low that even the Indians looked upon them with contempt. This was not all. They cheated and abused the Indians, until the latter were determined to exterminate them; and, it is said, actually formed a plot for that purpose. This coming to the knowledge of the Plymouth people, very much alarmed them; because they knew the Wessaguscus Colony would fall an easy prey to the Indians, and, fearing that might elate them, and so excite their insolence, that they would not spare any of the English. They therefore, in self-defence, as they argued, declared war against the Massachusetts Indians. This first and formal declaration of war in New England was made by the Government of Plymouth, on the 23d of March, 1623; and two days after, Capt. Standish, with some eight men, marched against them. After manoeuvring some time, by which he intended to get a large number together, and then to attack them, he succeeded in getting four into a house or wigwam. Two of these were noted war chiefs; by name, Wittuwamet and Peksuot. Standish ordered his men to fasten the door of the room in which they were; and then they fell upon the four Indians, and, after a desperate struggle, put them all to death. This was on the 27th of March. Standish soon after returned to Plymouth, carrying with him the head of Wittuwamet, which he set upon the fort. Seven Indians were killed during the expedition.

This rigorous proceeding of the people of Plymouth struck such terror into the rest of the Indians, in all directions, that they fled from their habitations, hid themselves in swamps and unhealthy places, and neglected their planting, until many of them perished from diseases thus contracted, and the want of the necessaries of life. Nor did they recover from the effects of this blow for a period of near fifty years; at the end of which period began the war with the Wampanoags, usually called King Philip's War.

In the mean time the country had been gradually filling up with white settlers; and numerous little settlements called towns dotted the landscape in every direction. The Indians became accustomed to their strange neighbors, and many of them were convinced that their own condition was made better by that people. Those who disliked them, and cared not to associate with them, were afraid to make their jealousy and hatred prominent; for they were aware of their superiority in the use of offensive weapons. However, several years before the war with Philip began, the Indians had, in various ways, supplied themselves with the guns of the English and French, and were apt in the use of them. In many tribes they had almost altogether superseded bows and arrows, and the war club. Laws were early made, and long continued, to prevent European arms being sold to the Indians; but it was quite impossible to enforce them effectually.

The natives who were possessed of any prudence well knew that it was not to their interest to engage in a war with their white neighbors, because they clearly saw the odds was vastly against them.

Although from 1623 to 1675 there was no general war with the Indians in New England, yet there were often and frequent disturbances,* some of the principal of which it is necessary to recount, as they had much influence upon the rise and progress of that war. There were also frequent quarrels and murders among the Indians themselves, with which the white people had nothing to do; though, after such occurrences, they sometimes espoused the cause of the party they considered injured, and used their endeavors to bring the offender to punishment. So when any wrong was done to any Indian by any of the settlers, justice was speedily extended to the injured party. Of course cases would often arise wherein, from conflicting evidence, the ends of justice were frustrated. This was oftenest the case when the English interfered with the Indians' private quarrels, or quarrels among themselves. They were bad lawyers; and it was difficult for them to understand the justice of such interference. Hence the party suffering by it often determined on taking the first opportunity to be revenged; or, as it used to be said, "to right themselves." In this way feuds and jealousies were perpetuated.

---

* No allusion to the Pequot War is intended, for I have prepared a detailed account of it, which remains in manuscript, and which I intend, at some time, to publish uniform with this. A very brief abstract of it may be seen in the HISTORY AND ANTIQUITIES OF BOSTON.

In 1631, Sergt. Richard Walker of Lynn, as he was upon watch, about midnight, was shot at by an Indian, and the arrow passed through his clothes. He gave an alarm, and a small cannon, called a culverin, was discharged, and nothing further was heard of an enemy.

On the 8th of August, the same year, about one hundred Tarratines attacked the Indians living at Agawam, since Ipswich, killed seven men, and carried away several captives. They also rifled a cabin established there by Mr. Matthew Cradock's men, who were employed in taking sturgeon, carrying off their nets and provisions. The Tarratines were eastern Indians, living beyond the Pascataqua.

On the 3d of October, one Walter Bagnal was murdered and robbed by an Indian. He had a trading stand near the mouth of Saco River; and it is said he had provoked the Indians by overreaching them in trade. Early in the winter following, 1631-2, the Tarratines, perhaps the same who had attacked Agawam, met with a boat belonging to Mr. Henry Way of Dorchester, in which were five men, one of whom was Mr. Way's son. All these they killed; and, to hide the evidence of their barbarity, they sunk the boat with stones. Some of the perpetrators were afterwards taken and hanged.

The next spring the Tarratines came again to surprise Agawam; but, through the prudent management of Sergt. John Perkins, they did not dare to land. This time there were twenty canoes full of them.

At the same time there was a war between the Narragansets and Pequots; and Canonicus, the Narraganset Sachem, came among the Massachusetts Indians to engage them to assist him against his enemies. Accordingly two of the Chiefs, Chikatanbut of Nepouset, and Wonohaqueham of Winnisemmet, each with about sixty men, engaged in an expedition. The result is not known.

In August, this year, two of Chikatanbut's men were set in the bilboes at Boston, "for assaulting some English people at Dorchester, in their own houses, and their Chiefs made to beat them;" but in what manner is not stated.

Sometime in the following month, one Reynold Jenkins of Dorchester, going among the Indians under Passaconaway to trade, is killed, while asleep in a wigwam, by one of them. The Chief pursued and captured the murderer, and, according to an agreement with the English, delivers him up for punishment. They doubtless executed him; but of that no record has been met with.

At the General Court at Boston, in September, it was ordered that Richard Hopkins should be severely whipt, and branded with a hot iron on one of his cheeks, for selling guns, powder, and shot to the Indians. At the same time the question was considered, whether persons offending in this way ought not to be put to death. But the subject was referred to the next court, which met on the 3d of October. It does not appear to have been then agitated: though Nicholas Frost, for stealing from the Indians at Damerill's Cove, and other less pardonable offences, had a like punishment inflicted on him. Instead of his head, a hand was to be branded: to be banished out of the colony; to be kept in bolts till his fine of five pounds was paid, and damages to Henry Way and John Holman of forty pounds. If ever he returned into the colony he was to be put to death.

In January, 1633, Poquanum, called by the whites Dlack Will, formerly sachem of Nahant, living at Richmond's Island, at the eastward, is seized by some Englishmen in pursuit of pirates, and hanged. It is said he was one of the murderers of Walter Bagnal.

During the autumn of this year the small pox destroyed great numbers of the Indians. About Pascataqua River nearly all perish. So about Boston; the Chiefs Chikatanbut, Montowampate, Wonohaqueham, with most of their people, die of it. About Plymouth, too, many are carried off by a malignant distemper; with which about twenty of the Pilgrims die also. In January following, 1634, it was reported that the small pox had swept over the Narragonset country, destroying in its course seven hundred of that nation, and that it was extending among those westward of them.

On the 4th of September, 1638, Arthur Peach, Thomas Jackson, and Richard Stinnings, (probably an Irishman,) were executed at Plymouth for the murder of a Narragonset Indian. Peach was said to have been "a young desperado, who had been a soldier in the Pequot War, and done notable service, being bold and forward in any desperate attempt." He was principal, and the other two accessories. After he came out of the service against the Pequots, instead of going to work, he set out to go to the Dutch settlement at Hudson's River, and enticed three others to run away from their masters and accompany him. As they proceeded southward, through the woods, they met with an Indian who had a quantity of wampum. They invited him to sit down and smoke with them, which he did. Peach proposed to his comrades to kill and rob him. They declined having any hand in the killing, but left it to Peach to do as he was inclined. He therefore, watching his opportunity, ran the Indian through the body with his rapier, leaving him for dead. But, though mortally wounded, the sufferer succeeded in reaching some of his countrymen, retaining strength enough to inform them who the assassins were, and then expired. Soon after, the Narragonset Sachems pursued and captured all the party of whites but one, and carried them to Rhode Island, where they were put into prison. Meanwhile the Narragonsets threatened to make war on the English, thinking they had authorized the murder. This they were easily induced to believe, because the Pequots had told them that, after the English had destroyed their nation, they would destroy them likewise. But when they saw the three white men executed they were amazed, and expressed themselves entirely satisfied. That three should be put to death for one Indian they could not well understand, knowing the deed was done by one man only. This some called "magnifying of justice," and the Indians may have thought it was paying for other murders of their countrymen in advance. However, the cause of war at this time was thus removed.

On the 25th of March, 1639, Massasoit, now known as Woosamequin, a name, perhaps, taken by him on the death of his brother, Quadequina, appeared at Plymouth, and desired to renew the treaty which he made on his first visit to Plymouth, in 1621. His son, then called Mooanam, came with him, and with him executed a new treaty, expressed in very strong terms of friendship and reciprocity. Woosamequin was influenced to appear at this time, very probably, from a fear of the Narragansets, who were jealous of him, because he had from the first been in high favor with the English. " Yet it is very remarkable," wrote a contemporary,* " that this Woosamequen, how much soever he affected the English, was never in the least degree any ways well affected to the religion of the English; but would, in his last treaty with his neighbors at Plymouth, when they were with him about purchasing some land at Swanzy, have had them engage never to attempt to draw away any of his people from their old pagan superstition and devilish idolatry to the Christian religion, and did much insist upon it, till he saw the English were resolved never to make any treaty with him more on that account; which when he discerned he did not further urge it." The old chief or sachem lived until about 1660,† at which time he must have been near eighty years of age; for in 1621 the Pilgrims say he was then a man " in his best years."

The period from 1638 to the disturbances which are usually considered as the immediate causes of Philip's War is full of deep interest. There was during that time a continued and unbroken chain of events, which led to the exterminating war between the Narragansets and Mohegans. Those events are closely interwoven with various impelling and conflicting interests of the English in the two colonies of Massachusetts and Connecticut, and have never yet been detailed with the justice and impartiality their importance demands. As many of the difficulties between those two great tribes grew out of the Pequot War, to the history of that war they will be properly deferred.

CHAPTER III.

Moonanam, Wamsutta, Alexander.—Charged with plotting against the English.—Ordered to appear at Plymouth, and refuses.—Is forcibly conveyed thither.—Conflicting Accounts as to the manner of Treatment in Captivity.—His Death.—Greatly Bewailed.—Philip succeeds him.—His Accession Celebrated, which causes Alarm to Plymouth.—He is sent for.—Makes a Treaty.—Family of Alexander.

For some time before his death " good old Massasoit " appears to have been quite inactive; and his elder son, Alexander, seems to have taken upon himself the affairs of the tribe, as some sales of lands were made by him before the death of his father. His name up to about this time was Wamsutta. At what date he threw off the name of Moonanam, and took that of Wamsutta, is not known; but it is very probable that on the death of his father he had it changed to Alexander. Accordingly, soon after that event,‡ he, with his younger brother, appeared at Plymouth, and requested the Governor to give

---

* The Rev. William Hubbard, in his *Narrative of the Troubles*, p. 8.

† Daggett's *Hist. Attleborough*, 13; I. Mather's *Relation*, 70-72; Morton, *N. E. Mem.*, Sub anno, 1662; Roger Williams, *Letter in Knowles*, 405.

‡ It is stated by some writers that Massasoit came with his two sons, and requested that they might receive English names; but Dr. I. Mather, *Relation*, 70, says the event was after the death of Massasoit. There is much confusion respecting this circumstance. Hubbard, *Narrative*, 8, speaks of Massasoit's going with Alexander and Philip, his sons, to Mr. Brown's, who lived near Mount Hope.

both of them English names. The Governor complied, calling one Alexander, and the other Philip. It had now become a custom for the Indians to take English names; which, when thus acquired, caused them much satisfaction.

Very soon after, or within a year certain, Gov. Prence* of Plymouth received information from Boston informing him that a plot was being laid by Alexander, which had for its object a hostile movement against the English of that jurisdiction. The Governor sent immediately to Capt. Thomas Willet,† who resided near Mount Hope, and requested him to confer with Alexander, to learn, if possible, what his grievances were, and to request him to appear at the next court at Plymouth, to give his reasons for proceeding in the manner alleged.

It is not certain that Alexander actually promised to appear, as requested; but, from what passed between him and Capt. Willet, the English expected him. Be this as it may, he came not to the court at Plymouth; but in the time of that court, it is asserted, he went over to the Narragansets, the very tribe he was charged with bringing into his scheme of offence against the people of Plymouth. This heightened their suspicions, and they resolved promptly to check any hostile design.

Thereupon the Governor and Council of Plymouth ordered Major Josiah, or, as then written, Josias, Winslow to take an armed force, and proceed to Mount Hope, and force the Indian Chief to come to Plymouth. This was indeed a highhanded measure on the part of that government, and would never have been attempted, but from a confidence in its own strength, and in the weakness of the other party. The Wampanoags were an independent power, such as it was, and had so been treated with from the first. And what renders this proceeding the more reprehensible is, that there does not appear to have been any real grounds for a suspicion that their Chief, at this time, was contriving any mischief himself, or was conniving with the Narragansets in any sinister design, at least against the people of Plymouth. However, Major Winslow, taking with him Major William Bradford, (both sons of governors of Plymouth of their respective names,) and about ten mounted men, well armed, proceeded for Sowams, or, as often written, Sowamset, now Warren, in Rhode Island.

To this point in the narrative there is no disagreement in the accounts of the contemporary writers: but respecting the capture, treatment, sickness, and subsequent death of Alexander, those writers differ very materially; and, as they seem to be very nearly on an equal footing for truth and veracity, there is no alternative for the more modern historian but to let each of them be heard in evidence in so important a cause.

"The person," writes Mr. Hubbard, "to whom that service was committed, was a prudent and resolute gentleman, the present [1676]

---

* Thus the governor always wrote his name. Here is a fac-simile, of 1650:—

† He was son of Thomas Willet who came to Plymouth in 1630; and the first English mayor of New York. He was ancestor of the late Col. Marinus Willet of the Revolution. See *N. E. Hist. and Gen. Regr.* ii. 576.

Governor of that colony, who was neither afraid of danger, nor yet willing to delay in a matter of that moment, he forthwith, taking eight or ten stout men, well armed, intended to have gone to the said Alexander's dwelling, distant at least forty miles* from the Governor's house: but, by a good Providence, he found him whom he went to seek at an hunting-house within six miles of the English towns,† where the said Alexander, with about eighty‡ men, were newly come in from hunting, and had left their guns without doors, which Major Winslow, with his small company, wisely seized and conveyed away, and then went into the wigwam, and demanded Alexander to go along with him before the Governor,—at which message he was much appalled; but, being told by the undaunted messenger, that if he stirred, or refused to go, he was a dead man, he was, by one of his chief counsellors,§ in whose service he most confided, persuaded to go along to the Governor's house. But such was the pride and height of his spirit, that the very surprisal of him so raised his choler and indignation that it put him into a fever, which, notwithstanding all possible means that could be used, seemed mortal. Whereupon, entreating those that held him prisoner that he might have liberty to return home, promising to return again if he recovered, and to send his son as hostage till he could do so. On that consideration he was fairly dismissed; but died before he got half way home. Here let it be observed, that although some have taken up false reports, as if the English had compelled him to go farther or faster than he was able, and so fell into a fever; or, as if he were not well used by the physician‖ that looked to him, while he was with the English; all which are notoriously false. Nor is it to be imagined that a person of so noble a disposition as that gentleman at that time employed to bring him, should himself, or suffer any one else, to be uncivil to a person allied to them by his own, as well as his father's league, as the said Philip also was. Nor was anything of that nature ever objected to the English of Plymouth by the said Alexander's brother, by name Philip, commonly, for his ambitious and haughty spirit, nicknamed King Philip."

Dr. Increase Mather speaks in quite as confident terms about what he narrates of the affair as Mr. Hubbard. His account is next in importance, and a little more circumstantial, which he gave to the public, as follows: "The immediate predecessor of Philip was not so faithful and friendly to the English as his father had been; for some of Boston having been occasionally [on some occasion] at Narraganset,

---

* It must be remembered that distances through the wilderness at that time were estimated by any very direct Indian paths.

† Believed to be at Munponset Pond, in Halifax, almost equidistant from Plymouth and Bridgewater, where it was known the Indians had a very desirable resort.

‡ A very great mistake; perhaps typographical. It should be eight, I have no doubt.

§ Dr. I. Mather says it was by the advice of a brother of John Sassamon. There was a Rowland Sassamon, brother of John.

‖ The first physician at Plymouth was Samuel Fuller; but he died in 1633. There was at Plymouth in 1640 a Dr. Matthew Fuller, who removed to Barnstable in 1652, and died in 1678. Five years before his death he was appointed Surgeon General of the military forces of Plymouth Colony. — Thacher. He was the attendant upon Alexander, as will also be here seen.

wrote to Mr. Prince, who was then Governor [1662] of Plymouth, that Alexander was contriving mischief against the English, and that he had solicited the Narragansets to engage with him in his designed rebellion. Hereupon Capt. Willet, who lived near to Mount Hope, the place where Alexander did reside, was appointed to speak with him, and to desire him to attend the next court in Plymouth, for their satisfaction and his own vindication. He seemed to take the message in good part, professing that the Narragansets, who, he said, were his enemies, had put an abuse upon him; and he readily promised to attend at the next court. But when the day of his appearance was come, instead of that, he, at that very time, went over to the Narragansets, his pretended enemies; which, compared with other circumstances, caused the gentlemen at Plymouth to suspect there was more of truth in the information given than at first they were aware of.* Wherefore the Governor and magistrates there ordered Major Winslow (who is since, and at this day, [1676,] the Governor of that colony) to take a party of men and fetch down Alexander. The Major considering that *semper nocuit differre paratis*, [when prepared to act delay is dangerous,] he took but ten armed men with him from Marshfield, intending to have taken more at the towns that lay nearer Mount Hope. But Divine Providence so ordered, as that when they were about the midway between Plymouth and Bridgewater, observing an hunting-house, they rode up to it, and there did they find Alexander and many of his men, all well armed, but their guns standing together without the house. The Major, with his small party, possessed themselves of the Indians' arms, and beset the house. Then did he go in amongst them, acquainting the sachem with the reason of his coming in such a way; desiring Alexander, with his interpreter, to walk out with him, who did so, a little distance from the house, and then understood what commission the Major had received concerning him. The proud sachem fell into a raging passion at this surprise, saying that the Governor had no reason to credit rumors, or to send for him in such a way, nor would he go to Plymouth but when he saw cause. It was replied to him, that his breach of word touching appearance at Plymouth Court, and instead thereof going, at the same time, to his pretended enemies, augmented jealousies concerning him. In fine, the Major told him that his order was to bring him to Plymouth, and that, by the help of God, he would do it, or else he would die on the place. Also declaring to him, that if he would submit, he might expect respective [respectful] usage; but if he once more denied to go, he should never stir from the ground whereon he stood; and, with a pistol at the sachem's breast, required that his next words should be a positive and clear answer to what was demanded. Hereupon his interpreter, a discreet Indian, brother to John Sausaman, being sensible of Alexander's passionate disposition, entreated that he might speak a few words to the sachem before he gave his answer.

(To be Continued.)

---

* On the other hand it might easily be inferred that the chief neglected to go to Plymouth, under the belief that he was to go there upon an idle errand; to communicate a rumor, the like of which was almost an every-day occurrence; and he did not care to have his own plans of hunting, or other employments, broken up to gratify people who had no right to make such demand upon him.

LEXINGTON, CONCORD, AND WESTON DOCUMENTS.

S. G. Drake, Esq., Editor *N. E. Hist. and Gen. Reg.*

Dear Sir,—Please find with this copies of four ancient papers in my possession. They are as follows :—

1. Lexington's Answer to the Petition of John Flint, Esq., and others, for a Separate Township.
2. Weston's Answer to same Petition.
3. Concord's Anti-Petition.
4. Concord's Rate List.

I am not aware that they have ever been published. Should you consider them worthy a place in your magazine they are entirely at your service.   Yours respectfully,   Jas. Lawrence Bass.

Boston, May 14, 1857.

LEXINGTON'S ANSWER.

To his Excellency Jonathan Belcher Esq' Cap' Gen'' and Governer in Chief in & over his Majesties Province of the Massachusetts Bay in New England, to the Hon'' his Majesties Council & the hon'''' house of Representatives in General Court Assembled at Boston Sep' 1735.

In answer to a Petition of Sundry of the Inhabitants & Proprietors of the Westerly Part of Lexington In Conjunction with Sundry the Inhabitants of Concord & Weston Exhibited to the General Court & Read in the house of Representatives July ye 2' 1735, & in Council Read & concur'd we a Committee of the town of Lexington humbly offer as followeth :—

1.—We are are Surprised the said Petitioners should offer to trouble this Hon' Court any further when their former petition was with so much reason & wisdom Dismissed.

2.—There is a greater number of families or persons Comprehended in the bounds of Land Petitioned for in Lexington who are averse to the prayer of the Petition than are Consenting to it as is certifyed under their hands.

3.—We have Sundry families who can make Stronger pleas to be Set off than these Petitioners, Lying upon worse roads & at a greater distance from our Meeting house & nearer unto other Meeting houses, besides these Petitioners chose their Distance for their own accomodations & every man cannot think to have a Meeting house at his own Door.

4.—They say they are obliged to Tarry at home, & we in answer say to their honor : They attend the publick worship as Constantly as other people.

5.—They object the Roads are Exceeding bad but we have lately been at Charge to Make them Good & we are Sure if they go off from us they will Exchange them for those that are Much worse.

6.—They say they were opposed by a Considerable number within said bounds in their former Petition so they are still & not without Good Reasons for it will aggravate their Charge and not lessen the Difficulty of their travel or Distance of way as to many of them.

7.—They say the number of Petitioners is now encreased but it is of very unqualified persons & with unreasonable importunity to the great regret of some of the subscribers.

8.—The Lands Petitioned for will make the teritory Larger than ours which is a thing unusuall in such Movements, their design then must be to make a fat benefice for some body, by Starving the towns they Depart from & Spoiling two or three towns to make their own great.

9.—They humbly pray your Excellency & honours will be pleased to take this Case Into your wise and serious Consideration & if our Case Come under the same wise and serious Consideration we are humbly of opinion this their Petition must be Desmissed as their former was, for there is the Same Reason for it in all Respects, save only they have over persuaded some to sign and join with them very much to their Disadvantage & which they have alredy Repented & will have more cause to do so afterward.

10.—They say we would not Consent to set them off, we say we Could not In Reason do it; for these very petitioners very lately were very forward to bring forward the Settlement of an assistant to the Reverend Mr. Hancock & we rejoiced In it but are surprised they should so soon meditate a remove & leave us under the Load of the augmented Charge which with the Charge of the Rebuilding the great Bridge at the Same time lyes heavy upon us (tho we abundantly acknowledge the favour of this Honble Court in their Grant to us on that account) & it will needs be with some reluctancy to the Late Settled Minister as well as to his Reverend Father to part with so many Good friends at once.

Finally, we humbly Claim the benefit of that paragraph in our Royal Charter page 6th wherein it is ordained that all Bodies Politick & Towns &c shall hold & enjoy such Grants & Bounds as have been made by any Generall Court formerly held & which gives us a right to Petition in the present Case & grounds to hope your Excellency & Hon^{rs} will deny the prayer of the said Petitioners, So shall we ever humbly pray for &c.

Lexington, 10: *of Sept* 1735.

FRANCIS BOWMAN,
JOHN MASON,
JOSEPH BOWMAN,

In the Name & behalf of the Town of Lexington—
  A True Copy.

     Examined per   THAD^r MASON Dep^t Sec^{ry}.

WESTON'S ANSWER.

To his Excellency Jonathan Belcher Esq Capt Gen^{rl} & Gover^{nr} In Chief in & over his Majesties Province of the Massachusetts Bay in New England & to the Honble the Councill & house of Repesentives in Genl Court assembled at Boston Septr 1735.

May It please your Excellencies & Hon^{rs}

In as much it was your pleasures at the Sessions in July Last past, upon the petition of Sundry the Inhabitants of the Easterly part of Concord & the Northerly part of Weston & of the Westerly part of Lexington, to order that the said petitioners Should Serve the towns of Concord Lexington & Weston with Copies of the Petition (wherein they pray to be Set off a Seperate Township as therein Expressed) to Shew Cause why the prayer thereof Should not be granted, The Town of Weston humbly offer their reasons as follows:—

1.—That the said Town of Weston is but small, Tho' about Seven Miles In Length from North to South, yet scarce Three Miles wide in the

Center & in Considerable parts not above half so much, & great part of the land very poor rocky and barren not Capable to be inhabited. That there are but about a hundred families in all & many of them in Low Circumstances.

II.—That the Said Town hath lately been at great Cost and Charges to build & finish a Decent Meeting house for the publick worship of God not only of sufficient Dimensions for the whole town, but it is not near fil⁴ when assembled together and this Meeting house stands by the great Road & as Surveyors find by the platt within a few Rods of the Centre of the Town. So that the Petitioners have little more Reason to Complain of the Distance or Difficulty than their Neighbours who live at the South End of the town.

III.—That iff the Said Petitioners Should be set off by the Large bound which they ask for it would be building their new town upon the Ruins of Weston, which we suppose is not doing as they would be Done by for that their South Bounds will Come Considerable nearer to Weston Meeting house than It is to the Center of the Lands they ask for, and the Meeting house in Weston would then be left so unequally Sittuated that the town will be in great Danger of falling into the fire of Contentions about Removing it or building a new one and providing new ways That may be needfull therunto.

IV.—That the Petition aforesaid Takes from Weston near Twenty families (tho severall of them do not subscribe) & Some of the best livings in the town, & yet Leaving those they would withdraw to grapple with the heavy Charge of Maintaining all the poor in the Town & of Maintaining their Bridges & especially the great Cart Bridge over Charles River in Watertown, Which from the Reason of things they ought to be proportionably subject to Besides the whole support of the ministry (whose family we must own) Reasonably requires more maintaisance than he hath ever received of Weston.

We further humbly observe that the Town of Weston Contains no other Bounds but the same that was formerly Granted to the Ancient Town of Watertown & by a Generall Clause In the Royal Charter P. 6 Confirmed to them Their heirs & Successors & for as much as Weston Descended from Watertown & hold by the Same ancient Bounds to Concord Sudbury & Lexington &c we humbly hope to Enjoy & hold the Same Bounds by which we were set off a Township, without Diminution or alteration which we apprehend will also be agreeable to the Law of this Province Made in the fourth year of the Reign of King William & Queen Mary entitled an act for Regulating of Townships. Among other things it is hereby Enacted that yᵉ bounds of all Townships Shall be & Continue as heretofore Granted & Settled Respectively &c For the which reasons the Town of Weston Humbly pray that their Northern Neighbours the petitioners may not be set off from them but Remain with them to do Duty & Receive Priviledges as here to for.

And the Respondents as In duty Bound Shall Ever pray &c.

Fra⁴ Fullam,
James Jones,
Josiah Brewer,

In the names & behalf of the Town of Weston.

A True Copy.

      Examined per   Thad Mason Dep⁴ Sec⁴.

CONCORD'S ANTI-PETITION.

These may Certyfie Whom it may Concern that we the Subscribers being Inhabitants and Proprietors of that par: of Concord which is Included in a Petition of John Flint Esq and others Prefered to the Genairil Court at theire Semioos in May 1735 praying that the Easterly Part of Concord and the Northerly Part of Weston and the Westerly Part of Lexington May be Set off a Seperate Town Ship.

Which if Granted will be Greatly to our Damage Sum of us who Dwoll with In the bounds set forth in Said petition being nearer to Concord Meating Hous then we can Soposo we shall be to the Meating House in said Township if Granted and the wayes to Concord being very good we most earnestly desire that their petition may not be Granted or that we may not be Included therein.

Samuel Hetwood	Eben^r Wheeler
Vathanel Ball	Noah Brooks
John Jones	Samuel Hartwell
Ebenezer Merriam	Joseph Brooks
Jacob Taylor	Wid Esther Whittamore
Sam^{ll} Minot	Hugh Brooks
Sam^{ll} Merriam	Ebenezer Lamson
Peter Harwood	Daniel Bruok*
Daniel Hoar	Thomas Brook*
Isaac Taylor	Job Brooks
Joseph Taylor	Nathaniel Whittamore
Joseph Wooley Jr	for two Liveings
Joseph Merriam	Joseph Wheate
Thomas Ball	Timothy Samson
Sam^{ll} Wooley	Joseph Billings
Sam^{ll} Fletcher	Sam^{ll} Billings
Eben^r Tayler	John Billings
Joseph Stratton	Sam^{ll} Brooks

A True Copy.

Examined per   Thad Mason Dep^t Secr.

On the back of this paper is the following :—

Note.—There are 19 of the Subscribers within-named who are not Inhabitants of that part of Concord pet^d for to be set off, but are all only prop^{rs} more or less of Small Woodlots in ye Same who pay out very little towards publick charges.

CONCORD'S RATE LIST.

THESE ON THE LEFT HAND ARE PETITIONERS.			THESE ON THE RIGHT HAND NON-PETITIONERS.			
Simon Dakin	9	0	Daniel Brooks	1	6	3
Edward Flint	17	11	Sam^{ll} Brooks	0	18	2
Thomas Wheeler	14	7	Thomas Brooks	0	17	0
Daniel Parks	0	0	Noah Brooks	0	5	11
Josiah Blancher	9	8	Hugh Brooks	1	4	0

* Daniel Brook and Thomas Brook the document has it, and I so give the names. They are undoubtedly meant for Brooks.—J. L. B.

PETITIONERS.				NON-PETITIONERS.			
Zacheus Parks		0	0	Job Brooks	0	18	11
Nathan Brown		13	5	Joseph Brooks	1	12	5
Daniel Brewer		10	0	Ephraim Heartwell	0	12	8
Jonathan Green		8	3	Samⁿ Heartwell	0	16	0
Joseph Parks		15	3	Nathan^{el} Whittemore	0	13	11
Josiah Parks		15	3	Widow Whittemore	0	5	5
Ephraim Parks		10	10	Ebenezer Lamson	1	12	7
Elizabeth Parker	1	3	4	Timothy Lamson	0	9	6
Daniel Adams	1	7	10	Benjamin Whittemore		14	5
Jonathan Dakin	0	9	2	Ebenezer Townsend	0	8	2
Abijah Wheeler		8	0	Joseph Wheat	1	3	11
John Fletcher		0	0	Daniel Whitney	0	8	9
Nathaniel Billing		0	0	Timothy Wesson	0	19	7
George Farrar	1	0	11	Stephen Wesson	0	15	8
Samuel Farrar	0	11	4	Ambros Tower	0	15	4
George Farrar Jun	0	12	6	John Baker	1	12	1
Nathaniel Whittaker		13	2	John Crosset	0	10	9
Benj^a Brooks	1	0	9	John Hackfarlin	0	10	9
Joshua Brooks	1	5	9	John More	0	9	
Joseph Wheeler		9	6	Sam^{ll} Hunt	0	7	8
Ebenezer Brooks	0	15	7	Ebenezer Hunt	0	19	1
Benjamin Wheeler	0	10	1	Daniel Billing	1	8	5
Jonathan Whitney for				Amose Heald	0	9	5
Ephraim Flint's Living		11	6	Sam^{ll} Billing	1	7	9
and his own Stock				Joseph Billing	0	11	2
William Hager		0	0	Benjamin Lull	0	14	11
				John Billing	0	12	2
				John More Junr	0	7	8
				George Crawford	0	7	8
				Eben Stow	0	7	8
	£17	3	7		£27	14	9

A True Copy of what the Respective persons above Named (Inhabitants of Concord) was Rated to the Province Tax in the year 1734.

Certified per   SAMUEL HEYWOOD Town Clerk.

A Copy.

Examined per   THAD. MASON Dep^t Sec^{ry}.

THE MIND AND THE STOMACH.

Dr. Nott, recently, in some remarks to the junior class at Union College, Schenectady, N. Y., stated that many years ago, when the students went to take their meals together in the subterranean portico of the South College, he was one day in the midst of an interesting lecture when the breakfast-bell rang, and symptoms of uneasiness were very evident among the class. Stopping in his lecture, he remarked, that " all who thought more of eating than of knowledge might leave." All left with the exception of two; one of them was the late Dr. Cuyler of Philadelphia, and the other the late John C. Spencer.—[20 Oct., 1855.

LETTER FROM S. SEVERANCE, 1775.

Newburyport, June 28, 1854.

Dear Sir,—If the following scrap of biographical history and letter you should deem worthy of insertion in your Register, they are at your disposal.

Yours, respectfully,	E. George Adams.

Samuel Severance, the writer of the following letter, was a native of Kingston, N. H. He enlisted in the Revolutionary army, and served about three months. He was in the battle of Bunker Hill, and brought home a small stone, which is now in the possession of my wife's family, as a memorial of that eventful day. The letter is addressed from Medford to his wife at Kingston. Her maiden name was Hannah Winslow. I have retained the spelling, &c., of the letter, and as a relic of those days that tried men's souls, I thought it would be interesting to your many readers. I will relate a little incident to illustrate the social life and the privation of those times. When the postman came round to convey letters from the inhabitants of Kingston, as well as any little necessaries from their friends, to the soldiers in the service, Mrs. Severance sent to her husband some green beans, with a piece of pork to cook with them, and some Indian meal to make him a pudding, while his little daughter, six years old, picked him a pint of berries to put in it; which he gratefully received, while the soldiers stood looking on with tears in their eyes, wishing they had a wife or children to send them a like present. Mr. Severance was taken sick with the camp disease, and was forced to return home. This little daughter's name was Hannah, and married Henry Adams of Newbury. When Mr. Severance returned to his home, he was so haggard, and pale, and changed, that this daughter, in her fright at the singular looks of a stranger, as she deemed him, fled, and hid herself behind the door. Henry Adams had a daughter Hannah who married Ebenezer Plumer of Newburyport, whose only child, Sarah Cobb Plumer, is my wife. I would state that though the spelling of the following letter is poor, the penmanship is very creditable.

E. GEORGE ADAMS.

THE LETTER.

madford July th 17, 1775,

these Lines comes to you, my loveing wife and dear children, hoping in the marcy of god that you are all well, and I hope in gods time I shall be restored home again; but if not, I beg of god that we may so live in this world that we may spend wone day in each others proasents in a world of glory, for I put noe trust in the arm of flesh, but my trust is in god alone for life and mearcy, and I hope in the mearcy of god that he will eary you throu all your troblo and dificiles that you have to pas throu in this life. my love to father and mother, to brother John and wife. I hope that you are all well, and the rest of my friends, to my wife; what money I send home to you, you may take care of it. if you have aney prosp'n of corn, I would have that old cow have a peas on her horns, so I have noe more at the present, so I remain your Loving housband til death pmrt.

Saml. Severance.

THE ELIOT BUREAU.

Jamaica Plain, July 17, 1857.

To S. G. Drake, Esq.

Dear Sir:—In my communication, addressed to you Sept. 1st, 1855, and published in the October number of the Genealogical Register, together with a drawing of the article of furniture in my possession, by James O'Bryan, which I then called the "Eliot Bureau," I gave a history of the manner in which it came into my possession, its condition at the time, and the alterations I had made upon it, so that its genuineness, in future time, might not be thrown into doubt. I also gave several items of testimony which seemed to establish the fact that the article was once the property of the revered Eliot, the Apostle to the Indians.

Since that time, I have received letters from several gentlemen who had read my former communication on the subject, and I send you some of these letters, together with extracts from others, relating to this question, so that, in view of all the evidence in the case, the public may come to a more satisfactory conclusion respecting its identity than they otherwise could.

The first extract I shall give you will be one contained in a letter from my old and respected friend, Gov. Levi Lincoln, whose opinion and judgment I learned to appreciate and respect most highly, during a long period of service in a public office under him. In a letter of Dec. 8th, 1855, he says :—

"In reference to the '*Cabinet*,' you have shown yourself a literary artificer of great excellence ; out of the rough and neglected materials, you have constructed *two* beautiful articles—one physical, the other intellectual. In both respects I think you have well made out ' the case,' and upon the evidence, I pronounce it the veritable ' Eliot Cabinet.' You must richly prize the article for its intrinsic and associate value."

Hon. Robert C. Winthrop replied as follows :—

"I thank you for a copy of your interesting account of the Eliot Bureau. I heartily wish it were in my power to add any thing to the strength of the testimony by which you trace up this relic of the olden time to the venerated Apostle to the Indians. But you have made a strong case of presumption, and I can hardly doubt that ' I. E.' designated John Eliot."

Mr. Winthrop intimates a doubt as to the significance of the letter "A." He says :—

"Whether the '*A*' stood for Anno, or for Anna, the name of Eliot's wife, you do not intimate. The wife's name, as you doubtless know, was Hannah Mumford ; but it is entered on the Roxbury records at least once as '*Ana*.' Our fathers were rather fanciful in their mode of combining the initials of husband and wife upon silver plate. I am not so familiar with marks upon furniture."

I will remark, in passing, that Mr. Winthrop, who doubtless gave the subject very careful consideration, and whose eminent fitness to express an authoritative opinion upon it is beyond question, scarcely doubts that the letters " I. E." designated John Eliot. As to his intimation that the letter "A" may have been the initial of his wife's name, because the initials of both husband and wife were often placed upon articles of plate, it may be said—first, the fact that the name of Eliot's wife was *Hannah*, is quite opposed to the idea of the use of the letter A to represent her name; for, although it may have been found on the Roxbury records "at least once" as Ann, it is quite unlikely that A would be used in the place of H upon this article of furniture, if the purpose was to designate her name. In the next place, this intimation does not apply to the Bureau, because the letters I and E are eighteen inches apart, upon the same horizontal line, and the letter A is nearly eighteen inches below them both. The figures 1681 are eight inches below the last letter, which clearly indicates that each had a distinct meaning, independent of its relation to the others.

Rev. Dr. LOWELL has communicated to me his opinion also, which is the more valuable by reason of his having made the sufferings and character of Eliot the subject of his distinct consideration, using the following language in reference to him, in a sermon preached at the dedication of a church in Natick, in 1828:—

"How interesting are the associations which are connected with this place, and this occasion! Nearly two centuries ago, this spot was first consecrated by the rites of religion. It was then that the apostolic Eliot imparted to the rude, untutored children of the forest, the light of Divine truth, and the wilderness echoed the voice of Christian prayer, and the songs of Christian praise. We revert with admiration to the wearisome pilgrimages, and the toilsome and perilous, though patient and persevering labors of this holy man. Imagination delights to go back through the long tract of time, and see him travelling on foot, with his staff and his Bible; or surrounded by his Indian children, with no altar but the trunk of the forest tree, and no canopy but the vault of heaven, yet cheered by the consciousness of devotion to the best of causes, and by the hopes of success. We honor thy memory, devoted servant of the Lord Jesus! Though no fruits of thy labor remain, thou hast erected a monument to thy praise in the hearts of the pious, in all times, who shall hear the story of thy toils and thy sufferings, and hast secured to thyself a portion with them who, 'having turned many to righteousness, shall shine as the brightness of the firmament, and as the stars, forever and ever.'"

In his letter to me he says:—

"I cannot doubt that I have, from time to time, acknowledged your kindness in sending me your interesting and valuable communications respecting your honorable and honored family, and the precious Eliot Antique, of which you are the favored possessor. You make out a strong case."

The next letter from which I shall extract will be that of the diligent antiquarian, J. WINGATE THORNTON, Esq. of Boston, a grandson of Judge Gookin, and connected by marriage with the Eliot family. He says:—

"I notice that on page 331, you make Capt. John Smith's hero, Daniel Gookin of Virginia, 1621, identical with the Major General of Massachusetts, but the latter was the son of the former."

As I have reason to think Mr. Thornton is correct, I am happy to state his remark here. As to the "Bureau," he says:—

"I rejoice that this memento of that Christian hero and apostle—ELIOT—is in the possession of one who can so well appreciate his greatness, and rightly value what is so blended with his memory, and I wish that every successive owner may preserve it with like sacred regard."

J. J. Clarke, Esq., late Mayor of Roxbury, says:—

"You seem to make it *almost certain* that this article of furniture once belonged to the Apostle Eliot. It is sufficiently well established to awaken, and keep alive, all the feelings which are inseparable from the contemplation of his many virtues; and that *alone is enough* to render it of great value."

The following letter from President Jared Sparks is quite gratifying:—

"*Cambridge, Nov. 30th, 1855.*

"My Dear Sir,—Please to accept my thanks for your kind attention in sending me your interesting account of the Eliot Bureau. Such a case scarcely admits of absolute demonstration, but it appears to me that the facts, as you have brought them together, give the highest degree of probability to the conclusion at which you have arrived. At any rate, you may fairly claim this curious specimen of antiquity to have belonged to the Apostle Eliot, till some person, more learned and ingenious than is likely to be found, shall prove the contrary.

"I am, dear sir, with great regard, very truly yours,

"Gen'l Sumner."　　　　　　　　　　　　　　Jared Sparks.

The next letter I give is that of Hon. Franklin Dexter of Boston:—

"I have received the copy you were kind enough to send me of your description of the Eliot Bureau. You are certainly very fortunate in possessing such a precious relic of antiquity; and I think no one can deny, that you fairly trace it, by presumption, to John Eliot, or at least to his son John,—and if to the son, then probably through him to the father, as it appears to have been of foreign workmanship, and therefore brought out by the venerable Apostle from England."

To the suggestion that the ownership of the Cabinet is traced through the son to the father, the chronological order of events in the history of the family is opposed, since the son died first, in 1668. This renders it probable that it came into the possession of the widow of John Eliot, Jr. subsequently, she being a daughter of Gen. Gookin.

As the last of the corroborative testimony, from the opinions of gentlemen eminently qualified to judge correctly upon the subject, I give an extract from a letter of John Codman, Esq. of Boston:—

"I have received, and read with much pleasure, your pamphlet on the subject of the Eliot Bureau. It is a matter of which I have no knowledge; but I think, to say the least, that you have made out a very fair case, and the presumption that you have a valuable relic of the Indian Apostle is very strong.

"That you have drawn out the very beautiful verses, at the close, I think a matter on which you may congratulate yourself.*

---

* By Mrs. Susan H. Todd, daughter of the late Aaron Hill, Esq. of Cambridge, and grand-daughter of Edmund Quincy. See Genealogical Register, Oct. 1855, page 333.

"I hope and think probable that you may meet with evidence which would establish your theory, as to the history of this Cabinet, even in a court of law."

Thus, in addition to the evidence which I have before adduced to support the opinion that the Cabinet belonged to Mr. Eliot, I have given the views of several eminent gentlemen, as above. But lest, upon investigation, it should be said by any one that it came from a man by the name of Scammon, in N. H., and not from the Gookin family, I am happy to be able to add direct testimony upon that point.

Mrs. HARRIET GOOKIN STORER, an elderly lady, now visiting at Mr. Steele's, her son-in-law, at Jamaica Plain, a daughter of Judge Daniel Gookin, says, in reference to the Eliot Bureau:—

"I very well recollect that when I was quite young, my father had an old piece of furniture, like the one I have seen at General Sumner's, besides many other articles of antique furniture, brought from England. I distinctly recollect that a Mr. Scammon, who worked for my father, and who lived at Stratham, which is doubtless the place where Dr. Swett obtained the Bureau, asked my mother to let him have it. She told him he might, and he took it away; but whether it was given to him, or he paid for it, I do not know. It was probably given to him, as my mother wanted to get rid of some of the old furniture which was in the way. I have no doubt that the Bureau or Cabinet which General Sumner has, is the identical piece of furniture that Mr. Scammon had of my mother, and that it came to my father's family from John Eliot, though I have no recollection of ever having heard any one say where it came from. There never was any other person connected with my father's family, or those of his ancestors, whose initials were I. E., except John Eliot."

This testimony of Mrs. Storer is strongly corroborative, and indeed seems to place the identity of the "Eliot Bureau" in my possession, and the article sold or given to Mr. Scammon, beyond a doubt, and at the same time confirms the statement of Dr. Swett, which was published in my former communication; for, although he was told by the people of whom he obtained it, "that the parents of one of them had owned it fifty years," he says also they were "very poor, and ignorant in proportion," and they were therefore not likely to be very accurate as to the date of the ownership. Mrs. Storer thinks it might have been in their possession forty years; and that period would carry the ownership back to the time when her mother parted with it. Mr. Scammon was not a relative of the Gookin family, as stated by Dr. Swett, he having been misinformed in that particular probably. Mrs. Storer states that Mr. Scammon lived in her father's family some time, and thus the idea may have arisen in Dr. Swett's mind that he was a relative of the family, or some of Scammon's descendants might have so understood it.

Having thus established, in my own opinion, the identity of the Cabinet as John Eliot's, the only article of furniture remaining that ever belonged to him, I have perhaps rendered it worthy of the acceptance of Harvard University or the Massachusetts Historical Society, to one of which I intend to devise it.

Respectfully, your ob't serv't,

WM. H. SUMNER.

NEWARK, ONE HUNDRED YEARS AGO.

[From the Newark Daily Advertiser.   Communicated by S. H. Congar, Esq.]

There are those, Mr. Editor, who doubt the correctness of your statement in introducing to your readers the article from Putnam's Magazine for June, that " the College was on what is now Washington Park."

We believe S. L. was "Samuel Livermore, A. M. LL. D., Col. Dart. 1792, in Cong. Amer. Deleg., Reip.   Neo. Hant, Cur. Sup. Jurid. Prin., et Gub. Cong. Rerumpub. Foed, Sen. et Repr." of the Catalogue of Nassau Hall, and a clever fellow of course. William Camp, at whose house S. L. boarded in 1752, was a great grand-son of that Wm. Camp, of Milford, who was married to Mary Smith, of New Haven, in 1661, by Deputy Governor Gilbert —the magistrate, not the minister, being in the opinion of that peculiar people the proper person to perform that ceremony. They came to Newark. Their son Samuel succeeded in the occupation of the old home lot. Nathaniel, one of the sons of Samuel, was the father of William, John, and Nathaniel.   William seems to have been a house-keeper, willing to make a trifle by keeping boarders, at 7 sh. per week, like others who it is said enlarged their dwellings to accommodate the Collegians.   He may have lived then in the ancestral mansion, but, where is the evidence?   In 1761, Camp's Dock, (the Stone Dock subsequently) was one of the improvements on the Passaic, and seems to have had its name from him as its constructor, or owner, he living in the vicinity.   He was engaged in mercantile pursuits. In 1762, we find him selling at the following prices :— 1-4 lb. pepper, 6d— 1-2 lb. tea 5 sh.—12 lb. nails, 10 sh.—208 feet pine boards, 18 sh. 8d.   In February, 1763, he purchased 248 lbs. Beef at 4 pence half-penny, York money. Clams, those excellent bivalves, were then 10d per 100— Salt Pork 6d per lb. Pigeons were a shilling the dozen, the gizzards included for medical purposes, and Spirits to wash down the substantials, 1 sh. per quart. Of his doings in 1760, we have a notice, with an official seal attached, as follows :

Port Perth Amboy.

Know ye that William Camp hath entered on board the Shallop Lovely Lass, Samuel Hays Master, Bound on a Cod Fishing voyage to the Eastward, Two Barrils of Beef, Six Barrils of Pork, One Ton of Bread, and Seven Barrils of flour for the Use of Seamen, Mariners and fishermen belonging to said Sloop. Dated at the Custom House, Perth Amboy, ye 12th May, 1766.   John Barberie, Coll'r.

After an absence of five months, the Sloop was permitted to return as follows :

Permit Samuel Hays to land the Sloop Lovely Lass, for New York, with Pick'd Fish. Dated at the Custom House, Canso, this 11th Day of Oct., 1760.   Jon. Binney, Coll'r.
To the Waiters.

Her Master, afterward Maj. Samuel Hayes, alias " Bark Knife," so called from the resemblance of his sword to that instrument, was associated with Joseph Hedden, Esq., and Thomas Canfield, (Hedden's brother-in law,) as Commissioners for the sale of forfeited estates during the war. All of them were particularly disliked by " the Loyalists," and all were surprised, and taken to New York. William Camp was also captured, in Nov. 1776, and died in New York, Jan. 3, 1777. aged 47.

Mr. Sol. Davis was doubtless thankful for the sixpence he received for bringing S. L.'s gown "from New York." Sixpences were not plenty as blackberries, in those days. Solomon Davis, four years after, was credited 4 sh. 6d. for his son Comfort Davis's driving plough six days. Comfort, however, probably found something comfortable on his employer's table, in addition to his sixpence per day. In 1754 "the Society of Newark Mountain" was about building "in the General after the model of the Meeting House in Newark." Justice Harrison, Deacon Freeman, Sam. Cundit, Stephen Dod, Joseph Harrison, and David Williams, had 3sh. 6d. per day for "taking down the Sealing of the Old Meeting House."— Deacon Freeman, Justice Harrison, William Crane, Thomas Williams, Samuel Cundit, Jun., Isaac Cundit, John Cundit, Stephen Dod, David Williams, Capt. Williams, and Isaac Williams, "laid sleepers," in the New Meeting House, at the same rate per day. The accounts also show that "a quart of rum and a quarter of sugar" was worth 1 sh. 3d., or, equal to one-third of a day's work, or S. L.'s board for one day.

S. L. also paid Dr. Turner 5 sh. for 5 days' board, the washing of 8 shirts, and "bringing up my chest." Dr. William Turner, besides making these apparently reasonable charges, we know wrote a fair legible hand, which is more than some physicians and lawyers were ever guilty of. He died Feb. 18, 1754, aged 42. His first wife, Mary, March 3, 1737–8, aged 25. His second, Rachel, in Sept. 1741, aged 16, according to the transcriber of the lines from her memorial—

> "God dealeth just, none may complain,
> Tho' Turner is left alone again."

His third wife was Mehetable, the widow of Benjamin Campfield. His step-son was a Jabez Campfield. A grandson, William, son of Daniel and Sarah Turner, died in 1775. Laid near his grand-parents, they inscribed on his memorial,

> "The Sweet Remains of Billie here may lay,
> Until ye Resurrection morn in peace."

In 1741, when Dr. Turner paid 38 sh. and 6d. for "the feed of the burying ground," he did not foresee that in a century after his decease, his professional brethren, perchance patrons of resurrectionists and skilful to cure, or kill, *secundum artem*, would lay the foundations of a theatre for their experiments amidst his crumbling bones, and, unlike Hamlet, never ask—Why may not that be the skull of a doctor?—if permitted to rob Turner's grave. There may be "peace" in the new well-protected cemeteries, where the sons hope to lie 'neath towering marble, but the fathers are neglected and forgotten.

S. L. paid E. Crane (Elijah or Elihu) for a "barrel of cyder" 14 sh., and I. Shippen, 40 sh., York, "towards the bottles." In I. Shippen we recognize the student who gives an account of President Burr's three days' courtship, and his marriage to a young lady, "rather too young, being only about twenty-one"—the President being then 36. (Vide Stearns, p. 192.) The writer for Putnam says, Jerseyman "may read with pride the evidence of the antiquity of a branch of industry that now reflects honor upon his State from all parts of the country," and fills many a champagne bottle, he might have added. Of its antiquity it may be said, that in the inventory of the estate of Matthew Campfield, of Newark, in 1673, we find "cyder"—and Deputy Governor Rudyard says, in 1683, "at a town called Newark, 7 or 8 miles hence, is made great quantities of Syder, exceeding any we can have from New England, or Rhod Island, or Long Island. I hope to make 20 or 30 Barrels out of our orchard next year, as they have done who had it before me; for that, it must be as Providence orders."

But where was the building in which S. L. was instructed by the President and Tutors of the College in Newark?   Was it upon "the upper Common," now Washington Park?   Some of those who witnessed the burning of the Academy, on that night memorable in the revolutionary history of Newark, when Joseph Hedden was taken from his residence, now No. 125 Broad street, in an arctic winter, and driven but half-clothed to New York, when questioned, have replied, that no College ever stood there to their knowledge. On March 8, 1774, the Town voted "that a School House may be built upon any of the Common Land in Newark, and the particular place shall be where a major part of the Subscribers in value shall appoint." On March 14, 1775, the Town "Voted unanimously, that one acre and a half of land in the Town Common, at the North End of the Town, may be taken up for the use of the New Academy, lately erected on said Land."

The ancient fillibuster, Aaron Burr, was born very near where now Alderman B. hands out "the wood," and his neighbor M. the candles to young fillibusters, and others.   There lived the President, and as he was never while the College was at Newark assisted by more than two tutors, that may have been the point to which the steps of S. L. were directed, whether boarding above or below.   Commencement exercises may have been held in the church, then standing on "the town Lot."   This appears to have been nearly finished in 1714, when it was voted that the old floor in the Meeting House, should "be made use of for the making a floor in the School House in the middle of the Town," and also, "that John Fford should have liberty to set a Mill below the old Mill, and that he should have a quarter of an acre of Land."   It does not appear, however, that John Fford tarried long in Newark. He seems to have kept on his way from "Qeonebog, up New London River," and died in Hunterdon, (now Morris county,) in 1721, the father of the Fords, of that county. These notices of contemplated improvements in our village, are gathered from lost Minutes of Town Meetings, recently recovered.   Where is the document that will give facts concerning the building occupied by the collegians, from 1748 to 1756, if one existed, other than the County Court House, in which, it is said, the public academical exercises were generally performed?   1857.

D.
T. M.
1713.

Stephen Davis was one of those who, in 1667, associated to "endeavor the carrying on of spiritual concernments, as also civil and town affairs, according to God and godly government," on the banks of the Passaic. His home lot of six acres was bounded by Aaron Blatchly's and Samuel Plum's, the river and Broad street.   It is written that in 1687, when John Brown, Jun., and Joseph Walters were appointed by the town to seal measures and weights, " it was agreed that Benjamin Baldwin's or Stephen Davis' half bushel shall be the standard which shall be thought most suitable, and all measures shall be sealed with an N, and all weights shall be tried with brass weights if they can be had, and if not, by Stephen

Davis's weights, which have been scaled in New York. And on Feb. 14th next every one as has measures or weights shall bring them to the prison, that they may tried and scaled, and for curing and scaling every measure they are to have three pence in money, or four pence in other pay, and for weights as they can agree. Stephen Davis was a prominent public man for more than twenty years. His sons were John, Thomas, and Jonathan.

Of the score of Davises whose names appear in our directories, some may feel interested in the ancestral mansion, and the mysterious initials which appear on its walls, since their covering has been removed. It, like those of the Bruens, Cranes, Camps, and others, built early in the last century, is to give place to the more splendid residences or churches, of those who know little and care less about the men, who, in their day, erected schoolhouses and churches, but now, to the disgrace of this city, are denied decent sepulchres. Even these are covered, that their site may be appropriated to purposes not contemplated by the grantors, or anticipated by the occupants.

Thomas Davis was born before the settlement of Newark, and died Jan. 26th, 1738–9, aged 78. Mary, his wife, died May 10th, 1732, aged 67. The initials of this married pair, according to the custom of those days, were graven upon the walls of their dwelling, as, after their death, their names and age were, upon the memorial placed to protect their bones from insult. The date, 1713, indicates that its foundations were laid before the Kitchells, Lindsleys, Cranes, Pruddens, and Canfields, the cotemporaries of Thomas Davis, had emigrated to the Western country, now Morris county, and while the red men where yet in the enjoyment of the rights reserved by them, in their bill of sale, fishing in the river, or hunting in the forests on its banks, Queen Anne being on the throne of England. The sons of Thomas Davis were Thomas, Jonathan, Stephen and James. His sons-in-law were John Vanderpool, the husband of Apphia, and Thomas Ball the husband of Sarah, who, it is said,

> " Had Rachel's Beauty, Leah's fruitful Womb,
> Abigail's Wisdom, Lydia's faithful Heart,
> Martha's just Trust, and Mary's better Part."

Those who now possess the houses and lands of the ancient inhabitants of Newark, may have a good title, but some of them seem yet to have to learn that they have not a right to make merchandise of their bones. Young America in sport mutilates the memorials of the founders of this city, unrebuked by men who hope for a part in the resurrection of the just, yet appear to prefer gain to godliness, calculate the value of their graves for building lots, and would gladly appropriate God's acre for a hospital yard and highway, while the public grounds, not allotted by the founders of the city for a sacred purpose, are carefully protected. Is it because those men desired to carry on civil and town affairs according to God and godly government, that these things are so, in this City of Churches?   M. P.

REV. ALEXANDER CAMPBELL.—A paragraph has been going the rounds of the papers, and been copied into this, which states that the Rev. Alexander Campbell, of Bethany, in Brooke county, died in New Orleans on the 27th ult. This is a mistake. The reverend gentleman who died was another and a different person. Alexander Campbell, of Bethany, the distinguished theologian, is not only not dead, but we are glad to learn is enjoying excellent health.—*Richmond Dispatch*, 25 July, 1855.

BLOUNT OF TENNESSEE.

[From papers in possession of Charles H. Morse, Esq.]

Clarksville, March 21, 1852.

Dear Sir—I received your letter making inquiry of the family of William Blount. I regret that I cannot give you as full a history of that family as I ought. My library has been open to my friends for twenty years, and Hayward's History of the State has been taken off, and other publications in relation to its early settlement, so that I have to rely in my statements mainly upon my recollection.

Jacob Blount was a member of the Provincial Assemblies called in 1775 and 1776, from Newbern, Craven County, and had four sons; and perhaps others, of whom I have not heard. William Blount, the eldest, was a member of the Assembly from Newbern in 1780—was sent to Congress in 1782-3; again to the Assembly in 1784-5, and again to Congress in 1786-7, and signed the Constitution of the United States. He was the Territorial Governor of Tennessee until the State was formed in 1796. He was then elected to the United States Senate, from which he was expelled in 1797 or '98, for an attempt to excite the Indians against the Spanish in Florida. I am unable to give you any of the particulars of the trial. Shortly after he left our State, and is said to have died in the Indian Nations, either in Georgia or Southern Alabama. (Died at Knoxville, 26 March, 1800, aged 56 years?) I knew two of his sons; William G. Blount, who was a member of Congress from Knoxville in 1827, shortly afterward removed to Paris, in the western district of Tennessee, and died without ever having been married. His other son was Richard G. Blount, who lived many years in this county; was exceedingly intemperate, spent his fortune and took his family off about twelve years ago to the Western District. In 1844 I last saw him at a little village called Yorke, where he was keeping a country school. He had some daughters also, one of whom was married to Gen. Gaines, and had several children. Two other brothers, John Gray Blount and Thomas Blount, continued in North Carolina, were said to be wealthy, large landholders in this State; and the latter was a member of Congress for six or eight years. The other brother, Willie Blount, came to Tennessee with William, and was his Secretary during the time he was Territorial Governor, and after removed to Montgomery County, Tennessee, where he married the daughter of Major Baker, a revolutionary officer, and was soon returned to the Legislature, and in the year 1809 was elected Governor of the State, and continued so until after the war of 1812; having served three successive terms, he retired with great popularity. In 1834 he was elected to the Convention that revised the Constitution of the State. He only had two daughters; one married Dr. Dabney, the other John B. Dortch. My wife's brother, both the girls and their husbands are dead; Dortch leaving two sons, Willie B. Dortch, now residing at Helena, Arkansas, the other near Port Royal, in this county. The oldest married the daughter of Gov. A. V. Brown, and the other married the daughter of Dr. Warfield, of Lexington. The Dabneys left daughters, all now dead; one leaving an infant. It is hardly probable that you could get any satisfactory information from any of the parties mentioned. Willie B. and John B. were infants at the death of their grandfather, Willie Blount, and of their father. Gov. Willie Blount died at the house of my brother, near this place, September 10, 1835, aged 68 years, whilst I was in Washington, leaving several large manuscript volumes in relation to the early history of the State, which my brother, not having leisure to examine, and not much taste for such things, handed them over to Dr. J. G. M. Ramsey, who resides at Mechlenburgh, Knox County, in this State, and is now understood to be engaged in preparing a full history of the State. I would refer you to him as the best source, from which to get information in relation to Gov. William Blount, who resided in or near the town of Knoxville. I have no reliable information in relation to the conspiracy, but you will perceive that the odium attached to it never affected the popularity of his brother and secretary, nor of his son or other members of his family. I imagine his object was to get up a war between the Indians and Spaniards, which would enable the United States to buy Florida, or compel them to take it. Such I find to have been the impression left on the minds of the early settlers. I imagine if you can get access to the American State Papers, published some years ago by Gales & Seaton, Title, Indian Affairs, you would find an account of it. The documentary History now publishing by Blair & Rives, should have progressed far enough by this time, to give us the whole of the papers in the offices at Washington connected with the conspiracy.

I am respectfully,

Your friend and servant,

C. JOHNSON.

Joseph B. Boyd, Esq., Maysville, Kentucky.

A REMARKABLE MAN.

A correspondent of the Kentucky Statesman, under date of November 26, 1855, gives the following sketch of an old citizen in Pulaski county, named Elijah Deny, who is perhaps the oldest man in Kentucky.

"He was 116 years of age on the 10th of September, and is as active as many men at forty. He works daily upon a farm, and throughout his whole life he has been an early riser. He informed the writer that he had never drank but one cup of coffee, and that was in the year 1848. He served seven years in the war of the Revolution, and was wounded at the siege of Charleston; he was also at the siege of Savannah, and at the battle of Eutaw Springs.

He was also present at the battles of Camden, King's Mountain, and Monk's Corner. He served under Col. Horry and Col. Mason, and was an eye witness of the sufferings and death of Col. Isaac Hayne, of South Carolina, an early victim of the revolution. He is sprightly and active, and would be taken at any time to be a man of middle age. He is a strict member of the Baptist church, and rides six miles to every meeting of his church. He has four sons and five daughters, all living, the eldest being now in his seventy-eighth, and the youngest in his fifty-first year. Such is a brief sketch of this aged soldier and republican, who is perhaps the only surviving soldier of Francis Marion, Sumpter and Horry."

Newbury 27 July, 1857.

DEAR SIR,

The following is an exact copy of an original document in the hand-writing of Tristram Coffyn senior which you may publish if you please, and oblige

Yours truly,
JOSHUA COFFIN.

"The Twentye first day of June 1660.

"These presents Doe wittnis yᵗ I Peeter folger of *Martaines vinyard
-did upon The Request of Tristram Coffyn Senior And with The Consent
-of Pattacohaunet, Sachem of tuckanuck devid The Island of Tuckanuck as
-followeth : The line Is to Run from a littell Round hill yᵗ lyeth a littell
-above the head of The pond yᵗ Is att The East Sid of the Iland ; And
-so to goe By the East northeast poynt of the Compas to The west South-
-west End of The Iland, And The Aforesaid Tristram Coffyn Senior Is
-to have The South Sid of The Iland according to This line And
-Pattacohaunet Is to have The North Sid.   Witness my hand

    Witness   Edward Sturbuck   Peter folger.
    Witness   Thomey Trappe

[*On the 21st of May, 1603, Gosnold having overshot the Vineyard Sound in the night, discovered an island which he named Martha's Vineyard. Not that since so called, but a small one, known as Nomansland, lying very near the southern extremity of the large island, since called Martha's Vineyard. Gosnold took the great island to be a part of the main land, but when it was found to be an island, the name conferred on its appendage, very naturally extended to it, and the name Martha's Vineyard has continued since the time of this discoverer.

*That the name *Martha's Vineyard* should be *Martin's Vineyard*, as some have surmised, is to be utterly rejected. The name was conferred by Gosnold himself, a year before the voyage of Pring. Why the name *Martha* was chosen is not known. It may have been the name of his own lady, or some other valued female acquaintance. Capt. Pring's christian name being *Martin*, it is easy to see how the surmise arose." *Hist. & Antiquities Boston.* p. 14.—*Editor.*]

REMARKABLE. — Died in Charleston, S. C., *Mrs. Ann Gourlay*, aged 99. Mrs. Gourlay has been a widow for half a century, and has outlived all her children and grandchildren, except one. In early life, at a hall in Maryland, her native state, she had danced with Gen. Washington, and perhaps was the last female in the United States who could claim this honor. All the acquaintance of not only her early days, but of maturer life, have long since been cut off by death ; and she has been for many years a stranger in the land, not only of her fathers, but even of her children. — *Paper of 1846.*

* If Martha's Vineyard was originally called Martin's Vineyard and so named, as it is said in honor of Martin Pring, when, why, and by whom was Martha substituted for Martin ! — *Editor.*

CHURCH RECORDS OF FARMINGTON IN CONNECTICUT.

Copied by the late Hon. Nathaniel Goodwin of Hartford.   Communicated by Daniel
Goodwin, Esquire.

[Continued from p. 328.]

John Norton's Children.

John Norton joined to our Church in October, 1661.

Hannah Norton, daughter of John Norton, aged about 12, baptized here,
immediately after her father's joining above mentioned.

Dorothy Norton, daughter of John Norton, aged about 10, was baptized
at the same time.

John Norton, aged about 8 years, was baptized at the same time.

Thomas Norton, son of John Norton, aged about 18 months, was baptized
at the same time.

Elizabeth Orvis, her Children.

Elizabeth Carpenter, was baptized on May 16, 1658, being aged about
14 years.

David Carpenter, baptized at the same time, aged about 11 years.

Mary Carpenter, baptized also, born August, 1650.

Samuel Orvis, born May, 1653,—baptized immediately after his mother's
entering into the Church.

Hannah Orvis, born in April, 1655.

Roger Orvis, born June, 1657.

Ebenezer Orvis, born February, 1659.

Margaret Orvis, born June, 1661.

Mary Orvis, born June, 1663.

All these were baptized here in Farmington;—the particular times at
which they were baptized, not easily to be come at.

John Lee.

John Lee and his wife Mary Lee, joined to the Church, anno : 1660.

John Lee, his son, born June 11, 1659.

Mary Lee, born August 14, 1664.

Stephen Lee, born April 2, 1667.

These 8 above-mentioned children, were baptized here.

John Wyatt.

Mary Wyatt, the wife of John Wyatt, was joined to the Church of Farmington, October 9, 1653.

Mary Wyatt, Jun., was baptized October 23, 1653, aged about 6 years.

John Wyatt, the same day, aged about 4 years.

Hepzibah Wyatt, the same day, aged about one year.

Dorcas Wyatt, together with the rest that follow, were baptized here ;
but the time of their baptism not registered. Their age may be computed
thus :—

Dorcas Wyatt, was 13 years of age, anno : 1668.

Sarah Wyatt, 9 years of age, anno : 1668.

Joanna Wyatt, 5 years of age, anno : 1662.
Elizabeth Wyatt, 3 years of age, anno : 1668.

Daniel Andrews.

Daniel Andrews, the son of Daniel Andrews, born March 9, ⅝,—baptized July 20, 1673.
Mary Andrews, born December 9, 1674. Baptized immediately after.
Joseph Andrews, born August 10, 1676. Baptized speedily after.
John Andrews, born June 10, 1680. Quickly after, baptized.
Martha Andrews, born July 17, 1682. Baptized soon after.

The Children of John Standley, Jun.

Esther Stanley, born December 2, 1674. Baptized immediately after.
John Standley, born April 9, 1675. Baptized immediately after.

The number of such as are in full Communion in the Church in Farmington, March 1, ⅚⅞.
1. Deacon Hart.
2. Deacon Judd.
3. Thomas Newell and his wife.
4. Capt. Standley and his wife.
5. Robert Porter.
6. Thomas Porter, senior, and his wife.
7. Richard Bronson, and his wife.
8. John Langton and his wife.
9. Thomas Barnes and his wife.
10. Moses Ventrus.
11. William Lewis, Jun., and his wife.
12. Thomas Orton, and his wife.
13. John North, senior and his wife.
14. John Andrews, senior, and his wife.
15. Isaac Moore and his wife.
16. John Norton, senior, and his wife.
17. Mr. Wrotham.
18. Samuel Hooker and his wife.
19. John Lee, and his wife.
20. William Judd, and his wife.
21. John Wadsworth and his wife.
22. Matthew Woodruff, Jun. and his wife.
23. Stephen Hart, Jun.
24. Samuel Coules and his wife.
25. John Root, senior, and his wife.
26. John Judd and his wife.
27. Thomas Hart and his wife.
28. John Thompson and his wife.
29. John Standley, Jun., and his wife.
30. Joseph Bird and his wife.
31. John Case and his wife.
32. Benjamin Judd and his wife.
33. Jo. Woodruff and his wife.
34. Jo Clarke and his wife.
35. Thomas Porter, Jun. and his wife.

36. Thomas Thompson.
37. Thomas Roll and his wife.
38. William Lewis, senior.
39. Jacob Bronson and his wife.
40. James Bird and his wife,
41. Thomas Judd, Jun. and his wife.
42. Obadiah Richards and his wife.
    Mr. Hawkins.
    Samuel Gridley's wife.
    John Orton's wife.
    Samuel North's wife.
    Richard Seymour's wife.
    Joseph Woodford's wife.
    Widow Warner.
    John Norton, Jun's wife.
    Edmund Scott's wife.
    Mehitabel Smith.
    John Warner's wife.
    Thomas Warner's wife.
    Joseph Hickcock's wife.
    Samuel Hickcock's wife.
    John Scovel's wife.

Thomas Gridley, joined to the Church here, Feb'y 6, 1681.

Philip Judd, joined March 6, 1681.

Debora Orvis, wife of Samuel Orvis, joined with the Church here, May 7, 1682.

Elizabeth Newell, wife Thomas Newell, Jun', joined May 14, 1682.

Thomas Porter, son of Robert Porter, joined in full Communion here, August 13, 1682.

The wife of Thomas Gridley, joined the same day.

Sarah Andrews, daughter to Robert Porter, wife of Abraham Andrews, joined in fellowship with us, July 15, 1683.

Isaac Bronson joined with us in full communion, May 25, 1684.

Lydia Smith, the wife of Joseph Smith, joined to us, August 3, 1684.

Richard Seymour joined here, May 31, 1685.

John Hart, and his wife, John Lee, the wife of William Lewis, Jun., Sarah, the wife of Matthew Woodruff, and Rebecca, the wife of Samuel Woodruff, joined here, November 24, 1686.

January 3, 1686. Benjamin Andrews and his wife, Samuel Porter and his wife, the wife of John Lee, Jun., the wife of Joseph (North,) and the wife Joseph (Bacon,) joined with us in full communion.

June 5, 1687. Samuel Newell and Elizabeth Laneton, joined with us in full communion.

December 11, 1687. Jonathan Smith, and the wife of Timothy Stanley, joined to the Church here.

William Lewis, joined to us, May 23, 1688.

John Hooker was added to us, October 13, 1688.

Sarah Barnes, wife of Benjamin Barnes, Mary Newell, wife of Samuel Newell, and Mary Bird, daughter of Joseph Bird, joined in fellowship with the Church here. January 2, 1689.

Joseph Gairlor, (Gaylord) and Mary Upson, daughter to John Lee, joined with us, June 9, 1639.

Joseph North entered full communion with us, May 25, 1690.

The same day, May 23, 1690, were joined to us,
Samuel Smith and his wife.
Samuel Colles and his wife.
The wife of John Orton.
The wife of Ephraim Smith.
The wife of Thomas Hancox.
The wife of Samuel Hooker, and
Susannah Hooker, the relict of William Hooker, and Joseph Barnes.

Thomas Judd, Jun., of Waterbury, joined with us, in full communion July 20, 1690.

Joseph Smith, joined to us, August 3, 1690.

Margaret Hart, relict of Deacon Hart, and Hannah Wadsworth, the wife of Samuel Wadsworth, joined with us March 17, 169½.

Benjamin Barnes and Thomas Judd, son of William Judd, both resident at Waterbury, joined with us, March 22, 169½.

Samuel Wadsworth, Sarah Root, the wife of Stephen Root, and Sarah, the wife of William Higgison, joined with the Church here, May 10, 1691.

Samuel Woodruff and Thomas North joined to us August 5, 1691.

Elizabeth Lewis, the wife of Samuel Lewis, joined to the Church here, September 27, 1691.

Thomas Bird and Mary his wife, joined with us, December 6, 1691.

Abigail Porter, the wife of Thomas Porter, son of Robert Porter, Elizabeth Hart, wife of Thomas Hart, and Sarah Hart, wife of Stephen Hart, joined to the Church here, February 2, 169½.

Thomas Barnes joined to the Church here, March 13, 169½.

Thomas Standley and his wife Anna, Joseph Root and his wife Elizabeth, and the wife of James Lewis, joined to us April 17, 1692.

Daniel Andrews, senior, and John Norton, jun. joined to us in fellowship with the Church here, May 24, 1692.

Mary Root, the wife of John Root, daughter of John Woodruff, joined to the Church here, October 30, 1692.

Elizabeth Thompson, the wife of Thomas Thompson, joined to us, December 7, 1692.

Joseph Woodford, John Cole, and Mary Woodruff, daughter of Matthew Woodruff, joined to us, March 14, 169½.

John Case, of Simsbury, and Thomas Newell, of Farmington, joined July 4, 1693.

Dorothy Moore, the wife of Deacon Moore, joined to the Church here, March 25, 169½.

Isaac Coules and his wife joined to us, August 11, 1696.

The wife of Caleb Root, joined to us March 30, 169½.

John Wadsworth and his wife, Elizabeth,—the wife of John Hooker, and the wife of Joseph Langton, were added to us May 30, 1697.

An account of Children Baptized in the Church of Farmington.

Joseph Lewis, son of Capt. Wm Lewis, baptized March 14, 167½. Born a few days before.

Elizabeth Coules, daughter of Samuel Coules, baptized March 21, 167½.
Obediah Richards, his children baptized March 21, 167½, viz:
John, 12 years of age,
Hannah, aged 8 years, November, 1679.
Mary, aged 10 years, January, 1679.
Esther, aged 6 years, June, 1679.

Elizabeth, 4 years old, July, 1679.

Sarah, 3 years old, April, 1680.

Obadiah, born October 1, 1679.

Elizabeth Steele, daughter of John Steele, baptized March 28, 16 79/80. Born a few days before.

Thomas Hart, son of Ensign Thomas Hart, baptized April 4, 1680. Born a few days before.

Hannah Clark, daughter of ——— Clark, baptized April 1, 1680. Born a few days before.

James Thompson, son of John Thompson, born May 30, 1680. Baptized the same day.

Elizabeth Gaylord, baptized November 21, 1680. Asa Arthur Thompson, son of Thomas Tompson, born October 17, 1680. Baptized speedily after.

Mindwell Bird, child of Joseph Bird, baptized February 27, 16 80/81.

Mary Judd, daughter of John Judd, baptized March 6, 16 80/81.

Philip Judd, son of Philip Judd, baptized March 13, 16 80/81.

Lydia Warner, daughter of John Warner, baptized March 13, 16 80/81.

Dorothy Cole, daughter of John Cole, baptized July 3, 1681. Born two or three days before.

John Gridley, son of Samuel Gridley, January 29, 1681.

Mehitable Bird, daughter of James Bird, March 12, 16 80/81.

John Hart, son of Ensign Thomas Hart, baptized April 23, 1682.

Margaret Woodruff, daughter of John Woodruff, baptized April 28, 1682.

Jonathan Bull, son of Thomas Bull, baptized May 14, 1682.

Benjamin Judd, son of William Judd, baptized at the same time, viz: May 14, 1682.

Deborah Orvis, daughter to Samuel Orvis, baptized May 14, 1682. Born April 17, 1681, or thereabouts.

Thomas Newell, son of Thomas Newell, Jun. baptized May 14, 1682.

John Standley, son of John Standley, of Mattatuck, baptized May 25, 1682.

Caleb Coales, baptized June 25, 1782. Born about five days before.

Daniel Lewis, son of Capt. Lewis, baptized July 16, 1682.

Martha Andrews, daughter of Daniel Andrews, baptized July 23, 1682.

Mary Thompson, daughter of John Thompson, baptized October 1, 1681.

Philoleatheros Thompson, son of Thomas Thompson, baptized November 12, 1682.

Elizabeth Hickcock, daughter to Samuel Hickcock, baptized November 12, 1682.

Susanna Woodford, daughter of Joseph Woodford, baptized December 3, 1682.

Hezekiah Wadsworth, son of mr. John Wadsworth, baptized December 24, 1682.

Mercy Seymour, daughter of Richard Seymour, baptized January 14, 1682.

On the same day that his child was born, the father, viz: Richard Seymour, went early into the woods to look for horses, 5, 6 or 7 miles off; found and followed one homeward:—but like to have perished ere he reached home.

INSCRIPTIONS FROM THE BURYING GROUND IN BRAIN-
TREE, NOW QUINCY.

[Communicated by William S. Pattee, M. D.]

[Continued from page 306, No. 4, 1857.]

1777, — In memory of Edmund Clark, son of Capt. James Clark, and Mary his wife, who died July 13 1777, aged 5 Years.

1799, — In memory of Capt. James Clark, who died Nov. 3 1799 aged 71 Years.

1822, — In memory of Mrs Mary Clark, wife of Capt. James Clark, who died March 1, 1822, aged 89.

> When such pure spirits yield to death,
> No fears the Christian mind Controul,
> 'Tis but resigning mortal breath,
> To reign immortal in the soul.

1827, — In memory of Henry H. Clark, who died July 12 1827, Æt 29.

1766, — Here lies Buried ye Body of Mrs Sarah Hall, wife of Lef. John Hall, who died Feb. the 23 1766, aged 60 Years.

1780, — In memory of Lieu^t John Hall, who died Sept 27 1780 in ye 83 year of his age.

1770, — Here lies Buried Mrs Sarah Vesey, the wife of Mr William Vesey, she died December, 15th 1770, aged 58, Years.

1787, — Here lies Buried the Body of Mr William Vesey, Who died the 23^d of May, 1787 Æt 79.

1802, — Erected in memory of Miss Sarah Vesey, who died July 29th 1802, aged 67 Years.

1802, — Erected in memory of Mr William Vesey, who died Ap^l 7, 1802, aged 63 Years.

1772, — Here lies interred the Body of Mrs Deborah Field, Consort of Mr Benjamin Field, who died Feb. 4, 1772, in the 21 Year of her age.

1790, — In memory of Mrs Mehitable Field, wife of Mr Joseph Field, who died June 23 1790, in ye 42 Year of her age.

1791, — In memory of Polly Brown, Daughter to Captain Samuel and Mrs Susannah Brown, She died May 15th 1791 aged 9 months.

1798, — In memory of Mr Samuel Brown, Junr who died September 29, 1798, Æt 23.

> Stop my Friend Come think on me,
> I once was in the world like thee,
> But now lie slumbering in the dust,
> In hopes to rise amoung the Just.

1794, — In memory of Mr Solomon Thayer, who Died August 8th 1794, aged 36 Years.

1797, — In memory of Susannah, Daughter of Mr Wilson and Susanna Marsh, who died April, 6th 1797 aged 4 Years.

1798, — In memory of Mr Wilson Marsh, who died May 20th 1798, Aged 48 Years.

1799, — In memory of Mrs Abigail Marsh, wife of Mr Wilson Marsh, who died April, 19th 1799, aged 83 Years.

1804. — In memory of Mrs Miriam Marsh, wife of Mr Jonathan Marsh, and daughter, of Mr Moses, and Mrs Pheebe Reed, of Abington, who died May 24 1804, aged 47 Years.

Inscription
Lean not on earth 't will pierce thee to the heart
A broken reed at best, and oft a Spear,
On whose Sharp point peace bleeds, and hope expires.

1814, — In memory of Mr Ambrose Marsh, who died June 25th 1814 aged 24 Years.

1814, — Ambrose son of Mr Jonathan, and Mrs Sophia Marsh, who died December, 15th 1814 aged 6 weeks.

1815, — In memory of Mrs Susannah Marsh, wife of Mr Wilson Marsh, who died June 1, 1815, Æt 50 Years.

1822, — In memory of Mr Jonathan Marsh, who died Nov. 6, 1822, aged 70 Years.

1828, — Sacred to the memory of Mr Wilson Marsh, who died July 7th 1828, aged 78 Years.

1827, — Sacred to the memory of Mrs Sophia Marsh, wife of Mr Jonathan Marsh, and daughter of Mr Seth and Mrs Abigail Spear, who died August 20 1827, Æt 37 Years.

1831, — Erected to the memory of Miss, Anna Marsh, Daughter of Mr Wilson and Mrs Susannah Marsh, who died July 29 1831 Æt 47.

Can the world one joyous thought bestow
To friendship weeping at the Couch of Woe?
No! but a brighter soothes their last adieu.
Soul of impassioned mould, she speaks to you!
Weep not she says, at nature's transient pain,
Congenial spirits part to meet again.

1841, — Sacred to the memory of Mrs Patience Marsh, wife of Mr Jonathan Marsh, formerly wife of Mr Whitman Bailey, and Daughter of Mr Henry and Mrs Elizabeth Crane, who died August 19th 1841, Æt 51 Years.

1845, — Sacred to the memory of Mrs Emily Marsh, wife of Mr Charles Marsh, and Daughter of Mr William, and Mrs Lucy Packard, who died Nov. 11 1845, Æt 25, Years.

In Memory
of
Elisha Marsh
Son of Wilson and
Susanna Marsh
Who Died
April 17th 1847
Aged 65
A kind husband
A firm friend
A valuable Citizen
Erected
By his wife
As a testimonial
of his virtues
And her affectionate
Remembrance.

" Then shall the dust return to the earth as it was : and the spirit shall return to God who gave it."

1855, — Susannah Savill Marsh Daughter of Wilson, and Susannah Marsh who died March 29th 1855 in the sixty first year of her age.*

1798, — In memory of Mrs Deborah Bent, wife of Mr Eben Bent, who died August 17th 1798 Æt 85 Years.

1803, — In memory of Susanna Curtis Daughter of Mr Noah and Mrs Abigail Curtis who died July 4th 1803 aged 1, Year 6, months.

1803, — In memory of Benjamin Curtis, son of Mr Noah, and Mrs Abigail Curtis, who died July 17th 1803, Æt 4 Years.

1804, — In memory of Mrs Abigail Curtis wife of Mr Noah Curtis who died Feb 7th 1804, Æt 29 Years.

1808, — Benjamin Curtis son of Mr Noah and Mrs   Curtis who died Sept. 27th 1808 aged 14 months.

1809, — In memory of Mr Adam Curtis who died Feb 25 1809 Æ 80 Year.

1811, — In memory of Mr Samuel Curtis, who died Jan 28th 1811, Æt 83 Years.

1814, — In memory of Ann Curtis, Daughter of Mr Noah and Mrs Ann Curtis, who died September 20th 1814 Æt 9 months.

1825, — Sacred to the memory of Mrs Elizabeth Curtis, wife of Mr Samuel Curtis who died April 6th 1825 Æt 90 Years.

In memory of Mrs Nelly Wife of Mr Jabez Wilson Died Oct. 11th 1804. Aged 28 Years.	Also Their Daughter Isabella Died Oct. 5th 1804. Aged 6 months.	Also Their Daughter Thirsey Died Oct. 6th 1804. Aged 2 Years.

Here lies a Mother and two Babes,
Who God has Shortly Called to their graves,
In Heaven we hope they are blest,
There to remain in eternal rest.

1807, — Sacred to the memory of Master Ichabod Johnson, celebrated Teacher of musick, who died Aug 5th 1807, aged 42 Years.

And let this feeble body fail,
And let it faint and die,
My soul shall quit this mournful vale,
And soar to worlds on high.
Shall join the disembodied saints,
And find its long sought rest,
That only bliss for which it pants,
In the redeemers breast.

---

* This numerous family of Marsh are the immediate descendants of Mr. Alexander Marsh, who died in 1804.   TRANSCRIBER.

FIRST BOOK EAST HADDAM LAND RECORDS.

[Continued from page 314, No. 4, 1857.]

PAGE 573.

[Th]omas the sone of Thomas ffuller and of Elizebeth his wife was Borne Apriell yᵉ: 5ᵗ: 1717.

Nathan yᵉ sone of Thomas ffuller and of Elizebeth his wife was Borne Apriell yᵉ: 20ᵗʰ: 1719

Hannah the daughter of Thomas fuller and of elizebeth his wife was born march yᵉ 21ˢᵗ: 1720

Jabez the sone of Thomas fuller and of elizebeth his wife was borne february yᵉ: 19: 1722

Jonathan the sone Thomas fuller and of Elizebeth his wife was borne January yᵉ 12ᵗʰ 1723

Elizabeth yᵉ 4ᵗʰ Daughter of Noadiah Brainerd and of hannah his wife Departed this Life June yᵉ 13ᵗʰ: 1733

Sybil yᵉ 5ᵗʰ Daughter of Noadiah Brainerd and of Hannah his [wife] was born June yᵉ: 7ᵗʰ: 1736:

Isaac Crocker and Ann Smith ware Joyned in marrage December yᵉ: 13ᵗʰ: 1718: [*Isaac Crocker was from Barnstable*]

Hannah yᵉ Daughter of Isaac Crocker and of Ann his wife was Born September yᵉ: 22ⁿᵈ: 1719

Ann the daughter of Isaac Crocker and of ann his wife was Born June yᵉ 29th: day 1722

Joseph the Sone of Isaac Crocker and of Ann his wife was born Decembʳ yᵉ 20ᵗʰ 1724

Noadiah Brainerd and Hannah Cone ware Joyned in mariage June yᵉ 4ᵗʰ 1721

hannah yᵉ daughter of Noadiah Brainerd and of hannah his wife was born apriell yᵉ 24ᵗʰ 1725

Jared the Son of Noadiah Brainerd and of Hannah his wife was born Septemᵇʳ yᵉ 17ᵗʰ Day 1739

Mary the davghter of Noadiah Brainerd and of hannah his wife was born apriell yᵉ 27ᵗʰ 1727

Noadiah the sone of noadiah Brainerd and of hannah his wife was borne march yᵉ 10ᵗʰ: 1729

Elizabeth yᵉ 3ᵈ Daughter of Noadiah Brainerd and of Hannah his wife was born August yᵉ: 12ᵗʰ: 1731. Elizabeth yᵉ 3ᵈ Daughter of Noadiah Brainerd and of hannah his wife Departed this Life Janu: yᵉ: 15ᵗʰ 1734

Elizabeth yᵉ 4ᵗʰ Daughter of Noadiah Brainerd and of hannah his wife was Born Jⁿʸ: yᵉ 27ᵗʰ 1734

John Wille and Elizebeth harvy ware Joyned in marrage october 1698

John yᵉ sone of John Wille and of Elizebeth his wife was born may yᵉ 24ᵗʰ   1699

Allin the sone of John Wille and of Elizebeth his wife was born September yᵉ 29ᵗʰ: 1700

Elizebeth the daughter of John Wille and of Elizebeth his wife was born december 29ᵗʰ   1701

mary the daughter of John Wille and of Elizebeth his wife was borne december yᵉ: 13: 1703

Joseph yᵉ sone of John wille and of Elizebeth his wife was born Apriell yᵉ 16ᵗʰ   1705

Lidea yᵉ daughter of John Wille and of Elizebeth his wife was born Apriell yᵉ: 15ᵗʰ: 1707

phebe y⁰ daughter of John Wille and of Elizebeth his wife was borne
January y⁰ : 6 :   1709

mahittabell the daughter of John Wille and of Elizabeth his wife was
born September y⁰ 14 :   1711

Leucretia the daughter of John Wille and of Elizabeth his wife was
borne June y⁰ : 7ᵗʰ   1713

Noah the sone of John Wille and of Elisebeth his wife was borne august
y⁰ 28ᵗʰ   1716

Hannah the daughter of Joseph selden and of Ann his wife was born
march y⁰ 15 : 1727

Elizebeth the daughter of Joseph selden and of Ann his wife was borne
november y⁰ 27ᵗʰ 1722

PAGE 577.

Mr Stephen hosmer & Mrs Sarah Long ware Joyned in marrage September y⁰ 29ᵗʰ 1702

Dorothy the daughter of Mr Stephen hosmer and of Sarah his wife was
born December y⁰ : 6ᵗʰ : 1703

Stephen y⁰ sone of Mr Stephen hosmer and of Sarah his wife was born
apriell y⁰ 24ᵗʰ 1711

Sarah the daughter of Mr Stephen hosmer and of Sarah his wife was
born September y⁰ : 8ᵗʰ : 1713

Zachariah y⁰ sone of Mr Stephen hosmer and of Sarah his wife was
borne January : 25ᵗʰ : 1714

Robert y⁰ sone of Mr Stephen hosmer and of Sarah his wife was borne
march y⁰ : 22ⁿᵈ : 1718

Grace holmes y⁰ daughter of John holmes and of mary his wife was
Borne August y⁰ : 4ᵗʰ 1717

Jonathan y⁰ sone of shuball fuller and of hannah his wife was born
september y⁰ 10ᵗʰ : 1724 : and departed this Life January y⁰ : 19ᵗʰ 1726

Rachell the daughter of shuball fuller and of hannah his wife born
february : 24th 1727

febe the daughter of Thomas Rowle and of mary his wife was born July
the : 13ᵗʰ   1719

Thomas Rowle aboue named departed this life october y⁰ 24ᵗʰ 1719

febe y⁰ aboue named y⁰ daughter of y⁰ aboue sd Thomas Rowle departed
this Life may y⁰ : 8ᵗʰ : 1719(20

PAGE 578.

Shuball ffuller and hannah Crocker ware Joyned in marrage December
y⁰ , 7ᵗʰ : 1708

Lydia the daughter of Shuball ffuller and of hannah his wife was borne
Septem' y⁰ first 1709

Ephraim y⁰ sone of Shuball ffuller and of hannah his wife was born september y⁰ : 8ᵗʰ : 1711

Thankfull y⁰ daughter of Shuball ffuller and of hannah his wife was born
July y⁰ : 10ᵗʰ : 1713

Zurviah y⁰ daughter of Shuball ffuller and of hannah his wife was born
march y⁰ : 29ᵗʰ : 1716 :

hannah y⁰ daughter of Shuball ffuller and of hannah his wife was born
Apriell y⁰ 29ᵗʰ : 1718

Shubale the sone of Shubale fuller and of hannah his wife was borne
January y⁰ 6ᵗʰ 1720(21

Richard purple and hannah Spencer ware Joyned in marrage September
y⁰ 20ᵗʰ 1717

Hannah the Daughter of Richard purple and of hannah his wife was Born march y⁰ 3ᵈ: 1719

Richard the sone of Richard purple and of hannah his wife was born march y⁰ 28ᵗʰ: 1721

Sarah y⁰ daughter of Richard purple and of hannah his wife was born apriell y⁰ 13: 1723

Esther the Daughter of Richard purple and of hannah his wife was born may y⁰ 3ᵈ 1725

Dauid the sone of Richard purple and of hannah his wife was born January y⁰: 17ᵗʰ: 1728(9

William Booge and dorithy Lord ware Joyned in marriage December y⁰: 6ᵗʰ 1720

Samuell y⁰ son of William Booge and of dorithy his wife was Born Sept⁰ʳ y⁰ 27ᵗʰ 1721

The sᵈ Samuell Booge departed this Life february y⁰ 10 day 172¼

PAGE 579.

[Torn off] e ye daughter of Jams ackle and of elizebeth his [w]ife was borne febeuary y⁰ 24ᵗʰ 1717(18

Elizebeth y⁰ Daughter of James Acley and of Elizebeth his wife was borne January y⁰: 16ᵗʰ; 1721(22

John y⁰ Son of Thomas Hungerford and of Elisebeth his Wife was Born March y⁰: 4ᵗʰ Day: 1718

Samuell olmsted and mary Rowle Joyned in marriage in y⁰ year 1697

Sarah y⁰ daughter of Samuell olmsted and of mary his wife was borne in y⁰ year 1699: in the: 29: day

mary y⁰ daughter of Samuell olmsted and of mary his wife was borne September y⁰ 18ᵗʰ: 1701

Samuell y⁰ sone of Samuell olmsted and of mary his wife was borne September y⁰: 8ᵗʰ: 1703

William y⁰ sone of Samuell olmsted and of mary his wife was borne nouember y⁰: 21ˢᵗ: 1705:

Sarah y⁰ daughter of Samuell olmsted and of mary his wife departed this life may y⁰: 10ᵗʰ: 1704

Jonathan y⁰ sone of Samuel olmsted and of mary his wife was borne Nouember y⁰: 9ᵗʰ: 1707

Dorraty y⁰ daughter of Samuell olmsted and of mary his wife was borne march y⁰: 21ˢᵗ: 1715

Abygall y⁰ daughter of Samuell olmsted and of mary his wife was borne in June y⁰: 10ᵗʰ: in y⁰ year 1716.

y⁰ Remainder is in the 3ᵈ book

Nemliah y⁰ sone of John warner and of mahittable his wife was born Janvary y⁰ 12ᵗʰ 1728(9

Joseph y⁰ son of John warner and of mahlttable his wife was born January y⁰ 13ᵗʰ 1731

PAGE 580.

Hannah the daughter of Lev⁰ Thomas Kno[ulton] and of Susanah his wife was borne may y⁰ 5ᵗʰ 1[torn off]

Hannah the daughter of John pick and of hannah his wife was born apriell y⁰: 13ᵗʰ: 1717

mary the davghter of Richard Skinner and of hannah his wife was born argust y⁰: 3ᵈ: 1725

Thomas the sone of Richard skiner and of hannah his wife died Janvary y⁰ 18ᵗʰ 1725(6

Richard the sone of Richard Skinner and of hannah his wife died January y 31 : 1725(6

mary the davghter of Richard Skinner and of hannah his wife died october y 21 : 1728

Ebenezer y Sone of Richard Skinner afores^d was borne october y: 22^d : 1728

Richard y son of Richard Skinner and of hannah his wife was borne January y 16: 1716: (17

Elizebeth the daughter of Richard Skinner and of hannah his wife was borne may y 20th : 1719

Thomas y sone of Richard Skinner and of hannah his wife was born september y: 11 : th 1722

John warner and mahittabell Richardson ware Joyned in marrage march y 21st: 1716 :

John the sone of John warner and of mahittabell his wife was borne December y: 19th: 1716

Daniell y sone of John warner and of mahittabell his wife was borne may y: 6th: 1717 [Quick work]

Nathaniell y sone of John warner and of mahittabell his wife was Born December y: 25: 1718

Jabez the sone of John warner and of mahittabell his wife was born November y 25: 1720

Lemuell y sone of Lemvell Richardson deceased and of mahitabell his wife departed this life march y: 9th: 1722

Elizebeth y davghter of John warner and of mahittabel his his wife was born Janvary y 25th 1724(5

Abraham the sone of John warner and mahittabel his wife was born february y 13th 1725(6

PAGE 581.

[Jer]emiah Selby and Susanah Dutton was Joyned in marrage June y 12th 1716

William y sone of Jeremiah Selby and of Susannah his wife was born June y: 5th : 1717

Susannah the wife of Jeremiah Selby departed this life may y: 3^d : 1718

Ebenezer Rolla the sone of William Rollo and of patience his wife was born feberary the 20th day 1717

John the sone of William Rollo and of patience his wife borne feberary y: 21st: 1720

Daniell Brainerd Ju Departed this Life September y: 28th: 1728

Hannah y Daughter of Daniel Brainerd Ju and of hannah his Wife was Borne april y: 17th 1729

Daniell Brainerd and hannah Seldin was Joyned in marrage feberay y second day 1715

Susannah the Daughter of Daniell Brainerd & of hannah his wife was borne November y 27th: 1716

Susannah y Daughter of Daniel Brainerd Junr and of Hannah his wife Departed this Life Sepr y 14th Day Anney Dom. 1751 :

hannah y daughter of Daniell Brainerd and of hannah his wife was borne November y: 28 : 1718

Daniell y sone of Daniell Brainerd and of hannah his wife was born february y 24th 1721(2

mary the Daughter of Daniell Brainerd and of hannah his wife was borne September y 24th 1723 :

Susanah the daughter of Daniell Brainerd Jun' was born august (9ᵗʰ) 1726

Three daughters of Daniel Brainerd Jun' departed this life february 1726 : mary the second day : Susanah yᵉ tenth day, and hannah the : 17ᵗʰ day : of the aboue sd month

Page 582.

Giddian the sone of James ackly was [born] aprie}l the 14ᵗʰ 1716

Bennjoh yᵉ Sun of James Ackley and of Elizabeth his Wife was Born July yᵉ 10ᵗʰ Day Anno Dom : 1729

Daniel Gates Departed this Life Nouember yᵉ 24ᵗʰ : 1761

Joseph the sone of nathaniell Beckwith and of Sarah his wife was born december yᵉ : 11ᵗʰ 1715

Elizebeth the daughter of Joseph Seldin and of Ann his wife was born November yᵉ 27ᵗʰ 1722

Joseph yᵉ sone of Daniell Gates was borne september the 7ᵗʰ : 1716

mary the daughter of Daniell Gates was Borne march yᵉ 29 : 1719

Joseph Selden and Ann Chapman ware Joyned in marrage decem' yᵉ 19 1706

Rebecah the daughter of Joseph Seldin Ju' and of ann his wife was borne July the 9ᵗʰ 1717

Eliakim yᵉ sone of Joseph Selden and of ann his wife was Born september yᵉ : 13ᵗʰ 1718

Ann the daughter of Joseph Seldin and of Ann his wife was born September yᵉ : 5 : 1720

Thankfull the daughter of Jabes Chapman and of easter his wife was borne august the 2' : 1715

Ruth yᵉ daughter of Daniell Gates and of Rebecka his wife was born yᵉ : 10ᵗʰ : day of august 1721

Ephraim the sone of Daniell gates and of Rebecka his wife was borne august yᵉ 18ᵗʰ 1724

Judah the sone of daniell gates and of Rebecka his wife was born august yᵉ : 2ᵈ : 1727

Page 583.

[John] Church and Elizebeth olmsted was Joyned [in] mariage feberary yᵉ : 5ᵗʰ : 1707 :

John yᵉ Sone of John church and of elizebeth his wife was borne July : 29ᵗʰ : 1711

mehittabell the daughter of John Church and of elizebeth his wife was [born] March yᵉ 7. 1714

William yᵉ sone of John Church and of elizebeth his wife was borne nouember yᵉ : 7ᵗʰ : 1716

Samvell yᵉ sone of John Church and of elizebeth his wife was borne July yᵉ : 5ᵗʰ : 1720

Sarah yᵉ daughter of John Church and of Elizebeth his wife was borne July yᵉ : 4ᵗʰ 1724

Joseph yᵉ sone of John Church and of Elizabeth his wife was borne January yᵉ 14ᵗʰ 1726

Elizabeth yᵉ Daughter of John Church and of Elizabeth his Wife was born august yᵉ : 8ᵗʰ 1709 [Query 1729]

Rachel yᵉ Daughter of John Church and of Elizabeth his Wife was Born September yᵉ 5ᵗʰ 1752

Elizebeth the daughter of Samuell andrus and of ellena his wife was borne aprie}l yᵉ : 15ᵗʰ : 1717

Ezra the sone of Samuell Andrus and of ellena his wife was Borne october y⁰ : 24ᵗʰ : 1718

Thomas the sone of Samuell Andrus and of elena his wife was borne march y⁰ third day 1720

Elizabeth y⁰ Daughter of Samᵘ Andrews and of Elena his wife departed this Life December y⁰ 24ᵗʰ 1751

Robert chapman and mary curch [Church] were Joyned in marriage march y⁰ 17ᵗʰ : 1726 ;

mary the daughter of Robert chapman was born January y⁰ 9ᵗʰ : 1726(7

Sarah the daughter of Robert chapman was born December y⁰ 8ᵈ : 1728

Deborah y⁰ Daughter of Robert Chapman & of mary his wife was Born october y⁰ 14ᵗʰ 1730

Hannah y⁰ Daughter of Robert Chapman & of mary his wife was born march y⁰ 26ᵗʰ 1733.

Look for y⁰ Remainder in the 5ᵗʰ Book Last End

PAGE 584.

Thomas knowlton Junʳ and Susanah Coud w[ere joined] In marrage December the 24ᵗʰ : 1724

James spencer and hannah Crippen was Joyned in ma[rriage] January y⁰ 14ᵗʰ : 1720

mary y⁰ daughtur of James Spencer and of hannah his wife was born september y⁰ 10ᵗʰ : 1722

hannah y⁰ daughter of James Spencer and of hannah his wife was born december y⁰ : 2ᵈ : 1724

micajah Spencer and Sarah Booge ware Joyned in marrage December y⁰ 27ᵗʰ 1722

Jonathan the son of micajah Spencer and Sarah his wife was borne November y⁰ : 4ᵗʰ 1723

Jedidiah the Son of micajah Spencer and of Sarah his [wife] was born January y⁰ 30ᵗʰ : 1725(6

Rachel the Daughter of micajah Spencer and sarah his [wife] was born march y⁰ 6ᵗʰ : 1726

Gideon the Sone of micajah Spencer and of Sarah his wife was born January y⁰ : 21ˢᵗ : 1729(30

Samuell dutton and Rachill Cone ware Joyned in marrage November y⁰ 17ᵗʰ 1726

Rachill y⁰ davghter of Samuell dutton and of Rachiel his wife was borne novemᵇʳ y⁰ 6ᵈ 1727

Samvell y⁰ Sone of Samvell dutton and of Rachlell his wife was born July y⁰ 27ᵗʰ 1729

Joseph y⁰ Sone of Samvell dutton and of Rachcell his wife was born June y⁰ 27ᵗʰ 1731

Ebenexer y⁰ son of samvell Dutton and of Rachell his wife was born January 22 1733

[The end of Records of births, marriages and deaths in the First Book of Land Records in East Haddam, Ct. Copied by D. Williams Patterson.]

East Haddam, Conn. Feb. 20, 1857.

I hereby certify that I have this day examined and compared with the original records, the foregoing copies made by D. Williams Patterson, and contained in seven sheets, to each of which I have attached my certificate, and that they are true copies of all the original records of births, marriages, and deaths contained in the first book of East Haddam land records.
                                        ALFRED GATES,
                                              Town Clerk.

ABSTRACT FROM THE EARLIEST WILLS ON RECORD IN THE COUNTY OF SUFFOLK, MASS.

[Continued from page 175.]

ALLICE GREEGSS, of Boston. Will. 20th: 5: 1662. Being now sick, In case my son. *James Greegss*, Come not, my will is that I giue to my grand Child, *William King*, one half of the ground, that half the barnes stands on, by the *Widow plantons* [Blantons ?] ground, and my will is, that my dau. *Sarah Hargiss*, shall haue the new end of the house and three rodd broad quite throw the loatt, alsoe the other old end of the house and the rest of all the ground belonging to it. My will is, that it shall be equally giuen to my daughters children; and my dau. *Sarah Burgiss*, shall haue the Cow, & in Case the Cow haue a Calfe the said *Sarah Hargiss*, is to keep him 5 werks and then to giue it vp to her sister, *Ann Joaness*. And all the rest of the moueables, wich are nott in my husbands will, due I giue equally to my tow dau' and to their Children, and my dau. *Sarah* is to haue the Better partt wich is to the vallue of 40s. 20 : 5 : mo. 1662

Witness to these.   Alice + Greegss.

Gamaliell Waite, Richard Price.

Richard + Gredle.

1 May 1663. Power of Administration to the estate of the late *Alice Griggs* is Granted to *Robert Lattimore*, in right of *Anne*, his wife, & to *Roger Burgis*, In right of *Sarah*, his wife, daughter to yt late *Alice Griggs*, according to the Imperfect will on the other side as their Guide.

         Edw. Rawson Recorder.

' Inventory of the goods and Chattels of *Alice Greegss*, widdow, deceased 26th 5th mo. 1663, prised by *Rich Gridley. Henry Allen*, 1 May 1663.

At a Meeting of the Magistrates and Recorder In Boston 5th Sep' 1665, (present *Fra. Willoughby* Esq' Dep' Gov', *Maj'r Leverett* & Recorder.)

Whereas *George Griggs*, Late of Boston by His Last will and testament gaue unto His sonne, *James Grigges*, his House & Ground about it, with the two acres of Land at Long Island, as also a Feather bed, Bolster, as in that will Date 4 July 1655 & prooued in Court 3 Aug' 1660, since when, *Alice Grigges*, His Widdowe, tooke vpon her to Make Her will & therein to make Diuision of the House and Ground amongst Her Daughters & their Children, on which the Courte 1 of May 1663 graunted Administration to the estate of the Late *Alice Grigges* to *Robert Lattimore* in Right of *Anne*, his Wife, & *Roger Burgisse*, in Right of *Sarah*, his wife, ordering the Imperfect Will of said *Alice Grigges* to bee their guide, since when, *Sarah Burgis*, Being Deceased, & *Robert Lattimore*, & *Ann* his Wife, Objecting against the Mothers Diuision and power to Make it, & no Certaine Information of the Death of the said *James Grigges*, though her hath Been absent for many yeares, & most probable that her is Dead, not being heard of for seuerall yeares.

The Magistrates Judged it meet to Graunt administration to the estate of *James Grigges*, to *Robert Lattimore*, in Right of *Anne*, his wife, & the Children of her Bodye, by her former & this Husband, to their vse & benefitte, & also to *Roger Burges*, in right of the children of *Sarah*, His laie wife, & her former Child, *William King*, and the children he Himselfe had by *Sarah*, His wife, in equall proportions. The House, Lands & goods of the s^d *James Grigges*, to be equally Diuided to the said *Robert Lattimore* & *Roger Burges* in Right & for the Benefitte of their seuerall Children as aboue, they giuing their owne Bonds, to value of £80 apeice, & obliging their seuerall Diuisions of Land & Housinge, to the Recorder of this Countye, on Condition that in case *James Grigges* shall euer appear in this Countery & Challenge His Just Right, they shall Respond the same to Him. And it is Desyred that *Ensigne John Hull* & *Richard Gridley* make a Just & equall Diuision of the Houseing, Lands & goods for the ends aforesaid & signifye the same to the Record^r to bee Recorded.

Edward Rawson Record^r.

[*Richard Gridlae* and *Henry Russ*, at the request of *Roger Burgisse* and *Anne Latimer*, prized a few articles, Amount £1. 18^s, Sep^t 6th 1665.

To this inventory *Roger Burgisse* " Deposed on his Corporall Oath," the same day.]

Boston Septemb^r 6th, 1665.

Wee whose names are heerunto subscribed, being appointed to Diuide a House & Land & Betwixt *Roger Burgesse*, in Behalfe of the Children of *Sarah*, his Late wife, Deceased, And *Robert Lattimore*, in behalfe of *Anne*, his said Wife & her Children, haue appointed as Followeth (uiz.) That *Roger Burgesse* shall haue for his part, the Dwelling house, & the East part of the Land, being in front to the Towne street, on the north, about 79 Foote. And Likewise Fronting on the towne Common to the East, 162 foot, & on the south, Bounded by the Land set out to s^d *Robert Lattimore* 150 Foote. The said *Robert* hath his p'tion appointed, fronting northward to the towne streete, about 98 foote, And on the west, Bounded by the Land of Widow *Phebe Mansen*, about 310 foote, And Southward by the towne Lane, about 268 foote, the Easterne & other northern side of the said Land abutteth vpon the Land of the s^d *Roger Burgesse* aboue expressed. All Being by Consent of all the said p'ties, who Haue likewise heervnto subscribed. And for the other small portion of goods being some Few tooles, a bed Blankett, Couerlead & Table, being Formerly all Valued but at 44^s, the said parties concerned haue ordered their parts to their Owne Content, This Being the summe of what seemeth necessarye relating to the premises, & the trust now Committed onto as by the Honoured Court, Wee make this o' Returne to y^r Worshippes now sitting in Court.

Resting y^r Humble Servants
{ *John Hull*,
{ *Richard* X *Gredler*.

The two Acres at Long Island is
Likewise by Consent to bee Kept   Consented as   { *Robert Lattimore*
Between Both P'artyes, not so   abous^d p'os.   { *Roger Burgess*.
Meete to Diuide.

HENRY BLAGUE. Inventry of the Goods, Chattells & Creditts of *Henry Blague*, of Boston, Brickburner, deceased, praised 2 Aug. 1662 by *Richard Collacott*, *Samuell Sendall*, and *Richard Gridley*. Am^t £461.12.09.

19 Aug. 1662. Power of Administration to the Estate of Henry Blague granted to *Elizabeth*, his Relict, in behalfe of herselfe & seven children. She deposed the same day.

4

JOHN JARVIS. Sep' 26, 1656. Inventorye of the Estate & wrightings of *Mr. John Jarvis*, deceased, being taken according to order of Co'——as also wrightings of other Gentlemen left in his Custody, w'h after viewing were delivered To the s'd Gentlemen. Imprimis—wrightings of *Mr. Rob't Patteshalls*, viz. Two Journalls, one Invoice booke, Two Ledgers, as also severall other Loose acco'' & bills of Lading belonging or referring to the s'd bookes, all w'h were delivered To the s'd *Mr. Rob't Patteshal*, "wompom & pege in the Hands of *Ann Carter*, about Eleven shillings." Whole am' of Inventory, £24.14.3½.

"Debtes owing by *Mr. Jno Jarvis*.—To *Wm. Blanten* for Diet 24 Weekes at 7' p' weeke," &c. &c. whole am' of debts, £19.06.09.

ELIAS PARKMAN. Inventory of the estate of Elias Parkman supposed to be deceased 28 of July 1662, prised p' *William Bartholomew*, *Thomas Rallings*, who deposed 30 : 5 : '62.　　　　　　　p' *Eliazer Lusher*.

Boston 20 Aug. 1662. One Request of *Bridget Parkman*, Relict of *Ellias Parkman*, of Boston, senio' & her Eldest sonne, as she affirmed, power of Administracon to the Estate of s'd *Ellias Parkman* is granted to *Thomas Rawlings*, in behalfe of the Children & Credito'', allowing the widdow her thirds in house & Lands, and the flocke bedd Rugg to value 2'b 10', s'd *Rawlings* Giving security to the Record' to Administer according to Law.　　　　　　　Edw: Rawson Record'.

[*Rallings* bond is on file, dated 25 Aug. 1662. Am' £32. Witnessed by *Joseph Hills, John Ferniside*.]

WILLIAM ROBINSON.—12 Sep' 1662. Pow' of Administracon ("to the Estate of *Wm. Robinson*, Late of *Barmudas*") is Granted to *Wm. Pearse*, in behalfe of the wife of said *Robbinson* & theire Children, & for paym' of his debts, &c.

William Robinson, of *Barmodus*, departed this life the third day of Sep'br 1662, in Boston in New England, having due to him the one third part of Twenty Barrells of Mackerell in partnership with *Richard Moore* and *Rich'd Toowills*, fishermen, the w'th share all charges of Boat hier, Salt Caske & bread deducted his partners value at £4.10' &c. Sum total £8.3' 2'.

Estate Deb' to *Richard Moore* & *Richard Toowill* for money Lent & provisions to him at the Eastward, 8' 9'; to *John Bateman*, for Indian dishes w'th he carryed to *Barmodus*, 6'; to said *Bateman* for goods out of his shop, 18'; to *William Pearse* for dyett; to Phisick to *Mr. Hale* and *Mr. Stone*, to Candle light in time of sickness; to Heare to them that Stretcht him forth; to the Pitman & toleing the Bell; wyne at his burryall, recording his death, money Lent him by *An Pearse*, &c. Whole am' £4. 13' 6'. Remains to ballance £3 09' 09'. *William Pearse* bound in the sum of £8 to Administer on the Estate.

JOHN HAZARD. Inventory of the Goods of *John Hazard*, who is supposed to be Cast away by shipwracke in *Mr. Hannifords* shipp. Prised y' 4'th of y' 7'm (62) by *Richard Gridly*, & *Henry Allen*.

10 ; 7'br (62.) Administracon to the Estate of *John Hazard* Granted to *Mary*, his Relict, who deposed.

RICHARD FLOOD. Inventory of the Estate of *Richard Flood*, deceased, prised 8 : 7'm 1662 by *Henry Allen*, and *Edward Drinker*. Am' £26 5' 6'.

Power of Administracon to the estate of the late *Rich'd Flood* Granted to *Joseph Gridly*, who marryed *Lydia*, the Relict of said *Rich'd Flood*.

The Court also ordered that the s⁴ *Joseph Gridly*, for his keeping the 2 Children of *Rich'd Flood* & his pᵗ of the Estate in Right of his wife, the said *Joseph* shall have the house & Land & all ther the Estate, he paying the fower Children of s⁴ *Floods* £4 apeece at age of 21 years. Reserving liberty to one or other of the children on theire being at Age to pay the said *Joseph Gridly* £22 in behalfe of himselfe & brothˢ, the s⁴ house to be theirs, otherwise not.

                                                    Edw: Rawson Record'.

)Then follows a list of "Things that are Left & not seene, but only Judged at from theire reports to vs."(

DAVID KELLY. Power of Administracon to the Estate of the Late *David Kellie* is Granted to *Elizabeth*, his Late wife, in behalfe of her selfe & children.

Inventory of the Estate taken by *Richard Davenport, Elias Maverick*, 22ᵗ 8ᵐ 1662. Amᵗ £286 5ˢ. *Elizabeth Kelly* Relict, deposed, 23 Oct. 1662.

At a County Court held at Boston 29ᵗʰ July 1663, *Elizabeth Kelly* sent in a Copie of hir husbands Inventᵒ'y & desireing a Just division of the estate, the house being burnt & much Goods, the Court on hir request mad yᵉ ordeʳ.

It being sufficently knowne that the house wherein the said *Elizabeth Kelly* lived tooke fier in the day time & was so furious in its burning, before help Could Come, as consumed at least fifty pounds of the goods in the Inventory Exprest, the which the Court Considering, on the motion of the Widdow for a Just division of that Estate. It is ordered that the fifty pounds in Goods mentioned, be deducted from the principle some, & the Widdow be allowed one third part of what Remaines, the rest to be divided amongst the fine children, the Eldest sonne to have a double portion, the rest, part & part alike.)Said Elizabeth with the house & land, in Boston, bound, for the security of the children's portion.(

SAMUEL ROBINSON. Inventory of the Chattells & Estate of *Samuell Robinson*, prized by *James Johnson, & John Lake*, 29ᵗʰ July 1662. Sume is £10 12 10⁴.

Inventory of Goods p'sented by *John Robbinson* Administrato' to the Estate of *Samuell Robbinson*, prized by *John Wiswall & John Lake*, 4 : 8ᵐ 1662.

John Robinson deposed 28 Oct. 1662.)He testified that there was an uncertainty as to the return given in, by reason of some claymes made for what he)Samuel Robinson(traded vpon, being vpon trust from my father and oth's, and also in p'tnership, cannot be resolued, vntill accounts be cleared, wᶜʰ being to be done in England must crave longer time."(

Mr. Thomas Robbinson came into the Court and Renounct his being Administrato' to the Estate of his late sonne, *Sam'll Robbinson*, wᶜʰ was accepted of by the Court, & he discharged. 28 Octʳ 1662.

DANIEL DOVENIES. Inventory of the Goods of *Daniel Dovenies*, deceased being in the keeping of *John Farnam* senio', praised by *Michaell Wills* & *Thomas Watkins*.

19 Dec. 1662. Power of Administration to the Estate of *Daniel Dovenies*

an Irishman. is Granted to *John Farnum* senio', in behalfe of the friends of the said *Dorenies. Jno Farnum* senio' deposed.)His bond is on file.(

2 Feb. 1662.)John *Farnum* testifies that, according to his understanding, it was stated – by some that vndertooke to plead *Benjamine Gillams* Case, that *Mr. Benjamine Gillam* by his Acco[m] vnder his hand, owned himselfe possesst of money belonging to the estate of *Dorenies* which was accordingly entered on the inventory, the same day.(

Joнn Marshall. 28 Jan. 1662. Power of Administration to the Estate of the Late *John Marshall*, of Barnstable, in old England, deceased is Granted to *John Sweete*, of Boston, in behalfe of the next of kinn.

An Inventory of the Estate apprised by *Richard Cooke, John Blake.* 18 Aug. 1662. Amt. £60 14 7½. Debts due to *John Sweete*,— (am' £7 1'.) who deposed at said time.)There is on file the bond of John Sweete to Edw[d] Hawson to the am' of £73.4.3, together with his house & land to be held for the faithful performance of said obligation. Signed by John Fernialde, W[m] Charde. 2d Feb. 1662.(

Thomas Houchine. 28 Jan. 1662. Pow' of Administracon to the Estate of *Thomas Houchine*, deceased, Granted to *John Sweete*, of Boston, in behalfe of the next of kinn.

Inventory of Estate apprised by *Richard Cooke*, and *John Blake*, 18 Aug. 1662. Amt. £19.18'. Debts due the deceased by the Estate of *Moses Row*, by *John Sweet*, from one *Carr* of Road Island. *John Sweete* deposed on the day above said.

Moses Row. 28 Jan. 1662. Pow' of Administracon to the Estate of the Late *Moses Row*, deceased, graunted to *Jno Sweete*, in behalfe of the next of kinn.)John Sweete's bond is on file to the amt of £36 7 9. 8 Feb. 1662.(

Inventory appraised by *Richard Cook* and *John Blake*, 18 Aug. 1662. Amt. £29. 5' 3[d]. Debts due from *John Sweete*, and *Henry Puddiford;* to *Jno Sweete, John Marshall, Thomas Houchine.*

John Sweete deposed 28 Jan. 1662.

John Samuel. Inventory of the Goods of John Samuel deceased the 8 10[m] 62, prized by *James Johnson, John Morse.*

Mentions "the Ende of a house Joyneing to *William Arvry*, £20"; in *Anthony Newlands* hands, £5; in *Goodman Lovells* hands, £1 3'; in *Pr. Peter Oliver's* hands, £3 2' 9[d].

Jabesh Eaton deposed 26 Feb. 1662.

Ralph Woodward. Inventory of the estate of *Ralp Woodward* of Hingham, deceased, as it was apprized by *Capt. Joshua Hobart & Deacon John Leavett*, of Hingham.

8 Acres of Land lying at a place Commonly called the world's end, £24; 4 acres to the east of *John Ferings* house lott, £12; 20 acres lying by glad tydings plaine, £20; one acre of upland bought of *Clement Bates*, £2; 6 acres by waie mouth River next *Thomas Huetts* land, £25; 2 acres one Warwill hill next *John Ferings* land, £6; salt marsh next *Thomas Linkcolns* land. bought of *Edmund Hobart* senior; marsh adjoining *John Towers* marsh, &c., &c.

11 April 1663. Power of Administration to the estate of *Ralph Woodward* graunted to *John Smith*, of Hingham, who married *Sarah* the only

Daughter of said *Ralph Woodward*, in bir Right and Right of their Children.   At the same time, *John Smith* deposed.

PETER GRAY. Accompt of the Debts of *Peter Gray*, late Deceased. who lined in the town of Brantre, and in the house of *John Basse*. Debts due to *M* *Allcocke* and others. Administration to the Estate granted to *Deacon Sam* *Basse* in his own & *Sam* & other Credito* behalfe. 28 April 1663. *Deacon Sam Basse* deposed on y* Daye abone said.

WIDDOW WILSON. An Inventory of what estate wee *William Alis* and *Francis Eliot* did find in Brantrey to belonge to the widdow *Wilson* late of Brantrey.

Money in hands of *David Walsbee*, put out to *John Woord* for 4 years: £4 in hands of *John Gurney*. *Francis Eliot*, of Brantre, deposed 30 April 1663.

The Court accepted the Care and Indeanors of *Francis Eliot & W* *Ellise* & order that y* Estate in the hands of said *Eliot* be p* Equally to the Children of said widdow *Wilson*, [charges deducted and a due proportion of the £4 allowed them with other creditors to y* late *John Gurney's* estate.]

JOHN OLIVER. The Estate of *M* *John Oliver*, deceased, by appraisment amounted in y* yeare 1646 to £180. Advanced since by Improvement £181 6 4. The Executrix has one third. *John Oliver*, the Eldest Son, a double portion, *Thomas Oliver* [deceased] ½ part, *Elizabeth Winsell*, ¼ part. The Estate of *Elder Thomas Oliver* disposed otherwise, soe that nothing Comes to this Estate from thence. The Executrix paid the Eldest son *John*, out of the produce of said Estate.

[A Division of £309 was then made between the executrix and heirs. Signed by *Peter Oliver* and *James Johnson*. The Court allowed the accompt and Division of the Estate, 14 May 1663.]

JOHN GURNEY. Brantry March 16* 1663. An Inventory of the Goods and Estate of *John Gurney* sen*, deceased, taken by *Gregory Belcher, Edmund Quincy, Thomas Faxon*. Am* £55 14 6. Debts due from Estate to Peter Brackett, Joseph Adams, Francis Nucomb, John Damit, sen., Goodman King of Waymoth, Goodman Italy, John Mills John Cleverly, Smith, Collins at Boston, &c., &c.

M *Sam. Broadstreet & M* *Richard Wharton* deposed to the Inventory given in to them by the widdow or friends of s* *Gurney* and subscribed by *Gregory Belcher* &c., w*h w*h they haue added a true Inventory of that Estate to their best knowledge.

JAMES BATHERSTON. 12 Dec. 1663. Pow* of Administration to y* Estate of *James Batherston*, late Mariner in y* Catch Returne, being not heard off for a six years, & supposed to bee dead, is Granted to *W* *Gibson*, his Kinsman, He Going security to Administe* thereupon According to Law, to Satisfy all debts, & to p*serve y* Remaind* fo* s* *Batherson* if ever he Returne. or otherwise, to such as shall Appeare to y* County Court to have most Rights therein.

[*James Batherston* was a partner with *Peter Oliver* in the Ketch Returne. *W* *Ballistine* demanded a letter of Atturney, which was granted.] *W* *Gibson* deposed 12 Dec. 1663.

[Bond on file of *W* *Gibson*, of Boston. shoomaker, and *Oliver Purchase*.

Hameronish, of Lynn, in the County of Essex. Witness, *Peter Oliver, Daniell Vernon.*]

ROBERT BILLS. An Inventory of the houshold staffe & goods pertaining to *Robert Bills,* who deceased Decemb. 15, 1635.

Mentions, *Goodman Hazard, goodman Kingman, James Clearke.*

A note of Charges attending his sickness and burial signed by *Ralph Sprague, Robert Hule.*

1 6 1638, *Samuell Peirce* affirmed vpon oath, that *John Knowls* married the widow of *Ephraim Davies* & so hee was alowed to administer of the estate of *Robert Bills* marriing his sister.

JOHN COGGAN. *Joseph Rock* bound in the sum of £200 to administer on the estate of *John Coggan,* and *Martha* his wife, 24 Feb. 1662. Witness, *Sam' Sendall, John Ferniside.*

WILLIAM JOHNS. 11th June 1663, Powe' of Administration to the Estate of *William Johns,* of Hingham, deceased, hauing no Relations left in y' Country as knowne, is Graunted to *Wm Woodcock,* in behalf of himself & such other's as the Court shall Judge to haue any Right therein, giuing security to Administer according to lawe. Edw. Rawson Record'. Inventory of the Estate taken 5 June 1663. Am'. £65 16 6. *Wm Woodcock* deposed 11 June 1663.

CORNELIUS THAYER. 3 [?] 3 1663. Invoice of the Goods of *Cornelius Tayer,* deceased taken by *John Holbrook, Thomas White.* Am'. £34.

25 June 1663. Powe' of Administration to the Estate of *Cornelius Thaier,* late of Weimouth, is Graunted to *Richard* and *Zacherius Thayer* his brethren in behalf of themselees & the Rest of his brethren & sisters. Estate creditor to the amount of $218 15 1. *Richard Thayer* deposed.

The names of M' Edward Ting, M' Braule, Rich: Wharton, goodman Kingam, goodman Barges, David Randall, goodman Fry, Gregory Belcher, are mentioned.

INSCRIPTIONS FROM SALEM, CONNECTICUT.

Shelburne, Franklin Co., Mass., July 25th, A. 1857.

MR. DRAKE.— Dear Sir:—

Whilst I was in Salem, Conn., about a year ago, I saw a few grave-stones in a large field, near the village of Salem (formerly Pogwonk, a parish of Colchester,) which were much time-worn; and which I, with much difficulty, was able to transcribe correctly. The inscriptions were the following, vis:—

"Capt. Sam" Gilbert died August 5th, 1733, æ. 70 years. Mrs. Mary Gilbert wife of Capt. Sam" Gilbert died Sept. 30th, 1736 in ye 91st year of her age. Mr. John Gilbert died Nov. 22d 1755 in ye 63d year of his age."

It appears by "Hinman's Catalogue," &c., that Capt. Gilbert was married in Hartford, in 1686, to Mary Rogers, daughter of Sam' Rogers of New-London.

I think the name of Gilbert became extinct in Colchester, as it does not occur on the Town Records, excepting Capt. S. G—'s name. I have supposed the Hon. Sylvester Gilbert, of Hebron, might have been a grandson of Capt. Sam", but do not know.

Yours, &c.,   CHARLES M. TAINTOR.

ANCIENT GRAVE YARD AT LEBANON, CONN.

[By Ashbel Woodward of Franklin, Conn.]

Lebanon originally consisted of several distinct grants or proprieties, the most important of which were the *one mile*[*] propriety and the *five-mile* purchase. The former was a grant from Owaneko, sachem of the Mohegans, to the Rev. James Fitch and John Mason, son of the famous Major John Mason, in 1695; and the latter was a purchase made of the same sachem shortly afterwards. Upon the one mile grant was a large cedar swamp, which, upon the principle of association, led Mr. Fitch to bestow the name of Lebanon[†] on the whole tract. The General Court gave the same name to the contemplated town in 1697. Lebanon was not incorporated till three years later. Having agreed upon a favorable location,[‡] the early settlers next provided themselves with a meeting-house, and installed their first minister, Rev. Joseph Parsons, in November, 1700.

About the same period, probably a few years earlier, the first burial ground was laid out upon an eminence in the valley of the Susquetonscot, half a mile east of their place of worship. This has been the principal cemetery of the town, or of Lebanon proper, for quite a century and a half. For the last fifteen years comparatively few new graves have been opened; an area of some two or three acres having been almost entirely appropriated to the dead of former generations.

The most ancient of the monuments were usually made of granite or of purplish slate. The former, being variable in quality, and often unsuited to such purposes, has suffered most from disintegration. We notice that the granite of a dark shade had changed least. Some of this description, although among the most ancient in the ground, were in a most perfect state of preservation.

This inclosure presents a circular plain, of limited extent, in its centre, with a gentle declivity to the south, and then slopes somewhat abruptly on all its sides to the level of the valley below. The part near and just above the southern slope, was first improved by the early inhabitants as a place of sepulture for their dead. In this locality we find the grave of the Rev. James Fitch, who was born almost as early as the embarcation of the Puritans for New England, and who was here interred in 1702. By his first wife, who was the daughter of the Rev. Henry Whitefield of Guilford, he had sons James and Samuel; by his second, who was a daughter of Major John Mason, he had sons Daniel, John, Jeremiah, Jabez, Nathaniel, Joseph, and Eleazer. The three youngest of the sons are interred near the father,—all of whom have monuments with inscriptions. We only give that of the father, which narrates the principal events of his life. It is in Latin :—

In hoc Sepulchro depositæ Sunt Reliquiæ Viri vere Reverendi D. Jacobi Fitch; natus fuit apud Boking, in Comitatu Essexiæ, in Anglia, Anno

---

[*] The one mile grant and the *five mile* purchase of Owaneko constituted the most southerly and easterly part of the town, and that first settled; the Clark and Dewey purchase, and the Whiting purchase, the northwesterly part.

[†] History of Norwich.

[‡] The site of the present church edifice is the same as that originally selected for the first house of worship.

Domini 1622, Decem. 24. Qui post quam Linguis literatis optime instinctus fuisset, in Nov Angliam venit Ætate 16 ; et deinde Vitam degit, Hartfordiæ, per septennium, Sub Instructione Virorum celeberrimorum D. Hooker & D. Stone. Postea Munere pastorali functus est apud Say-Brook per Annos 14. Illinc cum Ecclesiæ majori Parte Norvicum migravit ; et ibi cæteros Vitæ Annos transegit in Opere Evangelico. In Senectute, vero prae corporis infirmitate necessario cessabit ab opera publico ; tandemque recessit Liberis, apud Lebanon ; ubi Semianno fere exacto obdormivit in Jesu, Anno 1702, Novembris 18, Ætat 80.

A short distance to the west may be found the grave of Lieut. Samuel Huntington, who was an original proprietor, and who was born in Norwich, in 1665. He was a son of Dea. Simon of Norwich, and a grandson of Simon the emigrant, ancestor of the very numerous family of the name of Huntington in this country.

His own epitaph, and that of his wife, follow :—

Here lyes ye Body of
Lieut Samuel Huntington
Gentleman who died
May ye 19 1717 in y^e
52 year of his age

In memory of Mrs
Mary Huntington the wife
of Lieutenant Samuel Huntington
who died Oct. 5 1743
in the 77th year of her age

Near and a little to the south of the last, may be found the monument of Mr. Jonathan Metcalf, and that of his wife Hannah. They early emigrated from Dedham, Mass. His brief memoir was published in the Gen. Reg., vol. vii., page 168.

Here lies the body of Mr. Jonathan Metcalf
a virtuous, charitable & generous Merchant
and Benefactor to the Church* & First Society
in Lebanon, who having been long and Solicitously
Trading for the pearl of great price
exchanging this life in the hope of a
better & enduring Substance March
ye 5, 1738 in the 65 year of his age.

Low on the eastern slope is the grave of the venerable Duxbury minister, who, after serving about 40 years in his early field of labor, came here to end the evening of his days with his children. A sketch of the life of the Rev. John Robinson may be found in the Gen. Reg., vol. ix., page 339.

His monument of slatestone contains the following :—

Here lies the body of the Rev^d Mr. John Robinson
late Pastor of the Church of Christ in
Duxbury which charge having faithfully
and laudably sustained for the space of 39 years

---

* By his will, dated March 17, 1734-5, he gave twenty pounds to the First Church of Christ in Lebanon ; and farther declares, that the said legacy shall be understood to be of money according to the rate or value of Silver at 20 Shillings per ounce.

he removed to Lebanon & changed this life
for a better Nov. 14 A.D. 1745 aged 74.

Sic pater Sic, O, numerare Susae
Nos doce vitæ spatium caducis
Mens ut a curis revocata veri
Lumen honesti
Cernat ——— Duch* Psal.

With appropriate inscriptions, and at a cost of near $2000, a granite monument has recently been erected, in this cemetery, to the memory of the above, and to those of his descendants here interred.

We next notice the graves of two of the early graduates of Harvard,[*] who have rude monuments in the most ancient part of the ground.

Of the history of Isaac Bayley, H. C. 1701, we know nothing. Of Dr. Nathaniel Little, H. C. 1734, more is known. In 1740 he was a resident of Hartford, where he and wife Mabel had son Woodbridge born; in 1741, of Middletown, where he had daughter Theodosia born; and finally of Lebanon, where other children were born, and where he attained to an honorable position in his profession. From his monument we learn that the father and the once smiling infant unconsciously sleep on, side by side.

Here lies yᵉ body of that most
Ingenous & worthy Gentleman
Mr. Isaac Rayley yᵉ husband
of Mrs Mercy Bayley. He was a
Member of yᵉ Vnivercity in
Cambrid in New England
& Slept in Jesus August 23
A. Domin 1711 in yᵉ 30 year of his age

In memory of Mr. Nathaniel Little an happy and
Successful Physician & Surgeon who departed this
life April 5, 1753 in the 39 year of his age
Beloved by all for virtues Sake
Such virtue as the great does make
And worthy of immortal fame
If doing good deserves yᵉ same

On his left hand lies the body of Faith, his daughter, who died Oct. 27, 1753, aged 8 months.

Among these venerable relics, and those not unknown to fame, we find those also of the young wife and young mother occupying common ground and reposing side by side. Here Mary, (Gardiner,) the wife of Dr. Ebenezer Gray,[†] and the mother of his three children, found an early grave. The husband was a son of Samuel and Susanna (Langdon) Gray, and was born in Boston Oct. 31, 1697. The brief story of the wife is, that she was born at Gardiner's Island, September, 1702, being of the lineage of the ancient proprietor of that domain; that she was married at the age of 18, and died at 23.

---

[*] The date of their respective deaths has never been published in the *Harvard Triennial*; certainly not in the edition of 1851, which is before us.

[†] Dr. Gray was the first clerk of the courts in Windham County after its organization in 1726.

Two well preserved stones contain the following inscriptions :—

Here lies yᵉ body of Mrs.
Ann Johnson yᵉ wife of
Mr. Seth Johnson & daughter
of Mr. Thomas & Mrs. Lydia Eaton
She was a descreet and Virtuous
Woman & departed this life
in yᵉ comfortable hope of a
better April yᵉ 13ᵗʰ 1735 in the
23 year of her yong & tender age

Here lies interred the body of Mrs. Jerusha Mory
the dutiful & well Beloved consort of Mr. John Mory
who Dyed April the 24ᵗʰ 1736 & in the 26 year of her age
Memento Mori
Mors Vincent Omnia

For the sake of variety, and to furnish specimens of the grave-yard
literature that prevailed in early times, we subjoin a few epitaphs taken
almost at random.

Here lieth interred the
Body of Mrs. Abigail Tisdale
yᵉ late wife of Mr. James
Tisdale of Lebanon &
Daughter to Mr. John Colman
of Nantucket who died
yᵉ 18 of November 1726
& 45 year of har age
Har lis A virtuous loving wif
& ever she was kind
Unto har husband and har babes :
Whom she hath left behind

Here lies the Body of
Mr. James Tisdale* of Lebanon
The husband of Mrs. Mindwell
Tisdale.   He died May 3, 1727
aged 48 years
Here lies our faithful Loveing Friend
A Husband & A Father kind
Who hath rezind himself to God
And left his wife & babes behind

Here Lieth the Body of Mr. Abel Janes
yᵉ Husband of Mrs. Mary Janes, who
Died December yᵉ 18 1718 in yᵉ
73 year of his age
Leet Heavens Blessings rest upon
yᵉ Derling of my youthful dayes
& also one my children yong
To keep them all in wisdom' wais

---

* Probably Mr. James Tisdale, after the death of wife Abigail, married with Mindwell, who survived him.

Here lyes ye Body of y^t worthy
virtuous & pious Mother in Israel
wife to Mr. Abel Janes Mrs Mary
Janes by Name when she had
Lieved Long a holy and Patient Life
Dyed April 24 1735 in y^e
80 year of Har age

Farewell my Loving Children
My Neigburs & my Friends
Sarve God in Truth while in Your Youth
& Til Your Life doth end

In passing from the ludicrous to the sublime, we could not well do better than pause at the grave of the venerable Solomon Williams,* the veteran theologian of his time. He was a son of William Williams of Hatfield, and a grandson of Dea. Isaac, of Newton. He was ordained at Lebanon in 1722, three years after his graduation at H. C. He published many ordination and funeral sermons, the " Election Sermon " in 1741, and one for " Success in Arms " in 1759.

His character is elaborately given in his inscription upon a table of sandstone supported horizontally above his grave. That of his widow is also inscribed upon the same stone.

This stone covers the remains of that eminent Servant of God, the Revd Solomon Williams, D. D. late Pastor at Lebanon. Adorned with uncommon gifts of nature, learning, & Grace, he shone bright as the Gentleman, Scholar, Christian & divine, conspicuous for wisdom, warm in devotion, bold in the cause of Christ, excelling as a preacher, most agreeable in conversation, clear & Judicious in counsel, an ardent lover of peace & the rights of mankind, firm in friendship, Singularly hospitable & in all relations exemplary; having faithfully serv'd the interest of Christ, of Religeon & Learning at his Masters call, he calmly fell asleep in Jesus Feb. 28th 1776 in the 76th year of his age & 54 of his ministry.

Them that sleep in Jesus will God bring with him.

At the foot of the above we find the following inscription upon the marble head-stone at the grave of Dr. Thomas Williams. He was a son of the preceding.

Hic jacet
Thomas Williams
in expectione
Diei Supremi:
Quis erat
ille Dies declarabit
Natus 12th Nov. O. S. 1735
Obit 11th Feb. 1819

The immediate successor of the Rev. Dr. Williams was the Rev. Zebulon Ely. Their united ministry, including an interval of four or five years, covers a period of more than a century. The latter published

---

* Solomon Williams, D. D., the Rev. John Robinson, and Jonathan Metcalf, it will be remembered, were Prince's Subscribers. They have all been noticed in this article.

a sermon on the death of the elder Gov. Trumbull, in 1785, and of the second Gov. Trumbull, in 1809; also the election sermon in 1804. His Memoirs were written by his son, Dr. E. S. Ely. His inscription reads thus:—

Rev. Zebulon Ely
Died Nov. 28, 1824, in the 66 year
of his age and the 43 of his ministry.
He was born in Lyme; Grad. at Yale College;
and on Nov. 13, 1782, ordained Pastor of the
first church in Lebanon.

Although among the first who planted themselves here, and being also of the first generation that passed away, no allusion has yet been made to Capt. Joseph Trumble.* It has been thought more fitting that he should be noticed in connection with others, composing together a family group. He was a son of John², of Westfield, and a grandson of John¹, who was in Rowley, Mass., in 1643. He was born about the year 1679, and, at the age of 21 years, became a resident of Lebanon. He married a daughter of John Higley of Simsbury, and was the ancestor of a constellation of Revolutionary and later worthies, including among the number three Connecticut governors.

His plain inscription may be found upon his monument, just above the southern slope; also that of his widow.

Here lies the body of
Capt. Joseph Trumble
one of the Fathers of ye town and
just Friend to it, of a compassionate
kind disposition who after a short
illness departed this life in the hope
of a better June 16. 1755 in the 77ᵗʰ year of his age

Here are deposited the remains of
Mrs. Hannah Trumbull, late wife of
Capt. Joseph Trumbull, Doughter of John
Higley of Simsbury Esqur. who came from
Frimley in ye County of Surrey by Mrs. Hannah
Drake his first wife. She was born
at Windsor 22ᵈ April 1683, Died at
Lebanon 8ᵗʰ Nov. 1768, aged 85 years. 6 mo. & 15 days.

On the eastern slope is situated the Trumbull tomb, it being the only one in the cemetery. Concerning those here embosomed not much need be said. The celebrity of its tenants, including two governors, a signer of the Declaration of Independence, and one commissary general, is world-wide. In addition to a few of the inscriptions found upon the pedestal standing upon the tomb, we wish to note a single incident connected with the Revolutionary position of the first Gov. Trumbull. We

---

* This name was uniformly written Trumble till after 1755. There are now before the writer a number of autographs of the first Gov. Trumbull, some of which were of a date as early as 1740, and others as late as 1776. Those before 1755 were written Trumble; those later, Trumbull. The births of four out of five of Gov. Trumbull's children are recorded upon the town record Trumble; that of Col. John, born in 1756, is recorded Trumbull.

refer to the origin of the once New-England, but now national, soubri-
quet of " Brother Jonathan." It is understood to have come into use in
this wise :   Washington, whose resources were generally made equal to
any emergency, was, at some critical periods, greatly perplexed for the
want of troops, and that which was almost as necessary to insure success,
the munitions of war in general. It was then, when his own great heart
was almost ready to falter, that he unhesitatingly decided to fall back upon
Gov. Trumbull,* who was always reliable ; or, as he expressed it, " to
consult Brother Jonathan." Hence the origin of a name which has, in
the progress of our national existence, become almost as popular as that
of " Yankee," and which have, in a sense, come to be convertible terms.

Sacred to the memory of Jonathan Trumbull, Esq., who, unaided by
birth or powerful connections, but blessed with a noble and virtuous mind,
arrived to the highest station in government. His patriotism and firmness
during 50 years employment in public life, and particularly in the very
important part he acted in the American Revolution, as Governor of
Connecticut, the faithful page of History will record.
Full of years and honors, rich in benevolence, and firm in the faith
and hopes of Christianity, he died Aug. 9th, 1785, Ætatis 75.

Sacred to the memory of Madam Faith Trumbull, the amiable lady of
Gov. Trumbull, born at Duxbury, Mass., A. D. 1718. Happy and beloved
in her connubial state, she lived a virtuous, charitable and Christian life
at Lebanon in Connecticut, and died lamented by numerous friends,
A. D. 1780, aged 62 years.

Sacred to the memory of Joseph Trumbull, eldest son of Gov. Trumbull, and first Commissary Genl. of the United States of America. A
service to whose perpetual cares and fatigues he fell a sacrifice, A. D.
1778, Æt. 42.

To the memory of Jonathan Trumbull, Esq., late Governor of the
State of Connecticut. He was born March 26th, 1740, and died Aug.
7th, 1809, aged 60 years. His remains were deposited with those of his
father.

The following inscription is on a marble slab standing in front of the
tomb :—

The remains of the Hono. William Williams† are deposited in this
Tomb : born April 8th, 1731, died Aug. 2d, 1811, in the 81st year of his
age, a man eminent for his virtues and piety,—for more than 50 years he
was constantly employed in Public Life, and served in many of the most
important offices in the gift of his fellow citizens. During the whole
period of the Revolutionary war, he was a firm, steady, and ardent friend
of his country, and in the darkest times risked his life and wealth in her
defence. In 1776 and 1777 he was a member of the American Congress,
and as such signed the Declaration of Independence.

We should be without excuse if, in our gleanings, we passed the grave

---

* We believe that Gov. Trumbull was the only colonial governor who espoused
heartily the American cause.
† He was a son of Solomon Williams, D. D.

of " Old Master Tisdale,"* the great classical teacher of the age, and to
whose individual instruction so large a number of the distinguished men†
in our country owe their early training.

His inscription we copy :—

Reader,

as thou passest, drop a tear to the memory of the once eminent Academic
Instructor, Nathan Tisdale, a lover of Science. He marked the road to
useful knowledge. A friend to his country, he inspired the flame of
Patriotism. Having devoted his whole life from the 18th year of his age,
to the duties of his profession, which he followed with distinguished
usefulness to Society, he died Jan'y 5th 1787, in the 56 year of his age.

We will close this sketch with a brief notice of a few individuals who
participated in the Revolutionary struggle. More than five hundred men
from this town alone were in the army at one time. It is quite evident
that no inconsiderable aid was thus rendered to the patriot cause.

A short distance from the Trumbull tomb, on the west, may be found
the monument of the veteran Col. James Clark, who commanded a company on Bunker's Hill, and who was present at the laying of the corner-
stone of the Monument, just fifty years subsequent to the battle. The
old soldier was buried with military honors. His very chaste and appropriate inscription here follows :—

To the memory of
Col. James Clark
who died on the 29th day of Dec. 1826
aged 96 years and 5 mos.
He was a Soldier of the Revolution, and dared
to lead where any dared to follow. The
Battles of Bunker's Hill, Harlem Heights
and White Plains, witnessed his personal
bravery, & his devotion to the cause of his
Country.
He here in death rests from his labours,
For " there [is] no discharge in that war."

Near the same spot were interred the remains of Capt. Andrew Fitch,
who also served as a lieutenant on Bunker's Hill, and who was shortly
after promoted to the rank of captain, which command he held to the
close of the war, in the vicinity of New York, at Fairfield, and elsewhere.
He was a descendant of the Rev. James Fitch. We learn from his
modest inscription that he died Aug. 22d. 1811, aged 63 years.

In the central part of this ground may also be found a large sandstone
cenotaph, with the inscription which follows :—

---

* He m. the widow of Capt. John Porter, and hence there devolved upon him the
paternal training of her four children, besides the classical instruction of her youngest
son, John Porter 2d, a graduate of Y. C. 1776, secretary of Gov. Trumbull, transcriber
of Gov. Winthrop's Hist. of N. E., of the edition of 1790, and finally Comptroller of
Connecticut from 1794 to the time of his death, in 1802.

† Of these a few only will be mentioned, viz.: The 2d Gov. Trumbull, Col. Trum-
bull the painter, Rev. Wm. Robinson of Southington, Rev. John Robinson, Rev. Dr.
Lyman of Hatfield, Rev. Wm. Lyman of Glastenbury, Rev. Daniel Huntington of
Hadley, Hon. Jeremiah Mason, and Warren Dutton, Esq., both late of Boston, &c.

This monument is erected in Memory of Capt. Walter Hyde who was of approved integrity, a useful member of Society, a kind husband, an affectionate parent, a lover of his country & a firm Supporter of the rights of Mankind. Exempt from Military duty by former command, he nobly stept forth, raised and took the command of an Independent Company & with them proceeded to the neighbourhood of N. York A. D. 1776 in defence of the invaded rights of the United American States when he died at Greenwich on the 18th day of Sept. 1776 aged 41 years & was there buried & his grave undistinguishable from those of many other strangers. His death was greatly lamented by all to whom he was known.

We will add the names of a few of those who are known to have died in, or while connected with, the army. Perhaps some suffered martyrdom in the old Jersey Prison-ship. None were permitted to find a grave with their friends at home.

Aug. 12, 1776, Simeon Gray, Jr., died in the army in New York, age 12 years and 6 months.

Sept.	22,	"	Robert Gambell, in the army in N. Y.			age	30	years.
"	22,	"	Thomas Sloman,	"	"	"	"	34	"
Oct.	2,	"	Samuel Hyde,	"	"	"	"	51	"
"	14,	"	Daniel Brewster, at Durham,			"	25	"
"	29,	"	Ampb Clark, in the army in N. Y.			"	17	"
"	29,	"	Nathan Larnard,	"	"	"	"	21	"
Nov.	4,	"	Elisha Seabury	"	"	"	"	55	"
Jan.	3, 1777,	Asa Loomis, killed	"	"	"	"	22	"
"	21,	"	Jacob Gillett,	"	"	"	"	21	"
Feb.	11,	"	Lewis Gordis,	"	"	"	"	20	"
May	20,	"	Nathan Holbrook, of small pox, in do.			"	16	"
June	20,	"	John Babcock, in the army,			"	20	"
Aug.	22,	"	Capt. Judah Lewis,	"	"	"	25	"
Sept.	23,	"	Edward Webster,	"	"	"	21	"
Dec.	25,	"	David Barber, shot by a tory,			"	23	"
Jan.	20, 1778,	Jonathan Edgerton, in the army,			"	21	"
April	"	Edward Corsette,	"	"		"	20	"
Aug.	6,	"	Jacob Bettice, Jr.,	"	"	"	30	"

———— • ➤➤ • ————

REV. SAMUEL PARRIS.

[Copied from the Records of Stow by the Rev. J. L. Sibley, for the Register.]

"Stow Novembr 29 1697

At a meeting of yᵉ Inhabitns & Proprietrs of this Town being warned bye yᵉ Selectmen according to yᵉ direction of yᵉ Law in referance to yᵉ Reverend Mr Samˡˡ Parris his being helpful to this Towne in yᵉ Work of yᵉ ministry in preaching yᵉ word of God to this people

As alsoe to considr & conclud what is ferthr necessary to be done in referance to yᵉ proceeding to a Tryall about ye ministerial house.

furthermore to take sume ordr in what way ye Town may make theire adress unto yᵉ generall Court for help as to yᵉ suport of ye ministry in this small poore Towne

The Reverend Mr Samuel Parris according to yᵉ Townes desire have beene requested to Come to this Town to preach yᵉ word of God to this people in ordʳ. to his proseeding in said worke & to give ye Ihabits opportunity of hearing him in ordʳ to being helpfull to ym in yᵗ worke in this theire destitute condition.

The inhabitas & proprietrs being met did vote & unanimously agree to desire & request ye Reverend Mr. Parris to be forthʳ helpfull to ym in bareing on yᵉ worke of preaching ye word of God to this people.

And did also vote ordʳ & appoint Abraham Holman Tho: Whetney Benz Drown Samuel Hall & Thomas Steevens as a Comminee to Treate with him in reference to some monthes or other [2] time yᵗ if ther shal be a Concurrance & compliing there might be n further Treatye as the providence of God may dispose and ordʳ things And furthermore for ye Inciridgᵐᵗ of Mr Parris did vote and agree to give & pay him for his Labir and paines amongst vs thirty five punds pr annū but in case Mr Parris be not willing to except ye sᵈ sallerye ye Inhabitns did agree to pay fourty pounds per Annū as formerly though less able."

" Jan. 4. 1697 [8.] Voted & ye Saloctmen were ordʳd to make a rate of Ten pounds for Mr Parris oʳ present ministr for his Labor & paines amongst vs wch sᵈ rate is for one quartr ot £40 pr annū which is to be seasonably made & commited to ye Constable to collect."

" Stow Octobʳ 31. 1698
Recᵈ of Richᵈ Whitney Constable at sundry times ye just sum of ten pounds mony due to me for one quartʳ of a yeare Sallerye.
Witness my hand
Sᴀᴍ: Pᴀʀʀɪꜱ"

" At a meeting &c. July 4. 1698 It was voted & ordʳd yᵗ ye Selectmen doe take Care yᵗ there be a True invoice taken of all ye ratenble offects in this Towne ye heginning of August next and yᵗ they seasonnbly make n rate on ye inhabitns & proprietrs for their ministers [?] sallerye being 10 lbs for Mr Parris or present ministr except wtt is grante by ye Court may be procured to answer the same"

" Recᵈ. of Mr Joseph Daby of Stow ye full sume of Ten pounds for a qr of a years sallory due ye 31 Octobʳ last pr me Sᴀᴍ: Pᴀʀʀɪꜱ.

[Nᴏᴛᴇ.—There is a little obscurity as to this receipt but it seems probable that it is dated Jan. 26. 1698–9, and possibly may have been at Newton.]

" Nov 21. 1698 At a meeting of ye inhabitns & proprietors of this Town warned by ye Selectmen of sᵈ Town on Reference to several propoanlls made by ye Reverant Mr Samuel Parris in ordʳ to settlmt wch were del unto ye Selectmen in wrighting ye inhabitns being met together it being a very full meeting ye paps being rod severall times & ye severall priiculars wayd & considʳad ye inhabitⁿˢ doe not thinke ymselves in a Capassity to answere what is proposed in sd wrighting ye wholl matr boing put to voat it was voted in ye negatiue.

" It was also voted . . . to add to ye 40 lb formerly proffered" 5 lb more in fire wood or pay to procure ye same provided Mr Parris Take vp wth 20 lb pr Annū in monye & yᵗ othr Twenty pounds in good pay such as can be raised vpon ye place.

MR. JOSEPH BOYSE.

There is in the library of the Editor of the Register, a copy of "The Works of the Reverend and Learned Mr. Joseph Boyse, of Dublin. Being a complete Collection of all the Discourses, Sermons, and other Tracts, which have been already published. To which are added, several other Sermons; a Treatise of Justification; and, a Paraphrase on those Passages in the New Testament, which chiefly relate to that Doctrine."

This work is a very large folio, (two volumes bound in one,) and was printed in London, "for John Gray, at the Cross Keys in the Poultry. M.DCC.XXVIII." Several circumstances connected with this volume entitle it, in the opinion of the Editor, to a notice in the Register. Those circumstances are briefly these:—It was once the property of our great New England Antiquary, the Rev. Thomas Prince, as appears from his name and date of possession, being written with his own hand, upon the back of the title-page, thus,—" Thomas Prince. Boston. June 10. 1729." On the leaf pasted upon the cover facing the title-page, the same possessor wrote the following record:—

The Rev. and learned author of this excellent Collection, Mr. Joseph Boyse, was born at Leeds in Yorkshire, Jan. 11th, 1659-60.

His father was Mathew Boyse, a man of known piety, integrity and usefulness in his station, tho' exercised with considerable worldly losses: was an elder of the church of Rowley in New England, and one of their Deputies at Boston (during his abode there for about 18 years) and had at his coming thence an honourable testimonial of his being very serviceable, as well as exemplary in his behaviour.

He was in his early years under the care and tuition of a pious mother, to whom he bares this honourable testimony—" That few of her rank were superior to her in divine knowledge and serious Godliness, joined with great humility and modesty, and that she was every way a pattern of all the amiable virtues that are the truest ornament to her sex."

In 1675 he was put under the care of the Rev. Mr. Frankland who kept a private academy near Kendal, in Westmorland, with a view to his being trained up for the work of the ministry. Having continued 3 years with Mr. Frankland, he returned to his father's house at Leeds, where after a short stay he was sent to London to pursue his studies under the direction of that excellent divine Mr. Edward Veal, then teacher of a private academy at Stepney.

After he had studied 2 years with Mr. Veal and performed such preparatory exercises in private as were prescribed him by his tutor, he began to preach publicly about the year 1680, and was for some time assistant to the Rev. Mr. Edmond Trench, a worthy minister in Kent, of whose exemplary life and virtues he published an account in 1693.

In 1681 he was invited to be household chaplain to the late Countess of Donegall then at London, in whose family he past his time very agreeably about 3 quarters of a year.

The Countess breaking up house the following spring, he spent the next summer at Amsterdam, where he had an invitation to preach at the Brownist church, during the necessary absence of their minister in England, for about half a year.

After his return from Amsterdam he continued to preach occasionally at Leeds and some other places in that neighborhood till about midsummer, 1683; when upon the death of Mr. Timothy Haliday, a fellow student and intimate friend of his he had been for some time assistant to Dr. Williams, then pastor of this congregation (in Dublin) he received an invitation hence to succeed him in that station. Having taken the advice of friends, and sought direction from God, he came over hither in the latter end of the year 83, and was, after some trial, upon the call of this congregation solemnly ordained joint pastor with the Rev. Mr. Williams, and upon his removal for England became the sole pastor of it.

From thence to the time of his death (*which was about the 20th of November, 1728, at Dublin,*) he continued in the relation of a stated pastor to this church; and all that while discharged the duties of a faithful laborer and watchman, with so much diligence, reputation and success, as rendered him justly dear and valuable unto all that had the pleasure and advantage of attending his ministry.

The passages above, except those *in italic type,* I took out of Mr. Chappin's Funeral Sermon upon Mr. Boyse, wherein he gives him an extraordinary character, for piety, learning, charity, ministerial gifts and a large soul.

Dr. Increase Mather, in his Order of the Gospel, printed in 1700, page 50, has these words:—" Mr. Boyse, a worthy minister of the Presbyterian Judgement in Dublin, whom I have the rather taken notice of, because he was born in New England at Rowley, in which church his father, a man of eminent piety, was an officer."

If Dr. Mather was *not* mistaken as to the birth place of Mr. Boyse, then that very eminent Puritan divine was born in New England. But we are inclined to the opinion that Mr. Mather *was* mistaken, from the following reasons. His father, Mr. Matthew Boyes, was made a freeman of Massachusetts in 1639. That year was doubtless about the period of his arrival here. The father remained in the country " about 18 years." Hence he left *about* 1657; and as his son Joseph, the subject of this notice, was born in 1660, the probability is against his being born in New England. Mr. Boyse, the father, probably had children born here, and this fact being known to Mr. Mather, he took it for granted that Joseph was among the number. A letter from Matthew Boyes, Jr., dated London, " 29.3. 68," may be seen in our VIIth volume, p. 274. The father of Matthew, Jr. was then living in Yorkshire.

Mr. Boyse was a particular friend of the learned Mr. Ralph Thoresby, the historian of Leeds, and is frequently mentioned by him in his Diary, and in his Correspondence are many letters from him. In the former, date " July 4, Die Dom. 1680," is this entry. " Went to Newington-Green to hear Mr. Joseph Boyse preach, which I rejoiced in as the first fruits of our generation." To this passage, the Editor, the Rev. Joseph Hunter, F. S. A., has the following note:—" Boyse and Thoresby were born at Leeds the same year. He was educated for the ministry among the Nonconformists, in the academy which was conducted by Richard Frankland, one of the Silenced ministers. He was afterwards of Dublin, minister of a dissenting congregation there, and the author of many controversial works, a catalogue of which may be seen in the ' Biographia,' " Vol. 1, p. 48.

Under date 1699, Thoresby writes—" The learned Mr. Boyse, being come from Dublin, to his native place, lodged at my house till his marriage with Mrs. Rachel Ibbetson. The Sermon he preached relating to the sufferings of the French Protestants was very moving, there being once about 800 churches, in which the true worship of God was constantly celebrated, which are now demolished, 1,500 pastors banished, their flocks scattered, and many thousand families forced into exile, &c."

After Mr. Boyse had been settled in Ireland about twelve years, and had become quite famous by his writings, Thoresby importuned him for some account of his life. Among other brief items in his answer he says, "I am not very certain whether I was born January 59–60 or 60–61, though I think it was the latter, and could wish I knew the certainty, which I suppose might be learnt from the New Church Register in Leeds." Hence, that he was born in Leeds, he himself doubtless believed.

Notwithstanding Mr. Thoresby's great intimacy with the family of Boyse, and the celebrity of his special friend, he does not appear to have noticed either in his elaborate history of Leeds, where so much space is devoted to genealogies.

The family of Boyse, according to Sir William Pole, bore the name De Bosco, and occupied lands in Devonshire in the time of Henry the Second. The manor of Holberton had then been long in the family. The first mentioned is Ralph De Bosco, to whom successively succeeded William, William 2d, Sir William De Bosco, Kt. 3d, William 4, William 6, and John Boys, the last of the family in that place. There was another family at a place called Boyshele, in the parish of Modbiry, as early as the 1st of Edward the Second. Thomas Boys of that place granted Hele to Thomas Boys of Woode, (perhaps his son.) To him succeeded Thomas, Thomas, John, Thomas, John, &c. Some of these were probably the ancestors of the Yorkshire Boyses, among whom was the learned Dr. John Bois, born Jan. 3d, 1560, who had a considerable hand in the present translation of the Bible.—See Watson's *Hist. of Halifax*, 161; *Lane Fam. Papers, Reg.*, Vol. XI., INDEX.

Conn. Hist. Society's Libr., Dec. 2, 1857.

SAM'L G. DRAKE, Esq.:

Dear Sir :—At the suggestion of my friend Chas. Hoadley, Esq., State Librarian, I write to advise you that there is in the library of this Society a small volume of abstracts of sermons, in the MS. of Rev. Samuel Parris of Salem Village; a fact of which you may possibly like to take some notice in the Genealogical Register.

The volume contains series of sermons from Sept. 9, 1689, to May 6, 1694; and includes various curious discourses, one, with running title, "Christ knows how many Devils there are in his Churches, and who they are;" date "27, Mar. 169½ Sacrament day; and memo. at head, "Occasioned by dreadfull witchcraft broke out here a few weeks past, and one member of this church, and another of Salem upon publick examination by civil authority vehemently suspected for Shee-Witches, and upon it committed." Text, "Have not I chosen you twelve; and one of you is a Devil."

Another has this heading :—"Conc. 1 } 11. Sept. 1692. After ye condemnation of 6 Witches at a Court at Salem, one of the Witches viz: Martha Kory in full communion with our Church."

I understood Mr. Hoadley to say that the records of Salem Village were now in course of publication in the Register, and that the above facts would probably furnish a note at some point of the publication.

Very respectfully,   Your Ob't Serv't,

FRED. B. PERKINS, Librarian C. H. S.

CROOKER FAMILY.

[BY MISS MARCIA A. THOMAS.]

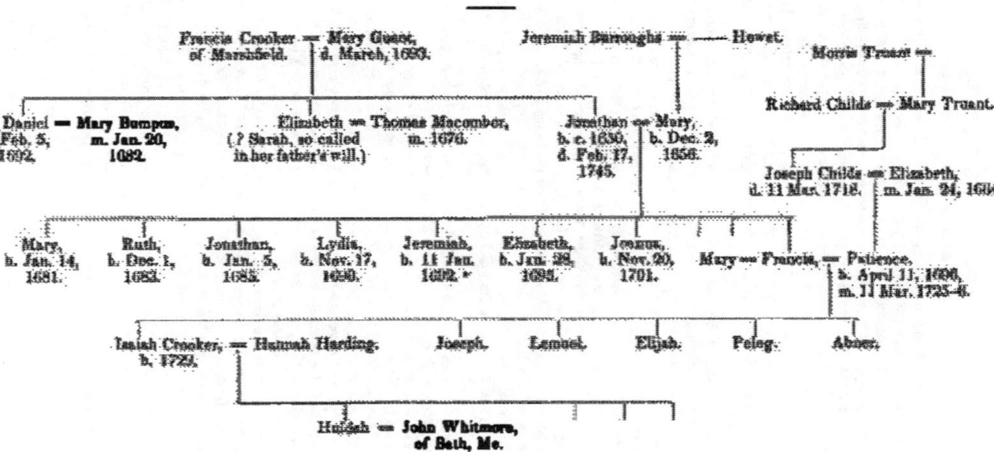

ROBERT AUCHMUTY, SENIOR.

[From the Norfolk County Journal.]

He, whose name stands at the head of this article, resided with his family in Roxbury for several years during the first half of the last century. His homestead has been carved into sites for many dwelling houses, few of the inmates of which are aware, perhaps, that such a person ever existed. Probably no other family in New England bore the same family name, and it has not been known here since the Revolution.

This gentleman of the old school was an eminent lawyer, and practiced in his profession in Boston early in the last century. He was contemporary with Gov. William Shirley, and probably they were personal friends, both before and after the elevation of the latter to the office of Governor.

On the 20th of August, 1733, he purchased the Scarborough estate in Roxbury, consisting of fourteen acres of land with a house thereon, situated on the road leading to Braintree, now Warren Street. The houses of worship of the Baptist and Methodist Societies both stand upon the estate. The price paid was three hundred pounds. His family, when he came to Roxbury, consisted of himself and wife, three sons and two daughters. His daughter Henrietta was the wife of John Overing, Esq., an advocate, and his daughter Isabella afterwards became the wife of Judge Pratt, Chief Justice of the Supreme Court of New York, and a graduate of Harvard University of the class of 1737. Mr. Knapp, in his sketch of the life of Judge Pratt, in his Biographical Sketches, says, "Pratt's highest ambition was gratified in his matrimonial connection, for he married a most accomplished woman, one who turned from the fashionable and elegant suitors around her, to whom by birth, fortune and female charms she had a full claim, to lavish her affections on him, enamored with his virtues and his intellect."

His son Samuel was a graduate of Harvard of the class of 1742. He settled in New York and was a rector of the English Church. Mention has been made of Robert in the Journal, on a former occasion.

Mr. Auchmuty, in the month of September following his settlement in Roxbury, was appointed Judge of the Admiralty Court for New England. There is but a solitary record book of the proceedings in that Court prior to the Revolution, now known to be in existence. The original papers are gone. This last relic of the King's Admiralty Court is mutilated, but it shows some curious things notwithstanding. It appears that Judge Auchmuty held a Court in Boston in April, 1740, and his judgments are entered from time to time until about the year 1742, when George Cradock appears to officiate as deputy Judge. (The daughter of this gentleman became the wife of Robert Auchmuty, Junior.) The record contains Gov. Shirley's sailing orders for the expedition to Louisburg, dated in 1744, the line of battle for the ships, and their names and orders for the impressment of seamen. History shows that this Louisburg expedition was a pet project with Gov. Shirley, and there cannot be much doubt that Judge Auchmuty took a lively interest in its prosecution, and rejoiced at its success.

In Smollett's History of England, (which, as it was written soon after this expedition, is in the following statement perhaps entitled to more than its usual credit,) it is stated that the most important achievement by the

English (in 1745) was the conquest of Louisburg on the Isle of Cape Breton in North America. * * * "The plan of this conquest was originally laid by Mr. Auchmuty, Judge Advocate of the Court of Admiralty in New England; he demonstrated that the reduction of Cape Breton would put the English in sole possession of the fishery of North America," * * * "employ many thousand families that were unserviceable to the public, increase the shipping and mariners, extend navigation, cut off communication between France and Canada by the River St. Lawrence; so that Quebec would fall of course into the hands of the English."

The records in Suffolk show that Shirley and Auchmuty had pecuniary transactions about these times. The latter went to England about the year 1741, and was there for several years, and March 12, 1745, he again presided in the Admiralty Court, and continued to preside until May, 1747, when the record ends. Within the period of about seven years covered by the record, Gov. William Shirley's genuine signature appears as Advocate General. John Overing, Esq., the son-in-law of the Judge, came into Court occasionally as an advocate.

In 1740, Judge Auchmuty was connected with the Land Bank Scheme, and 143 pages of one of the volumes in Suffolk Registry of Deeds are taken up with copies of mortgages relating to this scheme. It is mentioned in Hutchinson's History as follows :—"This was a revival of a project of a bank of 1714. The projector of that bank now put himself at the head of seven or eight hundred persons. A company was formed and were to give credit to £150,000 lawful money to be issued in bills, each person to mortgage a real estate in proportion to the amount he subscribed and took out. Ten directors and a treasurer were to be chosen. Every subscriber was to pay 3 per cent. interest for the sum taken out, and 5 per cent. of the principal, and he that did not pay in bills might pay in produce and manufactures. The pretence was, that by thus furnishing a medium, the inhabitants would be better able to procure the Province bills of credit for their taxes; that trade, foreign and inland, would revive and flourish." * * * "The company contrived to keep £50,000 or £60,000 abroad." * * * "The company was suppressed by act of Parliament, notwithstanding the opposition of their agent."

Judge Auchmuty died in 1751, and soon after his decease the estate was conveyed to Dr. Jonathan Davies, who probably some years afterwards erected the mansion now standing near Myrtle Street. He owned the estate for fifty years.

The will of Judge Auchmuty was made in 1741, just before he sailed for England. It is substantially as follows :—

"In the name of God, Amen.

"I, Robert Auchmuty, of Roxbury, in the County of Suffolk, Esquire, being bound to Great Britain, in the defence of the just rights of the Province of Massachusetts Bay in New England, in which, by the blessing of God, I hope to succeed, but considering the frailty of human life and the dangers of the sea, do therefore make this my last Will and Testament, with a spirit of Resignation to all the dispensations of Providence, trusting through the merits of Jesus Christ, my blessed Redeemer, that, after this troublesome life is ended, I may be a partaker of a blessed immortality."

And that he might not "sin in his grave," he adds, "And now in the first place I direct my Executrix to pay all my just debts." He then bequeathes "fifty pounds to his loving daughter, Henrietta Overing, wife of John Overing, Esq., in bills of public credit of the old tenor," the same sum to his son Samuel, to his daughter Isabella and his son Robert. He bequeathes to his son James Smith five pounds, " being sensible (he says) if he behaves himself well of the prospect he has of sharing a Benevolence of his God father, my very good friend, Mr. James Smith."

He then gives to his " truly loving and faithful wife Mary," the rest of his estate, " confiding (he says) in her great tenderness and affection to my children, which I have always experienced."

CONFISCATED ESTATES.
[From the Norfolk County Journal, 12 September, 1857.]

It is a well known fact that during the war of the revolution, an act of the Legislature of the State of Massachusetts Bay was passed, to confiscate the estates of a large number of persons who were favorably disposed to the government of King George III. This act was passed April 13, 1779, and was entitled " an act to confiscate the estates of certain notorious conspirators against the Government and Liberties of the Inhabitants of the late Province, now State of Massachusetts Bay," and recited that the persons therein named had justly incurred the forfeiture of all their property, rights and liberties holden under, and derived from the Government Laws of the State, and should be considered as aliens, and that all their goods and chattels, lands and tenements, should escheat and enure to the use of the Government and people of the State. Afterwards, in the same year, a Resolve was passed, directing the sale of the confiscated estates at public auction, and a committee was appointed for the purpose of carrying the Resolve into effect.

Not less than five of these estates in the town of Roxbury were sold by the committee. They had been owned under the Provincial Government by men of wealth, and in some instances by persons of high standing in society. It may prove interesting to the readers of the Journal to know where these estates were, and something about their former owners.

The old mansion house now occupied by Hon. Samuel Walker, near Dorchester Brook, and about 132 acres of land on both sides of Eustis Street, including the land where the mansion house of the late Gov. Eustis stands, was confiscated as the estate of Eliakim Hutchinson. This estate had formerly been the property of Gov. William Shirley, Royal Governor of Massachusetts from 1741 to 1749.

The mansion house on Bartlett Street, now occupied by Mr. Bradford, with about six acres of land, was confiscated as the estate of Robert Auchmuty, and sold to Increase Sumner, afterwards Governor of Massachusetts under the Constitution from 1797 to 1799. Gov. Sumner with his family occupied the mansion house as a place of residence until the time of his death in 1799. A fine steel engraving of the likeness of Gov. Sumner, with an interesting sketch of his life prepared by his son, W. H. Sumner, Esq., may be found in the April Number, 1854, of the New England Genealogical Register. He was born in Roxbury, 27th of November, 1746.

Robert Auchmuty became a resident of this mansion house about the year 1770. He was son of Robert Auchmuty, Judge of the King's Admiralty Court for New England, and on the death of his father in 1750, succeeded him in office. He was married in 1751 to Deborah Bradock, a great-grand-daughter of Mathew Braduck, who was chosen Governor of Massachusetts in 1628–9 by the Company in England for settling Massachusetts Bay, but never came to America. Robert Auchmuty, Jr. is represented as being a man of talent, and possessed of fine powers as a lawyer. He was associated with Adams and Quincy in the defence of Capt. Preston, in his trial for the Boston Massacre. His sister married Judge Pratt, Chief Justice of the Supreme Court of New York, and a graduate of Harvard University of the class of 1737. The elder Auchmuty was a resident of Roxbury from 1733 to the time of his death in 1750. His mansion house was on land purchased by him of Joseph Scarborough, on the Braintree road, now Warren Street, and which had been in the Scarborough family before the time of Queen Anne. The site of his dwelling house was probably near that of the house lately occupied by Jos. Adams. He was a lawyer, and was counsel for the Trustees of the Grammar School in a suit relating to land as early as 1716.

Benjamin Hallowell, with his wife and family, prior to the Revolution, occupied that mansion house now occupied by Dr. B. F. Wing, at the corner of Boylston and Austin Streets, at Jamaica Plain. The estate comprised about seven acres on the southwest side of Boylston Street. Mr. Hallowell's name was among those in the act of confiscation, and this estate was sold by the committee. It passed through several hands, and was purchased by Dr. Lewis Leprilite, in 1791. This gentleman was born in Nantz in France, and was a surgeon. Unfortunately for him the estate was owned by Mrs. Hallowell, and consequently the deed of the committee operated upon the life estate of Mr. Hallowell, in right of his wife, but did not convey the fee. Mrs. Hallowell died in 1795, and her husband in 1799. The heirs of Mrs. Hallowell recovered the estate of Leprilite by a suit in the United States Circuit Court. The remains of Dr. Leprilite, and those of his son, are buried on the estate, and the spot is indicated by a stone with a Latin inscription.

One of Benjamin Hallowell's sons was an Admiral in the British Navy, and was a knight; one of his daughters married Judge Elmsley of Montreal. Ward Nicholas Boylston, Esq., another son of Mr. and Mrs. Hallowell, by Royal License of King George III., took the name of Boylston, which was his mother's maiden name. He owned this estate for many years prior to his death. He was a gentleman of education, and had travelled in many parts of the world in early life. He gave considerable sums to Harvard College, and for other charitable purposes, in his lifetime and by his will.

Joshua Loring, Esq., Mandamus Counsellor of the late Province of Massachusetts Bay, as he is styled in the deed of the committee, was deprived of a farm of seventy-three acres, with two mansion houses and other buildings thereon at Jamaica Plain, bounded west by the county road leading by Jamaica Plain Meeting House.

Sir Francis Bernard's country seat, on the southwest side of Jamaica Pond, shared the fate of the other confiscated estates. This estate contained fifty acres. Sir Francis is described as a Baronet in the deed, but the committee made no allusion to his office under the crown, as was done in the case of Mr. Loring. Bernard was Governor from 1760 to 1769.

In addition to the places of residence already mentioned, which were lost by confiscation, Rev. William Walter, rector of Trinity Church, Summer Street, Boston, and Charles Ward Apthorp, whose residence was in Brookline, each lost tracts of land in Roxbury by the same summary proceedings. Several other estates in the present limits of Norfolk County were confiscated, including Gov. Hutchinson's estate in Milton.

[For the Register.]

"Broke by the share of every rustic plough :
So perish monuments of mortal birth,
So perish all in turn, save well recorded worth."

Mr. Editor—In a cultivated field in Newbury, as you approach the bridge at Old-town, is an ancient burial ground which seems to have been appropriated exclusively to the families of Dole, Illsley, and Plummer. Most of the graves are marked by stones with inscriptions, but three tablets are nearly all of them lying flat upon the ground and covered with the overgrowing turf. The owner of the soil is a thrifty farmer, and no doubt respects the spot, but, almost insensibly the plough, each succeeding year, creeps closer and closer to the resting places of the departed, and what remains of the dilapidated gravestones may soon give place to the march of improvement, and be sacrificed to the advancement of agriculture. That some memento of this spot may be preserved, I send for publication in the Register, copies of such inscriptions as yet remain.   H. G. S.

Here lies buried
in hop of a glorious
resurrection y⁰ body
of Mrs. Sarah Dole late
wife of Mr. Richard
Dole who died Septem⁰
y⁰ 1 1718 aged 62 years
& ten months.

Here lies buried in
hops of a glorys
resurrection the
body of Mr. Richard
Dole who died
August y⁰ 1 1723
in y⁰ 13 year
of his age.

Here lyes buried
y⁰ body of
Sarah Doolle the
wife of Mr
Abner Doole who
died • • • y⁰ 21
1770 in the • • •
• • • • •

Here lies y⁰ body of
Mrs Jane Plumer
wife of
Mr. Benjamin Plumer
daughter of Capt. William
& Mrs. Ruth Illsley
who died Dec⁰. 24
1774 in the 35 year
of her age.

Hear lies the
body of Mr.
Joseph Illsley who
died October y⁰
15 1704 in
the 76 year
of his age.

In memory of
Mr Richard Dole
died March 10ᵗ
1778
Aged 69 years.

Here lies the
body of Mr.
Jonathan
Plummer who
died September
y⁰ 27 1726
in y⁰ 59 year
of his age.

Here lyes the
body of Mr.
Stephen Dole
who dyed Jan⁰ʸ 28
174½ in y⁰ 56ᵗʰ
year of his age.

Here lies y⁰ body of
Mr. William Dole
who departed this
life August y⁰ 5ᵗʰ
1752
in y⁰ 69ᵗʰ year
of his age.

WALLER OF VIRGINIA.

Wildwood Plantation, Bolivar Co., Miss., May 14, 1857.

Editor N. E. H. & G. Register, Boston.

Dear Sir—It may be interesting to some to know the history of a good old family—I mean the *Waller* family.

Alured De Waller, of Newark, Co. Nottingham, d. in 1183, and from him descended David, Master of the Rolls to Edward III, for 30 years. He died with no heir. From John, his brother sprung Henry, father of *Richard*, the hero of Agincourt, and who was allowed to add the word Agincourt on a shield pendant from a walnut tree to his coat of arms. He left John who died in 1517, leaving William, having issue John of Beaconsfield, Co. Bucks, from which family sprung Edmund the poet, celebrated for his suit to Lady Sydney. Henry Edmund was issue of the Poet. William was succeeded by Sir Walter, Knt. of Groombridge; again by George, leaving Sir Hardress, who was a General in the Parliamentary Army, and Sir Thomas, Lieutenant of Dora Castle in James I., leaving William, Kt., celebrated as the commander in chief of the Western division of the Parliamentary Army. Thence sprung Thomas, father of Richard, leaving Thomas, who died in South Lambeth in 1781, and who left James, dying without issue in 1802.

Sir William's eldest son Wyadham came to the Colony of Virginia, where he engaged in planting. He died at or near the mouth of James River, where he had settled, leaving a son who engaged in a sea-faring life, and commanded a vessel from Boston to the South American coast. He settled in Greenbriar Co., Va., ultimately, and married a Miss Clifton. He left William and Bowker. William died in 1835 in Spottsylvania Co., Va. A Capt. Bowker Waller, who had married a Miss Chew, of Fredericksburg, Va., settled in the same county. He raised a numerous family of sons. John, who died in ———— at St. Francisville, Lou., and Byrd B., who died at the family seat in ————, leaving one son who is now a planter in the same county, Robert Beverley Waller, the sole survivor of so many noble men. Long will Bowker Waller's hospitable and generous welcome be remembered, and his many friends, now fast sinking beneath the sod of the valley, will join him on an unknown shore. May his many virtues be doubled in his son. He was an affectionate father, a kind husband, a Christian, and a true old Virginia gentleman.

Many of his daughters are married, and some remain near the old mansion, while others have sought homes amidst the fertile fields of the South and West.

Your ob't serv't,   P.

GENEALOGICAL AND ANTIQUARIAN RECORD.

[Communicated by Jeremiah Butler, of Sherborn.]

I find in the East Cemetery in Hopkinton, Mass., the following inscription:—

Aaron Butler was born at Hopkinton, June 4th 1762, and died April 23d, 1848, Son of Jeremiah and Martha, and Grandson of Thomas and Martha, and Great Grandson of William and Sarah Butler. Thomas was born at Ipswich in the County of Essex, September 15th, 1682, and removed with his family to Hopkinton, A. D. 1745.

FRANCIS BRINLEY

Was born at Datchet, in England, in 1632. He established himself at Newport, R. I., fourteen years after its settlement. In the year 1687, during the reign of James 2d, he was appointed a Judge of the Court of Common Pleas for Rhode Island. He occasionally resided in Boston, owning a large estate at the corner of Hanover and Elm Streets. He died there in 1719, at the age of 87, and was buried in a grave in the King's Chapel Burial Ground, on the spot where the family tomb now stands. As he survived his children, Col. Francis Brinley of Roxbury, his grand-son, and Mrs. Hutchinson, his grand-daughter, inherited his large estate.

The following Catalogue of his books is somewhat curious, and gives us an idea of the legal and other reading of a gentleman of the Province in those days. It is only *signed* by him; the writing somewhat tremulous, he then being about 80 years old.   F. B.

An account taken of my Books.—F. Brinley.—March 27. 1713.
IMPRIMIS LAW BOOKS.

1. Statute Booke.
3. Coke's Institutes.
2. Coke's Reports.
3. Croke's Reports.
1. Vaughan's Reports,
1. Dyer's Reports,
1. Shepard's Grand Abridgment.
1. Ditto Marrow of the Law.
1. West's Symbolography.
2. Dalton's Sheriff's Office.
1. Swinburn's—of Wills & Testam",
1. Orphan's Legacy.
1. Law of Executors.
2. Hobart's Reports.
2. De Jure Maritimo.
1. Interpreters, by Thos. Manley.
1. The New World of Words.
1. Of ye rise & Power of Parliam".
1. Power of Grand Juries.
2. Young Clerk's Guide,
1. Touchstone of Wills & Testaments.
1. Terms of ye Law.
1. The Law in use in her Maj" Plantations.
2. Reports in Chancery.
1. Law of Corporations.
1. The Compleat Attorney.
1. Law of Trespasses,
2. Of Courts Leet and Courts Baron.
2. Conveyancers.
1. Lex Vadiorum,
1. Practice of ye Court of K. Bench, &c.
1. Regula **Placitandi.**

1. The Infant's Lawyer.
1. King James's Laws.
4. King William's Laws.
1. Writs Judiciall, &c.
1. Pleas of ye Court of Chancery.
1. Ridley's View of ye Ecclesiastica Law.
1. Actions upon the Case for Slander.
1. Pleas of the Crown, by Sir Matthew Hale.
1. Laws against Bankrupts.
1. The Clerk's Cabinet, pr. Shepard.
1. Speciall Deductions, by Brownlow.
1. Sheriff's Acco". by Judge Hale.
1. Lex Customaria, or Law of Copy-Hold.
1. Perambulation of Kent, pr. Lombarde.
1. Original Writs, pr. Wm. Hughes.
1. Practicall Register, pr. Styles.
1. Directions for the Study of ye Law, pr. W. P.
1. Doctor and Student.
1. The Constable's Guide.
1. Mr. Perkins—of the Laws of England, by Wentworth.
1. Office of an Executor.
2. Book of Rates.
1. Tryalls, *per Pais.*
1. The new Natura Brevium, &c.
1. Bond's Justice.
1. Primitive Devotion.
1. John Down—his Works.
1. Philip of Mornay—his Works.

BOOKS OF DIVINITY.

1. Bible in ffolio.
1. Bible in Quarto.
1. Greek Testament.
1. Testament.
1. The Kingdom of God in y{e} Soul, by the Reverend Father John Evangelist.
1. Ecclesiasticall History Epitomized, by J. S.
1. The Exaltation of Christ, by Thos. Collier.
1. A Spiritual Journey of a Young Man, towards the Land of Peace.
1. Webster's Judgment Set.
1. Divine Teachings, in 3 parts, by R. Coppin.
1. The Song of Songs, by John Lloyd.
1. The Revelation of God, by H. N.
1. Terra Pacis, by H. N.
1. The Day Dawning, by Thos. Collier.
1. Free Grace, by John Saltmarsh.
1. The Originall of the Soul, by H. W.
1. Dawnings of Light, by John Saltmarsh.
1. Spare hours improved in Meditations, of Francis Quarles.
1. A. Testimony to the Glory that is near, pr. Jos. Spriggs.
1. An Infallible Way to Contentment.
1. Of the torments of Hell. by Saml. Richardson.
1. Comfortable Doctrine for Adams Offspring, pr. A. M.
1. Theologia Gramatica or Misticall Divinitie.
1. The Vision of God, by Giles Randall.
1. The Forbidden Fruit by August Elutherius.
1. Gospell Treasury opened by John Everard.
1. Sparks of Glory by John Saltmarsh.
1. A Guide to eternity by John Bona; now done in English by S{r}. Rog{r}. L'Estrange.
1. The Spiritual Guide by Dr. Michael de Malino.
1. The narrow Path &c. by Matthew Woyer.
1. Hermes Trismegistris by Dr. Everard.
2. Good Tydings for Sinners, by Rob{t}. Pernell.
1. The Life of Christ—Rich{d}. Coppin's works.
1. Christopher Gode's Works.
1. Christopher Cobb's Works.
1. Joseph Salmon's Works.
1. Tho{s}. Kempis, his Works.
1. Tertullians Apologie. pr. H. B.
1. The Testimony of Will{m}. Erbery.
1. Clement Cotton's Works.
1. Abraham Cowley's Works.
1. Natural History by F. Verulam.
1. Judge Hale's Contemplations.
1. Holy Flames and Discoverys, by John Saltmarsh.
1. Richard Winstanley's Works.
1. Treatise of Humane Reason.
1. (illegible) out of the Wilderness.
1. Ecclesiastical History.
1. Trumpet Sounding in the Wilderness, by Da: Leeds.
1. The Whole Duty of Man.
1. Origination of Mankind, by Judge Hale.

BOOKS OF SEVERALL SORTS, VIZT, PHILOSOPHERS, &c.

1. One Epicurus Morals.
1. Seneca's Morals.
1. Epictetus Morals.
2. Marcus Antonious.
1. The Life of one Pomponias Atticus.
1. Sir Tho{s}. More's Utopia.
1. The Jewel House of Art and Nature.
1. The Art of Husbandry.
1. Mr. Culpepper's English Physician.
1. An examination of a Book entitled Human Reason.
1. Justus Lipsius of Constancy.
1. The Fearful estate of F. Spira.
1. Ancient Funeral Monuments.
1. Whiston's Theory of y{e} Earth.

1. Destruction of Jerusalem.
1. Essays of Sr. William Cornwallys.
1. A new discovery of America, by L. Hennepin.
1. A, Ternary of Paradoxes.
1. Directions how to live after a Wasting Plague. By Thos. Dolittle.
1. A new description of the World, by Saml. Clarke.
1. A view of ye English acquisitions in Guinea.
1. The Compleat Gunger, by Mich. Dan.
1. A new Concordency by Vavasor Powell.
1. The History of Justin by Rich. Codrington.
1. An English History by P. Heylyn.
1. Of Gravitation or Non Gravitation of fluid bodies.
1. The difference betwixt Temporal and Eternal, by Eusebius Nuremburg.
1. A Vindication of the Protestant Religion, by Peter Des Maizeaux.
1. Councells Civill and Morall of Francis Ld. Verulam.
1. William Pasler's Works.
1. England's Improvement by Andrew Yaranton.
1. An History of the Low Country Wars by T. M.
1. Mr. John Arndt—his Works.
1. The Voyages of John Bapt. Tavernier.
1. John Guillim of Heraldry.
1. Latin Dictionary.
1. Greek Lexicon.
1. Latin Geographical Dictionary.
1. Burton's Democritus.
1. Of ye first, second, third and fourth Monarchys.
1. An Appeal to Cæsar by Rich?. Montague.
1. The Works of Jonnnis Cosin.
1. Peter Charron's Works of Wisdom.
1. The Testimony of ye twelve Patriarchs.
1. The History of *Prince* Ernstus.
1. Barton Holydays broll against disloyalty.

1. A preparation to the Sacrament.
1. Mr. Bollin's works.
1. The last words of ye Lady Margaret la (illegible)
1. Heaven opened by E. A.
1. The Protestant Religion maintain'd by the Ministers of ye Gospel in Boston.
1. The (illegible) corrected by George Keith.
1. John Napier's works.
1. Love and Gallantry by Nathl. Neel.
1. *Festiron's* Notes upon Don Quixote.
1. Eikon Bascilike.
1. The Portraiture of his Sacred Majesty King Charles in his solitude and suffering.
1. Edw?. Lyford's Works.
1. The ruins of Papacy by Peter de Moulin.
1. Mary Magdalen's tears wiped off.
1. The Mysteria of redemption by (illegible)
1. Kneeling of God by John Danforth.
1. The (illegible) of true love by Tho. Tuke.
1. A history of ye United Netherlands.
1. Aulus Persius Flaccus, his Satires.
1. A true history of ye wars of Ireland, Flanders &c.
1. Gallantry a la mode.
1. The Christian Temple, printed in Boston.
1. John Quarles' Poems.
1. The Compleat Statesman by the Earl of Shaftsbury.
1. Poems by John Hall.
1. Remains of the Royal Martyr King Charles.
1. Ceremony monger his Character.
1. Divine Poems by F. Quarles.
1. Iter Boreale by Rich?. Wild.
1. Mr. Everard Mainwaring's Doct?. of Physic.
1. A. Manual of Devout & Godly Prayers.
1. Concerning Witchcraft, by Increase Mather.
1. Divine Fancies digested by F. Quarles.

1. Chyrurgical Addresses made to S. Hartlit.
1. French Book.
1. History of the World.
1. Homer's Iliad.
1. The Young Clerk's Companion.
1. Plutarch's Lives.
1. Du Bartin his Works.
1. The Works of Virgil.
1. The Compleat History of Europe.
1. Sr. Henry Morgin of ye Bucaniora.

1. Joseph Glenville upon Witchcraft.
1. Nomenclature.
1. The Life of Florus—a Roman History.
1. Book of Characters.
1. Mrs. Broadstreet upon the (illegible.)
1. Rathbon's Surveyor.
1. The Dutch History of China.
1. Hopton's Concordance inlarged.
3. Jacob (illegible) Works.

(Signed)   Fra'. Brinley.

BOOKS AT ROXBURY.

1. Sir Walter Raleigh's H. of ye World.
1. The Civil Wars of France.
1. English Chronicles.
1. Greek Testament.

1. A Tomary of Paradoxes by Walter Charleton.
1. A Dutch Waggoner.
1. Latin Bible.
1. Euclid's Elements.

(Signed)   Francis Brinley.

GORDONIAN INCONSISTENCY.

The following instance of the want of consistency in Dr. Gordon's History, is very striking: Under the date of " Dec. 8, 1775," he says, " There is a general reluctance among the soldiers to inlisting afresh. The Massachusetts people show as much backwardness as the others. In short, they expect to be *hired*, and that at a very high price, to defend their liberties; and *choose* to be *slaves*, unless they can be *bribed* to be *freemen*. But yet, under the date of " Dec. 11, 1775," he says, " About 2000 militia arrived in camp, and 3000 more were expected every hour." Does this look like reluctance? Again, under the date of " Dec. 15, 1775," he says, " Let me now give you the following anecdote. Deacon Whitcomb, of Lancaster, (who was a member of the Massachusetts Assembly until the present contest, had served in former wars, and been in different engagements,) had served as a Colonel in the American army; but on account of his age was left out upon the late new regulation. His men highly resented it, and declared they would not inlist again, after their time was out. The Colonel told them he did not doubt there were sufficient reasons for the regulation, and he was satisfied with it; he then blamed them for their conduct, and said he would inlist as a private. A Col. Brewer heard of it, and offered to resign in favor of Col. Whitcomb. The whole coming to Gen. Washington's ears, he has allowed of Col. Brewer's resignation in Col. Whitcomb's favor, appointed the former Barrack-Master, until he can further promote him, and acquainted the army with the whole affair in general orders." Who but Dr. G. could have talked of " reluctance, and being raised," with such and many such instances before his eyes—instances which would have done honor to Romans—and which, had they been British, would have shone with lustre in the Doctor's pages.   A FREEMAN.

[*Centinel*, 1 *Aug.* 1789]

PERKINS FAMILY OF HAMPTON, N. H.[*]

[By Asa W. Brown, of East Rockport, O.]

Abraham and Isaac Perkins appear to have been among the grantees of Hampton. They were among the first to have their children baptized by Mr. Bachelor at that place. Abraham's son Abraham, born 2 Sept. 1639, baptized 15 Dec. 1639, is said to have been the first white *male* child born in Hampton. Two female children, namely, Mary, daughter of Robert and Lydia Sanderson, and Susanna, dau. of Thomas and Abigail Jones, were baptized 29 Oct. 1639. One of them was probably the first white child born there.

An old family bible, still preserved in Rye among the descendants of Abraham, gives the births of eleven of his thirteen children. Mr. Parsons of Rye favored me with the dates there recorded, and told me that Abraham Perkins, Jr. was the first male child born in Hampton, as stated above. This fact is either on record in the old bible, or has come down with it by tradition. This bible is the only one I have heard of, that gives the record of the first generation of any family in Hampton. By combining the dates from the bible and the town books, which vary, I have prepared the following record :—

I. ABRAHAM[1] PERKINS, born abt. 1611, d. 31 Aug. 1683; m. Mary ——, b. abt. 1618, d. 29 May, 1706. They had ch.: 1, *Mary,*[2] bp. 15 Dec. 1639, with her br. Abraham; m. 7 June, 1652, Giles Fifield, and removed to Charlestown, Mass. Her daughter Mary[3] was living in 1683.—2, *Abraham*[2] (ii) b. 2 Sept. 1639; m. Elizabeth Sleeper, 27 Aug. 1668; killed by the Indians, 13 June, 1677.—3, *Humphrey,*[2] b. 22 Jan. 1642; d. young.—4, *James,*[2] b. 11 April, 1644; d. young.—5, *Timothy,*[2] b. July, 1646; d. young.—6, *James,*[2] (iii) b. 5 Oct. 1647; 1st w. Mary; m. 2d, Leah Cox, 13 Dec. 1681; will dated 8 May, 1723, proved 9 Dec. 1731.—7, *Jonathan,*[2] (iv) b. 28 or 30 May, 1650, d. 20 or 21 Jan. 1689; m. at Exeter, 20 Dec. 1682, Sarah ——, who survived him, and m. in 1690 Josiah Sanborn. She d. at Hampton, 1 Sept. 1748, æ 85.—8, *David,*[2] b. 28 April or 2 Feb. 1653, living 1683. In 1691, Elizabeth Perkins, dau. of Francis Brown of Newbury, was living. *Qu.* Was this David's wife? and had he a son John?—9, *Abigail,*[2] b. 2 April, 1655; m. John Foulsham, 10 Nov. 1675.—10, *Timothy,*[2] b. 29 June, 1657, d. 29 Jan. 1660.—11, *Sarah,*[2] b. 7 or 26 July, 1659; living in 1683.—12, *Humphrey,*[2] (v) b. 16 or 17 May, 1661, d. at H. 7 Jan. 1712; m. Martha Moulton, b. 16 Nov. 1666, dau. of Lieut. John M.—13, *Luke,*[2] living in 1683.—The record shows that Abraham[1] Perkins had ten sons, of whom four died young; two more, Abraham,[2] Jr. and Jonathan,[2] became extinct in the male line; and two more, David and Luke, disappear from Hampton; (*Qu.* Did they remove to Bridgewater?) leaving only two sons, namely, James[2] and Humphrey,[2] whose descendants of the male line live in or near Hampton.

II. ABRAHAM[2] PERKINS (i, 2,) by wife Elizabeth, had ch.: 1, *Mercy,*[3] b. 3 July, 1671; m. 12 July, 1694, Samuel Chandler of Salisbury or

---

[*] A genealogy of this family was published in Vol. X. p. 215, which is not so full as this, the compiler of the former not having access to documents obtained by Mr. Brown.

Amesbury.—2, *Mary*,[2] b. 20 Nov. 1673; m. 26 Oct. 1692, John Moulton; d. 11 Aug. 1707; Hampton.—3, *Elizabeth*,[2] b. 9 April, 1676; m. 5 April, 1697, Jeremiah Dow, a quaker; lived at Salisbury and at Hampton Falls.

III. JAMES[2] PERKINS (i, 6,) had ch.: 1, *Jonathan*,[3] b. 6 May, 1675; d. young.—2, *Sarah*,[3] b. 3 Oct. 1682; m. Mr. Graves. Qu. Were they the Samuel Graves and wife Sarah who were living in 1722 at Nutfield? 3, *Mary*,[3] b. 2 Dec. 1686; m. 1707, Jonathan Taylor, who died in 1724, leaving his widow with 6 or 8 ch.—4, *Lydia*,[3] b. ab. 30 Jun. 1689; m. Joseph Clifford, 5 Jan. 1716; d. at Kingston, 8 Sept. 1723.—5, *Hannah*,[3] b. 18 Aug. 1691; m. Simon Moulton, 2 March, 1692; removed from Hampton (to Chester?) after 1730.—6, *Elizabeth*,[3] b. 1693-4; m. 26 Nov. 1719, Joseph Philbrook; d. 26 March, 1736, leaving 3 ch. at Hampton.—7, *James*,[3] (vi) b. 17 March, 1696; m. 22 Feb. 1729, Sarah Nason: d. 31 March, 1755, at Kensington.—8, *Moses*,[3] (vii) b. 30 July, 1698; m. 1st, Mary Marston, 26 Feb. 1730; m. 2d, Hannah Nay, 11 Feb. 1760; d. 14 Aug. 1765.—9, *David*,[3] b. 30 Nov. 1701; living 1728. Qu. Did he remove from H.?

IV. JONATHAN[2] PERKINS (i, 7,) by wife Sarah, had ch.: 1, *Abraham*,[3] (viii) b. ab. 1684; d. 14 April, 1715, æ 31; his widow, Mary, d. 6 Nov. 1738, æ 55.—2, *Abigail*,[3] b. 30 April, 1687.

V. HUMPHREY[2] PERKINS (i, 12,) had ch.: 1, *John*,[3] b. 12 March, 1688. 2, *Humphrey*,[3] b. March, 1690.—3, *Jonathan*,[3] b. 24 Nov. 1691; d. a young man.—4, *Mary*,[3] b. 28 Nov. 1693; m. 20 Dec. 1722, Samuel French; d. at Kensington, 14 Nov. 1766.—5, *James*,[3] (ix) b. 9 Sept 1695; m. 21 Dec. 1717, Huldah Robey; d. at Rye, 18 April, 1774.—6, *Martha*,[3] m. 16 Sept. 1720, Ephraim Leonard of Bridgewater.—7, *Sarah*,[3] m. 27 June, 1726, Stephen Flanders of Exeter.—8, *Abigail*,[3] m. Mr. Leonard of Bridgewater.—The last three children were bap. 7 Dec. 1712, eleven months after their father's death. I have no account of the sons, except James[3] Perkins of Rye.

VI. JAMES[3] PERKINS (iii, 7.)—His wife Shuah was, according to tradition, a remarkable woman. Theirs was one of the first families that settled at Kensington, and she endured privations of no ordinary kind. At her husband's death she was left with a large family, whom she supported by her own hands. Two of her sons, at their country's call, shouldered their muskets in '76, and died in its service. She was born 21 Nov. 1707, and d. 8 Sept. 1803. Their ch. were: 1, *David*,[4] d. 30 Jan. 1735-6 (?) of the throat distemper.—2, *Lydia*,[4] d. 17 Jan. 1735-6 (?) of the throat distemper.—3, *Jonathan*,[4] (x) b. 14 April, 1732; d. 14 Sept 1776, in the army; m. 3 Nov. 1757, Abigail Blake.—4, *Betsey*,[4] b. 1735; d. 5 Feb. 1736, of the throat distemper.—5, *Lydia*,[4] b. 14 April, 1737; m. 8 May, 1755, Caleb Brown, son of Josiah; d. at Kensington, 11 Nov. 1831, in her 95th year.—6, *David*,[4] b. 11 Feb. 1739. Qu. Did he m. Mary French of Kingston, 11 July, 1763?—7, *Abraham*,[4] b. 19 Dec. 1740; d. 10 Nov. 1748, of the throat distemper.—8, *Moses*,[4] (xi) b. 10 Sept. 1742; d. in the army, 26 July, 1776; m. 31 Oct. 1766, Betsey Sherburn.—9, *Betsey*,[4] b. 1744; d. 7 Sept. 1744.—10, *Simon*,[4] (xii) b. 22 Sept. 1745; m. 23 Nov. 1769, Abigail Blake.—11, *Shuah*,[4] b. 20 Dec. 1746; m. Benjamin Tilton, 30 Oct. 1765.—12, *Joseph*,[4] bp. 26 March, 1749. Qu. Did he m. Mary Gove of Weare?—13, *Benjamin*,[4] bp. 28 March, 1749; d. 26 Dec. 1757.—14, A child,[4] not named ou record; prob. d. at birth.—15, *Huldah*,[4] bp. 15 April, 1753; d. unm. at Kensington, 20 July, 1815.—16, A posthumous child,[4] of whom we had no record.

VII. Moses[3] Perkins (iii. 8) of Hampton, had ch.: 1, *James*,[4] (xiii) b. 23 Feb. 1731; d. 6 July, 1776; m. 1st, Abigail Knowles; m. 2d, Jane Moulton, 10 Dec. 1767.—2, *Samuel*,[4] b. 9 Jan. 1733; d. at Deerfield, 24 April, 1827, æ 94; m. 16 Oct. 1768, Lydia Kenniston.—3, *Sarah*,[4] b. 15 Feb. 1735; d. at Hampton Falls, 16 March, 1827, æ 89; m. 21 July, 1755, Isaiah Lane.—4, *Mary*,[4] b. 26 March, 1737; d. 9 or 12 July, 1738.—5, *David*,[4] b. 15 Jan. 1739; d. at Newbury, 14 March, 1805.—6, *Elizabeth*,[4] b. 9 Nov. 1740; m. 26 Nov. 1760, Josiah Lane; d. at Hampton, 25 Nov. 1810.—7, *Moses*,[4] b. 1 Nov. 1742.—8, *Jonathan*,[4] b. 15 June, 1745; d. 26 Nov. 1830, æ 85.—9, *Reuben*,[4] b. 5 Dec. 1747; m. Dolly Swain, 10 Nov. 1773.—10, *Mary*,[4] b. 24 June, 1750; d. 8 Dec. 1836, at H. Falls, æ. 86.—11, *John*,[4] b. 24 Feb. 1753; d. 21 Aug. 1754.

VIII. Abraham[3] Perkins (iv. 1,) had ch.: 1, *Keziah*,[4] b. 25 April, 1709; m. James Towle, 22 July, 1725; d. at Hampton, 12 Dec. 1794.—2, *Anne*,[4] b. 7 May, 1714; d. 7 May, 1715.

IX. James[3] Perkins (v. 5,) had ch.: 1, *Huldah*,[4] b. 28 Sept. 1718; m. 22 March, 1739, Elijah Lock.—2, *Anne*,[4] b. 21 Aug. 1720; m. 11 Nov. 1740, Stephen Page; d. at Hampton, 28 May, 1752.—3, *John*,[4] b. 8 Jan. 1723; m. 10 March, 1748, Ann (or Annis) Lock.—4, *Jonathan*,[4] b. 7 June, 1725; d. young.—5, *Abraham*,[4] bp. 27 Oct. 1728; m. 7 April, 1752, Mehitable Towle, and had a son Abraham[5] bp. 22 Jan. 1754.—6, *Martha*,[4] bp. 23 April, 1732; m. 1st, Henry Dow of Rye; m. 2d, Simon Lamprey of Northampton, 5 July, 1760.—7, *James*,[4] (xiv) bp. 5 Jan. 1735; m. 23 Feb. 1758, Abigail Lock.

X. Jonathan[3] Perkins (vi. 3,) had ch.: 1, A dau,[4] d. an infant.—2, *Mary*,[4] b. 5 July, 1759; m. 28 March, 1779, Samuel Longfellow; rem. to Maine.—3, *Betty*,[4] b. 26 Sept. 1761; m. 27 Nov. 1781, Edward Lock of Seabrook.—4, *Olive*,[4] b. 20 Dec. 1763; m. Thomas Bagley; rem. to Vermont.—5, *Abigail*,[4] b. 27 May, 1766; m. 4 Nov. 1784, Abraham Green; rem. to Weare.—6, *Jemima*,[4] b. 1 June, 1768; d. 10 Sept. 1769.—7, *Lucy*,[4] b. 28 May, 1770; m. Samuel Colby; d. at Weare.—8, *Jonathan*,[4] b. 1 Dec. 1772; m. Phebe ——; lived near Vienna, Vt.—9, *Dearborn*,[4] b. 30 May, 1775; m. Sarah Ring of Warner; d. at Danbury. ·

XI. Moses[4] Perkins (vi. 8,) had ch.: 1, *John*,[5] b. 19 Jan. 1767.—2, *James*,[5] b. 13 Sept. 1769.—3, *Samuel*,[5] b. 13 July, 1772; d. 5 July, 1773.—4, *Samuel*,[5] b. 27 April, 1774; d. 26 March, 1776.

XII. Simon[4] Perkins (vi. 10,) had ch.: 1, *Simon*,[5] b. 28 May, 1774; m. 12 Nov. 1795, Ann Greenleaf; d. at Kensington, 4 June, 1843.—2, *Meshack*,[5] b. 1 Sept. 1776; m. Rachel Prescott; rem. to Kennebec Co., Maine.—3, *Jemima*,[5] b. 9 Aug. 1781; living at Kensington unm.—4, *Sally*,[5] bp. 30 Aug. 1783; m. John Leavitt of Exeter.—5, *Samuel*,[5] bp. 12 June, 1791; m. and lives at Methuen.—6, *Polly*,[5] bp. 30 Aug. 1795; m. 4 Nov. 1816, Nathan Dow of Kensington.

XIII. JAMES[4] PERKINS (vii. 1,) had ch. by 1st w.: 1, *Moses,*[5] bp. 27 April, 1760; m. 2 Dec. 1787, Molly Palmer; d. at Hampton, 16 Jan. 1839.—2, *Abigail Knowles,*[5] bp. 28 March, 1762; d. 9 Oct. 1776.—He had also several ch. by his 2d wife.

XIV. JAMES[4] PERKINS (ix. 3,) had ch.: 1, *Mary,*[5] bp. 24 June, 1759; m. 1 April, 1777, Nathaniel Emery.—2, *Anne,*[5] bp. 12 Sept. 1762; d. young.—3, *John,*[5] bp. 18 Nov. 1764; m. 9 Feb. 1792, Joanna Elkins.—4, *Anne,*[5] bp. 24 May, 1767; m. 4 March, 1787, Jonathan Sherburn of Portsmouth.—5, *James,*[5] bp. April, 1769; m. Molly Perkins (6 Feb.?) 1791.—6, *Jonathan,*[5] bp. 16 Feb. 1772.—7, *Josiah,*[5] bp. 24 July, 1774.—8, *Huldah,*[5] bp. 25 May, 1777.—9, *Hannah,*[5] bp. 16 July, 1780.

XV. ISAAC[1] PERKINS of Hampton was apparently a younger man than Abraham[1]; and was probably born about 1612–13. He d. 13 Nov. 1685. His wife was named Susannah. His children were: 1?, *Lydia,*[2] m. 17 Oct. 1659, Eliakim Wardhall.—2, *Isaac,*[2] bp. 8 Dec. 1639; drowned 30 Oct. 1661.—3, *Jacob,*[2] (xvi) bp. 21 May, 1640; m. 30 Dec. 1669, Mary Philbrook.—4?, *Rebecca,*[2] m. 21 Sept. 1659, John Huzzey, and was mother of 16 ch.—5, *Daniel,*[2] d. 1 Aug. 1662.—6?, *Caleb,*[2] (xvii) m. 24 April, 1677, Bethiah Philbrook.—7, *Benjamin,*[2] b. 17 Feb. 1650: d. 23 Nov. 1670.—8, *Susan,*[2] b. 21 Aug. 1652; m. 1st, Isaac Buzwell of Salisbury, 12 May. 1673; m. 2d, William Fuller, Jr. of Hampton, 22 June, 1680.—9, *Hannah,*[2] b. 24 Feb. 1656; m. James Philbrook, 1 Dec. 1674; d. 23 May, 1739, æ 83.—10, *Mary,*[2] b. 23 July, 1658; prob. m. Isaac Chase of Hampton.—11, *Ebenezer,*[2] (xviii) b. 9 Dec. 1659; w. Mary.—12, *Joseph,*[2] (xix) b. 9 April, 1661; w. Martha.—I have found no will of Isaac[1] Perkins, nor any settlement of his estate; so that there is a possibility that *Lydia, Rebecca* and *Caleb* were not his children. I have little doubt that they were. It will be seen that one of the sons of Isaac,[1] namely, Joseph,[2] had a son Caleb. None of the descendants of Isaac[1] Perkins remained in or near Hampton excepting those of Caleb.[2]

XVI. JACOB[2] PERKINS (xv. 3,) had ch.: 1, *Isaac,*[3] b. 18 Dec. 1671.—2, *Jacob,*[3] b. 24 Dec. 1674.—3?, *Alice,*[3] m. John Marden. 16 Nov. 1699.—4, *Mary,*[3] b. 10 Aug. 1678.—5, *Benjamin,*[3] b. 12 Aug. 1692. We have no further knowledge of this family. *Qu.* Did they remove to York? Jacob Perkins of York m. Ann Linkfield of Wells, 17 Oct. 1717.

XVII. CALEB[2] PERKINS (xv. 6,) had ch.: 1, *Rhoda,*[3] b. 24 June, 1677; m. 24 May, 1700, Elias Philbrook, son of John of Greenland. She d. before 1722, leaving 3 ch., who were living in 1742, viz., Benjamin,[4] Caleb,[4] and Bethiah.[4] The latter was wife of Edward Palmer of Kensington.—2, *Benjamin,*[3] (xx) b. 11 May, 1680; m. 1 March, 1711, Lydia ——. He d. at Hampton Falls, 11 Feb. 1767.—3, *Anne,*[3] b. 19 March, 1682; prob. d. young.

XVIII. EBENEZER[2] PERKINS (xv. 11,) had ch.: 1, *Daniel,*[3] b. June, 1685.—2, *Abigail,*[3] b. 11 Aug. 1687.—3, *Jonathan,*[3] b. 10 May, 1691. This family probably removed from Hampton. On the 26 May, 1756, Jacob Kent was appointed administrator on the estate of Jonathan Perkins of Plaistow.

XIX. JOSEPH[2] PERKINS (xv. 12,) had ch.: 1, *Joseph,*[3] b. 28 July, 1689.—2, *John,*[3] b. 4 June, 1691.—3, *Caleb,*[3] b. 8 July, 1693. *Qu.* Did this family remove from Hampton?

XX. BENJAMIN[3] PERKINS (xvii. 2,) of Hampton Falls, had ch.: 1, *Joseph*,[4] (xxi) b. 5 May, 1712; d. 17 June, 1761; m. 31 Oct. 1734, Elizabeth Dow. A widow Perkins d. at Hampton Falls, 21 Nov. 1781.—2, *Lydia*,[4] b. 1 Nov. 1714; m. Gideon Dow, 12 Nov. 1735.—3, *Daniel*,[4] (xxii) b. 9 July, 1718; m. 28 May, 1741, Susanna Carr; d. in the army, 1755. His widow m. Daniel Carr, 26 Dec. 1757. The widow Carr d. at Kensington, 7 April, 1779.—4, *Mary*,[4] b. 19 April, 1721; m. Benjamin Robinson, 25 July, 1751.—5, *Jonathan*,[4] (xxiii) b. 30 Oct. 1723; m. Miriam True, 11 Dec. 1752.—6, *Abigail*,[4] b. 31 July, 1728; m. David Lowell, 26 Oct. 1749; d. at Epping, in 1825, æ. 97.

XXI. JOSEPH[4] PERKINS (xx. 1,) had ch.: 1, *David*,[5] b. 1 Oct. 1735; d. young.—2, *Lydia*,[5] b. 8 May, 1738; m. William Swain, 16 Feb. 1759.—3, *David*,[5] b. 3 Nov. 1740; m. Abigail Griffith, 22 March, 1764; d. 15 Aug. 1816.—4, *Sarah*,[5] b. 4 Jan. 1743.—5, *Benjamin*,[5] b. 17 Oct. 1746. *Qu.* Did he m. Elizabeth Creasy, 11 April, 1767?—6, *Hannah*,[5] b. 12 May, 1752.

XXII. DANIEL[4] PERKINS (xx. 3,) had ch.: 1, *Samuel*,[5] b. 22 Oct. 1741.—2, *Susannah*,[5] b. 4 Dec. 1743; m. Abraham Burnham, from Gloucester, Mass.; d. at Moultonboro', in 1779. He m. 2d, widow Lydia Fuller (a Bradley from Haverhill), who d. at Groton, Vt., aged 104 yrs. 9 mos.—3, *Mary*,[5] b. 29 Jan. 1746.—4, *Abigail*,[5] b 12 April, 1748; m. John Graves of New Andover.—5, *Daniel*,[5] b. 29 Sept. 1751.—6, *Mehitable*,[5] b. 26 Jan. 1755; m. Mr. Moulton of Moultonboro'.

XXIII. JONATHAN[4] PERKINS (xx. 5,) had ch.: 1, *True*,[5] b. 26 Oct. 1753.—2, *Jonathan*,[5] m. Rhoda Sanborn, 22 Feb. 1770, and had—1, Sarah,[6] b. 10 Jan. 1771; 2, Ezra,[6] b. 20 Aug. 1772; 3, Lucy,[6] b. 17 June, 1774; 4, Rhoda,[6] b. 13 Aug. 1776; 5, Mary,[6] b. 4 July, 1778, who m. James Brown of Chichester, 6 Oct. 1800.

THE TURN OF LIFE.

Between the years of forty and sixty, a man who has properly regulated himself may be considered in the prime of life. His matured strength of constitution renders him almost impervious to the attacks of disease, and experience has given soundness to his judgment. His mind is resolute, firm, and equal; all his functions are in the highest order; he assumes mastery over business; builds up a competence on the foundation he has formed in early manhood, and passes through a period of life attended by many gratifications. Having gone a year or two past sixty, he arrives at a stand-still. But athwart this is a viaduct, called the " Turn of Life," which, if crossed in safety, leads to the valley of " old age," round which the river winds, and then beyond without a boat or causeway to effect its passage. The bridge is, however, constructed of fragile materials, and it depends upon how it is trodden, whether it bend or break. Gout, apoplexy, are also in the vicinity to waylay the traveller, and thrust him from the pass; but let him gird up his loins and provide himself with a fitter staff, and he may trudge in safety, with perfect composure. To quit metaphor, " the Turn of Life," is a turn either into a prolonged walk, or into the grave. The system and powers having reached their utmost expansion, now begin to either close like flowers at sunset or break down at once. One injudicious stimulant, a single fatal excitement, may force it beyond its strength, whilst a careful supply of props, and the withdrawal of all that tends to force a plant, will sustain it in beauty and vigor until night has entirely set in.— *The Science of Life, by a Physician.*—Sept. 1857.

BIRTHS, MARRIAGES, AND DEATHS IN MALDEN.

[Continued from Vol. XI., p. 343.]

[Communicated by AARON SARGENT.]

BIRTHS.

Samuel,	son of	Unite & Lydia Cox	July 5, 1748
Mary,	dau. "	James & Mary Bucknam	" 16, "
Silas,	son "	David & Mary Parker	Aug. 6, "
Phebe,	dau. "	Joseph & Mary Lynde	" 15, "
John,	son "	John & Hannah Bucknam	" 20, "
John,	" "	John & Abigail Grover	Oct. 29, "
Asa & Elizab'h, s. & d. of Peletiah & Deborah Whittemore,			Nov. 19, "
Lydia,	dau. of	Ebenezer & Mary Brown	Dec. 1, "
Rebecca,	" "	Jacob & Rebecca Upham	" 2, "
Thomas,	son "	John & Phebe Knower	" 6, "
James,	" "	Robert & Anna Wilson	" 8, "
Hannah,	dau. "	Jabez & Hannah Burditt	" 10, "
Eunice,	" "	John & Judith Sprague	" 14, "
Thomas,	son "	Jacob & Mary Lynde	" 23, "
Edward,	" "	Edward & Sarah Oliver	Jan. 11, 1749
Sarah,	dau. "	Edward & Sarah Fuller	Feb. 9, "
Esther,	" "	Nathan & Esther Dexter	" 23, "
Ebenezer,	son "	Nath' & Abigail Paine	March 4, "
Stephen,	" "	Stephen & Catharine Tufts	" 28, 1749
Benoni,	" "	Benoni & Mary Vinten	" 31, "
Rebecca,	dau. "	Sam' & Rebecca Wayte	April 5, "
Daniel,	son "	Nathan & Tabitha Newhall	May 11, "
Samuel,	" "	Sam' & Sarah Blanchard	June 23, "
Mary,	dau. "	John & Susanna Sargeant	July 5, "
Sarah,	" "	Ezra & Eunice Green	" 11, "
Phineas,	son "	Joseph & Susanna Wayte	" 16, "
Mary,	dau. "	John & Elizabeth Oliver	Aug. 15, "
Rachel,	" "	Isaac & Deborah Wayte	" 17, "
Jonathan,	son "	Jon° and Mary Knower	" 22, "
John,	" "	John & Elizabeth Nichols	Sept. 16, "
Anna,	dau. "	William & Martha Gill	Oct. 4, "
Thomas,	son "	Thomas & Mary Wayte	" 6, "
Elizabeth,	dau. "	Solomon & Mary Townsend	Nov. 11, "
Hannah,	" "	Phineas & Hannah Sprague	" 19, "
Thomas,	son "	Joseph & Tabitha Burditt	Dec. 11, "
Mary,	dau. "	Benj. & Phebe Sprague	" 25, "
Thomas	son "	Thomas & Mary Sargeant	Jan. 17, 1749
Sarah,	dau. "	Jabez & Rachel Lynde	Feb. 19, "
Jemima,	" "	James & Mary Whittemore	" 19, "
Winslow,	son "	Silas & Mary Sargeant	" 26, "
John,	" "	John & Joanna Dexter	" 26, "
Lydia,	" "	Isaac & Sarah Hill	" 26, "
Mary,	" "	David & Mary Parker	March 12, "
Ebenezer,	son "	John & Esther Harnden	" 20, 1750
Elijah & Rebecca, s. & d. of Joseph & Bathsheba Caswell,			May 25, "

Elizabeth,	dau. of	Joseph & Mary Lynde	June 9, 1750
David,	son "	John & Hannah Bucknam	July 3, "
James,	" "	Sam' & Martha Wade	" 8, "
Loin,	dau. "	Sam' & Martha Sprague	" 13, "
Mary,	" "	Edw' & Sarah Fuller	" 27, "
John,	son "	Edw' & Dorothy Sprague	Aug. 20, "
Nathaniel,	" "	Nath' & Abigail Jenkins	" 21, "
Jabez,	" "	Jabez & Abigail Sargeant	Sept. 4, "
Barnard,	" "	Nathan & Tabitha Newhall	" 12, "
Rebecca,	dau. "	Unite & Lydia Cox	Oct. 26, "
Benjamin,	son "	Jabez & Deborah Burdin	" 26, "
Hannah,	dau. "	Peter & Hannah Edes	" 30, "
Bunker,	son "	Sam' & Elizabeth Sprague	" 30, "
Abigail,	dau. "	Daniel & Abigail Knower	Nov. 7, "
Aaron,	son "	Richard & Rebecca Dexter	" 11, "
Ann,	dau. "	John & Judith Sprague	" 20, "
Israel,	son "	Israel & Hannah Cook	Dec. 4, "
Anna,	dau. "	Stephen & Catharine Tufts	" 11, "
Mary,	" "	Timothy & Mary Upham	" 14, "
Elizabeth,	" "	John & Phebe Knower	" 21, "

MARRIAGES.

Jonathan Sargeant	and	Mary Lynde	Mch 13, 1700
Sam' Howard	"	Sible Lewis	
Joseph Lewis	"	Hannah Jones	
Benj Buronap	"	Elizabeth Newhall	
Eben' Harndell	"	Rebecca Alien,	
Ephraim Grover	"	Mary Pratt	in yᵉ year 1700
Joseph Green	"	Hannah Green	
Zachariah Hill	"	Judith Bucknam,	
John Green	"	Izeball Wiman	
Oliver Atwood	"	Anna Bets	
Sam' Tapan	"	Abigail Wigglesworth	Dec. 23, 1700
Obadiah Abba	"	Elizabeth Wilkinson	" 26, 1701
Thomas Waitte	"	Deborah Sargeant	" " "
Joseph Waitt	"	Lydia Sargeant	in yᵉ year 1701
Sam' Green	"	Martha Green	Feb. 12, 170¾
Joseph Townsend	"	Sarah Atwells	in yᵉ year 1702
Benj Whittemore	"	Elizabeth Cenecut	Dec. 17, "
William Sargeant	"	Mary Lewis	" 30, "
James Whittemore	"	Hannah ———	May, 1703
Phineas Upham	"	Tamzen Hill	Nov. 23, "
Moses Hill	"	Sarah Parker	Dec. 1, 1708
Steven Armstrong	"	Hannah Willcoxon	" 16, "
James Upham	"	Dorothy Wigglesworth	June 2, 1709
James Moulton	"	Bethiah Emes	" 31 (30?) "
Elias Totingham,	"	Rebecca Grover	Oct. 18, "
Joseph Chesse	"	Abignil Hill	Dec. 1, "
Abraham Cuzeas	"	Abigail Wilkinson	Jan. 4, 17½
Nath' Wilson	"	Martha Newhall	" 5, 17½
John Lereby	"	Elizabeth Jordan	Sept. 29, 1710
Zachrie Howard	"	Mary Jenkins	Dec. 27, "

Sam¹ Wilson	and	Margaret Chamberlin	Mch 6, 171¾
John Brintnall	"	Deborah Mellins	Aug. 28, 1712
William Johnson	"	Sarah Wilkinson	Nov. 6, "
Jonathan Waitt	"	Elizabeth Pratt	" 20, "
Benjamin Teele	"	Anna Jenkins	Dec. 31, "
James Hayes	"	Mehitable Sprague	Jan. 22, 171¾
Sam¹ Grover	"	Sarah Upham,	April 17, 1713
John Griffin	"	Mary Upham	May 28, "
Joseph Sargeant	"	Hannah Bucknam	June 4, "
Patrick Flinn	"	Mary Winsled	July 16, "
Sam¹ Newhall	"	Sarah Sargeant	Dec. 3, "
David Green	"	Martha Pratt	" 10, "
Joseph Lynde	"	Mary Sprague	Oct. 21, 1714
John Shute	"	Mary Wayte	" 27, "
Peter Edes	"	Martha Mudge	Nov. 16, "
Samuel Sargeant	"	Elizabeth Pratt	Dec. 2, "
Jonathan Howard	"	Anna Pratt	Jan. 13, 171¾
Sam¹ Upham	"	Mary Grover	Feb. 17, "
Sam¹ Mower	"	Elizabeth Sprague	Jan. 4, 171¾
Jabez Sargeant	"	Mary Lynde	Aug. 21, 1716
Jonathan Waitt	"	Abigail Wait	Sept. 26, "
Nath¹ Nichols	"	Ruth Upham	Jan. 22, 171¾
Sam¹ Sprague	"	Joanna Lynde	Mch 20, "
William Paine	"	Tabitha Waitt	Apl 18, 1717
Isaac Green	"	Mary Pratt	May 2, "
Eben¹ Upham	"	Elizabeth Blanchard	Oct. 10, "
Sam¹ Wason	"	Joanna Upham	Nov. 25, 1717
Jonathan Sargeant	"	Mary Sprague	" 26, "
William Sprague	"	Dorothy Floyd	Jan. 1, 171¾
Simon Grover	"	Mary Right	" 15, "
John Upham	"	Tamzen ong	May 7, 1718
Josiah Blanchard	"	Elizabeth Morison	Dec. 6, 1721
Richard Pratt	"	Joanna ong	" 19, "
John Burditt	"	Hannah Cole	July 5, 1722
John Sweetser	"	Martha Green	Oct. 2, "
Thomas Wayte	"	Abigail Heacy	Jan. 10, 1723
James Baldwin	"	Mary Stower	Feb. 7, "
John Coleman	"	Dorothy Upham	Apl 23, "
Abiathar Vinton	"	Lydia Green	" 30, "
Phineas Sargeant	"	Abigail Pratt	Dec. 31, 1724
Jacob Freese	"	Dorothy Moulton	Mch 31, 1725
Thomas Douglass	"	Mary Sargeant	June 10, "
Thomas Pratt	"	Lydia Lynde	" 24, "
Benj Blaney	"	Abigail Bucknam	Oct. 13, "
John Thomas	"	Elizabeth Nichols	Nov. 30, "
Phillip Sweetser	"	Mary Green	Dec. 30, "
Thomas Green	"	Martha Lynde	Jan. 13, 172¾
Joseph Green	"	Ruth Dexter	" 25, "
Thomas Blanchard	"	Judith Hill	Feb. 21, "
Timothy Wait	"	Mary Oakes	Apl 28, 1726
Jonathan Howard	"	Mary Harndall	June 1, "
Robert Snelling of Boston and Lydia Dexter of Malden,			" 30, "
John Woolson of Weston and Elizabeth Upham of Malden,			Oct. 6, "

Amos Putnam   and Hannah Lynde   Dec. 27, 1726
Daniel Floyd   "   Margaret Jenkins   Feb. 7, 1725
Jotham Tuttle   "   Martha Hall   Mch 1, 1727
Thomas Degrusha   "   Hannah Howard, but ye time not returned.
James Hill   "   Lois Upham   July 5,
Sam' Howard   "   Elizabeth Wayte   "   12,   "
Sam' Green   "   Lois Sprague   Feb. 15, 1727
Eben' Brown of Mendon & Mary Dexter of Malden   Apl 4, 1728
Abraham Lewis of Marblehead & Elizabeth Atwood of Malden Dec. 12, "
Daniel Newhall   and Tabitha Upham   Dec. 26,   "
James Barrett   "   Mary Bucknam   Feb. 13, 1728
Isaac Wheeler   "   Mehitable Sweetser   Apl 17, 1729
Richard Pratt   "   Rebecca Harnden   July 9,   "
John Emerson of Topsfield & Elizabeth Pratt of Malden   Oct. 23,   "
Thomas Burditt and Sarah Newhall   Dec. 4,
John Blodt of Boston & Sarah Nichols of Malden   Feb. 6, 1734
Robert Levenstone & Zabiah Sargeant   Mch 12,   "
John Hacy of Rumney Marsh & Abigail Dexter of Malden,   Nov. 17, 1730
Richard Perkins of Boston & Judith Bucknam of Malden,   Dec. 3,   "
Edward Hallowell of Malden & Huldah Farrington of Lynn   "   25,   "
Phineas Upham and Hannah Waite   "   "   "
Benjamin Tufts of Medford & Mary Hutchinson of Malden   Jan. 7, 1734
Samuel Wayte   and Elizabeth Pratt   Mch 16,   "
Jacob Burditt   "   Rebekah Brown   "   30, 1731
Thomas Parker, Jr. "   Mary Upham   Apl 5,   "
James Barrett of Killingley & Tabitha Hill of Malden   May 6,   "
Michael Sweetser and Mary Smith   Nov. 18,   "
Ezekiel Jenkins   "   Phebe Sprague   Aug. 3, 1732
Joseph Chadwick of Falmouth & Mary Jenkins of Malden   Nov. 2,   "
John Goddard of Roxbury & Mary Sprague of Malden   "   15,   "
Patrick Cowen of Malden & Jean Crawford of Lynn   Feb. 22, 1734
David Green of Reading & Hannah Marble of Malden   Mch 15,   "
Thomas Richardson and Ruth Bucknam   June 26, 1733
Thomas Mighills of Pomfret & Mary Howard of Malden   Sept. 6,   "
Benjamin Faulkner and Anna Green   Oct 25,   "
Nath' Paine   "   Abigail Hasey   Feb. 5, 1733
Ebenezer Harnden of Malden & Lydia Wade of Medford   "   25,   "
John Sprague of Malden & Judith Green of Stoneham   Apl. 11, 1734
David Pratt   and Mercy Upham   "   18,   "
Joshua Whittemore   "   Elizabeth Whittemore   "   25,   "
Asa Hill of Sherburne & Sarah Hill of Malden   May 29,   "
Ebenezer Barrett and Elizabeth Sargeant   Nov. 7,   "
Isaac Waite   "   Deborah Waite   "   28,   "
Samuel Evans of Reading & Sarah Marble of Malden   Nov. 3, 1735
Richard Whittemore of Killingley & Elizabeth Baldwin of
                                              Malden, Dec. 26,   "
Thomas Lynde & Joanna Parker,   "   27,   "
Benjamin Farnsworth of Groton & Rebecca Pratt of Malden May 19, 1736
William Deane of Cambridge & Mary Green of Malden   "   20,   "
Thomas Jenkins of Boston & Anna Sargeant of Malden   June 15,   "
Phineas Walker of Brookfield & Ruth Chadwick of Malden   July 3,   "
Samuel Sweetser & Mary Burditt   "   8,   "

[To be Continued.]

BOOK NOTICES

An Historical Discourse in commemoration of the One Hundredth Anniversary of the Formation of the First Congregational Church in Templeton, Massachusetts. With an Appendix, embracing a Survey of the Municipal Affairs of the Town. By Edwin G. Adams, *Junior Pastor. Boston, 1857. 8vo., pp. 175.*

The above able and interesting Discourse, containing an historical sketch of the early settlement of the town and of the Annals of the Church, was delivered on Sunday, Dec. 9, 1855. Its publication, however, was delayed till the present year, to enable the author to comply with the desire expressed, as he says, from many sources, to accompany it with some account also of the Municipal affairs of the town since its incorporation.

In the hundred years now closed there have been five ministers, three of whom are still living and two of them remain pastors of the Church. The ministry of the first, Rev. Daniel Pond, continued but three or four years. That of Rev. Ebenezer Sparhawk continued forty-four years till his death. The next in order, the present senior pastor, Rev. Charles Wellington, D. D., has recently preached his half-century Sermon,* receiving on the occasion gratifying testimonials of the respect and affection of those among whom he has so long lived and labored. Rev. Norwood Damon was settled as Colleague pastor in 1844, and remained a little more than a year and a half. The author of this Discourse was ordained as Colleague Jan. 13, 1847. He has faithfully given us in his Discourse the simple annals of the parish, a portraiture of its ministers, its statistics, and the varied changes of a Century. It seems to us a model of what such a Discourse should be.

The Appendix occupies 101 of the 175 pages of this valuable pamphlet, and yields not in interest to the Discourse itself. But being prepared in so short a time, it could not be expected to be sufficiently full and minute to fill the place of a town history. We hope Mr. Adams will continue his researches and investigations, and that by the time of the Centennial Anniversary of the incorporation of the town, which we believe will occur in 1862, he will be able to give the public a thorough and authentic History of the town, accompanied with genealogies of the families of the early settlers.   A.

Address of Hon. William G. Bates, *at the Laying of the Corner Stone of Westfield Academy, July 31st, 1857. Springfield, 1857. 8vo., pp. 20.*

Westfield has a written history, but it was published many years ago. That history, though small, is a corner stone on which another may be constructed. The history of an important institution in a town should form a chapter of great interest in its general history.

The Rev. Dr. Davis, in his few introductory remarks, carried back the ceremony of laying corner stones to a period of great antiquity. He said, "the friends of Job, who is supposed to have lived in the days of Abraham, asked him (Job, of course,) if he knew who laid the Corner Stone of the Earth?" But how Job answered that question, the Doctor does not inform us.

The Address of Mr. Bates is a historical document of great value, and must have been prepared with very considerable labor, as it is filled with names and dates.

Second Congregational Church in Berlin, [Ct.]—The Confession of Faith, Covenant, Ecclesiastical Principles and Rules, Forms of Admissions, etc., Historical Memoranda, Chronological Catalogue, and Alphabetical Index to September, 1857. Hartford: 1857. 12mo., pp. 94.

From works of this description, the future historians of towns must draw many of their most valuable facts   They are primary landmarks in the flood of time. The Second Church of Berlin is not an old one; dating back no farther than 1772, therefore it is not important to give any abstract of the work before us. It appears to be prepared with much care, and is published in a very neat manner.

---

* It was preached June 25, it having been postponed from Feb. 25, on account of his severe illness at that time.

The New Hampshire Annual Register for the year 1858.   By G. PARKER
  LYON.   Concord : 18mo. pp. 178.

This valuable little manual again greets us, and is heartily welcome. Our descriptions of it for previous years will give our readers a pretty good notion of what the work is for the present year; although its Editor is indefatigable in his labors to make every improvement which his long attention to the subject can suggest. No New Hampshire man should be without it.

*First Catalogue of Boscawen Academy, a Family Day School for Pri-
  mary, Academic, Normal and Collegiate Instruction, Boscawen, N. H.*
  JONATHAN TENNEY, Principal and Proprietor.   Concord, N. H. : 1857.
  8vo , pp. 16.

We do not recollect to have seen a more beautiful specimen of typography than is exhibited in this Catalogue of Mr. Tenney's School. Indeed the whole work discovers exquisite taste. Judging from his list of scholars, it is at least presumable that this Academy is in a flourishing condition. It is only necessary that the Principal should be known to insure him as large a school as he can wish.

*A Sermon in Commemoration of the 50th Anniversary of the Ordination,
  Feb. 25th, 1807, of the Author,* Rev. CHARLES WELLINGTON, *as Pastor
  of the First Congregational Church and Society in Templeton, Mass.*
  Boston: 1857.   8vo., pp. 39.

The venerable Author, in a prefatory note to his Sermon, tells us, that "The following Sermon is published neither by request, nor from a vain belief that it possesses any merits sufficient to entitle it to a publication; but only because it is an *Half-Century* Sermon; and because, as such, it may be regarded as a *injury* (though a trifling one) to the Author's parishioners and friends."
Besides being an excellent Discourse, it is an able comparative survey of the times of his ordination with the present. Mr. Wellington has appended to his Sermon a few valuable Notes; and no doubt every body who reads them will be very sorry they are so few.

The Early History of Florida.   An Introductory Lecture, delivered by
  GEORGE R. FAIRBANKS, Esq., before the Florida Historical Society,
  April 15th, 1857.   With an Appendix, containing the Constitution,
  Organization, and List of Members of the Society.   St. Augustine, Fla. :
  1857.   8vo., pp. 32.

In his Lecture, Mr. Fairbanks dwells chiefly upon the Spanish period of the History of Florida; and he has given us a very excellent summary view of that interesting period. The early English period of its history may be said to begin with the capture of St. Augustine by Sir Francis Drake in 1585. The fortress was manned at that time by about 150 Spanish soldiers, which was surrendered to Drake, and he carried thence to England fourteen pieces of cannon.
We hope to hear from time to time that the Florida Historical Society is flourishing, and that its members on the spot are busily engaged in rescuing the history of that State from oblivion.

DEATH OF TWO ENGLISH WRITERS.—Two persons, at one time intimately connected with newspaper literature in England, have recently died, viz.: Mr. John Black and James Silk Buckingham, the famous traveller. Mr. Black was for many years the editor of the Morning Chronicle, and Mr. Buckingham was the originator and first editor of the Athenæum. He once gave a course of public lectures in Boston, and made numerous addresses on Temperance in the United States.—*Newsp.* 20 *July*, 1855.

MARRIAGES AND DEATHS.

MARRIAGES.

Drake, Mr. John Robert, of Memphis, Tenn., (son of Mr. Samuel G. Drake of Boston) 24 Nov., to Miss Sarah H. Inman, youngest daughter of the late Henry Inman of New York, at Memphis, by the Rev. Dr. C. T. Quintard.

Porter, Josiah, Esq., of Cambridge, 21 Nov. 1837, at Boston, to Miss Caroline Hamilton Rice of Boston, by the Rev. Mr. Caleb Davis Bradlee.

Thaxter, Mr. A. Wallace, jr., of Boston, 25 May, 1837, at Boston, to Miss Mary Ellen Hill of St. Louis, by the Rev. Caleb Davis Bradlee.

Whiting, Mr. Wm. Henry, of Clark Co., Va., 3 Dec., to Miss Mary Jay, dau. of the late Judge Foote of Cooperstown, N. Y., in the city of New York.

DEATHS.

Alden, Mr. Simeon, Baltimore, Md., 9 Nov., æ. 64; formerly of Boston.

Barstow, Capt. Richard, jr., Havana, 5 Nov., in his 30th year; of yellow fever. He was master of the Sea Belle of Newport, R. I.

Bassett, Calvin, Belchertown, 1 Nov., æ. 80.

Beal, Mrs. Elsa, Lowell, 14 Nov., æ. 79, 7 mo.; widow of Mr. Benj. Beal of Hingham.

Birney, James G., Perth Amboy, N. J., 25 Nov., æ. 65; he was born in Danville, Ky., 1793; grad. Princeton and studied law with J. M. Dallas of Philadelphia. In 1808 he became a planter in Alabama, and owned 35 slaves, but soon after went to Huntsville in his native State, and entered upon the practice of his profession. He soon became a great anti-slavery advocate, freed his own slaves, and 21 which he induced his father to give him out of his patrimony. In 1834 he attempted to start an anti-slavery paper in Ky., but could get no one to print it; so he went over into Ohio and set one on foot, to which there was violent opposition. Prior to 1844 he was a resident of Michigan, and became the Liberty candidate for President of the United States. The movement of his party is believed by many to have been a great cause of the defeat of Henry Clay. His biography was published during his presidential campaign. He has a son at school in New Jersey, which occasioned his residence there. His second wife survives him, and is sister-in-law to the Hon. Gerrit Smith.

Bliss, Mr. John, Wilbraham, 23 Nov., æ. 76.

Bradley, Robert, Esq., Fryeburgh, Me., 11 Nov., æ. 83; formerly of Concord, N. H.

Burr, Mrs. Deborah, Salem, 13 Nov., æ. 83 yrs. 6 mo.

Burbank, Rev. William, Jefferson, Me., Oct., æ. 91.

Butler, Mrs. Huldah, Northampton, 12 Nov., æ. about 85; wid. of William Butler the founder of the Hampshire Gazette (1786) which he conducted some thirty years, and died in 1831. Mrs. B. was dau. of John Drown of Pittsfield, who joined the revolutionary army and was killed in the battle of the Mohawk, 1780. She was a teacher in early life, and was once a scholar of Master Elisha Ticknor of Boston. She had a sister Sally, wife of Dr. Hooker of Rutland, Vt. Henry C. Brown, many years High Sheriff of Berkshire, was her brother.—*Newspaper.*

Dozell, Mrs. Susan, Northwood, N. H., 9 Nov., æ. 81.

Castelaw, Patsy, (colored) New Bedford, 4 Nov., æ. 101 years. She was a slave for about 70 years to Alexander Cliff, of Hanover Co., Va., and was freed by him at his death. She came to New Bedford about four years ago, and lived with a daughter.

Clark, Capt. Joseph W., Charlestown, 11 Nov., æ. 78; formerly a shipmaster.

Clasby, Capt. Reuben, Nantucket, 16 Nov., æ. 80.

Collins, Daniel, M. D., Williamsburg, 8 Nov., æ. 77; a grad. of Williams College, 1803.

Davis, Mr. Charles, Jamaica Plain, 16 Nov., æ. 65, 4 mo.

Day, Mrs. Mary Ann Powers, 7 Nov., æ. 91; wife of Preston Day, Esq.

Dearborn, Mr. Samuel, Greenland, N. H., 11 Nov., æ. 85.

Derby, Mrs. Sarah, S. Danvers, 14 Oct., æ. 83 yrs. 6 mo.

De Visour, Prof. Francesco De, Savannah, Ga., 22 Nov., of consumption; a native of Cuba. He left Trinidad de Cuba when a youth, on account of political sentiments, and adopted the United States as his country; married Gertrude, the youngest daughter of Sumner Lincoln Fairfield. He was a great linguist, and for some time was a Prof. in the University of New York.

Dill, Mrs. Mary, Hull, 25 Aug., æ. 91; the oldest inhabitant of the town.

Doty, Mr. Jerathiel, South Wallingford, Vt., 14 Nov., æ. 83. Mr. D. was born in Rhode Island in 1764. He enlisted in the continental army when only fifteen years old, and served throughout the seven years' struggle. He was one of

the body-guard and escort of Lafayette to his native country. In 1812 Mr. Doty volunteered in his country's service, and took part in the operations at Plattsburg. He was buried on the 16th, with public honors, the people turning out en masse to manifest their respect for the departed veteran. The Declaration of Independence was read, an eulogy was pronounced by D. D. Nicholson, and the ceremonies closed by the Wallingford Rifle Company firing a farewell volley over his grave.— *Wallingford Local Spy.*

Dow, Mrs. Eliza, Beverly, 24 Nov., æ. 73; widow of the late Mr. James Dow.

Dutch, Miss Parmelia D., Exeter, N. H., 5 Nov., æ. 62; dau. of the late George and Abra Dutch of that town. w. p.

Dwinnel, Mr. Isaac, Tolland, Conn., 11 Nov., in his 76 yr.; Elder of the Baptist Church. He was the youngest child of Henry Dwinnel and Hannah Dargee of Millbury, and grandson of Jonathan Dwinnel and Mehitable Kenney, first settlers of Millbury (Sutton) in 1732, and great-grandson of Thomas Dwinnel and Dinah Brimsdell, the second son of Michael Dwinnel, one of the original settlers, and surveyor in laying out the town of Topsfield, Mass., previous to 1668.

Eames, Mrs. Mehitable, Wilmington, 31 August, æ. 99. She was a widow of the late Jonathan Eames, a soldier of the revolution. The deceased was possessed of a mild and amiable temper, which, together with her industrious and temperate habits, may account for her great longevity. She was mother of 6 children, 40 grand-children, and 64 great-grand-children.

Eddy, Mr. Caleb, Hancock, (at the United Society,) 20 Nov., æ. 72.

Edgerly, Joseph, Esq., Epping, N. H., Nov., æ. 81.

Ellsworth, Mr. Martin, Windsor, Ct., 2 Nov., æ. 74; son of the late Chief-Justice Ellsworth.

Fox, Mr. Ebenezer, Hollis, N. H., 6 Nov., æ. 73 yrs. 7 mo. An enterprising agriculturist, a most valuable citizen, and proverbially an honest man. (For his descent from Thomas Fox, see Worcester, Mrs. Zervier.)

Frost, Mr. Joseph, Dorchester, 23 Nov., æ. 74, 5 mo.

Frothingham, Dea. Nathaniel, 13 Nov., æ. 87. He was living in Charlestown in 1775, and escaped out of the town on the 19th of April; subsequently settled in Salem, and was an industrious mechanic, member of the General Court, &c.

Gammon, Mr. William, Stoneham, Me., 9 Nov., æ. 89.

Greaton, Miss Lucretia, Jamaica Plain, 12 Oct., æ. 88, dau. of the late Gen. John Greaton of the Revolutionary army.

Henderson, Mrs. Ann Maria, at Staunton,

Va., (residence of her son-in-law, Commander T. T. Craven, U. S. Navy,) 19 Oct., æ. 65, wid. of the late Dr. Thos. H., U. S. Army, and dau. of Com. Truxton.

Hersey, Mrs. Lydia, Pembroke, Me., 13 Nov., æ. 68.

Inches, Henderson, Esq., Boston, 9 Sept. 1857, æ. 83; long a retired merchant, a native of Boston, and a grad. of H. C., and the last survivor of the class of 1794. He was a highly respected citizen.

Josselyn, Mr. Jacob, Hanson, 18 Nov., æ. 83.

Keith, Royal, Esq., Grafton, 13 Nov., æ. 89.

Kettell, Mrs. Mary, Newburyport, 10 Nov., æ. 89, 9 mo.; wid. of Mr. Jonathan Kettell.

Lane, Mrs. Martha, Anisquam, 22 Oct., æ. 84; wid. of the late Mr. Aaron Lane.

Lane, Dea. Daniel, Norton, 1 Nov., in his 84th year.

Lane, Mrs. Sarah, Hubbardston, 2 Nov., æ. 83; wid. of Capt. Benj. I. Lane of Newburyport.

Little, Mrs. Mary Blake, Millwood, Clarke Co., Va., 21 Sept., æ. 76 yrs. and 1 mo. She was the dau. of Henry and Elizabeth Whiting, of Prince William Co., Va., and wife of Dr. R. H. Little.

Loring, Mr. Joshua, Marshfield, 7 Nov., æ. 84.

Marvin, Mrs. Thankful, East Berkshire, 6 Nov., in her 74 year; dau. of the late Samuel Barnard, Esq., of Deerfield, Ms.

Marston, Mrs. Susan, Salem, 23 Nov., æ. 79 and 9 mo.

Mayhew, Mrs. Eunice, Chilmark, 23 Oct., æ. 76; wid. of Mr. Abner Mayhew.

Moore, Mrs. Phebe, Amherst, 3 Nov.; wid. of Zephaniah Swift Moore, D. D., first President of Amherst College.

Morton, Capt. George, Adams, Ill., 10 Nov., æ. 76; formerly of Lynn, Mass.

Nason, Mrs. Eliza, Boston, 27 Nov., æ. 70; wid. of the late Mr. Joel Nason.

Nelson, Major Paul, Georgetown, Nov., æ. 83.

Otis, Mr. George W., Boston, 16 Nov., æ. 82.

Paige, Dea. Asbel, New Salem, 15 Nov., æ. 79.

Parker, Mr. Ebenezer, Cambridge, 13 Nov., in his 86th year. He was long the senior partner of the firm of Parker & Stevens,—of note some 40 years ago. Mr. P. was one of the enterprising merchants who built Colonnade Row, in Tremont Street, at the time the finest block of houses in the town.

Paine, Salmon, Charlotte, Vt., 23 July, 1857, in his 75th year. See Vol. III., page 349.

Perry, Mrs. Eunice, (widow,) Ashfield, Nov., æ. 87.

Pierce, Mr. Jeremiah, South Attleboro', 19 Nov., æ. 23 years, 7 mo. 14 days.

POOL, Mrs. Sarah, Rockport, 25 Oct., æ. 87½ years.

PRINCE, Mr. Thomas, Salem, 15 Nov., æ. 73.

PUTNAM, Mrs. A. B., Somerville, 11 Nov., æ. 67; she belonged to Andover.

RICE, Dea. Ebenezer, Leverett, 7 Nov., æ. 76; formerly of Rowe.

ROBINSON, Mr. Ebenezer, South Reading, Vt., 31 Oct., æ. 92 years and 8 months; a Revolutionary veteran.

ROBINSON, Mrs. Mary, Dorchester, 2 Nov., æ. 86; widow of the late Mr. James Robinson.

SHEAFE, Samuel, Esq., Portsmouth, N. H., æ. 72.

SLADE, Mr. William, Alstead, N. H., 25 Oct., æ. 100 yrs. 11 mos.

SOULE, Sarah, Middleboro', 18 Oct., æ. 87.

STEPHENSON, Mrs. Thomas, Belfast, Me., 30 Oct., æ. 88; a native of Cohasset, Ms.

STICKNEY, Mrs. Elizabeth, Newbury, 5 Nov., æ. 81½ years; widow of Richard Stickney.

SUTTON, Mrs. Mary, Boston, 10 Nov., æ. 77; widow of Mr. Abraham Sutton.

TABER, Susanna, Fairhaven, 15 Nov., æ. 94.

TENNEY, Mrs. Mary H., Dunbarton, N. H., 19 Nov., æ. 64; wife of David Tenney, Esq. and dau. of the late Rev. Dr. Harris of D.

THOMAS, Capt. Andrew, S. Weymouth, 12 Oct., æ. 81.

THORNTON, Agnes Winthrop, Brookline, 7 Nov., infant dau. of J. Wingate and Elizabeth W. B. Thornton.

UPTON, Mr. Josiah, Charlemont, 6 Nov., æ. 72.

WALKER, Capt. Simeon, Seekonk, 29 Oct., in his 81st year.

WATSON, Mrs. Hannah, Roxbury, 7 Nov., æ. 83.

WATSON, Rev. Elijah, East Andover, 3 Nov., æ. 80.

WEBB, Mrs. Sarah, Charlestown, 11 Nov., æ. 88 yrs. 4 mos.; widow of the late Nathan Webb, Esq.

WEED, Dr. Samuel, Portland, Me., 24 Nov., æ. 83 yrs. 3 mos.; born in Amesbury, Ms., 10 June 1774, son of Mr. Ephraim Weed, a respectable farmer. At 17, he entered Exeter Academy, and, about a year after, commenced teaching a village school. Bent on acquiring an education, Mr. Weed entered H. C. in 1796. After his graduation, Mr. W. took charge of an Academy at Framingham, Ms., then another at Medford. In the latter, Rufus Homer, his classmate, was associated with him. Here he studied medicine with Dr. John Brooks. He went to Portland in 1810, and there settled as a physician. In 1816, Dr. Weed married Miss Mary Condy of Medford, grand-dau. of the Rev. Jeremy Condy of Boston, and had by her three sons, the only survivor of whom is Edward Condy Weed of Boston. *Condensed from an article in the Portland Adv. of 27 Nov. 1857.*

WELLINGTON, Amos, Esq., Ashby, 20 Nov., æ. 87.

WENTWORTH, Enoch,[5] Cushing, Me., 23 Oct. 1857, æ. 91. He left (in Cushing) several children. He was born in that part of Stoughton which is now Canton, Ms., 9 May, 1766. He married in Friendship, Me., 4 Jan. 1791, Azubah Bradford, born in Truro, Nova Scotia, 21 May, 1765, and she died in Cushing, Me., 11 Nov. 1823. He was son of Zion[4] and Hannah (Pettingill) Wentworth, and grandson of Shubael[3] and Damaris (Hawes) Wentworth, who was son of John[2] and Martha ——, and grandson of the first settler, William,[1] of Dover, N. H.

WENTWORTH, Paul, at Pine Hill, Berwick, Me., 9 Nov. 1857, where he was born 9 June, 1760. On 15 Nov. 1807, he married his second cousin, Ruth,[5] dau. of Richard,[4] and grand-dau. of Thomas[3] and Mary (Knock) Wentworth. He was son of Samuel[4] and Lydia (Gowell) Wentworth, grandson of Ezekiel[3] and gr. gr. son of John[2] and Martha (Miller) Wentworth. John[2] was son of Ezekiel,[3] and gr. son of William, the emigrant settler.

WHITNEY, Mrs. Elizabeth, Westminster, 18 Nov., æ. 91 yrs. and 9 mos.; widow of the late Jonas Whitney, Esq.

WILLIS, Mrs. Sarah, Auburn, Me., Oct., æ. 97 yrs. 9 mos.; widow of Mr. James Willis.

WORCESTER, Mrs. Zervia (Fox), Salem, 23 Oct., æ. 78 yrs. 9 mos. 7 days; widow of the late Samuel Worcester, D. D. True to her obligations as a wife, a mother and a Christian, she lived beloved and respected, and died in full assurance of a blissful immortality. Her descent from Thomas Fox of Concord, Ms. was as follows, viz :—

Thomas Fox,[1] member of the church in Concord in 1640, freeman 1644, died Feb. 14, 1658. Md. 1st, Rebecca, d. March 11, 1647; md. 2d, Oct. 13, 1647, Hannah Brooks.

Eliphalet Fox,[2] named in the will of Thomas Fox[1] as his "eldest son," and a minor, in 1657; died in Concord, Aug. 15, 1711. Md. 1st, Oct. 26, 1665, Mary, dau. of George Wheeler; she died Dec. 24, 1678. Md. 2d, Sept. 30, 1681, Mary, widow of Isaac Hunt, and dau. of John Stone of Sudbury; she died about 1686.

Nathaniel Fox,[3] (Dea.), son of Eliphalet[2] and Mary 2d, born in Concord, Dec. 18, 1683; removed to Dracut in 1715, where he died about 1770. Md. 1st, Jan. 11, 1710, Hannah Merriam; md. 2d, Oct. 16, 1730, Elizabeth Brown.

David Fox,[4] third son of Nathaniel[3] and Hannah, born in Dracut, March 19,

1717; died in Dracut, 1758. Md. 1738, Mary Coburn.

Jonathan Fox,[3] (Dr.), 6th son of David,[2] born in Dracut, Feb. 1, 1754, studied medicine with Dr. Thom of Chester, N. H., was surgeon of a privateer in the war of the Revolution, afterwards settled as a physician in Hollis, N. H., where he died Oct. 26, 1782. Md. Nov. 20, 1777, Zeruiah, dau. of Hugh Jones of Dracut, born Dec. 23, 1755, died Feb. 18, 1816.

Zervia Fox,[4] only dau. of Jonathan,[3] born in Hollis, Feb. 16, 1779, died in Salem, Oct. 23, 1837. Md. Oct. 20, 1707, Samuel Worcester, D. D., born Nov. 1, 1770, died June 7, 1821. Eleven children, of whom Rev. Samuel M., D. D., Zervia Fidelia (Archer), Jonathan Fox, M. D., Elizabeth Lydia (Beaman), and Mary Maraden (Foster), are living.

Ebenezer Fox,[3] second son of Jonathan,[2] born in Hollis, April 6, 1783, died in Hollis, Nov. 6, 1857. Md. April 2, 1808, Susannah, dau. of Wm. Patterson of Salem, Ms. Eight children, of whom Ebenezer, John L., M. D., Surgeon U. S. N., Henry, Susan, Sam'l Worcester, and Wm. Emery, are living.　　J. F. W.

Wyman, Miss Lucena, Marlboro', Nov., æ. 85—burns to death by her clothes taking fire. It is remarkable that, many years ago, her mother perished by the same casualty, and in the same room.

Zachman, Mr. Charles, Philadelphia, Pa., Nov., æ. about 60; formerly a resident of Boston, and an eminent musician. He was the author of some popular works of music. Becoming entangled in the inexplicable mazes of spiritualism, so called, he committed suicide.

LINES

TO THE FAMILY FRIENDS OF MARY S. CARPENTER, WHO DIED IN BERNARDSTON,
MARCH 30, 1856.

Sorrowing mother! who thy grief can tell!
　　Another blow from Death's relentless hand
Has fallen where so recently one fell,
　　And thinned again thy cherished household band.

Stricken sister! who shall now thy sister be?
　　Though earthly friends may gather by thy side,
Earth offers none so near or dear to thee
　　As that fond one who lately drooped and died.

Mourning brothers! call ye this stroke severe?
　　To Heaven's all-wise decrees submissive bend:
Though short her date, no truth appears more clear—
　　"That life is long which answers life's great end."

O, friends, as down life's troubled stream ye glide,
　　With Faith's pure vision, upward lift your eyes;
This tribute is enough for mortal pride—
　　Your youthful friend has passed into the skies.

Bernardston, April 8, 1856.

THE DEARBORN MONUMENT.—The monument to the late Gen. H. A. S. Dearborn, an account of which we published some time since, has recently been erected upon the family ground, in the Forest Hill Cemetery, Roxbury. It is a Corinthian column of Italian marble, skilfully chiseled, and presents a beautiful appearance. It is a tribute from the citizens of Roxbury to the memory of one to whom, when living, they were greatly indebted for the lovely "city of the dead" which it now adorns. Upon the base, on each side of the monument, is an urn, surrounded by scroll work. Upon the front, engraved upon a tablet, are the following words:

"H. A. S. DEARBORN,
Died July 29, 1851,
aged 66 years."

On the opposite side is the following inscription:

"Ossa in Terra quam dilexit coluit, ornavit,
Cives et amici mœrentes condiderunt."

Newspaper, 31 May, 1852.

NEW ENGLAND HISTORIC-GENEALOGICAL SOCIETY.

CONSTITUTION.

[Revised and adopted, July 11, 1855.]

ARTICLE 1.—The Society shall be called THE NEW ENGLAND HISTORIC-GENEALOGICAL SOCIETY.

ARTICLE 2.— The objects of the Society shall be to collect, preserve and disseminate the local and general history of New England, and the Genealogy of New England families.

ARTICLE 3.—The Society shall be composed of Resident, Corresponding and Honorary Members, who shall be elected by ballot, having been nominated by the Board of Directors.

ARTICLE 4.—Every person elected a member of the Society shall become such by signifying his acceptance to the Corresponding Secretary, in writing; and any member may withdraw from it, at any time, by certifying his intention of so doing to the Recording Secretary, in writing, and paying all dues to the Treasurer.

ARTICLE 5.— Each Resident Member shall pay into the Treasury, on his admission, the sum of three dollars, and two dollars annually; and if he neglects or refuses to pay said tax for two years, he shall forfeit his membership, unless the Board of Directors shall otherwise order.

ARTICLE 6.—The Officers of the Society shall be a President; a Vice-President for each of the New England States; an Honorary Vice-President for each other of the United States as the Society, by vote, may determine; a Corresponding Secretary; a Treasurer; a Recording Secretary; a Librarian; and a Board of Directors.

ARTICLE 7.—The President, the Vice-President for Massachusetts, the Corresponding and Recording Secretaries, and the Treasurer, shall constitute the Board of Directors.

ARTICLE 8.— The Society shall meet quarterly in the city of Boston, on the first Wednesdays of January, April, July and October, to transact business; and at such other times as the Board of Directors shall appoint.*

ARTICLE 9.—The Officers of the Society shall be chosen at the January meeting, by ballot, and at any other stated meeting when a vacancy shall have occurred.

ARTICLE 10.—By-Laws for the more particular government of the Society, may be made or amended by a vote of three-fourths of the members present at any regular meeting thereof, notice of the same having first been given and entered upon the records at a previous meeting of the Society.

ARTICLE 11.—No alteration of this Constitution shall be made except at a quarterly meeting, on recommendation of the Board of Directors, and by a vote of three-fourths of the members present; notice of the proposed alteration having first been given and entered upon the records at a previous regular meeting of the Society.

BY-LAWS.

[Revised and adopted, October 3, 1855.]

ARTICLE 1.— To accomplish the objects of the Society, it shall be the duty of its members to seek genealogical and historical information by correspondence, to procure pamphlets, books, written communications, records and papers, ancient or modern, which may in any way contribute to the accomplishment of the end of its formation.

ARTICLE 2.— All donations shall be entered in the records of the Librarian, by specifying them, the time of their reception, together with the name of the donor;

[* The Board of Directors have appointed stated meetings to be held on the first Wednesdays of each month of every year, at 3 o'clock in the afternoon.]

and all such donations shall be acknowledged by the said Librarian, by letter, with a tender of the thanks of the Society for the same.

ARTICLE 3.— All written communications shall be deemed the property of the Society, unless the right to such be specially reserved by their authors or depositors.

ARTICLE 4.—No manuscripts shall be taken from the library of the Society, without permission from the Board of Directors.

ARTICLE 5.—The Corresponding Secretary shall conduct the general correspondence of the Society.

ARTICLE 6.— A publishing Committee, of three or more, shall be appointed in October by the Board of Directors.

ARTICLE 7.—The Society, at the annual meeting, shall choose two other Standing Committees, to consist of five members each: the first on Finance, and the second on the Library.   These Committees shall hold monthly meetings for the transaction of business.

ARTICLE 8.— The Committee on Finance, of which the Treasurer shall be, ex officio, a member, shall make a monthly examination of the books and accounts of the Treasurer; examine and report upon such motions involving the expenditure of money as shall be made at any meeting; and have a general supervision of the Finances of the Society.

ARTICLE 9.— The Committee on the Library, of which the Librarian shall be, ex officio, a member, shall solicit donations to the Library; determine what books may be taken from the room by the members; decide upon the arrangement of the books and pamphlets on the shelves, and upon the manner in which they shall be catalogued; oversee the cataloguing thereof; and have a general supervision of the Library and room.

With the consent of the Board of Directors, this Committee may make donations and exchanges with the duplicate books and pamphlets: but a full and particular record of the same shall be kept by the Clerk of the Committee.

ARTICLE 10.— An Historiographer shall be chosen at the annual meeting, whose duty it shall be to collect and preserve materials for a history of the Society, and for biographies of its members.   Whenever it is deemed advisable he shall prepare the same for publication.

ARTICE 11.— It shall be the duty of the Board of Directors to superintend and conduct the prudential and executive business of the Society, and to see that its Constitution be complied with, and that its By-Laws be duly enforced.

ARTICLE 12.— The January meeting shall be the time for the payment of the annual tax.

ARTICLE 13.— Resident and Life members only shall be entitled to vote at the meetings of the Society, to hold the office of Director, or be members of either of the Standing Committees.

ARTICLE 14.—No person who resides in New England shall hereafter be chosen a Corresponding member; and Corresponding members from other States, coming into New England to reside, shall cease to be such; but, on application, may become Resident members.

ARTICLE 15.— The payment of fifty dollars for that purpose, by himself or others, shall constitute any Resident, Corresponding or Honorary member, a Life member of the Society; and said Life member shall be free from assessments and entitled to all the rights and privileges of Resident members during his Life.

ARTICLE 16.—The Treasurer shall have charge of all moneys belonging to the Society; shall collect all fees and taxes; shall pay all accounts against the Society, when approved of by the Board of Directors; shall keep a full account of all receipts and expenditures, in a book belonging to the Society; and shall at each annual meeting, and at other times, if required by the Board of Directors, present a detailed report of the same, in writing.

ARTICLE 17.— The Librarian shall take charge of the books, pamphlets, manuscripts, and all other things belonging to the Society, or deposited for its use :

shall purchase books, under the instruction of the Board of Directors; shall make out a correct catalogue of the works belonging to the Society, keep a record of such as are taken out, and shall report at the annual meeting, and at such other times as the Board of Directors shall appoint, concerning the Library. He shall have charge of the rooms of the Society, and make, or cause to be made, all suitable preparations for holding its meetings.

ARTICLE 18.— A majority of the Board of Directors shall constitute a quorum.

ARTICLE 19.—The order of proceedings at the meetings shall be this, viz.:—
1. Read the records of the preceding meeting.
2. Announce donations.
3. Read letters received in correspondence.
4. Attend to unfinished business.
5. Read written communications.
6. Receive verbal communications.
7. Transact business specially introduced.
8. Propose candidates for admission.

ARTICLE 20.— All motions submitted at any meeting of the Society, shall, on the request of the presiding officer, be submitted in writing.

ARTICLE 21.—It shall be the duty of the Recording Secretary to keep a faithful and full record of all the proceedings of the Society at its meetings; and, to prevent omissions and misconceptions, it shall be the duty of the said Recording Secretary to keep a separate record of said proceedings, and to read it at the next succeeding meeting, that errors, should any appear, may not be entered upon the permanent book of the records of the Society.

[*Adopted January 7, 1857.*]

ARTICLE 22.— All elections to membership that are not accepted within one year from the date thereof shall be void, unless otherwise ordered by the Directors.

A true copy from the Records,

JOHN WARD DEAN,

BOSTON, November 13, 1857.　　　　　　　　　　　　　　　*Recording Secretary.*

N. B. Genealogical investigation being one of the principal objects of this Society, it seems desirable that some facts concerning its members and their family history should be preserved. Each member who has not already furnished such facts is, therefore, invited to send to the Historiographer, Joseph Palmer, M. D., his own name in full, and the place and date of his birth;—the names of his father and mother in full, and the places and dates of their birth, and (when dead their death;— and such other information of this kind as may be convenient. Relatives and friends of *deceased* members are invited to send the like information. adding the place and date of death.

PAYMENTS.—Payments for the Register for 1858, have been received from the following persons: *Belchertown,* Mrs. Doolittle; *Bernardston,* H. W. Cushman: *Boston,* N. Emerson, W. S. Leland, J. B. Loring, J. W. Thornton, T. Waterman: *Brookline,* W. B. Towne; *Cambridge.* C. D. Bradlee; *Gouverneur, N. Y.,* H. D. Smith; *Hartford,* C. J. Hoadly; *Hingham,* J. Richardson; *Litchfield, Ct.,* P. K. Kilbourne; *Lynn,* Joseph Moulton; *Marshfield,* M. A. Thomas; *Middletown, Ct.,* S. H. Parsons; *Natick,* E. Nason; *New London,* F. M. Caulkins; *New York, C.* C. Gardiner, W. H. Whiting; *Pensacola, Fla.,* W. H. Chase; *Philadelphia, N.* Chauncy; *Providence,* J. R. Bartlett; *Quincy,* E. Woodward; *Troy, N. Y.,* J. Edwards; *Waltham,* J. B. Bright; *Warren, R. I.,* G. M. Fessenden; *Westerly, R. I.,* C. H. Denison; *West Newton,* A. H. Ward; *Westford,* E. Abbot; *Woodbury, Ct.,* W. Cothren.

DENISON.—Are any descendants in the male line, of Major General Daniel Denison, formerly of Ipswich, Mass., now living? or of Edward Denison, of Roxbury, his brother?

Westerly, R. I., Nov. 1857.　　　　　　　　　　　　　　　C. H. D.

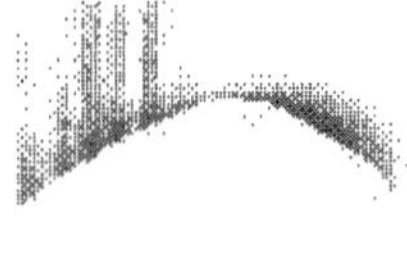

NEW ENGLAND

HISTORICAL AND GENEALOGICAL REGISTER.

Vol. XII.   APRIL, 1858.   No. 2.

AN ADDRESS

Delivered at the Annual Meeting of the New England Historical and Genealogical Society, held, by adjournment, at its Room, No. 5 Tremont Street, Boston, January 20th, 1858.

[By Samuel G. Drake, M. A., President of the Society.]

Gentlemen :—The few remarks I have to make will occupy but a small portion of the time of this evening ; and, with your kind indulgence, I will, in a plain way, without formality, proceed with them : observing, by the way, that it is quite embarrassing to be placed in the position I now happen to occupy,—a place so lately and so ably filled by the talented and eloquent gentleman who declines a further service.

In the first place, I beg to tender to you, gentlemen, my hearty thanks for this mark of your confidence and favor ; and while I accept the place of President of this highly important and extensively useful institution, I must at the same time observe,—I do so with very great diffidence ; but, gentlemen, you all well know, so far as you can know anything about it,—that the presidential chair of this Society was never sought by me. However, as your committee of nomination were disposed unanimously to nominate me, and as you have seen fit to confirm that nomination by an election, I feel it my duty to submit to the decision.

I was content to be a *common laborer* in the historical field, and to remain a soldier in the *antiquarian ranks*, but you have determined otherwise, and I acquiesce with no other protest than that which I am about to make. One nearly worn out in any service, can do little for its advancement. I therefore can promise little, nay, very little, though with your aid and encouragement I hope to do something.

We all have our fortes, or hobbies, if you will. All men are fitted by nature and training to fill certain spheres or stations in life, while at the same time it is wisely ordered that all men are not fitted for the same occupation. Some may be good mechanics, while others never can be. Some may be good public speakers, while others will ever appear to great disadvantage in attempts of that nature. So, one man may make an excellent soldier, but a very indifferent general. Long and tried services in the ranks, and even in the *forlorn hope*, may gain him just distinction, but it may give him small claim to the chief command.

This brings to my mind a circumstance which occurred many years ago, at a large dinner at which I happened to be present in Philadelphia. There were many speakers, young and old, called up, one after another. The night was far advanced, and the company much reduced in number, before Col. McKenny, who was among the guests, was called upon. The colonel had belonged to the army of the United States, and had seen service in the war of 1812. He began by remarking that, on looking around him, he was reminded of an army, after a battle by which its ranks had been greatly thinned; but that, he said, was no excuse for those who remained not to do their duty.

It is the reverse now here, for our ranks were never before so full; and although *we* may think it late in the day to be called upon, *we* shall nevertheless endeavor to do our duty.

And here I may not inappropriately refer to the origin of this Society. It is above thirteen years since it was formed, and all of the original members are living but one, and to this time but one of them has been called to preside as its chief officer. Of my own connection with the Society, I intend to say but a word. Throughout almost its whole course, I have been its Corresponding Secretary,—an office upon which considerable labor has naturally fallen, and by which much more has been unavoidably assumed, owing to circumstances not necessary to be mentioned. It was very important, in the outset of the Society's periodical, that the conductor or publisher of that periodical should be the Corresponding Secretary of the Society; hence the connection has been continued to the present time, with but a brief intermission.*

This Society is now large and flourishing, and perfect harmony prevails among its members. It is my sincere desire that this state of things may long continue. In large bodies of men differences may occur; they are perhaps more likely to occur than in smaller associations. Giving this due consideration, it will urge upon every one of us the duty of inculcating friendship among ourselves; to be careful to respect the opinions of those who differ from us, and not to judge hastily or rashly of the motives of any brother who may honestly, as he believes, differ from another brother.

Some may imagine that the Society moves too slow, while others may fear there is danger of its going too fast. Let us reflect a moment, and ask ourselves the question—Where is there a society which has accomplished as much as this in an equal space of time? It is easy to name societies which have existed a great

---

* For some particulars in the history of the Society, see the N. E. Hist. and Gen. Register, Vol. IX., p. 1, &c.

deal longer. Some of them have done much, but no one is known to me which has produced the amount of useful labor which this has accomplished, in twice as much time. It has not only produced valuable work, but it has produced authors,—authors who, but for the formation of this institution, would not have been authors. The members of this Society encourage capable persons to publish their labors; and to this encouragement the community is indebted for many excellent histories of towns, and other able historical and genealogical works, too numerous to be named at this time.

I have spoken of the Society as an institution of great importance; and I will take this occasion further to remark, that no society can have greater claims to that importance than this. If the question be asked, How happens this to be so? my answer is, in part, in another question. What society is there, to carry out the objects of which, every member finds a cord connecting his own person with all the rest? All societies should have the great object in view of elevating human nature. This can be done in no way so well as by dwelling upon the worth and virtues of those from whom we are descended. The first settlers of New England were, as a whole, preëminently virtuous. By showing that we are of their blood, that we are their production, we at the same time show that we have no excuse if we have not their virtues. We clearly trace to them, step by step, and there are no dark chasms, or dubious or broken threads. Hence a strong incentive to emulate ancestry. A merely historical society may be an institution solely for the collection of abstract historical knowledge. Of what value is such knowledge, leaving out the actors in historical affairs? That a band of men came from one place and conquered the people in another place, at a certain period, admitting it to be true, is historical knowledge. But of what importance is it unless we know the condition of the conquerors and conquered? who and what they were? the occasion of the action? &c. It is the details of history which make it interesting. Hence the reason why many historical students say they read only the notes to a historical work,—the work itself being dry and tedious, while the notes are never so.

For a moment I will advert to the collection of books and manuscripts in our Library. Of their value it is not necessary to say a single word. As I have referred to this collection, I wish particularly to impress upon the minds of all present, that they should encourage contributions of books, pamphlets, as well as manuscripts, of every description. For who can estimate the value a single pamphlet or letter may be to somebody at some time?

To illustrate this by a brief example. Several years ago, a gentleman was getting together materials for a history of an inland town of some importance. He knew that a few persons who had lived in the town had been authors of some small treatises. One work in particular, by an old revolutionary soldier, he very much desired to see; in fact, he could not make his history without the use of the work in question. It was a mere pamphlet of a few leaves, badly written, badly printed, and everything, it may be, bad about it. All that was nothing; the history could not be completed without it. The gentleman had applied to old residents for this bad pamphlet. They had all heard of it, many of them had read it years before, but not a copy could be found. At length a copy was heard of in possession of a great collector of books and pamphlets in a distant State, and a journey was resolved upon, as the only means of relief from the difficulty in which the writer of the history of the town found himself. This journey was prevented only by the accidental discovery of a copy nearer home. Thus a cost of some twenty dollars was avoided, which, but for the timely discovery, must have been incurred, merely for the privilege of a brief examination of an old and almost forgotten pamphlet.

Now, we may have a thousand pamphlets in our library intrinsically of more value than the one in question. Some person, at some day, may have as great a desire to see each of them, as the historian just mentioned did to see that which brought this circumstance to my mind. And the same may be said of the thousands yet to be deposited in these archives.

I have been influenced to remark upon this case, because some worthy members among us have been inclined to discourage donations, giving as a reason that we have already too much of what they have been pleased to term useless lumber in our way, and because much of what has been given does not contain historical or genealogical information. This should not be so; for every book, tract or pamphlet is, in itself, a historical item. Because one of this description has nothing about it immediately to our purpose, is no argument for its rejection by us. Somebody is the author or writer of every such work, and everybody belongs to somebody's genealogy. Hence, in preparing a history of a town, or a pedigree of a family, the person preparing such work will always be gratified to know if any individual, in either case, did ever produce a literary work of any kind; if so, such work is a part of the history of a town, and also of an individual. That we attach no value to such literary production, amounts to nothing at all. Self-constituted judges in such cases should remember that others have the same right to judge as ourselves, and that they will be very apt to reverse our decisions.

In this connection I would remark, concerning local histories, that writers of them should, as perfectly as possible, give lists of all printed documents concerning the localities of which histories are prepared. I do not think this has ever been attended to as it should be. How many persons, belonging to any town, do you suppose could answer this question—"How many works have been printed about your town and its people?"

A school book, a sermon, a controversial tract, a report of any society, school or corporation, or anything done in a town, belongs to its history,—and its history is the history of the individuals belonging to it. It was a primary object in view of the founders of this Society, to collect everything which could illustrate local as well as individual history—well knowing that from parts a grand whole is composed. And here I would ask, What can a general historian do without such parts? He may plod on like his predecessors, but his work will be comparatively useless. It may please for the hour by its style, but will never be preserved for reference.

I have been led to these remarks to prevent misconceptions, and to impress upon the minds of the members the importance of our collections already made, and that they may not remit their diligence in adding to them. There is no fear of their becoming too large; for the time will come when we, or our successors, will be enabled to assort, arrange and catalogue them, and thus make them available to all inquirers.

With respect to more suitable accommodations, I will only remark, that no one could be more delighted than myself to see such accommodations, and to see the wishes of the members fully gratified in that particular. But let us proceed in that matter with due caution. We are now in a healthy state of prosperity, which a single inconsiderate step might at once jeopardize. We shall have those accommodations. It is only a question of time.

Sooner than I would reject donations for the library, I would pack our apartment from floor to floor, and from wall to wall, until not even a mouse could find space to enter. Yes, I would sooner retire to the door-steps and entry, and hold our meetings there, than to reject donations; for you may rely upon it that such an accumulation will do much, indirectly though it may be, to provide itself with a shelter.

Even a fragment, or few leaves of a rare book or tract, should not be rejected; for it sometimes happens that, by two or three fragments, a complete work is made up. And let me tell you, gentlemen, that some of the rarest works in my own library have been obtained from imperfect or fragmentary works. I could give you some examples of this kind within my experience, which, if time allowed, would amuse if not astonish you. I will mention but one. Some twenty years ago there fell into my hands, among a large mass of pamphlets, a fragment of a little old quarto volume, printed in London "for Nath. Hillar, at the Princes-Arms, in Leaden-hall street, over against St. Mary-Ax, and Joseph Collyer, at the Golden Bible on London bridge," in the year 1700. This fragment consisted of but four leaves. These leaves contained the title-page and preface of Robert Calef's "More Wonders of the Invisible World." I need not mention for the information of antiquaries, that copies of the original edition of Calef's work have long been of very rare occurrence, and that copies bear a great price when they happen to be thrown into the market. And now for the sequel.

When I had kept this fragment of Calef some ten years or more, a bookseller in London forwarded to me for sale an invoice of scarce works. On casting my eye over the list, I found, marked at a trifling expense, "Calef's More Wonders of the Invisible World, bad copy and imperfect, *two-and-sixpence.*" On examining this "bad and imperfect copy," I found, to my agreeable surprise, that its *badness* consisted only in being a little dirty and water-stained, and its imperfection was precisely the very leaves I had had so long in my possession.

Every student in New England history knows that Calef's work is the standard authority respecting the "Salem witchcraft;" but every one may not know that the work was so unpopular here, when published, that not a bookseller in the town dared to keep it for sale!

In regard to the valuable books, tracts and manuscripts in the library, I will suggest, that while we would make them as free as is consistent with their safety, special regard should be had that they be used carefully, and not subjected to be lost through the carelessness of some, or the covetousness or cupidity of any. A suitable, and in every respect reliable custodian, is of the first importance. Such a person cannot be had without a fair compensation, and one of the first things to be done, in my judgment, is to find the means to compensate such an officer. Such a person should not only be a good custodian, but, to be fully equal to the office, he must be something of a scholar, must be one of us in interest, must possess order and neatness, and lastly, he should be a cultivator in our fields of research. Much, very much depends upon the gentleman entrusted with our archives. He sees more of the members of the Society than any other officer, being brought into daily intercourse with them in the way of his duty. He can do much for the Society in various ways. Strangers visiting the library constantly, gives him an opportunity to let them leave it with good impressions, and often with the good intention of adding to its collections.

If an institution is founded to be useful, it must have useful members—useful in some way. Hence, I say, the greater the number of members, the more good the institution can do. That a man can do as much work with one hand as he can with both, has always appeared to me a glaring absurdity; or that one man can do as much as ten men. For my part, I do not believe that any ten, even of our number, are quite smart enough to do as much as all of us together. Neither will any of you, gentlemen, believe that a few individuals associated together for historical purposes, however *smart* they may be, are yet quite sufficient to do all our historical and genealogical work for us. A small number may associate themselves together and hedge themselves about, entrench themselves behind any amount of self-importance, and argue that they can take care of the history of us all. That doctrine may do among the monks of Spain, even in the nine-

teenth century, but it is ill suited to the institutions of the *free*
States of America.

Now, historical knowledge is valuable or it is worthless. If
valuable, why try to limit and circumscribe its means of usefulness? This Society was formed, by its original members, in the
full belief that the knowledge brought to light by it, should benefit everybody who desired such knowledge. There were, therefore, no limits allowed to be set as to the number who might
incline to lend a hand in the undertaking; and hence, by en-
rolling their names, it might be known that they appreciated the
objects of it, and were ready to encourage it with whatever additional advantage their names and services might give it. It was
thought to be altogether too antiquated an idea to admit none
into their ranks until they themselves were dead.

No, gentlemen; instead of here and there an individual laborer,
a mighty army of antiquaries is necessary to rescue the perishing
records of the past. On a moment's reflection, every one of you
will admit this; for who of you undertakes an investigation, and
is not stopped almost in the very outset for want of the means to
pursue it? Who among you can clearly trace his progenitor to the
father land? It may be you may trace one line to the old world,
perhaps two, but most of us have at this time sixty-four lines to trace
them! I therefore confidently assure you that there is work
enough for us all, and all we can enlist to help us, even in this
single branch of inquiry, to say nothing of other branches.

This Society, it is extensively admitted, (though not as extensively admitted as the fact which I am about to mention is known,)
is more favorably and widely known abroad than any other Historical Society in New England, if not than any other in America.
To what is this owing? This is a question to which I propose to
invite the special attention of the Society for a few moments.

It is a question which deeply concerns every member of the
Society, if they are members interested in its advancement. It
being conceded that the Society has somehow acquired an importance, every member of it should feel that he has individually
done something for the acquirement of the merited distinction
which it holds.

Is it owing to the great names, and we have no lack of them,
upon our list of members? I distinctly state that this fact has
very little, almost nothing to do with it. Is it owing to our collection of books and manuscripts? To splendid apartments for our
meetings and our library? They are not extensive enough to
make any sensation abroad, and but little here. But let us recur
to the main question,—To what is this importance of the Society
owing? The answer, gentlemen, is very brief, and as simple as it
is brief. It *is* owing to a miserably supported periodical, now in
its twelfth year, published under the sanction of *this* Society,
called the New England Historical and Genealogical Register.
Gentlemen, I know this to be so. My connection with this peri-

odical, from its original inception to the present time, gives me the assurance with which I aver the fact. Nor am I alone in this estimate of the periodical to which your attention is called.

Such being the case, how important it is that this periodical should be sustained. Many valuable members of the Society have been introduced into it by their interest in that publication. They first became aware of the existence of the Society through that work. They had heard of it, subscribed for it, and thus became members of the Society.

From the nature of the work in question, it cannot be popular, and therefore cannot be profitable in a pecuniary point of view. To make it so would be to reduce it to a par with common magazines, and works suited to nurseries. No one can desire this. No one can wish to have its pages crowded with matter foreign to the objects of the Society. Every one knows how difficult it is to consult works containing all sorts of matter, especially as such works soon become repulsive from their bulky and overgrown appearance. A little consideration must satisfy nearly all of us that ordinary reading matter does not belong to its pages, and has, therefore, as far as possible, been excluded from them. As an illustration of this position, I refer you to the Gentleman's Magazine,—a periodical of which all of you must know something. That magazine has been published one hundred and twenty-seven years, and comprises two hundred volumes. Now, there is scattered through that work a vast amount of historical and genealogical information. But who of us can afford to possess those two hundred volumes? Yet, if all the articles to our purpose could be selected from them, and published by themselves, they would not, perhaps, extend to ten volumes. If this selection were made, (and no doubt it will be in coming years,) nearly all might secure them.

The Historical and Genealogical Register, gentlemen, although sustained almost entirely by individual effort, is not an organ of any particular persons, family or clique. Its' pages are open to all who contribute matter approved of by the Society's committee of publication. Should it not, therefore, be a primary object with every member of the Society to extend the circulation of its periodical? Is there any more direct way to extend the usefulness of the Society? I believe every gentleman who hears me will answer in the affirmative.

I have been thus particular, gentlemen, in speaking of this solitary periodical, because there are many, notwithstanding its age, who have scarcely any knowledge of it. I call it a *solitary periodical*, because there is not a similar one in the world; for the simple and very good reason, that *money* cannot be made by them. There have been similar works started in England, but, to use a periodical phrase, they died soon. Antiquarian and literary gentlemen of the present day in that country speak of the work with surprise and admiration,—surprise that such a work can be sustained in Republican America, and admiration at the extent of antiquarian and genealogical information contained in it; remarking, at the same time, that "such a work cannot live in England."

Gentlemen, they may well be surprised that such a work can be sustained here, and their surprise would be very far greater, if they knew *how* it is sustained. There are two gentlemen of the Society who have taken a few extra copies to help the work onward. Several others have done good service, by influencing their friends to become subscribers to it. The Society is under great obligations to all of these.

It will be remembered that it was by an unanimous vote of the Society, last year, determined to make a slight alteration in its name; that the President was made a Committee to petition the Legislature for that object. But the session of that body was so near at an end before he could attend to it, the matter was postponed. It will at once be attended to. For the benefit of new members, I will observe, that the name proposed is "The New England Historical and Genealogical Society." This is in conformity with the name of its Periodical. This name was immediately adopted in all ordinary transactions, as may have been observed. The name *Historic-Genealogical* was never agreeable to the original members. They, with a single exception, contended that it did not express fully their objects. "*Historic* Genealogy" covers but a small portion of the ground intended; whereas *History and Genealogy* was really what was considered to be comprehended by it.

Gentlemen, I have but a word more, and hope I have not broken down your patience. But let me again urge upon you the importance of harmonious action; let us not be sanguine in new projects, nor disturbed if they are set aside by others. The good of the Society is most likely to be with the intelligent majority, and it is the duty of the minority to acquiesce, and to work heartily with them.

As a last word, let me urge upon the officers of the Society the great importance of doing their duty, and doing it promptly. Let them remember that, with a society as with an individual, everything depends upon its straightforward course, and the harmony and integrity with which *all* of its officers do their duty. To understand the economy of such an institution, requires some experience in its service, and it is not to be expected but that gentlemen who have not had the opportunity to become informed, may draw conclusions unfavorable to its past and present progress. They may have a great many projects for the Society's advancement,—and they may be feasible projects under certain circumstances,—but let us move with caution, and do what we do understandingly. And, as I have before observed, our progress we know to be onward and our affairs healthy, and let us not jeopardize them by any doubtful experiments.

LETTER OF JOHN HANCOCK.

S. G. DRAKE, Esq.

Dear Sir:—I now enclose to you a copy of a family letter in my possession, directed "To Mrs Hancock at Worcester or Boston," which would not be a very definite direction at the present day, but seems to have reached her safely. The writer of it makes mention of Harry, Ned, and Joe, who were three of his black servants, one of whom lies under a gravestone in "the old Granary" burying-ground. This letter is chiefly interesting from the glimpse it affords us of the Governor's private life.

Yours faithfully,
J. GARDNER WHITE.

York Town October 18th: 1777.

My Dear Dolly—

I am now at this Date, & not a Line from you, nor a single word have I heard from you since your Letter by Dodd immediately upon your arrival at Worcester, which you may Judge affects me not a little but I must Submit, & will only Say that I expected oftner to have been the object of your attention.

This is my Sixth Letter to you, the former ones I hope you have Rec'd, by the Complection of those Letters you will, I dare say, be apprehensive that my Stay here was nearly Determin'd for the winter, & that I had thoughts of Soliciting your Return to me, my thoughts on that Subject were for a Season serious, but various reasons have occurr'd to induce me to Alter my Resolutions, and I am now to Inform you that I have come to a fix'd Determination to Return to Boston for a short time, & I have notified Congress in form of my Intentions. You will therefore please immediately on Receipt of this to Tell Mr Sprigs to prepare the Light Carriage & Four Horses & himself to be ready to proceed on to Hartford or Fairfield, as I shall hereafter direct to meet me on the Road, if my old Black Horses are not able to perform the Journey he must hire Two: The particular time of my Setting out & when I would have Sprigs come forward you shall know by Dodd the Express who I shall Dispatch tomorrow morning; my present Intention is to leave Congress in eight Days, but more particulars in my next.

I shall hope & must Desire that you will Take a Seat in the Carriage, & meet me on the Road, which will much advance your health, & you may be assur'd will be highly Satisfactory to me, & I have Desir'd Mr Bant to Accompany you in the Carriage, & when we meet he can take my Sulkey, & I return with you in the Carriage to Town. Mr Bant must hire or borrow a Servant to attend you on Horseback, as Harry & Ned are both with me, & Joe is not Suitable. my Dear, I hope your health will admit of your coming with Mr. Bant, I long to See you; I shall Close all my Business in three Days, & indeed have already nearly finish'd, & when once I set out shall travel with with great Speed, nothing will prevent my Seeing you Soon, with the leave of providence, but a prevention of passing the North River, I shall push hard to get over, even if I go so far as Albany. I need not Tell you there will be no occasion of your writing me after the Receipt of this.

My best wishes attend you for every Good. I have much to Say, which I leave to a Chearful Evening with you in person.

God Bless you, my Dear Dolly,

I am

Yours most Affectionately
JOHN HANCOCK.

EARLY RECORDS OF BOSTON.

[Continued from Vol. XI., p. 835.]

Braintree Births.

Martha Barritt Daughter of Thomas Barritt & of Francis his wife borne 17 : 7 : 56.

William Copeland sonne of Lawrence Copeland & of Lydia his wife borne 15 : 9 : 56.

Hannah Goole Daughtr of Francis Goole & of Rose his wife borne 18 : 5 : 55.

Jo° Goole sonne of Francis Goole & of Rose his wife borne 26 : 2 : 57.

Richard Poffer sonne of James Poffer & of Mary his wife borne 14 : 1ᵐ : 57.

Sarah Mills Daughter of Jo° Mills & of Elizabeth his wife borne 9 : 4 : 56.

Joseph Permenter sonne of Robᵗ Permenter & of Leah his wife borne 20 : 10 : 55.

Mary Twells Daughter of Robert Twells & of Martha his wife borne 6 : 8 : 56.

Jn° Permenter sonne of Robᵗ Permenter & of Leah his wife borne 23 : 8 : 53.

Elizabeth Permenter yᵉ Daughter of Robᵗ Permenter & of Leah his wife borne 22 : 8 : 57.

Rebecca Fackson Daughter of Tho: Fackson & of Deborah his wife borne 25 : 4 : 57.

Hannah Bracket Daughter of Peter Bracket & of Priscilla his wife borne 14 : 6 : 56.

Sarah Ruggles Daughter of George Ruggles & of Elizabeth his wife borne 29 : 7 : 45.

Mehitabel Ruggles Daughter of George Ruggles & of Elizabeth his wife borne 16 : 5 : 50.

Isaac Shefield sonne of Edmond Shefield & of Mary his wife borne 15 : 1 : 51.

Mary Shefield yᵉ Daughtr of Edmond Shefield & of Mary his wife borne 14 : 4 : 53.

Mathew Shefield Daughtr of Edmond Shefield & of Mary his wife borne 26 : 3 : 55.

Ebenezer Hoiden sonne of John Hoiden & of Susanna his wife borne 12 : 7 : 45.

Nehemiah sonne of Jn° Hoiden & of Susanna his wife borne 14 : 12 : 47.

Hannah Peniman Daughter of James Peniman & of Lydia his wife borne 26 : 3 : 48.

Abigail Daughter of James Peniman & of Lydia his wife was borne 27 : 10 : 51.

Mary Daughter of James Peniman & of Lydia his wife borne 29 : 7 : 53.

Samˡ sonne of James Peniman & of Lydia his wife borne 14 : 9 : 45.

Mary Saundʳs Daughter of Jn° Saundʳs & of Mary his wife borne 10 : 12ᵐ : 53.

Moses Paine sonne of Moses Paine & of Elizabeth his wife borne 16 : 6 : 46.

Elizabeth Daughter of Moses Paine & of Elizabeth his wife borne 5 : 6 : 48.

Sarah Daughter of Moses Paine & of Elizabeth his wife borne 30 : 11 : 50.

Moses 2ᵈ sonne of Moses Paine & of Elizabeth his wife borne 26 : 4 : 52.

Mary Daughter of Moses Paine & of Elizabeth his wife borne 12 : 1 : 55.

William yᵉ sonne of Moses Paine & of Elizabeth his wife borne 1 : 2 : 57.

Judith Newcome Daughtʳ of Francis NewCome & of Rachel his wife borne 16 : 11 : 45.

Peter sonne of Francis NewCome & of Ratchell his wife borne 16 : 3 : 48.

Abigail Daughter of Francis New Come & of Ratchell his wife borne 16 : 5 : 51.

Leah Newcome Daughter of Francis Newcome & of Ratchel his wife borne 30 : 5 : 54.

Mary Shed Daughtʳ of Daniell Shed & of Mary his wife borne 8 : 1 : 47.

Daniell sonne of Daniell Shed & of Mary his wife borne 30 : 6 : 49.

Hannah Daughter of Daniell Shed & of Mary his wife borne 7 : 7 : 51.

John sonne of Daniell Shed & of Mary his wife borne 2 : 1 : 54.

Elizabeth & Zechariah Shed yᵉ Daughter & Sonne of Daniell Shed & of Mary his wife borne 17 : 4ᵐᵒ : 56.

David Walsbee sonne of David Walsbee & Hannah his wife borne 29 : 7 : 55,

Hope Still Foster sonne of Tho: Foster & of Elizabeth his wife borne 26 : 1 : 48.

Joseph sonne of Thomas Foster & of Elizabeth his wife borne 28 : 1 : 50.

Hulda Daughter of Fardinando Thayre & of Hulda his wife borne 16 : 4 : 57.

Thomas sonne of Wᵐ Scant & of Sarah his wife borne 11 : 2 : 57.

Mary Daughter of Peter George & of Mary his wife borne 7 : 7 : 45.

Hannah Daughter of Peter George & of Mary his wife borne 7 : 7 : 48.

John sonne of Peter George & of Mary his wife borne 24 : 4 : 50.

Dependance French sonne of Jnᵒ French & of Grace his wife borne 7 : 1 : 48.

Temperance Daughter of Jnᵒ French & of Grace his wife was borne 20 : 1 : 51.

Thomas sonne of Jnᵒ French & of Grace his wife borne 10 : 1 : 57.

William sonne of Jnᵒ French & of Grace his wife borne 31 : 1 : 53.

Elizabeth Daughter of Jnᵒ French & of Grace his wife borne 29 : 7 : 55,

Dorothy Daughtʳ of Richᵈ Thayre & of Dorothy his wife borne 30 : 6 : 53.

Richᵈ sonne of Richᵈ Thaire & of Dorothy his wife borne 31 : 6 : 55,

Mary Daughter of John Hardman & of Sarah his wife 7 : 9 : 52.

John sonne of John Hardman & of Sarah his wife borne 10 : 9 : 54.

Isaac sonne of Thomas Thayre & of Hannah his wife borne 7 : 7 : 54.

John sonne of Thomas Thayre & of Hannah his wife borne 25 : 10 : 56.

Rachel Daughter of Sydrack Thayre & of Mary his wife borne 9 : 9 : 55.

Tryall Thayer Daughtʳ of Sydracke Thayre & of Mary his wife borne 7 : 12 : 56.

Samuell sonne of Edmond Sheffeild & of Mary his wife borne 26 : 9 : 57.

Delliverance Daughter of Wᵐ Owen & of Elizabeth his wife borne 15 : 12 : 54.

Ebenezer sonne of Wm Owen & of Elizabeth his wife borne 1 : 3mo : 57.

Sarah Daughter of Nath: Harman & of Mary his wife borne 3 : 1^m : 52.

Jonathan sonne of Nath Harman & of Mary his wife borne 24 : 4 : 54.

Ephraim sonne of Nath Harman & of Mary his wife borne 30 : 8 : 56.

Mary Daughter of Richd Fackson & of Elizabeth his wife borne 19 : 10 : 57.

Annah Daughter of Peeter Shooter & of Annah his wife borne 3 : 1 : 54.

Nath sonne of Nathaniell Mott & of Annah his wife borne 28 : 10 : 57.

John sonne of Thomas Holbrooke & Joan his wife borne 15 : 8 : 53.

Peter sonne of Thomas Holbrooke & of Joan his wife borne 6 : 7 : 55.

Johanna Daughter of Thomas Holbrooke & of Joan his wife borne 30 : 8 : 56.

Peter sonne of Christo: Webb & of Hannah his wife borne 10 : 10 : 57.

John sonne of Jno Downam & of Dorothy his wife borne 30 : 7 : 44.

Joseph sonne of Jno Downam & of Dorothy his wife borne 30 : 2 : 45.

John sonne of Jno Downam & of Dorothy his wife borne 7 : 1 : 52.

Mercy Daughter of Jno Downam & of Dorothy his wife borne 7 : 1 : 54.

Susan Daughter of Richd Chapman & of Mary his wife borne 25 : 12 : 47.

Hope sonne of Richd Chapman & of Mary his wife borne 30 : 11 : 54.

Mary Daughter of Richd Chapman & of Mary his wife borne 30 : 4 : 57.

Nath Thayre sonne of Richd Thayre & of Dorothy his wife borne 1 : 11 : 57.

Hannah Veasie Daughter of Wm Veasie & of Ellen his wife borne 18 : 1 : 44.

Solomon sonne of Wm Veasie & of Ellen his wife borne 11 : 3 : 50.

Elizabeth Daughter of Wm Veasie & of Ellen his wife was borne 13 : 8 : 53.

Elizabeth Daughter of Deerman Downam & of Elizabeth his wife borne 15 : 11 : 45.

John Downam sonne of Deerman Downam & of Elizabeth his wife borne 15 : 12 : 47.

Stephen Paine sonne of Stephen Paine & of Hannah his wife borne 8 : 1 : 52.

Sam^{ll} sonne of Stephen Paine & of Hannah his wife borne 10 : 4 : 54.

Hannah Daughter of Stephen Paine & of Hannah his wife borne 28 : 11 : 55.

Sarah Daughter of Stephen Paine & of Hannah his wife borne 1 : 9 : 57.

Sarah Daughter of Samuell Tomson & of Sarah his wife borne 27 : 8 : 57.

Hannah Daughter of Samuell Kingsly & of Hannah his wife borne 27 : 5 : 56.

Elizabeth Daughter of Samuell Kingly & of Hannah his wife borne 22 : 9 : 57.

Anna Daughter of Mr Wm Tomson & of Anna his wife borne 8 : 1 : 49.

Anna Daughter of Mr Henry Fliot & of Margery his wife borne 7 : 11 : 43.

Josiah sonne of Mr Henry Flynt & of Margery his wife borne 24 : 6 : 45.

Margart Daught^r of Mr Hen: Flynt & of Margery his wife borne 20 : 4 : 47.

Johannah Daught^r of Mr Hen Flynt & of Margery his wife borne 18 : 12 : 48.

David sonne of Mr Henry Flynt & of Margery his wife borne 11 : 11 : 51.

Seth sonne of Mʳ Hen: Flynt & of Margery his wife borne 2 : 2 : 53.

Ruth Daughter of Mʳ Henry Flynt & of Margery his wif borne 21 : 11 : 54.

Cotton & Jn° sonns of Mʳ Henry Flynt & of Margery his　　　borne 16 : 9 : 56.

Rachell Daughter of Francis Elliott & of Mary his wife borne 26 : 8 : 43.

Hannah Daughter of Fran: Elliott & of Mary his wife borne 8 : 11 : 51.

Jn° sonne of Jn° Saundʳs & of Mary his wife borne 23 : 9 : 57.

Samuell sonne of Wᵐ Savill & of Hannah his wife was borne 30 : 6 : 43.

Benjamine sonne of Wᵐ Savill & of Hannah his wife was borne 28 : 6 : 45.

Hannah Daughter of Wᵐ Savill & of Hannah his wife borne 11 : 1 : 47.

William sonne of Wᵐ Savill & of Sarah his wife borne 17 : 5 : 52.

Bethiah Daughter of Samˡˡ Deering & of Bethyah his wife borne 6 : 6 : 49.

Mary Daughter of Samˡˡ Deering & of Mary his wife borne 16 : 11 : 52.

Hannah Daughter of Samuell Deering & of Mary his wife borne 14 : 12 : 54.

Sarah Daughter of Samuell Deering & of Mary his wife borne 30 : 4 : 57.

Elizabeth Daughter of Jn° Francis & of Rose his wife borne 24 : 11 : 56.

Abigail Neale Daughter of Hen: Neale & of Hannah his wife borne 14 : 12 : 56.

Sarah Daughter of Georg Speere & of Mary his wife borne 11 : 3mo : 47.

Samuell sonne of George Speere & of Mary his wife borne 18 : 8 : 52.

Hannah Daughter of George Speere & of Mary his wife borne 30 : 1 : 52.

Jn° Aldridge sonne of George Aldridge & of Katherine his wife borne 9 : 2 : 44.

Sarah Daughter of Georg Aldridge & of Katherine his wife borne 16 : 11 : 45.

Peter Aldridge sonne of George Aldridge & of Katherine his wife borne 14 : 2 : 48.

Mercy Daughter of George Aldridge & of Katherine his wife borne 17 : 4 : 50.

Jacob sonne of Geo: Aldridge & of Katherine his wife borne 28 : 12 : 52.

Manithyah sonne of Geo: Aldridge & of Katherin his wife borne 10 : 5 : 56.

BRANTREY MARRIAGES.

John Mills & Elizabeth Shove were marryed 26 : 2 : 53 by Mʳ Bellingham.

Lawrence Copeland & Lyddia Townsend was marryed 12 : 16 : 53 by Mʳ Hibbins.

Farthenando Thayre & Hulda Hayward marryed 14 : 11 : 52 by Capᵗ Torrey.

Thomas Fackson & Deborah Thayre marryed 11 : 2ᵐ : 53 by Capᵗ. Lusher.

William Scant & Sarah Browne marryed 29 : 1 : 54 by Capᵗ Torrey.

Allexander Nah [Nash ?] & Mary Bellchore marryed 19 : 10 : 55 by Major Atharton.

JÁNSEN—WENDELL—QUINCY—FLINT—ORNE, ETC.

[Communicated by A. S. Oars.]

Observing in the Geaealogical Register, Vol. VII., p. 252, a notice of Gen. John Fiske of Salem, Mass., whose third wife was Sarah Gerry, widow of John Gerry of Marblehead, and daughter of John and Elizabeth (Quincy) Wendell of Boston, Mass., I will give this excellent lady's ancestral grandparents, also her descendants, beginning with her father's line.

1st.   Evart Jansen and —— Wendell, who came from Embden, East Friesland, Prussian Dominions, about 1645. He died in Albany, 1709, æ. 68.

2d.   John and Elizabeth (Staais) Wendell. She was daughter of Major Abraham Staais. He was born in Albany and died there Nov. 6, 1691, æ. 44.

3d.

4th b.   John and Elizabeth (Quincy) Wendell ; m. Nov. 12, 1724. He died in Boston, Dec. 16, 1762, æ. 60.

5th.   Sarah Wendell, m. 1st John Gerry ; he died in 1765, æ. 45. 2d. Gen. John Fiske, June 18, 1766 ; he died Sept. 28, 1797, æ. 53. She died Feb. 12, 1804, æ. 58.

On her mother's side.

1st.   Edmund and Judith (——) Quincy, m. —— ; came from England to Boston in 1633. He died about 1635, æ. 33. She died in 1654, having been m. to Robert Hull.

2d.   Col. Edmund and Elizabeth Gookin (Eliot) Quincy, m. Dec. 8, 1680. She died Nov. 30, 1700. He died 1698.

3d.   Hon. Edmund and Dorothy (Flint) Quincy, m. ——. He was born in Braintree about 1681 ; died in London, 1737, in the 57th year of his age, and was buried in Bunhill Fields. She died Aug. 29, 1737, in the 60th year of her age.

4th b.   Elizabeth Quincy, who married John Wendell, as before stated,

From the Browns.

1st.   Descent from Mr. John Brown, first of Plymouth, after of Rehoboth. Mr. John Brown's, Sen., will, dated April 7, 1662, mentions daughter Mary, wife of Thomas Willet ; his son, James, and wife, Dorothy, executors.

2d.   Mary Brown, m. July 8, 1636, Thomas Willet, first mayor of New York. He died Aug. 4, 1674, æ. about 64. She died Jan. 8, 1669.

From the Willets.

1st.   Thomas, as above.

2d.   Esther Willet, m. —— Rev. Josiah Flint. He died Sept. 15, 1680, æ. 35. She was born July 10, 1648 ; died July 26, 1737, æ. 89.

From the Flints.

1st.   Rev. Henry Flint and Margery (Hoar), m. ——. He died April 27, 1668. She died March ——, 1686–7. They rest in Braintree.

2d.   Josiah, as above.

3d.   Dorothy, as before stated.

From the Hoars.

1st.   John and Joanna (——) Hoar, m. ——. He died ——. She

died Dec. 21, 1664. Tradition says, relict of Mr. John Hoar, a wealthy banker of England.

2d.   Margory, as above.

Mrs. Sarah Wendell (Gerry) Fisk's descendants.

1st.   Sarah Gerry, m., Dec, 1785, Azor Orne ; he born March 1, 1762, died April 17, 1795, æ. 33. She died Nov. 11, 1846. He was son of Col. Azor Orne of Marblehead. She was grand-daughter of Thomas and Elizabeth (Greenleaf) Gerry, who was father of Elbridge Gerry, late Vice President of the United States.

2d.   John Gerry, Azor, Henry and Sarah Wendell Orne.

John Gerry and Ann (Stone) Orne, m. ——. He died Feb. 24, 1838. Their children were Francis Henry, Maria Eliza, Sarah Gerry, Charles Asaph, Joel Stone, and Caroline Frances Orne.

3d.   Maria E. and John P. Whiton, m. Feb. 1838. She died May 5, 1844. Their children are John Wilson and Charles Henry.

Sarah Gerry and Charles A. Page, m. Nov. 6, 1846. Their children, John Wilson, died, Anna Stone, Caroline Frances Orne.

3d.   Joel S. and Rachel Atwood (Brown) Orne, m. Oct. 1850. Their children are Maria Frances and Charles Parker.

2d.   Sarah Wendell and Maj. Loring Austin, m. 1818. He was born April 24, 1790, died ——. She died Aug. 27, 1846. One child, Loring Henry, who married Mary Jane Goodwin. Their children, Lilian Ivers, Loring Le Baron, Isabell Traotbie.

2d.   Judge Henry Orne m. 1st Frances Boyd Little (had Wm. Henry, d., and several who died young). 2d. Sempronia —— Little. One child, Franklin Boyd. Judge Orne died at Orneville, Maine, Jan. 1, 1853, æ. 61.

These are all the descendants, now living, of Mrs. Sarah Fisk. She had a daughter, Lydia, who m. Mr. George Lee, and had a daughter, Lydia, who died in Cambridge, æ. 5 yrs. 7 mos. Mr. George Lee m. 2d Miss Hannah Sawyer, a distinguished writer.

The ancestors of John Gerry, first husband of Mrs. Sarah Fisk, were first :—Thomas, who m. Elizabeth Greenleaf. She died Sept. 2, 1771, æ. 55. These on his father's side. On his mother's, as follows :—

1st.   Roger and Elizabeth Russell.

2d.   Samuel and Elizabeth (Elbridge) Russell, m. ——. He was born in 1645. She was born in 1653, June 19.

3d.   Rebecca Russell m. Enoch Greenleaf. She was born Nov. 6, 1692. It was their daughter Elizabeth who m. Thomas Gerry.

From the Elbridges.

1st.   Thomas and Elizabeth, m. ——.

2d.   Elizabeth, who m. Samuel Russell. Family tradition says that about the age of sixteen she was an orphan and had two brothers, John and Thomas. They had an uncle, a merchant in Bristol, England, who deceased and left them a large property. Their sister Elizabeth took her two little brothers and with them went to Europe to claim their fortune. She met with various romantic adventures, but accomplished her purpose, and returned safe. The family record of Samuel Russell, 2d, mentions " John and Thomas Elbridge of Bristol, England," his uncles, in 1706, December 24.

REMINISCENCES RELATING TO GENERAL WARREN AND BUNKER HILL.

[By Gen. WILLIAM H. SUMNER.]

Read before the New England Historical and Genealogical Society.

UPON the occasion of the inauguration of the statue of General Joseph Warren, at Charlestown, on the 17th of June, 1857, the different addresses then made contained very many interesting incidents illustrative of the life and character of that martyr of American liberty. The perusal of these has brought to my mind some additional facts connected with Warren's death which may be considered valuable as historical items. Desirous that nothing should be lost relative to one whose name shines so brightly on the historic page, I make the information in my possession the subject of this article; and in this connection it may be proper to remark that from my early boyhood I have been acquainted with different members of the Warren family. I was born within a fourth of a mile of Gen. Warren's house in Roxbury, and enjoyed familiar intercourse with his three brothers, his mother, and his aunt, and the patriot himself was one of my father's teachers in the Roxbury Grammar School. Thus, from my earliest recollections, associated with a family so honored in our country's history, many interesting facts and incidents came to my knowledge, some of which may be here embodied.

The unwavering patriotism of General Warren is well illustrated in an incident related to me by some one whose name I do not now recall. It is well known that the British commander was anxious to secure the services of American officers of known bravery for the government, and that tempting offers were made to Putnam to induce him to leave the provincials and join the royal army. The valuable acquisition which Warren would be to the royalists did not escape their notice, and (as the account was given to me) Dr. Jeffries, a surgeon in the British army and an intimate acquaintance of Warren, was conversing with him, a short time before the actual resort to arms, on a pile of boards near the Winnisimmet Ferry Ways, from which they had a full view of the British fleet. During this conversation, which naturally turned upon the hostile feelings which existed between the provinces and the mother country, Dr. Jeffries suggested that in his opinion Warren might receive a high commission in the British army, if he would accept of it. This was a fruitless suggestion.

But the main object of this communication is to bring out something more important in a historical point of view, although incidents like the one just related possess a value peculiarly their own, and which it would be difficult to overestimate.

Upon the anniversary of our nation's birthday, 4th of July, 1825, at the public collation given at the State House to the State and City authorities, I gave a toast, the sentiment of which was founded upon facts which I had collected as Adjutant General from some of the old soldiers who were engaged in the battle of Bunker Hill. They had been requested to meet at my office on the occasion of laying the corner stone of the Bunker Hill Monument, on the 17th of the preceding June, by the Marquis de Lafayette, to join in the procession on that occasion. A large number of them came, and at that time I inquired of them what they

Mr. Foster is a hale man of seventy-two, of respectable appearance, and gave his account of the events of the battle with great clearness both of recollection and expression. He is possessed of considerable property, I learn, and is a man of undisputed veracity. He represents that Dr. Warren was wounded when he addressed them, and spoke like a person in the greatest extremity, who thought all was lost, raising up his hands and saying " I am a dead man ;—fight on, my brave fellows, for the salvation of your country." I stated to Mr. Foster that it was generally supposed that Dr. Warren was shot in the head. He replied that it did not appear to him that he was wounded in the head at that time, but that his side was bloody.

Immediately upon seeing the communication of " Historian" in your paper, I addressed a letter to Mr. Foster, informing him that inquiry was made in a public manner of me for the authority I had for giving the sentiment as the dying words of Warren ; and requested him to furnish me with such further particulars as were within his recollection ; but, not having received a reply to my letter sent through the post office, with which the old soldier has probably but little connection, I have not chosen to wait longer in giving " Historian" the requested information, lest the delay might tend to confirm the doubts expressed in his communication.

My office, on the morning of the 17th, was crowded with revolutionary soldiers, who were requested to meet there before joining in the procession. Many anecdotes and old soldier's stories were related interesting to the " Historian," and never perhaps fifty years after any like event were so many witnesses of it present, face to face, shaking hands and reciting to each other their toils and perils and hair-breadth escapes as were collected together at the late celebration. Under the resolve of the Legislature, a small allowance for attendance and travel was allowed to each of them as " reported themselves at the Adjutant General's office on or before that day, and gave him satisfactory evidence of the fact of their having been in the battle of Bunker Hill on the 17th of June, 1775 ;" as far as the time allowed, such reports were made and the evidence received. My inquiries, therefore, relating to the events of that day, of the officers and soldiers who reported themselves, were not those of curiosity merely, but were a necessary means of obtaining the " satisfactory evidence " the resolve required. Such was the bustle of the morning, and the shortness of the time, it was impossible the purpose of the resolve could be accomplished, and the Legislature afterwards extended the time for complying with its provisions to the 4th of July, when one hundred and forty-one out of upwards of two hundred present, had applied and given the evidence required.

Impressed with the belief that posterity will consider the events of that conflict as of more importance than even the enthusiastic actors themselves attached to them, I availed myself of the opportunity thus afforded, which gave me the means of seeing the greater part of the living actors in those scenes, to make minutes of the important facts relating to what may have heretofore been considered as mysterious circumstances of the battle, and particularly such as respected the conduct and death of the first great martyr of American liberty. It was impossible to do this generally in the crowd of the morning of the 17th ; but, with regard to the important facts stated by Mr. Foster, this was not the case ; for that I took down in writing, and, in the presence of Gen. Patterson of Philadelphia, who was very attentive to the old soldier stories, spoke of the importance of the anecdote to Mr. Foster, and read my minutes to him, to ascertain whether I had recorded it correctly.

"Historian" calls on me "for further light on the subject," and has not left in obscurity the objects to which he wished my attention directed; but under the heads of "prevalent ideas" and "popular impressions" in some instances, and in others by direct assertions, conveys his own doubts of the great worth of Warren's services. He says that "after the battle began to rage there is no account whatever of him, except this given by the Adjutant General." That "the manner, time, and place on the hill where Warren fell is left uncertain." That he went there in his common clothes without uniform "to learn by actual observation how to command in battle on a future day." That "he was buried with the promiscuous slain in the common trench of the dead," which would not have been the case "if the British had known him," and that "even our own people did not seek out the body of their *fearless* patriot." (I have underscored the epithet, though I hope no slur was intended by your communicator when he used it.) That "the body taken up afterwards," which was near the place of the greatest slaughter of the Americans, "was mere conjecture." In fact, if I understand the drift of the communication, it is, that there is no evidence that Warren on that day did anything to distinguish himself.

When the sentiment of that dying hero was promulgated, it was without the least idea that it would invoke an inquiry into his general conduct; but, it is not to be regretted, if there is doubt in any mind, that the inquiry is instituted while many of the witnesses are living, as it must result like those respecting the conduct of other important actors in those scenes in the establishment of those great truths which have already emblazoned their names on the historic page.

There is no need of recurring to evidence in support of commonly received facts. Respecting such as are not generally known I will endeavor to cite the authority.

It is generally understood, I believe, that Warren, at the time of the battle, had not received the commission of Major General, to which office he was appointed on the 14th; that he left Watertown, where the Provincial Congress was sitting, on the morning of the 17th, and was present with the Committee of Safety in Steward Hastings' house, on Cambridge Common, where also Gen. Ward's head quarters were, when Major Brooks arrived from Charlestown and delivered Colonel Prescott's request for reinforcements. That he soon after left the Committee of Safety, of which he was Chairman, and walked a part of the way towards Charlestown, with Dr. Townsend, his pupil, and was spoken to by Judge Winthrop, before he reached the hill, in his usual dress, which was a light colored coat with a sprig on the button, as Gov. Eustis informed me. I have Gov. Brooks' authority for the fact of Warren's presence with the Committee of Safety, when he made his communication from Col. Prescott. He has often detailed to me the observations and opinions of that gallant officer at the councils of war, which were held before the message was sent to Cambridge, and the particulars of his own interview with General Ward first, and afterwards with the Committee of Safety, who sat in the adjoining room.

As it is probable I shall have no other so good opportunity, I can hardly refrain from mentioning one or two circumstances which I have learned in these conversations, although they are not immediately connected with

the object of this communication. After despatches had been sent over
to Mystic for Stark's and Reed's regiments, and other reinforcements
were ordered to march, messages were sent to the neighboring towns,
requesting them to bring in their own supplies of powder. As these arrived the Committee distributed themselves, and, seated on the tiller of the
carts, dealt out a gill of powder to each soldier, as he came up, some of
whom had powder horns, and others wrapped it up in paper. Meanwhile,
Brooks, who was not detailed with his regiment for duty the day before,
in consequence of his absence at Reading, (called home by the confinement of his wife with her first child,) but who on his return had the permission of the General to go as a volunteer, provided he would report at
head quarters in the morning, was collecting the two remaining companies
of his regiment, which had been on guard near the General's quarters.
It is well known that the General, apprehensive that the movements towards Charlestown were only a feint to cover a real attack of the main
position at Cambridge, was fearful of weakening his force at that place.
Brooks says to him, " now General, I have reported according to promise,
I hope you will let me march these men where they can be of some use."
To which he answered, " I am sorry I cannot comply with your request."
" But look at them, General," said Brooks anxiously, " they have got
bayonets—there are none scarcely on the hill, and I assure they will be
wanted there." " I shall want them here, sir," was the reply, which ter-
minated the interview, and he did not get orders to march until it was too
late for him to arrive before the retreat.

But to remove the uncertainty of the time, place, and manner of Warren's death, which " Historian" says exists, let us recur to the evidence ;
and, first, as to the time and place.

Upon his arrival at the redoubt, Prescott saw Warren, and supposing he
came to take the command, said to him he was glad to have assistance ;
to which Warren replied, as Mr. Wright (now of Beverly, then of Hollis,
who was in Prescott's regiment and heard it, says) " No, I did not come
to take the command, it is too late in the day; but I'll give you all the
assistance I can." Warren was afterwards seen conversing with Putnam,
who said to him in the presence of Lt. Col. Parker, who was wounded in
the knee, taken prisoner, and afterwards died, but whose wounds were
dressed by Dr. Jeffries on a fascine, to whom he related it, " they will
beat us from the work, I know ; but we shall do them infinite mischief,
though we must at last retreat." Col. Whitmore, then a Lieutenant in
Capt. Perkins' company, in Little's regiment, states that he was wounded
in the thigh *in the retreat from the redoubt ;* at the same moment Warren
fell, about six feet from him. Capt. Coburn, on *the retreat from the redoubt,* spoke to Warren, and Gen. Winslow saw him lying dead *about
sixty yards in the rear of the redoubt,* the morning after the battle, with
his hands under his head. Major Small of the British army, who acknowledged that he owed his own life to the humanity of Putnam on that occasion, in his turn attempted to save the life of his friend Warren, whom he
saw, as he entered the redoubt, and called to him to stand, or he would
be killed. This is his own relation to Dr. Jeffries, who went over with
the British troops as surgeon after the first attack. There can be no mistake about this, as Maj. Small and Dr. Warren were very intimate friends ;
and Dr. Jeffries, who was a professional rival of Warren's, used to meet
them frequently at Mr. Scollay's—and Dr. Warren had, a few evenings
before, offered him a place in the medical staff. Here is abundant evi-

dence, but more is at hand if needed, as, to avoid prolixity, I have omitted many minute particulars which would corroborate the facts, that Warren, although he was opposed to the plan of taking possession of the heights of Charlestown, thinking the Fabian policy the best in the condition the army then was, and though he was seen sick in his bed after he came from Watertown that morning with a nervous headache; when he heard Major Brooks' communication from Col. Prescott, requesting reinforcements and ammunition, left the Committee of Safety and repaired to the scene of action, was in various parts of the field, "*after the battle began to rage,*" *and was killed near the redoubt as the British entered it.*

Respecting the "manner" of his death, there is more uncertainty; though, to use the language of "Historian" to express one's own idea, "the popular impression" that he was wounded some time before he was killed, in the arm or side, gains strength from the circumstances and facts related by the witnesses who were assembled on the late occasion. Mr. Jonathan Clark, now living in Abington, 80 years old, but who then belonged to Boston, and was in Lock's company and Gardener's regiment, "who knew Warren, who had attended him as a physician," is positive in his testimony "that he was first wounded in the arm, and being pressed to retire, said he would never set the example of retreating to the "bloody backs." "The mortal wound," Mr. Clark says, "was in the head."

Gen. Warren's body had mouldered in the grave for ten months, when it was disinterred, which made it impossible at that time to ascertain the correctness of this supposition,—not so with the wound in the head. After the evacuation of Boston, Warren's friends were informed where he was buried. This was not as "Historian" says it was, "with the promiscuous slain, in the common trench of the dead;" though it was in the same grave with a person with a frock on. Warren's body was found stripped of its covering, while the other was buried in its common habiliments. Mr. Clark, above-named, as well as another soldier whose name I have forgotten, was here on the 17th, who assisted at the exhumation in the presence of the Doctor's two brothers, who were satisfied of the identity of the body, by many circumstances which they detailed. If stronger evidence of its identity were wanting, that afforded by Col. Revere, who set the artificial tooth, (which "Historian" says led to the "mere conjecture" that it was Warren's body,) and who recollected the wire he used in fastening it in, would afford it. One thing, however, is certain; that the skull was perforated by a musket ball in the upper part of the head, in such a place, as I am informed by professional gentlemen, would probably have produced sudden, though it might not instant death. "Historian" will observe that all these facts relating to the "*time,*" *place and manner* of Warren's death accord with the account which Major Small gave to Major Gordon, at the American minister's, in London, in the year 1791, when he told him that though he saw Warren fall, "life had fled before he saw his remains;" to Col. Trumbull, in 1786, at the time he was engaged in painting his celebrated historical picture, in which Major Small is represented in the exercise of the humane act which has been ascribed to him. (See Gordon's and Trumbull's printed letters.)

But "Historian" says "that according to the present popular impression, the probability is that the death of Warren was not known until after the British had buried all the slain of their opponents without knowing any sort of distinction among them." If it be the popular impression, it is time that this as well as some other "prevalent ideas" in "Historian's" communication was corrected. That Gen. Howe saw him *fell* is even to be inferred from Major Gordon's letter to Major Jackson of Philadelphia, above quoted, in which he relates the conversation between Gen. Howe and Maj. Small, at the time they supposed he fell, from the latter of whom he derived it; but that his *death* was known to the British commander is shown as well by that letter, as by the facts recorded in Dr. Jeffries' diary, of which, it is much to be regretted, great part was lost in a late fire, but from which leaf Samuel Swett had taken minutes, and the facts relating to which the present Dr. Jeffries, his son, perfectly recollects. The Doctor's story was that after the battle was over, while he was dressing a British officer, Gen. Howe came up to him and said, "Jeffries, there is a general officer fallen; do you know Warren?" "Do I know my right hand, you may as well ask?" says Jeffries. "Come here then," says Howe, "and let me know if the report is true that he is dead." Jeffries accompanied the General to the redoubt, and on the way Howe again asked him if he was certain he could identify the person; he replied anybody can do that, for he had a whitlow on a certain finger, naming it, by which he lost a nail; and he had also a particular artificial tooth. Howe soon pointed out the body, which was immediately recognized by Jeffries. When therefore "Historian" says that "Warren's body" could not have been known or he would have been buried with distinguished honors, even if he only was considered as a mason of a high order," he argues upon a probability against the truth. Not being a mason, I am not conversant of the customs of masons in this particular, (though I never heard of fallen enemies being buried with distinguished honors because they were masons; armies would have enough to do beside their "accustomed work" if this were the case,) and I am apt to think that "Historian" is in a similar cause with myself, as it appears that Warren was known, and was not only buried without any such honors; but, as it appeared at the time of the disinterment, the body was rifled of its covering.

If "Historian" thinks it is a "prevalent idea" that Warren could not have taken any important part in the events of that day, because he was dressed in his common clothes instead of his uniform; I should reply, that not being commissioned and qualified to act as an officer, he could not with propriety have worn a uniform, even if he was provided with one, which is not probable, for it is to be inferred from Gen. Ward's orderly book in my possession, that there was not a person in uniform nor an epaulette worn within the American lines till some time after Washington arrived at Cambridge. But that Warren was distinguished by his *coadjutors* as a "*courageous*" and "*fearless* patriot," besides other testimony, the toast that was given at a meeting of the field officers of the sixth brigade, under Col. Frye, who assembled two months after the battle at the house of Jonathan Hastings, to celebrate the memorable 4th of August, (repeal of the stamp act) is sufficient evidence. "Immortal honor to that *patriot* and *hero*, Doctor Warren, and the brave American troops who fought the battle of Bunker Hill on the 17th of June, 1775."

As "Historian" requested "such further light on the melancholy subject as the gentleman in question could give," I have mentioned these facts, and referred to the authority from which they are derived, as I did at the time I promulgated the words which it was said the enthusiastic patriot uttered, in the time of his country's greatest need, when the enemy seemed to be carrying all before them, and after he had received what he himself considered a mortal wound, "I am a dead man—fight on, my brave fellows, for the salvation of your country."

We have seen that it was not impossible, from the manner of his death, that he might thus have spoken, whether he was wounded once or twice before he fell. Those only, therefore, who are envious of the honors of the illustrious dead, will be eager to disprove the positive declaration of one who heard him. The evidence in support of the fact is of the highest authority. Let not his country, then, be deprived of the glorious example of the patriotic volunteer "without authority, yet whom none commanded," upon speculative surmises. The truth of the declaration ascribed to Warren is not only positively testified to, but the sentiment accords with his whole character. It is consistent with the account of his conduct at this particular crisis given of him by Col. Swett in his Historical Sketch of the Battle; of which, availing himself of the information collected at the late Jubilee, the public will be gratified to learn is preparing a new edition. "The chivalrous Warren," says he, "lingered to the last. His exalted spirit disdained, as a disgrace, a retreat the most inevitable. He animated the men to the most desperate daring, and when hope had fled he still disdained to fly." It is also perfectly compatible with the ardor of his feelings, when he said, "he would not set an example of retreating to the bloody blacks," and consistent to that fearless devotion to his country's cause, which led him previous to the battle to declare to Major Small, when doubting in conversation whether we should stick together, if the troops should be obliged to come to the last resort, (as I have the authority of Perez Morton, Esq., at that time Secretary of the Council, for asserting that he did,) "Depend upon it, my friend, whenever you pull a hostile trigger against my countrymen, you will find me among them."

The sentiment which he uttered in the hearing of Mr. Foster is a noble one. Though it does not increase Warren's fame, it adds something to his countrymen's pride; and no one that hears it can help throwing his thoughts back a few hours, to the interesting interview between him and Vice-President Gerry, to whose remonstrances against his exposing himself in the battle, Warren, perfectly aware of the necessity as well as the danger of it, so beautifully and prophetically replied, "Dulce et decorum est pro patria mori."

I send you Mr. Foster's letter in reply to my interrogatories, received while copying the above, which I beg you will consider as a part of this communication.

I am, respectfully,
Your obedient servant,
W. H. SUMNER.

Tewksbury, August 3, 1825.

Sir,—I have read the piece in the Patriot in which it is doubted whether the toast you gave on the 4th of July, as the words of Warren, are correct. They are strictly true, and stated exactly as I told you on the morning of the anniversary. I knew Dr. Warren before that day: had seen him among the troops at Cambridge, and am certain of the fact. His words made a lasting impression on my mind, and I have repeated them a thousand times. I was a private in Capt. Walker's Company, in Bridge's Regiment, and was on the ground all the night before, building up the works. After the old engineer had fixed his stakes, Eliakim Walker,

Jonathan Beard and myself, (who are both living I believe, Mr. Beard was
at the celebration with me) thought he had not got them quite straight,
and we moved one of them to square it up.

The day of the battle I was near the redoubt; we did all we could;
but were obliged to give up at last. The last time the British came up
we were moving off all in a hurry into the rear of the redoubt, to stop
them as they came up, and there it was that I saw Gen. Warren; his
clothes were bloody, when he cried out to us, "I am a dead man, fight
on, my brave fellows, for the salvation of your country." We had no
time to do much, but got off as soon as we could. I never saw Warren
after that. The British fired upon us both small and large guns on the
retreat, and more of us got off than could reasonably have been expected.

I knew Gen. Putnam and Col. Prescott, well. I saw Putnam riding
round, very active. I saw him ten times, at least, I should think. Putnam went off with David Baily and a number of others, and they took
tools with them to intrench on Bunker Hill, but a number of them came
back again. I was close by Asa Pollard when he was killed. He was
the first man that was killed. The ball struck the ground and hopped
along before it struck him. Mr. Benjamin Baldwin rolled him up in a
blanket, and they carried him off and buried him. I do not remember
anything more of very great importance. I saw a good deal, and remember a great deal, but it is not worth writing that I know of. I am willing
to tell all I do know. It appears to me the blood was running down his
(Warren's) arm or side when he spoke the words, but we were all in such
a hurry I wont be certain about that. I shall send an order for my
money under the resolve.

I am, Sir,
Your most obedient servant,
AMOS FOSTER.

General William H. Sumner.

(To be Continued.)

———— • ⟶ • ————

REMINISCENCES OF CANAAN, LITCHFIELD CO., CONN.

Albany, 4th Twelfth mo. 1857.

To the Editor of the N. E. Hist. and Gen. Register:
  Should the historical importance of the accompanying documents, relating to the
town of Canaan, Conn., entitle them to a place in your publication, it will be gratifying to the subscriber, and many others, who first saw the light in that town.

FRED. S. PEASE.

The following is a copy of a paper found with the papers of the late
Nathaniel Stevens, Esq. of Canaan, Conn.—

When Canaan was first settled, it was all a wild wilderness, except
three Dutch families, who lived on the Ousatonic river. The first family
of English that moved into the town was Samuel Bryant, from Stratford,
Ct. He came in May, 1738, and John Franklin drove his ox team. That
was the first ox team that was driven into the town. He settled down
near where the Blackberry river enters into the Housatonic. He had six
sons; and his seventh was the first English child that was born in Canaan.
It was James Bryant, Esq., that afterwards lived in Nobletown, York

State. The next families that moved into the town were those of Daniel Lawrence and Isaac Lawrence, and the Hewit family from Plainfield. They were eleven days on their journey, and they arrived the 2d day of June, 1738, with their families. They had to cut their way through from New Hartford to Canaan.

Daniel Lawrence had some boards. He set up some crotches, and made him a hut to shelter him. Isaac Lawrence unloaded his goods under a pine tree, and not a board to cover him but the boards of his cart. He had dug a hole in the side of a hill, and laid up some logs, ten feet one way and twelve the other. Next day he went to Sheffield and got some boards and covered it; and there he lived with his family one year, and ten men besides his own family lived with him. Then he built a large log house, by a fine spring, where he lived several years. And people kept moving into the town very fast from all parts of the country. The produce of the earth was very fine—exceeding good corn the first year, and pumpkins exceeding large; and everything seemed to flourish.

There were places where the Indians had planted corn, where the trees had grown very large, among the hills; and they ploughed up pestles and pots, very beautiful, made of free stone, and arrow pikes a multitude. And it was supposed there was a settlement of Indians in that place in times past. Isaac Lawrence dug up bones and ashes, when he was digging his cellar, about five or six feet from the surface of the earth. They were thought to be men's bones by people that saw them.

The first winter, there was a great deal of snow, and no rain all winter—but was a very forward spring and fruitful summer. The second winter was very moderate; but there was one man found dead in the snow. It was supposed that he sat down on a log, being in liquor, and fell asleep, and pitched down into the snow, where his breath thawed the snow so that it strangled him. He was found not far from Forb's iron works. His name was Blackbourn. He was the first person that died in Canaan. The third winter was very severe,—a vast deal of snow, and extreme cold, so that some cattle froze to death,—but it was a very fruitful summer after it.

Deer were very plenty about here, and some Indians lived about here that seemed to be very friendly. They belonged to Stockbridge and Barrington. One day the wife of Isaac Lawrence was up in her chamber, and she heard a noise. She looked out, and she saw thirty-three Indians coming up to the door. She gave herself up for lost. One of the Indians spoke to her, and told her not to be afraid, for they called to drink at the spring, and they were going to Stockbridge to a wedding, and that they were friends. But people were very much afraid of Indians all the time.

People kept settling so fast that, in the year 1741, they had a minister ordained—Mr. Elisha Webster from Farmington—and a great many people came a hundred miles to the ordination, and to see the country. And there was a man felling a tree to build the minister's house, and a limb struck him and crushed him into the earth. He was the second person that died in Canaan. His name was Richard Highsted. He left a wife and four children. The third was the wife of Thomas Hewit, with a fever.

In the year 1744, people began to be very much terrified about Indians, for there was a good deal of mischief done in the towns about by the Indians, so that our people bui't several forts in the town, and had a guard of soldiers in the town, which scouted the woods every day. But they never saw any signs of any enemy; but there were a great many alarms, but never any enemy appeared. Sometimes the forts would be crowded with people from other towns. In this situation we lived for two or three years.

Afterwards, the iron works were carried off by a flood; then rebuilt; and then, in the year 1750, they were burned to ashes, and a great many houses, and barns, and other buildings—eleven in all; and the same year the town was visited with great sickness among children. Thirty-three children and two old people died, almost all with the canker, and the next summer the dysentery carried off a great many old people. Thus the Lord hath visited us.

There were a great many bears killed about the town in 1760. There were five killed in one day. In the year 1765, there were five wolves killed in one day. There was a multitude of rattlesnakes on a hill that they call snake hill to this day. And Isaac Lawrence had a bitch that used to go out and be gone three days at a time; and she would come home all swelled up by being bitten by the snakes. Then she would dig a hole in the earth and bury herself up until it drew out all the poison; and then she would go out again. And thus she did till her hair all came off, and then they killed her.

The above named John Franklin was father to the late Silas Franklin, Esq.—the father of Charles W. Franklin, now (1857) living in Canaan.

THE PATENT OF CANAAN, LITCHFIELD COUNTY, CONN.

The Gouvernour and Company of his Majesty' English Colony of Connecticut in New England in America to all to whom these presents shall come, *Greeting.*

Whereas the Gouvernour an Company in General Court assembled on y* second Thursday of May one thousand seven hundred and thirty one—at Hartford—did order that the western lands on the east side of Ousatounack river—and north of the townships of New Milford and Litchfield, should be laid out into five townships, and appointed Messrs Edmund Lewis, John Bewell and William Judd a committee to lay out the same.

And whereas in pursuance of said order, the said committee laid out and surveyed the said five Townships—one of which in their survey aforesaid was called the Township of C. and bounded the same as follows (viz) For the south bounds of the township of C. they began at White Oak Pole at y* North West corner of the Township A. and run west nine and half North—four miles and half to Ousatounack River and made a monument for the south west corner of said Township of C. Then began again at said White Oak Pole which is the south east corner of y* said township—and ran north nineteen and one half degrees. East eight miles and one Hundred and forty six rods to the line of partition between the Province of the Massachusetts Bay and Colony of Connecticut and marked a small tree and laid many stones to it for a monument—Standing in or near the aforesaid line of Massachusetts and is the north east corner bounds of the township of C. and has these letters set on it (viz) E.L.W.H.R. and the said line from the said White Oak Pole—which also hath the aforesaid letters marked on it—is well set forth by marked trees and monuments—and from the above mentioned Spruce tree the north line of the township of C. runs West nine degrees and half north—four miles and half and one hundred and twenty nine rods to the Ousatounack River—where we made a monument for the north West corner of said Township of C. It being elm tree standing in the said Massachusetts line marked and stones laid to it and the letters I.H.F.L.W.H.B. set on it—Bounded north on the Massachusetts line South on the township of B. East on the township of D. and west on the Ousatounack River as by the returns made by s'd Committee bearing date October 15th AD. 1731 entered into the records of the aforesaid Colony of Connecticut Lib. 4 Vol. 503 in the secretarys office reference thereunto had more fully—and at large may appear.

And whereas the said Gouvernour and Company in Gen' Court assembled at Hartford on the tenth day of May 1783, did enact that the s'd Township among other Townships—then lately laid out should be disposed of and settled according to such time and regulations as the s'd assembly should order—And whereas the s'd Gouvenor and Company assembled in General Court at New Haven in the year of our Lord 1737, by their act did order that the s'd Townships should be divided into fifty three rights—Exclusive of all former grants of the General Court that were then surveyed and recorded in the Public Records of the Colony and lying in s'd Town—Of which fifty three Rights, one should be for the use of the Minister that should be settled in s'd Town according to the regulations in s'd act provided—One for the first Gospel Minister settled as aforesaid, and one other right for the support of the school in said Town—And ordered that fifty of s'd Rights should be sold, and that the other three Rights should be for the use aforesaid—and that the committee by s'd act appointed should sell, and in the name of the Gouvenor and Company aforesaid execute Deeds of Conveyance of the said several Rights to the purchasers thereof respectively with condition to such Deed annexed according to the directions in the said act contained.

And whereas in pursuance of s'd act the said committee have sold and by their several Deeds under their hands and seals, have granted unto William Roberts, Peter Hogeboom, John Beobe, Uriah Stevens, Daniel Lawrence Junior—and to the rest of the original purchasers of Rights or fifty third parts of s'd Township upon conditions as aforesaid—which Township is now called and known by the name of Canaan—And whereas Mr. Elisha Webster is in the ministry in s'd Town according to the directions aforesaid—and the several purchasers aforesaid—their Heirs or assigns having performed the conditions in the said Deeds expressed, and now moving for a more full congrmation of y' lands sold and granted them as aforesaid.

Now know ye, that y' said Gouvenour and Company by Virtue of the power granted unto them—by our late Souvreign King Charles the second of blessed memory—in and by his letters patient under the great Seal of England—bearing date of y' twenty third day of April—In the fourteenth year of his Majesty,' Reign have given and granted and by these presents, for themselves and their Successors—do give, grant, ratify and confirm unto them the said William Roberts, Peter Hogeboom, John Beobe, Uriah Stevens, Daniel Lawrence Junior—and to the said Mr. Elisha Webster who is the settled Minister in said Town and to the rest of the original purchasers or their respective heirs or assigns or legal representatives of such original purchasers to whom such original Deeds were made and executed—All the aforesaid Township of C. now called Canaan within the bounds and limits described by the survey aforesaid to be the bounds of the s⁴ Township of C. exclusive of the former grants—surveyed and recorded into the public Records aforesaid forever—together with all and singular the Woods, Timber, Trees, Underwood, Lands, Waters, Brooks, Ponds, Fishings, Mines, Minerals, and precious Stones—within and upon the s⁴ tract of land—and Township aforesaid hereby granted, mentioned or intended to be granted as aforesaid—and all and singular yᵉ Rights and Profits, privileges, and appertinances whatsoever of and within the said Township—and every part thereof to Have and to Hold yᵉ above said tract contained in the Township of Canaan aforesaid, with the privilege unto them the s⁴ William Roberts, Peter Hogeboom, John Beebe, Uriah Stevens, Daniel Lawrence Junior and yᵉ said Elisha Webster—and to yᵉ rest of the original purchasers, Their Heirs or assigns or legal Representatives of such original purchasers to whom such rights do belong and to their only proper use—benefit and behoof forever, as a good, sure, absolute—and indefeasible Estate of Inheritance in fee simple—without any condition, limitation, use or other thing to alter or make void the same—to be holden of his Majesty His Heirs or successors as of his Majestys Manner of East Greenwich in the County of Kent and Kingdom of Great Britton in free and Common soccage and not in Capite nor by Knights service—yielding and paying therefor unto our Sovereign Lord the King, His Heirs and successors forever only one fifth part of all the Ore of Gold and Silver which from time to time and at all times hereinafter shall be gotten had and obtained therein in lieu of all Services, duties and demands whatever.

In witness whereof we the s⁴ Gouvenour and Company have caused the seal of the said Colony hereunto to be affixed the Twenty eighth day of May. In the eighteenth year of our Sovereign Lord George the second by the grace of God of Great Brittain &c King Anno Dom. one Thousand Seven Hundred and forty and five—

By Order of the Gov. and Company of the Colony of Connecticut in General Court assembled May AD 1745.
  Signed)   Jon⁴ Law Gov.
George Wyllys, Secretary

Entered May 29th 1746 on the Records of the Colony of Connecticut Book no. 4 Vol. 575, 6–7 for Pattents, Deeds and conveyances of Lands.
     Attest   George Wyllys Secretary.

This Pattent is recorded in the Proprietors Book of Records in Canaan, page 75 and 76.
  By David Whitney,
     November 29th 1745.
       Proprietors Clerck:

When the Duke de Choiseuil, a remarkably meagre man, came to London to negotiate a peace, Charles Townshend being asked whether the French government had sent the preliminaries of a treaty, answered, "I do not know; but they have sent the outline of an ambassador."—*Newspaper.*

SERMONS BY REV. SAMUEL PARRIS OF SALEM VILLAGE.
1689—1694.

THE recent publication of the Danvers Church Records, in the Register, (Vol. XI., pp. 131 . . . . a notice of a volume of his manuscript sermons, preached at Salem Village, between his ordination in Nov. 1689 and May, 1694, ... Library of the Connecticut Historical Society. The volume . . . . . . neatly and carefully written, and numbered on the first page . . . . . . " of the writer's sermons. It commences with his ordination sermon, prefixed to which is the following note :—

"My poor and weak ordination sermon at the embodying of a church in Salem Village, on the 19. 9. 1689. The Rev⁴ Mr. Nicholas Noyse embodying of us: who also ordained my most unworthy self Pastor, and together with yᵉ Rev⁴ Mr. Sam: Phillips & the Rev⁴ Mr. John Hale imposed hands. The same Mr. Phillips giving me yᵉ right hand of fellowship with beautiful loveliness & humility."

The text is from Joshua, v. 9 : "And the Lord said unto Joshua, This day have I rolled away the reproach of Egypt from off you."

The remainder of the volume consists of sacramental sermons, in regular course, (with occasional omissions and reference to "these sermons in loose papers, 8vo.") the last of which was preached, May 6, 1694, in the afternoon.

Before the sermon of "27 Mar. 1691-2. Sacrament day" is this note : "Occasioned by dreadfull Witchcraft broke out here a few weeks past, & one member of this Church, & another of Salem, upon publick examination by civil Authority, vehemently suspected for Shee-witches, [& upon it committed.]*

The text is from John vi. 71 ; and the running title, "*Christ knows how many Devils there are in his church and who they are.*"

The two sermons of 11 Sept. 1692, preached "after yᵉ condemnation of 8 Witches at a Court at Salem, one of the Witches, viz. Martha Kory in full communion with our Church,"† and entitled, "The Devils & his Instruments will be warring against Christ & his followers," from Revel. XVII. 14, "These shall make war with the Lamb," &c.

In the "improvement" of this subject, Mr. Parris remarks, that "It may serve to reprove such as seem so to be amaz'd at the war the Devil has raised amongst us by Wizards & Witches against the Lamb & his Followers, that they altogether deny it. *If ever there were Witches, men & women in covenant with the Devil, here are multitudes in New England.* Nor is it so strange a thing that there should be such ; no, nor that some church members should be such. Pious *Bishop Hall* saith, The Devil's prevalency in this Age is most clear in the marvailous number of witches abounding in all places. Now hundreds (says he) are discovered in one shire ; & if Fame deceive us not, in a village of 14 houses in the North, are found so many of this Damned brood. Heretofore only Barbarous Desarts had them, but now the civilized & Religious Parts are frequently pestered with them : Heretofore some silly ignorant old woman &c., but now we have known them of both sexes, who professed much knowledge,

---

* These words added subsequently.   † Vol. XI., p. 134.

Holiness & Devotion, drawn into this damnable practice.—*Baxter's Apparitions & Witches, page 122.*"

With such lights to guide him, who can wonder that Mr. Parris went astray? We cannot be too often reminded that the witchcraft delusion was not of indigenous growth in America,—that it did not begin nor end at Salem Village,—or, as Mather states it, "that New England is not the only place circumvented by the wiles of the wicked and wiley serpent, in this kind."　　　　J. H. T.

COLD FRIDAY AND SATURDAY, JAN. 18 & 19, 1857.

From various sources we gather the following record of the two coldest days that have occurred the present century, as asserted by all observers. It is said that the winter of 1835 was as severe in the southern states, but in the northern nothing has exceeded it since 1800. The cold Friday of 1810 was a more blustering day, yet it did not freeze so hard. The time of the record is sunrise.

Location	Temperature
Boston, Mass.	16 *below* 0
Manchester,	37 "
Methuen,	32 "
Reading,	33 "
Cambridge,	25 "
Cambridgeport,	16 "
Roxbury,	23 "
Jamaica Plain,	25 "
Melrose,	32 "
Braintree,	24 "
West Sandwich,	25 "
Waltham,	28 "
Lanesborough,	30 "
Somerville,	24 "
West Newton,	30 "
Worcester,	28 "
Lowell,	30 "
Malden,	30 "
Hartford, Conn.	30 to 32 "
Coldest morning of this century.	
Portland, Maine,	29 "
Bangor,	44 "
Calais,	39 "
St. John, N. B.	28 "
Fredericton,	30 "
Quebec, Canada,	30 "
Northfield, Vt.	40 "
St. Johnsbury, mercury congealed.	
Norwich,	40 "
Montpelier,	50 "
Coldest ever known.	
Dover, N. H.	31 "
Keene,	24 "
Nashua,	28 "
Salem, Mass.	20 to 26 *below* 0
Springfield,	33 "
Mansfield,	36 "
Middleborough,	25 "
Bridgewater,	24 "
Taunton,	24 to 30 "
New Bedford,	20 "
Fall River,	26 "
Norton,	33 "
Easton,	28 "
Lawrence,	28 "
Attleborough,	30 "
Plymouth,	16 "
Hingham,	20 "
Providence, R. I.	25 "
North Providence,	32 "
Woonsocket,	35 "
Coventry,	32 "
Manchester, N. H.	35 "
Franconia,	49 "
Mercury solid; coldest ever known.	
Bath,	54 "
Vouched for by many individuals.	
Montreal, Canada,	35 "
New Haven, Conn.	27 "
Troy, N. Y.	26 "
Albany,	27 "
New York,	6 "
Philadelphia,	5 "
Washington,	8 "
Baltimore,	6 "
Alexandria, Va.	8 "
Charleston, S. C.	12 *above* 0
Tallahassee, Fla.	10 "

[*Taunton Republican.*

THE COLEMAN FAMILY.

[By William C. Folger of Nantucket, Cor. Member N. E. H. and Gen. Soc.]

In reply to the article on the Coleman family by Joshua Coffin, Esq. of Newbury, I will remark that Thomas Coleman was one of the Partners or purchasers of one twentieth part of the Island of Nantucket in 1659, being of those chosen by the first ten purchasers as partners. He must have moved here long previous to 1680, the time fixed upon by my friend Joshua Coffin, Esq. He had a house lot and other lands set off to him at different times, by the Committee for laying out lands. I find by the old Book of Records that he was on a jury, Oct. 20, 1673.

He deeded his lands, houses, &c., to his son Tobias,[1] to take effect after his death, dated Nov. 3, 1673, at which time he was, by his own declaration in the Deed, a resident of Nantucket, as well as his son Tobias, who had a wife Lydia and a son Thomas.[2] See the copy appended.

Tobias[2] Coleman had a daughter Deborah, born May 25, 1676. Vide Book of Record of Births, Marriages and Deaths, in the office of our Town Clerk. Of the other children of Tobias I know nothing, as he moved away.

Thomas and Tobiah Coleman, both inhabitants in the town of Sherburne, upon the Island of Nantucket, sell Samuel Bickford half a share of Land, Nov. 12, 1678.

<table>
<tr><td>In presence of
  Peter Folger.
  Wm Worth.</td><td>Signed Thomas ⊢ Coleman.
Tobias ·|· Coleman.</td></tr>
</table>

Of Benjamin Coleman[2] I do not know any thing.

Joseph Coleman[2] the son of Thomas[1] came to Nantucket and married Ann Bunker, daughter of George and Jane (Godfrey) Bunker. They had 2 children, viz.; Joseph,[3] b. Nov. 17, 1673, who was drowned when young, in the fulling mill pond, and Ann,[3] born Nov. 10, 1675, who married Edward Allen, and had 10 children, viz., 6 sons and 4 daughters. From 4 of the sons are descended many bearing the name of Allen in Nantucket and New Bedford and vicinity, and from the daughters are also many descendants, the writer being descended from Rachel Allen, who m. Thomas Starbuck.

Joseph Coleman[2] died in 1690, as Letters of Administration on his estate were granted Aug. 12, 1690. Book 2, Deeds.

Thomas Coleman[1] died in 1682, and Letters of Administration were granted to Tobiah Coleman, and Joseph also became a surety, Aug. 1, 1682.

John Coleman,[2] son of Thomas[1] and Joanna Folger, dau. of Peter and Mary (Morrell) Folger.

Their children were:—

John, Jr.,[3] b. Aug. 2, 1667, m. Priscilla Starbuck.

Thomas,[3] b. Oct. 17, 1669, m. Jane Challing, wid. of John.

Isaac,[3] b. Feb. 6, 1671-2, m. 1, Ann Reynold; 2, Jane Watson.

Phebe,[3] b.   1674, m. Gershom Cathcart of Bristol Co.

{ Abigail,[3] b.   1676, m. James Tisdale of Dighton, Bristol Co.

{ Benjamin,[3] Jan. 17, 1676, died young.

Solomon,[3] ——, m. 1, Mary Macy; 2, Deliverance Swett, dau. of Moses

Jeremiah,[3] —— m. Sarah Pratt, dau. of Joseph.

John Colman,[2] son of Thomas,[1] died at Nantucket, in 1715 or 1716, and Joanna, his widow, d. 18 of 5 mo. 1719.

The name of Coleman is now common among the names of Nantucket, there being many descendants now living of John Coleman,[2] Thomas,[2] Solomon,[2] and Jeremiah.[3]

Isaac Coleman,[2] son of Thomas,[1] is said by Benjamin Franklin Folger of this town, the genealogist, to have accompanied Thomas Macy in the autumn of 1659, in the boat, in his emigration to this island, he then being a boy, about 12 or 13 years old. By the Town's Record of Births, Marriages and Deaths, I find "John Barnard and Bethiah his wife and Isaac Coleman ended their days ye 6th June 1669 being drowned out of a canoe between nantucket & ye Vineyard, at the same time Eleazer Folger was preserved." This Bethiah Barnard who was drowned was a daughter of Peter Folger, and sister to Abiah Franklin.

The Joanna[2] Coleman mentioned in the article under consideration, I think must have been Joanna Coleman, wife of John,[2] and daughter-in-law of Thomas,[1] and not an own daughter. There was a Benjamin Coleman drowned in Hampton, 21 Oct. 1650; perhaps he was son of this Thomas[1] Colman. Isaac[2] Colman who was drowned in 1669 was the son of Thomas,[1] and was unmarried.

Isaac[2] Coleman, son of John,[2] left no children, though he was twice married. To give the names of all the descendants of Ann (Coleman) Allen[3], daughter of Joseph Coleman,[2] and of John Coleman,[2] would swell this article to a greater length than my time or ability will now permit. They are spread through many States and Territories of the Union. Being a descendant, both of Joseph Coleman[2] and of John Coleman,[2] sons of Thomas,[1] it will do for me to quote from some verses characterizing the different families of Nantucket, "A learned Coleman very rare." I believe that line, conveys the true characteristic of this family, although there have been very many worthy people among them.

[From Book 1st, page 23, County Records, Deeds.]
Copy of a Deed of Thomas Coleman.

"Be it known unto all men and by these presents be it declared that I Thomas Coleman of Sherburn on the Iland of Nantucket for divers good and weighty considerations me thereunto moving, do hereby freely give, grant, ratify and confirm unto my son Tobias Coleman, Ten Akers of land, part of it being that on which his house standeth, and the remainder on the north side of his house above the high way. This I give to him at present to have and to hold to him and his heirs forever. I also hereby give unto the said Tobias my son to enjoy the same after my decease, all my other land both upland and meadow upon this Iland of Nantucket with all the housing that is or may be upon it at the day of my death. Together with all my comonage or comonages, And also all other privileges that is or may be belonging to these my aforesaid Lands to him the said Tobias to have and to hold during the term of his natural life and to Lydia his wife to have and to hold after the decease of the sayd Tobias during the term of her natural life and after her decease to Thomas Coleman the son of the said Tobias to have and to hold forever, provided the said Tobias pay after my decease to his brother John Coleman five pounds and to his brother Joseph Coleman ten pounds, and also that his mother my now wife shall after my death enjoy the third of what I shall leave at my death, during the time of her life for her use and comfort, but not to sell or dispose of any thing, but only her bed and pewter and my bibel, which things I have freely given my wife. Al other goods and chattels that I shall leave at my death, I also freely give unto my son Tobias to him and to his heirs forever, only I except that my wife shall have the use of the mare as long as she liveth. This is my true act and deed as witness my hand and seal this third day of november one thousand six hundred and seventy and three.   Thomas Coleman.

<table>
<tr><td>Witness hereunto
peter foulger
the mark of
Margery N Coleman
Tristram Coffin.</td><td>This Estate mentioned in this deed was delivered in part by Thos Coleman to the aforesaid Tobias Coleman by turf & twig in presence of

        Tristram Coffin
        Peter Foulger."</td></tr>
</table>

[Book 2, in Registry of Deeds.]

" At the Court of Sessions the first day of August 1682. Lre of Administration on the Estate of Thomas Coulman are granted to Tobiah Coulman who bindeth himselfe to his Royall Highness in the sum of an hundred pounds starling to perform the trust in administering one his father's Estate and to bear the Court harmless according to law."

" Joseph Coulman doth bind himself together with Tobiah Coulman."

The Aprisers appointed }   Nathaniol Barnard
  by the Court are   }   Steven Coffin
                 Ric Swaine
                 Tho Looke."

" August the 12th 1690.

Letters of Administration on the Estate of Joseph Coleman are granted onto William Bunker and Stephen Coffin who bind themselves as followeth We William Bunker and Stephen Coffin Doe Bind ourselves Jointly and severally in the sum of an hundred pounds starling to performe the trust of an administrator on said Estate and to baire the Court harmless according to law.

                             William Bunker
                             Stephen Coffin"

Book 2, Deeds, &c.

ABSTRACT OF THE WILL OF ANDREW OSBORNE, OF LONDON, 1614.

Hartford, November 15, 1857.

Dear Sir,—I forward you an abstract of an early will;—from the original in the collection of the Connecticut Historical Society, handsomely engrossed on parchment and in good preservation, except the fold on which were the signatures and attestation, which has been cut off. I know nothing of the history of the document or of its line of descent to the place of its present deposit: but as the names of Osborne, Plympton, and Coffin were all represented, at an early period, in New England, the will may possibly supply important genealogical information to some of the descendants.

           Yours, &c.   J. H. T.

Andrew Osborne, " citizen and marchant taylor of London," by his will executed Nov. 20th, 1614, directs his body " to be buried within his Majesty's free Chappell Church of St. George wthin his highness Castle of Windsor," and gives his estate as follows :—

To his wife *Margaret*, the lease of his house " called the Garter house," within the castle of Windsor; the lease of his house called " the Bucks head" in Watling Street, parish of St. Augustine, city of London; and

the lease of a house where "now dwelleth one Robert Woodward, draper,"
in said Watling Street, "known by the name of the signe of the Lute and
Tunn,"—for her life, and at her death, the unexpired term to belong to
his three sons, *John, Charles* and *Edward* Osborne. Also, to his wife,
the use for five years after his decease, with the rents and profits of his
"five houses in Distaffe Lane," city of London; and of his "sixteen
houses scituate and being w^hout Temple Barr," in parish of St. Clement
Danes; and of one house in Gutter Lane; with remainder as before, to
his sons; and from the rents of these houses an annual payment of £200
to be made to *Andrew, Henry, Richard* and *Alice Plumpton*, the children
of his son-in-law, *Henry Plumpton*, citizen and salter of London, now
dwelling in Fryday Streets, city; and an annual payment of £100 to his
"cozen *Joane Center*."

Item. To *Margaret Center*, £20, in money.

Item. To his son *John*: "two houses in the Ile of Tennett," county
of Kent; 22 acres of arable land in Hallingburne parish, Kent, lately
purchased of Sir Thomas Flud (?); 16 acres, in Newington parish, Kent,
now "in tenure of John Osborne, gent."

Item. To son *Charles*, £250 in money.

Item. To son *Edward*, £250 in money.

Item. To the parish church of Hartlipp, county of Kent," where I
was born," 40 marks, for the poor of the parish.

The residue of his estate to his wife, who is made sole executrix: his
son-in-law, *Henry Plumpton* and *John Peerson*, notary public, named
overseers.

Executed in presence of *Philip Boles, William Hale, William Newman*, and *John Peerson*.

DEED FROM THE PROPRIETORS TO PETER FOLGER OF HALF A SHARE OF LAND ON NANTUCKET.

[Copied by William C. Folger, Cor. Memb. N. E. H. & Gen. Society.]

Nantucket 4th July 1663

These presents witnesseth that we whose names are underwritten do
give and grant unto Peter foulger, halfe a share of accommodations on
the Iland aforesayd that is to say half so much as one of the Twenty purchasers both in Respect of upland meadow, wood, & timber and all other
Appurtenances belonging to him & his heirs forever, on condition that he
com to Inhabit on the Iland aforesayd with his family within one year
after the Date hereof, likewise that the sayd peter shall atend the English
in the way of an Interpreter betwen the Indians and them upon al necessary ocasions: his house-lot to be lay^d out at the place commonly called
by the name of Rogers.field, so as may be most convenient: witness our
hands

Thos Macy	Tristram Coffin Sen; for myselfe and others
Edward Starbuck	being impowered by them, Peter Coffin Steven
John Swayn	Greenleafe
Robert Barnard	Tristram Coffin Jun;
Richard Swayn	William Pile for Two shares
John Holfe	nathaniel Starbuck
Tho Maybew	Thomas Coleman
	John Smyth　　[*Book* 1st *of Deeds*, p. 31.

JOHN ENDICOTT.

*What office did John Endicott sustain in Massachusetts, after his arrival
hither, Sept. 6, 1628, to his being elected, by the Company in London,
Governor of the same Plantation, April 30, 1629?*

At the former date, the Abigail arrives at Naumkeag, with her passengers and supplies. Of the colonists thus come to their new residence, was
Endicott, of whom Bradford wrote, he " brought over a patent, under the
broad seal, for the government of Massachusetts."

Here is one of the clearest and most pertinent statements which could
possibly be uttered to express the prominent ideas which its author most
evidently intended to communicate. It distinctly portrays on the tablet of
our perception a patent or charter, sanctioned by the King's seal, and for
the purpose of governing the emigrants, who dwelt in Massachusetts, under the administration of John Endicott. We might as well assert that
the daguerreotype of a man, impressed with a complete likeness on its
plate, is fully represented even after its head is erased, as to assert that
the image, made on our minds by Bradford's language, is full and exact,
in its original lineaments, when deprived of its royal patent. We have
never heard nor read that the author of such language varied a single
hair, either in its phraseology or signification, though he must have had
frequent suggestions to do it, had there been any need for it to be done,
while preparing his History of Plymouth Plantation, embracing various
concerns of its adjacent colonies, for the long period of twenty-nine
years.*

When Nathaniel Morton issued his Memorial twelve years after the
death of this honorable chief magistrate, in speaking of Endicott's arrival, he uses the same language and communicates the same thoughts,
which his uncle did, and thus made a literal quotation from the said history, then in manuscript. Care for the good fame of his uncle as an
accurate historian, and care for himself in a similar respect; his well
known regard for veracity, and his earnest desire for the truthful representation of his adopted country's character in its rulers, laws and transactions, would have naturally kept him from publishing such a passage,
and thus deliberately and consciously perpetuating a mistake—had he
known or even suspected that it was so at fault. His relations to Bradford, as a resident in Plymouth with him, from 1623,—and as Secretary of
State from 1645, under him for the years he was Governor, and otherwise in public and private concerns; and his own personal knowledge of
Endicott's political course to his decease in 1665,—leave not the shadow
of a probability that he would, with the most evident and fullest assurance,
have seconded, as he did, the plain and positive statement of his uncle,
that Endicott brought over a royal patent, unless he regarded it as an
undoubted and indubitable fact.†

Before the Memorial was issued by Morton, he submitted it to the supervision of John Higginson and Thomas Thacher, in order to have it
accompanied with their recommendation to the reader. These two ministers, from their long acquaintance with Bradford, Morton and Endicott,
were well qualified for the discharge of this office, and to judge of the
quotation made from the MS. of Bradford. Mark their language in the

---

* Bradford's Hist. Plym. Plant., 106.   † Morton's Memorial, Ed. 1721, p. 16.

address.* They assign as a reason why the production of Morton and others like it should be encouraged, is, " that there may be a furniture of materials for *true* and full history in after-time." They add, " the work itself is complied with modesty of spirit, simplicity of style, and *truth* of matter." Such caution and desire as here manifested on their part, as well as their acquaintance with Endicott in his political antecedents, is totally inconsistent with their suffering the quotation to remain unaltered, had it contained an essential error, as to a primary, prominent, and important matter of a royal patent, in the civil relations of Massachusetts.

In reference to this matter, Prince remarks,† " Governor Bradford and Mr. Morton seem to mistake in saying, ' he (Endicott) came with a Patent under the broad seal for the government of Massachusetts.' " He did this 108 years after the occasion of it, and 67 years from its publication by Morton, and confirmation of it by Messrs. Higginson and Thacher. What his reason was for the impression, so vaguely entertained and expressed, he did not assign, and thus came short of his extraordinary correctness. Suppose that one of our writers had stated, that Robert Gorges came over in 1623, as Governor-General of New England, and that he saw his commission for it, and this statement was repeated by another, and authorized by two more of credible qualifications,—but, many years after their concurrent testimony, an author arises and observes, that two of the first, just referred to, seemed incorrect in their statement, without so much as giving the lisp of a reason for his observation? Should we call this the presentation of facts and sound conclusions, which should lead us to disbelieve the relation of the two first authors? By no means. We should pronounce it insufficient to invalidate their testimony and set it aside.

That this is substantially the state of the case, the subsequent considerations are offered.

We look at the royal charter of Massachusetts, of 1628–9. This clearly narrates what took place, at different periods, in relation to such territory. It begins with the conveyance of it by James L., in 1620, with all the other territory, then comprised under the term of New England, to the Plymouth Company or Council. It then describes the sale of it in 1627–8, by this corporation, under their common seal, to six patentees, including John Endicott, and also the conveyance to the latter body of all authority to govern, and every other privilege essential to the regulation of a colony. The charter having so proceeded, notices the appearance of the royal grantor, so that he might secure to himself the fulfilment of a contract in which the Company or Council had promised him a fifth part of all gold and silver, obtained from any mines discovered in their jurisdiction, and, consequently, within the limits of Massachusetts. At this point a new relation is formed and assumed. The Council having given their deed to the patentees, did not continue their mineral obligation to the King, but passed it over to them. How do we know this? He states it himself. He declares, in the charter of 1628–9, that the patentees, having received the territory from the Council, do henceforth retain it " of us, our heirs and successors, in free and common soccage," and, as a collateral condition, they were to reserve a fifth of the gold and silver, obtained from mines, discovered within their bounds, as the Council had previously engaged to do. An exigency thus occurs, which demands some document

* Morton's Memorial.　　　† Prince, N. E. Chron., Ed. of 1736, note on p. 175.

or other, in order to preserve it and its conditions, subsisting between the King and the patentees. Who of these two parties should, according to rank and custom, take the lead in this matter? Evidently he, as their sovereign. In view, then, of nothing more than the nature of the case, he did do it and issue a document. What should we naturally expect this to be, coming from his order, short of a patent, describing the grant and all its privileges, and the mineral condition of them, under the royal or broad seal? Nothing. For his own security, he would do as much as this for the patentees, notwithstanding they had a deed from the Council under their common seal. In this state of the case, Endicott came over, and, from the preceding facts and considerations, with the declaration of Bradford and Morton, there is no reason to doubt that he brought such a document, as these two authors have described. The conclusion thus drawn is confirmed by the language of Johnson,* when referring to the emigrants of 1628, as "the much honored Mr. John Endicott come over with them to *govern*," and also by the letter of Dudley to the Countess of Lincoln. The last author states that, in 1628, "we procured a patent from His Majesty" for planting Massachusetts, "as also for the government of those who did or should inhabit within that compass, and, the same year, we sent Mr. John Endicott and some with him, to begin a plantation and to strengthen such as he should find there, which we [were?] sent thither from Dorchester and some places adjoining; from whom, the same year, receiving hopeful news." This passage plainly declares, that a patent was granted to proprietors of Massachusetts, by the King, for its government, and evidently denotes that the grant, so made, was before Endicott came to Naumkeag, and, therefore, must have been made to him and the other five patentees; and thus, with the testimony of Johnson, positively establishing the declaration of Bradford and Morton.

It is not unlikely that Prince may have formed his slight objection to the assertion of Bradford and Morton, just presented, from the subsequent passage in the letter of the Massachusetts Company in England to Endicott, dated April 17, 1629. "Since your departure, we have for the further strengthening of our grant from the Council of Plymouth, obtained a *confirmation* of it from His Majesty by his letters patent, under the broad seal of England, by which said letters patent we are incorporated into a body politic, with ample power to govern and rule all His Majesty's subjects that reside within the limits of our plantation."†

This may appear, in the minds of some, to suggest the two following questions: Does it not indicate that there was no patent under the broad seal, before its own existence, and, of course, none in 1628 for Mr. Endicott to bring over;—and that there was no government under him, because he had no such royal authority till 1629?

To the first question, we may truly reply, that to substantiate its affirmative, there is no conclusive evidence. Though only about a year passed between the Council's deed to the six patentees and the royal patent of 1629, yet this would not absolutely do away the need of a royal patent in 1628, so that these patentees, who had no prescience to foretell the speedy necessity of another similar document, might safely hold their settlement here of him, as the patent and charter of 1629 declares they did; and be still held them, instead of this Council, bound to him for the mineral stipulation;—nor dispense with the need of having a royal patent in 1629,

---

* Wonder Working Providence, 19.   † Hazard, I., 251.

because of the formation of a new company, including the six patentees, and properly requiring that the interests of their contract should be thus secured to them. While the quotation makes no denial of a royal patent, in 1628, it has the succeeding phrase, " for the *further* strengthening of our grant from the Council," which implies, rather than otherwise, that there had been already such confirmation by same document, aside from the Council's deed, which document might very properly be a royal patent.

As to the second question, we know that colonial government was exercised through the English and other territories of America, by settlers like those of Massachusetts, having patents from companies chartered by their kings. As one of the nearest instances, we may point to the Plymouth Colony, who had nothing more than patents from the Council for New England, and yet they enacted and executed laws for their Commonwealth down to their union with Massachusetts. Of course, then, though the quotation from the letter might, in the opinion of some, seem to deny colonial government to Massachusetts until the patent of 1629, it is directly contrary to well substantiated fact. With regard then to the two preceding questions, we perceive no cause to answer them any otherwise than in the negative.

The subject before us seems to have received the attention of Hutchinson, as intimated in the first volume of his history. It is probable that he was reminded of it by Prince, or his Annals, who was cotemporary thirty-one years, and long a townsman with him, after he graduated at Harvard College, and also by the quotation already adduced from the Company's letter. Referring to the arrival of Endicott, Hutchinson remarks, " The patent from the Council of Plymouth gave a good right to the soil, but no power of government. A royal charter was necessary."[*] This declaration seems not to comport with its author's usual carefulness. The Council had the right of government over Massachusetts, which they conveyed to the six patentees, comprising Endicott, in common with the rest of their jurisdiction, as plainly narrated in the charter of 1628-9. This is strengthened by the fact, previously mentioned, that a similar deed or patent from them to Plymouth Colony did invest these with such power, which they did exercise down to the day of their being united with Massachusetts.

In addition to this, there are other like proofs. Of these, we have room now only for the patent of 1622, to Robert Gorges, from the same Council, granting him a part of Massachusetts. This document, after reciting various interests conveyed by it to him, proceeds to confer upon him, his heirs or assigns, or " deputies, lieutenants, judges, stewards or other officers, all prerogatives, rights, jurisdictions, royalties, and power of judicature, in all causes and matters whatsoever, criminal, capital and civil, arising, or which may hereafter arise, within the limits aforesaid," with all the privileges and rights as claimed by the grantors. This language evidently signifies that the patent of the Council did bestow on the Colony, which Robert Gorges expected to settle within his boundaries, not only a claim to the soil, but also a power of government, and, consequently, overthrows the position of Hutchinson. Therefore, even if the supposition be made that Endicott did not bring over a patent or charter with the royal seal which Bradford and Morton say he did, he and his associates had one from the Council of New England, on his arrival at Naumkeag, who did

---

* Hutchinson, I., 3d Ed., 16. 7.

empower them to have government administered here, as they actually did Robert Gorges and the Colony of Plymouth in their respective jurisdictions.

Thus we have finished the course proposed. We have done it with the single purpose, to expose and reject the guises of error, and to discover and confirm the claims of truth.   J. B. FELT.

EXTRACTS FROM THE LEDGER OF DEACON JOHN PEAR-SON OF ROWLEY.

Extract from the Second Ledger of Deacon John Pearson of Rowley, kept during the years 1672–92.

This is the acounts of that monney that I spent when I went to
  bostan a depute to the genral court the 8 of May, '78
  monney   0— 9—9

2 agust '78   monney that I spent at the genral court for my self
  and my hols (horse) and ferey (ferry)   1—13—3

I went to the genral court the 4 of Janeware 1680 and I spent
  seuen weks wich the town owes me for.
  mor in other expenses that was not monney   0— 2—7

10 8 '83   I went to bostan depete to the genarl court and was
  2 weks and 4 days.

16 9 '83   I went to bostan a depute for the genarl court and
  spent thear a month and 5 days. al is—

I went to the genarl court the 5 day of May 1684—stayd thear
  thirten days : it comes to—monney—   1— 6—8

I John Pearson went to the genral court the 5 day of May 1684
  and stayd thear 13 days   1— 6—8

[These last two charges are evidently an example of *Double
  Entry.*]

I went to the genarl court the 27 of Janeware (1684) and
  spent near 8 days.

I went to the genarl court the 17 of March (168⁴⁄₅) and spent
  7 days.

  to court May the 6 day.

Thear is due to me for goeng to the generl court before this
  court of elexshon that was hould in May 27 '85 for thro weks
                          money,   2— 0—0

and I went to the court of elexshon the 26 of May '85 and
  spent near a hole month :—due in money,   3—13—4

I went to the general court 6 of Juley and stayd a wek :—
  money—   0—13—4

I went to the general court 20 july (1685) and spent a weke ;
  money   0—13—4

I went to the ganaral court the 12 of agust (1685) and spent
  near 4 days.   0— 8—0

I went to the genarl court the 15 of Septembr and spent 6 days 0—11—2

I went to the general court the 13 of Octobr and spent 2 weks
  lakeng oo day.   1— 5—1

I went to the (general court) the 16 of Novembr and spent on
  wek   0—13—4

I went to the general court the 16 of febereware and spent a
  weke: in money   0—13—4
I went to the genarl court the 10 of may '86 and spent 2 weks:
  in money   1— 6—8

It appears from the Colonial Records that John Pearson was chosen
deputy for Rowley for nine sessions of the General Court, viz.: for the
sessions commencing

8 May,	1678 ;	28 May,	1679 ;
4 Feb.,	1679–80 ;	19 May,	1680 ;
4 Jan.,	1680–1 ;	24 May,	1682 ;
7 Nov.,	1683 ;	27 May,	1685.
13 May,	1686 ;		

King James II. ascended the throne in 1685; this seems to have been
a busy year with the court.   J. P.
Schenectady, N. Y., Nov. 27, 1857.

PISCATAQUA, SEPT. 19th.—Yesterday several Gentlemen and others who
accompany'd Mr. *Elisha Plaisted*, on his Marriage to Mr. *Wheelwright's*
Daughter of Wells, designing to return they miss'd two of their Horses,
upon which three of the Company went out to see for them, viz., *Joshua
Downing, Isaac Cole*, and Sergeant *Tucker*, the former two the Indians
kill'd and the last they wounded and took Captive. Upon hearing the
Guns, Capt. *Lane*, Capt. *Robison*, Capt. *Herd*, Messieurs. *Elisha Plaisted*,
Roger Plaisted, Philip Hubbard, and *Joseph Curtis*, mounted each a
Horse, well arm'd that were ready first, ordering about a dozen soldiers
in the interim to run over the field a nearer way, in which their Horses
had been, to relieve their Friends, but before the Horsemen got to the
place intended, they were Ambuscaded by another party of Indians, who
slew Capt. *Robison* and dismounted all the rest by killing their Horses
under them, All of which made their escape from the Enemy, except
Mr. *Elisha Plaisted*, whom they took Captive. Upon this Disaster Capt
Harman and Capt. *Lane* rallyed their Men together, to the number of 70,
and engag'd the Enemy, but they being sheltred under covert of the
bushes, could not do any great execution upon them, but forced 'em to
retreat to a large Swamp, which gave cause of suspicion that they had
a further Strength that lay in Ambush, which caus'd our Men to draw off.
The Enemy are judged to be between 150 and 200 in number.—*Boston
News Letter*, No. 440, Sept. 15–22, 1712.

PISCATAQUA, SEPT. 26th.—Our last Advice from Wells say, That the
Indian Enemy projected the Destruction of the place by intercepting the
Inhabitants from the Garrison as they went to mow their marshes. The
Indians are now dispers'd into several small parties, being every where
seen, which very much retards the gathering in of the Harvest that bor-
ders on our Frontiers.—*The same*, No. 441, Sept. 29, 1712.

SALEM VILLAGE, JAN. 23d, 1712–13.—Last Wednesday was buryed
here Mrs. *Elizabeth Buxton*, an excellent Midwife, who dyed on Monday
last, in the 90th year of her age. She was exemplary in her Life and
very useful in her Generation. She lived to lay her Great Granddaughter
with several children, and left of her proper Posterity 163 Persons.—
The same, No. 458, Jan. 19–26, 1712–13.

THE DESCENDANTS OF PETER HILL OF YORK CO., ME.,

*With some Incidents relating to the French and Indian Wars,—gleaned
from old Manuscripts of the time.*

[By Usher Parsons.]

Peter Hill, a planter, was a member of the Assembly of Ligonia or
Ligonia in 1648. He probably settled in Biddeford, near the mouth of
Saco river, a few years previous to this date, with his son Roger, who was
admitted a freeman in 1653. New Hampshire, having sought admission
into Massachusetts, was soon followed by the settlers of York County, who
had become weary of the government of Thomas Gorges, and among
them was Peter Hill, who applied for admission in 1652. He died in
1667.

Roger Hill, the son of Peter, married Sarah Cross of Wells, and died
in 1696. Their children were Sarah, Hannah, John, Samuel, Joseph,
Mercy, Benjamin, and Ebenezer. Each of them will receive brief notice,
after which, our attention will be confined to the eldest son, John and his
descendants. This John, whom we are to notice, settled in Saco, and
after removed to South Berwick.

Joseph Hill resided in Wells, where he died in 1743. He married
Sarah, daughter of Joseph Bowles of Welles and sister of Mary, the wife
of Major Charles Frost of Kittery, who was killed by the Indians in 1697.
[See his Life in Vol. 3, No. 4, in the Genealogical Journal, 1849.]
Mr. Hill purchased the estate of Bowles. He had two sons, Joseph and
Nathaniel, to whom he bequeathed a large estate, and among the property
were several negroes. Joseph, Jr. died before his father, and left a large
estate, which he ordered to remain in the Hill family, to perpetuate the
name; and, if the two sons should die without issue, the real estate was to
pass over to their cousins John and Elisha Hill of Berwick. He provided liberally for teaching his children, and, indeed, it may be said that
all the immediate descendants of Roger Hill, were well educated for their
day. The estate was administered by his son, his son-in-law, Sawyer,
and his nephew, Hon. John Hill of Berwick. This Joseph Hill, senior,
served as a lieutenant under his brother, Captain John, at Saco fort, and
he held various offices in the town and parish, and was Collector of Customs.

Samuel Hill, the third son of Roger, was commander of a packet
that carried supplies from Boston to the forts eastward, in the time of the
Indian wars, and thus acquired the title of Captain. He was taken captive by the French and Indians about 1701, and detained some years
in Canada with his wife. In 1704, Oct. 7, he writes to his brother John,
from Canada:—

"Loving brother and sister,—My kind love with my wife's, hoping
these few lines will find you in good health, as they leave us at this time,
blessed be God for it. This is to give you to understand that we are not
likely to come home until next summer, when there will be a general exchange of prisoners, and the reason of my not coming home this fall is,
because our government sent no prisoners home, for those which this
governor sent by Livingstone, for which there was a great deal of reason to have done, and in the mean time we remain sufferers, whereas, if
the governor at Boston had sent them, I should have come home with my

family, and a great many others, nay, in so much that if the governor of Massachusetts had but sent one man for me, this governor would have let me had my family home with me. But I desire to wait, as Job did, for my appointed time is not come. I pray give my respects to Major Hammond and wife, cousin Pearce, Charles Frost, John Frost and their wives, and to Mr. Whittemore. Brother and sister Hill, (i. e. Ebenezer and wife) desire to be remembered to you both, and all friends, desiring your prayers, and of all God's people.

Your loving brother and sister,
Samuel and Elizabeth Hill."

The Governor of Canada sent this Capt. Samuel Hill to Boston to arrange an exchange of prisoners. From Kittery he writes to John Hill, at Berwick, May 10, 1705 :—

" Loving Brother,—These are to acquaint you of my health, and to let you know I have got leave of his Excellency at Boston to go to Wells and visit my friends there. Here are Brother and Sister Storer and Brother Hill (Joseph) come from Wells yesterday, with whom I intend to go thither in their boat, and I hope to return next week. The Governor has promised that I shall continue here till the messenger returns from Canada. Your loving brother."

The following year, Jan. 13th, 1706, Samuel writes from Portsmouth, thus :—

" Loving Brother,—After my kind love to you and to your wife, praying that you would be very careful of yourself in going into the woods, for the enemy will assuredly be skulking about to take all advantages, and I am afraid they are near at hand, for they did design mischief this winter, before I came out of Canada, and people's boldness and security denote sudden destruction, therefore I pray, let not people's carelessness be your danger."

Ebenezer Hill, a younger brother, being in Canada with his wife and child at the same time, writes from Quebec, March, 1704–5, to his brother John at Berwick, expressing great discontent in Canada, adding,

" Cousin Pendleton Fletcher," meaning his sister's son at Saco, " Mary Sayer, brother Joseph's daughter, and Mary Storer of Wells, with our other friends and neighbors here, are all well, and myself, wife and child are well, and send kind love to you all, begging your prayers that God would direct, protect and keep us, and in due time deliver us.

Your loving brother and sister,   Ebenezer and Abiel Hill."

Benjamin, the son of Roger, died in youth.

Ebenezer Hill, the fifth son, was, as may be seen above, a prisoner in Canada, and he was taken in the following manner :—" Several Indians in Saco, who professed to be friendly, and were frequently in the houses of the inhabitants, called at Mr. Hill's in the usual manner one morning and partook of some food which was offered them. They left the house, but soon after returned, and, finding Mr. Hill gone, told his wife they must make her prisoner. They proceeded to plunder such articles as they could carry away, and destroyed others. When Mr. Hill returned, he found his wife secured, having her arms pinioned, and the savages employed in emptying a featherbed. He gave himself into their hands, and the Indians decamped with their prisoners." They were carried to Canada, where they remained three years. Their oldest son Ebenezer was born in Canada, and was afterwards called the Frenchman. Ebenezer Hill resided at Saco, and died there in 1748, aged 69. He held many town and parish offices, and was deacon of the church. His children were Ebenezer, (born in Canada) Dorothy, Susanna, Benjamin, Lydia, Joshua, and Jeremiah. Jeremiah, the youngest, was justice of the peace, married a Miss Smith, daughter of Captain Daniel, and was father of the late Hon. Jeremiah Hill, collector of the port of Saco.

Sarah, the daughter of Roger Hill, married Pendleton Fletcher, a man of distinction in Saco. He died a prisoner in Canada, and his widow married William Priest.

Hannah, married Lieut. Joseph Storer, who was an active officer in the second Indian War in Wells, and had a garrison near the late Dr. Hemmenway's church. He was the ancestor of the Hon. Joseph, Clement and Woodbury, and of Commodore Storer, and Prof. D. H. Storer of Boston.

Mary married Daniel Littlefield, and their descendants are numerous in Wells and Kennebunk.

Leaving the other children of Roger Hill, our attention will now be directed chiefly to his oldest son, named John, and his descendants, and to the Indian war, with which his life was interwoven.

JOHN HILL was born in Saco, and there, like his brothers and sisters, received a good common-school education. In 1686 he entered into partnership with Francis Backhouse [modernized to Backus] in building a sawmill at a place called Backus's Creek, they owning equally. By the contract, Backus was to furnish timber, and Hill " to learn how to kilter the saws, and keep them in order."

In 1689 the Indian war broke out, called King William's war, which lasted nearly ten years. A military company was called into service this year, under the command of Edward Seargent, and John Hill was commissioned by Thomas Danforth its ensign. After this he was employed sometimes in scouting, but served mostly in the forts at Saco, Wells and South Berwick. In 1690 the settlement at Salmon Falls was destroyed and many killed or carried into captivity, and also the fort at Falmouth, near Portland. The neighboring garrisons drew off to Saco, and from thence the inhabitants mostly fled for protection to Wells, and among them the Hill family, where Joseph and Samuel, Hannah and Mary, with their parents, remained permanently. John, however, remained in the fort at Saco.

He had, the preceding autumn, received orders from Col. Benj. Church, the renowned Indian fighter, to scout, and " to command the twenty soldiers quartered at Saco garrison." It was ordered too, that " the 40 soldiers posted at Saco, Scarboro', and Spurwink, (Cape Elizabeth,) be in separate commands, but are to attend to the commands of Ensign John Hill, respectively, as they are concerned upon their scoutings."

Signed   " Benj. Church."

The mother of Ensign Hill probably remained in the fort with her son at Saco, as we find the following letter, written to her from Wells, the 7th of May, 1690, by her husband, Roger Hill :—

" Dear and loving wife,—These are to let you know that we are all well here, blessed be God for it, and all our children remember their duty to you. The Indians have killed Goodman Frost and James Littlefield, and carried away Nathaniel Frost, and burnt several houses, here in Wells, and I would have our son John Hill to hire a boat if he can, to bring you and some of our things by water, for I fear it is not safe to come by land. Son John, be as careful of your mother as possibly you can, for it is very dangerous times; the Lord only knows whether we shall ever see one another any more.   Praying for your prosperity,

Your loving husband, until death,

Roger Hill.

Remember my love to son Fletcher and daughter, and all their children, and to all my neighbors in general.

Son Storer and wife remember their duty to you, and love to their brother Fletcher and all cousins, and yourself."

The following year Mr. Hill was stationed at Wells, where he received the following note from the Governor's Secretary, dated Boston :—

" Ensign Hill at Wells "   " June 4—1691

These come to accompany 35 soldiers ordered for enforcing of the garrisons at Wells, who are to be put under your conduct until Captain Convers returns, within ten days.   Expecting you will carefully improve them for scouting to observe the motion of the enemy "——

On the 25th of January, 1692, the Indians surprised the town of York, killed seventy-five of the inhabitants, carried about the same number into captivity, and nearly destroyed the town.   On the 10th of June following a large force of more than two hundred French and Indians made a furious attack on the garrison at Wells, commanded by Captain Convers, who, with fifteen regular soldiers, aided by a few families collected there for protection, repulsed the enemy with a heavy loss.   This was considered the most brilliant achievement of the war.   Cotton Mather, in his " Magnalia," describes Ensign Hill's good conduct in the fight, and of his meeting a flag of truce of the enemy to hold a parley, and of his escape from an ambush the Indians had prepared to take him.   The people in the garrison, women as well as men, assisted bravely in passing cartridges and firing muskets at the enemy.

After this victory Hill was promoted to a lieutenant, and was stationed at Quampegan and Newichewannock, in South Berwick, under Major Charles Frost, who was stationed at Frost's Garrison, at Kittery, and commanded all the forts on the east side of the Pascataqua.   Spies were usually sent by the Indians to reconnoitre before the enemy approached places intended for destruction, who lurked about the woods, and required a constant ward and watch.   The following letter to Lieutenant Hill gives an idea of the vigilance and circumspection necessary to be observed in these trying times.

Leiut Hill   April : 2 : 1693

Last night a Litle after sun sett Noah Emory was coming from Kittery to Sturgion Creke & by the waie sid herd som crackling of stickes : & herd a man whissell : upon which he stopt under a bush : and went an other waie : John Smith coming after him saw a man nere Sturgion Creke bridge who ran a waie down the creke : Smith being on horse back came to my Garison—this morning I sent out som men who saw the Indian track at the same place where Noah Emerey herd him whissell—Kepe out scouts about the borders of the towne : I will send out from hence : all or souldiers at the banke are drawen of those yt belong to you are sent up : dispose of them to such garisons at present as you thinke fitt : I have given two of them liberty to goe home for a few dayes :

In hast I Remaine yor: lo: freind

[Superscribed]   Charles Ffrost major.
Ffor Leiut John Hill
　　　At Newitchawoneck
　　　　　Hast Post Hast

Hill's station was about five miles from Major Frost's Garrison and dwelling, where official duties required his frequent visits. A daughter of the Major, named Mary, attracted his attention, and soon after became his wife. Another daughter of Frost married Ichabod Plaisted, then in the legislature ; another married Lieut. Joseph Storer of Wells.

Towards the close of April, 1693, Hill received the following letter from three of the Council in Boston :—

" Capt. John Hill "

Sir, His Excellency hath been pleased to commissionate & appoint you to take the charge of a company for their Majesty's service, and pursuant thereunto hath sent you a Commission of Captain. By virtue of a Commission and Instructions given to us by his Excellency, with the advice and consent of the Council, we have ordered Capt. Convers to erect a garrison upon Saco River, where his Excellency intends to be, to give further orders and directions about the same ;—these are to order you to march, with such of your company as are suitable unto Saco, there to attend Capt. Convers's orders or such other orders as you shall receive from his Excellency Major Frost, or from us, from time to time. There are 80 men to be sent to Saco ; for dispatch, in erecting 3d garrison,—fifty whereof will be drawn off with Capt. Convers, to march East, in an expedition for their Majesty's service, and then the remainder, which will be 30, together with those posted at Wells, are to be your company, yourself to keep the post at Saco and see the garrison finished. Those at Wells to be left under the conduct of your lieutenant, Jeremy Storer. Signed,   Barth^w Gedney,
　　　　　　　　　　　　　　　　　　　　　　　Elisha Hutchinson,
　　　　　　　　　　　　　　　　　　　　　　　John Wally."

Immediately after John Hill's arrival in Saco, his brother-in-law, Ichabod Plaisted, writes to him, June 9th, 1693, " Last night we had four persons carried away from the Garrison by the Indians, and one wounded. The place was at Sturgeon Creek, and those carried away were Nicholas Frost's wife, and two children, and the Widow Smith."

Captain Hill was married to Mary Frost, Dec. 12th, 1694. He remained in the command of Fort Mary for many years, until 1700. His commission, of the same tenor as the former one by Governor Phips, was renewed in Sept. 1696, by Lieut. Governor Stoughton. The following letter was addressed to him by his father-in-law, Major Frost, soon after the cowardly surrender by Capt. Chubb of Fort Pemaquid, on the Kennebec, and when the combined force of French and Indians had devastated the whole province of Maine, with the exception of Saco, Wells, York, and Pascataqua, and when it was feared these must soon fall.

                                        Wells August 13th: 1696—
Sonn Hill

I am now at Wells with twenty horse Intending to Com over to you but hereing of severall guns about yor parts I have sent over three men to know how it is with you. I have an order from the governor to asist you in drawing of: and I have an order from the Leut gouvernor to draw of & bring a waie what can be transported by Land: & to hide the rest in the ground with the great guns: but or townes are son weake for want of men that if the enemie be about you we fere wee are to weke to com and bring you of: I was informed as I writ to you that Major Church was com to or assistants but it is not soo but tis said he is coming with three hundred men: & major Gidney with five hundred men to or assistants: or people are much troubled that yor fort should be Demollisbed: Capt Chubb gave up his fort without firing a gun against the Enemie. Let me here from you by the barer hero of my Love to yor selfe and wife: I pray god to keepe you from the Rage of the Enemie.   I Remaine
tis said six Indians   Yor Loving ffather in Law
were son here this day   Charles Ffrost

                        [Superscribed]
               To Capt. John Hill At Saco ffort
               Hast post Hast

The fort at Saco was not surrendered by Hill, although all the inhabitants of the town were driven away or killed, and many of Hill's soldiers were waylaid and murdered while venturing out of the fort.

Early this year, 1696, died Roger Hill, the father of Capt. John Hill. A division of the movable estate took place soon after, as appears by this receipt of the children.

"Wells December 18th 1696—Received of Capt. John Hill Administrator to father Hill's estate of the movables to our full satisfaction. Rec⁴ by us whose names are hereunder written,—Joseph Storer, Samuel Hill, Joseph Hill, David Littlefield, Pendleton Fletcher."

The real estate was divided among the children in Oct. 1702, by mutual agreement; John, the oldest son, taking a double portion, and the others all sharing equally. Previous to this, Pendleton Fletcher had died in captivity in Canada, and his widow had married William Priest, whose name appears among the signers of the agreement, and Ebenezer Hill was absent in Saco; otherwise the names were as in the former paper relating to movable estate.

The widow of Roger Hill made her home with her son John, and conveyed to him or his widow all her property at Berwick, in 1720, where she died soon after.

Captain Hill, while at Saco, acted as agent for Col. William Pepperrell, father of Sir William, in directing the building of vessels, to whom Pepperrell writes, Nov. 2, 1696—

"Sir,—With much trouble I have gotten and sent men for the sloop, and desire you to dispatch them with all speed. I think it may be safest to mast and bend her sails before you launch her. Desire you to hasten them night and day, for, sir, it will be dangerous tarrying there, and chargable keeping the men on pay. I shall send you a barrel of rum and a barrel of molasses, and there is a cask of wine to launch her with. So with my service to yourself and good lady, your humble servant,
                                        William Pepperrell."

Capt. Hill received the following sad tidings of the death of his father-in-law, Major Charles Frost, dated Wells, July 10, 1697, from his brother-in-law, Joseph Storer :—

" Brother Hill

It hath pleased god to take a way ; Major Frost—the Indens waylad him Last Sabbath day as he was cominge whom from meeting at night ; and Killed him and John Heards wife and Deacs Downing ; and John Heard is wounded ; the Good Lord santifie it to us all ; it is a Great Loss to the whole Province ; and Esposely to his famyley : and Last Monday the post that Cam to Wells as they went to goe whom the Indens Killed them a bout the marked tree : namly Nicbolas Smith Proper ; and Hennery Simson ; Brother misuress Frost is very full of sory ; and all her Children ; Cousen Charles and John was with there Father ; and Escaped wonderfuly ; and souerall others with them ; Capt Breken went with som of his Company a Monday by the way of Nechewanack and I went with them —and was there at the Major's Funerall ; and I see your wife full of greef : and your Child is well ; Mrs Frost and sister & all your Brothers & sisters Remembers theire loue to you ; and Ernesnly desires you to com over if you can possible without danger.

pray doe not venter In the day to Com ; Remember our Love to all our Brothers and sisters and Cousens ; and the good Lord Keepe us in these perreles times and santyfie all his Awfull dispensations to us noe more at present   praying for you

your uery Louinge Brother

Wells the ; 10th July 1697   Joseph Storer."

Major John March, who succeeded to the command after Major Frost's murder, writes to Capt. Hill :—

" Capt. John Hill   " Wells Aug' 3', 1697.

Sir,—My kind respects and service to yourself, hoping these will find you in health, as I am, blessed be God for it. Sir, I thought it good to write to let you understand I am now at Wells, and thought it convenient to inform you of my proceedings as to ordering out scouts from Wells to Saco to yourself, by reason of the inhabitants of Wells standing in much need of guards in marshes now in their hay season. I have ordered scouts to come every two days to you, but they shall come mounted and in the night, and stay with you the next day, and to return to Wells the next night. Likewise I have sent out two or three Englishmen with Lieut. Leatherby, with about 30 Indians, who have orders from myself to go out as far as Casco (Portland) and Black Point, and they are to lay out in ambuscade a week or ten days, I in hopes they will make some discovery of the enemy, or come up with them, and sir if they should have occasion for any provisions or any assistance by way of advice, pray sir supply and assist in the matter, and sir for what provisions they have, I will give you a receipt, and in so doing you will oblige

Your friend and servant to command
John March, Major.

(*To be Continued.*)

Mr. Lemuel Putnam Grosvenor, who died in Pomfret, Conn., on the 19th inst., has bequeathed to the Connecticut Historical Society the sword that was owned and used by General Israel Putnam during our revolutionary struggle.—*Jan. 27th, 1858.*

10

REV. THOMAS WATERMAN

Was born in London on the 31 December, 1774, became a member of Dr. Rippon's church in that city, and, for a short period previous to his immigration, he was a preacher of the Congregational order. He came to the United States in 1801, and having embraced the religious tenets of the Calvinistic Baptists, he was installed as the first pastor of the Baptist Church in Charlestown, Mass., on the 7th of October, 1802. On that occasion, the Rev. Dr. Stillman preached the sermon, Rev. Dr. Baldwin gave the charge, and Rev. Stephen Gano, the right hand of fellowship. Soon after his settlement he married Elizabeth, daughter of Archibald McNeil, Esq.; she died in Charlestown, in June, 1804, aged 25 years. Mr. Waterman's connection with the church in Charlestown was of short duration, only eight months, and in some respects unhappy, being for a time deprived of his ministerial office, yet afterwards restored and preached with great acceptance. Having lost his wife, and his pastoral relation dissolved as before mentioned, he left Charlestown and removed to Bow, N. H., where he was settled as pastor of the Baptist Church in that town, in the year 1804. While here he married Miss Mary Gault, a lady of great intelligence, possessing the virtues and graces of the Christian in an eminent degree; his success and happiness in after-life were in a great measure the result of her good management and kindness of heart.

On the 4th of July, 1806, Mr. W. delivered an address to the " Republican Citizens" of Concord, N. H. The celebrated Daniel Webster also addressed the " Federal Republicans," on the same day and in the same town. These addresses were printed, and both exhibit a candor and forbearance highly creditable to their authors, at a time when party spirit ran high in the community.

Mr. Waterman resigned his pastoral office in Bow in 1807, and it is supposed he was subsequently Preceptor of Addison Academy, as an individual of the same name held that office in 1810. In the spring of 1811, he removed to Woburn, Mass., where he was engaged to preach by the year, (he was not settled.) Besides attending to his ministerial duties, he kept a private school for boys, a position he was eminently qualified for, and in which he was very successful.

He died suddenly at Woburn, on the 23d of March, 1814, in the 40th year of his age. His wife survived him, and was living in 1854. One who knew him says, " he was a highly educated man, very eloquent and popular as a preacher; his death was deeply lamented by a large circle of friends, and by the community generally among whom he dwelt."

The following notice appeared in the Boston Weekly Messenger of April 1, 1814 :—" Died at Woburn, the 23d ult., in a fit of apoplexy, Rev. Thomas Waterman, aged 39, pastor of the Baptist Society in that town; a man of distinguished talents and honor, a blessing to the church of Christ, and universally esteemed."

His children were as follows, all by his last wife.—1. Thomas B., educated at Dartmouth Col., grad. 1826; emigrated to the West and d. young. 2. Alfred, died young. 3. Josephine, married Dr. J. M. Brodhead, and resides in the city of Washington.

HEZEKIAH CONANT, of Hartford, formerly a printer boy in Worcester, is reported to have sold the patent for his new breech-loading rifle for $80,000.—[*Newspaper*, 8 May, 1856.

CHURCH RECORDS OF FARMINGTON, CONN.

[Copied by the late Hon. Nathaniel Goodwin of Hartford. Communicated by Daniel Goodwin, Esq.]

[Continued from p. 35.]

He was so feeble that he remembreth [nothing after coming down the last mountain by sight, and memory and strength in a manner] gone; —but God who leadeth the blind in a way that they know not, directed him to John Norton, Jun., who was thrashing in his barn, who took him in and put him to bed,—called friends about him, who were diligent in the use of means for his recovery, after some time spent betwixt hope and fear, as not knowing whether he would die or live;—He lying in a sad manner, grating his teeth [and round in his hand that pleased God he exhibited and came to rights again.] The day in which this fell out was January 6, 1682,—a snowy Saturday,—especially the latter part of it.   Had the man not been directed home, in likelihood he had perished in the wilderness, and perhaps have been so far covered with snow as not to have been found 'till wild fowls or beasts had preyed on him.

Thomas Warner, son of John Warner of [Mattabuck], baptized May 6, 1683.

Rachel Richards, daughter of Obadiah Richards, baptized May 6, 1683.

Martha Orvis, daughter of Samuel Orvis, baptized May 6, 1683.

Thomas Judd, son of Philip Judd, baptized May 27, 1683.

Thomas Gridley, son of Thomas Gridley, baptized June 17, 1683.

Simon Newell, son of Thomas Newell, baptized June 24, 1683.

Nathaniel Judd, son of Benjamin Judd, baptized July 22, 1683.

William Porter, son of Thomas Porter, of Robert Porter, baptized October 28, 1683.

Sarah Steele, daughter of John Steele, baptized November 25, 1683.

Sarah Andrews, daughter of Abraham Andrews, by his wife Sarah, daughter to Robert Porter, baptized March 9, 168¾.

Abigail Woodruff, daughter of John Woodruff, March 30, 168¾.

John Norton, son of John Norton, baptized April 6, 1684.

Mary Warner, daughter of Thomas Warner of Mattabuck, baptized May 18, 1684.

Thomas Standley, son of John Standley of Mattabuck, baptized May 25, 1684.

Joanna Richardson, daughter of Thomas Richardson of Mattabuck, baptized there, April 8, 1684.

Isaac Brunson, son of Isaac Brunson of Mattabuck; John Brunson, son of Isaac Brunson; Samuel Brunson, Joseph Brunson and Mary Brunson, all children of Isaac Brunson of Mattabuck, baptized here June 29, 1684.

John Judd, son of John Judd, baptized August 3, 1684.

Joseph and Lydia Smith, children of Joseph Smith, baptized here, August 18, 1684.

John Gridley, son of Thomas Gridley, baptized October 5, 1684.

Hannah Judd, daughter of Philip Judd, baptized about October 19, 1684.

Sarah Hull, daughter of Thomas Hull, baptized November 8, 1684.

Hezekiah Hart, son of Thomas Hart, baptized November 23, 1684.

John Thompson, son of Thomas Thompson, baptized December 14, 1684.

Elizabeth Bird, daughter of James Bird, baptized November 23, 1684.
Ebenezer Thompson, son of John Thompson, baptized December 21, 1684.
Hannah Andrews, daughter of Daniel Andrews, baptized January 18, 1684.
Ebenezer Seymour baptized February 1, 1684.
Joseph Gridley, son of Samuel Gridley, baptized March 8, 16⅘.
Lydia Cole, daughter of John Cole, baptized March 22, Anno : 16⅘.
Stephen Hitchcock, son of Samuel Hitchcock, of Mattabuck, baptized April 12, 1685.
Johannah Smith, son of Joseph Smith, baptized April 12, 1685.
Hannah and Mary Andrews, twins, daughters of Thomas Andrews, of Milford, son-in-law to Robert Porter, baptized here, by virtue of communion of Churches, May 31, 1685.
Thomas Richards, son of Obadiah Richards, baptized August 9, 1685.
Samuel Orvis, son of Samuel Orvis, baptized October 25, 1685.
Abigail Woodford, daughter of Joseph Woodford, baptized December 27, 1685.
Esther Judd, daughter of Benjamin Judd, baptized February 14, 1685.
John Steele, son of John Steele, baptized March 7, 16⅘.
Samuel Gridley, son of Thomas Gridley, baptized March 21, 16⅘.
Thomas Brunson, son of Isaac Brunson, baptized April 11, 1686.
John Judd, son of John Judd, baptized June 20, 1686.
Sarah Standley, daughter of John Standley, baptized July 4, 1686.
John Porter, son of Thomas Porter, son of Robert Porter, baptized July 18, 1686.
Abigail Gaylord, daughter of Joseph Gaylord, of Waterbury, baptized November 7, 1686.
John Hart, son of John Hart, baptized November 27, 1686.
Isaac Hart, son of John Hart, baptized November 27, 1686.
John Lee, son of John Lee, baptized November 27, 1686.
Jonathan Lee, son of John Lee, baptized November 27, 1686.
Isaac Lewis, Ruth Lewis and Sarah Lewis, children of William Lewis, baptized November 28, 1686.
Isaac Brunson, son of Jacob Brunson, baptized November 29, 1686.
Josiah Hart, son of Ensign Thomas Hart, baptized December 6, 1686.
Mary Norton, daughter of John Norton, baptized November 21, 1686.
Paul Andrews, son of Daniel Andrews, baptized about January 2, 1686.
Mary Andrews, wife of Benjamin Andrews, and her two children Benjamin Andrews and John Andrews, baptized January 9, 1686.
Nathaniel Thompson, son of John Thompson, baptized June 16, 1686.
Mary Smith, daughter of Joseph Smith, baptized January 30, 1686.
Margaret Thompson, daughter of Thomas Thompson, baptized February 20, 1686.
Samuel Woodruff, son of Samuel Woodruff, baptized March 6, 16⅘.
Stephen Porter, son of Samuel Porter, son of Thomas Porter, April 10, 1687.
Jonathan Seymour, son of Richard Seymour, baptized April 17, 1687.
Susannah Newell, daughter of Thomas Newell, of Waterbury, baptized April 24, 1687.
Esther Gridley, son of Samuel Gridley, baptized May 15, 1687.
David Bull, son of Thomas Bull, baptized June 5, 1687.

Samuel Newell, son of Samuel Newell, baptized June 19, 1687.

William Judd, son of Philip Judd, baptized July 3, 1687.

Abraham Andrews, son of Abraham Andrews, baptized July 17, 1687.

Jacob Barnes, son of Joseph Barnes, born September 18, 1687. Baptized here immediately after.

Sarah Hart, daughter to John Hart, baptized December 11, 1687.

Mary Gridley, daughter of Thomas Gridley, baptized February 5, 1687.

Margaret Orvis, daughter of Samuel Orvis, baptized April 7, 1687.

Mary Orton, daughter of John Orton, baptized May 20, 1688.

Hannah Porter, daughter of Samuel Porter, baptized June 17, 1688.

Thomas Warner, son of Thomas Warner, baptized July 8, 1688.

Mary Andrews, daughter of Benjamin Andrews, baptized August 25, 1688.

William Lewis, son of William Lewis, baptized September 23, 1688.

Jonathan Judd, son of Benjamin Judd, baptized September 23, 1688.

Hezekiah Hooker, son of John Hooker, baptized October 20, 1688.

Jonathan Woodruff, son of Samuel Woodruff, baptized December 2, 1688.

Anna Thompson, daughter of Thomas Thompson, baptized February 10, 1689.

Hannah Bronson, **daughter of Jacob Bronson, baptized** October 28, 1688.

Sarah Norton, daughter of John Norton, baptized April 1, 1689.

Ebenezer Bronson, son of Isaac Bronson, baptized April 8, 1689.

Mercy Hiccok, child of Samuel Hiccock, baptized April 8, 1689.

Joseph Woodruff, son of Matthew Woodruff, baptized May 18, 1689, or thereabouts.

Mary Andrews, son of Benjamin Andrews, son-in-law to Robert Porter, baptized May 18, 1689, or thereabouts.

Joseph Newell, son of Thomas Newell, baptized June 2, 1689.

Rachel Steele, daughter of John Steele, baptized June 2, 1689.

Mary Porter, daughter of Thomas Porter, of Robert, baptized June 2, 1689.

Stephen Andrews, son of Daniel Andrews,—Stephen Upson and Mary Upson, children of Stephen Upson,—Benjamin Bevans and John Bevans, children of Benjamin Bevans, baptized here December 1, 1689.

Mary Orton, daughter of John Orton, baptized February 16, 1689.

Elizabeth Smith, daughter of Joseph Smith, baptized February 16, 1689.

Abigail **Barnes, daughter of Joseph Barnes, baptized** February 23, 1689.

Thomas Newell, son of Samuel Newell, baptized March 2, 1689.

Benjamin Judd, son of Philip Judd, baptized May 4, 1690.

Mary Lee, daughter of John Lee, baptized May 4, 1690.

Elizabeth Upson, daughter of Stephen Upson, baptized May 11, 1690.

Timothy Standley, son of John Standley, baptized about May 11, 1690.

Thomas Coales, son of Samuel Coales, baptized June 1, 1690.

Rachel Coales, daughter of Samuel Coales, baptized June 1, 1690.

William Smith, son of Samuel Smith, baptized June 1, 1690.

Susannah Hooker, daughter of William Hooker, baptized June 8, 1690.

Thomas Barnes, son of Benjamin Barnes, baptized June 8, 1690.

Ebenezer Clark, son of John Clarke, and Sarah Smith, daughter of Samuel Smith, baptized August 10, 1690.

Stephen Andrews, son of Benjamin Andrews, baptized September 28, 1690.

Giles Hooker, son of Samuel Hooker, baptized October 12, 1690.

Thomas Judd, son of Thomas Judd, of Waterbury, and Sarah Orvis, daughter of Samuel Orvis, baptized the same day 1.12. October 12, 1690.

Jonathan Gridley, son of Thomas Gridley, baptized November 2, 1690.

Matthew Hart, son of John Hart, baptized December 7, 1690.

Ephraim Smith, son of Ephraim Smith, baptized December 20, 1690.

Rebecca Woodruff, daughter of Samuel Woodruff, baptized February 8, 169⅟.

Benjamin Richards, son of Obadiah Richards, and William Judd, son of Thomas Judd, both of Waterbury, were baptized here, April 5, 1691.

James Gridley, son of Samuel Gridley, baptized May 3, 1691.

Timothy, John and Mary Root, children of Stephen Root, baptized May 17, 1691.

Margaret, Sarah and Elizabeth Higgison, children of William Higgison, baptized May 17, 1691.

Abigail Hooker, daughter of John Hooker, baptized May 31, 1691.

Ebenezer Richardson, son of Thomas Richardson, of Waterbury, baptized June 28, 1691.

Samuel Porter, son of Samuel Porter, baptized September 20, 1691.

Hannah Lewis, daughter of Samuel Lewis, baptized October 4, 1691.

Mehitable Smith, daughter of Jonathan Smith, baptized October 11, 1691.

Samuel Thompson, son of Thomas Thompson, baptized October 18, 1691.

Mary Bird, daughter of Thomas Bird, baptized December 27, 1691.

Mary Higgison, daughter of William Higgison, baptized January 10, 1691.

Nathaniel Porter, son of Thomas Porter, baptized March 28, 169⅟.

Hannah Norton, daughter of John Norton, baptized May 15, 1692.

Mary Huff, daughter of Jonathan Huff, baptized May 15, 1692.

Samuel Coales, son of Samuel Coales, May 22, 1692.

Samuel Lewis, son of Samuel Lewis, baptized May 29, 1692.

Elizabeth Root, daughter of Joseph Root, baptized June 26, 1692.

Samuel Hart, son of John Hart, baptized September 18, 1692.

Elizabeth Barnes, daughter of Joseph Barnes, baptized October 9, 1692.

Johanna Smith, daughter of Joseph Smith, baptized October 16, 1692.

Sarah Hart, daughter of Stephen Hart, baptized October 16, 1692.

Ruth Barnes, daughter of Thomas Barnes, baptized October 23, 1692.

John Orton, son of John Orton, baptized about December 4, 1692.

John Newell, son of Samuel Newell, baptized January 29, 169⅟.

Thomas Hooker, son of Samuel Hooker, baptized February 5, 169⅟.

Elizabeth Lee, daughter of John Lee, baptized February 5, 169⅟.

Ruth Woodruff, daughter of Samuel Woodruff, baptized February 26, 169⅟.

Ruth Smith, daughter of Samuel Smith, baptized February 26, 169⅟.

Joseph Root, son of John Root, grandchild to John Woodruff, baptized March 19, 169⅟.

Mary Woodruff, daughter of Matthew Woodruff, baptized March 19, 169⅟.

Stephen Hart, son of Thomas Hart, baptized July 30, 1693.

[*To be Continued.*]

BIOGRAPHICAL MATERIALS, COLLECTED FROM FUNERAL SERMONS.

(By Pliny H. White, Amherst, Mass.)

Brown.—Discourse at the Funeral of Daniel M. Brown, by Rev. Orville G. Wheeler. "Daniel M. Brown was a man of fine intellectual abilities. There was a capaciousness in his mind which enabled him to entertain a subject, make it a matter of well-directed thought, upon which was brought to bear a judgment, which, for one in his circumstances, was remarkably sound and discreet. His mathematical powers were extraordinary, and as to his knowledge of his mother tongue he surpassed most men of ordinary pursuits." He was drowned in attempting to cross the Lake from Plattsburgh, N. Y. to South Hero, Vt., May 28, 1849.

Bradford.—Discourse delivered at Francestown, N. H. on the last Sabbath in July, 1838, in commemoration of the character and usefulness of Rev. Moses Bradford, by Rev. Ephraim P. Bradford. Mr. Bradford was born at Canterbury, Ct., August 6, 1765. His parents were William and Mary Bradford. He was the fourteenth and youngest child of his mother, and a descendant in the fifth generation from William Bradford, second Governor of Plymouth Colony. He prosecuted his studies under the tuition of an elder brother, who was a man of a vigorous and cultivated mind, and an eloquent preacher; and he entered the senior class in Dartmouth College, after remaining in which institution a few months, he received a regular degree, with a good reputation for talents and scholarship, in 1785. He pursued the study of theology with his brother, then pastor of a Congregational Church in Rowley, Mass. He was married, Nov. 4, 1788, to Dorothy Bradstreet, who died June 24, 1792. His second wife was Sarah Eaton of Francestown, N. H., who survived him. He died at the house of his son in Montague, Mass., June 14, 1838.

Bennett.—Discourse on the Life and Character of Rev. Alfred Bennett, delivered at Homer, N. Y., May 18, 1851, by Rev. H. Harvey. Mr. Bennett was born at Mansfield, Ct., Sept. 26, 1780, and became a resident of Homer, N. Y. in 1803, commencing life there as a farmer. With great reluctance he entertained the idea of going into the ministry, and only decided to do so, after a severe mental struggle of two years. He was ordained pastor of the Baptist Church in Homer in 1807. During his ministry of twenty-five years at that place, he baptized 770 persons. In 1832 he became agent of the Baptist General Convention for Foreign Missions, and labored as such till his death in 1851.

Bennett.—Discourse delivered at the Funeral of Rev. Joseph Bennett, at Woburn, Mass., Nov. 22, 1847, by Rev. John W. Chickering. Mr. Bennett was born in Framingham, Mass., May 13, 1790, was graduated at Harvard College in 1818, and at Andover Theological Seminary in 1821. He was ordained at Woburn, Jan. 1, 1822, and in the following February married Mary Lamson. In 1846, in consequence of severe disease of the digestive organs, he became subject to extreme depression, with suicidal tendencies, which resulted in death by his own hand in November, 1847. His father, having fallen into a similar state of gloom, in consequence of an affection of the liver, and being seized with an impression that a famine existed, and that the only way to save his family from starvation was to starve himself, resisted for fourteen days all efforts and entreaties, and died of inanition.

Burnham.—Discourse delivered at the Funeral of Rev. Abraham Burnham, D. D., Pembroke, N. H., Sept. 23, 1852, by Rev. Daniel J. Noyes. Mr. Burnham was born in Dunbarton, N. H., Nov. 18, 1775. He was the son of Samuel and Mary Burnham, both of whom were eminent for their piety. At the age of fourteen he determined to procure a liberal education, but was not able to execute his purpose till after he had attained the age of twenty-one. He entered the Junior Class in Dartmouth College in August, 1802, being then 27 years old. The following was his division of time during the College course : " Six hours for close study, as close as my weak and pained eyes will admit ; six hours for deep thought, reflection, and mentally reviewing my lessons ; eight hours for sleep ; one for meals, and three for manual labor to pay for my board." He was graduated with honor in 1804, and taught the Academy at Bradford, Mass., from May 1805 till February 1807, when he commenced the study of Theology with Rev. Dr. Parish of Byfield, and after studying four or five months was licensed to preach the Gospel by the Essex Middle Association at Topsfield, Mass. March 2, 1808, he was ordained Pastor of the Congregational Church at Pembroke, N. H., and continued in that pastorate till Nov. 1850, when, " at his own repeated and earnest request, his people consented to receive a successor in his place." He was Secretary of the New Hampshire Home Missionary Society from 1822 to 1837, in which last year he was elected President of the Society and retained the office till his death. He was appointed Treasurer of the General Association of New Hampshire in 1809, and was never absent from one of its annual meetings till 1851, when feeble health prevented his attendance. The degree of D. D. was conferred on him by Dartmouth College in 1850. He died September 21, 1852.

Howe.—Discourse preached in Pepperell, Mass., July 21, 1840, at the Funeral of Rev. James Howe, by Rev. George Fisher. Mr. Howe was born in Jaffrey, N. H., Aug. 13, 1796, prepared for College at New Ipswich Academy, was graduated at Dartmouth College in 1817, taught a High-School at Concord, Mass. for one year, was graduated at Andover Theological Seminary in 1821, was ordained Pastor of the Church and Town of Pepperell, Mass., Oct. 16, 1822, and relinquished that connection in January, 1832, to become the minister of the Evangelical Congregational Society, then recently formed. He was recognized as minister of that Society by an Ecclesiastical Council, Feb. 1, 1832, and retained that relation till his death, which took place July 19, 1840. He married, Oct. 13, 1823, Miss Harriet Nason of Harvard, by whom he had six children. " He possessed a good, and in some respects a superior mind. It was a far-seeing and sagacious mind, a well-furnished and well-cultivated mind. Under his ministry the church increased from about seventy to nearly four hundred members.

If materials of this character are desirable for the Register, more will be furnished. [Let us have them, but older are more desirable.]

New Weapon of War.—We were shown a breach-loading rifle yesterday, which, for facility, the combined efforts of loading, safety, and self-capping, is, it strikes us, the most perfect weapon of its class we have seen. It is, moreover, in whole or in part, on the Minnie principle. It was invented by Mr. J. C. Day, but of what part of the country we did not learn.—[*National Intelligencer*, 1853.

ABSTRACTS FROM THE EARLIEST WILLS ON RECORD IN THE COUNTY OF SUFFOLK, MASS.

[Prepared by Mr. WILLIAM B. TRASK, of Dorchester.]

[Continued from page 54.]

WILLIAM BLAKE.—The last will* and testament of *William Blake* (being of perfect memory and vnderstanding, the good Lord God be blessed and praised therfore,) made the third day of September, in the yeare one thousand six hundred sixtie and one, as followeth.

Imp'mise: my will is, y[t] my body be desemly buried in hope of a ioyfull resurrection at the last day. li. I giue and bequeath vnto the towne of Dorchester, twenty shillings, to be bestowed for the repairing of the buring place, soe y[t] swine and other vermine may not aňoy the graues of the saints; p'vided it be repaired within one yeare after my deccase. The rest of my land, goods, and estate, after my funerall exspenses and debts discharged, my will is, and I doe giue and bequeth vnto my fiue children the one halfe of my lands, goods and estate, to be equally devided amongst them, by equall portions; not that I disrespect my eldest sońe, for he hath ben and is, soe dutifull a child vnto me as any of my Children, but, because he hath least need of it, and he hath noe Charge. The other halfe of my lands, goods and estate I doe giue and bequeth vnto my beloued wife, and doe make her sole executris of this my last will and testament: And I doe intreat my beloued brethren, brother *Edwarde Clapp*, and *John Capen*, y[t] they would be pleased to be the ouerseers of this my last will and testament, to se y[t] it be fullfilled and p'formed. Finally, my will is, y[t] my wife doe not dispose of any of her estate, left her by this my last Will and testament during the time of her life, without the advise and Consent of my ouerseers and my foure sońes, or the maior parte of them: yet neverthelesse, in her last will, she may dispose of it vnto whom shee please. In witnes hereof I haue herevnto sett my hand and seale: In the p'sence of *John Capen*.

Jn° *Minott*,

who deposed 2ª Jan. 1663.

William Blake

Inventory taken 6th Nov[r] 1663 by *William Sumner, James Humfrey.* Am[t]. £224. 12.

M[rs] *Agnes Blake* deposed 29th Jan. 1663, to this estate of her late husband.

———

JOHN MEARES.—Boston: 26: 7[m] 1663. I, *Jn° Merres*, lying sick—declare this as my last will, if no other after this doe appeare. I make my dear Vnkell, *James Johnson*, executor of this my last will. I giue to my wife, *Mary*, my dwelling house during her life, & if she marry, her next husband to give to her Child she now goes w[th], y° said house & ground, & after both her & her childs decease, then, to my two brothers, or y° survivor of them. Moreov[r], I giue to my beloved wife, y° bed I now ly on, wth all y° furniture thereto belonging, six greene Chairs, a round table, and two paire of sheets, besids them I had with her, with a Long table in the house. To my father *Meares*, my best suit and Cloak, and four Cord of wood, with my Weding hat. To my dear mother

———

* This is an entire copy of the will of William Blake, from the original, on file. T.

Mears, my Chest of drawers, two paire of sheets, and bed ticking. To
my brother, *Samuell Mears*, a pair of blew Curtains & my 2ᵈ suit and
Coat to *James Meers* with my musket and arms; to my wife, all the rest
of my estate.   John Meers.
Witness, *James Johnson, James Oliver.*

Moreov' wee, *Elizabeth Meers & Mercy Meeres*, testify yᵗ he declared
this to bee his meaning, yᵗ his child if it liue to yᵉ age of 20 yeares, or
att age, it shall injoy ½ yᵉ house during yᵉ Mothers life, & all after her
decease; in case of yᵉ childs death, *Mercy Meers* to have it for her life.

Capt James Oliver deposed, 5 March: 63.

Whereas it was desired by *Mrs Sands* & others of yᵉ friends of the
deceased *Jno Meares*, that there might be a meeting together Concerning
some expretions in his will, It was declared by both Capt. *James Johnson*
& *Elizabeth Mears*, yᵗ whereas it is expressed yᵗ yᵉ howse is giuen to his
wife dureing life and if she marry, her next husband to giue it her child
she now goes with, & after both her & her childes decease, to his two Brothers: yᵉ true words & minde of yᵉ deceased was howeuer not soe clerly
exprest, that his wife was to haue the howse dureing her life, & if she
should marry an other husband she should not haue power to giue it to
any other child she might haue, but it was giuen by this will to the Child
yᵗ she went then with, & to yᵉ issue of yᵗ child foreuer, & in case she
should liue longer then yᵉ childs coming to age, yᵗ at age he or she was to
haue possession of one halfe, but if she dies before yᵉ child comes at age
then yᵉ whole benefit to be to yᵉ vse of yᵉ child & his or her issue immediately after yᵗ decease.

I December, 1663.

This was done & expressed in yᵉ presence of *John Wiswall, Edw.
Hutchinson, Elizabeth Mears, James Johnson.*

Capt. James Johnson, Elizabeth Meares mother, & *Mary Meares* late
wife to *Jnᵒ Meares*, deceased, deposed 5ᵗʰ March 1663.

Inventory of the Estate prized 6ᵗʰ : 10 mo : 1663, by *John Lake, Edward Drinker.* Amt. £231. 01. 1. Mentions, "his Wedding Hatt, £1.
10s." "one Hatt Case, 1s. 6d." Capᵗ. James Johnson deposed, 5 March
1663.

THOMAS GULLIVER.—Power of Administration to the estate of the late
Thomas Gullife, of Brantrey, deceased, is graunted to *Prudence*, his relict,
& *Jonathan*, his elder son, they bringing in an Inventory of that Estate, &c.

ROBERT LINCOLNE.—Inventory of the Estate of Robert Linchorne late
of Winnisemet, within the p'cincts of Boston, deceased, prized by *Elias
Maxericke, Samuell Danids, Aaron Waye*, 16 : 3 mo : 1663. Amt. £192.
13s. 09d.

Anne Lincolne deposed 29 July 1663, to the estate of her late husband.

GEORGE DOD.—[Mary Dod's petition to the Court is on filo. In it she
represents that her husband, *George Dod*, "som yeares past departed
this life in London, in England, leving with me fouer smale Children to
take care for." She states that having made inquiry into his debts and
credits, she "finds that his debts far exceed his credits & estate," "his
Credits being all desperate debts, lying mostly in Virginia & som in New
England, but all of them in such hands as that he in his life time could
not get any of them." She therefore desires an allowance out of said
estate, &c.

31 July 1663. The Court allow her the best bed boulster, one pillow, one p' of blanketts, Rugg, bedsteed & Coard, & £5, in money. Administration on the estate was granted to *Richard Way* and *Edward Blake*, who gave a bond, which is on file, to the amount of £40. This obligation is witnessed by *Sarah Wilson* and *Peris Rawson*—date 11 Aug. 1663.]

Inventory of the goods & credits of *George Dod*, of Boston, marriner, deceased, praised by *Thomas Rallings, Richard Way, & Edward Blake*, 26th July 1663. Amt. £23. 13s. 10d. *Mary Dod*, relict of the late George Dod deposed, 31 July 1663.

SAMUEL MAVERICK, JR.—14th March 1663. Power of Administration to the estate of the late *Samuell Mauericke Jun'*, of Boston, is Granted to *Rebeckah Mauericke*, his relict, w^th *M' Moses Mauericke, M' John Wisewall, & M' Anthony Cheeckley*, in behalf of himself & children wth the Credito^r to that estate they bringing in an Inventory of said Estate, &c.

Inventory of said Estate apprised by *Mr John Winslow Senr & Jn' Farnham*, 28th March ‡‡. Amt. £127. 10. 2½. *M' Jn' Wiswall & M' Wm Bartholmew* deposed 4th Nov'. 1665.

28 : 6mo. 1665. Vpon Information from *Mr Jonathan Rainsford* that the Chamber Door was Broken up where some goods were left, whereof the Key was lost, &c. [Several articles are then enumerated.] 2 (7) 64. A note was made of what was wanting upon the reueiw of the Inuentory Immediately upon Mrs Mauerickes going out of the House, who was one of the Administrators, formerly. Amount £32. 8s. 4d.

ROBERT NANNY, of Boston, being weeke in bodie—make this my last will. 22 Aug. 1663. Debts and funerall Charges be discharged and in particular there being an estate in my hands in partnership betwixt my Vnckle, *Richard Hutchinson*, of London, and my selfe, my will is, that the houses and land I haue at Barbados, as also gouerner *Searle's* bills, of three hundred pounds maye be giuen and made ouer to my Vnclo, *Richard Hutchinson*, of London, to ballance all accounts betwixt us, only what is more then will pay him, as I hope thoro will, the ouerplus to be returned to my executrix. Unto *M' Maho, M' Madder*, and *M' Powell*, officers of the new Church in Boston, each 20s. Unto my wife, *Katherine Nanny*, one third of the rest of my estate—the other two thirds to my Children, vizt. son *Samuel*, and dauter *Mary*, and to the Child my wife now goes withall, being yet vnborne, to be equally deuided into fower partes, two partes to my sonne *Samuel*, the other two parts to my other two Children, to be equally deuided. In Case of the death of any of my Children, the Estate of such Child or Children to fall to my wife, who I leaue soll executrix, and desire her care in the bringing vp of my Children, for wch End I leaue there whole Estates in her hands, and she to haue the use of it for there education and bringing vp, untell they Come to the age of 21 yeares or day of marrage, wth Consent of there mother; and I request my honered father in law, the Reuorent *Mr John Whelewright*, Pastor of Salseborry, and my louing brother in law, *Mr Sam: Whelewright*, of Wells, to be ouerseores of this my will, and to assist my Exsequutrix what they Can in her business.   Robert Nanneye.

Samuel Hutchinson, John + *Stones* mark.
James Mattock.

Samuel Hutchinson and *James Mattock* deposed 7 mo : 63.

Inventory of the estate of *Robert Nanny*, taken 10th Sept. 1663. Amt. £1049. 14s. 4½d. Mentions " dwelling house, warehouse & wharfe, yards & other privillidges bellonging to the house neare the Draw Bridge, £300 ; the Red house and land neare to Charlestowne ferry, £200 ; one parcell of land neere adjoining to the said Red house lately Bought of leut *Wm. Phillips*, £60."

The property was aprised by *John Joyliffe* and *Robert Pateshall*, 6th of Oct. 1663. *Katherine Nanny* deposed, 31st Ocr. 1663.

———

Thomas Leader.—I, *Thomas Leader*, of Boston, 17 Ocr. 1663, make my last will. Vnto my wife, *Ales Leader*, the Dwelling house I use to lett out, ouer Against the house Called *Allcockes* house, with the yard as it is now fenced, with an Adititon of land to be more layd Vnto itt out of my Garden & Orchard, that is to say, from the outwardmost post of the Crosse fence next the lane to Draw a straight line quite Cross the Orchard through to my Neighbour *Sanfords* ground, I giue all the aboue mentioned, for her life, my son, *Samuell*, to sett and keepe the house and fencing in good Repayre all time of her life at my son, *Samuells* Cost, and after her Doccase, I giue all the aboue mentioned, vnto my Grand Child, *Thomas Leader*, the son of my son John, deceased, to him and his heires for Euer, and to haue it putt Into good Repayre for him by my said son *Samuell* ; further my will is, that my grand Child, *Thomas Leader*, shall pay out of it a legacie vnto my Grand Child, *Abigal Leader*, his sister, within one yeare after he poszrs the aboue mentioned premisses, the sum of fowre pounds. Vnto my son *Samuell Leadr*, all my now dwelling house, as also the New house adjoining, with all the appurtinances therevnto belonging, with Garden and Orchard and yard therevnto Bellonging, Excepting that part aboue mentioned wich I giue vnto my wife & grand Child, with this prouisiall, yt if my son *Samuell* Die without issue male, to ye next A kind [of kin?] in Case of Necessity, my son, *Samuell*, Finishing yt house Adjoyning to ye house I now dwell in. I give A liberty to sell either that or yt I now dwell in, wth halfe ye Ground, prouided the ground laid to what house yt he doe sell may bee laid out to as little damage to yt house & ground that shal bee preserved as may bee. Vnto my wife, £4, in Money & goods, to bee payd by my son, *Samuell*, within A yeare of my departing this world. Vnto *Rebecka Leader*, My Grand Child, £6 to bee paid by my son, *Samuell*, in Like paymt. in money & goods, wthin [a] yeer after my decease. Vnto my wife, ye best Shett, ye prouisions left in ye house, & five Cord of Wood. All my tooles & debts, & other Estate not Mentioned, I give Vnto my Son, *Samuell*, he Bestowing A decent Buriall Vpon this poore body of mine. My son, *Samuell*, sole Executor. My will is, that my executor should faithfully pay all ye Legacies & what I haue in my will Ingaged him to doe, or else, Vpon non paymt, My wife or Leagiees or their Assignes shall Enter Vpon what I haue given vnto him till they bee sattisfyed. *Jeames Penn*, ye Ruling Elder of Boston, overseer.

Witnesses, *Jer: Howchin.*　　　　　　　　　Thomas X Leader.

Jo. *Endecott*, Junior, Samll *Wheelwright*, who deposed 3d Novr. 1663. Inventory of *Thomas Leader*, prised, 5th Novr. 1663, by *John Button*, Tho. *Mattson*, Hugh *Drury*. *Samuel Leader* deposed, 29 Jan. 1663.

(To be Continued.)

A BRIEF SKETCH OF THE FAMILY OF REV. THOMAS WELLS, FIRST MINISTER OF AMESBURY, MASS.

[By D. W. Hoyt.]

Rev. Thomas Wells was settled as first pastor of the first church in Amesbury, in 1672 or 1673. Occasional preaching had been enjoyed in the "new town" for ten or twenty years before that time, but he was the first who was recognized as the town's minister. A committee were chosen, May 11, 1672, "to see if they can obtain Mr Weels to be helpfull to us in the work of the Ministry." He was admitted as a commoner in 1673–4, and was evidently a man of much influence and usefulness in the new town.

Various circumstances render it extremely probable, if not almost certain, that Rev. Thomas Wells was the Thomas Wells who was born Jan. 11, 1646–7, youngest son of *Dea. Thomas Wells* of Ipswich. The generations of the family are here numbered in accordance with that idea, Dea. Thomas being considered the first, and Rev. Thomas the second generation. If the above is the date of the birth of Thomas,^{2} he must have been 87 yrs. 6 mos. old at the time of his death. According to the inscription on his tombstone, he was then in his "87th year;" but that may have been intended to imply that he was between 87 and 88, though the expression, if properly used, would justify Farmer's statement, that his age was 86. Thomas^{1} Wells of Ipswich was "a gentleman of large property," and it has been supposed that he was a physician. He had land granted to him at Ipswich in 1635, and took the Freeman's oath at Boston, May 17, 1637. He died Oct. 26, 1666. From a branch of his family, the town of Wells, Me., took its name. Further particulars respecting him and his family may be found in vol. 4 of this periodical, pp. 11, 12.

By his will, Thomas^{1} made provision for his son's "going to College;" but his name is not to be found among the early graduates of any American college. Rev. Thomas^{2} Wells enjoyed the distinction, however, of being the first individual who received the honorary degree of A. M. from Harvard College. In the triennial catalogue of 1727, his name is put at the bottom of the class of 1669; in 1745, perhaps earlier, it was separated from the others by a line, and 1703 added. In 1830, the names of those who had received honorary and *ad eundem* degrees, were made a distinct division of the catalogue, and Thomas Wells was placed at the head of the list, under the year 1703. It is possible that he may have been at one time a member of the class of 1669; but if he received the degree in 1703, he must then have been 56 years old, and his name might have been placed under 1669 only because that class were near his own age.

A copy of the will of Rev. Thomas^{2} Wells is to be found on the Probate Records at Salem. It was dated Aug. 7, 1728, proved July 29, 1734. He there mentions four sons, three daughters, four daughters-in-law, and

---

Note. *Richard Wells* was one of the original proprietors and commoners of the town of Salisbury, and it would naturally be surmised that the Wells family of Salisbury and Amesbury were descended from him. "Dea. Richard Wells" died July 12, 1672, and we have no evidence that he left any children.

In a previous number of this magazine (July, 1850, p. 261), is found "Richard Wells, 56," and two or three other Salisbury names, among the "Passengers for Virginia," August, 1635, "in the Globe of London, Jeremy Blackman Mr."

two sons-in-law; three sons and one daughter-in-law having died before
that time. John Martin, the other son-in-law, is not mentioned. The
dates of the deaths of Mr. Thomas Wells and his wife, as given on the
town records, correspond with the inscriptions copied below, except that
the double date, 1726-7, is given. From the spelling and appearance of
the inscription, one would suppose Mr. Wells's tombstone to be of later
date than those around it.

Interred here the BODY of,
the Rev^d. M^r. THOMAS WELLS.
first Pastor, of the first Church
of CHRIST in Amesbury. who
Departed this life July ye 10th.
1734. in the 87th. year of his
Age, & the 62^d. of his Ministry,
having served his Generation by
the will of GOD, he fell on sleep, and
(we trust) enjoys a Prophets reward.
for tho' Israel should not
be Gathered, yet would
the faithfull ministers of
the Gospell, be glorious
in the Eyes of the Lord.

INTERRED HERE THE BODY
OF Mr MARY WELLS
DEC^s IANUARY THE 26th
1727 AGED 75 YEARS
LATE WIFE OF Mr THOMAS
WELLS

DEATH IS NOT DUMB IT BIDS US ALL
PREPARE BEFORE BY IT WE FALL
WE KNOW NOT HOW NOR WHERE NOR W
FIT NOW OR NEUR WE CANNOT THEN HEN

Children of Rev. Mr. Thomas[2] *Wells and wife Mary.*

(1)   I. John,[3] b. Feb. 2, 1672; prob. d. April 2, 1673.

(2)   II. Luke,[3] b. March 19, 1673-4; m. Wid. Dorothy Trull, of Haverhill, int. ent. Dec. 9, 1710 (11). Wife Dor. d. Sept. 29, 1715.

(3)   III. Titus,[3] b. March 14, 1675; m. Joanna ———— (14). A Titus Wells was an inhabitant of the West Parish in 1728.

(4)   IV. A Son,[3] b. ————. In his will, 1728, Thomas[2] mentions his daughter-in-law Rebecca Wells, late, " now Barrett," and his grand-daughter Rebecca, late Wells, " now Waters." These may have been the widow and daughter of a son who died previous to 1728. If so, the widow Rebecca m. ———— Barrett, and the dau. Rebecca[3] m. ———— Waters.

(5)   V. A Son,[3] b. ————; prob. d. before 1728, and without issue. John[3] is called the " 7th son," and hence there must have been two sons whose names are unknown to us, here numbered as 4 and 5.

(6)   VI. Abigail,[3] b. ————; m. Samuel Bartlett of Newbury, Feb. 6, 1704-5.

(7)   VII. Mary,[3] b. ———; m. John Martin of A., July 15, 1702.
(8)   VIII. Eliezer,[3] b. June 10, 1686; m. Deborah Worthen of A.,
          Nov. 17, 1714. (24).
(9)   IX. Elizabeth,[3] b. Dec. 17, 1688; m. Moses Chase, Jr., of New-
          bury, Oct. 12, 1709.
(10)   X. John,[3] b. Oct. 9, 1692; m. Dorothy[4] Hoyt of A., Feb. 5, 1712
          –3 (29). Will dated May, 1768, proved Dec. 24, 1776.
          Wife Dor. d. April 28, 1769, in her 77th year. (See p. 30,
          " Hoyt Family.") Thomas[3] mentions his " cousin," Philip
          Hoyt, in his will. We know not who is referred to, unless
          it be the brother of Dorothy, who was thus a brother of the
          daughter-in-law of Thomas.[3]

Children of (2) Luke[3] and Dorothy Wells.

(11)   I. John,[4] b. March 17, 1710–1.
(12)   II. Obadiah,[4] b. June 27, 1712; m. Judith ———. Chil.:
          Dorothy,[5] b. 1738; *Lydia,*[5] b. 1740; *Sarah,*[5] b. 1742;
          perhaps others. An Obadiah Wells m. Jemima Wiburn,
          Salisbury, May 25, 1749.
(13)   III. William,[4] b. Oct. 5, 1713.

Children of (3) Titus[3] and Joanna Wells.

(14)   I. Sarah,[4] b. July 30, 1698; m. Jonathan Farren, Dec. 10,
          1719.
(15)   II. Thomas,[4] b. March 4, 1699–1700; m. Sarah Hadley, Dec. 15,
          1720. Chil.; *Philip,*[5] b. 1721; *Benjamin,*[5] b. 1724;
          Winthrop,[5] b. 1726, perhaps others. A Thomas Wells,
          Jr., ent. int. marriage with Mary Sargent, 3d, both of A.,
          March 23, 1728–9.
(16)   III. Timothy,[4] b. April 16, 1704; m. Mary ———. He died
          before Aug., 1728, his wife surviving him.
(17)   IV. Titus,[4] b. Feb. 5, 1705–6; m. Mary ——— (39). (See
          " Hoyt Family," pp. 32, 44.)
(18)   V. Hannah,[4] b. Feb. 5, 1705–6.
(19)   VI. Philemon,[4] b. Sept. 3, 1708.
(20)   VII. Jacob,[4] b. Aug. 28, 1710.
(21)   VIII. Philip,[4] b. April 7, 1713; d. Feb. 2, 1714–5.
(22)   IX. Elizabeth,[4] b. March 11, 1716.
(23)   X. Abigail,[4] b. Dec. 18, 1718.

Children of (8) Eliezer[3] and Deborah Wells.

(24)   I. Moses,[4] b. Sept. 17, 1716.
(25)   II. Judith,[4] b. March, 1720.
(26)   III. Aaron,[4] b. Dec. 30, 1722.
(27)   IV. Hannah,[4] b. Jan. 5, 1722–3. (?)
(28)   V. Eliezer,[4] b. April 9, 1729.

Children of (10) John[3] and Dorothy Wells.

(29)   I. Rhoda,[4] b. Feb. 24, 1713–4; m. ——— Currier.
(30)   II. Electa,[4] b. April 7, 1715; m. ——— Currier.
(31)   III. Elizabeth,[4] b. Sept. 16, 1716; m. ——— Challis.
(32)   IV. Dorothy,[4] b. Feb. 16, 1717–8; m. Jonathan Bagley.
(33)   V. Christiana,[4] b. June 21, 1720; m. ——— Merrill.

(34) VI. John,⁴ b. Jan. 24, 1721–2; m. Rachel Currier, July 20, 1756.
He d. before May, 1768, leaving chil. : Levi,⁵ Hannah,⁵ Dorothy,⁵ and Rebecca.⁵
(35) VII. Mary,⁴ b. Feb. 14, 1723–4; m. John Currier.
(36) VIII. Thomas,⁴ b. Sept. 3, 1725; moved to Chester, N. H., previous to 1768.
(37) IX. David,⁴ b. March 14, 1729–30; d. Sept. 12, 1753.
(38) X. Rebecca,⁴ b. Oct. 28, 1731; d. Oct. 2, 1753.

    Children of (17) *Titus⁴ and Mary Wells.*

(39) I. Samuel,⁵ b. Aug. 16, 1736.
(40) II. Enoch,⁵ b. April 16, 1738.
(41) III. Mary,⁵ b. Dec. 15, 1739; m. Theodore⁵ Hoyt, the author's great-grandfather. (See " Hoyt Family," p. 44.)
(42) IV. Nathan,⁵ b. Aug. 5, 1741.
(43) V. Joshua,⁵ b. Feb. 7, 1744.
(41) VI. Hannah,⁵ b. Dec. 21, 1745.

TOWNSMEN OF DARTMOUTH, MASS.

Mr. Drake,—Will you please insert this in season to excite action in the next town meetings to save records particularly rich and hitherto unnoticed by genealogists.

      Yours,   Abner Morse.

" The names of the Townsmen of Dartmouth who had taken the oath of fidelity or freemen's oath."—*March* 24, 1686.

John Cooke	Ouice Jenny
John Russel sen'.	George Cadman
John Smith	James Trip
Samuel Jene sen'.	Samuel Jenny jun'.
Arthur Hathaway	John Hathaway
Wm Woode	Joseph Smith
James Samson	Joseph Russel
John Sherman	Hezekiah Smith
Seth Pope	Doliverance Smith
Joseph Tripp	———— Sherman
Jonathan Russel	———— Howland
Jonathan Delino	John Earl
Tho Tabor	Ralph Earl junr.
Samuel Cornwell	Stephen Peckum
James Sisson	Ralph Earl, son of Wm
John Spooner	Wm Macomber
Nathaniel Soull	Samuel Willcocks
George Soull	James Franklin
John Jene	Samuel Spooner
Eliazer Smith	Wm Wood
Return Badcock	Anthony Savory
Wm. Spooner	

Dartmouth then embraced, besides its present territory, Westport, New Bedford and Fair Haven; and her records, more shattered, probably, than those of any other town in Massachusetts, are essential to the early history of these towns, if not to that of the rise of Quakerism in New England; and it is hoped that public action will rescue them before it is too late. The Proprietors' records have not been committed to the clerk of Dartmouth, but remain in the hands of George Gifford, Esq., of Westport, son to their last clerk.

NOTES ON THE INDIAN WARS IN NEW ENGLAND.

CHAPTER III.

[Continued from page 16.]

"The prudent discourse of this Indian prevailed so far as that Alexander yielded to go, only requesting that he might go like a Sachem, with his men attending him, which, although there was some hazard in it, they being many, and the English but a few, was granted to him. The weather being hot, the Major offered him an horse to ride on, but his squaw and divers Indian women being in company, he refused, saying he could go on foot as well as they; entreating, only, that there might be a complying with their pace, which was done; and, resting several times by the way, Alexander and his Indians were refreshed by the English; no other discourse happening while they were upon their march, but what was pleasant and amicable. The Major sent a man before, to entreat that as many of the Magistrates of that Colony as could, would meet at Duxbury. Wherefore, having there had some treaty with Alexander, not willing to commit him to prison, they entreated Major Winslow to receive him to his house, until the Governor, who then lived at Eastham, could come up. Accordingly he and his train were courteously entertained by the Major. And albeit not so much as an angry word passed between them whilst at Marshfield. Yet proud Alexander, vexing and fretting in his spirit, that such a check was given him, he suddenly fell sick of a fever. He was then nursed as a choice friend. Mr. Fuller, the physician, coming providentially thither at that time, the Sachem and his men earnestly desired that he would administer to him, which he was unwilling to do; but by their importunity was prevailed with to do the best he could to help him, and therefore gave him a potion of working physic, which the Indians thought did him good; but his distemper afterwards prevailing, they entreated to dismiss him, in order to a return home; which upon [his] engagement of appearance at the next court, was granted to him. Soon after his being returned home he died. And this is the truth and substance of what concerns transactions with Alexander, concerning *Increase Mather* which so many fabulous stories have been spread abroad."

The remarkable particularity of this narrative gives it the first consideration, and is a very strong evidence of its truth. It fully corroborates Mr. Hubbard's account, so far as that author goes; and Mr. Mather, like him, was well aware that various other reports had gone abroad, and it is very clear that both of those gentlemen had inquired into the matter, and were fully convinced of the truth of what they had given. It is pretty evident, however, that Mr. Mather intended to make the most of his story; was willing his readers should think the number of Indians with Alexander was very large, while he took good care to keep within the bounds of truth, by making no statement as to their real number. This historical license cannot be defended, and is too easily seen through to have any very bad effect; as it only tended to exaggerate the danger the few English were in, and to make their conduct appear the more heroical. The Indians were surprised, with their guns standing outside of their wigwam; but nobody has said how many "guns" they had. Now it seems pretty clear that the company of Indians captured were upon a fishing design, upon the cool and beautifully shaded banks of the little lake before mentioned, and had not the remotest fears of being taken for enemies. Had they been upon any mischievous design, or had there been any plot undertaken, would they have allowed themselves in broad day to be surprised as is related? They doubtless saw the English approach, and had no suspicion that they were coming upon them as enemies.

Some time after this transaction, when its justice and propriety had been discussed in various quarters, the Rev. John Cotton* of Plymouth wrote to Dr. Mather of Boston concerning it, "lest you should," he observes, "through misinformation, print some mistakes." What he wrote, he says, was from Major Bradford's own mouth, the Major being one of the party who seized Alexander. Mr. Cotton remarks briefly that Alexander was found at Munpouset river, not many miles from Plymouth, "with about 8 men, and sundry squaws. He was there about getting canoes. He and his men were at breakfast under their shelter, their guns being without. They saw the English coming, but continued eating; on Mr. Winslow's telling their business, Alexander, freely and readily, without the least hesitancy, consented to go; giving his reason why he came not to the court before, namely, because he waited for Capt. Willet's return from the Dutch [at Manhattan,] being desirous to speak with him first. They brought him to Mr. [William] Collier's, that day, and Gov. Prince living remote, at Eastham, those few magistrates, who were at hand, issued the matter peaceably, and immediately dismissed Alexander to return home, which he did, part of the way; but in two or three days after he returned and went to Major Winslow's house, intending thence to travel into the Bay [Boston] and so home; but, at the Major's house he was taken very sick, and was, by water, conveyed to Mr. Bradford's, and thence carried upon the shoulders of his men to Tetehquet river [in Middleborough,] and thence in canoes, home; and, about two or three days after, died.'

This statement, though sent to Dr. Mather, had no influence, so far as known, to cause him to publish any modification of what he had already penned. The reader will judge for himself, whether Mr. Cotton's statement is to be taken for the whole truth.†

---

* Son of the Rev. John Cotton of Boston.

† The Rev. Samuel Niles, minister of Braintree in Massachusetts, from 1711 to his death in 1762, left a History of Indian Wars in New England in manuscript, which was published in 1837 in the 16th vol. of the Coll. Ms. H. Soc. This author's version of the death of Alexander differs very much from all others. It is brief, and in these words:—"That Alexander, after his father's death, became very surly and distempered toward the English people; for which reason the Court of Plymouth, which was then a distinct colony from the Massachusetts, suspecting him to have some treacherous purposes in view, brought him to Plymouth and put him under confinement; at which the fellow was enraged to that degree that he refused to eat, and even starved himself to death in this miserable manner."

"Where Mr. Niles obtained his information he does not tell us, but he seems to have paid no attention to what had been published upon this subject before he wrote; and yet he says, in his Introduction, that "the reader will find an exact narrative of the Indian Wars, as far as his intelligence had reached, and upon the best grounds he could obtain, from approved authors and otherwise."

Upon the death of Alexander, there was a remarkable solemnity among the Indians, and it was bewailed with great sincerity by his tribe. Multitudes of Indians from all parts, Chiefs and others, flocked to Mount Hope, and there, according to the ancient customs of that people, mourned his death for many days, by the practice of their strange rites and ceremonies. As soon as that was ended, a season of rejoicing and feasting succeeded, in honor of the accession of Philip to the Chieftainship.

This numerous assembling of Indians at Mount Hope, in view of what had happened in connection with the death of Alexander, alarmed the English at Plymouth. They were fearful that Philip had some evil design upon them. He was therefore required to come to Court, and to explain the cause of this seemingly strange conduct. The Court having met on the sixth of August, Philip soon after appeared, and was ready to renew the treaties already in existence, or make a new one. Accordingly a new treaty was drawn up and signed by Philip, Francis, Sachem of Nauset, and John Sausoman witnessed it.

Of the family of Alexander very little is known. That he had a wife and son has been mentioned in the extracts already given. His wife, whose name was Namumpum, survived him. She was afterwards called Weetamoo, and was Queen or Squaw-Sachem of Pocasset, and for a period was the wife of a somewhat noted Indian named Petananuet, which the English transformed into Peter Nunnit. Weetamoo espoused Philip's cause and perished in the war, in which she was conspicuous, and will be hereafter particularly noticed.

CHAPTER IV.

A glance at some opinions respecting the Origin of the Indians.—Gen. Gookin's views.—What he learned from the Indians themselves.—Dr. Cotton Mather's notions upon this subject.—Principal Tribes occupying New England.—A Digression concerning the Narragansets.—The Wampanoags.—Their description of the Pestilence of 1617.—The Massachusetts.—Pawtuckets.

ALMOST all of the early writers who touched upon the history of the aborigines of America, indulged in conjectures concerning their origin. It is not intended to revive the question in this narrative, having formerly, in another work,* given specimens of the opinions of various authors upon it. However, it may be interesting to general readers to know to what conclusion Major General Daniel Gookin came in regard to it; he having the best means of learning what the Indians themselves thought about it; therefore, before entering upon the business of this chapter, a few statements and observations will be given from the writings of that distinguished man,† to whom every historian must

----

* Book of the Indians, Book I.

† Maj. Gen. Daniel Gookin left several valuable works in MS. That here referred to is his *Historical Collections of the Indians in New England*. It has never been printed except in the Collections of the Massachusetts Historical Society. In that work it appeared in 1792; but its value is much impaired by its appearance in a modern dress. Whether the original is preserved, is unknown to the writer. There is much wanted a correct edition of it, in a volume by itself.

Daniel Gookin

be indebted for the best account of the numbers and condition of the Indiaus in New England previous to, and during the war with King Philip. He says, "I have discoursed and questioned about this matter with some of the most judicious of the Indians, but their answers are divers and fabulous. Some of the Inland Indians say, that they came from such as inhabit the sea coasts. Others say, that there were two young squaws, or women, being at first either swimming or wading in the water, the froth or foam of the water touched their bodies, from whence they became with child; and one of them brought forth a male, and the other a female child; and then the two women died and left the earth. So their son and daughter were their first progenitors. Other fables and figments are among them, touching this thing, which are not worthy to be inserted."

Of course, no intelligent person would put the least reliance on Indian stories of this nature. Like all ignorant people, the Indians delighted in the recital of marvellous stories, of which there was never wanting among them a host of inventors. They took much satisfaction in making up and relating improbable stories, especially when they found persons weak enough to be deceived by them.

But General Gookin's conclusion was, that they, the Indians, "were Adam's posterity." Hence, some wandering tribe of Asiatics or Europeans, by some means found its way into America; but *when*, it was as difficult to determine, as *how*. Gen. Gookin believed that all mankind were descended from one pair, and this was the general belief in his time. He seems to have been of opinion too, that the branch of the human race which had found its way into this continent, had got beyond the reach of christianity, or the gospel; and hence the inference, that, although men could not wander so far without divine assistance, that assistance immediately forsook them on their arrival here, and they were left to perish. But a reason for this conclusion was never satisfactorily given. Dr. Cotton Mather, however, finds no difficulty in supplying what may be supposed to have been, to himself, very satisfactory explanations of these difficulties; one or two of which, for their singularly characteristic qualities, are given.

Dr. Mather says, "The Natives of the Country now Possessed by the *New Englanders*, had been forlorn and wretched *Heathen* ever since their first herding here; and tho we know not *When* or *How* those Indians first became Inhabitants of this mighty Continent, yet we may guess that probably, the Divel decoy'd those miserable Salvages hither, in hopes that the Gospel of the Lord Jesus would never come here to destroy or disturb his *Absolute-Empire* over them. But our *Eliot* was in such ill terms with the Divel, as to alarm him with sounding the *Silver-Trumpets* of Heaven in his Territories, and make some Noble and Zealous Attempts towards outing him of his Ancient possessions here." *

The same author, in another work, remarks, that, "by the year 1636, it was time for the *Devil* to take the *Alarum*, and make some attempt in Opposition to the *Possession* which the Lord Jesus Christ

---

* The Life of the Renowned John Eliot, p. 74, ed. Boston, 1691.

was going to have of them *utmost Parts of the Earth.* * These *Parts* were then covered with Nations of Barbarous *Indians* and Infidels, in which the *Prince of the Power of the Air* did *Work as a Spirit;* nor could it be expected that Nations of Wretches, whose whole Religion was the most Explicit sort of *Devil-Worship,* should not be acted by the Devil to engage in some early and bloody Action for the extinction of a Plantation so contrary to his Interests, as that of *New-England* was." † But to return to the design of the present Chapter.

It is asserted that when the English first settled in New England, it was occupied by about twenty different nations or tribes of Indians.‡ These nations or tribes were generally independent of each other, but united sometimes for mutual protection, and the purpose of making war. In every tribe or clan there was a Chief or head man or head woman, to whom the rest paid a sort of deference; but these Chiefs had very little power, other than that bestowed upon them by nature. That is to say, Chiefs or Leaders became so usually, by being endowed with superior intellects, or great physical importance.

The principal tribes scattered over New England at the period of its settlement, were, according to General Gookin, the Pequots. Narragansets, Pawkunnawkuts, Massachusetts and Pawtuckets. Each of these was subdivided into many clans. There were also the Mohegans and Nipmuks. Some of these tribes are reported to have been very numerous. The Pequots were the most powerful at the time of the arrival of the white people; numbering about four thousand warriors. Their dominion extended from beyond Quinnipiack§ southwesterly, to the Narraganset country northeasterly. They exercised some jurisdiction over the Indians on a part of Long Island, and also as far inland on the main as the country of the Nipmucks.

Next in order of importance were the Narragansets. "They were a great people heretofore, and the territory of their Sachem extended about thirty or forty miles from Seaconk river and Narragansitt Bay, including Rhode Island and other islands in that bay, being their east and north bounds or border, and so running westerly and southerly unto a place called Wekapage, four or five miles to the eastward of Paweutuk river, which was reconed for their south and west border, and the easternmost limits of the Pequots." This tribe also exercised some sort of jurisdiction over a part of Long Island, and likewise over a part of the Nipmuck country, Block Island, Cawesitt, and other

---

* This and similar expressions were in constant use among the fathers of New England. See *New Eng. Hist. and Antiq. Jour.* vi. 52. Not only the Fathers who came first to New England used to speak of it as " The Ends of the Earth," but their children and even their grand children viewed it as such. And whatever their ideas may have been of its importance in a Christian point of view, it is pretty evident that they had no notion or conception that they were founding a great nation, such as we now see. Dr. Increase Mather says, in his *Election Sermon* of 1677, p. 75, ed. 1685—"Our Fathers did not in their coming hither, proposed any great matter to themselves respecting this world," &c. Here they believed was the place where Christ was to take up his abode while on earth, at his " second appearing." And as the Saints would be few in comparison to the rest of the human race, His kingdom would require but a small corner of the American Continent. It is evident too that the pious founders did not wish or desire a great nation composed of those who were not believers; and when such came among them, they took measures to send them away again. This course they continued to until they were overwhelmed by numbers.

† *Magnalia Christi Americana,* Book VII., p. 41.
‡ *Mather's Life of Eliot.* p 74.
§ At the close of this work I propose to give a list of all the Indian names of places, and their corresponding English names.

places. The Pawkunnaukuts or Pokanokets (Wampanoags) stood
much in fear of the Narragansets, and were threatened by them with
war, when they found the Wampanoags were treating with the white
people who came to settle at Plymouth. Canonicus was then Sachem
of the Narragansets. He was a Chief of extraordinary capacity, and
doubtless saw that mischief might accrue to his people by this lodg-
ment of strangers upon the Indian territory. Therefore he determined
to see what kind of people they were, whether they were warlike, and
if they would fight should they he attacked. To ascertain with certainty what the character of the intruders was, in these particulars, in
the month of February, 1622, he sent a challenge to them. This challenge was brought by an Indian named Tokamahamon, and consisted of a number of new arrows, which were wrapped in a rattle-
snake's skin. These the messenger left at Plymouth without any
explanation, but Tisquantum explained them to mean a challenge for
war. The English took the snake's skin and, filling it with powder
and ball, sent it back to the Chief, with a message, to the purport that
they had never done any wrong to the Narragansets, and desired to
live in peace with them ; but, if they were determined on war, to begin
as soon as they had a mind to ; nor would they find the English un-
prepared. This message was delivered with an air of defiance, and
they rejected the returned snake's skin, probably from a superstitious
fear of its contents ; nor would they allow it to remain among them ;
every one casting it from his neighborhood, until at length it was
returned to Plymouth with all its contents.*

The prompt action of the English seems to have awed the belligerent
Narragansets into a respectful silence, as they issued no proclamations
of war against the English for a long period. Canonicus was then
aged, but he lived until the fourth of June, 1647, supposed then to have
been about eighty-five years old. His decease was observed by all the
Natives as a great and sad event.

Mention has already been made of the Wampanoags. Of them
General Gookin says, " their Chief Sachem held dominion over divers
other petty Sagamores: as the Sagamores upon the island of Nan-
tuckett, and Nope, or Martha's Vineyard, of Nawsett, of Monnamoyk,
of Nawkattukett, Nobsquasitt, Matakees, and several others, and some
of the Nipmucks. Their Country, for the most part, falls within the
jurisdiction of New Plymouth Colony. This people were a potent
nation in former times, and could raise, as the most credible and
ancient Indians affirm, about three thousand men."

▸ The estimate of Indians of their former numbers and importance is
to be taken with allowance ; and according to the accumulated knowledge of them now available for a comparative view, it is reasonably
doubtful whether any of the great tribes of New England were as
numerous as was formerly believed. General Gookin speaks of the
pestilence already noticed, by which " these people were sorely smitten
by the hand of God, but what this disease was, that so generally and
mortally swept away, not only these but other Indians, their neighbors,
I cannot well learn. I have discoursed with some old Indians, that

---

* Winslow's *Good News*, (in Young's Collection,) p. 281. See, also, *Old Indian Chronicle*,
p. 54-6.

were then youths, who say, that the bodies all over were exceeding
yellow, describing it by a yellow garment they showed me, both before
they died, and afterwards."

The same author says of the Massachusetts,—they were the next
great people northward of the Wampanoags, and "inhabited principally about the Massachusetts Bay. These were a numerous and
great people. Their Chief Sachem held dominion over many other
petty governors; as those of Weechagaskas, Neponsitt, Punkapaog,
Nonantum, Nashaway, some of the Nipmuck people, as far as Pokom-
takake, as the old men of Massachusetts affirmed. This people could,
in former times, arm for war, about three thousand men, as the old
Indians declare. They were in hostility very often with the Narragansets, but held amity, for the most part, with the Pawkunnawkutts
and with the Pawtucketts."·

The Pawtuckett, Gen. Gookin continues, "is the fifth and last great
Sachemship of Indians. Their country lieth north and northeast from
the Massachusetts, whose dominion reacheth so far as the English
jurisdiction, or colony of the Massachusetts, now doth extend, and had
under them several other smaller Sagamores, as the Pennacooks, Aga-
womes, Naumkecks, Pascoraawayes, Accomintas, and others." The
Pawtuckets were anciently about equal in numbers to the Massachusetts, namely about three thousand men, and were generally in amity
with them. But the pestilence, before described, "almost totally
destroyed them, so that, at this day," says our author, "they are not
above two hundred and fifty men, besides women and children."

CHAPTER V.

The fate of Races.—Internal Troubles of the Indians.—Philip's circumstances at the time of Alexander's Death.—Did not intend a general War with the English.—Prudence was duly exercised to
  prevent the War of 1675.—Philip's authority limited.—Said to have wept at the news of hostilities.—
  Indians had feeble means to counteract evil reports of them.—False reports became permanent.—
  Philip assumes a bearing corresponding to that of the English.—His sales of territory.—Brief
  account of them.—His Counsellors.—Presented with a Horse.—His Expedition to Nantucket.—
  Other sales of land.

As the settlements of the Europeans advanced, the Indians receded
and shrunk away; but they did not go without a struggle, though it
were indeed against fate itself. And why they could not withstand
the current which they saw sweeping them along, they could not tell;
nor could they comprehend that this current was soon to plunge them
down a cataract, from the vortex of which there was no escape! The
instability and fate of human races was not within the scope of their
philosophy.

Besides the disturbance given to the Indians of New England by the
English settlers, one tribe continually harrassed another, and diseases,
unknown in the country before the Europeans came, were added to
the destructive use of fire-arms and spirituous liquors to hasten their
destruction.

The manner of the death of Alexander unquestionably had considerable effect upon Philip, who was ready to believe anything unfavorable to the Plymouth people. He had seen that they exercised authority over his father and brother; an authority which was inconsistent with the natural freedom of the Indians. Nor could he understand the grounds of such an assumed authority; inasmuch as his tribe were independent, and had not been subdued by the English. He was at this time a young man, scarcely twenty-two years of age perhaps, and when he was in the presence of the venerable Pilgrim Fathers he could not summon courage enough to deny any of their demands; but when he was in his native forests he remembered his promises as matters at too great a distance to be of any special account, as it respected his actions.

Although the Massachusetts, Narragansets, Mohegans and other tribes were engaged in frequent wars with Indians bordering upon them, there is no account that Philip was ever actively engaged in any war until that called by his name. And it appears pretty evident that he never contemplated a general war with the English. What are called his aggressions upon them were only intended by him as retaliatory for wrongs which he believed he had received from them. But by this course affairs soon got beyond his control. Had prudence been exercised on both sides, war might have been avoided; at least in 1675. Had the white settlers been assured that the Indians were more than a match for them in war, they would have had much greater forbearance towards them. It was far otherwise. They despised the Indians, looked upon them as inferiors in almost every respect, and were haughty and overbearing on numerous occasions. Revenge is the consequence of such relations of man to man.

It is also pretty evident that many of the chiefs of the small clans of the Wampanoags desired a war with the Plymouth people. These, although they were under or within the Sachemdom of Philip, were not controlled by him, in any such sense as a European king controls his distant subjects. But when war did come, Philip was accounted at the head of it, and he could not escape its responsibilities, or avoid its disasters.

It was told,* at a time when the truth could scarcely be mistaken, that Philip was averse to the war in which his young men had plunged him by their blind rage for revenge and plunder. "All the histories," says Mr. Callender, "from Mr. Hubbard and Dr. Mather, make Philip to be the spring and mover of the war; but there is a constant tradition among the posterity of the people, who lived next to him, and were familiarly conversant with him, as also with the Indians who survived the war, that both Philip, and his chief old men, were utterly averse to the war, and they show the spot (Kikemuit Spring, in a farm belonging to Stephen Paine, Esq. in Bristol) where Philip received the news of the first Englishmen that were killed, with grief and sorrow, and wept at the news; and that a day or two before the first outrages,

---

* By the Rev. Mr. Callender, in his Centennial Discourse on the Civil and Religious Affairs of Rhode Island, p. 73. This excellent Author holds a place in the same rank with our Prince; and had he lived to apply himself as Mr. Prince did, he might have been his equal in knowledge of New England history. He wrote in 1738.

he had protected an Englishman the Indians had captivated, rescued him from them, and privately sent him home safe."[*]

It must be remembered that it was not a day of Newspapers then. A story often gained much of its wildness and improbability in its passage through a wild and savage country. The Indians had very scanty means to counteract any reports concerning them, however absurd they may have been. There was a very general prejudice against them, and hence a readiness, on the part of the English in general, to credit stories and reports against them. Boston was the great centre where all reports found their way. Here they were talked over, and probably lost nothing as they passed from mouth to mouth. Letter writers took up these reports, and hence they acquired a permanence detrimental alike to truth and to the Indians. Specimens of such letters will be given in the progress of this narrative.

It is asserted that Philip intended to begin a war with the English from the time he came in to be Chief, and was only waiting for a good opportunity. This assertion does not appear to be well supported. It is however very clear, that by the year 1674, he became convinced that a war could not be avoided, and that towards the close of that year he began to enlist as many in his cause as he could. Up to this period there appears nothing in his actions which cannot be accounted for without the imputation of treachery or a covert design of mischief. Until then he went from tribe to tribe in a friendly way, sold land to the English, and appeared proud of the consequence they imputed to him; dressed himself up in a rich and gaudy manner, called the King of England his brother, and assumed something of the haughtiness of the English themselves.[†]

He was so fond of the goods of the English that he sold off his territory rapidly, which was as rapidly occupied and improved by them. His lands were of small value to him, but under the improvements of the English he saw they were immediately increased in value. It is probable, therefore, that this may have been a cause of irritation; and, when too late, he felt a dissatisfaction with himself for his imprudence, and perhaps fancied himself overreached by those with whom he traded.

The people of Dedham had been negotiating for about five years for the tract of land now Wrentham, but were not able to obtain it until 1662. In that year they succeeded in purchasing it of Philip. The tract was then called Wollomonopoag, was six miles square, and cost twenty-four pounds and ten shillings.

---

[*] *Historical Discourse*, 73. At the breaking out of the war of 1675, two of Hugh Cole's sons were made prisoners by the Indians and taken to Philip's head-quarters at Mount Hope. Philip ordered them set at liberty, because their father had always been his friend. He also sent word to Mr. Cole, that as he could not control his young warriors, he advised him to remove at once to Rhode Island. Mr. Cole did so, and saw his house in flames before he had left it an hour.—Fessenden's *Hist. Warren*, 39. Col. R. Cole, of the 4th generation from Hugh, gave me a similar account in 1814. See Church's *Hist.* p. 339.

[†] John Josselyn saw Philip at Boston about 1659, and thus describes him:—"His coat and buskins were thick set with beads [Wampampeague] in pleasant wild works and a broad belt of the same. His accoutrements were valued at twenty pounds."—*Two Voyages to New England*, 148. Josselyn says, "their beads are their money; of these there are two sorts, blue and white; the first is their gold, the last their silver. These they work out of certain shells, so cunningly, that neither Jew nor Devil can counterfeit them."

In 1661 he sold Mattapoisett to the Hon. William Brenton of Newport. In the deed he is styled "Pumetacom alias Philip, Chief Sachem of Mount Hope, Cowsumpsit and of all territories thereunto belonging." He then had a wife, whose name appears with his upon the deed. Her name was Wootonekamuske. In this transaction John Sassamon was interpreter and a witness, and his brother Roland Sassamon was also a witness. Of the former there will be special occasion to speak hereafter.

Philip had constantly about him several men who became very noted in the course of the war, and all perished in it. They were chiefs of clans or small tribes of Wampanoags, and are called Counsellors to King Philip. Some of the most noted of them were Watutspaquin, often called by the English the Black Sachem; his son, William; Uncompoin; Umnathum or Munashum, more generally known by the name of Nimrod; Annawon; Pecbe,* and several others. The most of their names appear frequently to sales of land; sometimes as principals, but more frequently as witnesses.

In 1665 Philip gave a sort of quitclaim to Acushena and Coaxet. The same had been sold by his father. For this he received ten pounds; but this sum included Philip's services in "marking out the bounds" of the old purchase. The same year the Court of Plymouth made him a present of a horse.

In May of this year Philip made an excursion to Nantucket, partly, as tradition reports, to punish an Indian who had spoken disrespectfully of his father, and partly to assert his authority over the Indians of that Island. The name of the offending Indian was Assasamoogh, called by the English John Gibbs. He was a preacher to the Indians on the island. Philip intended to surprise and kill him, but Gibbs' friends had notice of Philip's design, and the object of his wrath had barely time to escape by leaping a precipice. Philip however was not to be thwarted in this manner, and demanded the delivery of his victim into his hands. Meantime search was continued for him without effect. At length a negotiation was entered into for his ransom. Philip's demands were exorbitant, but were eventually complied with, and amounted to nearly all the money upon the island. Assasamoog was thus saved from destruction, and was living there about ten years afterwards, and had thirty members belonging to his Church.

In 1666, by a written instrument Philip gave to Watuckpoo and Sampson power to sell certain lands, but where they were situated does not appear. In 1667 Philip sold to Constant Southworth and others, "all the meadow lands from Dartmouth to Matapoisett," for the sum of fifteen pounds. The same year he sold to Thomas Willet and others, "all that tract of land lying between the River Wanascattaquett and Cawntoquissett, being two miles long and one broad." For this he received ten pounds sterling. Pawsaquena, counsellor to Philip, and Tom, alias Sawsuett, an interpreter, witnessed the sale.

In 1669, "Philip Pometacom and Tatamumaque, alias Cashewashed, sachems," for "a valuable consideration" sold to several English a

---

* Phebe's Neck in Rhode Island was doubtless so named from that Chief, who had his residence there.

tract of some square miles, adjacent to Pokanoket. Among the witnesses were Sampointeen, alias Tom, and Nananuntnew, son of Thomas Plants. The same year Philip and Uncompawen having laid claim to a part of New-Medows-Neck,* alleging it was not intended to be conveyed in a former deed by Philip's father and brother, Ousamequin and Wamsutta, to remove any cause of complaint it was re-purchased by those who had before purchased it; yet they protested that it was, according to the record, comprehended in the former purchase. This quitclaim, however, cost but eleven pounds. The purchasers were Capt. Thomas Willet, Mr. James Brown and John Allen, "in behalf of themselves and the rest." To this conveyance the names of Philip and his wife seem to be represented as "Philip Nanuskooke." Nimrod and Tom Sansawest were witnesses. In 1669 Philip sold to Hugh Cole and others, 500 acres of land in Swanzen, on the west side of the river now known as Cole's River, so called from this proprietor.†

These sales are but a few specimens of many made by Philip and his chief men, and are introduced to show the progress the English made in acquiring the Indian territory. It was so in every direction, and continued until the natives had very little left. Seeing this when too late, it was, as before remarked, a cause of irritation and dissatisfaction, and had something to do in preparing the way for more serious troubles.

CHAPTER VI.

Government among Indians.—Philip and the Narragansets.—Murder of an Englishman.—Its consequences.—King Philip implicated.—Arguments for and against him.—Continued complaints against Philip.—Plymouth appeals to Massachusetts to interfere.—Philip consents to attend a Conference at Taunton.—The meeting.—Transactions at the Conference.

THE nature of government among the Indians must not be considered like government among the white people. The authority of Indian Chiefs was so unlike any government among civilized people, as to amount to almost no government at all. For mutual safety they would sometimes appear in force, and so if a few of them planned any important expedition, volunteers joined it, as it promised plunder, or a chance of revenge for former injuries, either to themselves or their friends or kindred. A distinguished leader could always obtain followers; and these would stand by him as long as he was successful, and he had no authority to keep them longer.

It is said that King Philip endeavored early to engage the Narragansets against the English, but this does not very clearly appear, until war had actually broken out. But it is certain that the Narragansets had been enemies to the settlers of Massachusetts ever since the war between the former and the Mohegans. The part they took in that war, which ended in the capture and death of Miantonimo, was a sufficient cause for the Narragansets to hate the English, and especially

---

* In Barrington, R. I.   † Fessenden, Hist. Warren, 59.

those settled in and about Boston. That they ever after hated them is to be seen through all the records of the United Colonies, as troubles were continually occurring. Hence, when the Wampanoags took offence to the English, the latter had the best reason to apprehend a union with the former, although they knew they were enemies to each other; that both the Narragansets and Wampanoags laid claim to the same portion of the Nipmuck country, only a short time before the war began with Philip, and that jealousies and difficulties had always existed between them.

It is wrong, therefore, to infer that the Narragansets joined Philip in the war merely because he desired them to do so, or from any affection they had for the Wampanoags. Either could have been, at almost any time, influenced to make war on the other, if they could have enlisted allies who could ensure them success. It was as much as Roger Williams could do, with all his philosophy and philanthropy, to prevent an open war between them at different times.

These introductory observations and details being understood by the reader, will enable him to proceed understandingly with the events of the war. It is pretty certain that, as early as the year 1671, there was cause of apprehension on the part of the English settlers, that the Wampanoags intended mischief. This alarm probably grew out of a murder which was perpetrated by some Indians in "Dedham woods," in the month of April of that year. With this affair Philip's name was immediately connected, though it does not appear that he knew anything about it. The circumstances attending the murder were these. Zachary Smith, a young man, in travelling through Dedham, stopped for a night at the house of Caleb Church, a millwright, then residing there. He left, the next morning, and, when he had been gone about half an hour, three Indians came along, and went the same way which Smith had gone. As they passed Church's house they behaved insolently, throwing stones and using insulting language. They were known to the English, having been employed as laborers among them in Dorchester, and had said they belonged to King Philip. These Indians, on overtaking Smith, killed him for some little effects which he had about him, and his body was found "near the sawmill" in Dedham soon after. Search was then made for the three Indians; it being suspected that they were the murderers. They were in a few days found and taken into custody. At their trial but one of them was found guilty, and he was executed on the gallows on Boston Common. After the execution his head was cut off and set upon the gallows, where it was remaining at least five years afterwards. This Indian was the son of Matoonas, Sachem of the clan of Nipmuks living at Pakachoog. Of him there will be occasion to say more hereafter. It was remarked by the best historian of that age, that this son of Matoonas, "being vexed in his mind that the design against the English, intended to begin [in] 1671, did not take place, out of their malice and spight against them, slew an Englishman travelling along the road." *

(To be Continued.)

BIRTHS, MARRIAGES, AND DEATHS,

Contained in the volume lettered " Original Distribution of the Town of Hartford (Ct.) among the Settlers, 1639."

[Transcribed by LUCIUS M. BOLTWOOD of Amherst, Corresponding Member of Hist. and Gen. Society.]

PAGE 1.

Mary Smith daughter of Arter Smith was born Febuary the —— one thousand six hundreth for[ty] & fower.

John Pratt sunn of William Pratt was borne Febua[ry] the twenty & three one thousand six hundreth forty & fo[ur]

Abigail Kelsea, daughter of William Kellsea, was bor[ne] Aprell the nineteenth one thousand six hundreth forty & [   ]

Daniel Steel sunn of John Steel was borne Aprell the twen[ty] nyne in the yeare of o' Lord one thousand six hundreth forty & fi[ue]   Received Nou' [ ] 1646.

Mary Lawes daughter of William Lawes Junio' was borne sixth of May one thousand six hundreth forty & fiue.

Elizabeth Wadsworth daughter of William Wadswor[th] was borne May y° seuenteenth one thousand six hundr[ed] forty & fiue.

Sara Gibbins daughter of William Gibenes was b[orn] August the seuentene one thousand six hundreth forty & [   ]

Loues Standla daughter of Timothy Standla was b[orn] August twenty and three one thousand six hundreth forty & [   ]

Elisabeth Baysa daughter of John Baysa was baptised Augu[st] the twenty and three, one thousand six hundreth forty & fiue.

John Blomfilld sun of William Blomfilld was baptised August the twenty & three, one thousand six hundreth forty & fi[ue]

Mary Bunc daughter of Thomas Bunc was borne Septm seuentem one thousand six hundreth forty & fi[ue]

Joseph Whightting sun of M' William Whightting was borne abought October the seckond, one thousand six hundreth forty & fiue.

Samiwell Patreck sunn of —— Patreck was borne October the fifteneth one thousand six hundreth forty & fiue.

Jacob Whight sun of John Whight was borne October the eyghten (?) one thousand six hundreth forty & fiue.

Samewell Andrews sun of William Andrewes was borne October twenty* one thousand six hundreth forty & fiue.

Samiwell Addams sun of Jerrymy Adams was baptised November the twenty & three one thousand six hundreth forty & fiue.

PAGE 2.

Elisabeth Allcock daughter of Thomas Allcock was baptised Decm the seuenth one thousand six hundreth forty & three

Isack Bruneson sun of John Bronsun was baptised Decem the seuenth, one thousand six hundreth forty & fiue.

Daniel Hubberd sunn of George Hubbard was baptised the seuenth of Desem one thousand six hundreth forty & fiue.

John Peck sunn of Paul Peck was borne Decm the twenty & two one thousand six hundreth forty & fiue.

Thomas Bur sunn of Beniamin Bur was borne the twenty & sixth of Jenruary one thousand six hundreth forty & fiue

Ilanna Kicharell daughter of Samiwell Kecherell was born the forth of January one thousand six hundreth forty & fiue.

Elizabeth Samford daughter of Robbard Samford was borne Febuary the nynetenth one thousand six hundredth forty & fiue.

Debory Barttlett daughter of Roberd Bartlett was baptized March the eyghteth one thousand six hundreth forty & fiue.

Mabell Haynes daughter of Ma[r] John Haynes Esq[r] was borne March the ninetenth one thousand six hundreth forty & fiue

John Roott sunn of Thomas Rotte was horne the tenth of June one thousand six hundreth forty & six

Thom Silldeu sun of Thomas Silldin was baptized August y[e] thirtieth one thousand six hundreth forty & fiue.

John Whittmore sun of Thomas Whitmore was baptised Septem the sixth one thousand forty & six. [*sic.*]

Eli[zabeth] Koerbe daughter of John Koerbe [was . . . .] the eaighten (or eaighteth?) of September one thousand six hundreth forty & six.

PAGE 3.

John Andrewes suun of Francis Andrewes was baptised Sepm. the twenty and seuen on thousand six hundreth forty and six

Joseph Stone, sunn of Mr. Samwell Stone was baptised October the eaigteneth one thousand six hundreeth forty and six.

Samiwell Wadsworth sun of William Wadsworth was bapti[sed] Octobr. the twentyth one thousand six hundreth forty and six.

Samiwell Wrislea, sun of Richard Wrislea was baptised November the first one thousand six hundred forty and six.

Samiwell Holten, sun of William Holten was baptised Novem[r] the first one thousand six hundred forty and six.

John Felowes, sunn of Richard Felowes was baptised Novem[r] the first one thousand six hundreth forty and six.

Thomas Morrells son of Thomas Meeriels was baptised Nov[r] the first one thousand six hundreth forty and six.

Mary Olmsted daughter of Nicholas Olmsted was borne Noumb[r] the twentieth one thousand six hundreth forty & six.

Mary Steell, daughter of John Steel Jun[r] was borne Nov[r] the twentith one thousand six hundreth forty and six.

Mary Catteling was baptised Novem[r] the twenty and ninth one thousand six hundred forty and six.

Philip Lawes sun of Will. Lawes Jun[r] was baptised Desem the thortenth one thousand six hundreth forty and six.

Pheabe Disborow, daughter of Nicholas Disborow was baptised Desem 20th one thousand six hundreth forty and six.

Bazelels Tomsun daughter of Thomas Tomsun was baptised Jenouary the saunenth one thousand six hundreth forty and six.

Joseph Marsh, sunn of John Marsh was baptised Jenouary the twenty and forth one thousand six hundreth forty and six.

Daniel Garrod, sunn of Daniel Garrod was baptised Jenouary the twenty and forth one thousand six hundred forty and six.

PAGE 4.

Ruth Judg, daughter of Thomas Judg and Sara Coll, daughter of John Coll, both of Farmington ware baptised on Feabruary y[e] scuenth one thousand six hundreth forty and six.

Sara Crow, daughter of John Crow was borne March the first in the yeare of o[r] Lord one thousand six hundred forty and six.

Joseph Stanten, sunn of Thomas Stanten was baptysed March the twenty one in the yeare of o' Lord one thousand six hundred forty and six.

Samiwell Ellmer sun of Edword Ellmer was baptised March the twenty and one in the yeare of o' Lord one thousand six hundreth forty and six.

Sara Hulberd, daughter of William Hullberd was borne y° tenth of July one thousand six hundreth forty and seuen

Samewell Bloumfild sun of William Blomfilld was borne July the twelfth one thousand six hundreth forty and seuen.

Samewell Gridla, sun of Thomas Gridle was born y° twenty and fifth of Noue' 1647.

Abriham Brunson was baptised Noum the twenty and eaight one thousand six hundreth forty and seuen.

Siuon Kellsa sunn of William Kellsa was baptised Nouem' the seuenth one thousand six hundreth forty and seuen.

Sara Whitmore daughter of John Whitmore was born Deuem the sixteenth one thousand six hundreth forty and seuen.

(To be Continued.)

LETTER OF THE REV. JONA. PARSONS OF NEWBURYPORT.

Middletown, Conn., Dec. 12, 1857.

My Dear Sir:—I herewith send you, for insertion in your "Genealogical Register," a letter written at Newburyport, Mass., October 20, 1769, by the Rev. Jonathan Parsons to his son, Samuel H. Parsons of Lyme, Conn., giving his reminiscences of family history, which may, perhaps, interest some of his descendants. I give the whole letter, verbatim et literatim. You can publish what you please. I am

Very respectfully yours, &c.,
Samuel Holden Parsons.

Dear child :

I am glad to hear by yours of y° first & 10ᵗʰ Instant y' your health is restored, & pray God to give y° a heart to serve him in newness of Spirit. Sorry am I to find y° Ch⁸ are thrown into Confusion, & y° more so, as I understand much of y° Controversy is whether y° Children of those Parents who do not come to y° Lord's Table shall be baptized or not? My Judgement is y' no minister or Ch⁸ has a right to deny Baptism to those Children whose Parents openly profess good principles & lead a moral life, even tho' they do not come to y° Lord's Table. & I am very sorry D' Bellamy & others have stirred up Strife ab' y' Matter. I think they may be easily answered, and were I a minister in your Colony I believe I should think it my duty to enter y° List. I am persuaded if the Seperatists from Mr Edwards had an able Leader, Mr Edwards must either be convinced or removed. Mr. Bird is not his Match & perhaps those y' superate do not desire him if he was. I should be loth to stand in a special connection with a particular Church that goes into y' new Scheme. The like controversy gave great disturbance to y° protestant Church about 150 years ago, but was happily calmed by some ab'e Penn.

You write y' one Samuel Parsons from Martinico desires to know from w' part of England our Ancestors came. I will tell you as near as my Memory enables me, (as I have no records of the matter but what I heard from my Parent) I suppose my Great Grandfather Parsons came from Great-Torrington about 20 or 30 miles from Tiverton, and not far from Exeter. He came over and brought my Grandfather Benjamin Parsons and other children about 130 years ago, perhaps 140. I believe

y⁰ Record of my Great Grandfather and Grandfather might be found
either at Great Torrington or Tiverton, & by y' means it might be known
whether we & Samuel Parsons are descended from one Stock. My
great Grandfather Marshfield came from Exeter, and brought my Grandfather when he was ab' 4 years old. My Grandfather Marshfield's
name, I think was Samuel, and my great Grandfather's name Josiah ;
They came over about the same time with my great Grandfather Parsons
and his family. I should be glad if the history of the families could be
traced back as far as those y' first came over, for it might be of service
to some of their Descendants.

My love to my children and grand children & am your careful Father
    Newbury Port, Oct. 20. 1769.   J. Parsons.
      (addressed) Samuel H. Parsons Esq,
          Lyme,
            Connecticut

Benjamin Parsons, the grandfather of the Rev. Jonathan Parsons, mar-
ried Sarah Vore, October 6, 1653, the daughter of Richard Vore of
Windsor, Conn., and died in Springfield, Mass., August 24, 1689. [See
Gen. Reg., Vol. I., for July, p. 269.]

Samuel Marshfield (the maternal grandfather of the Rev. Jona. Parsons)
was the son of Thomas Marshfield, who is mentioned in 1640 as an
owner of lands in Windsor, Conn., but removed from Windsor about
1642. His son, Samuel Marshfield, married, March 18, 1651, *Hester*
Wright, the daughter of Deacon Samuel Wright, who settled in Springfield, Dec. 12, 1639, and had children : Sarah, d. May, 1653 ; Mary, b.
June 10, 1653 ; Thomas, b. Sept. 6, 1654 ; Sarah, b. Feb. 2, 1656 ;
Samuel, b. Aug. 20, 1661, m. Joseph Dedortha, July 24, 1634.

Hester, the wife of Samuel Marshfield, died at Springfield, April 3,
1664, in childbed, leaving a daughter, Abilene, b. April 2, 1664, who m.
Thomas Gilbert, Aug. 15, 1646. And on the 28th Dec., 1664, Samuel
Marshfield m. for his 2d wife, Mrs. Catherine Gilbert (the widow of
Thomas Gilbert), by whom he had four children, viz. :

    1. Josiah, b. Sept. 29, 1655 ; m. Rachel Gilbert, Sept. 22, 1686.
    2. Hester, b. Sept. 6, 1667 ; m. Ephraim Cotton, March 26, 1685.
    3. A child stillborn, Nov. 17, 1669.
    4. Margaret, b. Dec. 3, 1670 ; m. Ebenezer Parsons of Springfield,
the father of the Rev. Jonathan Parsons. [See Gen. Reg., Vol. I., p. 270.]

Mrs. Catherine Gilbert, the 2d wife of Samuel Marshfield, was the
daughter of Deacon Samuel Chapin, who removed from Braintree to
Springfield before the year 1643. She m., in 1646, Nathaniel Bliss of
Springfield, son of Thomas Bliss of Hartford, by whom she had four
children. She became a widow ; and, July 3, 1665, m. Thomas Gilbert,
who removed from Windsor to Springfield about 1655, Jan. 30, by whom
she had four children, and again became a widow ; and in 1664 m. Samuel Marshfield for her 3d husband, by whom she had four children, as
above mentioned.

Samuel Marshfield frequently represented the town of Springfield as a
deputy to the General Court, and held many important offices. He died
at Springfield about 1692. His son, Josiah Marshfield, on the 23d Dec.,
1692, presented an inventory of his estate before the Hon. John Pynchon,
Esq., Judge of the Probate of Wills, which is recorded at Northampton,
Mass., Vol. III., p. 3.

BOOK NOTICES.

*Remarks on Currency and Banking; having reference to the present
Derangement of the Circulating Medium in the United States. By
NATHAN APPLETON. Third Edition. With an Appendix. Boston:
1857. 8vo., pp. 63.*

[Prepared for the January number of the Register, but was crowded out by other matter.]

Mr. Appleton's pamphlet was published, in a first edition, in 1841, just as the country
was beginning to recover from the great pressure of 1837. That work was widely cir-
culated, and probably very extensively read, and therefore, had we spare, it would not
be necessary now to go into any analysis of its contents.

There has been a great deal written, and our newspapers have literally teemed with
"Causes of the Revulsion in Financial Affairs," and under similar captions; but the
real cause of the present depression may be set forth in a few words. *It is solely owing to
the credit system;* at the bottom of which lies banking. Hence it is very hard for any
one in the banking interest to set forth the real share which banks have in causing the
troubles in question. There is, therefore, much mystification in nearly every attempt of
a bank writer to explain the difficulty. By bank accommodations people can go on and
manufacture, import goods, and build palaces, until there are five, ten, twenty, &c.
times as many goods, houses, &c. &c. at cost value, as there is money in the country to
pay for them. Every man in any way engaged in business of the wholesale kind,
knows, or would know this on a few moments' reflection. The more extensive a man's
business, the more easy he can get credit, so long as he promptly meets his engagements. He gradually gets into the credit of various banks and firms, and borrows of
one to pay the other, until his expenses and discounts swallow all his profits. Then the
day is not far off in which he must fail; and his failure brings with it others; numerous,
or otherwise, according as his business is extended.

*Memorials of the Chaunceys, including President Chauncey, his Ances-
tors and Descendants. By WILLIAM CHAUNCEY FOWLER. Boston:
1858. 8vo., pp. 304.*

This work is an enlargement of the account of Chauncey given in the Register. The
additions are many and important, and have involved long and untiring research of
gentlemen every way capable of making it worthy of the subject. In the closing portion of his preface, the Editor (Prof. Fowler) mentions several gentlemen of the Chauncey Family who have promoted the undertaking; but from what we know of two of
them, namely, Nathaniel Chauncey, Esq. of Philadelphia, and William Chauncey, Esq.
of New York, he could with more propriety have given these gentlemen a more conspicuous place, as the prime movers in the matter; the former for his long and extensive research in England as well as America, and the latter for his liberality in obliging
the world with one of the most important genealogical works which has yet appeared.
But the Editor has no doubt said all they would allow him to say in those regards, as
they are gentlemen who do a good work for the art itself, and not for any praise from
others.

Some may think Mr. Fowler has rather overloaded some parts of his work from the
learned lore of the early days of the Chaunceys in this country. But every one must,
we think, acknowledge, that he has given us a volume of great interest and value. The
several tabular folding pedigrees of different branches of the family add very much to
the value of the work. And as to the mechanical part,—that is very beautiful, as all
the work from Messrs. Dutton & Son's press is, where they are allowed sufficient latitude
for the purpose.

*A Historical and Genealogical Record of the Descendants of Timothy
Rockwood. Born in Medway, July 5, 1727. Died in Holliston,
Feb. 21, 1806. Compiled from Authentic Sources. By E. L. Rock-
wood. Boston: 1856. 12mo., pp. 148. Index, &c. 5.*

The writer of the Rockwood Genealogy has chosen an admirable motto for his title-
page—"Children's children are the crown of old men; and the glory of children are
their fathers." *Proverbs,* 17 : 6.

It is rather singular that this family traces no farther back than 1695. It may be owing to the change of name; for this author tells us that "the Rockwoods, during the last part of the 16th and the first part of the 17th centuries, were called Rockets. Their names were pronounced Rocket and written Rocket in the old records." He begins with a Samuel Rocket, but in a note says the father and mother of this Samuel were John and Bethia of Medfield. "This Samuel," he continues, "was born a Rocket, lived a Rocket, but died a Rockwood." For aught we know to the contrary, Rocket may be as legitimate a surname as Rockwood.

This record of the Rockwood Family is a valuable accession to our New England Genealogies. It is printed in an intelligible manner, though we think not in the most approved form for such records. Its only references are by generations. In so small a book, this can be managed without much loss of time; but it would be a serious defect in an extensive work.

All persons engaged in compiling Genealogies for publication might very profitably consult the pages of the New Eng. Hist. & Gen. Register. In it they will see almost every mode of drawing up such work, and be able easily to choose those most experienced in such labors.

A Genealogical Chart of the Descendants of Gregory Dexter. By S. C. Newman, Member of the R. I. Historical Society, and Genealogical Secretary of the Blackstone Monument Association. Providence: 1857.

The above title is partly our own; the sheet containing the Dexter Genealogy, not having a special title. From the valuable information contained in the chart before us we learn that Gregory Dexter was born at Olney, County of North-Hampton, England, in 1610; that he was a printer in London, but gave up that business and came to New England with Roger Williams in 1644; that while a printer in London he printed for Mr. Williams his Indian Dictionary, [Key into the Indian Language.] Settling in Providence, Mr. Dexter became a preacher, and was the fourth Pastor of the First Baptist Church there. He died in the year 1700. The Christian name of his wife was Abigail, but her surname is not given. Mr. Dexter had children, Stephen, 1647; James, 1650; John, 1652; Abigail, 1655; and Peleg, 1658.

What this Chart or Table contains, is very clearly laid down, but there are some important omissions. It does not show who any of the individuals married; nor is the month or day of month of birth or death given. Indeed the Author's plan could not well admit them. If he had taken the ancient legal method, (which is unquestionably the best which has yet been devised for a Chart,) all these omissions could have been inserted in a space not more extensive than the facts on this sheet require.

We are heartily glad that Rhode Island has so able a genealogist in the field as Mr. Newman has shown himself to be, but it is our opinion he would satisfy himself and friends better, if he should adopt another plan for the display of his genealogical information.

History of the Town of Dorchester, Massachusetts. By a Committee of the Dorchester Antiquarian and Historical Society. No. 7. Boston: 1858. 8vo.

This number of the History of Dorchester carries the work to 438 pages. It is one of the most interesting of the series, and we hope the Publisher will not feel obliged to close the volume, so long as matter of so much interest remains to be had. The History of the Schools of that town is thoroughly gone into in the present part, and should interest every one in New England, as we have no doubt it would, could it be brought to the knowledge of all. This paper alone ought to ensure a place for the History of Dorchester in every School Library in New England.

*A Genealogical History of the Rice Family: Descendants of Deacon Edmund Rice, who came from Berkhamstead, England, and settled at Sudbury, Massachusetts, in 1638–1639; with an Index.....*By Andrew Henshaw Ward, A. M., Member of the New Eng. Historical and Gen. Soc., &c. &c. &c. Boston: 1858. 8vo., pp. 379.

Among our ablest, best qualified, and most industrious genealogists is the Author of the book before us. To recommend a work coming from his hand would be a labor of supererogation. What has been remarked respecting the Genealogical work on the Cushman Family applies well to this, with the exception of the numbering for reference from one individual to another, and the want of the means to designate the generations.

In all matters of reference, the Cushman genealogy is perfect. Mr. Ward has numbered his families. This we do not think important.

The Rice Family is beautifully printed, while it is at the same time economically printed; and shows at once that the printers, Messrs. Dutton, have experienced and careful men who not only superintend their work properly, but also that those employed by them are masters of their business. If the paper used was fully equal to the typography, there would have been little indeed to complain of.

The Life and Times of Alexander Hamilton. By SAMUEL M. SMUCKER, A. M., Author of " The Court and Reign of Catherine II.," " Emperor Nicholas I.," " Memorable Events in French History," etc. Boston and Chicago: 1857. Pp. 408.

At this distance from the closing scenes of the life of Alexander Hamilton, his course ought to be viewed by his biographer without bias or prejudice; but it is very difficult, if not impossible for any of us entirely to free ourselves from the influence of our early impressions. We have been taught to view Hamilton as a saint, and Aaron Burr as the impersonation of Satan himself. This view of the two men is undoubtedly wrong. The one was not so faultless as is generally imagined, nor the other so wicked as to prevent a rational inquiry into his motives and his actions. It may be safely said that if Hamilton had killed Burr in the fatal duel, the world would now look upon the two characters in an almost reversed relation. Time softens asperities, but time will not blot out the wrongs of one man towards another.

Our Author has given us a readable and authentic narrative of the *Life* of Hamilton, but we are rather of the opinion that he has claimed a little too much for him, notwithstanding his insertion of active partiality. We readily allow that it is much easier to make a saint of Hamilton than of Burr, while we do not believe that either of them had very strong claims to that character.

Messrs. Crown & Co. have published their work in a very handsome manner, and accompanied it with a fine portrait of Hamilton.

The Genealogy of the Descendants of Several Ancient Puritans, by the names of Adams, Bullard, Holbrook, Rockwood, Songer, Wood, Gross, Goulding, and Twitchell. By Rev. ABNER MORSE, A. M., Member of the N. E. Historical and Gen. Society. Boston: 1857. 8vo., pp. 355.

If Mr. Morse's remuneration is equal to his industry, it will be greatly to the credit of the numerous families for which he has labored so incessantly, and so successfully. It is a mystery to those acquainted with Mr. Morse, how he can possibly find time to perform so much labor; labor requiring the closest application, and the minutest scrutiny into conflicting statements, and examinations of Records often made by incompetent persons, and imperfect in themselves.

The volume before us is almost entirely made up of names and dates; therefore if there are errors in it, they ought to surprise no one; and we apprehend they should rather wonder there are so few. The work is illustrated with a large number of well executed lithographic portraits.

In his future works on Genealogy, we hope Mr. Morse will adopt the universally approved method of printing them together, so often recommended in the Register.

Oration, Poem, Speeches, Chronicles, &c., at the Dedication of the Malden Town Hall. On Thursday Evening, October 29th, 1857. Malden: 1857. Pp. 52.

The Oration on this occasion was by Gilbert Haven, Esq; the Poem by Dr. John L. Sullivan, and the Chronicles by C. C. P. Moody, Esq. The Orator took a wide range in his remarks; from Plymouth Rock to the Pyramids of Egypt. After the Poem, Mr. Wm. A. Richardson made some appropriate home remarks, as did several others. But Mr. Moody's "Chronicles" must have set gravity at defiance. If any one doubts our opinion, let him procure a copy of this curious pamphlet and decide for himself.

Proceedings of the Kilbourn Historical and Genealogical Society. 1857. 8vo., pp. 4.

This Association continues its activity, and judging from the " Proceedings " of the late meeting at " Kilbourn House," in the town of Milton, Ct., it was as interesting as any of its predecessors.

Charlemont as a Plantation.—An Historical Discourse at the Centennial Anniversary of the Death of Moses Rice, the first Settler of the Town, delivered at Charlemont, Mass., June 11, 1855. By Joseph White. Boston: 1856. 8vo., pp. 48.

The town of Charlemont has done a good act in taking the occasion of the death of its first Settler to have that event duly commemorated by a Discourse. This Discourse gives a very excellent outline of the History of the town, which was settled by Moses Rice in the Spring of 1743, and portrays in a clear and forcible manner the hardships to which the early settlers of the towns in New England were exposed.

Mr. White has been unable to ascertain from what circumstance the town received the name of Charlemont. Can any of our readers inform him? It was doubtless so named from a place of that name in Ireland or in France. Probably from that in the former country.

The American Almanac and Repository of Useful Knowledge, for the year 1856. Boston: 1857. 12mo., pp. 376.

The Proprietors and Publishers of this valuable, or we should rather say invaluable annual, contrive to keep it in a reasonably sized volume, and yet comprehensive enough for all practical purposes. It is an important recommendation to the American Almanac, that it progresses without any considerable change of its important features.

An Address delivered at West Springfield, August 25, 1856. On occasion of the 100th Anniversary of the Ordination of the Rev. Joseph Lathrop, D.D. By WILLIAM B. SPRAGUE, D.D., his Colleague and Successor in the Pastoral Office. With an Appendix. Springfield, Mass.: 1856. 8vo., pp. 101.

This effort of Dr. Sprague is exceedingly interesting, and as eloquent as it is interesting. About half of the pamphlet is occupied by the Appendix, chiefly in giving the proceedings of the occasion. Much valuable information was elicited from the various speakers, among whom were the Rev. Dr. Vermilye, Rev. Mr. Hawks, Mr. Wm. M. Lathrop, Rev. John Woodbridge, Rev. Erastus Hopkins, Rev. Dr. Osgood, Rev. A. A. Wood, Rev. Dr. Davis, Prof. Fowler, Rev. Henry M. Field, Judge Terry, &c.

A Sermon, in Two Parts, delivered on the Sabbath, June 28, 1856. The close of the 50th year of his Ministry, as Pastor of the First Church and Parish in Hingham, by JOSEPH RICHARDSON. Hingham 1856. 8vo., pp. 48.

In this very excellent Discourse, we have a notice of the predecessors of Mr. Richardson. Four only had been settled over that Church before him. Their names were Peter Hobart, John Norton, Ebenezer Gay, and Henry Ware. Mr. R. was ordained in 1806. Hence, in the fifty years now closed, he could say, as he does towards the end of his Sermon,—"Few remain in life with me to remember that day."

In the course of Mr. Richardson's time he has published a large number of Sermons and other tracts, and we hope to see a complete collection of them in the library of the N. England, &c. Society; of which Society he is a member.

Report of the Industrial Exhibition held in the Town of Waltham, Mass., Sept. 24, 1856. Boston: 1857. 8vo., pp. 79.

This is an exceedingly neat performance in all respects. The title of the work is a sufficient indication of what its contents are, and the names of the superintending Committee are good assurance that all parts were well performed. These gentlemen were J. B. Bright, Thomas Hill and Josiah Rutter. Mr. Banks, our present able Governor, was the principal speaker on the occasion.

The New Jersey Historical Society has issued Proposals to publish, "on the obtainment of a sufficient number of Subscribers," the 5th Vol. of its Collections. To contain "An Analytical Index to the Colonial Documents of New Jersey in the State Paper Offices of England; with Notes and Explanations and additional

References to Manuscripts in other depositories, by Wm. A. Whitehead, Corresponding Secretary of the Society."

This Circular contains a specimen of the manner in which the volume is to be executed. Judging by this, the work cannot fail to be one of great value, and of interest to many besides the inhabitants of New Jersey. The volume will contain about 600 pages, and be afforded at three dollars. But a small edition will be printed.

History of Cape Cod.

The Rev. Frederick Freeman, of Sandwich, is engaged upon an elaborate work, the title of which we learn is to be "The Annals of Barnstable County, and its several Towns, Sandwich, Barnstable, Yarmouth, Eastham, Harwich, Chatham, Falmouth, Truro, Provincetown, Wellfleet, Dennis, Orleans and Brewster, including the District of Mashpee." Any one will readily perceive, that Mr. Freeman has upon his hands work enough for the present; but we are happy to learn from him that he has his work in a forward state, and is desirous to begin to print in a short time.

New England Society of Quincy, Illinois.

The 22d of December last was appropriately observed by the New England people, residents of the flourishing city of Quincy. The supper, speeches and music, were, judging from the reports, all of a high order. Upwards of three hundred were assembled at the Quincy House on the occasion. The festivity was closed with dancing, which was probably kept up till a pretty early hour; for a reporter said the next day, " they were dancing then, for ought he knew."

LETTER OF GEN. WARREN.

CAMBRIDGE 24 APRIL 1775
In Committee of Congress

Gentlemen

The Committee of Congress have paid due attention to the Proposal of his Excellency to the Inhabitants of Boston & the Vote of the Town consequent thereto.

We cannot but commend the Generosity & Clemency of his Excellency's Disposition wh: inclines him to such a proposal, and approve the Wisdom of the Town in readily accepting the terms proposed,—respecting the poor Inhabitants of Boston, we cannot but repeat our advice that the Committee of Donations would employ the monies lodged in their Hands to facilitate their Removal; and when apprized of the time allowed for the departure of our suffering Brethren from the devoted Metropolis, we shall not fail to lend them our best assistance, by recommending to our friends in the Country to furnish Habitations to the unhappy fugitives on the lowest terms; respecting those who incline to seek a retreat in the Town of Boston, we shall exert our best Endeavours that they may pass with their Effects without Injury or Molestation.

We are Gentlemen
with great Esteem &
Affection
Your most obedient Humble Servant
JOSEPH WARREN   *Chairman*

To the Selectmen, and other respectable
Inhabitants of the Town of Boston

MARRIAGES AND DEATHS.

MARRIAGES.

DUDLEY, Mr. Elbridge Gerry, to Miss Martha A., third dau. of the late Stephen Child, Esq., 19 Nov. 1857, by the Rev. E. E. Hale, all of Boston.

EDGERLY, Mr. Norman F., to Miss Mary Emma, eldest dau. of the late Alexander Gibbs, 31 Jan., by the Rev. D. M. Graham, all of New York.

FILLMORE, Hon. Millard (late President of the United States, and Honorary Vice-President of the N. England Historical, &c. Society) to Mrs. Caroline C. McIntosh of Albany, at Albany, 10 Feb.

PUTNAM, Schuyler, Esq., (only surviving grandson of Gen. Israel Putnam,) of Elyria, Ohio, to Mrs. Demafoot of Dover, O., 6 Dec. 1857, at Jamestown, Chatauque Co., N. Y., by the Rev. J. W. Allen.

SANBORN, Joseph H., M. D., to Miss Hannah M. Mendy of Gilmanton, 9 Oct. 1857, at Concord, by the Rev. Jacob Sanborn, father of the bridegroom.

WHITMORE, Mr. J. W., to Miss Lizzie E. Lane, Aug. 1857, at Hampden, Me., by the Rev. Joseph Whitmore.

WHITMORE, Capt. Parker M., to Miss Mary E. Blair, both of Richmond, Me., 1 Dec. 1857.

DEATHS.

ABBOTT, Mr. Herman, Andover, 3 Feb., æ. 86 yrs. 11 mos.

ALDEN, Capt. Amasa, Dedham, 7 Dec., æ. 86.

ALGER, Mr. Abiel, Winchendon, 24 Jan., æ. 85 yrs. 7 mos.

ANDREWS, Mr. Daniel, New Salem, 7 Dec., æ. 85. He had lived with his wife (still surviving) sixty years.

ARNO, Mr. Jonathan, Foxcroft, Me., 1 Aug., æ. 85.

BAILEY, Dea. Josiah, Fitchburg, 5 Jan., æ. 89 yrs. 11 mos.; formerly of Townsend.

BELKNAP, Andrew Eliot, Esq., Boston, 23 Jan., æ. 78. He was son of the Rev. Jeremy Belknap, the eminent historian; also fond of historical studies, and frequently made communications relative to past men and things in Boston to the newspapers, which he signed "Boston Boy."

BENJAMIN, Mrs. Catharine, North Adams, 22 Jan., æ. 71.

BINNEY, Mrs. Lydia, E. Cambridge, 23 Jan., æ. 84 yrs. 3 mos.; widow of the late Benjamin Binney.

BLAKE, William, Woburn, 1 Feb. He was born in Boston, 28 Feb. 1776, son of James and Elizabeth, and was a lineal descendant, in the sixth generation, from William and Agnes Blake, who settled in Dorchester in 1630. He died suddenly, in consequence of an injury received by a fall five days previous, and was interred in Boston.

BRADFORD, Mr. Isaac, Woonsocket, R. I., 5 Jan., in his 74th year; formerly of Plympton, Ms.

BROWN, Mr. Josiah, Bennington, Vt., 20 Jan., in his 82d year.

BUTLER, Mr. Charles Paxton, Charleston, S. C., 16 Jan., ae. 95; a native of Boston, but for 70 years a resident of C.

CARPENTER, Miss Anna Banks, Keene, N. H., 9 Jan., ae. 86.

CATRELL, James, Rochester, 24 Jan., aa. 70 yrs. 6 mos.

CHADWICK, Mrs. Abigail, Hopkinton, N. H., 21 Jan., ae. 83 yrs. 7 mos.

CHANDLER, Mrs. Margaret, Hopkinton, N. H., 21 Nov., ae. 81; widow of the late Josiah Chandler.

CHILD, Stephen, Esq., Boston, 3 Feb. 1857, ae. 89 yrs. 11 mos.

CHILDS, Mr. David, New Salem, 13 Jan., ae. 97.

CHIPMAN, Capt. Ward, Salem, 20 Jan., ae. 78 yrs. 3 mos.

CLEVELAND, Mr. Ezra, Edgerton, 9 Aug., ae. 81.

COBB, Mrs. Rebecca B., Dorchester, at the residence of her son, Moses G. Cobb, Esq., 15 Jan., ae. 50.

COFFIN, Mrs. Sophronia Richards, Brookline, 18 Jan., ae. 54; wife of Capt. George Coffin.

COLBURN, Mrs. Catharine S., Groton, 18 Jan., æ. 77 yrs. 7 mos. 15 days; widow of the late Calvin Colburn of Boston. She was the last and youngest of eleven children of Isaac and Mary (Lawrence) Lakin of Groton.

COOK, Mr. Zebedee, Framingham, 24 Jan., æ. 72; formerly an enterprising citizen of Boston. He was a native of Newburyport, where he was born 11 Jan. 1786. He came to reside in Boston in 1810. Several years he served in the Legislature. In 1838 he removed to New York. Last summer he took up his residence in Framingham, having retired from active business.—*Daily Advertiser.*

CRANE, Larra, Esq., South Boston, 4 Feb., æ. 73 yrs. 10 mos.; a well known citizen. He had been in the Common Council from Ward 3, 1830-2, and in the Board of Aldermen in 1843 and 1844.

CURTIS, Joseph, Esq., Jamaica Plain, 13 Feb., æ. 86 yrs. 6 mos. "Few men have passed through life more honorably, and few leave behind them a more unblemished reputation."

DEAN, Mrs. Sarah A., Roxbury, 27 Jan., æ. 76; widow of the late Wm. S. Dean.

DEARBORN, Mr. Reuben L., Nashua, N. H., 24 Oct.; a soldier of the war of 1812.

DEGAN, Mr. Patrick, Portland, Me., 19 Oct., æ. 100; a native of Ireland.

DODSON, Mr. John, Newburyport, 25 Dec., æ. 94 yrs. 6 mos.

DRAKE, Mrs. Eunice, Fiskdale, 30 Jan., æ. 79; wife of Mr. Simeon Drake, formerly of Easton.

DUNHAM, Mrs. Mary Ann, South Boston, 16 Feb., æ. 61; widow of the late Josiah Dunham, Esq., and dau. of Capt. Wm. Elmer, deceased.

ECKERLY, Joseph, Esq., Epping, N. H., 28 Oct., æ. 91. He was many years a member of the Legislature of that State.

EVERETT, Mr. William, Everettville, 7 Dec., æ. 92 yrs. 7 mos. William, Joshua and Rhoda Everett, with an adopted girl, were the only children of their father's family. They always lived within a few miles of each other. Joshua died in Feb. 1851, æ. 84; Rhoda in 1853, æ. 83; Mrs. Whitney, their adopted sister, in Oct. 1857, æ. 92; William as before mentioned. Their united ages were 331 years.

FILLEBROWN, Mrs. Mary, Watertown, Dec. 1857, æ. 79; widow of Mr. John Fillebrown.

FOLSOM, Martha J., Cambridge, 13 Jan., æ. 16 yrs. 5 mos.; only dau. of Nathaniel Folsom of Gilmanton, N. H.

FOOTE, Mrs. Mary Wilder, Salem, 24 Dec., æ. 47 yrs. 12 days, wife of Hon. Caleb F.

GALE, Mrs. Anna, Hopkinton, N. H., 22 Dec., æ. 76; a native of Amesbury, Ms.

GIBSON, Mr. Joseph, Great Barrington, 25 Jan., in his 84th year.

GOLDTHWAIT, Mr. Luther, Salem, 11 Oct., æ. 71 yrs. 9 mos.

GRAFTON, Rev. Benjamin C., Cambridge, 12 Jan., æ. 77.

GREEN, Mrs. Eunice, Lowell, Jan., æ. 87; widow of the late Rev. Aaron Green of Andover.

HACKET, Mrs. Zilpha, Middleboro', Ms., 31 Aug., æ. 92 yrs. 10 mos. 4 ds.; widow of George, by whom she was a pensioner. Mrs. H. was a dau. of Jonathan Shaw of Carver, and married, first, —— Coggeswell. She received two pensions in right of both husbands, for services in the war of independence.

HATHAWAY, Hon. Elnathan P., Freetown, 23 Jan., æ. 50; a respected member of the Bristol bar.

HATHAWAY, Mr. John, Watertown, 27 Dec., æ. 71; formerly of Boston.

HAYDEN, Mr. Samuel, Shelburne, 11 Feb., æ. 92 yrs. 6 mos. 24 ds.

HINCKLEY, Mrs. Esther, Milton, 3 Jan., æ. 79; widow of the late Capt. Robert Hinckley.

HOYT, George Ann, M. D., Framingham, 15 Oct., æ. 52 yrs. and 32 days; son of Dr. Enos H. of the same town. He was b. in Northfield, N. H., 13 Sept. 1825, grad. D. C. 1847, took his degree of M. D. at Harvard C. 1851, after which he practiced medicine successfully, in connection with his father, in Framingham. He was a much beloved young gentleman wherever he was known, and in his practice discovered a wonderful insight into the causes of disease. No obituary can do him justice in our confined limits.

HUBBARD, Mrs. Lucinda (Noble), Hadley, 29 Oct. 1858, æ. 83 yrs. and 5 mos., wid. of the late Elisha Hubbard. Her descent from *Thomas Noble* of Boston, Springfield and Westfield, is as follows, viz:

Thomas Noble, was adm. an inhabitant of Boston, Jan. 5, 1652, (doubtless 1652-3) removed the same year to Springfield, and about 1669 to Westfield, where he d. Jan. 20, 1704. M. Nov. 1, 1660, Hannah Warriner, b. in Springfield, Aug 17, 1643, only dau. of Wm. Surviving Mr. N., she m. Jan. 24, 1705, Dea. Medad Pomeroy of Northampton, and d. prior to May 12, 1731.

Thomas Noble, deacon, second son of Thomas and Hannah, b. in Springfield, Jan. 14, 1666; d. in Westfield, July 29, 1750, æ. 84; m. Dec. 19, 1695, Elizabeth Dewey, who d. Oct. 2, 1737, doubtless dau. of Thomas, and b. in Westfield, Jan. 10, 1676.

Thomas Noble, eldest son of Thomas and Elizabeth, b. in Westfield, Sept. 10, 1696; d. in Westfield, Feb. 18, 1775, æ. 78. M. (1) Sept. 1, 1722, Sarah Root, b. in Westfield, March 9, 1702, dau. of John and Sarah. She d. July 19, 1760, æ. 58; m. (2) about 1761, (published April 11, 1761,) Sarah Belding of Hatfield. She d. in Westfield, Aug. 17, 1763, æ. 62.

Stephen Noble, second son of Thomas and Sarah, b. in Westfield, April 14, 1727; d. in Westfield, April 2, 1761, æ. 64; m. March 7, 1753, Bath Church, b. in Springfield, July 11, 1733, dau. of Dea. Jonathan. She d. in Hadley, July 6, 1794, æ. 61.

Lucinda Noble, youngest child of Stephen, b. in Westfield, Jan. 27, 1774; d. in Hadley, Oct. 29, 1857. M. Feb. 9, 1797, Elisha Hubbard, b. in Hadley, June 6, 1766, son of Edmund and Margaret. He d. Feb. 24, 1837, æ. 58. She had seven children, all of whom survived her. L. M. B.

HUDSON, Mr. Daniel, West Stafford, Ct., 19 Dec., æ. 69.

HUNT, Mrs. Sarah, Longmeadow, 23 Jan., æ. 90.

KINNICUT, Hon. Thomas, Worcester, 12 Jan., æ. 58; Judge of Probate for Worcester County.

KINGMAN, Gen. Joseph, Coraville, Me., 25 Dec., æ. 77.

LAMSON, Mr. Asa, Salem, 6 Feb., æ. 75.

LEONARD, Mr. Henry, Springfield, 31 Jan., æ. 59.

LUNT, Deac. Ezra, Newburyport, 29 Dec., æ. 78.

McLANE, Hon. Louis, Baltimore, Md., æ. upwards of 70; he was U. S. Senator from Delaware in 1827. In 1829 he was appointed Minister to England; in 1831 was made Secretary of the Treasury of the U. S.; in 1833 Secretary of State, and succeeded Mr. Everett as Minister to England in 1845.

MARSH, Mr. John, South Danvers, 29 Jan., in his 80th year.

MARSH, Mr. Moses R., Quincy, 26 Dec., æ. 73.

MINOT, Mrs. Louisa, Boston, 21 Jan., æ. 70; wife of William Minot, Esq.

MITCHELL, Mr. Louis, Newport, R. I., 28 Dec., æ. 92; a native of France.

MOORE, Mrs. Sarah Fiske, Boston, 4 Feb., æ. 71; wife of the Rev. Martin Moore, and dau. of Mr. Moses Fiske of Natick. They were married in 1814.

MORSE, Dr. Elijah, Watertown, 9 Jan., a. 96 yrs. 11 mo. "Dr. Morse was a native of that part of Shrewsbury now W. Boylston, and came to Watertown more than fifty years ago. At one time in his life he owned the only packet then running between Boston and London, a ship called the 'Galen.' The destruction of a large amount of his property on sea by the French, gave him a claim upon the government, which he has prosecuted with great pertinacity during the latter part of his life. His age was 96 yrs. 10 mos. and 25 days, as inscribed on the plate on his coffin. His funeral took place from his late residence yesterday afternoon. The services were conducted by the Rev. Mr. Bradford of the First Unitarian Church, at which the deceased was a constant attendant during his life-time, and by the venerable Dr. Francis of Harvard University, who, in the fulfilment of a promise exacted from him years before his death, came to speak at his funeral. The remains were deposited in the family tomb in the old burying ground in this town, and were followed to their final resting place by his only remaining relatives.—*Journal*, 13 Jan., 1858.

NORTON, Rev. Jacob, Billerica, 17 Jan., (Sunday morning,) æ. 93 years, 11 mo. 5 days.

"Mr. Norton was the son of Samuel Norton; was born in Abington, Mass., on the 13th of February, 1764. He graduated with distinction at Harvard in 1786; and at the time of his death was the oldest surviving graduate of the College. He was ordained over the Congregational Church in Weymouth, on the 10th of October, 1787, where he continued his pastoral labors for thirty-seven years, until 1824, when he resigned his charge, and a few years afterwards removed to Billerica, where he resided during the remainder of his long life. Mr. Norton retained his mental and physical powers to a remarkable degree until past the age of 90. For the last year or two he spent most of his time during the day reading, and without glasses, which he never used, with the exception of a short time, and then laid them aside as useless."—*Daily Advertiser.*

OSGOOD, Mrs. Elizabeth, Marblehead, 22 Jan., æ. 76.

PARMENTER, Mrs. Martha, Boston, 4 Feb., æ. 69; widow of Mr. George P., formerly of Webster.

PARROTT, Mr. James, Lynn, 9 Aug., æ. 87.

PARSONS, Mr. James, Boston, 23 Dec., æ. 85; Pilot for many years in this port. He leaves a wife, one dau., numerous grand and great-grand children, and also six great-great-grand children.

PARSONS, Mrs. Sabra Bicknell, Cambridge, 27 Jan., æ. 48; widow of the late William Parsons of Boston.

PATTERSON, Mr. Chester, Newark Valley, Tioga Co., N. Y., 22 Sept. 1857, of dropsy, æ. 73.

He was oldest son of Amos and Anne (Williams) Patterson; was born in Richmond, Mass., Sept. 24th, 1777, and removed with his father to Union, Broome Co., N. Y., where he arrived 23 Feb. 1793.

He was Sheriff of Broome County from 1809 to 1813; represented the County in the State Legislature from 1819 to 1821 inclusive; and was one of the Presidential Electors for the State of New York in 1824, giving his vote for John Quincy Adams. He was Town Clerk of Union for many years, and otherwise much engaged in the service of the town.

In 1839 he removed with his family to Newark Valley, where he spent the remainder of his life. He was a man of great liberality—a friend to the poor—earnestly interested in every work of improvement, and of unflinching honesty and integrity.

PEARSON, Mrs. Martha, South Lancaster, 13 Jan., æ. 94; widow of the late Joseph Pearson, formerly of Sterling.

PERRY, Mrs. Elizabeth Champlin, Newport, 11 Feb., æ. 67; widow of Commodore Oliver Hazard Perry, widely known for her unassuming Christian character, as well as for her being the widow of one so distinguished in American annals. Since her husband's death, in 1820, she has resided in Newport, occupying the same mansion that her husband purchased at the close of the war of 1812. She had for her neighbor and friend the widow of the lamented Lawrence of the Chesapeake, still living. A daughter of Mrs. Perry is wife of the Rev. Dr. Francis Vinton of Trinity Church, New York.

PHIPPEN, Abraham, Salem, 5 Dec., æ. 58.

PIERCE, Mrs. Lucy (Tappan) Brookline, 12 Feb., æ. 90 yrs. 7 mo.; widow of the late Rev. John Pierce, D. D. She is descended, according to the Franklin memoranda, published in vol. xi, p. 19, from Mary, sister of Dr. Benj. Franklin.

PILLSBURY, Mr. Caleb, Neponset, 31 Jan., æ. 77; formerly of Candia, N. H.

PUFFER, Mr. Jepthah, W. Cambridge, 13 Dec., æ. 69.

PYNCHON, Mrs. Mary, Great Barrington, 4 Feb., æ. 90; widow of Mr. Walter Pynchon.

RANDOLPH, St. George, Charlotte Co., Va., 4 Dec. 1857; nephew of John Randolph of Roanoke.

RIPLEY, Miss Damaris, Oakham, 19 Jan., æ. 90 yrs. 11 mo.

RIPLEY, Mrs. Tabitha, North Adams, 3 Feb., æ. 87; widow of Mr. Eleazar Ripley.

ROBINSON, Mr. Zachens, Southboro', 17 Jan., æ. 93; a revolutionary soldier.

SANBORN, Miss Abbie J., East Kingston, N. H., 27 Oct. 1857, æ. 20 yrs. 5 mo. 11 days, dau. of Stevens S., Esq. She was a teacher of great merit, and her death caused not only regret, but genuine sorrow for a loss which all felt could not be made up to them.

SANBORN, Miss Laura A., Epping, N. H., 13 Oct., of quick consumption, æ. 25 yrs., dau. of the late Jeremiah Sanborn, Esq.

SANBORN, Rev. Peter, Reading, 6 Aug. 1857, æ. nearly 90 yrs. He was born at Kingston, N. H., 13 Aug., 1767; son of Lt. William S., b. 1 May, 1723, who was son of Deac. Tristram S., b. 1683, who was 40 years Deac. of the Congregational Church of Kingston, N. H. The Rev. Peter S., æ. 1st, Polly Stimpson of Reading, 26 May, 1798, b. 7 Jan., 1781, d. 15 Oct., 1818; m. 2d, Martha Wakefield of Dublin, N. H., 10 Nov. 1819; she was b. 11 April, 1768, d. 2 May, 1847. Mr. Sanborn was ord. pastor of the 1st Cong. Ch. in Reading, 7 June, 1790. He was a grad. D. C., 1768; had 14 children. Two of his sons succeeded him in the ministry. The Rev. Ivley Fiske Sanborn settled in New York, and the Rev. George Edwards S. is pastor of the Congregational Church in Georgia, Vt.

SALTONSTALL, Mrs. Mary Elizabeth, Salem, 11 Jan., æ. 70; widow of the late Hon. Leverett Saltonstall. She was dau. of Thomas Sanders, Esq., merchant of Salem.

SECOMB, Mr. John, Salem, 5 Dec., æ. 83.

SHERMAN, Mrs. Delight, North Dartmouth, 2 Feb., æ. 98 yrs. 4 mo., widow of Zoeth Sherman.

SNOW, Capt. Anthony, Dighton, 4 Jan., in his 71st year.

SMITH, Deac. Isaac, Hopkinton, N. H., Jan. æ. 91 yrs., 6 mo., a native of Rowley, Mass.

SMITH, Seth, Amherst, Dec. 15, 1856, æ. 81 yrs. and 5 mos. His descent from Lt. Samuel Smith of Wethersfield and Hadley, is as follows:

Samuel Smith, sailed "the last of April 1634" from old England for New England in the Elizabeth of Ipswich, resided in Wethersfield and Hadley, in both of which places he was a leading man "in church and state," and died in Hadley, Dec. 1680 or Jan. 1681, æ. about 82: M. Elizabeth ———, who d. March 16, 1685, æ. 90.

Philip Smith, son of Samuel, born in England; d. in Hadley, (where he had been deacon, lieutenant, representative, &c.) Jan. 10, 1684–5, "murdered by a hideous witchcraft," according to Cotton Mather. M. Rebecca Foot, b. about 1634, dau. of Nathaniel of Wethersfield, Conn. Surviving Mr. Smith, she m. 1688, Dea. Aaron Cook of Northampton, and died April 8, 1701.

John Smith, deacon, 2d son of Philip, b. in Hadley, Dec. 16, 1661, died in same place, April 16, 1727, æ. 65. M. Nov. 29, 1683, Joanna Kellogg, b. Dec. 8, 1664, dau. of Joseph and Joanna.

John Smith, eldest son of John, born in Hadley, 1684; lived for a time in Hadley, but removed thence to South Hadley, where he d. Dec. 25, 1761, æ. 77 yrs. M. Esther Colton, b. Oct. 23, 1687, dau. of Ephraim. She died about 1771, æ. about 84.

Eleazer Smith, deacon, son of John, b. Jan. 27, 1725–6, resided in Longmeadow, Peru, Wilbraham and Amherst, dying in Amherst, Jan. 4, 1816, æ. 90. M. (1) Lydia Thomas, b. in Lebanon, Ct., Jan. 29, 1725. M. (2) Abigail White, b. in Longmeadow, Feb. 8, 1733. She d. in Amherst, June 24, 1812, æ. 77.

Seth Smith, only son of Eleazer and Abigail, b. in Wilbraham, July 12, 1775; d. in Amherst, Dec. 15, 1856. M. Feb. 21, 1798, Levina Jackson, b. in Woodstock, Ct., Oct. 1, 1771, dau. of Nehemiah and Esther. She d. in Amherst, Dec. 26, 1852, æ. 81.   L. M. B.

STEVENS, Ebenezer, M. D., Hopkinton, N. H., 15 Jan., of disease of the heart; for many years a practising physician in South Boston, and for a time held a place in the Custom House. He was a native of Henniker, N. H.

STICKNEY, Capt. Amos, Auburn, N. H., 17 Jan., æ. 69; a native of Beverly, Ms.

STOCKTON, Francis B., Purser U. S. N., Baltimore, 5 Jan., æ. 68.

STRAIGHT, Henry, Springfield, Ashtabula Co., O., 10 Jan., æ. 97; a native of Warwick, R. I., where he was b. 3 July, 1760. At 14 years of age he enlisted into the army of the Revolution, and served throughout the war. He also served in the war of 1812, as a lieutenant, and was in the battle of Plattsburg, and other skirmishes.

SWEETSER, Mrs. Hannah, Boston, Dec., in her 86th year; widow of the late Samuel Sweetser of Athol.

TAYLOR, Danforth, Esq., Stoddard, N. H., 4 Jan., æ. 88.

TAYLOR, Mrs. Mary, Ashfield, 26 Jan., æ. 92; widow of the late Ezekiel Taylor.

THOMPSON, Mrs. Abigail, Middleboro', Ms., 21 July, æ. 91 yrs. 5 mos. 27 days; wife of Mr. Moses Thompson, who survives her, at the age of 95 yrs. on 1 July last. He is of the fourth generation from Lt. John Thompson, the ancestor of all the Thompsons in Middleboro', &c. She was the dau. of Capt. Thomas Sampson of Halifax, gr. dau. of Thomas, and gr. gr. dau. of Benjamin, who was son of George, a first settler of Plympton. Mr. Moses and Abigail had lived in married relation 75 years. w.

TINKHAM, Mr. Levi, Middleboro', Ms., 17 Sept., æ. 91 yrs. 9 mos. 29 days. He was the youngest child of the seven sons and three daus. of John, jr. and Jerusha (Vaughan, dau. of John, jr.) His emigrant ancestor was Ephraim[1] Tinkham of Plymouth, whose eldest child, Ephraim,[2] jr., m. Estar Wright before 1680, and came (with most or all of his brothers with him, or afterwards) to Middleboro', where he died 13 Oct. 1714, æ. 55. His eldest child, John,[3] whose birth is not in the O. C. records, but in the Middleboro' proprietors' records—20 Aug. 1680—was grandfather of Mr. Levi.[5] John[4] m. Hannah Howland, 1716, and died 14 April, 1766, æ. 85 yrs. 8 mos. His widow died 25 March, 1792, æ. 97 yrs. 5 mos. She was long blind, but retained her mental powers. On the mention of the Mayflower, she would say, "I know all about that." By her request, she united (at her house) with the First church, Middleboro', in 1788. [See Descriptive Catalogue, No. 395.]

Mr. T. m. in 1793, Mary, the dau. of Thomas Foster, and gr. dau. of Rev. Peter Thacher of Middleboro'. She died 19 March, 1826, æ. 60½ yrs. They had three sons and three daus., all of whom have families in M., excepting the second son, Boland, who died 2 May, 1854, æ. 56½ years.

Mr. T. passed a life of much regularity and industry,—not neglecting the improvement of a gifted mind,—by judicious reading and research, so far as compatible with his daily engagements as a mechanic in wood, and a farmer.

He was a subscriber for Rees' Encyclopedia. Whatever he did as a mechanic—and people thought he could make anything—was ingeniously and well done. w.

TREADWELL, Mrs. Dorothy, Salem, 29 Jan., æ. 80 yrs. 11 mos.

TURNER, Mr. William, Provincetown, 24 Dec., æ. 77.

VAN RENSSELAER, Miss Adeline, Cherry Hill, near Albany, 16 Jan., eldest dau. of the late Gen. Solomon Van Rensselaer.

WADLEIGH, Mrs. Nancy D., Laconia, N. H., 9 Dec., æ. 52; wife of Col. Simeon Wadleigh.

WARNER, Andrew F., Cromwell, Ct., 24 July, 1857, æ. 35 years; son of Andrew Warner of Haddam, Ct. He was a gentleman much respected for his intelligence, enterprise and public spirit—qualities which led him to enter warmly into plans for the improvement, material, moral and intellectual. He highly approved of the objects of the New England Historical, &c. Society, and was one of its promising members. His loss is severely felt among all who knew him.

WAINMAN, Rev. Ebenezer, Racine, Wis., 29 Dec., æ. 65; a native of Hardwick, Ms.

WASHBURN, Mrs. Sylvia, Portland, Me., 4 Jan., æ. 84.

WEED, Hon. Jared, Petersham, 6 Aug., æ. 74.

WELLINGTON, Mr. Amos, Ashley, 20 Nov., 1857, æ. 67 yrs. 7 mos. 15 days. [See Bond's Watertown.]

WHEELOCK, Col. Hiram, Boston, 16 Aug., æ. 63.

WHITMORE, Harriet Elizabeth, Hingham, 31 Oct. 1857, æ. 44 yrs. 7 mos.; wife of Henry Whitmore.

WHITTEMORE, Mrs. Deborah, Malden, 12 Dec. 1857, æ. 75; widow of Benj. Whittemore, formerly of Bennington, N. H.

WHITTLESEY, Mr. Henry N., Roxbury, 12 Feb., æ. 30 yrs. 4 mos. 20 days. He leaves a wife and one child.

WINSLOW, Mrs. Henrietta, Roxbury, 24 Jan., æ. 70; widow of the late Isaac Winslow.

WINSOR, Capt. James, Duxbury, 21 Dec., æ. 68.

WORCESTER, Mrs. William, Fitzwilliam, N. H., 5 Feb., æ. 98.

WYATT, Mrs. Sophia, Georgetown, 31 Dec., æ. about 78; wife of Mr. Samuel Wyatt, the well known hotel keeper of Dover, and recently of the Marlboro' hotel, Boston. Mrs. W. published, not long before her death, some account of her experience in instituting temperance hotels, &c., in a 12mo. volume.

WYETH, Mrs. Elizabeth J., Cambridge, 20 Jan., æ. 90; widow of the late Jacob Wyeth.

Officers of the New England Historical and Genealogical Society for the Year 1858.

President,
SAMUEL G. DRAKE, Esq., of Boston.

Vice Presidents,

Massachusetts.   Hon. FRANCIS BRINLEY of Boston.
Maine.   Hon. WILLIAM WILLIS of Portland.
New Hampshire.   Hon. NOAH MARTIN of Dover.
Vermont.   Rev. JOHN WHEELER, D. D., of Burlington.
Rhode Island.   Hon. WILLIAM R. STAPLES of Providence.
Connecticut.   Rev. LEONARD BACON, D. D., of New Haven.

Honorary Vice Presidents,

New York.   Hon. Millard Fillmore of Buffalo.
New Jersey.   Hon. Joseph C. Hornblower of Newark.
Pennsylvania.   Hon. Samuel Breck of Philadelphia.
Maryland.   S. F. Streeter, Esq., of Baltimore.
North Carolina.   Edward Kidder, Esq., of Wilmington.
South Carolina.   Rev. Thomas Smyth, D. D., of Charleston.
Ohio.   Hon. Elijah Hayward of McConnellsville.
Michigan.   Hon. Lewis Cass of Detroit.
Indiana.   Hon. Ballard Smith of Cannelton.
Illinois.   Hon. John Wentworth of Chicago.
Wisconsin.   Cyrus Woodman, Esq., of Mineral Point.
Iowa.   Rt. Rev. Henry W. Lee, D. D., of Davenport.

Corresponding Secretary,
Rev. SAMUEL H. RIDDEL of Boston.

Recording Secretary,
WILLIAM M. CORNELL, M. D., of Boston.

Treasurer,
Mr. ISAAC CHILD of Boston.

Librarian,
Mr. EDWARD HOLDEN of Roxbury.

Historiographer,
JOSEPH PALMER, M. D., of Boston.

Standing Committees:

On Publication.	On Finance.
Rev. William Jenks, D. D., of Boston.	Sylvester Bliss, Esq., of Roxbury.
Hon. Francis Brinley of Boston.	Mr. William E. Baker of Boston.
Hon. Timothy Farrar of Dorchester.	Jacob Q. Kettrile, Esq., of Boston.
Mr. John Ward Dean of Boston.	Mr. C. Benj. Richardson of Boston.
Mr. William H. Whitmore of Boston.	Mr. Isaac Child of Boston, (*ex officio.*)

On the Library.
Mr. Thomas J. Whitmore of Cambridge.
William Makepeace, Esq., of Boston.
Horace G. Barrows, M. D., of Boston.
Mr. Edward S. Rand, Jr., of Boston.
Mr. Edward Holden of Roxbury, (*ex officio.*)

New England Historical and Genealogical Society.

OFFICERS.

Presidents,

*Charles Ewer, Esq., of Boston, Mass. — Jan. 1845, to Jan. 1850
Rev. Joseph Barlow Felt, LL.D., of Boston, — " 1850, to " 1853
William Whiting, Esq., of Roxbury, — " 1853, to " 1856
Samuel Gardner Drake, M. A., of Boston, — " 1856.

Vice Presidents,

Lemuel Shattuck, Esq., of Boston, — Jan. 1845, to Jan. 1850
Rev. Lucius Robinson Paige, of Cambridge, — " 1850, to " 1851
Nathaniel B. Shurtleff, M. D., of Boston, — " 1851, to " 1853
Hon. Timothy Farrar, of Boston and Dorchester, — " 1853, to " 1855
Hon. William Willis, of Portland, Me. — " 1855.
Hon. Noah Martin, of Dover, N. H. — " 1855.
Rev. John Wheeler, D. D., of Burlington, Vt. — " 1855.
Hon. William R. Staples, of Providence, R. I. — " 1855.
*Hon. Nathaniel Goodwin, of Hartford, Ct. — " 1855, to May, 1855
Rev. Leonard Bacon, D. D., of New Haven, Ct. — Aug. 1855.
Hon. Francis Brinley, of Boston, — Jan. 1858.

Honorary Vice Presidents,

Hon. Millard Fillmore, of Buffalo, N. Y. — Jan. 1855.
Hon. Lewis Cass, LL.D., of Detroit, Mich. — " 1855.
Hon. Elijah Hayward, of Columbus and McConnelsville, O. — " 1855.
Hon. John Wentworth, of Chicago, Ill. — " 1855.
*Rev. John Lauris Blake, D. D., of Orange, N. J. — " 1856, to July, 1857
Hon. Samuel Breck, of Philadelphia, Pa. — " 1856.
Sebastian Ferris Streeter, Esq., of Baltimore, Md. — " 1856.
Edward Kidder, Esq., of Wilmington, N. C. — " 1856.
Rev. Thomas Smyth, D. D., of Charleston, S. C. — " 1856.
Hon. Ballard Smith, of Cannelton, Ind. — " 1856.
Cyrus Woodman, Esq., of Mineral Point, Wis. — " 1856.
Rt. Rev. Henry W. Lee, D. D., of Davenport, Iowa, — " 1856.
*Andrew Randall, Esq., of San Francisco, Cal. — " 1856, to July, 1856
Hon. Joseph C. Hornblower, of Newark, N. J. — " 1858.

Corresponding Secretaries,

Samuel G. Drake, M. A., of Boston, — Jan. 1845, to Jan. 1850
Nathaniel B. Shurtleff, M. D., of Boston, — " 1850, to " 1851
Samuel G. Drake, M A., " " — " 1851, to " 1858
Rev. Samuel H. Riddel, — " 1858.

Recording Secretaries,

John Wingate Thornton, LL.B., of Boston, — Jan. 1845, to Mar. 1846
Rev. Samuel H. Riddel, " " — Apr. 1846, to Jan. 1851
Charles Mayo, Esq. " " — Jan. 1851, to " 1856
Hon. Francis Brinley, " " — " 1856, to " 1857
David Pulsifer, Esq. " " — " 1857, to Aug. 1857
John Ward Dean, Esq. " " — Aug. 1857, to Jan. 1858
William M. Cornell, M. D., " " — Jan. 1858.

Treasurers,

William Henry Montague, Esq., of Boston, — Jan. 1845, to Jan. 1851
Frederic Kidder, Esq., " " — " 1851, to " 1855
John Ward Dean, Esq., " " — " 1855, to " 1857
Isaac Child, Esq., " " — " 1857.

Historiographer,

Joseph Palmer, M. D., of Boston, — Jan. 1856.

Librarians,

Edmund Batchelder Dearborn, Esq., of Boston, — Jan. 1846, to Jan. 1849
David Pulsifer, Esq., of Boston, — " 1849, to " 1851
Thomas Bellows Wyman, Jr., Esq., of Charlestown, — " 1851, to " 1852
William Blake Trask, Esq., of Dorchester, — " 1852, to Aug. 1854
Rev. Luther Farnham, of Boston, — Aug. 1854, to July, 1856
Thomas B. Wyman, Jr., Esq., of Charlestown, — Sept. 1856, to Jan. 1858
Edward Holden, Esq., of Roxbury, — Jan. 1858.

* Deceased.

ACTIVE MEMBERS,

From the formation of the Society in 1844, to March 1, 1858.

* signifies deceased.
  †   "   membership changed.
  ‡   "   ceased to be a member.

The residence given is that of the individual at the time of joining the Society.
When no State is named, Massachusetts is understood.

LIFE.

1857.
Benjamin V. French, Braintree.

1858.
Edmund B. Dearborn, Boston.
Thomas B. Wyman, Jr., Charlestown.
William B. Trask, Dorchester.

RESIDENT.

1844.
*Charles Ewer, Boston. [*1858
 Lemuel Shattuck, do.
 Samuel G. Drake, do.
 William H. Montague, do.
 J. Wingate Thornton, do.

1845.
 James S. Loring, Boston.
*William Ingalls, do. [*1851
 Samuel H. Riddel, do.
‡Frederick P. Tracy, Williamsburg, [‡1846
 Nathan'l B. Shurtleff, Boston.
 Charles Deane, do.
‡Chandler Robbins, do. [‡1851
 Edward Tuckerman, Cambridge.
 Lucius R. Paige, do.
 Andrew H. Ward, West Newton.
 Wm. W. Greenough, Boston.
 Horatio G. Somerby, do.
 Wm. Reed Deane, do.
‡David Reed, do. [‡1851
‡Jonathan Mason, do. [‡1852
*Samuel T. Armstrong, do. [*1850
‡John Henshaw, Cambridge, [‡1847
†Benjamin V. French, Braintree, [†1857
 William H. Sumner, Jamaica Plain.
‡William J. Adams, Boston, [‡1847
‡Thomas Bulfinch, do. [‡1848
‡John G. Palfrey, do. [‡1850
‡Charles H. Stedman, do. [‡1849
 William P. Mason, do.
*William P. Greenwood, do. [*1851
‡Thomas Whittemore, Cambridge, [‡1853
*Frederick T. Gray, Boston, [*1850
 Solomon Lincoln, Hingham.
*William T. Harris, Cambridge, [*1854
‡Amos Phelps, Boston, [‡1848
 Joseph Willard, do.
†Edmund B. Dearborn, do. [†1858
‡Waldo Higginson, do. [‡1858
*David Hamblen, do. [*1858
‡Francis N. Mitchell, do. [‡1858
 Adolphus Davis, do.
‡William H. Kelley, do. [‡1858

1846.
‡James M. Robbins, Milton, [‡1851
‡George Winslow, Boston, [‡1850
 Edward Everett, do.
*Caleb Bates, Hingham, [*1857
 Nathaniel W. Coffin, Boston.
‡Wm. I. Buddington, Charlestown, [‡1848
 Thomas C. Smith, Boston.
‡Josiah F. Leach, do. [‡1850
 Isaac Child, do.
 John H. Blake, do.
 Samuel Swett, do.
‡Garland Tarou, do. [‡1859
 Zachariah Eddy, Middleboro'.
*Abbott Lawrence, Boston, [*1855
‡George Livermore, Cambridge, [‡1851
‡Samuel A. Eliot, Boston, [‡1851
 Jared Sparks, Salem.
‡Caleb Eddy, Boston, [‡1849
‡Horatio N. Otis, New York, N.Y. [‡1849
 Joseph W. Wright, Boston.
‡William T. Andrews, do. [‡1852

1847.
*William Cogswell, Boston, [*1850
†*Daniel F. Parker, do. [*47, *50
*Theodore Lyman, do. [*1849
‡Charles M. Ellis, Roxbury, [‡1849
‡Edward E. Hale, Worcester, [‡1851
 Fred. W. Lincoln, Jr., Boston.
‡Wm. T. G. Morton, do. [‡1848
 Martin Moore, do.
 T. Larkin Turner, do.
*William Savage, do. [*1851
‡Charles Stoddard, do. [‡1852
‡Andrew Bigelow, do. [‡1850
 Albert Fearing, do.
 William Hayden, do.
‡Joseph B. Felt, do. [†‡1855
 William Parsons, do.
 George B. Upton, do.
‡Alex. W. McClure, Malden, [‡1853
‡Charles C. F. Moody, Boston, [‡1854
 Richard Frothingham, Jr., Charlestown.
‡William Thomas, Boston, [‡1849
‡Stephen P. Fuller, do. [‡1849
*Enoch Train, do. [*1855
*Harrison G. O. Colby, N. Bedford, [*1853
‡Charles J. F. Binney, Boston, [‡1853
 Amos A. Lawrence, do.
‡Horatio H. Hunnewell, do. [‡1852
 Benj. P. Richardson, do.
*Simon Greenleaf, do. [*1853
‡Edward F. Hodges, do. [‡1850

William Sutton,   Salem.
‡Theodore L. Howe,   Boston,   [‡1849

1848.

*Ralph Haskins,   Roxbury,   [*1853
*Daniel Gilbert,   Boston,   [*1849
‡Baron Stow,   do.   [‡1854
Andrew Johonnot,   do.
*Nathaniel M. Davis,   Plymouth,   [*1848
Thomas H. Leavitt,   Boston.
*Artemas Simonds,   do.   [*1854
George W. Messenger,   do.
David Pulsifer,   do.
Samuel Andrews,   Roxbury.
‡Charles Mayo,   Boston,   [‡1856
‡Pliny Nickerson,   do.   [‡1852
‡Justin Winsor,   do.   [‡1852
*Israel P. Proctor,   do.   [*1851

1849.

Frederic Kidder,   Roxbury.
‡Nathaniel Hamlen,   Boston,   [‡1852

1850.

‡Thos. B. Wyman, Jr.,   Charlestown,   [‡'58
‡B. Homer Dixon,   Boston,   [‡1857
John Ward Dean,   do.
‡Samuel H. Jenks,   do.   [‡1853
Henry Davenport,   Roxbury.
Eleazer F. Pratt,   Boston.
Isaac Winslow,   do.
John G. Locke,   do.
Timothy Farrar,   do.
Joseph Moulton,   Lynn.
*Elisha Fuller,   Worcester,   [*1853
Marshall P. Wilder,   Dorchester.
William M. Wallace,   Boston.
J. Huntington Wolcott,   do.
‡Samuel J. Bridge,   do.   [‡1853
Alonzo H. Quint,   Dover, N. H.
Frederic W. Prescott,   Boston.
‡William W. Cowles,   do.   [‡1853
J. B. Bright,   Waltham.
Lucius M. Sargent,   Roxbury.
George H. Lyman,   Boston.
Charles G. Loring.   do.

1851.

‡William I. Brown,   S. Reading,   [‡1857
‡Amasa Walker,   Boston,   [‡1854
Francis Brinley,   do.
Henry C. Brooks,   do.
Jacob Q. Kettelle,   do.
John Wells Parker,   Roxbury.
Guy C. Haynes,   Boston.
William G. Brooks,   do.
Daniel C. Colesworthy,   do.
John R. Rollins,   do.
Sylvester Bliss,   do.
‡William Lincoln,   do.   [‡1856
John I. Baker,   Beverly.
‡John Doane, Jr.,   Charlestown,   [‡1855
Isaac Davis,   Worcester.
‡Henry B. Wheelwright,   Taunton,   [‡1856
‡William B. Trask,   Dorchester,   [‡1856
*Henry H. Fuller,   Boston,   [*1852
Addison Child,   Medford.
William S. Thacher,   Boston.
Luther M. Harris,   Jamaica Plain.
Samuel Jennison,   Worcester.

1852.

William Whiting,   Roxbury.
Joseph Palmer,   Boston.
Thomas Waterman,   do.   [*1853
Henry K. Jones,   do.   [*1848
Thomas Prince,   do.   [‡1854
*Moses Plimpton,   do.   [*1854
Stephen T. Farwell,   Cambridge.   [*1848
Henry Bright,   Northampton.
‡Richard Pitts,   Dorchester,   [‡1855
‡Eben S. Stearns,   W. Newton,   [‡1853
George Adams,   Boston.
A. Bronson Alcott,   do.
William B. Towne,   Brookline.   [‡1856
‡Charles S. Lincoln,   Somerville,   [‡1852
Charles Adams, Jr.,   Boston.   [‡1855
Lyman Mason,   do.   [*1851
John G. Metcalf,   Mendon.
John P. Healy,   Boston.
Alfred Poor,   Groveland.   [‡1852
Almon D. Hodges,   Roxbury.
Alex. L. B. Monroe,   Medway.

1853.

William H. Chace,   Pensacola, Fla.
Bowen Backman,   Woburn.   [‡1853
‡Joseph W. Ward,   Boston,   [‡1855
Frederic A. Whitney,   Brighton.
Samuel Nicolson,   Boston.
Paul Willard, Jr.,   Charlestown.
Sam'l G. Wheeler, Jr.,   Boston.
‡A. W. Conant,   do.   [‡1856
Ithamar W. Beard,   Lowell.   [*1855
Stephen M. Allen,   Jamaica Plain.
Ira B. Peck,   Woonsocket, R. I.
Charles A. Ranlet,   Charlestown.
Hiram Wellington,   Boston.   [‡1855
Bichford Pulsifer, Jr.,   Charlestown.
‡John Haskins,   Roxbury,   [‡1854
‡George M. Champney,   Woburn,   [‡1855
‡Christ'r C. Andrews,   Boston,   [‡1854
‡Roger N. Pierce,   do.   [‡1854
‡D. M. Huckins,   do.   [‡1855
‡William Jones,   do.   [‡1856
John M. Bradbury.   do.
Nathan Appleton,   do.
Manning Leonard,   Southbridge.
Edmund Boynton,   Boston.
Daniel Draper,   do.
Nathaniel Whiting,   Watertown.
Josiah Newhall,   Lynnfield.
‡Peter S. Wheelock,   Boston,   [‡1854
William D. Ticknor,   do.
John S. Barry,   Hanover.
B. F. White,   Boston.
‡Sam'l H. Gilbert,   Gage Town, N.B. [‡'54
Josiah Dunham, Jr.,   Boston.
*Chas. Fred. Adams, Jr.   do.   [*1856
‡James M. Chase,   Cambridge,   [‡1854
Henry Clark,   W. Poultney, Vt.
Elias S. Hawley,   Buffalo, N. Y.
Charles H. Peaslee,   Boston.
John R. Kimball,   do.
Lloyd Glover,   do.

1854.

Luther Farnham,   Boston.
‡*Thomas Hopkinson,   do.   [‡1855, *'56

Charles Atwood, Boston.
‡ Alonzo B. Chapin, S. Glastenb'y, Ct. [‡'5?
Wm. H. Whitmore, Boston.
Daniel N. Haskell, do.
*Thomas S. Pearson, Peacham, Vt. [*1856
*Gorham Brooks, Medford, [*1853
William S. Bartlit, Chelsea.
Dean Dudley, Boston.
Horatio Powers, do.
Lemuel Little, do.

1855.

Charles H. Morse, Cambridgeport.
Sam'l S. Kilburn, Jr., West Newton.
Tho's J. Whitemore, Cambridge.
Joseph Allen, Northborough.
Amos Otis, Yarmouth Port.
Tolman Willey, Boston.
Uriel Crocker, do.
William S. Morton, Quincy.
John A. Boutelle, Woburn.
William J. Reynolds, Roxbury.
Alexander Blaikie, Boston.
George Lunt, do.
Franklin Haven, do.
Laban M. Wheaton, Norton.
Alexander Beal, Boston.
Stephen M. Weld, Jamaica Plain.
Robert C. Winthrop, Boston.
Jeremiah F. Jewett, Lowell.
Samuel Hall, Boston.
C. H. B. Caldwell, Jamaica Plain.
James W. Clark, Framingham.
S. C. Simmons, Boston.
George O. Smith, do.
Amos Sargent, Jr. Somerville.
Charles C. Jewett, Roxbury.
Israel Thorndike, New York, N. Y.
Isaac Parker, Boston.
Charles K. Dillaway, Roxbury.
Richard K. Swift, Chicago, Ill.
Henry Rice, Boston.
Philip H. Sears, do.
Thomas C. Amory, Jr. do.
William M. Lathrop, do.
Ephraim G. Ware, do.
G. Quincy Thorndike, New York, N. Y.
Horatio N. Bigelow, Clinton.
G. D. B. Blanchard, Malden.
Alvah A. Burrage, Boston.
Charles Hudson, Lexington.
Lewis H. Webb, Rockingham, N. C.

1856.

John W. Proctor, South Danvers.
James D. Green, Cambridge.
Elias Nason, Natick.
John W. Warren, Boston.
William Makepeace, do.
Henry Austin Whitney, do.
Samuel Hooper, do.
Thomas E. Graves, Thompson, Ct.
*Andrew F. Warren, Cromwell, Ct. [*1857
James H. Means, Dorchester.
Francis De Witt, Ware.
Samuel L. Wheeler, West Newton.
Calvin E. Stowe, Andover.
William Mason Cornell, Boston.

Caleb Davis Bradlee, Cambridge.
Samuel B. Noyes, Canton.
Oliver Carter, Boston.
William Phillips, do.
Elihu Yale, New Haven, Ct.
Gardner B. Perry, Groveland.
Leverett Saltonstall, Brookline.
William L. Weston, Danvers.
Abijah W. Draper, West Roxbury.
Day O. Kellogg, Brooklyn, N. Y.
William H. L. Smith, Boston.
Alfred E. Giles, do.
C. Benj. Richardson, do.
Jacob W. Reed, South Groveland.
Nathan H. Chamberlain, Cambridge.
Frank W. Bigelow, Weston.

1857.

David W. Hoyt, Brighton.
Henry M. Brooks, Salem.
Enoch C. Rolfe, Boston.
Luke Brooks, Salem.
George T. Thacher, Dorchester.
John L. Fox, Charlestown.
Jasper H. York, Boston.
Wm. W. Whitcomb, do.
Wm. A. Richardson, Lowell.
Matthew Harvey, Concord, N. H.
James W. Crooks, Springfield.
Charles Banker, Roxbury.
Alfred A. Prescott, Reading.
Samuel Burnham, Rindge, N. H.
Edward S. Rand, Jr. Cambridge.
Dean W. Talmarr, Charlestown.
Ariel I. Cummings, Roxbury.
Joseph Richardson, Hingham.
Edward Holden, Roxbury.
George Minns, Reading.
Edward G. Russell, Cambridge.
Hiram Carleton, West Barnstable.
Edwin R. Hodgman, Lynnfield Center.
And Emerson, Boston.
John Barstow, Providence, R. I.
James M. Wilder, Boston.
Horace G. Barrows, do.
James W. Merriam, do.
Daniel Denshaw, do.
William E. Baker, do.
Daniel R. Curtis, Dorchester.
Jeremiah Colburn, Boston.
Ezra Wilkinson, Dedham.
Winslow Lewis, Boston.
Elisha Copeland, do.
Henry A. Scudder, do.
Francis L. Harding, do.
David Thayer, do.
Peter E. Vose, Dennysville, Me.
Henry A. Miles, Boston.
George White, Quincy.
Daniel J. Coburn, Boston.
Angus. C. L. Arnold, Charlestown.

1858.

Rufus Wyman, Roxbury.
Thaddeus Allen, Boston.
S. Benton Thompson, do.
Calvin Guild, Jr., Dedham.
Richard Briggs, Boston.

William S. Leland,	Roxbury.		W. Elliot Woodward,	Roxbury.
Calvin P. Hinds,	Boston.		John S. H. Fogg,	South Boston.
Charles Stearns,	Springfield.		Francis B. Hayes,	Boston.
David Bryant,	Boston.		Thomas T. Richmond,	do.
J. Ripley Osgood,	do.		Joseph H. Ward,	do.
Langford W. Loring,	do.		Josiah Quincy, Jr.,	do.
Francis S. Drake,	Dorchester.		Alexander H. Rice,	do.

Present number of Active Members, 264.

PAYMENTS.—*Albany, N. Y.,* R. Townsend, G. H. Thacher, E. S. Stearns; *Albion, N. Y.,* L. C. Paine; *Beverly,* J. I. Baker; *Boston,* J. H. Dexter, L. Shattuck, E. Nute, S. Walker, Jon. Palmer, F. A. Bartlet, J. W. Warren, Mrs. A. Lawrence, J. Quincy, W. H. Prescott, D. Sears, E. Child, J. W. Plimpton, A. Sargent, Jr., N. Appleton, J. Aiken, S. Andrews, E. Brooks, J. M. Bradbury, J. Bryant, T. C. Amory, Jr., J. Savage, G. W. Messinger, W. M. Lathrop, G. Bates, Boston Library, J. R. Osgood, Mrs. Adams, J. L. Richards, E. Pearson, W. G. Brooks, J. Stevens, J. H. Wilkins, T. A. Neal, B. Abbot, Z. Hosmer, E. Mason, A. A. Lawrence, J. W. Paige, Merc. Lib. Assoc., W. Hayden, S. Swett, C. G. Loring, I. Tarbox, Mrs. Parker, W. Pierce, J. K. Hall, J. F. Baldwin, H. Davenport, E. S. Erving, S. T. Snow, F. A. Hall, J. Henshaw, C. Adams, Jr., D. Barnard, J. Brock, W. T. Andrews, C. F. Adams, W. B. Bradford, J. W. Clarke, L. P. Cook, G. T. Thacher, T. C. Smith, J. Richardson, I. Harris, M. F. Cook, P. Kelly, R. Choate, A. W. Thaxter, T. W. Pierce, J. G. Locke, J. W. Dean, S. Child, W. Whiting, F. W. Prescott, J. Merriam, L. Shaw, E. J. Browne, R. C. Winthrop, M. P. Wilder, Jona. Phillips; *Bridgewater,* W. Latham; *Brighton,* F. A. Whitney; *Brooklyn,* D. O. Kellogg; *Burlington,* S. Sewall; *Cambridge,* L. R. Paige, N. Cotton; *Canandaigua, N. Y.,* H. W. Taylor; *Carlton,* W. S. Bartlett; *Chester,* C. Clement; *Cleveland, O.,* J. Wade, Jr., A. S. Sanford; *Duxbury,* J. F. Wadsworth; *Elmira, N. Y.,* A. T. Thurston; *Fitchburg,* K. Brooks; *Georgetown,* S. Nelson; *Groton,* J. Greene; *Hampton, O.,* J. Clarke; *Jamaica Plain,* L. M. Harris; *Lawrence,* S. Blaisdale; *Leominster,* D. Wilder; *Lowell,* F. White; *Milwaukie, Wis.,* J. S. Buck; *Natick,* A. Bacon; *New Haven, Ct.,* T. R. Trowbridge, H. White; *New York, N. Y.,* Edgerly, J. E. Bulkley, O. Hoyt, G. Q. Thorndike, H. S. Otis; *Northampton,* H. Bright; [*Original Subscribers whose names are not on the Publisher's list,* Henry Gale Dunnell, M. D., New York; F. S. Pease, Albany, N. Y.;] *Pawtucket, R. I.,* W. Tyler; *Philadelphia, Pa.,* C. D. Cleveland, H. Bond; *Portsmouth, N. H.,* A. R. H. Fernald; *Providence, R. I.,* J. Barstow; *Quincy, Ill.,* S. H. Emery, W. Keyes, C. A. Savage, C. H. Howland, N. E. Society; *Quincy, Ms.,* I. Marsh; *Randolph,* E. Alden; *Schenectady, N. Y., U. College,* J. Pearson; *Sherburne,* C. W. Tainter; *South Glastonbury, Ct.,* A. B. Chapin; *Springfield,* O. B. Morris, J. G. Chase; *Tipton, Iowa,* W. H. Tuthill; *Troy, N. Y.,* A. J. Skilton; *West Amesbury,* D. Sargent; *West Brattleboro, Vt.,* S. Clark; *West Winstead, Ct.,* D. W. Patterson; *Woburn,* B. Buckman; *Zanesville, O.,* E. Abernathy.

N. F. Edgerly, of New York City, is collecting materials for a full genealogy of the Edgerlys in the United States. All communications will be thankfully received, from persons possessed of any facts concerning them, especially those of an early date. The co-operation of those of the name is respectfully requested.

Inquiries.—Who was Capt. Edward Edgerly, attached to Col. Benjamin Ford's Maryland Regiment, received his commission 10 Sept., 1779, and entitled to half pay?

Joshua Edgerly joined the Revolutionary Army when quite young and served through the War. Married Mary, dau. of Dyer Weeks of Greenland, N. H. Lived during the latter part of his life in Wakefield. Whose son was he and where was he born?

Address N. F. Edgerly, No. 158 Ninth Street.

The Rev. Mr. Nason, of Natick, Mass., read before the New England Historical and Genealogical Society a very interesting paper on Sir Charles Henry Frankland, of whose romantic history many have heard, but of which little was known. Mr. Nason is preparing a more extended Memoir of that distinguished individual, and will be glad to receive any information concerning him, in the shape of original letters or otherwise. Address Rev. Elias Nason of Natick, Mass.

MEMOIR OF THE LATE SIR JOHN BURKE, K. H., AUTHOR OF "THE PEERAGE."

[By his son, Sir John Bernard Burke, Ulster King of Arms at Dublin.]

THE family from which John Burke, Esq., the author of "The Peerage," paternally sprang, was seated in high repute for several successive generations at the Castle of Meelick, in the west of Ireland, an inheritance conferred on its immediate founder, John Burke, by his father Richard, second Earl of Clanricarde. Maternally, Mr. Burke had an equally honorable ancestry, deriving, through his mother, who was cousin-german of the eminent law reporter, Richard Vaughan Barnewall, and of the late Sir Robert Barnewall, Bart., from the distinguished Anglo-Norman house of Barnewall of Crickstown Castle, the parent stock whence issued the noble families of Kingsland and Trimlestown.

Mr. Burke's grandfather, John Burke, was an officer of the Austrian service; and his father, Peter Burke, Esq. of Elm Hall, in the county of Tipperary, was for many years an active magistrate for that and the King's county. In politics a moderate whig, Mr. Peter Burke held himself always aloof from the agitation going on around him, and on more than one occasion proved of great service to government in preserving the peace of his district. He lived on terms of friendship with the late and the present Earls of Rosse, with Colonel Bernard of Castle Bernard, and, indeed, with all his fellow-magistrates, by whom his sense, his rectitude and his independence were duly appreciated and respected. Mr. Peter Burke married Anne, daughter and co-heir of Matthew Dowdall, Esq., M. D. of Mullingar, an eminent physician, by Bridget his wife, daughter of Robert Barnewall, Esq. of Moyrath, county of Meath, and had issue, John, the subject of this notice; Joseph, late a poor-law commissioner in Ireland, from which office he recently retired with a pension, and Bridget, the widow of M. Hoey, Esq.

The elder son, John Burke, was born the 29th of November, 1786. His father, after securing him a good classical education, wished him to attach himself to mercantile affairs. He therefore, in pursuance of this desire, became a merchant, and for some years continued busily engaged in commercial pursuits. The occupation, however, was not to his taste. Naturally endowed with a mind that excelled in the excitement of politics and literature, he felt no pleasure in any other employment. While thus situated, and yet very young, he married his cousin, Mary, second dau-

ghter of Bernard O'Reilly, Esq.[*] of Ballymorice, in the county of Long-
ford, a woman of beauty, talent and amiability, to whom he was ever
after devotedly attached. With her he came to London. Once there,
Mr. Burke gave vent to his genius. His first essays in writing were
strictly political. Articles of his, of course anonymous, appeared in
many newspapers, and particularly in the Examiner, then at the height
of its popularity. One squib he inserted against Mr. Canning was so
sensitively felt by the minister, that, long after, he took occasion to notice
it and to express his unforgiveness of it.

Mr. Burke was also a poet; a little volume of verses which he published, partly also in a political vein, had an immediate and rapid sale.
It would now be difficult to enumerate the many productions of this nature
he at that period of his life successfully, though anonymously, brought
out, in prose and verse. Through these, and subsequently the fruits of
his attention to the more purely literary periodicals of the day, he always
maintained a respectable position, and continued to rear and educate
liberally a large family.

After having profitably edited an edition, with a continuation by himself, of Hume and Smollett's History of England, he happily thought of
a new work, in improvement of the pitiful volumes called peerages at
that time published. This idea brought him into connection with Mr.
Colburn, and it is but justice to that eminent publisher, now deceased, to
say that he at once fostered the speculation, and joined liberally and
energetically in its advancement. The first edition of Mr. Burke's Peerage and Baronetage was published in 1826. The merits of that most
popular and useful book are now universally known. Its success, from
the beginning, was very great indeed, and that success has since gone on
increasing. The last edition was the nineteenth, and it now sells an
edition of at least fifteen hundred copies every year. After some few
prosperous issues of the Peerage, Mr. Burke was assisted by his son,
John Bernard Burke, then but just returned from college. Their united
labors have since produced the History of the Landed Gentry, the General Armory, and the Extinct Peerage and Baronetage—works of the
greatest value to the historian and genealogist.

The cheering prosperity attending these pursuits, and his own friendly
disposition, led Mr. Burke into the habit of seeing much company. His
hospitality was unbounded, and many, too, of note and station were the
visitors who spent frequent and pleasant hours under his social roof.
But it was the will of Providence that the joys of his domestic life should
not remain unchequered. Within the space of two years, Mr. Burke had

* The O'Reillys of Ballymorice descended, in a direct and unbroken line, from the
O'Reillys, Princes of Brefay, derived more immediately from the marriage of Terence
O'Reilly, Esq. with Rose, sister of Philip O'Reilly, Esq. of Ballymorice. Mr. Burke's
uncle, the late John O'Reilly, Esq. of Anneville, married Ellis, sister of Dr. Chevers,
one of the Irish Catholic bishops, and left two sons—Christopher of Anneville, and
John, late consul-general at Guatimala, and two daughters, of whom the elder, Anna,
became the wife of Sir David William Smith, Bart. of Alnwick. Mrs. Burke's father,
Bernard O'Reilly, Esq., though a younger son, succeeded to the ancient patrimony of
Ballymorice. He married Mary, another daughter and co-heir of Dr. Dowdall, mentioned in the text, and had by her numerous issue. All the sons are now dead. Mrs.
Burke's eldest sister, Mrs. Somers, resident at Rinrown, county Meath, was a lady
of talent and literary reputation in Ireland, and a friend of Miss Edgeworth's. Among
other works, Mrs. Somers was the author of a very popular production, entitled,
" Selections from the Modern Poets of France," which contains some beautiful trans-
lations in verse. She died a few years ago.

the agony to see die three of those children to whom he was so fondly
devoted—one of the three who thus perished in their youth was a boy
of extraordinary ability and promise. That death the parents never entirely recovered from, but Mr. Burke's cup of bitterness was not yet filled.
His wife, who had been the life and soul of his existence; she whose
ready wit and perpetual good humor had charmed and won for him so
many friends, who, in fact, made his home a paradise, died, after a severe
and lingering illness, on the 17th of November, 1846, to the inexpressible
grief of all around her. From that day his heart and spirit failed him.
After attending her funeral, when he remarked to a relative near him
that the pedestal of his life was gone from under him forever, he relinquished all his labor to his son, and retired to the Continent.

He for some time sojourned at Bruges, and latterly at Aix-la-Chapelle,
where he was much courted and respected by the English residents. On
the morning of the 26th of March, 1849, Mr. Burke went, in apparent
health and spirits, to attend divine service. On his return from the
church he was struck with apoplexy, and never rallied after. He lingered
until the following evening, when he expired, in the sixty-second year of
his age. The two physicians who were with him, Dr. Velten and Dr.
Straaten, both distinguished practitioners at Aix, declared they never witnessed a more awfully sudden or hopeless case. Mr. Burke was interred
with much ceremony in the cemetery at Aix-la-Chapelle, the English
residents being present at the funeral. Mr. Burke left three children,
viz.: a daughter, Mary Clarinda, and two sons—Peter, a barrister on the
Northern circuit, author of various legal and other works, and John Bernard, the present editor of the Peerage and the Landed Gentry, now Sir
John Bernard Burke, Ulster king of arms, knight attendant of the order
of St. Patrick, and keeper of the records in the Binningham tower of
Dublin Castle.

AMES'S ALMANACS.
[From the Boston Gazette, January 14, 1760.]

"In a *Connecticut* Paper was advertised Almanacks for 1760, with my
Name thereto, to be sold by some of the Booksellers in Boston; and also
some to be sold at New Haven, at the low Price of *Two Shillings* per Dozen;
and having seen [? some] of them in Boston, it appears that said almanack
is a notorious Cheat and Imposition: The Chief Design was (as given out
by some who had Honor, Honesty and ingenuity enough to assist in Coun-
terfeiting) to destroy the Credit my Almanack had gained, and prevent its
having such Credit for the future: To which Purpose they have endeav-
oured to render my performance as despicable as possible, by omitting the
Preface, Ephemeris, Verses, &c. also what is of Service, Interest Tables,
Value of Coin, the several Roads and Stages; and further to make me appear still more contemptible omitted ALL the Week Days in the whole
Year and above 50 Days in the Months, and fixed in some Places the wrong
Dominical Letter: Surely such a Conduct is to the last Degree, Base!

"☞ I therefore advertise again, That those Almanacks printed in Boston from my Copy have the Printers name thereto, and none others: And
I hope that the Defence of my Reputation, in thus advertising, which at
this Time seems necessary, will be a sufficient Apology to my Country-
man, whose Good I seek, and on whose Good-will I depend.

NATHANIEL AMES.

"*Boston, Jan.* 8, 1760."

BIRTHS, MARRIAGES, AND DEATHS,

Contained in the volume lettered "Original Distribution of the Town of Hartford (Ct.) among the Settlers, 1639."

[Transcribed by LUCIUS M. BOLTWOOD of Amherst, Cor. Mem. of H. and G. Soc.]

[Continued from page 175.]

John Stanla sunn of John Standla was borne Nom the third or forth one thousand six hundreth forty and seuen.

Thomas Andrewes sunn of Frances Andrewes was baptised Jeneuary the second one thousand six hundreth forty and seuen,

Lodea Stone daughter of Mr. Samiwell Stone was borne Jeneuary the twenty and two one thousand six hundreth forty and scuen.

PAGE 5.

Samiwell Maruen sun of Matthew Maruen was baptised Feb. the sixth one Tousand six hundreth forty and seuen.

Izack Standla sunn of Timothy Standla was borne March tenth one thousand six hundreth forty and seuen.

Samiwell Rusco sun of Will. Rusco was born March the twellth one thousand six hundred forty and seuen.

Rebecka Ollmsted was borne March the twell one thousand six hundreth forty seuen, wich is y' daughter of Nicholas Ollmsted.

Ezeckell Samford sunn of Robberd Samford was borne March the thirteenth one thousand six hundred forty and seuen.

John Gillbertt sun of John Gillbart was borne Jeneuary the sixteenth one thousand six hundredth forty and seuen.

Elizabeth Spencer daughter of Thomas Spenser was baptised March the twenty and six one thousand six hundreth forty and eaighti.

Mary Sellden daughter of Thomas Sillden was baptised March the twenty and six one thousand six hundreth forty and eaighti.

Samiwell Lanes sun of Will: Lanes was borne Augusi the eaighteth one thousand six hundredth forty and eaighti.

Richard Risla sunn of Richard Risla was baptised Augusi the twenty and one one thousand six hundreth forty and eaighti.

Sara Willcock daughter of John Willcock Jun' was borne October the third one thousand six hundreth forty and eaighti.

Sara Barnard daghter of Bartellmaw Barnard was borne Desember the third one Thousand six hundreth forty and eayght.

Mara Webb daughter of John Webb was borne the fifth of Febuary one Thousand six hundreth forty and seuen,

Abigail Disborow daughter of Nicholas Disborow was borne Febuary the first one thousand six hundreth forty and eaighti.

Johanna Smith daughter of Gylles Smith was baptised March the twenty fivo one thousand six hundreth forty and nyne.

Jonathan Bull sun of Thomas Bull was baptised March the twenty and five one thousand six hundreh forty and nyne.

—— Stone sunn of Mr. Samuel Stone was baptised Aprell the twenty and nyne one thousand six hundreth forty and nyne.

John Culleck sun of Mr. John Clleck was borne May the forth one thousand six hundreth forty and nyne.

Mary Catling daughter of Thomas Cattelling was baptised May the sixth one thousand six hundreth forty and nyne.

Anna Crow daughter of John Crow was borne July the thirtene one thousand six hundreth forty and nyne.

Joseph Marsh son of John March was baptised the fifteene of July one thousand six hundreth forty and nyne.

Elizabeth Ellmer the daughter of Edward Ellmer was baptised July ye fifteene one thousand six hundreth forty and nyne.

Leden Ensign daughter of James Ensigne was baptised August the Ninteenth one Thousand six hundreth forty and nyne.

Philip Judd sun of Thom Judd was baptised Septemr the seckond one thousand six hundreth forty and nyne.

Sara Wodford daughter of Thomas Wodford was baptised Septm the seckond one thousand six hundredth forty and nyne.

PAGE 7.

Mary Gilberd, daughter of Jonathan Gilberd was baptised Desem the seuenteoth one thousand six hundreth forty and nyne.

John Olmsted sunn of Richard Olmsted was baptised Desember 30 in the yeare one thousand six hundreth forty and nyne.

Rachel Maruen daughter of Mathihew Maruen was baptised Desem^r the 30 one thousand six hundreth forty and nyne.

John Stelle, sunn.

John Allcock sunn of Thomas Allcock was baptised Febuary ye third one thousand six hundreth forty and nyne.

John Olmsted sunn of Nickolas Olmsted was baptised Febeuary ye third one thousand six hundreth forty and nyne.

Sary Wadsworth daughter of William Wadsworth was baptised March the seuentene one thousand six hundreth forty and nyne.

Anna Hulberd daughter of William Hullberd was baptised March the seuenteoth one thousand six hundreth forty and nyne.

John Pantree sunn of John Pantree was baptised March the seuenteenth one thousand six hundreth forty and nyne.

Joseph Hilles, sunn of William Hilles was baptised March the seuenteenth one thousand six hundretho forty and nyne.

Elizabeth Seger daughter of Richard Seger was borne June the ——— one thousand six hundreth aud fifty.

Daniel Kelsa sunn of William Kelsa was borne the ——— one thousand six hundreth and fifty.

Abbigall Stone daughter of Mr. Samiwell Stone was borne Septm 9th one thousand six hundreth and fifty.

John Russell sunn of Mr. John Russell was baptised Septm the twenty and three one thousand [six] hundreth and fifty.

Gorg Hubberd sunn of Gorg Hubberd was baptised Desem the fifteene one thousand six hundreth and fifty.

Joseph Peck sunn of Pall Peck was baptised Desem the twenty and two one thousand six hundreth and fifty.

John Willcock sunn of John Willcock Junr was borne Oc[to]ber the twenty and nyne one thousand six hundreth and fifty.

Thomas Healle son of Thomas Healles was baptised Jeuneuary the nyotent^h one thousand six hundreth and fifty.

Thomas Gridla sun of Thomas Gridla was borne the first week in August one thousand six hundreth and fifty.

Mary Felowes daughter of Richard Felowes was baptised Febuary the ninth one thousand six hundreth and fifty.

Daued Bull sun of Thomas Bull was baptised Febua^r the ninth one thousand six hundreth and fifty.

Rebocka Keeler daughter of Ralph Keeler was baptised Febeuary the ninth one thousand six hundreth and fifty.

Arther Smith son of Arther Smith was baptised Apell the twentyeth one thousand six hundred fifty and one.

Sary Whiyhtmore daughter of Thomas Whytmore was baptised Aprell the twentyeth one thousand six hundred fifty and one.

Esther Selden daughter of Thomas Selden was baptised the third day of March one thousand sixe hundred forty and nyne.

John Selden sonn of Thomas Selden dyed in the month of May one thousand sixe hundred and fifty.

Esther Selden daughter of Thomas Selden dyed in the month of June one thousand sixe hundred forty and one.

Joseph Selden the sonn of Thomas Selden baptised the second day of November one thousand sixe hundred fifty and one.

Elizabeth Culleck daughter of Captaine Mr John Culleck born July the 15th one thousand sixe hundred fifty twoe.

John Gilbert the sonn of John Gilbert borne the 19th day of February 1652.

Hannah Spencer the daughter of Thomas Spencer borne the 25th of Aprill 1653.

PAGE 9.

Dorothy Lord daughter of Mr Thomas Lord borne the 17th day of August one thousand six hundred fifty and three.

Jonathan Gilbert the sonn of Jonathan Gilbert borne the 15th of December one thousand sixe hundred forty eight.

Sarah Gilbert the daughter of Jonathan Gilbert borne the 25th day of July one thousand sixe hundred fifty one.

Lydia Gilbert the daughter of Jonathan Gilbert borne the 3 day of October one thousand sixe hundred fifty four.

Marah Spencer the daughter of Thomas Spencer borne the 18th of May one thousand sixe hundred fifty fyve.

Mary Graves the daughter of Isaack Graves born the 5 day of July one thousand sixe hundred forty seeven.

Isaak Graves, son of Isaack Grave born the 21st day of August one thousand sixe hundred and fifty.

Rebeckah Graves the daughter of Isaack Graves born the third day of July one thousand sixe hundred fifty twoe.

Samuel Graves the son of Isaak Graves born the first day of October one thousand sixe hundred fifty fiue.

Elizabeth Gilbert the daughter of John Gilbert was borne the twelfh day of February one thousand sixe hundred fifty fiue.

Joseph Grannis the sonne of Edward Grannis was born the 31st day of March one thousand sixe hundred fifty six.

Martha Spencer the daughter of Thomas Spencer born the 19th day of March one thousand sixe hundred fifty seven.

Hannah Stockin the daughter of Samuel Stockin of Middle Towne borne the 30th of October one thousand sixe hundred fifty four.

Samuel Stockin the soon of Samuel Stockin of Middle Towne, born October the 29th one thousand six hundred fifty six.

Judith Ambeck the daughter of Mr Johannes Ambeeck born the fifth of December one thousand sixe hundred fifty four.

(*To be Continued.*)

FAMILY MEETING OF KELLOGGS.

The following account of the gathering of the descendants of the late Hon. CHARLES KELLOGG, of Kelloggsville, N. Y., is copied from the *Auburn American*, of October 9th, 1857, having been furnished to that paper by a clergyman, who was a guest on the occasion. As such meetings are full of interest to families composing them; and this was marked by the unusual circumstance of eleven brothers and sisters, whose united ages averaged forty-nine and one half years, and whose ranks had never been broken by a single death, it is hoped it will come within the objects of this Register.

A Member of the N. E. Hist. & Gen. Soc.

I designed before this to have given you an account of the Kellogg reunion, which was enjoyed at the "American," in this city, on Tuesday of last week. The family made no parade of their gathering, and none of them have thought to publish it; but it seems to me that such an occasion is of too much interest to be kept from the public. As one who has long known them, and who shared their hospitality that day, I will give your readers an account of the family, and of their recent meeting.

The Kelloggs are of Scotch descent, and they trace an interesting and honorable genealogy. Charles Kellogg, father of the present family, was born in Sheffield, Mass., Oct. 3, 1773. At the age of fourteen he removed to Galway, Saratoga Co., N. Y., where his father had settled as a pioneer seven years before. At twenty-one he married Mary Ann Otis, a descendant of the Pilgrims, and two years after, with their eldest son, then an infant, and with an outfit but little more than willing hands and stout hearts, Mr. and Mrs. Kellogg sought a new home in central New York. Their conveyance was a sled and oxen; their road was through woods which they had to open some portions of the way; and after a fatiguing journey of fifteen days they arrived at their first home in Marcellus, on the western shore of Skeneateles Lake. They erected a log cabin, made a clearing in the forest, remained one year, sold their improvements to a wealthier immigrant, and purchased a second home in Aurelius, (now Owasco,) resided there two years, again sold out, and in the autumn of 1799 removed to the third forest farm, in Sempronius, (now Niles,) where they resided forty years.

These changes enabled them at each remove to enlarge their possessions, and at this home, for many years known as Kelloggsville, their family history chiefly transpired. Before the new farm was fully cleared, Mr. Kellogg added merchandizing to farming, and acquired a moderate fortune. The writer of this remembers when the farmers of Sempronius drew their grain on sleighs to Albany and returned with goods for Mr. Kellogg's store. He was the second justice of the peace appointed in that town, and was supervisor for several years. In 1808 he was elected to the State Assembly, and received a re-election the following year. He subsequently held the office of judge of the county courts. In 1812 the village post-office was established, and he was the first postmaster, while his own name was given by the postmaster general to the office, and since then the village has been called Kelloggsville. In 1821 and 1822, he again represented Cayuga Co. in the Assembly; and in 1824 he was elected a representative in Congress, and took his seat in Dec. 1825,— the first Congress under Mr. Adams' administration. In all his services as a legislator, he was more a man of deeds than words, and held a high position as a man of eminent justice and practical common sense. In all his offices, and in all his life, he secured the highest confidence and warmest esteem of the public.

Returning from Congress, he gave his chief attention to his farm for the next ten years, and then sold the old homestead and removed to Ann Arbor, Mich., where four of his children were settled. He died in May, 1842, aged 68, leaving the example of as fine and as happy a christian manhood as one often sees on earth. Mrs. Kellogg, who was in all respects worthy of such a husband, survived him only two and a half years.

They had eleven children, six sons and five daughters, all of whom are alive and happy now.

They are, 1, Day Otis, b. Aug. 7, 1796, of Brooklyn, N. Y.; 2, Dwight, b. Oct. 4, 1797, of New York; 3, Dor, b. Feb. 8, 1799, of Ann Arbor, Mich.; 4, Delia, (Mrs. C. Whitwood of Auburn,) b. April 7, 1803; 5, Abigail Ann, (Mrs. E. A. Warden of Auburn,) b. June 10, 1804; 6, Charles Harvey, b. Sept. 19, 1808, of Lansinburgh, N. Y.; 7, Electa Semanthy, (Mrs. Abell, a widow, of Peekskill;) b. July 28th, 1810; 8, Dan W., b. March 26th, 1812, of Brooklyn; 9, Dorlinka, (Mrs. Backus,) b. Jan. 17, 1816, of Peekskill; 10, Frances Louisa, (Mrs. Otis, of Almond, N. Y.,) b. March 6th, 1818; 11, John Quincy, b. March 24th, 1823, of Yonkers.

The brothers and sisters now have thirty-one children, twenty-three sons and eight daughters.

The sons are, all but one, engaged in mercantile pursuits, and a more capable family of merchants I have seldom found. The daughters are not behind their brothers in mind or heart, while their marriage connexions are excellent. The eldest son, Day Otis, has been a member of the State Assembly, Mayor of Troy, Paymaster General of N. Y. State Militia, and U. S. Consul at Glasgow, Scotland; to all of which offices he gave character and honor. The youngest daughter, Frances, resided for a time with her husband on a consulship in Switzerland.

This excellent family were never all together but twice in their lives. In 1836, they all met for the first time in the old homestead at Kelloggsville, when their father and mother blessed them. Their second reunion was last week, (Sept. 29th.) The sun took their pictures in a group of excellent photographs, after which they dined at the American. Their wives and husbands, (with three exceptions,) were present, as were also a number of their children, with two or three guests. Hon. Day Otis Kellogg read an interesting sketch of their history, and addressed to them a few very tender and eloquent remarks on the character of their parents, on their reunion, and their family hopes and loves and duties. They sang family hymns, and related both sad and mirthful stories of early life. They intended to visit the old homestead together the next day, but were prevented from going. During the feast of reunion they received message after message of joy and love, by telegraph and otherwise, from absent children and old friends.

Here, sir, is a family, remarkable at least for numbers and fine health, and for a general resemblance of features and characters, with some finely drawn lines of personal dissimilitude; a group of good heads and faces, on each of whose characters and in each of whose lives and fortunes, the light of the best parental influence and christian education may be traced. And though I have enjoyed many happy occasions, I remember none that brought hearts to a warmer glow of gladness, or will shed a sweeter light on the future, than this last reunion of the Kellogg family.

Auburn, N. Y., Oct. 8, 1857.   D. K. L.

GENEALOGICAL ITEMS OF THE KELLOGG FAMILY.

[By D. O. Kellogg, a member of the N. E. Hist. Gen. Soc.]

There seems a propriety in introducing the name of Kellogg into this "Register," as the earliest history of the family locates them in New England, and connects them with its annals. For several generations they are believed to have remained there, though now the name is found in many parts of the United States, and their descendants have become numerous. The name is found in the early records of the first settlements on the Connecticut River, but no connected history of the family of those days has been discovered.

It is not pretended that these fragments embrace more than a brief record of a portion of the family, and it is admitted that they are entirely deficient in relation to the immigration of its progenitors from Europe, as well as to the history of their early descendants. Much remains to be known before a complete genealogy can be written. It is, however, hoped that this beginning may stimulate some one having leisure, and feeling sufficient interest in the research, to continue the subject, until a full record shall be published.

The present writer has been unable, in the limited investigations his pursuits have permitted, to trace back the progenitors to their first settlement in America, or to their European home immediately prior to their immigration. An existing similarity of name, now in Scotland, gives a probable clue to their early history. Tradition relates that they were originally Scotch, and that, being partizans of James VI., of Scotland, they came with that prince to England when he ascended the throne of Great Britain as James I.—where they remained until their settlement in New England. They came here soon after the landing of the Pilgrims at Plymouth, and settled somewhere in Massachusetts.

The Herald's College, London, records two ancient families in Scotland, bearing the name of KELLOCK. One was of the nobility,—the head of which was a duke. No trace of such rank now remains. The other were commoners, having a heraldic claim to the distinction of a *coat of arms*, the description of which is, for the present, omitted. The simplicity of American institutions suggests that the claim of descent should be based on the latter.

Late inquiries in Scotland, by the writer, led to the discovery of two families, now residing there,—one in Fifeshire, the other in Dumfriesshire,—there may be others, of the same name as that in heraldry. The Gaelic idiom justifies the belief that, originally, the name was written KILLOCH. The guttural sound given by the Scotch to the letter *h*, at the termination of words, is very nearly the American sound of *g*, and accounts for the change of spelling in this country. When surnames were first introduced into Britain, the names of cities, towns, manors, estates, and local objects were often adopted by families. This suggests a probable explanation of the origin and meaning of the name. In the Gaelic language, KIL is a burial place, and LOCH a lake. Thus KILLOCH indicates *Lake Cemetery*, or the family of the *Lake Burial Ground*. In process of time the name has become KELLOCK, in Scotland, and KELLOGG in the United States.

Materials now at hand serve only to give an imperfect account of that branch of the family settled in western Massachusetts, a century and a half ago, and of such of their descents as were among the early emigrants to the State of New York.

(1) STEPHEN KELLOGG,[1] resided in Westfield, Mass., on the river of that name, in the early part of the eighteenth century, and is believed to have been a farmer. Particulars of his birth, marriage and family have not been ascertained.

(2) SILAS,[2] son of Stephen, was born in Westfield, in 1714, married Ruth Root, daughter of Josiah Root, of the same place, b. March, 1722. They settled in Sheffield, Mass., in early life, and were among the first settlers of that then frontier town. He was clerk of the land office established there by the proprietors of Sheffield, embracing the present town of that name, and the town now known as Great Barrington. He was a man of high social and religious character, and died about 1790. His widow survived him many years, and d. there in 1818, at the advanced age of 96. They had four sons and five daughters, all of whom married, and most of them lived to old age, viz. :

(3)   I. EPHRAIM,[3] b. in 1740 ; resided in Sheffield ; a farmer.
(4)   II. ENOS,[3] b. in 1742 ; resided in Sheffield ; a farmer.
(5)   III. ASA,[3] b. Feb. 19, 1745 ; m. Lucy Powell of S., who was b. Feb. 27, 1746 ; d. Nov. 9, 1816 ; settled in Galway, Saratoga Co., N. Y., during the revolution; was a farmer; held the offices of justice of the peace and captain of the militia,—then important stations ; was a deacon in the presbyterian church, and universally respected. He d. June 4, 1820, aged 75.
(6)   IV. ELEANOR,[3] b. 1747 ; m. Joab Austin ; set. in Sheffield ; d. in Homer, N. Y., Aug. 20, 1835.
(7)   V. RUTH,[3] b. 1749 ; m. Solomon Kellogg ; set. in New Hartford, Ct. ; removed to Paris, Oneida Co., N. Y. ; d. at an advanced age ; had 12 sons.
(8)   VI. RHODA,[3] b. 1753 ; m. Moses Kellogg ; set. in New Hartford.
(9)   VII. MIRIAM,[3] b. 1755 ; m. Dr. Lewis Beebe ; set. in Pawlet, Vt.
(10) VIII. SILAS,[3] b. 1757 ; m. Rhoda Root of Sheffield ; resided in that town through life, and represented it for several years in the Legislature ; was a member of the Convention of 1821, for amending the Constitution of Massachusetts ; served much in public life, and was highly respected. He d. at an advanced age, leaving sons and daughters.
(11)   IX. ANNA,[3] b. in 1760 ; m. James Hickok ; set. in Lansinburgh, N. Y., and d. in old age.

Asa,[3] (5) who m. Lucy Powell, had 7 sons and 2 daughters, who lived to mature age.

(12)   I. FREDERICK,[4] b. in Sheffield, Sept. 27, 1766 ; m. 1, Polly Phelps ; 2, Tryphena White ; 3, Mrs. Brown. Left Galway in 1803 ; set. in Brutus, Cayuga Co., N. Y. ; a farmer ; d. in Auburn, Oct. 16, 1832, leaving the example of a well spent life. Had a large family of sons and daughters.
(13)   II. EZRA,[4] b. in S., June 26, 1769 ; m. Abigail Olmstead ; set. in Galway ; d. Oct. 13, 1836. Had sons and daughters.
(14)   III. MARTIN,[4] b. in S., June 22, 1771 ; m. Rhoda Smith ; set. in Mexico, Oswego Co., N. Y. ; d. Jan. 27, 1854. Had 3 sons and 1 daughter.

(14½)   IV. CHARLES,[4] b. in S., Oct. 3, 1773; m. Mary Ann Otis, daughter of David Otis of Galway, Oct. 21, 1794,—a direct descendant of John Otis, one of the English colony who settled Hingham, Mass., in 1635. She was b. Nov. 3, 1774. They set. in that part of Sempronius, Cayuga Co., N. Y., now known as Kelloggsville; resided there about forty years, then removed to Ann Arbor, Mich. He d. there May 11, 1842, aged 68; and she, Oct. 14, 1844, aged 70. He was a farmer, and for many years a merchant also; was much in public life, having been a member of the New York Legislature, four years; a representative in Congress two years, and for several years a judge of the county courts, besides serving many years in minor offices. In his public employments he secured the confidence and esteem of the people. Through life he maintained a consistent religious character, and left an unsullied name and many excellent examples, a precious legacy to his descendants. Had six sons and five daughters.

(15½)   V. ASA,[4] b. in S., Nov. 12, 1777; m. 1, Margaret Stewart, b. April 18, 1796; d. June 11, 1819; 2, Ann Stewart, b. May 15, 1794; d. April 17, 1843. He d. Aug. 23, 1836; was an estimable and successful merchant, first in Milton, N. Y., then for many years in Troy, N. Y. Had sons and daughters.

(17)   VI. LUCY,[4] b. Nov. 11, 1779; m. 1, David Westcott; 2, Reuben Hewett; d. in western New York, April 13, 1851.

(18½)   VII. WARREN,[4] b. in Galway, June 2, 1783; m. Abigail Paine of Troy, b. Nov. 6, 1790, who survives. He d. Feb. 23, 1835; was an honorable and successful merchant in Troy. Had sons and daughters.

(19)   VIII. ALEXANDER CRAUS,[4] b. in G., June 22, 1785; m. 1, Ann Sayles; 2, Ann Hinman Davis, now living. He was many years a merchant in Troy; removed to Connecticut, and d. in Bridgeport, June 13, 1846. Left two sons and two daughters.

(20)   ELECTA,[4] b. in G., May 6, 1788; m. Alanson Kennedy. They settled in western New York. She d. Sept. 1839.

Frederick,[4] (12) who m. 1, Polly Phelps; 2, Tryphena White, had

(21)   I. SILAS,[5] b. in G., June 6, 1789; m. Martha Simpson of Brutus; farmer; resides in Ira, N. Y.; has sons and daughters.

(22)   II. POLLY,[5] b. in G., June 6, 1790; m. William G. Beach, res. in Dexter, Mich.

(23)   III. LUCINDA,[5] b. in G., Aug. 10, 1791; m. David Dixon. She is a widow; res. in Lima, Mich.

(24)   IV. ALVAN,[5] b. in G., Jan. 12, 1793; m. Sylvia Stow, formerly a cloth dresser, of whom Ex-President Fillmore learned that trade; is now a farmer; res. in Scott, N. Y.; has been many years a justice of the peace, supervisor, &c., and has served in the legislature. Has sons and daughters.

(25)   V. WEALTHY,[5] b. in G., Oct. 24, 1794; m. Milo Phelps. Is a widow; set. in Painesville, O.; now res. in Ladoga, Wis.

(26)   VI. AMANDA,[5] b. in G., Aug. 24, 1796; m. Henry Perine; res. in Ira.

(27) VII. FREDERICK,[5] b. in G., Nov. 26, 1797; m. 1, Sally Everst; 2,
—————; set. in Scott; cloth dresser; d. in Alleghany Co.,
N. Y., Dec. 25, 1857. Had sons and daughters.

(28) VIII. ASA,[5] b. in G., April 26, 1800; m. Sarah St. John; resided
in Calhoun Co., Mich.; farmer; d. May 7, 1854.

(29) IX. LUCY,[5] b. in Brutus, June 1, 1803; m. Amos Carter; r. in Ira.

(30) X. ISRAEL PHELPS,[5] b. in B., Oct. 24, 1808; m. 1, Eliza Whiting; 2, —————; farmer; r. in Wyocena, Columbia Co.,
Wisconsin.

(31) XI. HARRIET,[5] b. in B., Dec. 10, 1810; m. Hicks P. Phelps; res.
in Wyocena, Wis.

(32) XII. CHARLES WHITE,[5] b. in B., May 21, 1815; m. Demmis D.
Comstock of Fort Ann, merchant, New York; r. in Brook-
lyn; has one son, *Peter Comstock,*[6] and two daughters,
Gertrude,[6] and *Fanny.*[6]

Ezra,[4] *who m. Abigail Olmsted, had, all b. in Galway—*

(33) I. EZRA POWELL,[5] b. March 18, 1795; m. Margaret Anderson;
res. in Galway; has one son.

(34) II. MERCY CROSBY,[5] b. May 12, 1797; d. Aug. 13, 1805.

(35) III. CLARISSA H.[5] b. June 12, 1799; m. Samuel Dauchy; r. in
Troy.

(36) IV. JONATHAN CROSBY,[5] b. Dec. 18, 1801; d. Oct. 12, 1810.

(37) V. ABIGAIL ANN,[5] b. Jan. 9, 1804; m. Sears E. Smith; res. in
Cleveland, O.

(38) VI. SYLVESTER TRUMAN,[5] b. March 22, 1806; m. Lucy Ann
Lindsley, merchant in New York; res. in Yonkers; has
sons and daughters.

(39) VII. RUTH ANN,[5] b. June 11, 1808; m. Lewis Goodrich; d. Feb.
5, 1833.

(40) VIII. LUCY,[5] b. May 2, 1811; m. R. F. Gillet; r. in Cleveland.

(41) IX. MARY,[5] b. July 10, 1813; m. Rev. Charles S. Renshaw; d.
Sept. 26, 1839.

Charles,[4] (15) *who m. Mary Ann Otis, had—*

(42) I. Day Otis,[5] b. in Galway, Aug. 7, 1796; m. 1, Ann Eliza
Smith of Lansinburgh, b. Feb. 26, 1797, d. Aug. 3, 1829;
2, Mary Ann Dimon of Fairfield, Ct., b. Dec. 31, 1804, d.
May 17, 1840; 3, Harriet Walter Odin of Boston, b. Oct.
27, 1804. A merchant, first in Owasco, N. Y., then 23
years in Troy, now in New York, resides in Brooklyn, N.
Y. Has occasionally served in public life, having been a
member of the New York Legislature, Mayor of Troy, and
U. S. Consul at Glasgow, Scotland. Has five sons.

(43) II. DWIGHT,[5] b. in Marcellus, N. Y., Oct. 4, 1797; m. Minerva
Annable, who d. —————; settled in Ann Arbor, Mich.;
res. now in New York. Has five sons, *Charles Annable,*[6]
Calvin Whitwood,[6] *Don W.,*[6] *William Henry,*[6] and *George
Dwight,*[6] and one daughter, *Julia.*[6]

(44) III. DON,[5] b. in Aurelius, N. Y., Feb. 8, 1799; m. Lucretia Annable; res. in Ann Arbor. Has served as a justice of the
peace, and in other offices.

(45) IV. DELIA,[5] b. in Kelloggsville, April 7, 1808; m. Calvin Whitwood; res. in Auburn, N. Y.

(46)   V. Abigail Ann,[4] b. in K., June 10, 1801 ; m. Ethan A. Warden ; res. in Auburn.

(47)   VI. Charles Harvey,[4] b. in K., Sept. 19, 1808 ; m. Frances Amelia Parmelee of Lansinburgh, where they now reside ; merchant and manufacturer in Troy ; has four sons,— *William P.,[5] Warren T.,[5] Francis Pelatiah,[5]* and *Henry Parmelee;[5]* and three daughters, *Mary Frances,[5] Amelia L.,[5]* and *Harriet Odin.[5]*

(48)   VII. Electa Semantha,[4] b. in K., July 28, 1810 ; m. Col. William A. Abell of Ann Arbor ; a widow ; res. in Peekskill, N. Y.

(49)   VIII. Dan W.,[4] b. in Galway, March 26, 1812 ; m. 1, Esther A. Bull of Troy ; 2, Kate Pake of Lansinburgh ; 3, Emma S. Congdon of Syracuse.   Was two years secretary of the Michigan Senate under Gov. Woodbridge's administration ; merchant in New York ; res. in Brooklyn.

(50)   IX. Dorliska,[4] b. in K., Jan. 17, 1816 ; m. Dr. Cyrus Backus ; res. in Peekskill.

(51)   X. Frances Louisa,[4] b. in K., March 6, 1818 ; m. Seth T. Otis of Chicago, Ill., who has been U. S. Consul to Basle, Switzerland ; res. at Almond, Allegany Co., N. Y.

(52)   XI. John Quincy,[4] b. in K., March 24, 1823 ; m. Helen Mary Dauchy of Troy ; merchant in New York ; res. in Yonkers. Has one son, *George Abel,[5]* and two daughters, *Fanny Louisa,[5]* and *Clara Dauchy.[5]*

Asa,[4] (16) *who m.* 1, *Margaret Stewart* ; 2, *Ann Stewart* ; *had, all b. in Troy :—*

(53)   I. Eliza,[4] b. July 27, 1805 ; d. Sept. 8, 1806.

(54)   II. Warren Stewart,[4] b. March 1, 1807 ; m. Lucy Ann Rawdon of New York ; res. in Hempstead, L. I. ; has sons and daughters. *Ralph Rawdon,[5]* d. at two years old ; *Edward H.,[5] Lucy Ann,[5] Margaret Anne,[5] Leavitt Rawdon,[5] Warren S.,[5] Isaac Merritt,[5] Susan A.,[5] I. Newton Phelps.[5]*

(55)   III. Edward Asa,[4] b. June 15, 1808 ; d. Oct. 20, 1809.

(56)   IV. Edward,[4] b. Jan. 20, 1810 ; m. Sarah Hastings, who d. ——; res. in Independence, Mo.   Has sons and daughters.

(57)   V. Asa,[4] b. July 2, 1811 ; never married ; d. 1848.

(58)   VI. Eliza,[4] b. Aug. 5, 1813 ; d. Sept. 15, 1815.

(59)   VII. Margaret Ann,[4] b. March 1, 1821 ; m. Francis Newlands ; resided at West Point, N. Y. ; d. Feb. 20, 1858.

(60)   VIII. Jane Eliza,[4] b. April 27, 1822 ; d. July 15, 1823.

(61)   IX. Jane Eliza,[4] 2d, b. Sept. 26, 1823 ; m. James S. Knowlson ; resides in Troy.

(62)   X. Mary,[4] b. Aug. 12, 1826 ; m. George Redfield of Troy ; d. 1847.

(63)   XI. William,[4] b. Aug. 25, 1829 ; d. Nov. 15, 1830.

(64)   XII. Henry,[4] b. Aug. 25, 1829 ; m. Sarah May ; resides in Westminster, Vt. ; has children.

(65)   XIII. Caroline,[4] b. May 6, 1833 ; d. Sept. 15, 1835.

Warren,[4] (18) *who m. Abigail Paine, had, all b. in Troy :—*

(66)   I. George William,[4] b. Feb. 27, 1812 ; m. Charlotte Elizabeth Cobb of Albany ; was a merchant in Troy ; d. April 15, 1849 ; left one son, *Sanford Cobb,[5]* and one daughter, *Frances Southwick.[5]*

(67)   II. John Paine,* b. Oct. 11, 1814; unmarried; merchant in New
          York.
(68)   III. Henry Lyman,* b. April 28, 1817; graduate of Washington
          College, Ct.; m. Frances A. Wilson of Troy; merchant in
          Cleveland, O.; has two sons, *Lewis Southwick*,* and *Wil-
          liam Cooper*,* and 3 daus., *Elizabeth Homer*,* *Mary Lyman*,*
          and *Ellen Wheeler*.*
(69)   IV. Mary Elizabeth,* b. Oct. 11, 1818; d. March 8, 1820.
(70)   V. Frances Lucretia,* b. Jan. 25, 1821; m. Maj. George H.
          Thomas, U. S. A.; res. at Fort Mason, Texas.
(71)   VI. Julia Augusta,* b. Dec. 6, 1822; unmarried; res. in Troy.
(72)   VII. Charles Augustus,* b. March 26, 1825; graduate of Har-
          vard University, 1845; studied law in Montgomery, Ala.;
          practised in New Orleans; removed to New York in 1851;
          now a merchant there.
(73)   VIII. Samuel Cobb,* b. April 23, 1828; d. Sept. 24, 1828.
(74)   IX. Caroline Louisa,* b. Oct. 25, 1830; d. Dec. 3, 1830.
(75)   X. Ellen Maria,* b. Sept. 17, 1831; d. Aug. 27, 1832.
(76)   XI. Homer Hall,* b. Dec. 9, 1833; d. May 23, 1837.

Day Otis, now of Brooklyn, has five sons.*

(77)   I. Dorr Smith,* b. in Owasco, Aug. 5, 1826; m. Kate Curtis
          of N. White Creek, N. Y.; merchant in New York.
(78)   II. Charles Day,* b. in Troy, June 4, 1828; m. Mary Elizabeth
          Cobb of Boston; merchant in B.; resides in Brookline, Ma.
(79)   III. George Dixon,* b. in Troy, July 13, 1833; graduated at the
          University of Vermont, 1853; m. Harriet A. Sanborn of
          Peru, N. Y.; counsellor at law; office and residence, N. Y.
(80)   IV. Theodore Dwight,* b. in Troy, April 17, 1835; settled in
          Ida County, Iowa.
(81)   V. Day Otis, 2d,* b. in Troy, March 31, 1837; graduated at
          Hobart College, Geneva, 1857; resides in Boston.

HOUSEHOLD REGULATIONS OF HENRY VIII.

The following extracts have been transcribed from a *Manuscript* of the time of *Henry
VIII.* They relate to the Household regulations of this noted English sovereign.

We give the literal reading with an amended orthography.

Its design may have been to caricature certain customs common in high places at
that day.

Quaint and inelegant though these extracts may appear, and meagre intrinsically as
a historic record, as they confessedly are, yet from the great antiquity of the paper,
(1537,) it may possess some interest, if from no other cause.   A. W., of F., Ct.

"His Highness's attendants are not to steal any locks or keys, tables,
forms, cupboards, or other furniture, out of Nobleman's or Gentlemen's
houses where he goes to visit.

There shall be no romping with the maids on the staircases by which
dishes and other things are often broken—Care should also be taken of the
pewter spoons, and that the wooden ones, used in the kitchen, be not
broken or stolen.

The pages shall not interrupt the kitchen maids;—and he that is guilty
of seduction shall pay a fine of two marks to his Highness, and have his
allowance of beer withheld for a month."

INSCRIPTIONS FROM THE BURYING-GROUND IN HULL, MASS.

[Transcribed, July, 1857, by W. S. BARTON.]

THIS collection comprises *all* the inscriptions, which are at all legible, found upon the various stones and monuments in the only burying-ground in Hull. There are a few rough stones, partially broken or buried in the ground, upon which inscriptions once existed, but are now too much defaced and weatherbeaten, where exposed to the elements, to allow their various memorials to be even partially decyphered. Two or three dates, only, are preserved from the fragments of stone found in the enclosure; one, with the *title* of a name, " Capt.," and the date, " Died April ye 2d 1708," the earliest date found; one with the date only of " April 30. 1718," and another of " Sept 30. 1759." The burying-ground is situated towards the easterly part of the town, on the west side of the road so constantly frequented in the summer season by parties visiting Nantasket Beach, and is but a short distance from the Marine telegraph station at Hull, and the coast in the vicinity of the lower light in Boston harbor. The number of deaths recorded in this collection is one hundred and three, and the different inscriptions are given *verbatim*, as near as may be, the names of individuals and families being alphabetically arranged, so far as the inscriptions would allow.

The writer was engaged one summer afternoon only in transcribing these interesting memorials, and may have occasionally failed in *literal exactness*, but, in the main, believes his record to be faithfully accurate and reliable.

DINNEY.

1. In memory of Jonathan son to Mr. Benjamin & Mrs. Jane Dinney, who died Oct. ye 20. 1792, in his 11th year.

2. In Memory of Mrs Rebeca Widow to Capt. Amos Dinney She Died May ye [1?]5th 1798 In her 86th year.

3. In Memory of John Dinney son of Mr. Spencer and Mrs Molly Dinney, died Septr. 9. 1810 aged 9 years 7 m, and 21 days.

> ' He is not lost,
> ' He is only gone before us.'

4. In Memory of Mr. Spencer Dianey died Jan 20. 1811 Aged 53 Years.

> ' Our life is ever on the wing,
>   And Death is ever nigh,'—

[two additional lines, illegible.]

5. In memory of Miss Rebecca Dinney who died June 26. 1819 in the 83 Year of her age.

> ' My threescore years and ten are past,
>   And Christ has call'd me home at last,
>   From all my sufferings here below,
>   To dwell with him, and angels too.'

6. In memory of Miss Jane Rinney, daugr of Spencer & Molley Dinney who died Sept. 13. 1819 in the 23 year of her age.

> Stop youthful gay, and loving mate,
> Read here your step to eternal state
> Through lingering long, I sum'd to stay,
> More sudden you may pass away.

7. In Memory of Mrs. Molly Binney, Relict of Mr. Spencer Binney, died Dec. 16. 1823; Aged 51 years.

> Farewell my friends, & children dear,
> I've left this world of pain,
> May virtue be your practice here,
> Till we do meet again.

BRUCE.

8. In Memory of Mrs. Lydia Bruce wife of Jonathan Bruce Junr. & daughter of Jonathan & Lydia Loring, who died Dec. 14. 1828. aged 37 years.

> She was a tender Parent, a dutifull Wife,
> Call'd from this world in the meridian of life,
> While here she slumbers, underneath this clod,
> She will ne'er awake but by the Trump of God.

COLYER.

9. Thomas Colyer ' deceased July 25. 1719.'

CUSHING.

10. { In memory of Perez Cushing, died in the West Indies 1794,
          aged 46 ; &
11. { Ruth Cushing his wife died in this Town April 12, 1830 Aged
          77. [Same stone.]

12. In memory of Mr. Benj⁺ Cushing, died June 12, 1810, aged 70 years.

13. Robert C. Cushing son of Mr. Robert V. and Mrs. Mary Cushing, died May 12, 1816, aged 17 months 10 days.

> Friends and physician could not save,
> The mortal body from the grave.

14. Lydia Cushing daughtr of Robert Vinal & Mary Cushing, died Nov. 4. A.D. 1822 aged 3 years & 9 months.

15. Robert Y. Cushing died March 10 A.D. 1827, aged 45.

16. William L. Cushing died at Boston, Sept 25. AD. 1827, aged 45.

17. Sarah Cushing died May 7th 1828, aged 78.

18. In Memory of Mrs. Jane Cushing, who died Dec 25, 1829, Aged 83.

19. In memory of Mr. David Cushing, died July 17, 1832. Aet. 58.

20. In memory of Mr. Pyam Cushing, died April 9. 1841. Aet 63 years.

> Thy form now mouldering back to native clay,
> Must here remain till the great rising day,
> Surviving friends who did thy friendship prove,
> Erect this stone—a token of their love.

21. In memory of Mrs. Olive Cushing, Relict of Mr. Pyam Cushing, died Jan. 6, 1848, Aet 64 years.

> When the last trumpets awful voice,
> This reading earth shall shake,
> The opening graves shall yield their dead,
> And dust to life awake.

22. Judith S. Cushing dr of R. V. & Mary C. d⁴ June 24 1855 aged 33 yrs 6 mos.

> Dear Judith—thy mother consecrates this stone,
> A mark of friendship and of love sincere,
> While in her memory ever thou shalt bloom,
> And in her heart forever will be dear.

23. Mary Cushing, daughter of Robert V. & Mary Cushing died Feb. 9, 1856, aged 41 years 4 mos.

> Tranquil she left this transitory scene,
> With joyful triumph and a look serene
> By faith she fixed her ardent hopes on high,
> In Jesus' merits, and in him did die.

24. Jane L. Cushing, d. of Robert V. & Mary Cushing died July 31. 1856, aged 39 yrs 6 mos. & 13 days.

> While weeping friends bend o'er the silent tomb
> Recount her virtues and their loss deplore,
> Faith's piercing eyes dart through the gloom,
> And hail her blest where tears shall flow no more.

DILL.

25. { In memory of Sally Daug. of Mr. Saml. & Mrs. Susannah Dill, who died April 5. 1808 aged 2 years, 8M, 22 days. [Also on the same stone,]

26. { In memory of Alonzo son of Mr. Saml. & Mrs. Susannah Dill, who died Aug. 5. 1808 aged 3 months.

27. Susan M. Dill, Daught. of Solomon Dill, died July 18, 1838, AET. 19 years.

GOOLD.

28. In memory of Mr. Elisha Goold, who died Dec. 24, 1816, Et. 73.

29. In Memory of Mrs. Martha Goold, wife of Mr. Elisha Goold, died Sep. 4. 1819 Aged 74 Years.

> Reader stand still and drop a tear,
> Think on the dust that slumbers here;
> And when you read the state of me,
> Think on the glass that runs for thee.

30. Sacred to the Memory of Bitha T. Goold, Wife of John Goold, Who died May 31st. 1830, Aged 38 years.

> Farewell vain world, with all thy various ties,
> I go to prove my mansion's in the skies,
> My time of suffering ceased with my breath,
> I die to live, for I have liv'd for death.

GOULD.

31. In Memory of Mr John Gould, died August 4. 1810, aged 37 years.

> Quick snatch'd from time and sense,
> Here must my body lay,
> Till Jesus call me from the [grave !]
> To see that last Day.

32. In Memory of Miss, Mary Gould, Daur of Mr. Sam¹ & Mrs. Mary Gould died July 11. 1818, aged 16 years.

> Yet kindred breasts regret her early end,
> And mourn a lovely daughter, sister, friend,
> Submissive, fond, affectionately dear,
> Her memory nurtured by a tender tear.

33. In memory of Elisha Gould, son of Sam¹ & Mary Gould, who died in Boston, June 4. 1824, Et. 16.

> Why should we mourn departed friends,
> Or shrink at death's alarms,
> 'Tis but the voice that Jesus sends,
> To call us to his arms.

34. William Brewster, son of Rev. Robert and Rebecca L. Gould, died Oct. 8. 1842, aged 7 years.

> "He cometh forth like a flower, and is cut down."

35. Thomas Lincoln, Member of the Sophomore Class, Wesleyan University, and son of Rev. Robert and Rebecca L. Gould, died at Middletown Con. Sept. 23, 1847, aged 20 years.

> "Thy Brother shall rise again."

36. Sacred to the memory of Mrs. Mary G. Gould, wife of Samuel Gould, Died Oct. 22, 1848, Aged 73 years.

> Home thou art gone; thy lips declared
> The Hope that strong inspired thy breast;
> A life well spent, through lengthened years,
> Secure[s] the promised home of rest.

GREENLEAF.

37. In memory of Bathsheba Greenleaf, died Dec. 2, 1825, æt. 83. [This and the following, enclosed by a wooden fence.]

38. John Greenleaf died Dec. 23, 1827 AEt. 54.

HUNT.

39. Sacred to the Memory of Mr. Matthew Hunt, died May 16. 1797, in the 43 year of his Age.

> Quick, snatched from time and sense,
> Here must this body lay,
> Till Jesus calls me from the dust,
> At the great rising day.

40. Sacred to the Memory of Mrs. Winefred Hunt, Wife of Mr. Matthew Hunt, died Feb. 12, 1842 AEt. 68 years.

> Our life how short, a groan, a sigh,
> We live—and then begin to die,
> But Oh! how great a mercy this,
> That death's a portal into bliss.

KNIGHT.

41. Susan P. Knight, daught of Joel and Jane L. Knight, died Nov 26. 1840, AEt. 6 Years.

> "Them which sleep in Jesus, will
> God bring with him."

42. Sacred to the Memory of Rev. Joel Knight, 13 Years a traveling minister of the M. E. Church. Born at Sudbury Mass. May 4. 1804, closed his labours and his life in Providence R. I., Aug'st 13. 1843, Aged 39 Years 3 Months & 9 Days.

> "And I heard a voice from heaven saying unto me,—Write, Blessed are the dead which die in the Lord, from henceforth; yea, saith the Spirit, that they may rest from their labours, and their works do follow them."

43. Timothy Tabor, son of Joel and Jane L. Knight died Oct. 18, 1843, AEt. 1 Year, & 4½ Months.

> "Suffer little children to come unto me, and forbid them not, for of such is the kingdom of Heaven."

KNOX.

44. In memory of Mrs. Content Knox, Relict of Mr. Thomas Knox, Died Oct. 3, 1825, Æt. 65 years.

LORING.

45. Here lyes yᵉ body of [*Elijah*] Loring. [* * *] He died Sept. yᵉ 9. 1715. [This, and the next stone, are much defaced.]

46. Here lyes y° body of Benjamin Loring, aged 72 years, Died March y° 10th. 1716.

47. Here Lyes y° body of Mr. John Loring, died February y° 29. 1719, in y° 49th. year of his age.

48. In memory of Jane, Dau' to Mr. Samuel Loring Jur. & Mrs. Huldah his wife.   She died Sept y° 5th 1791, aged 16 months & 19 days.

49. In memory of Mrs. Jane wife of Mr. Samuel Loring.   She Died Oct. y° 19th 1795, in her 73d year.

50. In Memory of Capt. Daniel Loring died Nov. 2, 1801, aged 46 years.

    May Guardian angels watch the sleeping dust,
    Till time shall have the rising of the Just.

51. In memory of Elisha Loring, son of Mr. Jon° and Mrs. Lydia Loring, died March 20, 1810, Aged 14 years.

52. In Memory of Eliza Loring, Daughter of Mr. Jona. & Mrs. Lydia Loring, died March 16, 1811, aged 16 years.

    Now here my body silent lays,
    And moulders back to dust,
    But Jesus call'd my soul away,
    To live among the just.

53. William D. Loring, son of Mr. James C. & Mrs. Mary Loring, died Feb. 14. 1813 Aged 34 Days.

54. In memory of Mr. Samuel Loring, died Sept 19, 1813, Aged 92 years.

55. In Memory of Sarah Loring, Daugh. of Mr. John G. & Mrs. Martha Loring, died June 2, 1815, Aged 4 months & 28 Days.

56. In memory of Lucy N. Loring, Daught. of Mr. Samuel & Mrs. Lucy Loring, died May 29, 1816, aged 14 months, & 1 day.

57. In Memory of Mrs. Martha Loring wife of John G. Loring, who died April 18, 1817, Æt. 33.

    In faith she dy'd, in dust she lies,
    But faith foresees her dust shall rise,
    When Jesus with Almighty word,
    Calls sleeping saints to meet their Lord.

58. In Memory of Mrs. Huldah Loring, wife of Mr. Samuel Loring, died July 23, 1820 Æt. 70 years.

59. In Memory of Miss Harriot Loring, Daught. of Mr. Daniel & Elizabeth Loring, died Sept. 17, 1826, Æt. 42.

    We part to meet in heaven.

60. Sacred to the memory of Mr. John Loring, who died Jan. 18, 1828, in his 77 year.

    May these few lines engraver'd stand,
    In Memory of your departed friend ;
    When Christ commands, we all must go,
    And bid farewell to all below.

61. In memory of Mr. Jonathan Loring who died July 6, 1830, Æt. 71.

62. In Memory of Mrs. Mehitab" Loring, wife of Mr. John Loring, died Feb. 5, 1834, Aged 88 Years.

63. In memory of Mr. Samuel Loring died June 14, 1840, Æt. 86 years.

> "For me to live was Christ, and to die is gain."
> Patriarch and friend of peace, we seek thy shade in vain,
> Yet allege thy memory to the lips of penury and pain,
> Thy memory is on the spot, where thy fresh childhood grew,
> By living intellect, embalm'd with ever fragrant dew.

64. In memory of Mrs. Sophronia S. Loring, wife of Aboer D. Loring, who died Dec. 20. 1841, aged 25 years.

> Ordained to lose the partner of my breast,
> Whose virtue warmed me, and whose beauty bless'd,
> I yet remember that the parting sigh,
> Appoints the good to slumber, not to die,
> The starting tear I check; I kiss the rod,
> And not to earth resign her; but to God

65. In memory of Rachel C. Loring, daughter of Samuel and Lucy Loring, born Aug. 4, 1827, died Dec. 19, 1843.

> Peace to her dust; for surely peace her gentle spirit knows,
> Around her narrow house on earth, the night wind sadly blows,
> But heavenly airs, that through the trees of life forever play,
> Are breathing on her spirit's brow, to dry her tears away.

66. Sacred to the memory of Mrs. Elizabeth Loring, who died Dec. 22, 1851, aged 95 years, 4 months.

> Life's labor done, as sinks the clay,
> Light from its load the spirit flies,
> While heaven and earth combine to say,
> How blest the righteous when he dies.

LOVELL.

67. In memory of James Goold son to Mr. Samuel and Mrs. Olive Lovell, he Died Dec. ye 31. 1796, Aged 18 months.

68. Sacred to the memory of Mr. Samuel Lovell, died Aug. 7, 1807, aged 54 years.

> Friends and Physicians could not save
> My mortal body from the Grave,
> Nor shall the grave confine me here,
> When Christ commands me to appear.

69. { In memory of Mr. Caleb G. Lovell, died Aug. 6, 1828, Æt. 37
      years. [Also upon the same stone,]
70. { And his son Caleb G. Lovell, lost at sea Oct. 25, 1839, Æt. 24
      years.

71. Sacred to the memory of Mrs. Olive Lovell, Relict of Mr. Samuel Lovell, died Aug. 25, 1844, Æt. 87 years.

MITCHELL.

72. In Memory of Mrs. Hannah Mitchell, wife of Mr. John Mitchell, died July 15, 1825, Æt. 29 years. She was a native of Carlscrona, Sweden.

73. In memory of Lucy S. Mitchell, obt. July 25, 1839, aged 18 years, 7 mo.

74. Elizabeth Mitchell, Daught. of John Mitchell, died July 27, 1840, Æt. 17 years.

Newcomb.

75. Sacred to the memory of Mrs. Harriet, Wife of Mr. Bryant Newcomb, died Jany 31st, 1808, A.E. 20.

> May these few lines engraven stand,
> In mem'ry of your departed friend,
> When Jesus calls, we all must go,
> And bid farewell to all below.

76. In memory of Mrs. Elizabeth Newcomb, Relict of Mr. Oliver Newcomb, died Sept. 6, 1821, Aged 60 years.

77. Sacred to the memory of Mr. Peter Newcomb, who died April 22, 1833, Aged 52 yrs.   [Also, on same stone.]

78. Also Simon P. Son of Peter & Margaret Newcomb, died May 20, 1826, Æt. 2 yrs.   [Also, the following.]

79 and 80. And 2 Infant children.

> No pain nor grief, nor anxious fears,
> Invade thy bounds; no mortal woes
> Can reach the peaceful sleepers here
> While angels watch their soft repose.

[This inscription is upon a marble stone, enclosed by an iron fence.]

Reed.

81. In Memory of Mrs. Bessy Reed, wife of Mr. John Reed, died March 24, 1815, Aged 45 Years.

82. In Memory of Mr. John Reed Jr., who died April 17, 1828, Aged 31 Yrs.

> Stop my young friends, and on this Grave,
> Pray cast an eye without delay,
> My Wife and Children for me do mourn,
> For I to them, can near [ne'er] return.

83. To the memory of John Reed, who died Mar. 5, 1832, In the 85th year of his age.

> Rest sleeper rest, thy toils and pains,
> No more shall press thy weary soul,
> That peaceful shore where Jesus reigns,
> Is thine while endless ages roll.

84. In Memory of Mrs. Martha, wife of Mr. John Reed, who died Dec. 29, 1838 aged 58 years.

> Thirty four years by faith in Christ she trod,
> The blissful path that leads from sin to God,
> Reader, believe the Saviour's words, and fly,
> From every sin, then rise to joys on high.

85. In memory of Mr. Samuel Reed, who died Feb. 29 [?] 1853, Aged 87 Years.

> Like shocks of corn that's fully ripe,
> He to the grave is borne,
> Of earthly things a perfect type,
> Then let us cease to mourn.

Sirowich.

86. Esther, wife of Nicholas Sirowich, died Aug. 18, 1844, aged 36 years.

87. John L. died Feb. 16, 1835, aged 2 yrs. 6 mos.;

88. Angelino A. died Aug. 9, 1843, aged 11 mos.;

89. Mary & Esther, twin daughters, died Dec. 30, 1828, aged 4 days.

90. Children of Nicholas & Esther Sirowich.

[All in one inscription upon a marble stone.]

SOUTHER.

91. In memory of Capt. Daniel Souther, he died March y⁰ 26. 1797, in his 71ˢᵗ year.

92. In memory of Mrs. Judith, widow of Capt. Daniel Souther. She died Feb. 25ᵗʰ 1801, in her 67ᵗʰ year.

SPEAR.

93. In memory of widow Sarah Spear, who died March 12, 1823, Æ. 65.

> Reader, If love of worth thy bosom warms,
> If virtue please thee, or if friendship charms,
> On this cold Grave, O! drop a pensive tear,
> For, Friendship, virtue, worth, lay buried here
> Can bounteous heaven a greater solace give,
> Than that which whispers friends departed love, [* *, the rest
> [illegible.]

SPRAGUE.

94. Sacred to the memory of Miss Joanna Sprague, died Nov. 13, 1837, Aged 81 Years.

SWAIN.

95. Martha Swain, Daug'r of Mr. William & Mrs. Martha Swain, died March 25, 1810, aged 9 months.

96. In Memory of Mr. William Swain died July 23. 1813, Aged 39 Years.

THOMPSON.

97. Mrs. Sarah Ann Augusta, wife of William Thompson, died Feb. 14, 1837, aged 24 Years.

> We will not mourn, or even pour
> For her the sorrowing tear,
> But rather joy that she has 'scaped,
> A dread sojourning here,
> And though from earth this fond one's risen
> We trust through Christ to meet in Heaven.

TIRRELL.

98. In Memory of Jane Dau'tr of Mr. Gideon Tirrell, & Mary his Wife She died May [11th?] 1802, in her [7th?] year.

99. In Memory of Nancy Dau'tr of Mr. Gideon Tirrell, & Mary his Wife. She died May 14ᵗʰ 1802, in her 16ᵗʰ year.

100. In memory of Mrs. Mary, wife of Mr. Gideon Tirrell, who died Feb. 4. 1809, Æ. 52.

101. In memory of Mr. Gideon Tirrell, who died Feb. 28, 1823, A. E. 70.

TURNER.

102. In Memory of Mrs. Elizabeth Turner, died April 15, 1831, Æt. 44 years.

103. In Memory of Mrs. Elisha Turner, who died Aug. 16. 1849, Æt. 65 years.

> My flesh slumber in the ground,
> Till the Arkangel tramp shall sound,
> Then burst my bounds, in glad surprise,
> And in my Saviour's Image rise.

A BRANCH OF THE WHITNEY FAMILY.

[Communicated by Dr. L. M. Harris.]

On looking over the genealogy of the Whitney Family, as given in two late numbers of the Register, I find that the family name of the wife of John,[2] son of John[2] and Ruth (Reynolds) Whitney, was not known, either to Dr. Bond, or H. A. W.

Robert Harris, my emigrant ancestor, was married, Jan. 24, 1642–3, to Elizabeth Boughey, at Roxbury. Their eldest child, Elizabeth,[2] was born Nov. 9, 1644. Their next child, John,[2] was baptized Aug. 8, 1647. Elizabeth,[2] dau. of Robert II. m., (probably) in 1669, John[3] Whitney; and John,[2] son of Robert II. m., Sept. 20, 1670, Mary, b. 26. 7. 1650, dau. of Richard Sanger of Watertown. Now, by reading the will of Robert Reynolds, Vol. IX., p. 137, Gen. Reg., you will find that Ruth, the mother of John[2] W., and Mary, mother of John[2] II.'s wife were both dau. of the said Reynolds.

To make this more intelligible, I give the names of the Patriarch Robert's children in full, and in some order.

Robert Harris m., Jan. 24, 1642–3, Elizabeth Boughey.

Children of Robert and Elizabeth (Boughey) Harris.

1. Elizabeth, born Nov. 9, 1644, m. 1669, John[2] Whitney of Watertown.
2. John, baptized Aug. 8, 1647, m. Sept. 20, 1670, Mary, b. 26. 7. 1650, dau. of Richard Sanger of Watertown.
3. Timothy, born July 9, 1650, m. April 2, 1697, Abigail, b. March 30, 1681, dau. of Thomas and Susannah Morey of Roxbury.
4. Daniel, born May 14, 1652, m. June 14, 1682, Joanna Brown. Parentage not ascertained.
5. Priscilla, born Oct. 7, 1653, died Jan. 2, 1718, unm. Have a copy of her will, made Dec. 31, 1717.

I find no record of the Patriarch, Robert's, death; but his signature to a deed, May 19, 1698, is yet in existence; and a legacy, to be paid two years after his decease, to his dau. Elizabeth Whitney, is receipted for by herself and husband, Jan. 14, 1702–3, which makes it probable that he died in Jan. 1700–1.

John Whitney, the grandson of John and Elinor Whitney, the first settlers, was made freeman in May, 1684, and d. March 4, 1726, aged 83. "Elizabeth Whitney owned covenant at Roxbury chh. 30. 2. 1671." The name of John W. appears in the list of members of the 2d chh. in Roxbury, when gathered by "ye Rev. Nehemiah Walter, Nov. 2d, 1712," and, doubtless, he had previously been a member of the first chh. in Roxbury. His houselot, containing nine acres, was situated in that part of Roxbury called Jamaica Plain; and lying on the right as you pass up Pond St. to the south part of Brookline, which town was called *Muddy River* until the year 1705.

Whitney's lot extended back from the street, westerly, to the line separating Roxbury from Brookline. The late Major Benjamin Weld of Roxbury, who died in 1852, being then in his 86th year, told me, a short time before his decease, that he well remembered the Whitney house to have been standing in his boyhood. The old tabernacle has, probably, been among *the things that were*, from 75 to 80 years. Within the last 14 years, two hollows, marking the places of the cellar and well have

been visible; but the plough has since passed over, and obliterated all
marks of them. The dwelling-house of Robert Harris stood about six
rods over the line into Brookline; and the two houses—Harris's and
Whitney's—were about ⅛ of a mile apart, following the road that leads
into Brookline. In the rear of the spot where the old Whitney mansion
stood, the ground descends on a gradual slope for several rods to a narrow strip of meadow, through which runs a pleasant little brook. Beyond
the meadow, the ground rises abruptly to an elevation many feet higher
than the front of the lot; and still rises, gradually, forming a slope of
considerable dimensions, and extending westerly to its boundary on
Brookline. All that part of the lot lying west of the brook is covered
with a fine grove of forest trees. On the removal of the Whitneys, the
property came, by purchase, into the possession of the Child Family,
whose premises it joined, and was by them retained until about four years
since, when Mr. Stephen Child of Boston, lately deceased, sold the lot to
Mr. Abel Adams. On the elevated plain in the rearward portion of his
lot, Mr. Adams has erected a magnificent stone edifice, in the Eliza-
bethan style of architecture, which fairly *out-gables* Hawthorne's Pynchon
house.

The numbers given in parentheses refer to the same persons mentioned
in the Whitney Genealogy, as given in Vol. XI. of the Register, beginning on page 113, and continued on page 225.

John Whitney[e] (13) the grandson of JOHN and ELINOR, m. Elizabeth Harris, probably in 1649. He was admitted freeman, May, 1684,
d. March 4, 1726, aged 83.

ISSUE.

1. (77) *Elizabeth*, b. Sept. 9, 1670. 2. (78) *John*, b. April 1, 1672;
probably d. young. 3. (79) *Ruth*, b. Aug. 31, 1674, m. April 24, 1701,
Joseph Adams, son of Mary and Roger Adams. They lived in Brookline, where she d. Nov. 19, 1762, aged 88 years. 4. (80) *Timothy*, b.
April 16, 1678. See below. 5. (81) *Daniel*, b. Dec. 3, 1681. See
below. 6. (82) *Sarah*, b. Aug. 2, 1684. A Sarah Whitney d. July 4,
1689.

Timothy Whitney,[e] (80) m. Margaret Bacon, June 12, 1706. He
purchased land of the Prentice family, in Newton, in 1728, where he
afterwards resided. See Bond, p. 964. His children, as here given,
were born in Roxbury.

ISSUE.

(211)   I. *Sarah*, b. Feb. 28, 1707.
(212)   II. *Caleb*, b. April 7, 1711, m. Hanoah Cheney. See below.
(218)   III. *Moses*, b. June 20, 1714, m. Rebecca Hyde. See below.
(232)   IV. *Joseph*, b. Feb. 1, 1716, m. Mary Hastings. Children—1.
         Abigail, b. Dec. 18, 1749. 2. Martha, b. May 31, 1752.
         3. Ann, b. Feb. 10, 1755. 4. Samuel, b. Aug. 7, 1758.
         5. Lois, b. Sept. 5, 1761.
(240)   V. *Timothy*, b. April 30, 1720, or 1721.

Daniel Whitney,[e] (81) m. in Roxbury, June 21, 1704, Susanna
Curtis.

ISSUE.

(242)   I. *John*, b. May 23, 1705.
(243)   II. *Elizabeth*, b. Feb. 4, 1706–7.
(244)   III. *Susanna*, b. Feb. 21, 1708–9.

(245)   IV. *Daniel*, b. March 25, 1711, m. in Roxbury, Sarah Gray,
              March 7, 1709.
(246)   V. *Ann*, b. April 4, 1713.
(247)   VI. *Elijah*, b. Jan. 15, 1715, wife Hannah.   See below.
(248) VII. *Ruth*, b. Dec. 5, 1719.
(249) VIII. *Elisha*, b. Oct. 15? 1722, m. Abigail Dana.   See below.
        IX. *Esther*, bapt. July 11, 1726, (2d Ch. Rec. Roxbury,) m.
              John White, March 8, 1745, (2d Ch. Rec.)

CALEB WHITNEY,[2] (212) (son of Timothy and Margaret,) m. HANNAH
CHENEY, in 1756, dau. of Joseph and Sarah (Wiswall) Cheney of Newton.

ISSUE.

    I. *Hannah*, b. March 3, 1737, m. Nathl. Parker, 1772.
   II. *Caleb*, b. June 17, 1740, m. Elizabeth Hyde.   See below.
  III. *Sarah*, b. Oct. 23, 1743, m. James Richards, Jr. 1769.   She
              d. 1771.
   IV. *Thaddeus*, b. July 10, 1747, m. Temperance Hyde.   See
              below.

MOSES WHITNEY,[2] (218) (son of Timothy and Margaret,) m. REBECCA
HYDE, in 1739, dau. of Ensign Timothy and Rebecca (Davis) Hyde of
Newton.

ISSUE.

    I. *Margaret*, b. May 8, 1741.
   II. *Moses*, b. April 9, 1743, d. in the Revolutionary Army.
  III. *Mary*, b. Feb. 1, 1745, m. Edward Richard of Cambridge.
   IV. *Timothy*, } b. Feb. 12, 1747, m. Mary Hyde.   See below.
    V. *Stephen*, } b. Feb. 12, 1747, d. in the Army.
   VI. *Elizabeth*, b. May 30, 1749, m. Asa Payson, 1777.   Had
              Asa and 2 daughters.
  VII. *Ephraim*, b. June 16, 1751, m. Ann Fuller, 1774, and d. in
              the Army.
 VIII. *Rebecca*, b. March 17, 1751, m. Wm. Buzzard, 1780.   Chil.
              Betsey, Clara.
   IX. *Relief*, b. Dec. 29, 1756, m. John Woodward of Brookline,
              1783.
    X. *Gershom*, b. July 25, 1758, d. 1759.
   XI. *Persis*, b. Feb. 19, 1760, m. James Richards, 1797.
  XII *John*, b. April 8, 1762, m. Polly Pope, 1785.   Children—
              Moses, Asa, and 2 daughs.   He d. suddenly, Aug. 28,
              1816, aged 54.

(247) ELIJAH WHITNEY,[2] (son of Daniel and Susanna,) m. HANNAH
              ——.

ISSUE.

    I. *Elijah*, b. Sept. 23, 1744.
   II. *Elisha*, b. Oct. 6, 1747, m. Abigail Dana.   (See below.)
  III. *John*, b. Nov. 29, 1749.
   IV. *Hannah*, b. June 13, 1756.

CALEB WHITNEY,[4] (son of Caleb and Hannah,) ELIZABETH HYDE, 1765.
    I. *Oliver*, b. March 9, 1766, d. unm.
   II. *Amariah*, b. Nov. 18, 1767.
  III. *Ruth*, b. May 31, 1773.
   IV. *Sarah*, b. June 4, 1774.
    V. *Abigail*, b. Sept. 10, 1775.

THADDEUS WHITNEY,[5] (son of Caleb and Hannah,) m. 1772, TEMPER-
ANCE HYDE, dau. of Lieut. Noah and Ruth (Seger.)   He d. 1832, aged
85. She d. 1842, aged 89.
ISSUE.
   I. *Temperance*, b. Sept. 2, 1774, m. Jona. Cook, Jr. 1795.
   II. *Ruth*, b. 1776, m. —— Worcester.
   III. *Hannah*, b. April 9, 1778, m. David Wardwell.   No chil.
   IV. *Thaddeus*, b. Sept. 1, 1788, d. 1823, unm.

TIMOTHY WHITNEY,[6] (son of Moses and Rebecca) m. MARY HYDE,
1773. He d. 1821. She d. 1828.
ISSUE.
   I. *Stephen*, b. prob. 1774, m. May 5, 1803, Ruth Whittemore.
     Has children.
   II. *Timothy*, b. prob. 1776, m. Peggy, dau. of Lott Thayer, 1821.
   III. *Polly*, b. prob. 1778.
   IV. *Peggy*, b. prob. 1780, m. Elijah Whitney.
   V. *Anna*, b. prob. 1782.
   VI. *Elisha*, b. prob. 1784, d. young.

ELISHA WHITNEY,[6] (son of Elijah and Hannah,) m. ABIGAIL DANA of
Brookline. His portrait, painted by Stuart, is in the possession of his
grandson, Benj. Duick Whitney.
ISSUE.
   I. *Experience*, b. March 1, 1776.
   II. *Abigail*, b. April 10, 1778.
   III. *Elisha*, b. Feb. 4, 1780, m. Sarah Heath.   (See below.)
   IV. *Asa*, b. May 18, 1782, m. Mary Hammond.   (See below.)
   V. *Pede*, b. July 20, 1784, m. Col. Joseph Dudley of Roxbury.
     See Vol. X., p. 342, Gen. Reg.
   VI. *William*, b. June 17, 1788.
   VII. *Elizabeth*, b. March 3, 1793.

ELISHA WHITNEY,[7] (son of Elisha and Abigail,) m. Feb. 26, 1804,
SARAH HEATH. He d. Feb. 12, 1823.
ISSUE.
   I. *Abigail*, m. a son of Amasa Gay. *John*, m. a daughter of
     John Skinner, and had 2 sons. *Sarah*, unm. *William*,
     unm. *Caroline*, bapt. Jan. 6, 1814. *Nathl. Davis*, bapt.
     Dec. 15, 1816. Order of births not known.

ASA WHITNEY,[7] (son of Elisha and Abigail,) m. MARY HAMMOND, dau.
of Phineas and Mary (Gay) Hammond. He d. March 4, 1826.
ISSUE.
   I. *Benj. Duick*, b. Nov. 6, 1807; grad. H. C. 1828; m. Eliza-
     beth Williams, and have had 8 children, of whom Stephen
     Williams, b. 1841, is now of the class of 1861, H. C.
   II. *Daniel Hammond*, b. Oct. 7, 1809, d. Oct. 6, 1817.
   III. *Sarah Hammond*, b. May 23, 1812, d. June 23, 1817.
   IV. *Mary*, b. May 5, 1815, d. April 12, 1815. She m. Professor
     Cornelius C. Felton of Harvard University.
   V. *Emily*, b. Sept. 27, 1817, m. Joseph Sargent, M. D. of
     Worcester.
   VI. *Asa Hammond*, b. June 17, 1819, m. Laura Henshaw of
     Leicester. Graduated H. C. 1838. Five children.
   VII. *Sarah*, b. July 13, 1822; m. Frederic W. Gale of Worcester.
     They were both lost in the steamer Arctic, Sept. 27, 1854.

VIII. *Catherine Dean*, b. Dec. 17, 1824, m. Henry Sargent, M. D.
She d. Sept. 9, 1849.   He d. 1858.

NOTES.—The ages of John and Elinor Whitney, and of their children, as recorded, at the time of their embarkation for New England, in April, 1635, (see Vol. X., Third Series, Mass. Hist. Coll., p. 24,) and, as stated in the beginning of the Whitney Genealogy, were doubtless incorrect. It is probable that they were several years older than this record would make them appear.

Samuel Whitney of Brunswick and son Samuel taken prisoners, to Canada, July 24, 1751, and sold for 126 livres.   He had a wife and 6 children.   He since made his escape.

Solomon Whitney made his escape from the Indians, and died at Hospital, Nov. 18, 1750.   Timothy Whitney was bought for £315. Per "Revolution" Book, Vol. 74, (VIII.) pages 46 and 59, at State House, Massachusetts.

* * *

THE HONG KONG MONTHLY MAGAZINE.—Newburyport is somewhat celebrated for the great number of publishers and editors it has produced. They are scattered all over the Union, and we can call to mind enough to supply a whole state with publications; but we were not aware till Monday, when we received No. 4 of the above-named Magazine, edited by Mrs. Annie E. Bercher, (formerly Miss Annie E. Goodwin,) at Norooba's office—Oswold's Terrace, Hong Kong, that a native of Newburyport was editing for the Chinese. It is a Magazine of 48 pages, very creditable to the editor, who had gained some celebrity as a writer before enlisting as an American missionary in that distant land.—*Newburyport Herald*, 28 *Dec.*, 1857.

* * *

" Salem April 23ª.   Last Lords-Day dyed and this day was buried the Honourable Madam *Ann Bradstreet* aged 79 years ; She was the relict widow of Governour *Bradstreet*, and a Gentlewoman of good Birth and Excellent Education, being Daughter to *Emanuel Downing* Esq ; and Sister to the Honourable Sir George *Downing* Bart, sometime Envoy Extraordinary from King Charles the II. at the Hague : But that which rendered her one of the Excellent ones of the Earth was her known Eminence in Religion both as to the knowledge and power of it, with which were happily joyned many rare Endowments of mind, and a most agreeable Conversation : she was born in London, and came very young to New-England, was first Marryed to Capt *Joseph Gardner* of Salem, and afterwards to Governour Bradstreet, but left no Issue by either."— *Boston News Letter*, April 20–27, 1713.

* * *

"*Marlborough Aug.* 20, 1711

" On the 15th Instant dyed here Mr *Edward Rice* born at Barkhamsteed in Hertfordshire, South Britain, Anno Dom 1618, from whom by one Wife (who still survives) are descended 142 Persons of which 119 are now living.   And an Elder Brother Mr *Henry Rice* who dyed in 1711 at Framingham has left as numerous a progeny, being both Men of virtuous lives."—*From the Boston News Letter*, No. 436, *of August* 18 *to Monday* 25, 1712.

THE FAMILY OF PADDOCK.

[Communicated by Z. Eddy, Esq.]

1. *Robert Paddock*, the Pilgrim ancestor, was settled in Plymouth in 1634, and probably several years before and after that time.* He afterwards settled in Duxbury, and is noticed in Windsor's history of that town. He died in 1650. See Reg., vol. 8, p. 316. He had a son Robert, who lived in Dartmouth; and John Eddy, son of Samuel, the Pilgrim, married his daughter, Susanna, Nov. 30, 1665. He had also a son John, and there are families of his descent now in that region. Also, Zechariah, brother of said John Eddy, married " Alice Paddock, daughter of Robert Paddock of Duxbury, May 7, 1663. It is probable she was the daughter of the first Robert, who also left a son, Zechariah, born in the " fore part of the year," May, 1636; also George and John. George married Sarah Ricard in 1657. John married Anna Jones; he was born in 1643. Mary, his daughter, m. Thomas Roberts, 1656; she was born in 1638. Alice was born March 7, 1640.

II. *Zechariah Paddock*, son of the first Robert, lived in Yarmouth, (Cape Cod,) and died there May 1, 1727. A very full and favorable account is given of him in the Register, vol. 8, p. 251, taken from the N. E. Weekly Journal, of June 5, 1727. He married Deborah Sears, (1650,) who survived him, and left " of his own posterity, forty-eight grandchildren and thirty-eight great-grandchildren. " He obtained the character of a righteous man." The most of his descendants were through his son Zechariah, born in 1664.

III. *Zechariah Paddock.* Of his personal history little is known. Two of his sons emigrated to the town of Middleborough,—Ichabod and Thomas. No doubt the records and graveyard, at Yarmouth, afford the account of his birth, death, and those of his children.

IV. So, of his son, *Thomas Paddock* of Middleborough; there are records and grave stones which give an account of his numerous family. Two of his sons, Thomas and Adino, are remembered. Thomas lived in Middleborough, and was distinguished, physically, as the most powerful and robust man in town. Adino lived in Boston, and had a store in Tremont Street, and planted the large elm trees in that street, near Park Street Meeting-house; was captain of a company then called " the Train Artillery;" was a loyalist, and left Boston with the British troops, when evacuated by them in 1776. He was called Col. Paddock.

Of *Ichabod*, son of Zechariah, jr., we have a more full account. He was born in Yarmouth, June 1, 1687; married Joanna Faunce, daughter of Elder Faunce, son of the Pilgrim John Faunce, and had born to him, in Yarmouth, Bethiah, b. Sept. 21, 1713, d. same year; Priscilla, b. Oct. 1, 1715; Jane, b. Aug. 1717; Joanna, b. June 15, 1719; Ephraim, b. April 15, 1721. He removed to Middleborough in 1722, and had born to him there, Thomas, May 5, 1723; Zechariah, b. Feb. 20, 1725; Patience, b. Nov. 6, 1727, and James, b. April 11, 1730.

He was unfortunate in his removal, having the sole money of his farm stolen from the vessel in which he sailed to Plymouth; and having driven all his neat cattle to his new farm, and feeding them with fresh meadow hay, they all died, having before been kept upon hay from the salt marsh;

---

* He lived in Plymouth, 1643, he also d. there. See Reg., vol. 4, p. 255.

and English hay at that time was very little cultivated. He and his wife were both active and respectable members of the First Church in Middleborough. He died August 5, 1750, aged 63; and she died May, 1758, aged 68.

V.   1. *Priscilla*, daughter of Ichabod, married Thomas Savery, by whom she had a large family of sons and daughters. One, Dea. Thomas Savery, is remembered as a man of sound sense and shrewdness, and of eminent piety. One daughter married a Burbank, and another, Capt. William Stephens of Plymouth.

2. *Jane*, married Gideon Bradford, Esq., of Plympton, a descendant of Gov. Bradford, of whose genealogy there is a full account in the Register, vol. 4, p. 337, and the names of her seven children are there given. They were all heads of numerous families.

3. *Joanna* married Lewis Harlow, and lived in Woodstock, Vt., and had a large family of children.

4. *James*, son of Ichabod, had a family and lived in Holland and in Brimfield, Mass.

5. *Thomas*, son of Ichabod, lived in Middleborough ; m. Hannah, dau. of William Thomas. Had sons, William and Stephen, and daughters, Mary and Sally. Mary m. Holmes Cushman, and Sally m. Samuel Eddy. They all had large families in the State of Vermont.

6. *Ephraim*, son of Ichabod, m. Sarah Bradford, sister of Gideon, who m. his sister. They lived in Pembroke. See Reg., vol. 4, p. 49.

7. *Zechariah*, son of said Ichabod, and great-grandson of said Zechariah, first named, m. Martha Washburn, lived in Middleborough, and was an extensive manufacturer of fishermen's hooks and women's glove-shoes. She was a descendant of the Pilgrim, Joshua Pratt. He lived on the ancestral lands inherited through his mother from Elder Faunce. He d. June 4, 1795, aged 70 years. He was a well read and well informed man, and had a good report in the church to which he belonged. She d. April 10, 1819, aged 87, long well reported and distinguished for her piety. They were married in 1748, and had a family of ten children. These are their names.

VI.   1. *Jane*, b. July 20, 1752. She m. John Faunce of Duxbury, a descendant of the Elder, and d. young, leaving one or two children.

2. *Elisha*, b. May 5, 1754. He enlisted in the revolutionary army, and died in the retreat from Ticonderoga.

3. *Lydia*, b. July 22, 1756. She m. Capt. Joshua Eddy, of the army of the revolution, April 19, 1778. An account of their family is given in the Register, vol. 6, p. 203. He died in 1833; she d. in 1838. He was 86 years of age ; she was 82.

4. *Gaius*, b. Nov. 2, 1758. He was a revolutionary soldier, and d. on his farm in the State of Illinois, aged about 70 years, leaving a numerous family. His wife's name was Polly Wood.

5. *Apollos*, b. Sept. 8, 1760, also a revolutionary soldier ; he lived in the State of Vermont, and died at the age of 77, leaving a number of children.

John, b. June 3, 1763 ; m. Lydia Cushing of Plympton, daughter of Col. Cushing ; lived in Middleborough and had eight children, all daughters, some of whom have large families. He was a carpenter and died at the age of about 70. Distinguished for his *practical* jokes.

7. *Peter*, b. July 3, 1765 ; d. at the age of two years of accidental death.

8. *Joanna*, b. July 21, 1767 ; m. Oliver Cushman of Plympton ; lived in Plainfield, Conn., and in Brookfield ; removed to the State of Illinois, where she died, leaving two sons and two daughters.

9. *Joanna*, —— ; was betrothed to Isaac Thompson, Esq., but died unmarried. She was born in the year 1750, being the eldest of the family.

10. *Zechariah*, a bachelor, who died about 40 years of age.

NOTES AND QUERIES.

Mr. Editor,

Among your " Notes and Queries," be pleased to insert the following, and oblige
Yours, respectfully,   W. J.

Not far from the beginning of this century, and while several of the spoils of revolutionary Europe were brought under the hammer in America, an elaborately sculptured marble bust of Pope Nicholas V., in pontifical dress, was sold by the auctioneer, T. K. Jones, then keeping his rooms at the corner of Kilby and State Streets.

This Pope was the Founder of the Vatican Library ; and the inquirer wishes to ascertain to what quarter his bust was transferred, and where it is now preserved. This inquiry is of some literary interest, of course ; but it will not be thought unimportant if it tends to keep alive or to resuscitate the memory of a benefit conferred on literature and science by a pope—so rare, unhappily, is such a record !

A recent historian, or biographer, thus characterizes him :

" Nicolas V. [Tommaso de Sarzana, who died March 24, 1455,] was one of the brightest ornaments of the pontifical throne. In the exercise of authority over the ecclesiastical dominions, he exhibited a happy union of gentleness and firmness. Purely disinterested in his views, he did not lavish upon his relatives the wealth which the prudent administration of his finances poured into his coffers ; but appropriated the revenues of the church to the promotion of its dignity. The gorgeous solemnity which graced his performance of religious rites, evinced his attention to decorum and the grandeur of his taste. In the superb edifices which were erected under his auspices the admiring spectator beheld the revival of ancient magnificence. As the founder of the Vatican Library he claims the homage of the lovers of classic literature. His court was the resort of the learned, who found in him a discriminating patron and a generous benefactor. It was the subject of general regret, that the brief term of his pontificate prevented the maturing of the mighty plans he had conceived for the encouragement of the liberal arts. When his lifeless remains were consigned to the grave, the friends of peace lamented the premature death of a pontiff, who had assiduously labored to secure the tranquillity of Italy ; and they who were sensible of the charms of enlightened piety regretted the loss of a true father of the faithful, who had dedicated his splendid talents to the promotion of the temporal as well as the spiritual welfare of the Christian community."

Shepherd's Life of Poggio Bracciolini, pp. 462, 3.

May 10, 1858.

PEDIGREE OF THE ODIN FAMILY.

1. JOHN ODIN, 1722. The first of the family in Massachusetts, New England, was a native of Kent County, England; b. Aug. 10, 1722. A part of the family to which he belonged resided in the city of London, England, and a part in Greenwich, Kentshire. Some of his sisters were settled in the latter. He was the commander of the ship " Morning Star," and made voyages from Boston to Charleston, S. C., and from thence to London, as was the usual route, before the currents of the Gulf Stream were as well understood as now. He married *Margaret Sherman* of Boston, Mass., Nov. 20, 1745. Died at Charlestown, Mass., Feb. 15, 1757, æt. 35 years. *Margaret Sherman*, his widow, born May 18, 1721; died 1797, æt. 76 years.

    I. *John Odin*, born Aug. 25, 1746; died Sept. 23, 1749, æt. 3 years 29 days.

    II. *Margaret Odin*, born March 14, 1748; died May, 1745, æt. 17 weeks.

    III. *John Odin*, born March 15, 1749; married *Esther Kettell*, dau. of *James Kettell*, magistrate of Malden, Mass., Aug. 22, 1773; died in Boston, July 25, 1798. *Esther Kettell*, widow of *John Odin*, born Jan. 13, 1752; died in Boston, May 8, 1805.

    IV. *Margaret Odin*, born Aug. 3, 1752; married *Joseph Darr*, had several sons and daughters.

    V. *Elizabeth Odin*, b. Sept. 12, 1753; married *Robert Fairservice*; had no children.

    VI. *Timothy Cutler Odin*, born April 18, 1756; sailed for Europe; never heard of after.

2. JOHN ODIN, 1749. Married *Esther Kettell*, of Charlestown, Mass.

    I. *John Odin*, born June 19, 1774; married *Harriet Tyng Walter*, daughter of Rev. *William Walter*, D. D., rector of Christ Church, Boston, Jan. 4, 1804, and died Aug. 28, 1854, æt. 80 years, one of the oldest and most respected merchants of the city.

    II. *Timothy Cutler Odin*, born Aug. 6, 1777; died Nov. 26, 1777, æt. 3 months.

    III. *Timothy Cutler Odin*, born Jan. 29, 1779; died Jan. 23d, 1787, æt. 3 years.

    IV. *James Odin*, born Aug. 12, 1781; died Jan. 7, 1787, æt. 5 years and 5 months.

    V. *Timothy Cutler Odin*, b. March 10, 1788; died Sept. 1, 1788, æt. 6 months.

    VI. *George Odin*, born Jan. 21, 17—; merchant, Boston.

3. JOHN ODIN, 1774. Married *Harriet Tyng Walter*, daughter of Rev. *William Walter*, D. D. *Harriet Tyng Walter*, wife of *John Odin*, born May 16, 1776; died Oct. 14, 1847.

    I. *Harriet Walter Odin*, born Oct. 27, 1804; married *Day Otis Kellogg*, merchant, New York, N. Y., Sept. 16, 1841.

    II. *Esther Kettell Odin*, born March 14, 1806; married Rev. *Benjamin Darr*, D. D., rector of Christ Church, Philadelphia, Penn., July 12, 1827; died Dec. 20, 1857, æt. 51 years.

III. *John Odin*, M. D., born Jan. 16, 1808; married *Ann Frances*,
  daughter of *James W. Vose*, merchant, of Boston, Feb. 28,
  1839; married *Louisa Hayward*, daughter of *James W. Vose*,
  Aug. 6, 1851.
IV. *Amelia Matilda Odin*, born Oct. 28, 1809; married *Benjamin
  H. Currier*, notary public, July 12, 1834; died Sept. 15, 1850,
  æt. 40 years.
 V. *Charlotte Maria Odin*, born Jan. 25, 1813; married *Reuben
  Richards*, merchant of Boston, Oct. 27, 1841; died Feb. 16,
  1846, æt. 33 years.
VI. *Mary Maynard Odin*, born May 13, 1815; died April 16, 1847,
  æt. 32 years.
VII. *Louisa Brown Odin*, born Jan. 18, 1818; married *Reuben Rich-
  ards*, merchant, July, 1848; died Dec. 23, 1852, æt. 31 years.
VIII. *George Walter Odin*, born April 12, 1821; died at Winter Hill,
  Charlestown, Aug. 22, 1822, æt. 1 year and 4 months.

4. JOHN ODIN, 1808. Married *Ann Frances Vose*, born Dec. 4,
  1818; died July 19, 1850, æt. 33 years.
  I. *John Odin*, born Nov. 16, 1839; died Jan. 11, 1845, æt. 5 years
    and 2 months.
  II. *Ann Frances Odin*, born May 24, 1842.
  III. *Louisa Vose Odin*, born Jan. 15, 1846; died Dec. 8, 1852, æ. 6
    years and 11 months.
    Married, 2d, *Louisa Hayward Vose*, born June 12, 1824.
  IV. *Harriet Walter Odin*, born April 30, 1852; died Sept. 14, 1852,
    æt. 4 months and 2 weeks.
  V. *Harriet Louisa Odin*, born April 29, 1854.
  VI. *Esther Kettell Odin*, born at Scituate, Mass., July 9, 1857.

OLD AGE IN WOBURN.— *Woburn, March 17, 1858.* Mr. Editor : I saw
in one of the daily papers a few days ago a notice of an old man living
in Woburn, named Converse, and thought I would give you a further description of the family.

  Jesse Converse, the oldest man in Woburn, was 93 years old last Feb.
He was the third of seven sons, children of Josiah Converse. (His two
older brothers were in the revolutionary war, one of whom was at the taking of Burgoyne.) He is hale, hearty and bright. He has a brother,
Joshua Converse, living about a mile from him, who was 91 years old last
January, and who would, at reaping or binding stalks of rye, put many a
man of half his years to thinking seriously whether he might not come out
second best in a trial. He was a member of the Legislature in 1836. He
has another brother, Luther Converse, who resides about half a mile from
him, who was 81 years old last January, who is also smart and bright.
They are all moral and temperate, but not total abstinents. In their religious opinions they are Calvinist Baptists. The oldest brother is a deacon.
The second brother don't want that office, and the third won't have it.
Politically they are hunker democrats of the straightest sect, and they can
either of them give strong reasons for the faith that is in them, either religious or political. If there are three brothers in any town in the State,
so old, bright, smart, moral and temperate, let us hear from them.
                                        Yours,   C. D.

REMINISCENCES OF GEN. WARREN AND BUNKER HILL.

[By Gen. William H. Sumner.]

[Continued from p. 122.]

The evidence in support of the questioned fact contained in the preceding communication, and in the letter of Amos Foster, was so conclusive that another article appeared in the Patriot of the 15th of August, 1825, acknowledging the successful vindication of the authenticity of the toast given upon the preceding 4th of July. This article, although without any signature, was universally attributed to Dr. Waterhouse, and the internal evidence points to that source, for even here is an apparent unwillingness to allow to Warren the honor he so richly merited.

The article referred to is in these words:—

BATTLE OF BUNKER HILL—ONCE MORE.

History is under obligations to the Adjutant General for his successful elucidation of a doubtful point, referred to by "Historian." It would have been well had the like pains been taken 50 years ago, as it regarded the Battle of Bunker Hill: but alluring fashion, instead of heightening the charms of truth, injures her dignified simplicity. The partizans, amongst the "Sons of Liberty," following, in that day, the fashion of monarchies, were not contented with a *glorious battle*, fought by the *people*, but must needs have some particular leader or *Hero*,—some Leonidas, who might, for what we know, have been in the rear of his 300 Spartans. Our Fathers, like all those of the whole world, deemed it expedient to emblazon victory by some well known name or some man of rank, as the Dukes of Cumberland or York, though dead weights on their respective armies. The good Washington, when he last visited Boston expressed his pain and uneasiness at having so much credit given TO HIM, during our seven years' contest, and so little to the patriotic army and officers which he commanded. The noblest democratic battle fought was that at Bunker Hill, where each man did that which seemed good in his own eyes.

It is a mistake to suppose that the writer grudged the great credit due to Dr. Warren. In proof of it we cannot help subjoining, that if any one should think fit to attach to Warren the epithet of "chivalrous," we hope he will add it to no other valiant American who fought on that day. Before the revolutionary contest ended, there were some *chivalrous* British and French who fought bravely under our banners; but Warren stepped forth as a private citizen, in a more serious and solemn manner. The error has been in calling him a *General*, instead of an illustrious and fearless *patriot*, as was likewise Judge Winthrop, who was slightly wounded, and among the very last who retreated.

The serious question is—why sink the names of Gardiner of Cambridge,—Parker of Chelmsford,—McClary of New Hampshire,—More of ——, who all had commissions, and lost their lives, to elevate the name of one *Bostonian* who had none? Our *country people* have thought, feeling and pride, and have talked all these things over their mugs of cider, on winter evenings, for half a century past; and, take them collectively, they generally think right; and when they come to know more of John Paul Jones they may think more justly of some other foreigners; more lightly of some of our people. Truth is eternal and unbending. It allows of no tamperings, humorings, intrigues, barters or exceptions, and is not at the caprice of times, places and persons. It depends not on particular lights or positions. In studied dress, or dishabille,—in every attitude and look, Truth is the same; equally captivating and commanding. Historics composed of ingredients of this high quality come forth but rarely; for few can produce them. A work of elastic spirit and commanding genius, which has all the mastery of a ruling mind, appears but now and then in the long course of centuries; and when it does it commands all before it, like that voice from the dominion of thought, which philosophers, real politicians and historians have considered the Vox Dei. That is the history which alone teaches philosophy by example.

On this general subject it may not be amiss to make a particular and illustrative remark, viz., that every account, and among them this of Gen. Sumner's, tends to confirm the narrative of the Battle of Bunker Hill, written by Major Gen. Dearborn, especially the incidental or circumstantial observation of Amos Foster, who, in his letter to Gen. Sumner, says: "I know Gen. Putnam (he should have said *Colonel*) and Col. Prescott well. I saw Putnam riding round, very active. I saw him ten times at least, I should think. *Putnam went off with David Baily and a number of others; and they took tools with them to intrench on Bunker Hill;* but a number of them came back again," (to Breed's Hill, where the battle was raging.)

This is precisely Gen. Dearborn's account of it, which has been corroborated by Governor Eustis, and confirmed by his friend the late Mr. Andrew Cragie, who were both together on the hill, and assisted in burying Asa Pollard; and who saw Col. Putnam, "*very active, riding about.*" Truth is a spirit too close for confinement.

That first military lesson which was given to Gen. Howe, on the 17th of June, 1775, was emphatically *the battle of the people.* Col. Prescott was the first and most commanding character in it; yet if you cast your eye on that apocryphal painting of the battle by Mr. Trumbull, you will see Col. Prescott represented more like the driver of a baggage-wagon than a soldier, while the British officers appear in all their flattered pomp of Victory and *Humanity!* We cannot denounce too strongly, nor castigate too severely, false medals, false statuary, and false pictures, or value too highly faithful ones, because of their durability.

Perhaps there will be no more appropriate place than this to introduce one or two incidents relating to Bunker Hill which came within my personal knowledge. While I was Adjutant General, I learned that Gen.' Ward's Order Book was in the hands of Mr. Ward of Brookfield, a relative of the Gen., who was the Commander of the American forces at Cambridge till the 3d of July, when Gen. Washington assumed the command. I obtained the loan of that Order Book, and found it so interesting that I caused the whole volume to be copied and placed in the Adjutant General's office, where I left it when I resigned, lest the original should be lost. In the same volume there was also made a copy of Gen. Thomas's Order Book at Roxbury. That volume is now, I presume, where I left it. My chief solicitude to obtain the Order Book of Gen. Ward was to ascertain what order he had given for the fortifying of Bunker Hill. I also wanted to read his account of the battle. I found nothing of the kind; but, on the margin of the book, against the seventeenth of June, there was this memorandum: "The battle of Charlestown was fought this day. Killed, 115; wounded, 305; captivated, 30; total, 450." Gov.

Gage, in his account, acknowledged a loss on the part of the British, of 1051, of whom 226 were killed, 828 wounded, including 19 officers killed and 28 wounded. It is remarkable that no full account of the battle was recorded by Gen. Ward, because hereafter everybody will inquire for his Order Book to learn about the battle. It does not appear from that book that either Putnam or Prescott made any report; nor does there appear any order approving the conduct of the troops in the battle. This omission may be accounted for by the fact that the troops were not organized, and that Gen. Ward had as yet no regular staff.

Another interesting matter that occurs to me relates to the fortifications on Bunker Hill. After my appointment, in 1818, to the office of Adjutant General, by Gov. Brooks, his staff was completed by the appointment of Samuel Swett, Benjamin Pickman, and Theodore Lyman, as aids. About this time Gen. Dearborn made a publication respecting Gen. Putnam, in which his bravery in the battle of Bunker Hill was doubted. He also, in connection with the publication, gave a "plan" of the redoubt, the breast-work and the rail fence, behind which he stated that Col. Stark's regiment, in which he was a Captain, was stationed. The plan struck Gov. Brooks as being erroneous; and he said to Col. Swett and myself, "Gentlemen, I have not been on to that ground since the battle, and if you will accompany me I will go there and examine it."

It must be recollected that Brooks returned to Cambridge on the 16th of June, the day before the battle of Bunker Hill, and that the battalion of Bridge's regiment, in which was his company, was left at Cambridge, and not ordered to Charlestown. As the troops were about to march to Charlestown, Brooks applied to Bridge for leave to go with his company, among the other troops, to Charlestown. Bridge said he had no authority to allow it, and referred him to Gen. Ward. On applying to him he replied to Brooks, "I did not order your battalion of Bridge's regiment to Charlestown, because I want to have troops here that I can rely upon, in case the enemy should consider that the main position at Cambridge is so weakened by the expedition, that they can safely make their main attack here." This may account for Brooks not being in the battle, when a part of his regiment was there; but, as he had obtained permission from Gen. Ward to go as a volunteer, under a charge to return to his command in case of necessity, he went as a volunteer, without his company, and was engaged all the night before the battle, in counselling Putnam, and Gridley the engineer, about the position of the works that were to be thrown up. He left early in the morning, with a message from Col. Prescott to Gen. Ward, requesting a reenforcement. His recital of the position of the works at Bunker Hill must be of the highest authority.

According to assignment, the Adjutant General and Col. Swett, his first aid, met the Governor on the hill, in the beginning of the month of June, 1818, for the purpose of examining the works and comparing them with Dearborn's plan. We went into the redoubt together. After looking about him and examining the ground, the Governor said, "Gentlemen, where is the sallyport? I do not see where it was. Let us look about and see if we can find it." We found an excavation in the lines of the fort on the side opposite to that where we afterwards found it had been when the works were thrown up, the night before the battle. "Gentlemen," said the Governor, "can we verify this? For," continued he, "the fact is, the breastwork ran in a northerly or northeasterly direction from the sallyport; and if we can ascertain where that breastwork was

we can identify the true position of the sallyport." He requested Col.
Swett and Major Swan, (who came down with the Governor from Medford, and whose father owned or leased the ground) to go several rods in
a direction which he pointed out; then to turn and walk at right angles to
the course they had before taken, to see if they could find where the old
breastwork was, which had probably been ploughed down. The grass
was high, and it could not be seen until the gentlemen, wading the grass,
came into a hollow place and ascended a little height, and then passed
down into another hollow on the other side. The gentlemen exclaimed,
" We have found it." Gov. Brooks said, " I thought you would ; let us
examine a little further. Take the same course, and go down a short
distance and see if you find there the same evidences of its position."
They did so, and satisfied the Governor that they had discovered the place
where the breastwork was built, and thus verified the fact, that the sallyport was originally in the place where he had indicated that it ought to be
found.

It was plain to the observer that if the breastwork ran in the direction
indicated by Gen. Dearborn's plan, it would puzzle the commander to tell
on which side of it his men should be placed, in order to defend the main
position. Thus it appears, from Gen. Brooks' recollection of the ground,
that the plan which Gen. Dearborn had published, in connection with
his work impeaching Gen. Putnam, *was not a plan of the ground, as it
was on the 17th of June,* when the battle was fought. The explanation
of these facts is probably this : that Dearborn's plan was that of *the works
after the retreat of the American forces, and the consequent change of the
relative position of the two armies.*

For, if the works had not been thus changed, it would have been easy
for the Americans, if they designed to re-take the fort from which they
had retreated, for those of them who were posted on Winter Hill and
Prospect Hill to pass over Charlestown neck, and for those on Cobble Hill
to cross the mill-dam over the creek, or, in winter, to go over the millpond on the ice, and thence to march up the hill unmolested from the
breastwork.

After finishing the examination of the works on the hill, the Governor
pointed out the place where those who were on the ground at the time,
stated to him that Warren was killed. It was about three or four rods
northwesterly from the work, near a young elm tree which had grown up
since the battle. The location of the " rail fence " was also pointed out.

The American redoubt was about eight rods square. Notwithstanding
the firing from the Lively, man-of-war, which commenced early in the
morning, the men continued to labor steadily upon the breastwork for
some time. At dawn, the officers and men on the decks of the British
vessels in the harbor were seen, with their spy-glasses, taking observation.
As their firing upon the works continued, with some intermissions, at
length one man fell mortally wounded. The name of the man who was
thus killed was Coburn. The others were so much alarmed that they
hesitated to work in that place. Prescott, to show that there was not so
much danger of being killed as they supposed, mounted the parapet in
his banyan gown, and, strutting backward and forward upon it, he raised
his " *three-cornered scraper*," as his cocked hat was called, and in raising
it turned his queue around so that it hung over his right shoulder, giving
him a quite ludicrous appearance ; and, swinging his hat in the air, with
loud exclamations he shouted to the British, " Hit me if you can." The
men still hesitated to work while the body of Coburn was lying there, and

Prescott accordingly ordered it to be buried immediately. It was interred at once, a little in the rear of the redoubt. When the order was given for the man to be buried, some one exclaimed, "What! bury a man without prayers?" Of this, Prescott took no notice.

Gen. Dearborn, in his publication, states that he saw Gen. Putnam carrying off spades and other intrenching tools when he should have been directing the forces. Dearborn, it should be noticed, was stationed behind the rail fence, which was not a favorable position for making observations. Putnam was as active as any man that morning. He saw how much necessity there was for reinforcement, and went to Cambridge to urge Gen. Ward to send it. That act Dearborn considered as retreating from the field.

From Gen. Ward's order-book, it appears that Gen. Washington took the command at Cambridge July 3, 1775, and that the first order respecting military operations which he gave, was one approving of the sentence of the court-martial upon Capt. Callender, which broke him. It is dated July 7th. Gen. Washington says:—

"It is with inexpressible concern that the General, upon his first arrival in the army, should find an officer sentenced by a general court-martial for cowardice; a crime of all others the most infamous in a soldier, the most injurious to an army, and the last to be forgiven, inasmuch as it may, and often does happen, that the cowardice of a single officer proves the destruction of an whole army. The General, therefore, with great concern, (and more especially as the transaction happened before he had the command of the troops,) thinks himself obliged, for the good of the service, to approve the judgment of the court-martial with respect to Capt. John Callender, who is hereby sentenced to be cashiered. Capt. John Callender is accordingly cashiered, and dismissed from all further service in the Continental army as an officer."

The justice of this sentence was universally acknowledged. It should be stated, however, to the credit of Capt. Callender, that he was so much mortified by the decision, that he determined to restore himself to favor; and for this purpose, he joined his company as a volunteer private, and fought bravely in every action in which his company was engaged. At the battle of Long Island, after both the captain and lieutenant of the company were killed, by the request of the company he took the command. He continued in the service, and distinguished himself on many occasions.

It is a very singular circumstance, that Gov. Gage had determined to take possession of Dorchester heights on the same day that the battle of Bunker Hill took place; but the demonstration by the Provincials, in taking possession of Breed's Hill, diverted him from that purpose. In the following year, we took possession of Dorchester heights ourselves. At the time they were taken possession of, as I have received the impression from some person—whose name I do not now recollect—Washington had but little ammunition. In order to conceal from the soldiers the true state of the army in that respect, he ordered powder casks to be filled with sand, and that several loads of them should be carried to the heights by the way of Roxbury, where the right wing of the army, under Gen. Thomas, was posted. By this deception, the soldiers were satisfied that the army was in a condition to defend itself, notwithstanding the reports that the supply of ammunition was nearly exhausted.

After possession was taken of the heights, hogsheads were filled with earth, and so placed that they could be rolled down upon the enemy to break the columns, if they should dare attempt to march up the hill.

As my intentions in this article were limited to facts and incidents connected with Gen. Warren, I will forego the recital of other items which crowd upon my recollection, and which may form the basis of some future communication.

REMINISCENCE OF GEN. WARREN.

Dr. David Townsend, June 17, 1775, in the morning, went to Brighton to see Mr. Carnes's family of Boston. About one in the afternoon, Mr. Carnes came and reported that there was hot work. The British at Boston, with their shipping, were firing very heavy on our men at Bunker Hill. Dr. Townsend said he must go and work for Dr. Warren. He was very young, and a student with Dr. Warren, who was appointed Major General on the day previous. Gen. Warren left him in Boston to protect his effects, and he had just before come to Cambridge from Brighton to Gen. Ward's quarters, and found Cambridge quiet as the Sabbath,—all the troops gone, and no one at Ward's quarters but Gen. Warren, who was sick with one of his oppressive nervous headaches, and, as usual, had retired to rest, and taken some camomile tea for relief. Mrs. Hastings said no one else was in the house. Gen. Warren told Dr. Townsend that if he would wait he would accompany him to Bunker Hill immediately. He took tea and walked with him as far as the road to Milk Row, in Cambridge. People said there were some wounded soldiers there, brought away, and Warren remarked that Dr. Townsend had better remain and dress their wounds, which he did. The British ship Glasgow was firing across. Gen. Warren had presided in the Provincial Congress that morning, and was decorated very much. He wore a light cloth coat with covered buttons worked in silver, and his hair was curled up at the sides of his head and pinned up. He was very cheerful and heartily engaged in preparation for the battle, which was just commencing, and the muskets must have begun firing when he arrived. When Warren left Dr. Townsend he had a cane only. Dr. Foster of Charlestown was principal surgeon to the troops. Dr. Eustis, probably Dr. Hart, and Dr. Bricken, who was Lieutenant Colonel, and Dr. Townsend were at the hospital, the first house on the north side of Bunker Hill, known as the Sun Tavern. Col. Patterson's regiment was at Jack Tufts's storehouse, near down to the road leading to Milk Row. Dr. Townsend took dressings and instruments with him. He was rather of opinion that there was a battery in Mystic River. He saw nothing of Gen. Ward or his aids. All the troops, except Patterson's, went upon Bunker Hill. Col. Gardner was wounded with a musket ball, and carried home by four men with a blanket and poles. The wound was just plastered together before he arrived at the hospital. He did not remain there. Dr. Church did not belong then to the hospital. There was very little organization of that department. Col. Small and Gen. Warren were very well acquainted with each other, and both were remarkable for very fine manners. Dr. Warren cheerfully avowed his presentiment that he was destined to fall in the conflict. The truth of this presentiment, alas, was soon to be recorded in his heart's blood! A nobler heart never panted after immortality.

J. e. L.

GENEALOGY OF THE McKINSTRY FAMILY, WITH A PRE- LIMINARY ESSAY ON THE SCOTCH-IRISH IMMIGRATIONS TO AMERICA.

[By Hon. WILLIAM WILLIS, of Portland, Me.]

The McKINSTRYS originated in Scotland. The first of the name who emigrated to Ireland was Rodger, who had lived in the neighborhood of Edinburgh, and emigrated thence to the north of Ireland about the year 1669. I propose, as a preliminary to the history of this family, to give a brief account of the Scotch emigration to Ireland, and from that country to America previous to our Revolution.

During the Irish rebellions in the reign of Elizabeth, the Province of Ulster, embracing the northern counties of Ireland, was greatly depopulated, and it became a favorite project with her successor, James I., to repeople those counties with a protestant population, the better to preserve order, and introduce a higher state of cultivation in that portion of his dominions. To promote this object, liberal offers of land were made, and other inducements held out in England and Scotland, for persons to occupy this wide and vacant territory. The project was eagerly embraced; companies and colonies were formed, and individuals without organization were tempted to partake of the advantageous offers of government. A London company, among the first to enter upon this new acquisition, established itself at Derry, and gave such a character to the place as to cause it to be afterwards and forever known as the renowned city of Londonderry.

The first emigration from Scotland was chiefly from the Highlands, where agricultural resources were scanty and often wholly cut off, and where the fruits of labor were gathered from a stern soil. Sir Hugh Montgomery, the sixth Laird of Braidstone, a friend and follower of King James, was among the earliest to obtain possession of forfeited land in the county of Down, and laid his rough hand upon many broad acres. The coast of Scotland is within twenty miles of the county of Antrim in Ireland, and across this frith or strait flowed from the northeast a population distinguished for thrift, industry and endurance, which has given a peculiar and elevated character to that portion of the emerald island. It is said that the clan McDonald contributed largely to this emigration, and was among the first of the Scottish nation to plant upon its shores. They scattered chiefly in the counties of Down, Londonderry and Antrim, and greatly assisted to build up Newry, Bangor, Derry and Belfast, the principal cities of those counties.

This was the first protestant population that was introduced into Ireland, the Presbyterians of Scotland furnishing the largest element; and they have maintained their ascendancy to the present day, against the persevering efforts of the Episcopalians on the one hand, and of the Romanists, bigoted and numerous, by whom they were surrounded, on the other. The first Presbyterian church established in Ireland was in Ballycarry, in the county of Antrim, in 1613.

The Clan Alpine, otherwise called the McGregors, in the latter part of the 17th century, had made themselves very obnoxious to government and the neighboring clans by a wild and reckless course of life. Argyle, the chief of the Campbells, their inveterate enemy, who was high in court favor, procured a decree of extermination against them, extending even to the obliteration of their name and place of residence. Heavy penalties were proclaimed against all who bore the badge of the clan. To avoid this withering persecution, many sought refuge in the neighboring islands; many changed their names and fled to remote parts of their own country or to other countries. Descendants from this clan are now found in the United States and elsewhere, under the names of Grier, Greer, Gregor, Gregory, &c., the Mac being dropped. Thus we shall probably find that a distinguished Judge of the Supreme Court of the U. States, residing in Pennsylvania, Judge Grier, derives his origin from the same wild tribe, which, under the guidance of Robroy McGregor, was the terror of the high and low lands of his native soil. Nor was the change of name confined to that clan; for we are assured that the Mackinnons, from the isle of Skye, are now McKenna, McKean, McCannon; that McNish has become McNiece, Menzas, Munnias, and Monies; and Graham is Graeme, Grimes, Groom, &c.

Although the rebellions of 1715 and 1745, against the House of Hanover, made large additions to the Scotch population in the north of Ireland, yet by far the largest accessions to this colonization were occasioned by religious persecutions in the time of the latter Stuarts. That fated race, blind to the dictates of justice and humanity, and devoted with sullen bigotry to their peculiar notions in religion and politics, pursued a system of measures best calculated to wean from their support subjects the most devoted to their cause. The Scottish race was bound to the Stuarts by a national prejudice and a sincere affection. But they were imbued with a religious enthusiasm, inspired by Knox their great apostle, which ruled their consciences, and rendered the sanctions of a higher law superior to their patriotism, or their attachment to their native sovereigns. Rather, they believed that true patriotism consisted in maintaining the religion transmitted by their fathers.

When, therefore, the Charleses and James II. endeavored to introduce prelacy among them, and to force it upon their consciences by arbitrary laws and the iron hoofs of the dragoons of Claverhouse, very many of these hardy, persistent and enduring Presbyterians, having suffered to the bitter end of cruelty and oppression, abandoned the land of their birth, the home of their fondest affections, and sought an asylum among their countrymen in the secure retreats of Ulster, or fled across the ocean. They carried their household gods with them; and their religious peculiarities became more dear in their land of exile, for the dangers and sorrows through which they had borne them.

Presbyterianism was transported from Geneva to Scotland by John Knox, who composed his first Book of Discipline, containing the substance of his intended policy, in 1561. In 1566, a general assembly approved the Discipline; and all church affairs, after that time, were managed by Presbyteries and General Assemblies. They did not at first formally deprive the bishops, who had ecclesiastical jurisdiction, of their power, but they went on gradually and steadily doing it, as they acquired confidence and strength. In 1574, they voted bishops to be only pastors of one parish; in 1577, they decreed that bishops should be called by their own names without title; and the next year they declared the name of bishop to be a nuisance. In 1580, they pronounced with one voice, in the General Assembly, that diocesan episcopacy was unscriptural and unlawful. The same year, King James and his family, with the whole Scotch nation, subscribed a confession of faith, embracing the "solemn league and covenant," obliging them to maintain the protestant doctrine and presbyterian government. Thus, in the space of twenty years, grew up this formal, extensive and powerful institution, twining itself over the Scottish mind with stern and inflexible bands, which death only could sunder; and for which, home, country, life—all things beside—were freely given up.

James had hardly become secure and easy on his English throne when he began his attack upon the religious system of his early life, and of his native country, and his successors followed it up with a pertinacity worthy of a better cause. The attempts to establish the church of England over Scotland, and destroy the religious system so universally established and so dearly cherished by that devoted people, was pursued by the Charleses and James the 2d, by persecutions as mean, as cruel, and savage, as any which have disgraced the annals of religious bigotry and crime. And they did not cease until they had greatly depopulated Scotland, and were stripped of their power by the happy revolution under William and Mary, which restored repose to a distracted and long suffering people.

Scotland, a country no larger than Maine, with a population at the close of the seventeenth century of a million, and in 1800 not so much as the present population of Massachusetts and Maine; with agricultural and other resources by no means equal to ours—of which a writer in a recent number of the Edinburgh Review, on the Highlands, says, " at the end of the 17th century the chief social feature of the Highlands was famine, and another was emigration." Yet this country has contributed largely, by emigration, to furnish numerous and prominent settlers for many other lands; to the nation with which she is connected, profound statesmen, brilliant writers, and men the most renowned in every department of scientific and philosophical research.

This is the race, composed of various tribes flowing from different parts of Scotland, which furnished the materials of the Scotch-Irish immigration to this country. By their industry, frugality and skill, they had made the deserted region into which they had moved a comparatively rich and flourishing country. They had improved agriculture and introduced manufactures, and by the excellence and high reputation of their productions had attracted trade and commerce to their markets, so as to excite the jealousy of government in the reigns of Anne and the first George, notwithstanding that by their efforts and example the prosperity of the whole island had been promoted. The patronizing government began to recognize them, in the shape of taxes and embarrassing regulations upon their industry and trade. The same jealousy controlled that government afterwards, in regard to the American Colonies, by which the commerce and enterprise of their subjects on this side of the ocean, were, in like manner, hampered and restricted, so that they were hardly permitted to manufacture articles of the most common necessity, but were driven to import them from the mother country, as glass, nails, hats, cloths, &c.

These restrictions occasioned general distress, not only in the north of Ireland, but throughout the whole island. To this, Douglass (p. 368) says, " was added an extravagant advance in rents by landlords, whose long leases were now expired." The energetic and self-willed population of the north of Ireland, animated by the same spirit which subsequently moved the American mind, determined no longer to endure these oppressive measures; and they sought by another change to find a freer verge for the exercise of their industry and skill, and for the enjoyment of their religion.

One of their spiritual leaders, the Rev. Mr. McGregor, in a sermon which he preached on the eve of the departure from Ireland, assigned the following reasons for their removal to America: 1, to avoid oppressive and cruel bondage; 2, to shun persecution; 3, to withdraw from the communion of idolaters; 4, to have an opportunity of worshipping God according to the dictates of conscience and his inspired word. He looked at it chiefly from a religious point of view; others, from a material and commercial stand point. It was undoubtedly suggested and promoted by a variety of motives gradually operating upon the mass of the population, which brought them to the determination, solemn and painful, to sunder the ties which had bound them firmly to their adopted country, and impelled them to seek new and doubtful homes in a wild, unexplored, and far-distant land.

The first immigration of these people to this country was to the Middle and Southern Colonies. As early as 1684 a settlement was formed in New Jersey, and in 1690 small groups were found in the Carolinas, Maryland and Pennsylvania. But it was not until the reigns of Anne and George I. that large numbers, driven by oppressive measures of government and disastrous seasons, were induced to seek, even in the wilderness, a better home than their old settled region could give them. Gordon says, "Scarcity of corn, generally prevalent from the discouragement of industry, amounted in 1728 and the following year almost to a famine, especially in Ulster. Emigrations to America, which have since increased, drew above 3000 people annually from Ulster alone." Dr. Boulter, afterwards Archbishop of Armagh, who labored strenuously in 1728 to divert the horrors of famine in Ireland, wrote to the English ministry, March 7, 1728, that there were seven ships then lying at Belfast that "are carrying off about 1000 passengers; most of them can neither get victuals nor work at home." He also says, "3100 men, women and children went from Ireland to America in 1727, and 4200 in three years, all protestants." The principal seats of these emigrations were Pennsylvania and the Middle States. New England was found not so favorable to their farming and other interests. Douglass, who wrote at Boston in 1750, says, "at first they chose New England, but being brought up to husbandry, &c., New England did not answer so well as the Colonies southward; at present they generally resort to Pennsylvania." By Proud's history of Pennsylvania, we find that in 1729 near 6000 arrived in that Colony; and before the middle of the century nearly 12,000 arrived annually for several years. These were protestants and generally Presbyterians; few or no Catholics came, until some time after the Revolution.

In the summer of 1718, the first organized company of this class of immigrants, of which we have any knowledge, left the shores of Ireland in five vessels, containing 120 families, for the new world, and arrived safely in Boston, August 4, 1718. Here all was new, the wilderness and the world before them. Imagine this little colony, strangers in a strange land, seeking new homes and not knowing whither to turn. There they lie at the little wharf at the foot of State Street in the town of Boston, which then contained about 12,000 inhabitants, taking counsel where to go, and how to dispose of themselves and their little ones, to begin the world anew. With their wonted energy, they were soon astir. One brigantine, with a company of twenty families, sought their fortunes at the eastward, among whom were Armstrong, Means, McKean, Gregg;—they spent a hard and long winter in Portland harbor, and then fled westward, most of them, to join their companions in founding their new Londonderry. Another portion went to Andover and its neighborhood, led on by their pastor McGregor; another to Pelham, Mass., under the lead of the Rev. Mr. Abercrombie; another remained in Boston, under their pastor the Rev. John Moorhead; and still another sought refuge in Worcester and its vicinity. Wherever they went, this devoted people first of all planted the Presbyterian church, adopting the discipline and usages of the church of Scotland. Mr. McGregor and his flock finally established themselves at Nutfield, in N. H., and built up a town which they called, from their venerated city in Ireland, Londonderry. Here they founded a colony, which, like a fruitful mother, has been sending forth from its prolific bosom men and women, of their hardy and enlightened stock, to instruct and adorn society. And here were gathered the McGregors, McClintocks, Starks, Reid, Bell, Morrison, Anderson, McKean, and others, who have given vigor to our varied institutions.

The society in Boston established the Presbyterian church, which continued for more than half a century to worship in their meeting-house on the corner of Long Lane and Bury Street, where Dr. Gannett's church now stands, under the pastoral care of Rev. John Moorhead, familiarly called Johnny Moorhead, whose ardent and impulsive temper often led him into embarrassments, but who faithfully ministered to his people until his death in 1773. He was succeeded by the Rev. Robert Annan, a Scotch presbyter, who occupied the pulpit until 1786, when the people cast off Presbyterianism, assumed the Congregational form of government, and, in 1787, settled the excellent and learned Dr. Jeremy Belknap. In 1745, they established the first Presbytery, consisting of twelve churches, called the Presbytery of Boston.

This company introduced into Boston the cultivation of the potato, which had not before been known in the country, and the flax spinning wheel, the familiar domestic instrument of their native households. The latter had quite a run in Boston; schools were established to teach the art of spinning, and ladies of the first quality were found among the votaries of this useful art.

The party which went to Worcester fared worse than any other; they encountered a severe persecution, and were not permitted to erect a house of worship of their peculiar order. In one attempt of the kind, the structure was entirely demolished by a mob. A great prejudice was enlisted against them, both from their religion and their country; they were called *Irish*, a term they greatly resented. Mr. McGregor wrote, " We are surprised to hear ourselves termed Irish people." The Worcester immigrants struggled awhile against a bitter opposition, and finding repose there hopeless, they abandoned the place, some for Pelham, others for their head-quarters in Londonderry, and some to plant themselves at Unadilla, on the banks of the Susquehanna in New York. In the Worcester company were the names of Clark, McKinstry, Gray, Ferguson, Crawford, Graham, Barbour, Blair, and Thornton; Mathew, then a child, became the distinguished patriot and statesman of New Hampshire, and a signer of the declaration of Independence.

In 1719 and 1720, five ships, under the conduct of Capt. Robert Temple, who had previously explored the country, landed several hundred families from Ireland on the shores of Kennebec River and Merry Meeting Bay. Temple was of a distinguished family in Ireland, and the ancestor of the numerous and respected family of the late Lt. Governor

Thomas L. Winthrop of Boston, who married his grand-daughter Elizabeth Bowdoin.

Dummer's Indian war broke up this colony, and the larger part of them went to Pennsylvania. After the war was ended, other companies of this race occupied various points in Maine, as Topsham, Brunswick, Boothbay, Pemaquid, and the Waldo patent, which region contained a larger number of this description of immigrants than any part of New England. They were entirely under the religious government of Presbyters and Assemblies, until the eve of the Revolution, when large accessions of Congregationalists or Independents mingling among them, a struggle took place between the two orders for the government of the church. This resulted in the overthrow of Presbyterianism and the establishment of Congregationalism over the churches of the State. There is not now a Presbyterian church in Maine. Once it boasted of Murray, famed for his eloquence,—of Rutherford, Blair, Boyd, Dunlap, McLean, Urquahart, Whittaker, Strickland,—none remain, and hardly a record of them. The same struggle took place in Massachusetts, until Synod, Presbytery and Church disappeared, and now only the feeble Presbytery of Londonderry remains in New England to record and perpetuate the religious characteristics of that great race which sought refuge on these shores, and has done so much to advance the honor and prosperity of the country. Their power as a sect is most prevalent in the Middle States.

Independency or Congregationalism was not introduced into England until 1616. But Puritanism, which embraces both orders of dissenters, had its origin in Elizabeth's time, in her attempts to cause subscriptions to be made to the liturgy, ceremonies, and discipline of the Church, in 1564. Those who refused subscription and preferred a simple worship, were called Puritans by way of reproach. When the doctrines of Arminius began to prevail in the English church, the Puritans adhered to the system of Calvin, and were defined to be men of severe morals, Calvinists in doctrine, and non-conformists to the ceremonies and discipline of the Church. The first Presbyterian church was established in England, near London, in 1577, by a few scattered brethren; and both these branches of dissenters, Independents and Presbyterians, made at first but slow progress; and although agreeing in doctrine, they differed from each other on the form of government as widely as they both did from Episcopacy.

The Independents or Congregational brethren were small in number in the Westminster Assembly, although they increased prodigiously afterwards under Cromwell. They made a bold stand against the proceedings of the high Presbyterians. They maintained "that every particular congregation of Christians" has an entire and complete power of jurisdiction over its members, to be exercised by the elders thereof within itself." They add, "this they are sure must have been the form of government in the primitive church."—*Neal*, 3, 157.

The system of the Independents was attacked by the rigid Presbyterians with great severity, "as tending to break the uniformity of the church, under the pretence of liberty of conscience." But one of their number, Mr. Herle, the prolocutor of the Assembly, with great candor and good sense, remarked, "The difference between us and our brethren who are for Independency, is nothing so great as some may conceive; at most, it does but ruffle the fringe, not any way rend the garment of Christ."

Yet the quarrel continued and has continued with more or less violence to the present day; the sound of the controversy, even in this country, is now ringing in our ears; in the last century it was discordant and harsh throughout our churches in the ambitious struggle for power. The controversy then related to church government, for in doctrine there was a substantial agreement. The Savoy confession of 1658 proceeds upon the plan of the Westminster Assembly; the preface declares, "that they fully consent to the Westminster confession, for the substance of it." The disagreement was not in matters of faith, but only in matters of form.

It is not my intention to trace further the migrations of these people upon this continent. Having accompanied the earliest colony to Massachusetts, which contained the first of the McKinstry family who came to America, I leave the nation to follow the fortunes of the individual.

[*To be Continued.*]

EARLY SETTLERS OF WESTERLY, RHODE ISLAND.

[Communicated by J. D. CHAMPLIN, Jun., of Stonington, Conn.]

The town of Westerly was settled in the year 1661 by a colony from the island of Aquidneck, (now Rhode Island,) and mostly from the town of Newport. Its Indian name appears under the various orthography of Misquamocuck, Swampecot, Squamicun, Squamicuck, &c. For a particular account of the first purchase and settlement, see Potter's Narraganset, Vol. III, Collections Rhode Island Historical Society. The following list of " free inhabitants " is a literal transcript from the first volume of town meeting records, and although bearing date, 1669, was probably not entered until 1682–3, as may be inferred from the following, recorded on the next page, immediately after the list :—

" The records of the acts and orders of the Inhabitants of the towne of westerle—

whereas it hath pleased the Honnored Gennerall Assembly of his Majesties Collony of Rhod Island and Providence plantations and Kings province Sitteinge att Newport May the fift 1669 :

To grante unto us the Inhabitants of the towne of westerle the Liberty And Authority of Carrieing on our affairs in Condition as A Towne

As it may Appeare :

In persuance where of

wee the Inhabitants of the towne Aforesaid have Judged it expedient for the upbuulding of peace and Concorde Amonge our Selves and such as shall be Leagally admitted Inhabitants Amonge us and for the prevention of the Contrary hereof for the future ;

To make sundery orders hauth formerly and lately which have been exposed to delaye being only Committed into Loose papers, (and partly by Reasons of the Changes of Governments we have been passing under) for the prevention whereof for the future the haveing provided,

A Book

And att a Towne meeting held by the ffree Inhabitants in the towne of westerle on March 22. 1681

Voted.	Mr. Jeffree Champion [*Champlin*] Chossen Moderator—

Voted.   That the laws and orders of this Towne shall by the Towne
Clerk be Recorded in the Towne Book, and Mr. Tobias Saunders and
Leiftanante Joseph Davell are Appointed And Authorized to be Assistants
to the towne Clerk in the orderly placeing of them :"

"A List of the free Inhabitants of the towne of westerle" may the 18—
1669 :

John Crandall	March 3 16⁶⁹
Tobias Saunders 17 lot	Joseph Davell 42 lot
Edward Larkin	Joseph Crandall 14
Robert Burdick 36	James Lewes 1 lotu
Stephen Willcox	James Pendleton
John Randall	Joshua Holmes 39 lot
John Lewes	Hope Chapman 31 lot
John Mackoon	John Masson Jun. 12 lot
James Cass	Benjamin Burdick 15 lot
John Sharp	Joseph Masson 29 lot
Johnathan Armstrong	James Babcock Jun. 48 lot
Danniell Stanlon	Hennery Halle Jun. 6 lote
John Masson 10 lote 34	Edward Larkin Jun. 33 lot
James Babcock Sen	Thomas Rennolds 28 lote
Jeffree Champion Sen.	John Davis 8 lot
Thomas Painner	John Babcock 27 lot
John ffairfield 30 lot	Joseph Pemberton 10 lot
James Babcock Jun. 35	Thomas Stephens 20 lot
Danniell Cromb 23 lot	Joseph Clark Jun. 43 lot
John Babcock	James Halle 13 lot [Landpheare
Nickolas Cottrell 21	Caleb Pendleton 41 lot given to Georg
Job Babcock 45 lot	George Browne 4 lot
Shubaell Painter	Daved Lewes 5 lot
Joseph Clark 18 lot	Izreall Lews 16 lot
Sept. 1679.	Richard Landfeare 11 lot
Georg Landfeare 32 lot	Nicolas Satterle
Richard Swait	Thomas Wells Jun. 47 lot
Jeffree Champion Jun.	Thomas Wells sen. 40 lot
HenneryHalle sen.	Samuell Lews 38 lot
John Lews Jun. 9 lot	Thomas Burdick 37
Gershem Cottrell	Edward Wilcox
William Champion 49 lot	John Enos 2 lot
Petter Crandall 19 lot	Shendrak Landfeare 24 lot
Christopher Champion 22 lot	John Maconne 26 lot
James Crandall	John Larkin 46 lot

In the above list, Lews and Lewes, same as Lewis; Cromb—Crumb ;
Champion—Champlin.   Pemberton is probably a distinct name from Pendleton.

One Thousand Funerals.—Rev. J. Rebaugh, in a funeral sermon
which he preached on the occasion of the death of Mr. George Cushwa,
which took place week before last, stated that he (Cushwa) was the
thousandth person he had buried in the course of his ministry.   Dr. Rebaugh is not an old man, and we believe has never preached in a city,
which makes the matter astonishing.—*Greencastle (Pa.) Ledger*, 12 Oct.
1857.

BIRTHS, MARRIAGES, AND DEATHS IN MALDEN.
[Continued from page 87.]

[Communicated by AARON SARGENT.]

MARRIAGES.

Theophilus Burrill of Lynn & Mary Hills of Malden	Sept. 24, 1736
Samuel Grover & Abigail Oakes	Nov. 8, "
Samuel Bleigh of Boston & Mary Tufts of Malden	" 12, "
Nathaniel Townsend of Lynn & Margaret Chamberlane of Malden	Dec. 9, "
Daniel Marnsfield of Lynn & Mrs. Elizabeth Tufts of Malden	Jan. 6, 1739
Samuel Sprague & Martha Hills	" 11, "
David Howard & Sarah Degresha	" 20, "
Samuel Newhall & Martha Upham	Mch 18, "
Timothy Sprague & Mrs. Mary Legg	Apl 14, 1737
Samuel Hasey of Boston & Sarah Upham of Malden	May 9, "
Charles Lemoyne & Mary Marble	" 19, "
Timothy Green & Dorothy Wayte	Nov. 8, "
Joseph Burditt & Tabitha Paine	Dec. 16, "
Moses Gleeson of Oxford & Deborah Whittemore of Malden	Feb. 2, 173¾
Stephen Sweetser & Elizabeth Mudge	" 8, "
Benj. Faulkner & Anna Sprague	Mch 22, 1738
John Mudge & Mary Waite	May 4, "
Robert Wilson & Anna Jackson	July 12, "
John Sweetser of North Yarmouth & Elizabeth Stevens of Malden	Nov. 16, "
Reuben Derbe of Pomfret & Zibillah Howard of Malden	Dec. 27, "
William Waite & Deborah Bucknam	" 28, "
Jona. Oakes & Martha Bucknam	Feb. 1, 1738
Timothy Dexter & Sarah Bucknam	Mch 22, "
Abraham Skinner & Anna Emmes [Eames]	" 13, 1739
Joseph Barrett & Phebe Waitt	Apl 27, "
Daniel Merritt of Boston & Lydia Sweetser of Malden	Dec. 11, "
Jonathan Lynde & Elizabeth Mower	" 21, "
Jabez Burditt & Hannah Sargeant	Feb. 7, 1739
Daniel Goffe & Mrs. Mary Upham	Mch —, 1740
Nathan Richardson of Woburn & Lydia Whittemore of Malden	Apl 3, "
Joseph Lynde & Mary Lynde	July 4, "
John Sargeant & Hannah Wadkins	" 24, "
David Parker & Mary Upham	Sept. 5, "
John Nichols & Agnes Leveston	Dec. 11, "
Ezra Green & Sarah Hutchinson	Feb. 12, 1743
Ichabod Clark of Stoughton & Sarah Whittemore of Malden	Mch 30, 1741 *
Samuel Wade of Medford & Martha Newhall of Malden	Dec. 2, "
Joshua Tucker of Woodstock & Mary Wright of Malden	Feb. 11, 1744
Nathan Sargeant of Leicester & Mary Sargeant of Malden	June 24, 1742
James Dunbar of Malden & Rebekah Woods of Boston	Jan. 11, 1744
Joseph Mudge & Phebe Green	" 19, "
Wm. Barnes of Boston & Mary Mansur of Malden	" 26, "
Joses Bucknam & Mary Sprague	June 8, 1743

John Hoyle of Providence & Anna Wayte of Malden	Aug. 11, 1743
Samuel Sargeant & Lois Wayte	Oct. 25, "
Nathan Newhall & Tabitha Wayte	" 26, "
Benjamin Bucknam & Rebecca Parker	Nov. 12, "
John Wayte of Chelsea & Sarah Faulkner of Malden	" 25, "
Benjamin Sprague & Phebe Lynde	Mch 20, 1744
Samuel Shute & Elizabeth Pratt	May 23, 1744
James Whittemore & Mary Sherman	June 4, "
James Milliner of Mansfield & Ruth Peirce of Malden	" 12, "
Nathan Dexter of Malden & Esther Brintnall of Chelsea	" 26, "
Benj. Rice of Brookfield & Sarah Upham of Malden	" 30, "
Edward Sprague & Lydia Howard	July 4, "
John Dunten & Mercy Johnson	Aug. 17, "
Israel Cook of Boston & Hannah Upham of Malden	Jan. 11, 1744
Bartholomew Flag & Susanna Marble	Mch 27, 1745
John Goddard & Sarah Sargeant	Aug. 3, "
John Marten & Sarah Mansur	Sept. 18, "
Charles Crouley of Charlestown & Mary Marks of Malden	Oct. 1, "
Thomas Purten & Jemima Brintnall	Dec. 4, "
Thomas Boston & Anna Taylor	Jan. 7, 1745
John Burditt & Jemima Green	Feb. 6, "
Silas Sargeant & Mary Winslow	" 14, "
David Bucknam of Salem & Mrs. Esther Sprague of Malden	Mch 4, "
John Dexter & Abignil Hill	Apl 18, 1746
Nathaniel Jenkins & Abigail Baldwin	May 1, "
Abraham Hill & Abigail Upham	" 8, "
Moses Collins of Roxbury & Lydia Whittemore of Malden	" 20, "
Thomas Wayte & Mary Sprague	June 13, "
John Knower & Phebe Sprague	" 17, "
Jabez Sargeant & Rachel Wayte	Oct. 9, "
Joseph Sargeant & Hannah Whittemore	Jan. 20, 1746
Benjamin Wayte of Malden & Barbary Unthank of Chelsea	Mch 20, "
William Thomas & Mary Hill	" 28, 1747
Ebenezer Pratt & Elizabeth Knower	May 7, "
Nathaniel Jenkins & Catharine Grant	June 19, "
John Sargeant & Hannah Knower	Oct. 1, "
John Bucknam & Hannah Lynde	Nov. 12, "
Joseph Sprague of Dudley & Phebe Hutchinson of Malden	Jan. 7, 1747
Jacob Upham of Malden & Rebecca Durnin of Reading	" 19, "
Thomas Shute & Sarah Baldwin	" 21, "
John Dexter & Joanna Lynde	Mch 15, "
Edward Oliver of Malden & Sarah Wayte of Chelsea	" 23, "
John Nichols & Elizabeth Burditt	Apl 21, 1748
James Bayley of Boston & Mary Wayte of Malden	May 16, "
Ebenezer Upham of Leicester & Lois Waite of Malden	Oct. 28, "
Thomas Sargeant & Mary Wayte	Jan. 17, 1748
William Gill & Martha Flinn	Mch 9, "
James Sargeant & Elizabeth Upham	Apl 25, 1749
Jabez Burditt & Deborah Richardson	Jan. 16, 1749
Samuel Sprague & Elizabeth Wade	" 24, "
Jacob Breeden of Chelsea & Hannah Floyd of Malden	Mch 2, "
Nathan Sprague & Mary Hovey	Apl 17, 1750
Thomas Hills & Mary Shute	" 26, "

Jonathan Oakes & Esther Bucknam   Sept. 13, 1750
Thomas Hurrage of Lynn & Anna Wayte of Malden   Nov. 15, "
Jacob Shute & Mary Pratt   Dec. 27, "

MARRIAGE INTENTIONS (*Marriages not recorded.*)
Samuel Bucknam & Elizabeth Wyman of Woburn   July 21, 1738
Pellitiah Whittemore & Deborah Kendall of Dunstable   " 30, "
Timothy Upham & Mary Cheever of Lynn   Sept. 29, 1739
Joseph Newhall & Mary Bradshaw of Medford   Dec. 29, "
Benj. Howard & Abigail Wallion of Reading   Jan. 13, 17⅜
Rev. Mr. Thomas Skinner of Colchester & Mary Newhall   June 15, 1740
Amos Upham & Lois Green of Reading   Oct. 5, "
John Newhall & Dorothy Newhall of Leicester   June 10, 1741
Elkanah Hitchens & Phebe Baldwin   Aug. 15, "
Richard Dexter & Rebecca Peabody of Boxford   Oct. 24, "
Jabez Lynde & Rachel Parker   Nov. 4, "
Benj. Parker & Phebe Green of Stoneham   "   4, "
Jabez Green of Stoneham & Mary Lynde   " 11, "
Samuel Wade of Medford & Martha Newhall   " 15, "
Ralph Merry of Lynn & Sarah Knower   Jan. 3, 174¾
Aaron Burden of Medford & Thankful Wellcom   " 31, "
John Oliver & Elizabeth Pratt   Feb. 10, "
Joseph Hopkins of Charlestown & Margaret Hills   Aug. 18, 1742
John Goold & Susanna Harndel   Sept. 15, "
John Harndel & Esther Parker   Oct. 13, "
Joseph Baldwin & Mary Potter of Lynn   " 27, "
Peter Hayse of Stoneham & Lydia Lynde   Dec. 1, "
John Sargeant & Susanna Chamberlaine of Chelsea   "   8, "
Thomas Pratt & Mary Ausgood of Reading   Feb. 9, 174¾
Jabez Sargeant & Abigail Mower of Worcester   Oct. 4, 1743
Isaac Hill & Sarah Haven of Framingham   Nov. 20, "
Ezra Green & Eunice Burrill of Lynn   Feb. 22, 174¾
Rev. Daniel Emerson of Dunstable & Mrs. Hannah Emerson Oct. 17, 174¾
Samuel Polle of Medford & Anna Nichols   Jan. 20, 174¾
Sam'l Blanchard & Sarah Cuner of Medford   Feb. 10, "
Unight Cox & Lydia Faulkner   July 1, 1745
Thomas Hills & Sarah Burrill of Lynn   Oct. 20, "
Samuel Wayte & Rebecca Sweetser of Charlestown   Mch 3, 174¾
Jacob Lynde & Mary Goold of Stoneham   " 28, 1746
John Polle of Medford & Jemima Nichols   July 1, "
Stowers Sprague & Rebecca Deal of Boston   Feb. 14, 174¾
James Bucknam & Mary Goddard of Roxbury   Aug. 19, 1747
Nathan Eaton of Reading & Sarah Collman   Oct. 7, "
William Pratt & Abigail Pell of Lynn   Nov. 5, "
Stephen Tufts & Catharine Taylor   July 17, 1748
Phineas Sprague & Hannah Goold of Stoneham   Sept. 21, "
Jonathan Knower & Mary Wilson   Apl 15, 1749
Edward Sprague & Dorothy Skinner   Nov. 4, "
Daniel Knower & Abigail Whittemore   " 25, "
John Upham & Deliverance Fowll of Lynn   Apl 27, 1750
Jonathan Wiles of Lynn & Tamzen Upham   June 17, "
Daniel Welich & Elizabeth Berry   " 24, "
Aaron Bucknam & Alice Skinner of Lynn   Oct. 14, "
Israel Persons of Leicester & Hannah Wayte   Dec. 22, "

DEATHS.

Richard, son of Richard & Abigail Upham	Sept. 4, 1700
Joanna, dau. of Richard & Lydia Shute	" 12, "
Judith Townzen	Feb. 5, 1701
Robert Callo	" 15, 1704
Elizabeth Lamson	June 10, 1703
Timothy, son of John & Winefred Dexter	Aug. 20, "
Benjamin Whittemore, Jr.	Oct. 7, "
John Sprague	Dec. 16, "
Christopher Lewis	Feb. 6, 1703
Thomas Skinner	Mch 2, "
Timothy, 8th child of John & Winefred Dexter	Oct. 17, 1704
Joseph Floyd	Jan. -, 1705
Joseph Wilson	" 14, "
Lydia, wife of John Greenland	" 20, "
Rev. Mr. Wigglesworth, Pastor of the Church at Malden	June -, 1705
John, son of William Bucknam	" 14, "
John, son of John & Winefred Dexter	July 4, "
Ezekiel Jenkins, Sen.	" 30, "
Tryall Newbury	Dec. 9, "
William Green	" 30, "
Michael, son of Richard & Lydia Shute	Apl 10, 1706
Mary, wife to Thomas Upham	" 21, 1707
Susanna, wife to John Lynde, Jr.	Sept. 9, "
Dea. John Green	Oct. 16, "
William, son of Samuel & Deborah Bucknam	Feb. 10, 1705
Tabitha, dau. of John & Elizabeth Wilson	Jan. 4, 1708
Mary, dau. of Samuel & Sarah Sprague	Oct. 26, "
John Green	Mch 22, 1709
Sarah, dau. of David & Sarah Parsons	June 8, "
Marcy, dau. of Samuel & Sarah Sprague	Aug. 8, "
Rebecca Sprague *alias* Brown	July 8, 1710
Nathaniel Evens, Sen.	Dec. 16, "
Zebediah, son of Phineas & Tamzen Upham	Apl 28, 1712
Tamzen, dau. of " " "	June 13, 1713
William, son of William & Elizabeth Green	July 25, "
Lemuel Jenkins, Sen.	Dec. 20, "
Elizabeth Jenkins	Mch 11, 1713
Abigail Jenkins	" 15, "
Samuel, son of James & Deborah Hovey	" 17, "
Daniel, son of Nathaniel & Mary Upham	Sept. 1, 1714
Joseph Baldwin, Sen.	Nov. 23, "
Edward Sprague	Apl 13, 1715
Sarah, wife of Nathaniel Upham, Sen.	Oct. 14, "
Abigail, wife of William Ireland	Nov. 21, "
Mary, wife of Samuel Green, Sen.	" 22, "
Lydia, widow, relict of John Sprague	Dec. 11, "
Abigail, dau. of Richard & Abigail Upham	Jan. 7, 1715
Abraham, son of Abraham & Abigail Hills	" 8, "
Dorcas, dau. of Richard & Abigail Upham	" 22, "
Jabez, son of Joseph & Hannah Green	July 13, 1716
John Sargeant, Sen.	Sept. 9, "
Mary, wife of Jonathan Sargeant	Nov. 19, "

Sarah, dau. of John & Lydia Sargeant	Dec. 5, 1716
Abigail, wife of John Upham	Aug. 23, 1717
Henry Green	Sept. 19, "
Nathaniel Upham	Nov. 11, "
Simon Grover, æ. 73	" 17, "
Sarah, widow, relict of Capt. John Green	Dec. 1, "
Luke, son of Richard & Abigail Upham	May 6, 1719
Jacob, son of John & Tamzen Upham	Sept. 2, "
Ruth, dau. of John & Lydia Sargeant	Oct. 28, "
Sarah, dau. of Samuel & Sarah Blanchard	Mch 30, 1720
Caleb, son of Simon & Sarah Grover	June 4, "
Isaac, son of Isaac & Mary Greene	Sept. 19, "
Dea. Phineas Upham	Oct. 19, "
Sarah, dau. of Jonathan & Sarah Knower	Sept. 7, 1722
Jonathan Knower	Oct. 15, "
Sarah, wife of Jonathan Knower	" 22, "
Dea. John Dexter	Dec. 14, "
Samuel, son of Samuel & Martha Green	May 9, 1724
Samuel Green, Sen.	Oct. 31, "
Phebe, dau. of Nathaniel & Mary Upham	Apl 4, 1725
Joseph Wayte	" 9, "
Lydia, dau. of Joseph & Lydia Wayte	" 27, "
Joseph Wilson	" 29, "
Dea. Nathaniel Nichols	May 10, "
Mary Nichols	" 13, "
Joseph, son of Samuel & Sibel Howard	" 18, "
Rebecca, wife of Thomas Newhall	" 26, "
Abigail, dau. of Samuel & Abigail Stowers	" 29, "
Martha, dau. of Nathaniel & Mary Upham	" 31, "
John Lawson	July 14, "
Thomas Green	Aug. 24, "
John, son of John & Dorothy Coleman	Nov. 3, "
John, son of John & Abigail Paine	Dec. 2, "
Hannah, widow of Abraham Skinner	Jan. 14, 1724½
Sarah, widow of Simon Grover	Feb. 16, "
Benjamin Whittemore	July 16, 1726
Elizabeth, widow of Benjamin Whittemore	" 18, "
Elizabeth, wife of John Wilson	Sept. 15, "
David, son of Samuel & Sarah Newhall	Dec. 23, "
Dorothy, widow of Capt. Edward Sprague	Mch 29, 1727
in 58th year of her age, and was the only wife of said Sprague.	
Timothy, son of John & Mary Tufts	Apl 29, "
Sarah, dau. of Simon & Sarah Grover	Sept. 18, "
Jacob, son of Thomas & Mary Wayte	Oct. 1, "
Mary, dau. of Timothy & Mary Wayte	" 12, "
Joseph, son of John & Elizabeth Knower	Dec. 20, "
Lemuel, son of Nathaniel & Sarah Jenkins	" 20, "
Nathan, son of Samuel & Anna Wayte	" 26, "
Mehitable, dau. of Joseph & Lydia Wayte	" 31, "
Lydia, " " " "	Jan. 9, 1727½
Samuel, son of Thomas & Hannah Degresha	" 22, "
Caleb, son of Samuel & Sarah Blanchard	" 30, "
Benjamin, son of Samuel & Sarah Grover	May 24, 1728

Marcy, wife of Richard Pratt — May 28, 1728
Left. Thomas Newhall — July 13, "
Simon, son of James & Mary Whittemore — Sept. 14, "
Dea. John Greenland — Oct. 17, "
Amos, son of John & Sarah Stower — Mch 28, 1729
Thomas Burditt — June 20, "
Peternell, wife of Samuel Whittemore — Aug. 23, "
Mary, dau. of James & Margaret Wilson — Nov. 14, "
Mary, dau. of John & Mehitable Pratt — Jan. 5, 1730
John, son of " " " — " 14, "
Phebe, wife of David Pratt — " 20, "
Phebe, dau. of Stower & Phebe Sprague — " 21, "
Phebe, dau. of Nathaniel & Lydia Howard — " 22, "
Mary, wife of Samuel Greene — " 24, "
Nathaniel, son of Nathaniel & Lydia Howard — " 25, "
Edward, son of Samuel & Peternell Whittemore — Feb. 24, "
Lydia, widow of John Sargeant — Mch 2, 1730
John Whittemore — " 4, "
John Sprague, in the 75th year of his age — " 8, "
William, son of Richard & Sarah Dexter — May 30, "
John Marble — June 2, "
Sarah, dau. of Samuel & Sarah Blanchard — July 6, "
Elizabeth, dau. of Jonathan & Mary Knower — " 22, "
Benjamin, son of " " " — Aug. 1, "
James, son of John & Mehitable Pratt — Sept. 9, "
Hannah, wife of Bartholomew Gidny — " 21, "
Sarah, wife of John Stower — Oct. 2, "
Sarah, dau. of Joseph & Elizabeth Lynde — " 14, 1731
John, son of John & Ann Wellcom — July —, 1732
Thomas Oakes, husband of Sarah Oakes — Sept. —, "
Dea. Joseph Green — Nov. 28, "
Stephen, son of Dea. Joseph & Hannah Green — Feb. 3, 1734
Nathaniel, son of John & Dorothy Coleman — Mch 29, 1733
Lieut. Samuel Newhall — Apl 17, "
Lydia, wife of Benjamin Faulkner — May 26, "
John Upham — June 11, "
Elizabeth, wife of Joseph Lynde, æ. 73 years — " 20, "
Ruth, wife of John Mudge — Oct. 17, "
John, husband of the above Ruth Mudge — " 29, "
Uriah, son of Uriah & Deborah Oakes — Dec. 18, "
Ruhama, wife of James Green — Jan. 10, 1734
Sarah, dau. of David & Sarah Upham — " 21, 1734
Anna, dau. of John & Ann Wellcom — June 18, "
Martha, dau. of Joseph & Mary Chadwick — Aug. 30, "
Samuel, son of Nathaniel & Sarah Eustis — Dec. 18, "
Dorothy, wife of John Coleman — Jan. 24, 1734
Benjamin, son of Thomas & Mary Wayte — June 2, 1735
Waldon, son of Joseph & Mary Emerson — July 8, "

Samuel, son of Nathaniel & Sarah Nichols, and hus-
    band to Jemima Nichols
John, son of Nathaniel & Sarah Nichols, and husband
    to Agnes Nichols
     } in ye year 1725

(To be Continued.)

DANVERS CHURCH RECORDS.

[Continued from Vol. XI., p. 321.]

3 That they in publick do consent to the Coven^t. propounded unto y^m by our Pastour in these words (or words to ye like effect)—

You—A. B. do before y^r holy Assembly acknowledge ye only Living and true God to be y^r God, & do give up y^rself to him to love, fear, serve him, and to be happy in the enjoyment of him forever.

You do also acknowledge ye Lord Jesus Christ the Eternal son of God to be your only Saviour and Redeemer; and (under a sense of y^r sin and misery & need of him) do give up y^rself to him to be saved by him from sin and from the wrath of God.

You do also acknowledge the Eternal Spirit of God to be your only Sanctifyer, and do give up y^rself to him to be sanctifyed, comforted, and guided by him to Glory.

You do also submit to the discipline and government of Jesus Christ in ye Chh, and do promise y^t you will live in ye use of all means y^t so you may be fit to come to all ye ordinances of Christ in his Church.

This was first voted by the Chh.

4 We do also consent y^t the children of such persons be baptized provided the parents publickly give y^m up to God, and promise y^t if God shall spare their lives they will see such their children educated in the nurture and admonition of ye Lord.

This was voted by itself—and there was none that manifested any dissatisfaction—but all gave their consent to each particular.

Blessed be God for such a peaceful meeting."

1701, June 18. "A day of Publick Thanksgiving. God smiled on ye season, ye work of ye day was carryed by Mr. Noyes (who prayed) & Mr Pierpoint preach^t, & concluded." The reasons for the Thanksgiving were, 1. Y^t God has so far discovered ye wiles of ye Devil which might have been more hurtfull and distructive to us, if God had not in judgm^t remembred mercy. 2. Y^t when ye people were farthest from peace & unity y^t God was pleased to hear prayers & unite us, & especially to hearken to those prayers y^t were put up here on a day of publick fasting & prayer by Mr. Hale & Mr. Noyes, from wch day God was pleased to succeed all publick endeavours for a peaceable settlem^t. 3. & y^t God has now for some years continued peace and prosperity to us. & 4. that he has been carrying on his work in ye midst of us, &c."

Oct. 19. "The Pastor read a Letter to the Church at B..verly, to desire our assistance in ordaining Mr. Blower—& three messengers were chosen with ye Elder &c."

Oct. 29. "We assisted in Mr. Blowers ordination, all impediments removed."

1702. December. "The Pastor spake to ye Chh. on ye Sab. as followeth Brethren I find in ye Chh book a Rec^d of Martha Corys being excommunicated for witchcraft.—And ye Generality of ye land being sensible of ye errors y^t prevailed in y^t day—some of her friends have moved me sev^l times to propose to ye Chh whether it be not our duty to recall y^t sentence y^t so it may not stand ag^t her to all Generations and I myself being a stranger to her & being ignorant of what was alledg'd ag^t her—I shall now only leave it to your consideration, and shall determine the matter by a vote ye next convenient opportunity."

Jan. 13. " We kept a day of fasting and prayer on account of yᵉ
small pox, &c."

Feb. 14. " The Pastor moved yᵉ Chh to revoke Martha Corys excom-
munᵘ.—but sevⁿ dissented and there was not a full vote for yᵉ revoking
it, tho' a majᵗʸ."

1706. Aug. 25. " Recᵈ Ann Putnam to full communion.

The confession of Anne Putnam when she was received to commu-
      nion: 1706.

I desire to be humbled before God for yᵗ sad and humbling providence
that befell my fathers family in the year about 92, yᵗ I then being in my
childhood should by such a providence of God be made an instrument for
yᵗ accuseing of severall persons of a grievous crime wherby their lives
were taken away from them, whom now I have just grounds and good
reason to believe they were innocent persons, and yᵗ it was a great delusion of Satan yᵗ deceived me in that sad time, wherby I justly fear I have
been instrumental with others tho' ignorantly and unwillingly to bring
upon myself & this land the guilt of innocent blood Though what was said
or done by me against any person I can truly and uprightly say before
God & man I did it not out of any anger, malice, or illwill to any person
for I had no such thing against one of them ; but what I did was ignorantly being deluded by Satan. And particularly as I was a chief instrument of accuseing of Goodwife Nurse and her two sisters I desire to lye
in the dust & to be humbled for it in that I was a cause with others of so
sad a calamity to them & their familys, for which cause I desire to lye in
yᵉ dust & earnestly begg fforgiveness of God & from all those unto whom
I have given just cause of sorrow & offence, whose relations were taken
away or accused.   (Signed)   Anne Putnam.

Yᵉ confession was read before yᵉ congregation together with her relation Aug: 25. 1706. & she acknowledged it.—J. Greene. Pastʳ."

1702–3, Feb. 14. " The majʳ part of the brethren consented to yᵉ following &

Whereas this Church passed a vote Sept. 11. 1692 for the excommuni-
cation of Martha Cory, and that sentence was pronounced agᵗ her Sept.
14 by Mr. Samˡˡ Parris formerly the Pastour of this Church ; she being
before her excomⁿ condemned & afterwards executed for supposed witchcraft : and there being a record of this in our Chh book page 12. We
being moved hereunto do freely consent & heartily desire that the same
sentence may be revoked, and that it may stand no longer agᵗ her for we
are thro' Gods mercy to us convinced yᵗ we were at that dark day under
the Power of those errours which then prevailed in the land ; and we are
sensible that we had not sufficient grounds to think her guilty of that crime
for which she was condemned & executed ; and yᵗ her excomⁿ was not
according to the mind of God ; and therefore we desire that this may be
entred in our Church book, to take off that odium that is cast on her name
and that so God may forgive our sin, & may be atoned for the land, & we
humbly pray that God will not leave us any more to such errours and sins,
but will teach & enable us always to do that which is right in his sight.

There was a majʳ part voted—& 6 or 7 dissented. J. G. Pʳ."

[I know not by what accident this entry—1702–3—is thus transposed
to the end of the year 1707—but so it stands in the Church Book. W.
T. H.]

1717, June 5. Wednesday. Rev. Peter Clark ordained. " Rev.
Elders and Messengers of yᵉ Chhs of Salem, Beverly, Wenham, Tops-

field, & Reading convened.   Rev. Mr. Gerrish gave y⁰ Charge, ordaining him a minister of y⁰ Gospel, Pastor of the Chh in Sal: Village &c with y⁰ consent of y⁰ Chh & y⁰ Inhabitants—and Rev. Mr. Curwin gave to him y⁰ Right Hand of Fellowship, and to this Chh."

1717–18, Feb. 13.   "This Day was kept as a Day of Solemn Fasting & prayer to God, occasioned by a Sore Visitation, by Sickness & mortality; some of y⁰ neighboring Elders assisted &c."

1718, Oct. 3.   "At a Chh meeting before y⁰ Sacram⁴ was read a Letter from y⁰ first Chh in Salem to request y⁰ presence & assistance of y⁰ Pastour & messengers at y⁰ Ordination of y⁰ Rev⁴. Mr. Fisk on y⁰ 8ᵗʰ of Octob: 1718.   The two Deacons & Capt. Jonath: Putnam were chosen as messengers by a vote of y⁰ Chh.

1719, April 5.   "A Letter from y⁰ Chh newly gathered in Salem was read, wherein was desired y⁰ presence & assistance of y⁰ Pastour & messengers at y⁰ Ordination of y⁰ Rev⁴. Mr. Staunton on y⁰ 8ᵗʰ of April 1719." Same messengers as in last extract chosen.

May 6.   "A Contribution being made by this Chh & Congregation on y⁰ Publick Thanksgiving Dec. 11. 1718. on y⁰ account of the *Brief* for y⁰ Propagating & maintaining y⁰ Gospel ministry &c. amounting to y⁰ sum of 5 lb was transmitted & put into y⁰ hands of Edward Bromfield Esq. according to y⁰ Directions of s⁴ Brief.   By y⁰ Pastor of s⁴ Chh."

1720, April 10.   "A Letter from y⁰ neighbouring Society at Lyn–End who had entred upon y⁰ foundation of a Chh State, was read, requesting y⁰ assistance of y⁰ Elder & messengers in y⁰ proceeding to an Ordination on Apr. 13.   The two Deacons & Mr. Cheaver were chosen as messengers by a vote of y⁰ Chh."

June 19.   "A Letter from y⁰ Chh newly gathered in Reading North Precinct desiring y⁰ assistance of y⁰ Elder & messenger of this Chh in joyning wᵗʰ those of other neighbouring Chhs in y⁰ Ordination of y⁰ Rev⁴. Mᵣ Danˡˡ Putnam, was read, & y⁰ two Deacons & Capt. Putnam were chosen as messengers by a vote of y⁰ Chh."

1723, Nov. 28.   "A Letter from y⁰ Chh in Reading North Precinct was read, to desire y⁰ presence & assistance of y⁰ Elder & messengers in Council with y⁰ Rev. Elders & messengers of other Churches, in order to y⁰ composing some matters of difference among y⁰ to be held Dec. 3. 1723. & Deac⁰ Edward Putnam & Mr. Ezekiel Cheaver were chosen as messengers by a vote of y⁰ Chh."

1727, Oct. 29.   "Being Lord's Day, at night, between 10 & 11 oclock, y⁰ happened a very Great Earthquake accompanied with a terrible noise & shaking wᶜʰ was greatly surprizing to y⁰ whole Land y⁰ rumbling noise in y⁰ bowels of y⁰ Earth with some lesser trepidation of y⁰ Earth has been repeated at certain intervals divers weeks after."   [Church Records, between Jan. 7th & Jan. 14th, 1727–8.]

1728, May 12 (?)   "A Letter from y⁰ Chh of Christ belonging to y⁰ East Parish in Salem was read, desiring y⁰ presence & assistance of y⁰ Elder & messengers at y⁰ Ordination of y⁰ Rev⁴ Mʳ. Wᵐ. Jenison, appointed to be on May 22, 1728.   The two Deacons & Brother Ezekiel Cheever were chosen as messengers by a vote of y⁰ Chh."

Nov. 24.   "A Letter from y⁰ Chh of Christ in Topsfield was read, desiring y⁰ presence & concurrence of y⁰ Elder and messengers with those of other Chhs, in y⁰ Ordination of y⁰ Rev⁴. John Emerson Nov: 27. 1728.   The two Deacons & Capt. Jon⁰ Putnam were chosen as messengers on y⁰ occasion."

1729, Nov. 18. " A Letter read from y* Chh of Christ in Middleton, requesting y* presence & assistance of y* Elder & messengers to joyn with those of other Chhs in y* Ordination of y* Rev* M* Andrew Peters Nov: 26, 1729. The two Deacons & M*. Ezekiel Cheevers were chosen as messengers on y* occasion by a vote of y* Chh. At y* same time were propounded y* Desires of several of y* brethren & sisters of y* Chh to be dismist to y* Chh of Christ in Middleton, whose names are as follows, Viz. *Males.* Henry Wilkins, Dan* Kenny, Jon*. Fuller, Joseph Fuller, Isaac Wilkins, Ezra Putnam, Edward Putnam, Benj*. Wilkins. *Of y* Females.* Sarah Fuller, Mary Fuller, Sarah Putnam, Eliz*. Putnam, Mary Wilkins, Mary Kenny, Susanna Fuller, Eliz*. Nichols, Mary Wilkins, Hannah Carril, Margery Wilkins, Eunice Lambert, Eliz*. Eliot, Penelope Wilkins, Susanna Fuller, Susanna Hobbs. In complyance with whose desires Letters of Dismission were granted y* with consent of y* brethren."

1731, Aug. 15. " A Letter was read from y* Second Chh in Lynn, requesting y* presence of y* Pastour & Delegates to joyn with other Elders & Delegates in Council upon y* affair of y* dismission of y* Pastor M* Nath*. Sparhawk. The two Deac** & Joseph Hutchinson were chosen as Delegates. To meet Thursday, Aug: 19, 1731."

1732, Dec. 31. " A Letter from y* Chh of Christ in Wenham was read, desiring y* presence & assistance of y* Elder & messengers in orders to y* Ordinations of y* Rev* M* John Warren, Jan: 10. 1732-3. The two Deac**. Edward & Nath** Putnam & Brother Joseph Hutchinson were chosen as messengers by a vote of y* Chh."

1736, Dec. 5. " A Letter read from those Brethren of y* Chh of y* First Parish in Salem meeting in y* ancient place of publick worship, requesting y* presence & assistance of this Chh by y* Elder & messengers with y* Elders & messengers of other Chhs, in y* Ordination of M*. John Sparhawk to y* Pastoral Office, on Decemb* 8**, & also a Letter from y* Rev*. M*. Sam* Fisk & his adherents of y* First Chb in Salem objecting ag* our proceeding in that affair."

Dec. 6. " A concurrence" with the request of the *first* letter abovementioned " was voted by a considerable majority of y* Brethren present; and y* two Deacons present & Cap* Jon* Putnam & Brother John Putnam were chosen as messengers of y* Chh on y* occasion."

1737, May 8. " A Letter read from y* Brethren of y* Fourth Chb in Salem requesting y* presence & assistance of this Chh by y* Elder & messengers, with y* Elders & messengers of other Chhs, in y* Ordination of M* James Diman to y* Pastoral office over y* on May 11**, 1737. Accordingly the Brethren consented, & y* Deacons & Cap*. Jon*. Putnam were chosen messengers on y* occasion."

1837-8, Jan. 1. " A Letter from y* brethren of y* Chh in Marble Head lately under y* Pastoral care of y* Rev* M* Edw* Holyoke was read, desiring y* presence & assistance of this Chh by y* Elder & messengers, with y* Elders & messengers of other Chhs, in y* Ordination of M* Simon Broadstreet Jun* to y* Pastoral Office over them; on Jan. 4. 1737-8, in compliance with w* request Deac* Whipple, Cap* Jon* Putnam, and Cap* Tho* Flint were chosen messengers by y* vote of y* Chh."

(To be Continued.)

NOTES ON THE LOMBARD FAMILY.

FIRST GENERATION.

1. Bernard Lombard, of Scituate, 1633 ; freeman, 1636 ; Barnstable, 1640 ; married ———, and had
[3.] 2. Joshua, b.
[4.] 3. Jabez, bapt. July 4, 1641 ;
    4. Martha, bapt. Oct. 2, 1639 ; m. John Martin, 1657.
    5. Mary, bapt. Oct. 8, 1657 ; m. George Lewis, jr., 1654

Margaret Lumbard m. Edward Coleman of Boston, Oct. 27, 1648.

2. Thomas Lombard of Barnstable, 1641 ; m. ———, and had
[5.] 6. Jedidiah, bapt. Sept. 19, 1641 ;
[6.] 7. Benjamin, bapt. Aug. 5, 1643 ;   8 Caleb ;
[7.] 9. Thomas.

SECOND GENERATION.

3. Joshua Lombard m. Abigail Linnett, May 27, 1651, and had
    10. Abigail, b. Apr. 6, 1652 ;   11. Mercy, b. June 15, 1655 ;
[8.] 12. Jonathan, b. April 28, 1657 ;
[8½.] 13. Joshua, b. Jan. 16, 1660 ;
He joined the church, March 14, 1646.

4. Jabez Lombard m. Sarah Derby, Dec. 1, 1660, and had,
    14. Elizabeth, b. June, 1663 ;   15. Mary, b. April, 1666 ;
[9.] 16. Bernard, b. April, 1668 ;
    17. John, b. April, 1670 ;   19. Mehitable, b. Sept. 1674 ;
    18. Mathew, b. Aug. 28, 1672 ;   20. Abigail, b. April, 1677 ;
[10.] 21. Nathaniel O., b. Aug., 1679 ;
    22. Hepzibah, b. Dec. 1, 1681.

5. Jedidiah Lombard m. Hannah Wing, May 20, 1668, and had
    23. Jedidiah, b. Dec. 25, 1669 ; m. Hannah Lewis, Nov. 8, 1699 ;
    24. Thomas, b. June 22, 1671 ;   25. Hannah, b. Aug., 1673 ;
    26. Experience, b. April, 1677.

6. Benjamin Lombard m. Jane Warren, Sept. 19, 1672, and had
    27. Mercy, b. Nov. 2, 1673 ;
[11.] 28. Benjamin, b. Sept. 27, 1675 ;
    29. Hope, b. March 26, 1679 ;
His wife dying Feb. 27, 1682, he m. 2d, Sarah Walker, Nov. 19, 1683, and had
    30. Sarah, b. Oct. 29, 1688 ;   32. Mary, b. June 17, 1689 ;
    31. Bathshua, b. May 4, 1687 ;   33. Samuel, b. Sept. 15, 1691.
She died Nov. 6, 1693, and he married, 3d, widow Hannah Whetstone, May 24, 1694, and had
    34. Temperance, b. May 25, 1695 ; 35. Martha, b. Dec. 28, 1704.

7. Thomas Lombard m. Elizabeth Derby, Dec. 23, 1665, and had
    36. Sarah, b. Dec. 1666.
[12] 37. Thomas, b. March, 1667.   42. Patience, b. May, 1676 ;
    38. Elizabeth, b. Sept. 1668 ;   43. Bethiah, b. July, 1680 ;
    39. Mary, b. April, 1669 ;   44. Bathshua, b. Aug. 1682 ;
    40. Hannah, b. Dec. 1671 ;   45. Rebecca, b. Sept. 1676 ;
    41. Jabez, b. Feb. 1673, d. 1673 ; 46. Patience.

THIRD GENERATION.

8½. Joshua Lombard m. Hopestill Bullock, Nov. 6, 1682, and had
    47. Mercy, b. Mar. 16, 1684 ;   48. Hopestill, b. Nov. 15, 1686;
[13.] 49. Joshua, b. Aug. 5, 1688 ;
    50. Samuel, b. June 1, 1690 ;   53. Elizabeth, b. Apr. 22, 1700;
    51. Abigail, b. Jan. 2, 1692 ;   55. Jonathan, b. April 16, 1703.
    52. Mary, b. Nov. 22, 1697 ;

8. Jonathan Lombard m. Elizabeth Eddy, Dec. 11, 1683, and had
    56. Jonathan, b. Nov. 20, 1684 ;   58. Ebenezer, b. Feb. 1, 1648 ;
    57. Alice, b. Oct. 19, 1686 ;   59. Abigail, b. July 12, 1691.

9. Bernard Lombard, m. ———— and had
    60. Joanna, b. Dec. 1692 ;   63. Maria, b. Oct. 1700 ;
    61. Mehitable, b. Mar. 18, 1694 ;   64. Bethiah, b. Sept. 1702 ;
    62. Mathew, b. Jan. 15, 1698;   65. John, b. April, 1704 ;
[14.] 66. Solomon, b. March 1, 1706.

10. Nathaniel Lombard m. ————, and had
    67. Sarah, b. Aug. 2, 1710.

11. Benjamin Lombard, jr. m. Hannah Treddeway, May 23, 1711, and had
    68. Jonathan, b. March 29, 1712; d. 1712.
    69. Hannah, b. Sept. 8, 1714.

12. Thomas Lombard m. Mary Newcome, Oct. 4, 1694, and had
    70. John, b. Jan. 5, 1694 ;
[15.] 71. Jedidiah, b. Feb. 16, 1696 ;
[16.] 72. Thomas, b. Aug. 3, 1698.

FOURTH GENERATION.

13. Joshua Lombard m. Sarah Parker, Dec. 14, 1715, and had
    73. Sarah, b. Sept. 28, 1716 ;   74. Parker, b. Dec. 24, 1718.

14. Solomon Lombard m. Sarah ————, and had
    75. Anna, b. Sept. 26, 1725 ;   81. Solomon, b. May 15, 1738 ;
    76. Jedidiah, b. Apr. 8, 1728 ;   82. Mary, b. Sept. 9, 1740 ;
    77. Sarah, b. June 8, 1730 ;   83. Richard, b. Feb. 23, 1743-4;
    78. Hannah, b. May 11, 1732;   84. Ebenezer, b. Mch 26, 1745;
    79. Susanna, b. Aug. 5, 1734;   85. Hezekiah, b. Sept. 30, 1746;
    80. Salome, b. June 10, 1736;   86. Calvin, b. May 25, 1748.

15. Jedidiah Lombard m. Mary ————, and had
    87. Joseph, b. May 1, 1717 ;   94. John, b. Aug. 4, 1727 ;
    88. Jedidiah, b. June 28, 1718 ;   95. Simeon, b. Nov. 29, 1729 ;
    89. Mary, b. Dec. 13, 1719 ;   96. Elizabeth, b. Feb. 2, 1731 ;
    90. Susanna, b. May 14, 1721;   97. David, b. May 24, 1732 ; d.
        d. May 24, 1721 ;   Sept. 7, 1732 ;
    91. Benj., b. Mch 23, 1722 ;   98. Joshua, b. May 13, 1733 ;
    92. Susanna, b. Apr. 30, 1723;   99. Rebecca, b. Sept. 26. 1734 ;
    93. Mathew, b. Mch 28, 1725;   100. Thomas, b. March 26, 1737.

16. Thomas Lombard m. Elizabeth Binney, of Hull, April 1721, and had
    101. Eliza., b. Feb. 17, 1723 ;   105. Isaac, b. Aug. 5, 1734 ;
        d. Dec. 15, 1793 ;   106. Caleb, b. Oct. 20, 1736 ;
    102. Simon, b. Oct. 8, 1725 ;   107. Peter, b. March 23, 1739 ;
    103. Thomas, b. Nov. 16, 1727;   108. Rebecca, b. July 6, 1741 ;
    104. Samuel, b. May 1, 1731 ;   109. Paul, b. Aug. 16, 1743.

[17.] 110. Israel, b. April 17, 1746.
His wife d. June 19, 1825.

FIFTH GENERATION.

17. Israel Lombard m. Jemima Atkins, Nov. 29, 1770, and had
   111. Binney, b. Sept. 9, 1771 ;
   112. Jemima, b. Oct. 23, 1773 ; d. Dec. 29, 1849 ;
   113. Israel, b. March 14, 1776. d. April 26, 1821 ;
   114. Elizabeth, b. July 17, 1778 ;
   115. Ruth, b. Dec. 6, 1780, d. Feb. 1847 ;
   116. Rebecca, b. Sept. 24, 1783 ; m. John Ayres, Nov. 15, 1803 ;
       d. Dec. 25, 1852 ;
   117. Thomas, b. Oct. 25, 1786 ;
   118. Sarah, b. July 13, 1789 ;
   119. Joseph A., b. May 10, 1792 ; d. 1799.

The following families I cannot clearly trace to their proper places, but the record may be convenient for reference.

Children of Daniel and Mary Lombard :—Thomas, b. May 24, 1749 ; Daniel, b. June 22, 1751 ; Hannah, b. June 14, 1753 ; Mary, b. Dec. 31, 1757.

Children of Simeon and Experience Lombard :—Ruth, b. Sept. 15, 1773 ; Hannah, b. July 2, 1777 ; Jemima, b. Feb. 17, 1782 ; Jane Atkins, b. Jan. 2, 1784 ; Richard Paine, b. Sept. 12, 1788.

Children of Ebenezer and Bethiah Lombard :—John, b. Aug. 3, 1728 ; d. 1748 ; Bethiah, b. June 27, 1736.

Children of Caleb and Thankful Rich Lombard, m. Nov. 10, 1760 :—————, son, b. May 20, 1761 ; Thankful Rich, b. June 16, 1763.

Children of Ephraim and Huldah Lombard :—Ebenezer, b. Aug. 22, 1769 ; Ephraim, b. Aug. 3, 1771 ; Huldah, b. July 14, 1774 ; Margaret Hopkins, b. July 3, 1776 ; Freeman, b. May 2, 1779.

Children of Lewis and Elizabeth Lombard :—Lewis, b. Aug. 10, 1767 ; Elizabeth, b. Sept. 12, 1771 ; James, b. May 15, 1769 ; Anna, b. Aug. 7, 1772 ; Sarah, b. April 11, 1774 ; Jane, b. Dec. 23, 1775 ; Hannah, b. Aug. 20, 1779.

Children of Solomon and Rebecca Lombard :—Mehitable, b. Sept. 1, 1789 ; Hannah, b. May 18, 1791.

Children of Simon and Ruth Lombard :—John, b. July 8, 1791 ; Solomon, b. ————, 1793.

Children of Daniel and Thomasine Lombard :—Mary, b. Feb. 6, 1780 ; Rachel, b. June 10, 1782 ; Thomasine, b. June 12, 1785 ; Thomas, b. Aug. 22, 1787 ; Daniel, b. Feb. 9, 1790.

Children of John and Bethiah Lombard :—John, b. Jan. 22, 1739 ; Experience, b. July 18, 1741 ; Hannah, b. June 16, 1747 ; Jemima, b. Sept. 11, 1750.

Children of Thomas and Mary Lombard :—William, b. Jan. 25, 1700 ; Simon, b. Nov. 28, 1701 ; Hannah, b. Jan. 16, 1703 ; Keziah, b. June 30, 1705.

Children of Jedidiah and Abigail Lombard :—Ruth, b. Sept. 22, 1744.

Children of James and Elizabeth Lombard :—James, b. Mar. 31, 1731 ; Sarah, b. July 6, 1733, d. Aug. 6, 1734 ; Hannah, b. Nov. 15, 1737 ; Elizabeth, b. July 4, 1735 ; Lewis, b. March 17, 1740 ; Jane, b. April 22, 1742 ; Ephraim, b. June 13, 1744 ; Sarah, b. Sept. 15, 1745.

Children of John and Elizabeth Lombard :—Phebe, b. Sept. 19, 1768; Jedidiah, b. Jan. 1, 1770.

Children of Cornelius and Rebecca Lombard :—Benjamin Parker, b. Dec. 6, 1776; Apha Freeman, b. Oct. 6, 1779.

Children of James and Elizabeth Lombard :—Rachel, b. April 2, 1749; Mehitable, b. April 11, 1751.

Children of Ephraim and Joanna Vickery Lombard, m. Feb. 27, 1746. Hannah, b. Oct. 16, 1746; Mary, b. Dec. 17, 1748; Joanna, b. June 11, 1751; Ephraim, b. May 18, 1753; Susanna, b. Feb. 13, 1759; Salome, b. May 1, 1761; Ruth, b. Aug. 12, 1755; Jedidiah, b. June 1, 1763.

Children of Simeon and Margaret Lombard :—Jedidiah, b. May 4, 1757; Hannah, b. March 12, 1759; Simeon, b. March 2, 1761.

Children of Samuel and Mary Lombard :—Jerusha, b. June 1, 1752; Mary, b. Dec. 2, 1753; Thomas, b. Aug. 22, 1756; Samuel, b. June 1, 1758.

James Lombard m. Thankful Dyer, March 28, 1754—Children:—Elizabeth, b. July 9, 1754; Thankful, b. June 18, 1756; Abigail, b. Sept. 7, 1758; Thankful, b. Nov. 3, 1760; Jane, b. March 31, 1763; Hannah, b. April 7, 1765; Mehitable, July 26, 1767; ——, b. Aug. 25, 1770.

Children of John, jr. and Rebecca Lombard :—Nathaniel, b. May 23, 1764; Bethiah, b. June 1, 1766; Rebecca, b. July 3, 1768; Barzilla, b. Aug. 29, 1770; Elizabeth, b. Aug. 29, 1770; Atkins, b. Aug. 5, 1772; Harding, b. Dec. 1774.

Children of Ephraim and Mehitable Lombard :—Ephraim, b. Sept. 9, 1775; James, b. April 9, 1777; Mehitable, b. Oct. 7, 1779; Hannah, b. April 29, 1781; Nat. Knowles, b. Nov. 29, 1784.

Children of Thomas and Mary Lombard :—Daniel, b. Sept. 20, 1776.

Children of Timothy and Lydia Lombard :—Thankful, b. Sept. 28, 1763; Lydia, b. Oct. 31, 1787.

———

Lewis	Lombard m.	Sarah Barker, Nov. 16, 1741.
Daniel	"	" Mary Avery, July 14, 1748.
Lewis	"	" Sarah Paine, March 1, 1753.
James	"	" Thankful Dyer, March 28, 1754.
Thankful Rich	"	" Perez Bangs, Feb. 23, 1786.
Simeon	"	" Rebecca Paine, Aug. 8, 1781.
Sarah	"	" Thomas Hopkins, Oct. 27, 1785.
Solomon	"	" Rebecca Knowles, ——, 1786.
Sarah	"	" Richard Rich, 3d, March 10, 1768.
Mary	"	" Henry Atkins, Oct. 24, 1768.
Ephraim	"	" Huldah Ryder, Nov. 10, 1768.
Joanna	"	" Jesse Dodge, Oct. 3, 1769.
Mary	"	" Thomas Dyer, March 25, 1771.
Jerusha	"	" Job Avery, March 27, 1771.
Hannah	"	" Ephraim Rich, April 16, 1771.
Rachel	"	" Benjamin Collins, jr., Jan. 23, 1772.
Mehitable	"	" Zaccheus Atkins, March 12, 1772.
Ruth,	"	" Samuel Atkins, Feb. 17, 1774.
Thankful	"	" Joshua Harding, April 7, 1774.
Susanna	"	" Joseph Freeman of Wellfleet, Apr. 7, 1772.
Hannah	"	" John Salew, July 12, 1774.
Ephraim	"	" Mehitable Knowles, Nov. 17, 1774.
Sarah	"	" Nehemiah Harding, March 22, 1770.

Cornelius	Lombard m.	Rebecca Freeman, May 30, 1775.
Sarah	" "	Wm. Myrick of Eastham, Jan. 4, 1777.
Hannah	" "	Peter Wells, March 28, 1765.
Simeon	" "	Experience Lombard, April 22, 1766.
Rebecca	" "	Richard Rich, Nov. 19, 1761.
John, jr.	" "	Rebecca Smith, Dec. 3, 1761.
Rebecca	" "	Abiah Harding of Eastham, Jan. 28, 1758.
Hannah	" "	John Pike, Dec. 13, 1758.
William	" "	Mrs. Hannah Green, Jan. 22, 1761.
John	" "	Rebecca Varril, Feb. 10, 1763.
Lewis	" "	Hannah Paine, April 9, 1781.
Jedidiah	" "	Mary White, Sept. 25, 1717.
Elizabeth	" "	George Pike, ——, 1758.
John	" "	Bethiah Harding, ——, 1737.
Hannah	" "	Jonathan Paine, jr., ——, 1740.
Ebenezer	" "	Bethiah Mayo, ——, 1727.
Jane	" "	Thatcher Rich, April 19, 1764.
Bethiah	" "	James Webb, Oct. 4, 1764.
Lewis, jr.	" "	Elizabeth Pike, March 27, 1766.
Rebecca	" "	David Smith, April 9, 1767.
Jedidiah	" "	Sarah Snow, ——, 1798.
Simon	" "	Ruth Knowles, Nov. 25, 1789.
Elizabeth	" "	Isaiah Paine, Dec. 22, 1789.
Sarah	" "	Zaccheus Knowles, ——, 1791.
Huldah	" "	Ambrose Snow, ——, 1791.
Timothy	" "	Annie Rich, ——, 1791.
James	" "	Hannah Snow, ——, 1792.
Ebenezer	" "	Mary Lewis Paine, ——, 1792.
Annie	" "	Jeremiah Grose, ——, 1792.
Anna	" "	Joshua Paine, Sept. 4, 1789.
Simon	" "	Ruth Knowles, April 18, 1789.
Elizabeth	" "	Isaiah Paine, Nov. 16, 1789.
Rebecca	" "	Saml Hinckley of Bowdoin, Sept. 16, 1790.
Elizabeth	" "	Samuel Dickerman Munson, Dec. 4, 1788.
Anna	" "	Joshua Paine, Nov. 5, 1782.
Ebenezer	" "	Bethiah Mayo, June 15, 1727.
Sarah	" "	Richard Collins, Jan. 25, 1733.
William	" "	Mary Gaines, Aug. 3, 1721.
Daniel	" "	Thomasine Cobb, April 15, 1779.
Susanna	" "	Nathaniel Snow, March 29, 1781.
Salome	" "	Obadiah Rich, Jan. 22, 1781.
Jedidiah	" "	d. Sept. 12, 1739.
Mrs. Hannah	" "	" April 25, 1743.

—————————————

REMARKABLE LONGEVITY.—Mrs. Anna Pope, widow of the late Rev. Joseph Pope, of Spencer, Mass., and mother of the late Joseph Pope, Esq., of Portland, is said to be the oldest white inhabitant in the Commonwealth of Massachusetts. She was *one hundred and three years old* on the 16th day of the present month, and is still in the enjoyment of good health. She makes it her home with her son, William Pope, Esq., of Spencer.— *Dec. 29th,* 1857.

NARRATIVE OF COL. JOHN ALLAN.

To the Editor of the New Eng. Hist. and Gen. Reg. :—

I send you for publication in the Register, the following extracts from an unfinished manuscript, written toward the close of the last century, by Col. John Allan, who, during the war of the Revolution, was an agent of the American government among the Eastern tribes of Indians. All of whom (both agent and Indians) rendered important service to the country in the times "that tried men's souls."

Danville, Dec. 1, 1857. **Peter E. Vose.**

After a geographical description of the country inhabited by the Eastern tribes of Indians, and an account of the facilities for communication with each other, the writer says,—

I shall now attempt briefly to notice the different transactions and Opperations, with the Indians from the commencement of the revolution, which have come within my knowledge—before my leaving Nova Scotia in 1776. It was suggested by some persons in Government to encourage the Indians to take an active part against the United States, as a check upon the Inhabitants of the Province, (a great proportion of whom were attached to the Interest of America) and to aid and Influence the Indians more Westward to harrass and disturb the Eastern settlements of Massachusetts, so as to annex those parts to that Colony. In consequence of this I despatched couriers to the different Villages thro' the Mickmack country. And previous to my departure, met a large body ; among them were deputies from St. John and other parts adjacent. A long and tedious conference took place, and a satisfactory explanation given of the dispute between America and Britain. It was concluded by a lengthy speech from them and a solemn declaration made, that if from situation and distance they could not assist, they would not injure or molest the Americans. A chief from Merrimachi spoke for the whole,—they were all as one,— no distinction made between the different tribes. Being compelled to leave that country suddenly, the business was soon communicated to the Council at Boston.

Mr. Bowdoin, then President, entered very minutely into particulars, and pressed my departure to the southward. General Washington approved of the proceedings and desired me to lay it immediately before Congress, that steps might be taken to retain their friendship. As the nature and extent of the business was fully understood by the several official departments, to whom it was communicated, the Agency, appointed for this purpose, comprehended the whole, Eastward and Northward of Connecticut River,—making no exceptions in what nation or country the Indians resorted.

Previous to my appointment there were several negociations, by order of the Massachusetts and Genl Washington. Letters and speeches are now to be seen among the Indians,—great encouragements and promises made them.

In May 1777 I arrived on the river St. John ; where a number were collected—the business was communicated and myself accepted as an agent. We soon had a general meeting composed of deputies from different parts, including the whole tribes of St. Johns and Passamaquoddy. It was agreed and concluded, that Peace and Friendship be now established permanent and Lasting, between the United States and the several Tribes, that such of them as were in the proximity of the States, should immediately withdraw and assist in the defence of the country, which lay within the jurisdiction of the United States,—that any individual belonging to those tribes whose situation would not permit publicly to take an active part, were admit'd to join with those who did—that those employed should be supported during their service and the widows and children of those who died in the time, to be taken care of 'till otherways provided for. That they should be forever viewed as brothers and children under the Protection and Fatherly care of the United States and enjoy every right and privilege according to the difference of situation, in proportion with others. They should enjoy the free exercise of religion, agreeable to their profession, a clergyman of that denomination be furnished, and a suitable residence be provided for him, on which a place of Worship was to be erected. They were to have an exclusive right to the beaver hunt, or if not consistent with the rights of others, necessary steps were to be taken, as to prevent a destruction of the dams and other enormities, committed by the white hunters, by which conduct a great diminution of that ancient and profitable support has been the consequence—that in times of difficulty and distress, or by any unforeseen calamity those who live within the territory of the United States, should be furnished with ammunition for Fowling, &c. in proportion as their necessitys required,—that trade was to be so regulated as to prevent impositions,—that an agent should constantly reside as near them as possible, to whom they might apply for redress: to assist in the transacting of business among the inhabitants and such other necessary matters as their situation required.

These were the principal objects at this time; but in the course of the war the Indians of St. Johns and Passamaquaddy, resigned to the United States, their particular claim to lands known to be within their haunts, on condition that the United States would confirm to them the ancient spots of ground which they have hitherto occupied, and a suitable tract for the use of all Indians, which might have occasion to resort there.

How far these people have complied with their engagements our present possessions eastward of Penobscot might be a sufficient proof, as it is acknowledged by all acquainted with that country, that their assistance was a principal support in its defence; but in justice to them I would take the Liberty to mention a circumstance among many others, which must evince the zeal by which they were actuated. Some time after my arrival in St. Johns, Lieut. Gov't Franklin, British Super Intendent arrived with a strong Land and Sea Force furnished with every requisite to allure the Indians. Our quarters were within eight miles; only two white persons remained with me. Conferences every day alternately on both sides—and after using every stratagem and art to gain them and make me a prisoner, they (the Indians) in a body of 128 canoes, containing near five hundred men, women and children, left the River with me at the end of Ten days, only a few Families remaining to keep up a claim and give intelligence. There was not more than a weeks provisions for the whole. They left their little plantations well improved, and a good prospect; with a great part of their clothing; After 28 days Journey I arrived at Machias, suffering many hardships and difficulties by excessive heats and the lowness of the streams; which greatly obstructed the Canoes.

Their zeal and attention during the war, from the attempt made by the British under Sir Geo. Collier, is so well known in that country that it needs no comment. Their uniform conduct both in respect of humanity, as submitting with patience under every difficulty was not inferior to the most disciplined troops, and even when imposed on at a time of intoxication and fleeced of the little they had, they always sat down contented and resigned without the appearance of resentment or malice.

At the close of the war, a circumstantial account of the whole proceedings was laid before the Government of Massachusetts and Congress and approved of by them. As the Constitution invested the latter with the management of Indian affairs, they of course fixed the agency on a peace establishment, and comprehended, as before, the whole tribes eastward of Connecticut river: the appointment took place in June, 1783. In September it was communicated to the Indians, in the several parts, who signified their satisfaction. The treaty of 1777 was then confirmed and an arrangement for Future Conduct. The Indians at this time endeavored to prevent the English from making a settlement at St. Andrews, and did actually seize some persons, who attempted to survey the Lands. In January 1784 it was suggested to Congress from the Massachusetts that such an appointment was improper. (The plan adopted would have prevented much trouble and expense and given security to the country.) Consequently as no steps were taken to controvert it, the Agency was dissolved in March following. From that time it does not appear, that any notice has been taken of them (the Indians) to the Eastward of Penobscot.

The Indians notwithstanding the treatment and neglect continued sometime in the vicinity of Passamaquoddy expecting when the hurry and confusion arising from the war were subsided, notice would be taken of them, but nothing encouraging coming to view, they began to withdraw in small bodies, to their former settlements destitute of necessarys to subsist, and of friends to protect them. In this indigent state those of St. John suffered much and they felt the resentment of the Loyalist for their attachment and assistance to the United States. For near two years wandering about from Place to Place—disquieted and unsettled, they at length began again to embody, and consult more generally respecting their situation. Still attached to this country, they repeatedly apply'd to me, for a settlement, and to procure a clergyman, if nothing else could be done. I evaid'd the business—they continued their solicitations. I finally gave them for answer, it was not in my power, and recommended to make application themselves to the head of Government, but in January 1791 a message came from the several Villages on St. Johns, and repeated their demands, and delivered it in such a manner, as allarmed me, consequently I consented to meet and consult with them. (this may be thought Timidity, but it is a maxim with me, never to live near Indians, except in a state of defence, without a certainty of their Friendship either in Peace or War) At a large Council it was agreed, among other things, to address the Bishop of Baltimore, praying to be considered as brothers and children of the United States, and to take them under his care as their Spiritual Father and requesting a Clergyman to reside among them.—that an address be presented to the General Court of Massachusetts, to lay out a suitable Settlement as a resort for themselves, and a residence for the Priest, the former of these were answered to their sanguine expectations and the clergyman arrived among them in October 1792—a man who appeared well qualified for the mission. In March 1793 a Speech was presented to the General Court and Commissioners were appointed, who met the Indians in October following, but their power was so Limited, that no satisfactory agreement could be made. "The Indians at this time appeared very thoughtfull and anxious about the business, and the proceedings rather opperated to our disadvantage.

"In November the Indians sent for me to attend. I was with them five days, in which time we had several public and private conferences. After recapitulating their Treaties and promises made them,—their conduct during the war, their sufferings, &c.,—and they demanded a fullfillment of their Promises, particular Lands for settlement, which, if refused, they should view themselves free from all engagements, and be at liberty to treat and accept of any Proposals made to them by any other Power, and in future to pursue in their own way what they thought consistent with their right and interest; but would wait to the beginning of February to know what would be done for them in Boston.

"A report prevailed this summer that the British were endeavoring to draw the Indians into New Brunswick; and in November, when at the village, I received authentic advice and information of the particulars.

"The British in those parts found it necessary to bring the Indians over for the defence of the Country, as the Marching Troops were ordered off to assist against the French; also, should any rupture take place with this Country, to secure their interest betimes. For this purpose preparations have been making since August last, supply's of all kinds have been laid in, and many things distributed among them. Several letters have been sent the Priest, promising every attention and a satisfactory compensation. During my visit a letter was received, and a vessel detained some days at St. Andrews for him. I remonstrated against his going; he promised not, as long as he could retain any Indians and procure subsistance, as he had suffered hitherto; but in April it appears that himself and the residue of the Indians had removed to St. Johns, a few straggling ones excepted. This is the true state and situation of the Indians in that country. . .

"If the foregoing statement be confided in and intelligible, it may be seen that there is no distinction to be made, but if there was, the Passamaquoddy Tribe comparatively have the least claim, both as to numbers and attention in time of difficulty, and in the Late Transaction there were five others to one of them."

ANCIENT FAMILY RECORD.

SALEM, Feb. 11, 1858.

SAMUEL G. DRAKE, Esq.

Dear Sir,—In an old Bible (which has recently come into my possession) of the year 1601, "Imprinted at London by Robert Barker Printer to the Queenes most excellent Majestie," I find the annexed family record, which I have copied and send, that you may, if you think best, publish it in the N. E. Hist. and Gen. Register.

Yours very truly,   IRA J. PATCH.

"Mem.

"John Raisbeck of the Parish of Basildon and Mary Haines of the Parish of Bradfield were married at Basildon Novr 20th 1759."

"John the Son of John Raisbeck and Mary his wife was baptized March 6th 1761. (St Lawrence Wooton, near Basingstoke, Hants."

"Mary the wife of the s^d John Raisbeck died—after a lingering Illness June 28 1762. Æt 26. and was buried at St. L. Wooton."

"John Raisbeck Rector of Dymchurch in Kent, and Sarah Bradley of the Parish of Northington, were married at Northington, Hants, May 20th 1765. Sarah the Wife of John Raisbeck died July 4th 1778,—and was buried in the Chancel at Dimchurch."

THE DESCENDANTS OF PETER HILL OF YORK CO., ME.

*With some Incidents relating to the French and Indian Wars,—gleaned
from old Manuscripts of the time.*

[By Usher Parsons.]

[Continued from page 145.]

The number of soldiers in the garrison at Fort Mary, in February,
1699, was sixteen, including officers, viz., Capt. John Hill, Lt. Joseph,
his brother, Corporal Ebenezer Hill, do., Pendleton Fletcher, nephew of
the Hills, Thomas Harvey, Samuel Smith, Edmund Leverett, John
Crocker, Benj. Mayers, Humphrey Deering, Shubael Henning, John
Sweeting, Henry Taylor, David Jones, Mark Round and Jeffry Merry,
two thirds of whom, exclusive of officers, could not write their names,
as appears by the pay roll.

The following letters are worthy of preservation, as illustrative of the
history of the times.

In August, 1699, the Earl of Bellamont writes to Capt. Hill :—

"His majesty's council of this province and I have agreed that it will
be for his majesty's service, that you do with all possible speed give notice to the Sagamores of the Eastern Indians, that they come hither to
Portsmouth, N. H. to make their submission, and give such assurance of
their fidelity and allegiance to his majesty as shall be required of them,
and that they be herewith on the 10th of this present month of August.
I desire therefore you will not fail to dispatch messengers to the said
Sagamores accordingly.

I am your friend and serv't,

"I desire you will employ some people   Bellamont."
to collect some Balm of Gilead, and I will
reward their pains that gather it, and be
thankful to you."

Again, Oct. 19, 1699, the Governor writes :—

"Captain Hill,—I hope you will not fail to be extremely secret in the
business I now commit to you; if Bradish and Wetherby, the two pirates
that escaped out of the jail of this town, be not taken and brought back
by the last day of this month, I desire you will then send this inclosed
letter of mine to the French Jesuit or Frier, that is with the Indians, at a
fort called Norocomecock, and that by some very trusty Indian, to whom
you must give a double reward, and charge him to deliver my letter to
the Friar privately, that nobody may see him deliver it, if he can. If
you manage this matter prudently, I doubt not but Bradish and his companion will be retaken and brought back, and your chief care must be to
keep it secret that I have written to the Friar, wherein you will oblige

Your friend and servant,

Bellamont."

[Copy of the letter.]

de Boston, de 19 l'Octobre, 1699.

Monsieur,—L'on me donne avis aujourdui que deux Pyrates Anglais
nommez Bradish et Wetherby qui se sont eschappez hors de la prison de
cette ville il y a plus de trois mois, se sont retirez au Chateau des Indiens

appella Norocomecock ou vous tenez votre residence a present. Je ne
crois pas que vous pretendiez garentir in couvrier deux Siclerats de la
main de la justice, et sivous piquez d'eu faire de bons Catholiques Romans je suis seur que vous vous y tromperez comme Jesuis persuadé que
des gens comme ces deux liqui sont capables de Piraterie (que jéstime
le dernier des crimes) se rendroient de main ou Juifs ou Mahometains,
pourveu quils peuvent se sauver la vie. Vous vous ferez donc plus
d'honneur et eu mene temps plus de service au bon dieu, enfaisent re-
noyer ces deux Siclarets in à Boston a fin quils recoivent le chatiment
qui leur es dû. Je donneray deux cent escus de Bradish, et cent escus
de Wetherby, a celui qui me les rameneront, et de plus j pacmay les frais
du voyage. J'ose dire que Monsieur de Calliere Gouverneur de Canada
vous feza ses remerciments du service que vous jerez au public en
m'accordant la grace on plútost la justice que je vous demande peut estre
aussi pourray. Je trouver l'occasion de vous en rendre une pareille,
quand je ne manqueray pas de vous marquer que je feray

Mon^r

A Monsieur   Votre tres humble serviteur
    le Pere Missionaire   Bellamont.
        Norocomecock.

[Translation.]

Boston, 19th October, 1699.

Monsieur,—I am informed to-day that two English pirates, named
Bradish and Wetherby, who escaped from the prison in this town more
than three months ago, have taken refuge in the Indian post called Norocomecock, where you now reside. I do not believe that you intend to
screen two criminals from the hand of justice; and if you please yourself
with the hope of making them good Roman Catholics, I am sure that you
will be deceived, for I am persuaded that such fellows as these, who are
capable of piracy (which I consider the worst of crimes), would turn
Jews or Muhammedans on the spot if they could save their lives by it.
You will then do more credit to yourself, and a better service to the good
God, by sending back these two criminals to Boston, that they may receive the punishment due to them. I will give two hundred crowns for
Bradish, and a hundred crowns for Wetherby, to any one who will bring
them back, and will pay the expenses of the journey in addition. I have
no doubt that M. de Calliere, the Governor of Canada, will thank you for
the service you will do to the public by granting me the favor, or rather
the justice, which I ask. Perhaps, moreover, I shall find an opportunity
to make a like return, when I shall not fail to testify that

I am, Sir,

To Monsieur   Your very humble servant,
    the Missionary Father,   Bellamont.
        Norocomecock.

Secretary Addington to Captain Hill :—

" Boston, Feb. 8, 1699.

" Sir,—I am commanded by his Excellency to acquaint you that by
letters from Governor Winthrop of Connecticut and a narrative given to
him by Owoneco, Sachem of the Mohegans, the Indians have been abused
by a malicious and lying report insinuated to them, that the king of England is sending over forces to cut off and extirpate them, which has
instigated them to enter into a combination against the English, and to

send presents one to another to engage them thereto. And it is said some of the new Roxbury Indians are drawn off and gone eastward. It is thought necessary that you be advised hereof, that as you have opportunity you may endeavor to undeceive the Indians and to give them to understand there is nothing in said report, but that they stand in good terms with the king's government whilst they continue peaceably and orderly, and may expect protection from them. So it will be prudent to us to use all vigilance and circumspection, to observe their motions and behaviour, and to endeavor the preventing of their taking advantage by any surprise which you are directed to take care of at the garrison under your command, and to avoid all occasions of giving them any provocation. You are not ignorant of their insults and falseness; wherefore they are to be the more strictly observed and watched over. My lord has received letters from Albany dated the first of this month which advise him that all things are well there.

> Your friend and humble ser^t
>
> Isaac Addington, Secretary."

Subjoined is the following:—

"Capt. Hill, Sir,—I made bold to open your letter because there came a report that the Mohegan Indians intend to fall on the English forthwith, but since I looked into it I hope there is no great danger as yet. The Good Lord fit us for his own will.

> Your brother,   Joseph Hill.

Feb. 21, at sunset, 1699."

From I. Addington:—

> "Boston, Nov. 28th, 1699.

"Capt. Hill,—I am commanded by his Excellency and Council to signify unto you that upon information given them by Capt. Sylvanus Davis, lately come from Casco Bay (Portland), of a considerable number of Indians gathered together in those parts, in expectation of receiving some supply for trade, and that they had brought with them stores of peltry for that purpose; the Governor and Council have thereupon thought fit to order a vessel with suitable goods, provisions, &c. to be forthwith dispatched into those parts for the supplying of and trading with the said Indians; of which you are to forward the speedy notice unto the said Indians by some prudent person belonging unto the garrison under your command, to the intent the said Indians may not draw off in disgust, looking at themselves to be neglected by the government.

> I am Sir your your obed^t ser^t
>
> Isaac Addington, Secretary.

Another:—

> "Boston, March 12, 1699.

Capt. Hill, Sir,—I am commanded by his Excellency and Council to acquaint you by several credible informations from divers parts they are persuaded to believe that the Indians of Pennicooke &c. are forming a devilish design of raising a new war upon the English and that they are hastening to begin to put it in execution, possibly in the moonlight nights now drawing on, and to direct that you forthwith put all things in good order within the garrison under your command, and be very careful of keeping good watches and lookouts, and observant of the behaviour and carriage of the Indians, especially of those that resort unto you on the account of trade, that they gain no advantage for the perpetrating of any mischief or surprise, withal avoiding the giving them any just provocation or beginning a quarrel with them. You are not unacquainted with their stratagems, and it is believed your prudence will direct you to do what shall be necessary for the safety of yourself and those under your command and the public peace.

I am with respects y^r hum^e ser^t

I. Addington, Secy.

In November, 1699, Capt. Hill, having served through the war—over ten years—resolved to resign his commission and retire to private life. The Governor, in compliance with his request, granted him permission "to visit Boston to adjust his accounts," and in the following April received his resignation.

By his Excellency the Earl of Bellamont.

"Whereas, upon your request to be discharged from his majesty's service, I have thought fit to appoint and commissionate George Turfrey Esq. gent. to be captain of his majesty's Fort Mary, at present under your command.

You are therefore hereby ordered, upon receipt hereof (which I send by s^d Captain Turfrey) to surrender and deliver up to him the said Turfrey's charge and command the said Fort Mary, and all the guns, artillery, ammunition, stores, provisions and appurtenances thereunto belonging, and the soldiers now posted in garrison there: as also to deliver unto his custody all such Goods and Effects remaining unsold in your hands of what was committed to you for trade with the Indians. Taking the said Turfrey's receipt for what you shall deliver to him. Hereof fail not, For which this shall be your sufficient warrant. And you are upon receipt hereof accordingly discharged from his majesty's service.

Given under my hand at Boston the eighth day of April 1700, and in the 12th year of his majesty's reign.

Bellamont."

To Capt. John Hill
Commander of his Majesty's
Fort Mary at Saco.

Capt. John Hill removed from Saco to Berwick, and built a house a quarter of a mile west of Great Works' falls. His brother-in-law, Ichabod Plaisted, resided between him and the falls. Mr. Hill followed the occupation of a planter, and owned mills. He was succeeded by his son, Hon. Judge Hill, who, after his father's death, built the house opposite the old residence, which is now occupied by his great-grandson, Captain Benjamin Gerrish.

The children of Captain John were—

1. Hon. JOHN HILL, just mentioned, who, as will presently appear, became a judge, representative and senator in the legislature, major and councillor. He was born March 2, 1703; married Eliza ——, who died Jan. 2, 1763. His second wife was the widow of Rev. John Blunt, and daughter of Hon. John Frost, the son of Major Charles Frost, who was killed by the Indians. [See Frost's life, in Genealogical Journal, 1849.]

2. *Abigail*, born Dec. 15, 1706.

3. *Elisha*, born Feb. 3, 1709, and died June 1, 1764, aged 54. He had a son Elisha, who died Aug. 6, 1785, aged 68.

4. *Eunice*, born Nov. 1, 1712, who died single, 1737.

The children of Judge John Hill and Eliza were—

I. *Abigail*, born July 31, 1729. She m. Thomas Wallingford. Their children were Thomas, who m. Hannah Lyman of York; John, who m. a March; Margaret, who m. a Tate; Mary, who m. Gen. Ichabod Goodwin; Elizabeth, who m. Capt. Ebenezer Ricker; Abigail, who m. Dr. Jacob Kittredge, and Andrew, who died young.

II. *John*, born Feb. 25, 1730, died July 14, 1737.

III. and IV. *Margaret* and *Eliza* (twins), born July 22, 1733. Margaret and her brother John died of throat distemper, 1737. *Eliza*, the other twin, m. Capt. Ben. Gerrish, son of Timothy. They had four children, viz: 1. *Nathaniel*, b. June 2, 1754, died single. 2. *Elizabeth*, b. June 24, 1756, m. Capt. John Furness, and had three children, viz: Thomas, who died in Algiers a prisoner; Betsy, who m. Capt. Eliot Raynes of York, and the third died in infancy. Mrs. Furness afterwards m. Nathaniel Raynes of York. 3. *Benjamin*, b. July 23, 1758. He m. Miriam Rait Ferguson, commanded a vessel, and died in Havana in 1792, aged 33. His widow died in 1835, aged 72. They left two children— Betsey, who died in 1835 unmarried, and Capt. Benjamin Gerrish, who m. Abigail, daughter of Col. Daniel Lewis of Alfred. The captain resides in the house of his great-grandfather, Judge Hill, S. Berwick. 4. *Mary*, who m. Richard Lord, and had nine children, viz: Benjamin, Eunice, Betsey, Sabina, Sophia, Prudence, Abigail, Mary and Caroline.

V. *Charles*, the fifth child of Judge Hill, born Aug. 15, 1734. He resided many years with his father, Judge Hill, at Great Works. Being unsuccessful in lumber trade, he removed to Conway, N. H. In his later years he lived with his sons in Fryburg, Lyman, and elsewhere. He died at Meredith, N. H. in 1819, aged 85. He was a justice of the peace, a man of great conversational power, and deeply imbued with religious feeling. He m. Sarah Prentiss of Cambridge, who died in April, 1802. She was the mother of fourteen children, viz: 1. John; 2. Sarah; 3. Sarah, 2d; 4. Charles; 5. Henry; 6. Sarah, 3d; 7. Elizabeth; 8. Leavitt; 9. Thomas; 10. George; 11. John, 2d; 12. Amos A.; 13. Thomas P.; 14. Mary. Five of these died in infancy. Charles died in July, 1819, at Lyman, aged 57; Henry in 1801, aged 40. Sarah, 3d, m. Moses Yeaton, a farmer in Berwick. Elizabeth m. Elijah Clemmens, and had, Leavitt, born 1770; George, born March 7, 1774; Amos Adams, born Feb. 22, 1778; Thomas P., born May 13, 1781, a physician in Hanover, N. H. Mary m. John Evans, a farmer in Fryburg.

Charles Hill, the son of Charles and grandson of Hon. John, had four wives. By the first (Martha Day) he had one son, named Charles, born in 1788, and settled in Lyman. By the second wife no children. By the third he had eight children, viz: Martha, m. J. W. Roberts, Lyman; John, a printer, died in Louisiana in 1819; Deborah, m. Solomon Drown, Lyman; Abigail, died March, 1812; Leavitt, resides at Sacarappa, Me.; Sarah P., m. Seth Whitten, Kennebunkport; Simon, died in 1833; Amos A., a mechanic, Dorchester. By the fourth wife he had Henry Hill, a farmer in York, Me.; Samuel P., merchant, Charlestown; Lucy, died in 1818, an infant.

Henry Hill, son of Charles and grandson of Hon. John, had six children, viz: Sarah, Henry, Hypsebath, Elizabeth, Amos A. and Thomas P.

Sarah Hill, 3d, daughter of Charles Hill, the son of Hon. John Hill, married Moses Yeaton, and had eleven children, viz: Lucy, Alice, Cyrus, Mahalah, Mary, Elizabeth, Susan C., Caroline S., Leavitt H., Sarah P. and Moses.

Leavitt Hill, son of Charles and grandson of Hon. John, m. Miss Russell, and had eight children, viz: Sarah, John, Abigail, Eunice, Thomas, Mary, Leavitt and Charles.

George Hill, son of Charles Hill, great grandson of Hon. John, married Penhope Parker, and had eight children, viz: Mary, Caleb m. and settled in Dorchester, Samuel in South Carolina, Naomi, Sally, Joshua, Betsy and James.

Thomas P. Hill, son of Charles Hill, born May 23, 1781; married, 1818, Sophia —— of Conway, by whom he had one child, born Oct. 1819. He was married the second time to Mrs. Phebe C. Marsh of Bath, Me.

Mary Hill, daughter of Charles Hill, the son of Hon. John, born 1785, married John Evans of Fryburg, Me. 1804, and had ten children, viz: Henry H., Thomas S., John, Charles, Amos, James O., Prentiss H., Sarah E., Stephen and George.

Hon. John Hill, son of Capt. John who commanded at Saco, was born, as before stated, in 1703, and married Eliza ——. He was commissioned as ensign in 1727 by Gov. Dummer, and in 1729 as lieutenant; as first lieutenant by Burnet in 1729; as captain by Belcher; again as captain in 1744 by William Shirley, and in 1754 as major by Shirley.

He was elected to the house and senate of the legislature of Massachusetts, and was a member of the governor's council from 1755 to 1771. He was appointed a justice of the peace, and associate justice of the court of common pleas, and chief justice of the same, also judge of probate for a brief period.

He was distantly related to, and an intimate friend of Sir William Pepperrell, who reposed every confidence in him, and made him the depositary of his will for many years before his decease. When appointed judge of the court, Sir William notifies him from Kittery point by letter, thus:—

" Hon. Sir,—If you will come next Saturday and take a fish dinner with me, I will deliver you your commission for one of the judges, and do what I can to qualify you, not pretending to add anything to your qualifications, but to assist in administering the oaths.

With the best respects to our reverend and worthy friends, Mr. Wise and lady,

Your sincere friend and servant,

Wm. Pepperrell."

Major Hill performed a vast amount of business as justice of the peace. He often received orders from Pepperrell respecting the training of his company. One of them, dated Sept. 18, 1746, soon after Sir William's return from Louisburg, reads thus:—

" Sir,—There is a talk of a French fleet being on our coast; if so you may depend there will be an army of French and Indians upon our backs. Pray be careful and direct all the captains in Berwick to see that all the men are provided arms and ammunition, and let there be a good watch kept in your town and be much upon your guard.

Your affectionate friend,

Wm. Pepperrell."

One from Governor Shirley, dated July 12, 1745, says:—

"This comes to give you intelligence that the French Indians have already broke out in the western part, and have killed two of our men and scalped them. This intelligence you must send to all the exposed places near you, that so all persons may be upon their guard to prevent a surprise. I am not without hope that when the Eastern Indians find that we have succeeded at Louisburg, they will not be forward to break with us.

Your friend and servant,   W. S."

When Sir William's son-in-law, Sparhawk, was compelled, by the pressure of the times in 1758, to go into bankruptcy, he entreated Major Hill with great earnestness to act as one of the commissioners to settle the estate, which he accordingly did, and in the following year he attended the baronet's funeral as pall bearer. He died March 2, 1772, aged 69.

Major Hill seems to have been a man of stern integrity and of extensive influence and usefulness. He was deeply interested in religion, and a leading man in the church and in high public stations.

The other children of Hon. Judge Hill were—

VI. A child, stillborn.

VII. *Eunice*, born April 19, 1739, married Capt. George March of Stratham. Their children were, Elizabeth, who married John Wallingford of Berwick; Eleanor, who married Dr. Fogg of Deerfield; Eunice, who married James Haggens of Berwick; John and Patty, who died unmarried.

VIII. and IX. A son and daughter, stillborn.

X. *Mary*, born Dec. 6, 1748, died April 14, 1754, of throat distemper.

ELISHA HILL, brother of the judge, left one son and perhaps more. This son, named Elisha, resided at Great Works near his father and grandfather, Capt. John. He had twelve children who followed him to his grave—six sons and six daughters. Of the sons, except John the oldest, we have no account. Their names were John, Elisha, Jeremiah, Samuel, Ichabod and James. The daughters m. Deacon Dominicus Goodwin, a Mr. Morrill, a Mr. Ladd and afterwards Rev. Dr. Buckminster, a Mr. Cutts of Saco, a Mr. Fernald in or near Saco, a Mr. Widden of Portsmouth, and a Mr. Taylor of Canada.

Deacon John Hill, the eldest son of Elisha, Jr. above mentioned, was a justice of the peace and member of the legislature, and died in 1810, leaving three or four children. He was much respected for his useful and exemplary life.

The foregoing account of the Hills was gathered chiefly from manuscripts found in an old chest in the garret of Capt. Gerrish in S. Berwick, where they had been nailed up seventy years. All the commissions held by the Hills, both civil and military, were among them, and forty letters from Sir William Pepperrell, some of which were used in writing his life. I have also gathered some important facts from Folsom's history of Saco.

GLEANINGS.

Mr. Editor:

Dear Sir,—I hand you herewith a number of unconnected memoranda, some referring to subjects already discussed in the Register, and others suggesting new topics of a similar nature, none of them being sufficiently long to form a distinct paper.

W. H. W.

1.

Your success in examining J. Boyse's correspondence with Ralph Thoresby (see January No., 1858) has led me to examine the book in relation to the Rayners.

I find that, in 1677, Thoresby lived at London with Mr. Dickinson, whose wife's sister was Mrs. Madox, mother of the antiquary. This I presume to be the John Dickinson, Jr., of the Lane Papers.

Oct. 22, 1680, he went to "Brotherton and visited old Mrs. Rayner, being my great grandfather's father's third wife, now a great age, having lived to see many of her grandchildren's grandchildren."

Feb. 28, 1682. "Most of the day spent in company at the marriage of Mrs. Mary Sykes with Mr. Thomas Rayner. This was the elder sister of Thoresby's wife, whom he married Feb. 25, 1685."

May 9, 1695. "Rode with relations to Ledsham, to the funeral of my brother Rayner's father, an excellent person."

How to explain this Mrs. Rayner being his great great grandmother is difficult. He was son of John and Mary (Idle), grandson of John and Grace (Cloudesly), great grandson of George and Isabel Curtis, and great great grandson of Ralph Thoresby, whose wife's name is not given in the Ducatus Leodosensis. His mother's pedigree is also untraced there.

His brother-in-law, Thomas Rayner, was of Beghall, and had issue: John, Thomas, Joshua, Elizabeth, Mary, and Sarah.

About 1695 he commenced to write the life of Rev. —— Rayner, of Lincoln, "who was born in this neighborhood," and lived in Halifax, Pudsey and Woodchurch, from his own diaries and letters. The next year Mr. H. Sampson writes that this MS. is in Mr. Disney's hands, and he hopes soon to receive them. [Query, was this life ever published?]

2.

Knowledge and Practice: or, a plain Discourse of the Chief Things necessary to be Known, Believed, and Practised in order to Salvation. Useful for Private Families. The Third Edition, revised and corrected. By Samuel Cradock, B. D., Rector of North Cadbury, in Somersetshire. London: 1673.

The History of the Old Testament Methodized according to the Order and Series of Time wherein the several things therein mentioned were transacted; to which is annexed a Short History of the Jewish Affairs, by Samuel Craddock. Folio, calf. London: 1683.

Samuel Cradock. Apostolick History, containing the Acts, Labors, Travels, Sermons, Miracles, Successes, and Sufferings of the Holy Apostles, from Christ's Ascension to the Destruction of Jerusalem by Titus. Folio: 1672.

Bury, Samuel (of St. Edmond Bury). Funeral Sermon on Rev. Samuel Cradock, Rector of North Cadbury, Somersetshire, interred at Wickham Brook, Suffolk. 8vo., old calf. 3s. 1707.

3.

As to Joseph Boyse (see January No., 1858), a passage in the Lane Papers makes it clear that his father returned to England 'early in 1657, or late in 1656. This confirms your conjecture that Joseph was not born in this country.

I find by the Thoresby Papers that he had a brother Elkanah; a brother Samuel, who had a daughter, Dorcas; sisters Priestly and Fenton; nephew Wm. Jackson; and cousin Hickson. He died in 1728, leaving an only son, Samuel, the spendthrift poet, and friend of Johnson, of whom a good biography is given in Chalmer's General Biog. Dict.

4.

The elaborate pedigree which Mr. Pavor of York, Eng., sent you, contains a reference to the same Boyse's family and its offshoots. Elizabeth, daughter of Henry Hobson of Unflete, married John Johnson, Rector of Sutton-upon-Darwent, who died in 1657.

5.

[From the original, in my possession.]

These are to Certifie all whome it may concerne, that John Hudd, Son of John Hudd of Sherborne in the County of Dorsett, Victualer, was baptized the 22 day of May A'no Dom'i. 1631. And that Joane Hudd, daughter to the sayd John Hudd the elder was baptized the 11th day of February A'no Dom'i 1636. And Jeremiah Lodge of Sherborne aforesayd was Married to the sayd Joane Hudd the daughter, the 16 day of May 1669.

As appears by the Register of Christenings and Marriages kept in the p'ish Church of Sherborne in the County of Dorsett, in England; as witness our Hands the fourth day of March A'no R'i Jocobi, d. Aug. &c. primo Anoque Dom'i 1664 John Hinchman, Vicar; Alexander Williams, Robert Whetcom, Church-wardens; John Horne; Reynald Pond; George Pennington; Will. Thornton; George Dyer, parish-clarke.

Married	1703	Dec 28	Benjamin Tolman Ruth Fletcher	
"	"	" 30	Joseph Kettle of Charlestoun Elizabeth Long	
"	"	Jan. 4	Peter Ellickson Joanna Borma	
"	"	" 6	John of Beverly Betty of Boston	Negroes
"	"	" 27	Samuel Green Elizabeth Barger	
"	"	" "	William Moor Sarah Milton	
"	"	Feb. 8	Daniel Stone of Framleagham Abigail Wheeler	
"	"	Mch 1	Ebenezer Ager Abigail Skinner	

By C. Mather.

6.

Extracts from the Diary of Thomas Seccom of Medford.

1736 July 18 Mr Timothy Symms of Cituate preached
1736 Oct 17 Mr Coalman preached
" " 24 Mr Shearjashub Brown preached
" Nov 11 Thanksgiving Day.
" Dec 12 Mr Manning our schoolmaster preached
1737 Jany 23 Preached by my brother
" " 30 " " Mr Hooper
" June 19 " " Mr Gardner the man that is Chosen at Menottomy
" Oct 23ᵈ Sermon by Mr Hobby of Reading
1738 Feb 12 " " Mr Burt of Boston, the Gold Smith's Son
" April 23 Sermon by Mr Rogers fellow of yr Colledge.
" May 7 I first sett in Uncle Joh Willis' Pew
" " 28 Sermon by Mr Aaron Cleaveland
" June 11 " " Mr Cook
" " 26 " " Mr Whipple minister of
" July 16 " " Mr Joshua Tufts
" " 30 " " Mr Goss
" Sept 3 " " Mr Man
" " 17 " " Mr Rand, a young man : lives between Charleston and Cambridge, he is going to Carolina
" Oct 8 Governour Belcher was at meeting here
" Nov 23 Thanksgiving Day ; fair & very cold
" Dec 24 Sermon by Mr Thoˢ Skinner
1739 Mch 29 Fast Day
" April 29 Sermon by Mr John Sparhawk of Salem
" June 17 " Preached on ye accᵗ of Coll. Isaac Royalls Death, by the Desire of the Remaining family, which Desired Mr Turill to Preach a Sermon Suiteable to the Condition. Yᵉ Coll Died Thursday June ye 7 in ye fore noon, and was Buried at Medford Saturday June 16, and was Carried the same night to Dorchester to his Marble Tomb
" June 24 Sermon by Widdow Towl's son of Charleston a young Preacher.
" Aug 5 Sermon by Mr Maning, Doctor.
" Sept 16 " " Mr Welsted of Boston
" Nov 11 " " Mr Ebenʳ Bridge of Boston a Blacksmith's son.
1740 Jan. 20 Sermon by Mr Pattishall a young man belonging to Boston
" Feb 3 Sermon Preached on ye accᵗ of the Death of the Revᵈ Mr Hancock Junʳ of Lexington, who dyed last week of yᵉ throat Distemper.
P. M. Richᵈ Waite dyed last Saturday morning in a Pitt verry suddainly.
" Feb 24 Sermon by Mr John Seccomb
" March 2 Preached on ye accᵗ of ye Death of Good Old Deacon Whitmore who Dyed Fryday Feb. 22, 1739—40, aged 57 years
" Mar 16 Sermon by Mr Fowle of Charleston a young man Mr Turill Preached at Lexington
" April 13 Sermon by Mr Emerson of Malden

1710 June 15 "   " one Mr Lewes who lives somewhere down at
                 the Cape
  "   Aug 31 Sermon By Mr Richardson of Woburn
  "   Oct   5 By Mr Andᵛ Eliot of Boston, a young man.
  "   Nov 13 Thanksgiving Day; a verry cold day indeed, and snowey
                 all Day
  "   Dec 28 By Mr Rogers a young man, a Stranger
1741 Feb 21 Saturday, the Revᵈ Mr Gilbert Tenant, preached 2 Ser-
                 mons in our Meetinghouse.
  "   April 5 Young Frances Whitmore and his wife were taken in to
                 Church
  "   Apl 19 By Mr Abbot of Charlestown
  "   May 17 " Mr Osgood of Stoneham
  "   "   31 " Mr Appleton of Cambridge
  "   June 7 " Mr Turell, 2 Excellent Discourses
                 A Collection was made to day for South Carolina,
                 their Distressing Circumstances on ye accoᵗ of a Grate
                 fire.
  "   July   5 By Mr Symes of Haddom in Connecticutt
  "   "   26 " Mr Belcher Hancock. Mr Turell is gone to Newberry.
  "   Aug   30 By young Mr Gardner of Boston son to ye Lether Dresser
  "   Sept 27 By young Mr Bucknam of Malden
  "   Oct   4 " Mr Jackson of Woburn. Mr. T. was not well
  ". Nov   12 Thanksgiving Day, fair and not very cold
  "   Dec   27 By young Mr Hill who kept school at Weston
1742 April 18 Wᵐ Whitmore, Ebenᵣ Oakes, Sarah Tufts, wife to Jona.
                 Tufts Jr, Martha Whitmore, and Sarah Dunton; were
                 Taken into Church
  "   July 11 By Mr Green of Barnstable, a worthy Minisᵗ
  "   Aug   1 Preached on yᵉ accoᵗ of the Extraordinary Lightning and
                 Thunder, last Fryday night
  "   Nov   11 Thanksgiving; a cold Day and Night following
  "   "   21 I was at home all Day by reason of a Grate Cold & Soar
                 throat
  "   "   28 By Mr Bowers that married Sarah Newell
1743 Feb. 13 Capt Ebenᵣ Brooks dyed last Fryday about sun down, he
                 was well at Lecture the samo week on Wednesday
  "   April 3 The forenoon Sermon was very Excellent
  "   July   3 These Texts were chosen on accᵗ of a Worm that Pre-
                 vails among us & Destroys the Grass & Corn
  "   Aug   28 By Mr Boardman our School master
  "   Sept 25 Preached on accoᵗ of a Council of Churches lately Held
                 at Concord on accoᵗ of a Difference between Mr Bliss
                 & some of his People, which is now settled by said
                 Council
  "   Oct   13 A Thanksgiving Day, The ocasion of which is a follows:
                 It having pleased Almighty God, on whose sovereign
                 & gracious Providence all Events entirely depend, to
                 grant signal Success and Victory to his Majesty's Arms
                 at the late Battle on the River Mayne in Germany, and
                 to preserve his Majesty's Person, when greatly en-
                 dangered in the Heat of Action, &c.

7.

Incorporation of the Town of Lexington.

The records of the town of Lexington commenced March 30th, 1713. Previously the records stand in the name of Cambridge Farms, or Cambridge Precinct; but a year or two previous to the above date, it had been decided that an order of incorporation should be obtained if possible. The following terms were offered to the town of Cambridge to secure her consent to the separation, viz.: 1. that the inhabitants of the precinct would pay one third part of two thirds of the cost of the maintenance of the great bridge until there should be a new establishment of court; 2. that they would pay their proportion of twenty-five pounds to clear off the arrearages of the town. The following order was accordingly made:—

At a Great & General Court or Assembly for Her Majesty's Province of the Massachusetts Bay in New England, began & held at Boston upon Wednesday the 20th of May 1712 & Continued by several Prorogations unto Wednesday the Eighteenth of March following in the same year 1712 (3). being their fifth session

The following Order pass'd in Council & Concur'd by the Representatives, viz

Whereas upward of Twenty Years since the Inhabitants or farmers dwelling on a certain Tract of Out Lands within the Township of Cambridge in the County of Middlesex, living remote from the Body of the Town towards Concord, Obtained Leave of the General Court with approbation of the Town to be a Hamlet or separate Precinct & were set off by a Line, viz beginning at the first run of Water or Swampy place, over which is a kind of a Bridge in the Way or Rhode, on the southerly side of Francis Whitmore's House towards the town of Cambridge aforesaid, across the neck of Land lying between Woburn Line & that of Watertown side, upon a Southwest and Northeast Course, commonly called the Northern Precinct, & being now increased, have obtained Consent of the Town & made Application to this Court to be made a Separate & distinct Town, upon such Terms as they & the Town of Cambridge have agreed upon,—That is to Say that the sd Northern precinct when made a Township shall bear such a part of the two thirds of the Charge of the Great Bridge over Charles River in Cambridge as shall be according to their proportion with the Town of Cambridge annually in the province Tax, And they shall annually pay to the Treasurer of the Town of Cambridge their part of the Charges as aforesaid.

And such other Articles as the sd Town & the Precinct have already agreed on by their Committees

Ordered that the aforesaid Tract of Land known by the Name of the Northern Precinct in Cambridge be henceforth made a separate & distinct Town by the Name of Lexington; upon the Articles & Terms already agreed on with the Town of Cambridge & that the Inhabitants of the said Town of Lexington be entitled Have, Use, Exercise, & Enjoy all such Immunities, Powers, & Privileges as other Towns of this Province have & do by Law Use, Exercise & Enjoy

And the Constable of the sd Precinct is hereby directed & empowered to Notify & summon the Inhabitants duly qualified for Voters to Assemble & meet together for the Choosing of Town Officers.

Consented to   J Dudley

A true Copy Exam'd   Pr   Simon Frost Depu' Sec'

In accordance with the above, on March 30th, 1713, a meeting was held and the following officers appointed :—

Mathew Bridge
Capt Reed
Lt Fransize Bowman } Selectmen.
Ensign Joseph Simonds
Deacon John Miriam

James Willson } Constables,
John Mason

Lt Fransis Bowman
William Munroe } Assessors.
Samuel Stearns

Lt Thomas Cutteler
Mr Thomas Bloggitte } Tithingmen.
Mr Samuell Whittmore

Town Clerk Mathew Bridge.

Mathew Bridge Town Treasurer.

Joseph Teed, Senler of Weights & Measures.

Sherebiah Kibbe Scaler of Leather.

Isaac Stearns
Thomas Cutteller } Surveyors.
John Poulter

All the above gentlemen were sworn but Mr Whittmore.

Mr Benjamin Muzzy } Fence Viewers.
Mr Phillip Russell

Nathaniell Bunktline
John Muzzye
Jonathan Robinson
Sam. Russell } To take care of swine that be yoked &
Josiah Hubb Jr.   ringed.
John Cooper

It was voted to build a pound, and also a pair of stocks, and to provide the town with weights and measures. Four hundred and sixteen pounds were voted to defray the cost of the new meetinghouse. The cost of the pound and stocks which were made by Mr. Wellington was four pounds. The expenses of the committee to the General Court were six pounds six shillings and eight pence. Widow Whitney was excused from paying the minister's rate for 1711 ; and Mary Addams was provided with clothing at the town's cost. Thomas Meads, Nathaniell Dunklin, Joseph Phasit, Phillip Burdoe, Thomas Kendall and Widdow Lidia Teed, were granted the use of the highways enclosed by them, in consideration of their paying a certain sum to the town as an acknowledgement.

LONGEVITY IN SALEM.—Since the commencement of the present year sixty Salem persons have died who had passed the age of three score years and ten. Of those, 26 were males and 34 were females. Of the whole number, 35 were between 70 and 80, 17 between 80 and 90, and 8 between 90 and 100. Of the most advanced in years, two were 82, six 83, two 86, one 87, two 89, one 90, one 91, one 92, two 93, two 94, and one 98.—*Salem Register, Dec. 28, 1857.*

SANBORN GENEALOGICAL HISTORY.

[By Dyer H. Sanborn.]

Most of the matter that follows was furnished by John S. Sanborn, Esq. of Sherbrooke, Canada East, member of the Provincial Parliament, copied from the Government Archives at Toronto, Canada West.

Extracts from Robson's British Herald of English Nobility and Gentry, relating to the name " Samboure," or " Samborne :"

(1.) Samborne, Moulsford, Berks ; Hants ; and Somers.

Arms, ar. a chev. az. between three Mullets gu.

(2.) Samborne, (same arms,) Crest, a dexter hand holding a sheaf of arrows, ppr.

(3.) Samborne, [Worc.] ar. a chev. between three mullets pierced, gu.

(4.) Samborne, Sa. (another az.) a lion rampant.

Explanations of the preceding contractions :

(1.) Samborne, the name is found in Moulsford, in Berkshire ; also, in Hamshire and Somersetshire.

Arms, argent, a cheveron, sable, between three mullets, gules.

(2.) Samborne, (arms found to be the same,) the Crest consists of a dexter [right] hand holding a sheaf of arrows [ppr.] (purpura,) purple (color.)

(3.) Samborne, (name in Worcestershire.)   Arms, argent, (silver,) a cheveron between three mullets, pierced gules (red.)

(4.) Samborne, Sable, (another azure,) a lion rampant.

Explanations of technical terms used :

A cheveron is an ordinary, representing two rafters joined together in chief, and descending in the form of a pair of compasses to the extremities of the shield.

The mullet is supposed to be the rowel of a spur, and should consist of five points only, whereas stars consist of six.

A mullet pierced is where the groundwork is gules, or red ; there are small white spots where the field is seen through it.   The ground-work is silver, and is a five-sided figure.

The cheveron, the rafters inside of this figure, is black ; the mullets are red ; the Crest a right hand standing upright holding in the clenched hand five arrows.   There are two coats of arms belonging to the name. The other is a lion rampant.   The field, or ground-work, is black, (sometimes azure,) and the lion, gold.

The name is spelled Sambourne in Berkshire ; Samborne without the letter u in the other counties.

In Sims' Index to the Pedigrees and Arms containing the Herald's Visitations, and other Genealogical manuscripts in the British Museum, is found of the pedigrees in Somersetshire—

" Samborne, of Timsbury, 1141, fo.* 88 ; 1385, fo. 70 ; 1445, fo. 122b ; 1559, fo. 85.

In Berkshire, is found

Sambourne, of Moulsford, 1097, fo. 9 ; 1483, fo. 186b ; 1530, fo. 71b ; 1332, fo. 96b ; 1982, fo. 96b ; 1982, fo. 115b ; 5865, fo. 16 ; 6173, ff. 86b, 87, add Mss. 4961, ff. 30b, 31, 14 ; 283, ff. 30b, 31, 14 ; 284, p. 102.

Sambourne, 4108, fo. 5."

---

* Fo. for folio ; ff. for folios.

County Genealogies in Hampshire, taken by William Berry, from the Visitations of the British Museum, in 1634.

John Rogers married the daughter of John Sisley, after the decease of Sir Thomas Sisley, Knt. S. P.

John Brocas married Anne, daughter of John Rogers.

Elizabeth, daughter of John Rogers, married Nicholas Samborne.

John Sanborne of Berkshire married Dorothy Tichborne about the year 1600. She was a descendant of Sir Roger Tichborne who was knighted some two generations prior to the time of Edward III.

———

It appears from the examination of early town, church, county, and State records, that the sons of our progenitor John Samborne of Derbyshire, England, Lieut. John, William, Esq., and Stephen, spelled their name Sumborne, and not Sanborn. The letter e was dropped in the 3d generation. The writer, in a recent examination of the Church and Town Records of Kingston, N. H., found the name Capt. Jonathan Samborn, (15.) b. May 25, 1672, of the 3d generation; Dea. Tristram Samborn, (30.) b. in 1643, and the primitive members of the Congregational Church registered Samborn. In the 5th generation the name in most instances is spelled Sanborn, some exceptions. Dr. William Prescott, the New Hampshire Antiquarian, this winter, at Salem, Mass. furnished me the following record, found in examining the "Old Norfolk County Records," which embrace Essex County and the county of Rockingham, N. H. This record of births, marriages, and deaths has been legibly transcribed by order of the Essex County Commissioners. These records extend from 1640 to 1680, inclusive, and contain much that cannot be found in Town Records prior to 1660.

Wherever our name occurs in these records it is invariably spelled Samborn.

———

Issue of Stephen Samborn, (4.) third son of John of Derbyshire, England, and his wife Sarah.

THIRD GENERATION.

1. Sarah Samborn, b. June 4, 1651.

2. Dorothy Samborn, b. March 2, 1653.

No record is found when Stephen was married, nor what Sarah's surname (maiden) was before marriage. Since Stephen returned with his grandfather, Rev. Stephen Bachilor to England, in 1654, probably his wife and daughters accompanied him; and the births of his then living children were registered in Norfolk County Records for preservation.

"The ancient Stephen Bachilor of Hampton, N. H., died at Hackney, a Village and Parish in Middlesex, two miles from London, in 1660, in the one hundredth year of his age."

1. Abial, (7.) Sanborn Gen. in these records is plainly written out Abigail, b. Feb. 23, 1653.

2. Richard, (8.) b. *Feb.* 4, 1655, instead of Jan. 4, 1655.

3. Stephen, (11.) b. Nov. 12, 1661.

4. Sarah, (20.) b. Feb. 12, 1667, instead of Feb. 10, 1667.

It seems that the name Samborne and Sambourne were not uncommon in Somersetshire and Berkshire, in the Parishes of Timsbury and Moulsford. It is, also, found in Hampshire, Shropshire, and Worcestershire, but not in Derbyshire.

ABSTRACTS FROM THE EARLIEST WILLS ON RECORD IN THE COUNTY OF SUFFOLK, MASS.

(Prepared by Mr. WILLIAM B. TRASK, of Dorchester.)

[Continued from page 144.]

EDMUND GROSSE.—I, *Edmund Grosse*, of Boston, giue the bigger halfe of my now Dwelling house to my son, *Isaack*, and the lesser halfe of my house to my wife, Bieing the better p' thereof, for my wife to Inioy her life time and then to Returne to my daughter, *Susan*. I giue my best suit & cloake to my son, *Isaack* ; my dau, *Susan*, my second Cloake ; my best sease coat to my wife ; my sixe acres of marsh & ten acres of upland that lyeth at Rumney marsh, Equeally to be diuieded bettweene my son, *Isaake*, & my dau. *Susan*. I giue my 50 acres of land that lyeth at mudey Riuer to be equally deuieded betweene my wife and fiue Children, proportionably.

Wittnesses—*Edmund Jackson*,			Edmond Grosse.
	Francis Hudson, Edward Yeomanes.

9 May 1655. Power of Administration to the Estate of *Edmund Grosse*, In Behalfe of the widdow & Children, grnunted to *Mr Jeremy Houchin* & *Lesse James Johnson*. *Edmund Grosse*, creditor, 29th April 1655 to *Capt James Oliuer*, & *Mr William Cotton*. In his account he mentions Mr Edmunds, Mr Simeon Kemthorne, John Barnes, Cornelius, Tho: Watkins, Mr Ting, Lieuet Bud, Mr Waldrone of Newichanneck, Mr Colchester of London. William Hubbom, " my sister *Mary Grosse*," " my Brother *Edw : Weeden*."

———

JOHN STONE —I, *John Stone*, of Hull, being sick—make this my last will—to my wife, *Jone Stone*, My house & housing, w'h all my Lands, Cattle, bonta, debts, & whatsueu' estate I have, making her my sole executrix. My will is, y' my wife shall pay out of my estate, £60, to my broth' *Simon Stones* Children, w'h sometime lived in Crusingtone, in Sumersetsheire, in old England, In consideration of same Acco' that was betwene him & I, when I Lived in England, w'h I know not whether it was all paid o' not, & this £60 to bee p' to y' three Children, £20 Apeece ; but if any of them bee dead & leave neither wife nor Children, then to be paid to y' other, w'hin one yeare after my Decease, Vpon lawfull demands.			5th of May 1659.
	Wittnesse, *Nica: Baker, Nathani ll Bosworth.*			John + Stone
	27 Jan. 1663, *Nathaniell Bosworth*, deposed,

Inventory of the Estate of *John Stone* who Deceased December 23' 1663, as apprised p' us who subscribe, Jan. 13th, *Nathaniell Bosworth, Nathaniell Barker*. Amt. [£369. 7.] Debts owing by John Stone, " in England," " to our minister," " to Charles Kymball, Mr Lewes, Henry Chamberlaine, Goodwife Druin, Mr Luke, widow Johnson. Armatage the Taylor, John Tuker, John Faroh, Thomas Dyer. [in all, £70. 14s.] June 8th 1665, *Joane Stone*, deposed.

[In the appraisement are mentioned 9 Acres of Land at alder point, Sagamore Hill, 12 Acres at petocks pond, Brusters Iland ; a Bill of *John Balmans*, a Bill of *Thomas Joyes*.]

———

CHARLES GRICE.—I, *Charles Grice*, of Braintree, being very weake of Body but of p'fect Memory, make this my last will. All my goods unto

my wife, *Margery Grice*, during her life for A support & succor to her
in her old Age, whom God hath continued w{th} mee now this Thirteene
yeares to bee help full & serviceable to me in my Aged & helplesse Condition.   My Will is, that when it shall please God to take my beloved wife
out of this wourld that then I give Unto *William Owen* all my Imovable
estate, for y{e} space of three yeares, as A token of my love for his filliall
care & love exprest to me in my Aged condition, in w{ch} three yeares my
son may prepare & come hither, if he like my Motion.   My will is, y{t} y{e}
contents of this my will, be sent into England, to my son, *David Grice*,
Vnto whome (after three yeares injoyment of my estate by son in law,
William Owen) I doe give all my Immovable estate, provided he doe
come ov{r} to New England for it, w{th}in y{e} space of three yeares After y{e}
death of my s{d} wife, *Margery*.   My will is, y{t} if my sone, *David Grice*
doe Refuse to Come to New England, that then it bee certified to My
Brother *John*, o{r} *William Grice*, y{t} if one of their sons doe Come ov{r} to
New England, that then he y{t} Cometh over shall Injoy all My imovable
estate, But if Neithe{r} of My Brothers sonnes doe Come, within y{e} space of
three yeares, after Notise, that then I doe give All My Imovable estate
Vnto My son in law, *William Owen*, his heires & Assignes for ever.   I
doe make my wife, *Margery*, my sole executrix.
    9{th} Novemb{r} 1661.

In y{e} p{r}sence of us,   Charles X Grice.
                                                              his mark.
Peter + *Brackett*, *Barnabas* X *Dorifield*,
David X *Wallsbe*.
        12{th} of Nov{r} 1663, *M{r} Henry Flint* and *Peter Brackett* deposed.
        Braintry, 9{th} : 9{th} : 1663.   Inventory of the Goods & Estate of
Charles Grice, Deceased 10{th} of October 1663, attested by *Samuell Bass*
and *Edmund Quinsey*.   Amt. £92. 13s. 6d.
    12 Nov{r} 1663, *Margery Grice*, deposed.

————

    ROBERT GAMLER, late of Roxbury, being sicke, make this my last will.
Vnto my son, *Benjamin Gamlen*, all my house & Lands in Roxbury to
him & heires for ever to possesse Imediately After my decease, vpon y{e}
Conditions hereafter expressed.   I doe hearcby Injoyne my sonne to lay
into y{e} farme yearely so much good hay, at his own charge, as shall
sufficiently winter two Cowes, & Also liberty for two Cowes to goo freely
into any of y{e} s{d} Land to pasture, at all such times as is conuenient for
feeding, winter & summer, & also liberty of housing & yard to keep y{e}
said Cow for y{e} use of my wife, *Elizabeth*, so long as my s{d} wife shall
live.   I injoyne my son to deliuer unto my said wife, yearely, twelve
bushills of good Merchantable wheat, two bushills of pease, & six bushills
of Indian Corn, also, to provide & lay down by my dwelling house so
much wood as my wife shall need to burn, also my wife to Injoy all y{e}
dwelling house, except y{e} new end of y{e} said house, during y{e} time of y{e}
life of my said wife, Also halfe of y{e} orchard.   My said son is to pay
my son in law, *Isack Cheurey*, soo much as one Acre of my salt Medow
shalbee valued at.   I doe order my said sonn, *Benjamin*, to have my two
oxen & my Mare as his owne, w{th} this provisall, that my said wife have
y{e} vse of y{e} said Mare to Ride vpon as oft as shee shall need her, this said
Mare & oxen to bee praised in y{e} Inventory, & my will is, y{t} if my wifes
necessity should call for y{e} value of y{e} Mare & oxen, all or parts of it,
by y{e} advice of mine ov{r}seers it shalbee paid vnto my said wife, by my

moon, *Benjamin*. All y⁰ rest of my Moveable goods I give vnto my said wife, *Elizabeth*, whom I make my sole executrix. I request my beloved friends, *William Parke & John Bowls* to bee ov'seers of this my will. Thus have finished my will, in y⁰ best Manner as I Am Able, this 3 day of August 1663.

In y⁰ p'sence of *Christopher Peake*.   Robert + Gamlin.
        Edward Morris, who deposed 28 Jan. 1663.

Inventory taken 22 : 9 : 1663, by *William Parke, John Bowles, Robert Searcr*. Mentions land " neer y⁰ house of *Abraham Hows*," " neere *Ed. Bridges* house." *Elizabeth Gamlen* deposed, 28 Jan. 1663.

———

WILLIAM WARDELL.—A Contract made between *William Wardell* on the one p'te, & *Elizabeth Gillit*, Widdow on the other p'te, before their ioyning in mariage, being the fourth day of December 1657, is as followeth :—First, that what estate the said *Elizabeth* was possessed of before her mariage was to bee at her disposeing at the time of her death or at the mariage of any of her children, and for the howse and land that now the said *William Wardell* & *Elizabeth*, his wife, doth possess, it follow by course of law to *Hannah Gillis*, daughter to *John Gillis*, who was the former husband to the abouesaid *Elizabeth*, now the wife of the said *William Wardell*. The said *William Wardell* did then ingage for and in Consideracon of the said howse & ground to traine vp the said *Hannah Gillis*, being then about two yeares old, that at the day of her marriage, or at the day of the said *William Wardells* death, to give vnto the said *Hannah* the value of sixteen pounds, which was then to the full vallue of the said howse & ground, the howse beeing much decayed & ready to fall ; this is truth, as witnes our hands.

Witnesse, Seth Perry, John Perry.   William + Woodells
        3 Nouember 1663.   Elisebeth + Woodell

The Court allowed of this Couenant only w'th Consent of *W'm Wardell* ; ordered y' said *W'm Wardell* in full sattisfaction of y⁰ old house, y⁰ Ground of s' *Gillett* to be held & Converted to the vse of said *Wardell* & his heires ; ordered that he bring vp *Hannah Gillet* & when she comes to be of age shall pay hir twenty one pounds for the same.

                              Edw : Rawson Recorder.

———

JEREMIAH STEVENS.—15'th of October 1663. At a meeting of the magists. who being Informed by *dacto' Clarke* y' y⁰ late *Jeremiah Stevens* desird that Administration to his estate might be Graunted to *S' Thomas Temple* & *M' Jn° Jalyffe* that so they might take Care of his Estate & Convey it to his father. [Administration was Graunted to said individuals.]

Inventory of the Estate of *Jeremiah Stephens* deceased taken in Boston, 17'th Ocr 1663, by *Hezekiah Usher, scitnas', Tho. Lake*. Amt. £72. 4. 11½ ; of this amount, £68. 17. 5. were in books, 122 in number. The names of 38 are given.—*John Jaylyffe* deposed, 28'th of Ocr 1663, *Sir Thomas Temple*, 3' Ocr 1663.

———

DAVID ABERCROMBY.—5'th March 1663. Power of Administration to y⁰ Estate of y⁰ late *David Abercromby* is Graunted to *Amos Richardson*, in behalf of himself & other Credito's &c.

                    (*To be Continued.*)

SAVAGE'S GLEANINGS.

[Correction explanatory.]

S. G. Drake, Esq., Editor "N. E. Gen. Reg.,"—

Sir,—In "*Gleanings for New England History*," by James Savage, Esq. ("*Mass. Hist. Soc. Coll's*;" 3d ser., vol. 8th, pp. 316 and 317), I find the following passage :—

"Examination of a Register of the diocese of Sarum, from early in the 13th century, printed by Sir Thomas Philips, a distinguished Antiquary, but never published, helped me to one or two of our New England divines from Wiltshire; Williclmus Noyes p. m. at the church of Choldrington 1602, and Nathaniel Noyes p. r. Wm Noyes at the church of West Chaldrington 1621. I conjecture the meaning of p. m. here to be, by removal; and p. r. pro rectore."

Mr. Savage's conjecture was not a happy one; but, fortunately, a communication from Sir Thomas Phillippa* enabled him to correct the error into which he had fallen, and he has done so (same series, vol. 10th, p. 133) in his second interesting collection of "*Gleanings*." He therein informs us that "'p. m.' is an abbreviation for *per mortem*, and 'p. r.' for *per resignationem*." Before reading Mr. Savage's correction I had inserted the following note, opposite the erroneous passage, in my copy of the "*Collections*." The mistake, made by so old and distinguished an antiquary, induces me to believe that the information will prove serviceable to others who may have occasion to examine registers of the English clergy.

A clergyman was presented to a benefice, made vacant by the death, or resignation, or other avoidance of the preceding incumbent. The character of this voidance was usually expressed, in the registers, in abbreviated terms. Occasionally the sentence was fully written out. I will give a few examples of the latter class, which will render all the customary abbreviations easily intelligible. They are as follows: "Gul. Watson, Cler. 1. Nov. 1662. vacavit per amotionem A. Burgess, propter Nonconformitatem."—"vacari per mortem Walteri Finseeys ult. Rect."—"quem nuper obtinuit Dus. J. Burdett, vacantem per ejus assecutionem Archidiaconat Cestrie."—"vac. eo quod Mr. John de Severley adeptus est dignitatem, viz. Archd. Wig."—"vac. per occasionem ult. incumbentis."—"vac. per negligentiam dni. Ric. Kylner," (in not paying his "teaths.")—"vac. per deprivacionem."—"vac. per legitimam deprivacionem."—"vac. per resignationem."—"vac. per lapsum tempori,"—finally, in cases of exchange of benefices,—"permutavit cum—." These are all the different examples I found, in the examination of many lists of the clergy, in "*Dugdale's Warwickshire*," 2d Edit. by Thomas, 1730. As *removal, death, promotion, surrender, negligence, deprivation, resignation* and *delayed-acceptance* are included among the causes of vacancies, the summary seems to be quite complete.

Trusting that the above may be thought worthy of a place in your valuable and interesting "Register," I remain, very respectfully, &c.,

Robert Townsend,

Albany, N. Y., June 3d, 1858.　　　Cor. Mem. "*N. Hist. and Gen. Soc.*"

---

* Sir Thomas Phillipps, Bart., F. R. S. and F. S. A., of Middle Hill, Worcestershire, possesses the finest private library in the British empire. It is exceedingly rich in Heralds' Visitations and other genealogical collections. Sir Thomas is known as an eminent antiquary and an accomplished scholar. J. O. Halliwell, Esq., F. R. S., F. S. A., the celebrated antiquary, literary editor and author, married Sir Thomas' eldest daughter.　　　　　R. T.

BOOK NOTICES.

*The Vinton Memorial, comprising a Genealogy of the descendants of
John Vinton of Lynn, 1648; also Genealogical Sketches of several
allied Families, namely, those bearing the names of Adams, Alden,
Allen, Boylston, Faxon, French, Hayden, Holbrook, Mills, Niles,
Penniman, Thayer, White, Richardson, Baldwin, Carpenter, Safford,
Putnam, and Green. By John Adams Vinton. Boston: 1858. 8vo.
pp. 534.*

This work bears evidence of thorough research, and in many particulars may be
recommended as a model genealogy. Some of the Sketches, as the author terms them,
are fuller than many genealogies that have been published in separate form. In his
Appendix he has given a very good history of the introduction of the Iron Manufacture
into New England; and scattered through his pages are curious and interesting illustrations of the manners and customs of other days.

In the Preface Mr. Vinton offers some conjectures upon the native country of his
blood, and the origin of his name. The materials he has collected are scanty; and of
these he seems not to have made that earnest use, which marks his labors in genealogy.
Having caught the echoes of a tradition among his aged relatives, that their ancestors
emigrated from France, and found the name of Petrus de Vintonne, at Rouen, in 1336,
he forgets the great mass of testimony adduced in his subsequent pages, leading to a
diverse conclusion. We admit the probability that John Vinton of Woburn, came from
France, and that his ancestors may have fled from intolerance there. But we shall
proceed to show that long before the exodus of the Huguenots, before St. Bartholomew's, before Protestantism itself, men bearing the name Vinton were found not only
in France, but in many parts of England and Scotland. The French Vintons were,
therefore, but one branch of a family widely diffused; or else, the name was adopted in
various countries, by men bearing no blood relationship to each other.

To arrive at some satisfactory conclusion, let us examine the meaning and origin of
the name. Mr. Vinton rightly connects it with Winchester, without seeming to perceive the precise mode and degree of the connection. That it is far closer than a mere
" Latinizing " of that name, may easily be shown. In the " Codex diplomaticus ævi
Saxonici,"* the name of that city, is found more than seventy times, occurring in
ancient charters, of the ninth, tenth, and eleventh centuries. But the forms of the name
are as various, as of all others discovered through the mist of the middle ages. They
may be arranged in the order of their resemblance to Winchester, as Wintancastro,
Wintanceastre, Wentana, Wintonia, Vintonia, Wynton, and Winton.

It is easy to see that Wintancastre is Winte-castrum, that is, the camp at Winte, or
Wenta, or Venta. For, Venta was the Roman name of Winchester, as may be seen
on maps of Britain; and it is so ("Οὐέντα) mentioned by Ptolemy, the Greek geogra-
pher, 130 years after Christ. Mr. Vinton quotes from a Celtic dictionary (by J. B.
Bullet,) the assertion " Vinchester est l'ancienne Vintonia, grande ville située dans une
île formée par un partage de l'Itching Vin, rivière, town, partage." " Prodigious as
the erudition is which Bullet summons to his aid, the judgment he exhibits is not equal
to his scholarship; nor do we know less satisfactory authority than the Dictionnaire
Celtique." We are not inclined to accept this etymology; for it seems more probable
that the second syllable was formed, as we have indicated, through the corruptions the
name endured from popular use, in a barbarous age. Certainly the original Celtic word
was Went, (meaning river,) which is still preserved in Caerwent, and Derwent. From
this the Romans, having no W, formed Venta, a noun of the first declension. The
monks afterwards changed this to Wintan, for more distinctness of sound, as we are in
two of the forms given above. Bullet's hypothesis is built on the occurrence of the
syllable ton, in many names; as Winton, Ilveston, Taunton, and the like, where the
meaning is said to be " habitation." But if, as he says, " town " means " partage,"
(division,) and Winchester was named from the branching of the Itching, then a similarity of circumstance occurring elsewhere, might occasion the same name to be given
in other places. Wherever a stream was divided by an island, in Celtic countries, a
Winchester might arise, (or rather, if no castrum stood near, a Venta might be built,)
the town taking its name from the local situation. There are, in fact, two other towns

---

* By Thomas Wright, of the English Historical Society.

of this name, on Roman maps of Britain, suggesting the probability that there might have been more, not mentioned by Latin writers. Winchester, the "grandville" in Hampshire, was called Venta Belgarum, to distinguish it from Venta Icenorum, the present Norwich, and from Venta Silurum, now Caerwent in Wales.* In this last name we see the ancient Venta still preserved, with the prefix "Caer," meaning habitation. In all three we have the presence of a river, the Itching at Winchester, the Yare at Norwich, and the Wye (?) at Caerwent.

The syllable Vin, or Ven, followed by a dental, was in fact of very frequent occurrence in British geography. On maps of Roman Britain, we find in the south of the island, Vindomum, (now Silchester,) Vindomes, (now White-Church), and Vindogladia, (now Gussage.) In the north were Vindalana, Vindobala, Vindomora and Vinovia. Other cases are those in which the order of syllables is inverted; as Bennaventa, Glanoventa, Derventio and Magloventum. On the continent, were Ventium, and Ventiponte, Vindo, Vindobona, Vindomagus and Vindonisum.

Remembering how easy it is to make ludicrous blunders in ancient and foreign etymologies, we preach no farther in this Celtic field. But we submit that there must have been a common idea at the root, blossoming into these analogies at the top, and we feel an impregnable confidence, that at least in Britain, the syllable Vint, or Vent, possessed an extreme antiquity and a wide diffusion. The name Vintred occurs on many old British coins, and Vint still survives among the gentry of Essex.

The city of Winchester, a thousand years ago, possessed much more than its present relative importance. Edward the Confessor held very extensive lands in its vicinity. In early Norman times, moreover, it was often the regal residence. Henry III., in the battle of Evesham, (1265,) saved his life by exclaiming, "I am Henry of Winchester, your king." The survey of the royal lands, made in the time of Henry I., (1101–1135) is still known as the "Winton book." It was also quite a matter of course, that the Earls of Winchester, should write themselves Winton, when they could write at all, for such was the common abbreviation of Wintonensis; and the priors, bishops and cardinals named from that city, who certainly could write, would use no other signature. We do not mean to contend that the family name, Vinton, originated thus; for these were mere official designations. But in very early times we meet with names which certainly are not official, but names of persons called after their estates, or place of abode. Such was Robert de Winton, precentor of York, in 1250, and Robert de Winton, prior of St. Andrews, in 1255. Such also was Taleferris de Wynton, who died in 1332, and Roger de Winton, prior in Southwark, in 1304. Mr. Vinton enumerates no less than thirteen de Wintons, mentioned in local histories, as living prior to Henry VIII. He might have added to his list the names of Peter de Wintonia, mentioned by Rymer, as "clericus garderobe," from 1257 to 1273, and of Johannes de Wintonia clericus, appended to an instrument dated 1306. The preposition de at length disappeared from most names in which it occurred, and in the fifteenth century we meet with the name Vinton standing alone.

There is no need of supposing that all who bore this name were connected with Winchester. The numerous names of places identical or similar to the ancient form of this, show that the family name might have been adopted from estates elsewhere situated. Beside the village of Venton, in Cornwall, there still remain Winton in Suffolk, Winton in Cumberland, Winton in Yorkshire, and Allwinton in Northumberland. The name, also, of the Scottish Chronicler, Andrew of Wynton, as well as Richard of Winton, found in the Rotuli Scotiæ, render it probable that such a place existed in Scotland. The name of " Peirus de Vintonor, chanoine de Reims," in 1396, makes it probable that the name was also attached to the soil of France. But the great mass of evidence adduced above, unites with national feeling, to make us prefer the English origin of the name.

One thing, we own, seems unaccountable to us—the almost utter absence of the name from all English lists of persons. Except a few in London, and in Glasgow, Mr. Vinton is not able to find his family in England or Scotland. In the south of Ireland we have heard the name is common. In this country it is somewhat extended, and the ancestor, to whom a great number have been traced, seems to have sprung from a family who had resided in France. We incline to think they were emigrants from England in a distant age. No claim to distinction can be advanced in favor of the race; but we think there is something venerable in a name rooted in the geography of Britain, and traceable in its elements back to the time of Christ.   * *

---

* At all these places, Roman ruins have been found.

Collections of the Massachusetts Historical Society. Vol. iv. of the
Fourth Series. Published at the charge of the Appleton Fund. Boston: 1858. 8vo. pp. 514.

The Committee of Publication for this volume consisted of Richard Frothingham, Jr.,
Thomas Aspinwall, George Livermore, and Lorenzo Sabine. In our opinion, no volume of Historical Collections, or any publication of ancient records, (issued only for reference) need or require to be got up, any better than this volume. It is occupied, mainly, with a "Correspondence, in 1774 and 1775, between a Committee of the Town of Boston and Contributors of Donations for the Relief of the Sufferers by the Boston Port Bill." For the editing of this part of the volume, the Chairman of the Committee, Mr. Frothingham, is peculiarly qualified. Indeed the whole volume bears evidence of his care, diligence and accuracy, and is alike creditable to his good taste and sound judgment.

Besides the important Correspondence above mentioned, the volume contains a variety of other articles from unpublished materials of great value; among which may be mentioned letters from Samuel Adams, Joseph Hawley, Andrew Eliot, a Petition of Roger Williams, Phinehas Pratt's Narrative and Petition, &c. &c. All these are elucidated by Mr. Frothingham with judicious notes. An Index, or suitable table of contents, would greatly facilitate the examination of the volume. As usual, probably, in such cases, nearly the whole labor of editing the work fell upon the Chairman of the Committee. In this case he has done all that could, in reason, be required of him; and we hope the editor of the next volume of the Society's Collections, will, in accepting his charge, make it a condition that those associated with him, shall prepare an Index to their work.

The Life of John Fitch, the Inventor of the Steamboat. By Thompson
Westcott. Philadelphia: 1857. 12mo. pp. 415.

We did not imagine that so much interesting matter could be found about John Fitch, as we find in the volume before us. In the Preface is plainly told what the reader may expect in regard to Fitch's claim to the discovery of applying steam to propel vessels. He says, "By the general voice, Robert Fulton has been most unjustly lauded as the inventor of the steamboat. Honor is paid to his memory by statesmen, orators, and writers, and 'poor John Fitch,' if ever alluded to, is spoken of as one who knew not how to produce the effects which he was ingenious enough to conjecture were possible. Perhaps a stronger instance of the tendency of mankind to elevate the fortunate and degrade the unfortunate, cannot be adduced."

John Fitch was truly a man who had to struggle with misfortune, and we can heartily recommend this attempt to do justice to his memory to our readers. The Fitch family to which John belonged, came from near Braintree, County of Essex, England, and settled in Connecticut. There is in the volume a pretty good genealogy of the family.

*Third Annual Report and Collections of the State Historical Society of
Wisconsin, for the year 1856.* Vol. 3. Madison: 1857. 8vo. pp. 547.

Few works of the same extent contain a more valuable body of Western History than the one before us. Its list of Papers or Articles occupies a page in small type— so numerous that our limits will not allow of their enumeration; nor can we give some of them without seeming to do injustice to others. We observe many valuable notes, illustrative of the various papers, from the hand of the corresponding Secretary of the Society. The Hon. Lyman C. Draper, a gentleman to whom the West is under great obligations for his persevering efforts in recovering materials for its history.

A Genealogy of the Descendants of David Goddard. By William Austin Goddard. Worcester: M. Spooner, Printer: 1833. 8vo. pp. 39.

This work may be fairly termed one of the pioneers in the great field of genealogy, and would even now be considered very creditable to the author. Of course there is a lack of that system which now characterizes books of this nature, but the reader will find little trouble in holding all the threads of the pedigree in his hands. It is a singular proof of the necessity of a Genealogical Association and Journal, that this book has so long eluded the search of the collector. It has already been availed of by the authors of the "Watertown Genealogies" and the "Rice Family;" and their mention is sufficient proof of the accuracy and fidelity with which the author fulfilled his task. w. s. w.

Annals of the Minnesota Historical Society, 1856, *containing Materials for the History of Minnesota.* Prepared by EDWARD D. NEILL, Secretary of the Society. Saint Paul : 1856. 8vo. pp. 141.

Books without some kind of pictorial illustrations, now-a-days, appear in a sort of unfinished state. The spirit of illustration is extensively abroad, and an author can hardly expect his work to sell, however good it may be, without pictures to set it off. Even historical collections are beginning to partake of the spirit of the age. This volume of the Minnesota Society has many neat and appropriate wood engravings. The headings of some of its chapters are— "Who were the first men?" Gov. Ramsey's Address at the Second Annual Meeting of the Society. "Early Notices of the Dakotas." "Louis Hennepin." "Sieur du Luth." "Explorer of the Minnesota River," and a great number of other topics, chiefly illustrative of the Dakotah Indians and their country.

We are indebted to Mr. William H. Kelly of St. Paul, (formerly of Boston,) for a copy of the Annals here noticed.

The Paine Family Register, or *Genealogical Notes and Queries.* Nos. 5 & 6. Albany : Jan. and May. 1858.

Though confined principally to the Paine race, this work forms a highly interesting miscellany, to those engaged in kindred pursuits. No. 5 opens with a neat account of Robert Treat Paine, the signer of the Declaration of Independence, tracing his pedigree to his emigrant ancestor, who came into Plymouth Colony in 1621. Every connection of the family should patronize the work. It is conducted by Dr. Henry D. Paine of Albany, to whom, if one dollar be remitted, he will forward to the address of such patron four numbers of the work.

The Sheldon Magazine, No. IV. October. Or, a *Genealogical List of the Sheldons in America, with Biographical and Historical Notes, and Notices of other Families with which they Intermarried. Embellished with Portraits and Fac-similes.* By the Rev. HENRY OLCOTT SHELDON. Sidney, O., 1857. 8vo. pp 33.

The character of this number of the Sheldon Magazine not differing from its predecessors, it will be necessary only to refer our readers to previous notices, for our opinion respecting it. We are glad the editor is encouraged to continue the work, and hope he will soon complete it, so that we can bind the numbers in a permanent volume.

Memoirs of the Historical Society of Pennsylvania. Vol. VI. Philadelphia : 1858. 8vo. pp. 429.

This volume is entitled "Contributions to American History, and the expense of its publication is defrayed by a fund; to which fund, any person contributing twenty dollars, entitles such person to all the publications issued by the Society during life. The first article in the volume under notice is "Some Account of the Society of the Cincinnati." 2. Journal of the Meeting of the Society in 1784. 3. The Insurrection in the Western Counties of Pennsylvania. 4. Presentation to the Hist. Soc. of Pa., of the Belt of Wampum delivered by the Indians to William Penn, at the great Treaty under the Elm Tree in 1682, Penn's Letters to the Indians, &c. 5. The Acadian Exiles. 6. The case of Major André. There are several fine illustrations in the volume. Among them a curious representation of the Belt before mentioned. The paper, typography, &c., is fully equal to any volume of historical collections issued by any of the historical societies in the country.

A History of the Rise, Progress, and Present Condition of the Bethlehem Female Seminary. With a Catalogue of its Pupils, 1785—1858. By WILLIAM C. REICHEL. Philadelphia : 1858. 8vo. pp. 464.

This is a very large as well as a very magnificent volume, illustrated with a great number of fine plates ; consisting of Views and Portraits. It is, altogether, the most superb work of the kind which has fallen under our notice. It contains many pieces, prose and verse, by pupils, or those who have been such, which do them much credit, and reflect honor upon the conductors of the institution.

*A Sermon on the Re-opening of Christ Church, Cambridge, Mass.,
preached on the 24th Sunday after Trinity, Nov. 22, 1857; with an
Historical Notice of the Church. By the Rev. NICHOLAS HOPPIN, Rector. Boston: 1858. 8vo. pp. 79.*

Everything about this production is excellent; an excellent sermon, valuable historical notes, fine engravings representing the church edifices in 1761 and 1858. The
original petitioners for a church (1759) embrace the since well known names, Henry
Vassal, Joseph Lee, John Vassal, Ralph Inman, Thomas Oliver, David Phips, Robert
Temple, James Apthorp. The first minister was the Rev. East Apthorp, who was born
in Boston, and was the fourth son of Charles Apthorp, Esq., an eminent merchant.

*Memoirs, Counsels, and Reflections. By an OCTOGENARY. Addressed to
his Children and Descendants, and printed for their use. "The father
to the children shall make known thy truth."—Is., xxxviii. 19. Cambridge: Metcalf and Company, printers to the University. 1857. 8vo.
pp. 119.*

This work of the venerable Rev. Dan Huntington of Hadley, consists of two sermons
and notes, an autobiography, and a brief genealogy of the Huntingtons. We do not
presume to make any extracts from the former, as they treated of private affairs. The
genealogy is brief, and the author, by assuring us that the Rev. E. B. Huntington of
Stamford, Conn., has an elaborate work on the subject, soon to appear, relieves us from
the task of reviewing the present book at length. We trust soon to report the appearance of the new book. W. H. W.

American Annual Obituary.

There is in press, and soon to be published, a volume, entitled "Annual Obituaries."
This work has been undertaken by the Hon. NATHAN CROSBY of Lowell, Mass., for the
editorship of which he is well calculated; and, judging from the facilities at his command, and the industry which he has bestowed upon it, the volume must be highly
valuable to the public. We understand that Phillips, Sampson & Co., are the publishers.

*The Morse Monument, erected at Medfield, Mass., April 27, 1858, by
their Descendants in reverence for their Memories, and gratitude for
their Benefactions.*

Such is the inscription upon a fine lithographic print, representing the Morse Monument. This monument is wrought out of the most durable stone, and consists of three
square obelisks or columns, united at the base. The centre column is thus inscribed:
"To the Memory of Seven Puritans, who emigrated from England to America in 1635
-9." On a tablet on the same column below is this:—"Samuel Morse, born 1585;
settled in Dedham, 1636; died at Medfield, 1654. Joseph Morse settled at Ipswich,
where he died, 1646." The other two columns represent two other families of Morses.
On the one:—"John Morse, born 1604; settled at New Haven, and died at Wallingford, Ct., 1707, æ. 103." On the other: Anthony Morse, born at Marlboro', England,
1606; died at Newbury, 1686. William Morse, born 1608, died 1683, at N. Hubert
and Peter, their brothers, settled and died in New Jersey"
In justice to the Rev. ABNER MORSE, it should be stated, that it is through his untiring exertions, that this Monument, at a cost of 300 dollars, has been erected.

A VIGOROUS OLD AGE.—Mrs. Lucy Osgood, of Salisbury, who is now in her 87th
year, for two years has attended the "Cattle Show" in this city. A year ago she
stopped at the north end with her friends, and after walking three quarters of a mile,
stood for two hours about the mall to see the balloon ascension, and then walked back.
When the stage called for her in the evening, she for some time declined entering it,
because it was crowded, saying she could walk to Salisbury, which was some three
miles. This year she walked from the north end and visited the Fair, apparently no
more fatigued than half the girls who had never seen twenty summers. Since she was
ninety years old, she has walked from Salisbury, and experienced no inconvenience
therefrom.—*Newburyport Herald, Oct.*, 1857.

MARRIAGES AND DEATHS.

MARRIAGES.

DANDRIDGE, Philip P. of Virginia, to Mrs. Betty Taylor Bliss, dau. of the late General Z. Taylor and wid. of the late Major Bliss.

DIXON, R. H., at the Cathedral, Toronto, on the 8 May, by the Hon. and Rt. Rev. the Lord Bishop of Toronto, assisted by the Rev. Richard Mitchell, M. A., Rector of York Mills, B. Homer Dixon, K.N.L., eldest son of the late Thomas Dixon, K.N.L., K.L., to Kate McGill, second dau. of the Hon. Chief Justice Macaulay.

LEE, Mr. William P., Salem, to Miss Hannah G., dau. of Hon. J. Thomas Stevenson.

WENTWORTH, Mr. John A. of Wentworth, Iowa, to Miss Rachel A. Griffis of Fredericton, N. B., at Boston, 1 March.

DEATHS.

ABBOT, Mrs. Polly, Westford, 3 March, æ. 93 yrs. 2 mos. 11 ds.; widow of Mr. Jacob Abbot.

ADAMS, Col. Chester, Natick, 15 March, æ. 72; many years a member of the General Court, and one year a member of the Council.

ADAMS, Mr. Thomas, Halifax, Vt., 14 April, æ. 90.

AIKEN, Mr. Robert, Boston, 25 April, æ. 77.

AINSWORTH, Rev. Laban, Jaffrey, N. H., 17 March, æ. 100 yrs. 2 mos. 28 ds. He had been a pastor of the Congregational church in that town seventy-four years.

BABBITT, Mr. Isaac, Jamestown, N. Y., 5 Feb., æ. 75.

BALDWIN, Mrs. Margaret D., 19 May, æ. 89; wid. of the Rev. Dr. Baldwin.

BALFOUR, Mrs. Mary, Charlestown, 99 May, æ. 72; wid. of the Rev. Walter Balfour.

BATCHELDER, Mrs. Hannah, Salem, 17 April, in her 87th year. She had kept a dry goods store on Essex Street above sixty years, and by her business accumulated a handsome fortune. Her integrity and honesty are proverbial.

BATTLES, Mr. Benjamin, Chelmsford, 18 Feb., æ. 67 yrs. 7 mos.

BENTON, Hon. Thomas Hart, Washington, 10 April, æ. 76 yrs. and 1 mo. wanting four days. He was a native of North Carolina, passed his youth in Tennessee, settled in Missouri in 1815, and was one of that State's first U. S. Senators, in which office he was continued thirty years. He married Elizabeth, dau. of Col. James McDowell of Rockbridge Co., Va. His surviving children are, Mrs. William Carey Jones, Mrs. Ann Benton Fremont, Mrs. Sarah Benton Jacob, and Madame Susan Benton Bolleau, now at Calcutta, wife of the French consul-general. Col. Benton lost his wife in 1854, after which event he visited no places of amusement or festivity.

BIGELOW, Mr. Convers, Weston, 25 Feb., of apoplexy, æ. 73 yrs. 3 mos.

BLAKE, Col. Solomon, Brewer, Me., 4 May, æ. 93.

BORDEN, Mrs. Alice, Fall River, 12 March, æ. 99; wid. of Joseph Borden.

BOUTELLE, Mrs. Molly, South Reading, 22 March, æ. 90 yrs. 4 mos.

BOYNTON, Mr. Daniel, South Deerfield, 27 May, æ. 82.

BRECKENRIDGE, Mrs. Mary H., Louisville, Ky., (at the residence of her son, the Rev. W. L. Breckenridge), 26 March, in her 90th year.

BROWN, Charles H., Esq., Boston, 1 April, æ. 66. He was a native of Newburyport, but has resided in Boston thirty-six years. For the last six years he has been president of the Atlas bank.

BROWN, Mrs. Rowena, Wilmington, N. C., 28 March, æ. 49 yrs.; wife of Asa A. Brown, Esq., and dau. of the late Milton Cushing of Putnam, Muskingum Co., Ohio, and great-grand-dau. of General Rufus Putnam of the Revolution.

BULLARD, Mrs. Anna, Framingham, 4 April, æ. 77; wid. of Josiah Bullard.

BULLARD, Mr. Samuel P., New Orleans, 7 Feb., æ. 58; a native of Providence, R. I., of the firm of Toulmin, Bullard & Co.

BURK, John Erie, Bernardston, 23 March, æ. 48 yrs. Deacon Burk was the fourth generation from "Hon. Major Burk," one of the first settlers of Bernardston, and quite a distinguished man in that section of the State for thirty years before the Revolutionary war, both in civil and military affairs. He was first commissioned by Gov. Shirley, under King George II., 1 March, 1747, as "Ensign of a company of Volunteers raised for his Majesty's service for the defence of the western frontiers." He was subsequently commissioned as lieutenant, then captain, and finally as major, by Gov. Pownal, in 1760, in the thirty-third year of the reign of King George II. He was in active service in the French and Indian war, and was at the surrender of Fort William Henry, Aug. 10, 1757, at which time he narrowly escaped from massacre, losing all his clothing except his deerskin breeches and his silver watch. He lost property at that time valued at £828 8s., continental currency—probably about $50 in specie. He died at Deerfield while attending the public service, in 1784, æ. 67 yrs. The following is the inscription on his grave-stone in the old burying-ground in Bernardston:

"Were I so tall to reach the pole,
  Or grasp the ocean with my span,
I must be measured by my soul—
  The mind's the standard of the man."

The following are the ancestors of the subject of this notice: Maj. John Burk, above mentioned, who died in 1784; John Burk, 2d, died in 1796, æ. 54; John Burk, 3d, died in 1812, æ. 28; John E. Burk, the fourth generation and the last male descendant of his distinguished ancestor.

Deacon Burk was ever esteemed and trusted in the community in which he lived. For many years he was a deacon of the Baptist church in Bernardston, a selectman of that town in 1850, a representative in the legislature, a justice of the peace, and, on the first Monday of March last, was elected by the town one of the trustees of Powers Institute.
                                    s. w. c.

BUTLER, Miss Ann C., Boston, 16 May, æ. 80.

BURTON, Mr. Jonathan, North Danvers, 5 March, æ. 92 yrs. 2 mos. 23 days.

CHAMPLIN, Mrs. Rebecca, Warren, R. I., 4 March, æ. 81; wid. of Capt. William Champlin of Bristol, R. I.

CHAPMAN, Mr. Albert Pierce, Palmer, 19 Feb., æ. 31; a native of Peterboro', N. H., resided some five years in Boston, and was highly respected as a business man. A younger brother, Walter D. Chapman, died in Boston about four weeks later, æ. 72.

CLAPP, Capt. Samuel, Marshfield, 9 Feb., æ. 89.

CLARK, Stanford R., West Brattleboro', Vt., 3 April, æ. 44; a grad. of Amherst, 1853. He was son of the Hon. Samuel Clark of W. Brattleboro', Vt.

COFFIN, Mrs. Frances Cutler, Lynn, 17 April, æ. 54; widow of the late Edward L. Coffin, M. D. She was the daughter of Samuel Cutler, Esq., and born at Cambridgeport, Mass., 27 May, 1802; married to Dr. Coffin 14 June, 1831. He died 31 March, 1845, leaving her with two small children,—an only son and an only daughter,—whom she has brought up in a manner that bespeaks much for her wisdom, prudence and Christian influence.   W. P.

COLMAN, Dr. William, Pittsfield, 17 April, æ. 92.

CONKLIN, Mrs. Rebecca Browning, Leicester, 9 Feb., æ. 87.

COTHREN, Willie Steele, Woodbury, Ct., 26 April, æ. 20 months; only child of the Hon. William Cothren.

CROSWELL, Rev. Harry, D. D., New Haven, Ct., in his 83d year; had been Rector of an Episcopal (Trinity) church there 43 years. To Jan. 1, 1856, he had officiated at 2,553 baptisms, 873 marriages and 1,842 burials. He was father of the late Rev. Dr. Wm. Croswell of Christ church (Boston), and Sherman, for many years editor of the Albany Argus, and Frederick, many years judge of the Probate court of New Haven. A newspaper, called the Balance, published at Hudson, was edited by him from 1803 to 1809, making 6 vols. in 4to. A copy of this work is in the Editor's library. It was rather a violent anti-Jefferson paper. For some of his remarks on Mr. Jefferson's conduct, Mr. Croswell was prosecuted for a libel. An account of his trial was published.

CURTIS, Mrs. Ann, Somerville, 24 Feb., æ. 73 yrs. 7 mos.; widow of the late Noah Curtis, Esq. of Quincy.

CURTIS, Joseph, Esq., Jamaica Plain, West Roxbury, 13 Feb., æ. 85 yrs. 4 mos. 20 days. His great-great-grandfather, William Curtis, with his wife Sarah and four children, came from England to America in the year 1632, and settled on a farm lying on Stony river in Roxbury, where he had four more children born to him. His youngest child, Isaac, born in 1642, inherited the homestead, with the condition that he should take care of his parents in their old age. The emigrant, William, died 8 Dec. 1672, æ. 80. His wife, Sarah, died 20 March, 1673, æ. 73. The old homestead is now in possession of the fifth Isaac C., who has also a son of that name.

The eldest Isaac had a son Samuel, born 2 Sept. 1668, who married, 6 June, 1711, Hannah Gore of Roxbury. In 1712 he purchased twenty acres of land on Jamaica Plain, bounding on the pond, and, in 1722, built the house yet standing on the premises. By two later purchases he increased his premises to thirty-one acres, which constituted the original Jamaica Plain farm. Samuel and Hannah (Gore) Curtis had eleven children, of which number Joseph and Benjamin, twins, were born 11 Jan. 1721-2. Samuel C. died at J. P. 19 Feb. 1772, æ. 84. His wife, Hannah, died there 13 Oct. 1775, in her 88th year.

Joseph, twin brother of Benjamin C., remained at home with his father, Samuel, until the age of 21, when he purchased a negro man and horse, and began farming on his own account. He was the first person who sent vegetables to Boston market in a cart—they having been previously carried in panniers. He came into possession of the family estate by buying out the other heirs, paying one half of the purchase money at the decease of each parent, and agreeing to support them comfortably during their natural lives. He lived a bachelor until the age of 66. His house was the seat of hospitality for his relations and friends, and the poor and needy were refreshed by his bounty.

He married, 3 July, 1771, Katherine, born May, 1745, youngest daughter of Timothy and Mary Parker of Jamaica Plain, Roxbury. She was a very superior woman, possessed of a strong, discriminating mind, with great wit and turn for repartee, and was universally beloved by old and young for her cheerfulness and benevolence.

Joseph Curtis, Sen. was born in the house built by his father, Samuel, in 1712, and died there 28 Jan. 1792, æ. 70. His wife, Katherine, died there 16 June, 1802, æ. 67. Their eldest son, Joseph, Jr., was born in the ancient house 23 Sept. 1772, and there married, 27 May, 1800, Bethiah Allan, daughter of Jeremiah and Abigail Parker of Roxbury. He inherited the homestead, and, from time to time, added to its dimensions. He also inherited the kind and benevolent dispositions of both his parents. [*From Miss C. P. Curtis's manuscript genealogy of the descendants of William Curtis.* c. w. h.

DAVENPORT, Mrs. Dimis Loomis, Boston, 23 April, æ. 83; wld. of Asher Davenport.

DENNY, Mrs. Lucretia, Leicester, 12 April, æ. 90; widow of the late Mr. Thomas Denny.

DICKINSON, Mr. Joh, Grand Rapids, Mich., 11 April, æ. 86; a native of Granby, Ms.

DORR, Sullivan, Esq., Providence, 2 Mar., a native of Boston, and father of the late Thomas W. Dorr. He had resided in Providence more than fifty years. The grave of Roger Williams is said to be included in his estate.

DRAKE, Richard G., Esq., Philadelphia, Pa., 20 February; of the well-known law firm of Chapman & Drake of Hartford, Ct.

DREW, Charles, Esq., Duxbury, 4 Feb., æ. 88 yrs. 10 mos.

BROWN, Mrs. Isabella, Rye, N. H., 22 March, æ. 72 yrs. 4 mos.; widow of Mr. Henry Brown.

EASTMAN, Mr. Phineas, Manchester, N. H., 24 May, æ. 67; formerly of Canaan, N. H.

EATON, Rev. Asa, D. D., Boston, 74 Mar., in the 80th year of his age; long Rector of Christ church in this city. His funeral took place on the 25th. He was a grad. of H. C. 1803.

EATON, Mrs. Ruth, North Reading, 5 March, æ. 10 yrs. 4 mos. 2 days.

ELWELL, Mrs. Betsy, Gloucester, 9 Feb., æ. 77 yrs. 8 mos. 11 days.

EDES, Mrs. Dorothy C., 14 March, æ. 84.

EMERSON, Mrs. Esske, Westbrook, Me., 17 Feb., æ. 68 yrs. 9 mos.; widow of the late James R., Esq., formerly of Bridgeton, Me.

FARMAN, Mr. Dehonacr, Boston, 14 March, æ. 54 yrs. 5 mos.; formerly of N. H.

FLINT, Mrs. Sally, South Danvers, 22 Feb., æ. 84; widow of Capt. Hezekiah Flint.

FLINT, Mr. Isaac, Greenwood, Me., 12 April, æ. 76½ yrs.; one of the first settlers of the town, and a native of Mass.

FOLGER, Mr. Aaron, Nantucket, 24 April, æ. 82.

FORBES, Mr. Amasa, Portland, Me., 17 Feb., æ. 81; a much esteemed citizen of Westbrook, Me.

FREEMAN, Rt. Rev. Geo. W., Little Rock, Ark., 29 April, æ. 68. He was one of a family of twenty children, all of whom arrived at mature years. The Rev. Frederick Freeman of Sandwich is his brother. The deceased was bishop of Ark.

FRENCH, Dr. Otis, Gilmanton Iron Works, N. H., 9 April, æ. 53; a native of Sandwich. He received his medical degree at D. C. 1827, was in practice in Gilmanton nearly thirty years, where he acquired a deservedly high reputation, as well as a man and citizen, as a physician. He represented the town in the General Court in 1843-4, and held other offices of trust; all of which he discharged with honor to himself and advantage to the community.

GARDNER, Capt. Joseph, Woburn, 9 April, æ. 78 years, 6 mos.

GARDNER, Mr. Samuel, Winchester, 15 April, æ. 83.

GILCHRIST, Hon. John, Washington, 29 April, æ. 49 yrs. 9 mos. 13 ds.; judge of the U. S. Court of Claims. He grad. H. C. in 1828, was a lawyer in Charlestown, N. H. Married a dau. of the late Ex-Gov. Hubbard, became judge of the Supreme Court of N. H., and finally of the Court of Claims of the U. S., as above stated.

GILMAN, Rev. Samuel, D. D., Kingston, 9 Feb., in his 67th year; of Charleston, S. C., a grad. at H. C. 1811.

GARY, Mrs. Susannah, Lincoln, 21 Feb., æ. 84.

GUILD, Benjamin, Esq., Boston, 30 March, æ. 72 years 10 mos.; a gentleman endeared to a wide circle of acquaintances, among whom his urbanity of manners and intelligence were highly appreciated. He graduated at H. C. in 1804.

HALL, Dea. Jonas, Woburn, 23 Feb., æ. 77.

HAMILTON, Mrs. Mehitable, Conway, 9 April, æ. 68; wife of Micah Hamilton.

HARE, Robert, M. D., Philadelphia, 15 May, in his 77th year; noted for his discoveries in chemistry, electro-magnetism, &c.

HARRIS, George, Esq., Boston, 20 May, æ. 76 yrs. 5 mos.

HASKELL, Mrs. Lois, Ipswich, March, æ. 84; wife of Mr. Daniel Haskell.

HINMAN, Mrs. Martha A., Newbury, Vt., Feb., widow of the late Dr. C. T. Hinman, first president of the Northwestern University, near Chicago, and oldest dau. of the Hon. Timothy Morse of Newbury.

HOARE, Mr. Joseph, Waterboro', Me., 10 March, æ. 84.

HUNT, Mr. Freeman, New York, 2 March, æ. 53; publisher of the Merchant's Magazine. He was a native of Quincy, Mass., where he was born, 21 March, 1804; son of Nathan and Mary (Turner) Hunt.

HUSSEY, Mr. Charles F., Nantucket, 22 May, æ. 68.

JEWETT, Mrs. Rebecca, Pepperell, 10 April, æ. 90.

JONES, Mr. Anthony, Hopkinton, 11 Jan., æ. 67. He was the son of Isaac, b. 1757, who was the son of Anthony, who was the son of John, Esq., who came from Boston to Hopkinton, and joined the church there in 1727. He m. Hannah, daughter of Savill Simpson, one of the wardens of King's chapel, who took up 611 acres of land in Hopkinton in 1693. The children of John and Hannah were John, Simpson and Anthony. The latter m. Elizabeth Alden, 1742, and had Nathaniel, b. 1748; Hannah, b. 1742; Elizabeth, b. 1750; Anthony, b. 1743; Jesse, b. 1755; James, b. 1757, d. 1818; Samuel, b. 1759; Lydia, 1762; Anna, 1764; Elisha, 1768; Mehetable, 1770. Isaac m. Martha Barker, 1781, d. 1818, and had Isaac, Simpson, Anthony, Patty and Henry. Anthony m. Sophia Loker of Natick, d. 1837, and had Lucy Ann, who m. Charles Watson; and Sophia N., who m. Joseph Hanson Walker.—R. Nason.

JONES, Archibald, Esq., Frankfort, Me., 6 Feb., æ. 81 yrs. 4 mo., a native of Worcester, Ms., whence he emigrated in 1803.

JONES, Mr. Cyrus, Belmfield, 16 Feb., æ. 92.

KIMBALL, Mr. Benjamin, Littleton, 27 May, suddenly, æ. 74.

KERR, Mr. John, Leicester, 24 May, æ. 81 years, 7 months, 25 days.

LINCOLN, Capt. Jacob, Eastport, Me., 14 March, æ. 81; a native of Hingham, Ms. He was clerk of the first town meeting in Eastport, held Mar 11, 1798. A brother of his is living in Hingham, over 60, and a sister at Cohasset, aged 94.

LORING, Mrs. Rachel, Great Barrington, 17 April, æ. 89; widow of Levi Loring.

LUNT, Mrs. Rebecca, Newburyport, 24 Feb., æ. 61; widow of Capt. Joseph C. Lunt.

MARSH, Mrs. Sarah, Heath, 9 April, æ. 100 years, 6 months, 7 days.

MASON, Mrs. Mary, Boston, 10 April, æ. 80; wid. of the well-known lawyer, Jeremiah Mason.

MANLEY, Mrs. Mary Bull, 31 Dec. 1857, æ. 81, wid. of Milton M., Esq., lawyer of Beaufort, S. C. Mrs. M. died at the residence of her son-in-law, Rev. Chas. Ed. Leverett, Rector of Prince William's Parish.

Major Gen. Stephen Bull, the father of this venerable lady, held the high rank of a Colonial Commander in the Revolutionary War. Inheriting a large estate, he nobly perilled it for the defence of his country. In revenge for his brave and vigorous partisanship, his splendid residences at Sheldon and Laurel Bay were burnt, the first named by the British Gen. Prevost, on his march from Savannah to the siege of Charleston, 1779, and the plantations connected with them ruthlessly ravaged and destroyed. For his adoption of the American side he was disinherited of another family estate, Ashley Hall, on Ashley River, by his uncle, William Bull, the loyalist Governor of South Carolina during the revolution. Gen. Bull was grandson of the first governor, William Bull, 1738–1743, and gr. grandson of the Hon. Stephen Bull, a cavalier emigrant in the earliest days of South Carolina. C. E. L.

MAXWELL, Mrs. Olive, Heath, 9 March, æ. 81, widow of Mr. Hugh Maxwell.

MAYNARD, William, Esq., Chilmark, **27** Feb., æ. 89.

MAYO, Mrs. Huldah, **widow**, Hampden, Me., 4 Feb., æ. 95.

MEADE, Mrs. Mary M., Dinwiddie, Va., March, æ. 80; mother of the Hon. Richard Kidder Meade, U. S. minister to Brazil.

MEARS, Mr. Elijah, Boston, 2 Mar., æ. 90.

MELLEN, Mr. Joshua, Weyland, 22 Feb., æ. 94; father of Chief Justice Mellen.

MESSERWOOD, Mr. Jonathan, Canton, 17 April, æ. 80½ years.

MITCHELL, Mrs. Anna, Nantucket, 6 Feb., æ. 81; widow of the late Mr. Moses M.

MORSE, Mrs. Nancy H., Boston, 25 April, æ. 78 years, 11 months.

NASH, Mr. James, Abington, 18 March, æ. 72.

NEWELL, Moses, Esq., West Newbury, March, æ. 63; one of the most prominent men in the County of Essex.

NEWHALL, Mrs. Elliot, Malden, 3 March, æ. 64 years, 4 months.

NEWHALL, Mr. Jabez, Conway, **2 April**, æ. 81.

NORRIS, **Capt. Nathan, Salem, 17 March**, æ. 75.

O'BRIEN, Hon. Jeremiah, Machias, Me., 30 May, æ. 80.

OSBORN, Rev. Elihu, Fairton, N. J., 1 Mar., in his 100th year, a soldier of the Revolution, and for 70 years a minister of the Gospel. He would have been 100 had he lived till August next.

PALMER, Mr. Earl, Boston, 16 March, ae. 76 years, 5 months.

PARKER, Mrs. Mary, Newburyport, 14 March, ae. 91 ys. 9 mo., wid. Deacon Silas P.

PARSONS, Mrs. Abigail, Hinsdale, 8 May, ae. 94.

PATTERSON, Enoch, Esq., Dedham, 17 March, ae. 85.

PATTERSON, Mrs. Mary, Dedham, 19 May, ae. 78; widow of the above.

PEABODY, Mrs. Abigail, Salem, 8 April, ae. 95 ys. 9 ds.; widow of the late Samuel Peabody. Supposed the oldest person in the city.

PEARSON, Mr. Moody, Newburyport, 22 Feb., ae. 71.

PECK, Rev. John Mason, D. D., Rock Spring, near St. Louis, Mo., 15 March, in his 69th year; a native of Litchfield, Ct. He was a Baptist minister, and as early as 1818 he took up his residence at St. Louis, Mo., and originated the first Baptist Society in that city. Mr. Peck became a writer, and his works discover a vigorous mind, and were deservedly popular; especially his books about the West. In 1852, Harvard College gave him the degree of D. D. The date of his birth is Oct. 31, 1789.

PERRY, Com. Matthew C., New York, 4 March. He was a younger brother of the late Commodore O. H. Perry.

POMEROY, Mrs. Fidelia, East Hampton, 18 May, ae. 78.

POMEROY, Mrs. Susan, Pittsfield, 15 May, ae. 78.

POWELL, Mrs. Mary, Boston, 21 March, ae. 93.

RANDALL, Capt. Heathersby, Bowdoinham, Me., 17 April, ae. 93.

RICH, Mrs. Elizabeth S., Portsmouth, N. H.; 3 March, ae. 66.

RICHARDSON, Mr. Lemuel, Woburn, 12 Feb. ae. 72 years, 6 months.

SACKETT.—The Bar of this city has sustained a severe loss in the death of two of its most worthy and respected members, the brothers, C. D. and G. A. Sackett. The elder brother, C. D. S., died yesterday afternoon, of congestion of the lungs. His brother died this morning of apoplexy, a consequence of the excitement and grief which the decease of his brother had induced. They were most estimable men; their relations through life had been singularly close; they lived together, worked together, and died together. The elder brother was married, and died in his 60th year; the younger was a bachelor, and died in his 54th year.—N. Y. Ev. Post, 8 March.

SEARS, Mrs. Achsa, Monument, 16 Feb., in her 83d year.

SLACK, Mr. Ruggles, Chelsea, 13 April, ae. 65; a gentleman well known in Boston, where he had been employed in connection with the Boston Post for many years. He was the father of Charles W. Slack, Esq., and of the Rev. Samuel R. Slack, of Newark, Del., an Episcopal clergyman.

SOUTHWORTH, Mr. Nathaniel, the well known miniature painter, on his way home to Hingham from the Steamer Canada, in which he had just returned from Europe. He was buried on the 27th of April.

STARK, Mrs. Betsey, Bow, N. H., 14 May, ae. 87; wife of Lt. John Stark.

STARKWEATHER, Dr. Robert, Chesterfield, 6 May, ae. 92.

STEWART, Mrs. Mary, Blanford, 20 Feb., ae. 94.

SWIFT, Mrs. Ruth, Wareham, 16 March, at the residence of her dau., Mrs. P. S. Crocker, ae. 75.

TABER, Mr. David, Deer Isle, Me., 10 March, ae. 81.

TILDEN, Mr. Thomas, Roxbury, 12 May, ae. 83; many years a respected citizen of Roxbury.

TODD, Mr. Elias, Newburyport, 17 Feb., ae. 78.

TOWNE, Mrs. Nancy F., Brookline, 3 May, ae. 40 ys. 5 mo.; wife of Wm. B. Towne, Esq., and eldest daugh. of Mr. Jeremiah Hill. She was b. at Boston, 26 Nov. 1817, and was a descendant of the seventh generation, commencing with Ralph Hill, sen., an inhabitant of Billerica, at the incorporation of the town in 1655, and who died there, 29 d. 3 mo. 1663.

TRASK, Miss Rachel, Beverly, 24 March, ae. 80.

TROWBRIDGE, Mrs. Anna, Newton Corner, 28 May, ae. 76 years, 5 mo.; widow of Col. Wm. T.

TERRY, Mr. William, Portland, Me., 19 March, ae. 93. He was in active service in the Revolutionary War, and was intimate with Talleyrand, when that celebrated Frenchman was in Portland.

TYLER, Rev. Bennet, D. D., East Windsor, Ct., 14 May, in his 74th year, after an illness of only ten hours; late President of the Theological Seminary at that place. Mr. Tyler was an able theologian, and noted for his controversial writings. He grad. at Yale in 1804, was President of Dartmouth College, 1822-8, succeeded Dr. Payson in Portland, Me., in which place he continued till 1834, when he was elected at East Windsor. He had a large family; his eldest dau. was the first wife of Dr. C. E. Stowe; another dau. m. the late Philip Greely, Jr., formerly Collector of Boston. Edward Tyler, Esq., Cashier of the Suffolk Bank, is his son; another is a missionary in Africa.

TYLER, Mrs. Esther, East Windsor Hill,

Ct., 23 May, æ. 72; widow of the above, whom she survived but ten days.

Tyng, Rev. Dudley Atkins, Brookfield, near Philadelphia, 19 April, æ. 33. He was accidentally caught by his dressing-gown in a cornshelling machine which he was viewing, which so injured one of his arms that amputation was necessary, but his life could not be saved. He was a son of the Rev. Dr. Tyng, and was b. in Prince George County, Md., in 1825.

Vincent, Mr. Wm. E., Dorchester, 12 Apr. æ. 45; teller of the State Bank, Boston.

Wade, Mr. Benj., senr., Natchez, Miss., 9 May, æ. 62; a native of Massachusetts.

Wadsworth, Mrs. Priscilla S., 16 Feb., æ. 87; widow of Wait W., Esq.

Ward, Thos. W., Esq., Boston, 3 March, æ. 71; a well known and wealthy citizen.

Warren, Mrs. Abigail, Charlestown, 19 May, æ. 89 yrs. 1½ mo., widow of Isaac W., Esq.

Warren, Mrs. Mary, Plymouth, 24 Mar., æ. 87; widow of Henry Warren.

Wateman, Mr. William, Williamstown, 26 Feb., æ. 73.

Weaver, Ruth, Prescott, 20 Feb., æ. 82.

Wellington, Mr. Albert K., Lexington, 5 March, æ. 40 yrs. 9 mo. and 5 days; son of the late Mr. Benj. O. Wellington of Lexington.—(Bond's Watertown.)

Wellington, Mrs. Hannah, Waltham, 16 April, æ. 76; widow of Richard Wellington.

Wells, Mr. George, Sevier County, East Tennessee, 9 April, æ. about 94; "one of the remnants of the days of the revolution." He was accidentally killed by a tree, which, in its fall, struck the log-cabin in which he was, knocking a piece of it against his head, causing a wound of which he died. He is said to have been the father of 21 children.

Wells, John B., Esq., Boston, 18 March, æ. 75.

Wentworth, Miss Elizabeth L., Roxbury, 29 March, æ. 62; formerly of Canton.

Wentworth, John Paul, only son of the Hon. John and Marie (Loomis) Wentworth of Chicago, Ill., at the residence of his maternal gt.-father, Riley Loomis of Troy, N. Y., on the 27th March, æ. 6 mo. 9 days.

Warrs, John, Skowhegan, Me., 10 April, æ. 92.

Whiton, Mrs. Emma, Hingham, 4 March, æ. 83; widow of Capt. Kara Whiton.

Williams, Mrs. Harriet Harding, Mosul, East Indies, 25 Dec.; dau. of the Rev. Sewall Harding of Boston. She had recently arrived upon her field of missionary labors.

GROTON EPITAPH.

Inclosed I send you a copy of the oldest inscription in the Groton burying place. Mr. Butler, in his History of Groton, page 253, thus alludes to it:—"It is supposed that the first settlers buried their dead in this place, though there is no monument bearing an inscription, to tell whose dust lies there, earlier than that of James Prescott, 1704. This is an unwrought flint stone, the name, age and time of death indented with a common pick." He was the son of Jonas and Mary [Loker] Prescott, and was born March 16, 1684. See Butler's History, page 426.

S. A. G.

Here-Lyeth-The
Body-of-James-Pres
cot-Hee-Dyed-the-
9-of-May-1704
aged-20-and 7 wee[ks?]
yeres-old

A LINEAL DESCENDANT OF DEFOE.—Walter Savage Landor and Charles Knight have discovered a great-grandson of Defoe, the author of Robinson Crusoe. He is seventy-eight years old, living in London, in a state of destitution. Landor has addressed an appeal to every school-boy, and every one who has ever been a school-boy, to subscribe one penny each for his immediate relief. James Defoe is a box-maker and undertaker; has had a family of eight children—two of whom are yet living—James and Priscilla. Mr. Knight has received and expended about £50 during the year for him.—*19 November, 1855.*

PAYMENTS.—*Albany, N. Y.*, E. E. Kenrick, J. F. Winslow, H. D. Paine, R. Woodward; *Amherst, N. H.*, P. Dodge; *Adrian, Mich.*, N. F. Spofford; *Andover*, N. Farrer; *Boston*, P. Willard, H. Lee, Jr., J. R. Kimball, R. Palmer, T. Parker, A. Child, D. W. Holmes, W. Parsons, J. A. Lowell, P. Butler, H. Rice, W. Adams, T. L. Turner, C. C. P. Moody, O. Tufts, A. Beale, F. Haven, A. D. Hodges, W. R. Deane, F. W. Lincoln, J. G. Chandler, J. H. Blake, W. Lewis, C. C. Jewett, D. A. Boynton, L. M. Sargent, J. A. Stearns, N. T. Farwell, Mrs. White, D. Draper, G. B. Upton, A. Davis, J. Willard; *Baltimore, Md.*, W. E. Mayhew; *Boscawen, N. H.*, W. Temple; *Harrington, N. H.*, J. N. Fernald; *Beverly*, C. T. Leach; *Buffalo, N. Y.*, L. K. Haldock, N. K. Hall, E. S. Hawley; *Braintree*, H. V. French; *Brighton*, D. W. Hoyt; *Cleveland, O.*, W. A. Otis, E. Wade, T. Beck; *Cincinnati, O.*, H. Emerson; *Canton*, R. Ames; *Conway*, A. Howland; *Cambridge*, C. H. Morse, G. Livermore, Harvard College, W. G. Stearns, C. Francis; *Castine, Me.*, D. Johnson; *Chicago, Ill.*, E. S. L. Richardson, E. Lane, J. Wentworth; *Chelsea*, S. Bassett, O. Merriam; *Evangeville, Me.*, P. R. Vose; *Dover, N. H.*, N. Martin; *Dedham*, W. Bullard, E. Wilkinson; *Dorchester*, H. Vose; *East Haddam, O.*, D. H. Warner; *East Rockport, O.*, A. W. Brown; *Ellington, O.*, F. W. Chapman; *Framingham*, G. N. Bigelow; *Fitchburg*, F. Perkins; *Gloucester*, J. J. Babson; *Galena, Ill.*, A. M. Haines; *Haverhill*, Mrs. Merrill; *Hartford, O.*, J. H. Hosmer, J. H. Trumbull; *Hingham*, S. Lincoln; *Hatfield*, G. W. Hubbard; *Jersey City*, S. Alofsen; *Jamaica Plain*, C. P. Curtis; *Jaffrey, N. H.*, J. Melville; *Indianapolis, Ind.*, A. G. Willard; *Lynn*, A. Rhodes, W. Bassett, R. S. Johnson; *Lowell*, J. Avery, N. Crosby; *Lenox*, H. Taft; *Lynnfield*, J. Newhall; *Lawrence*, J. R. Rollins; *Litchfield, Ct.*, G. H. Hollister; *Monson*, J. R. Flynt; *Medford*, A. T. Wild; *Milwaukee, Wis.*, J. F. Birchard, E. D. Holton; *Meadon*, J. G. Metcalf; *Middletown, Ct.*, R. Stearns; *Manchester, N. H.*, S. D. Bell, M. H. Bell, City Library; *Manhattanville, N. Y.*, T. M. Peters; *Marlboro'*, N. H. Phelps; *New York*, H. M. Smith, J. H. Redfield, C. Swan, B. W. Bonney, S. Wetmore, B. Pomeroy, J. Lenox, G. W. Pratt, E. H. Davis, Merc. Library, R. J. Lansing, A. W. Griswold; *Nashville, Tenn.*, C. W. Smith; *Northfield, Vt.*, H. M. Bates; *New Haven, Ct.*, W. S. Porter; *Northampton*, C. A. Dewey; *New London, Ct.*, T. W. Williams, R. Hallam; *Norfolk, Ct.*, R. Battell; *Norton, O.*, G. F. Clarke; *Norwich, Ct.*, S. Bliss; *Putnam, O.*, A. Kingsbury; *Peoria, Ill.*, C. H. Deane; *Portland, Me.*, H. K. Hinckley; *Providence, R. I.*, H. T. Beckwith; *Philadelphia, Pa.*, J. Jordan, Jr.; *Rockingham, N. C.*, S. H. Webb; *Roxbury*, J. Dudley, J. W. Parker; *Salem*, M. A. Stickney; *Springfield*, J. W. Crooks, C. Stearns, R. D. Morris; *Sturbridge, Me.*, J. R. Thornton; *St. Paul, Min.*, W. H. Kelly; *Stonington, Ct.*, J. D. Champlin; *South Reading*, L. Eaton; *Stockbridge*, D. D. Field; *Shawneetown, Ill.*, J. Bowler; *Taunton*, H. L. Danforth, W. A. Sproat, E. H. Reed; *Troy, N. Y.*, I. M'Conihe; *Westerly, R. I.*, C. H. Denison; *Worcester*, C. B. Whiting, A. H. Wilder, B. F. Haywood, J. S. Farnum, W. H. Bigelow, I. Jenison, C. Allen; *Woonsocket, R. I.*, I. B. Peck; *Westfield*, J. H. Snow, Jr., J. Fowler, E. Davis; *Watertown*, N. Wilding, B. Dana, Jr.; *Wilmington, N. C.*, A. A. Brown; *West Waterford, Vt.*, A. B. Carpenter; *West Newton*, C. Pierce; *Warwick, R. I.*, G. A. Brayton.

QUERY.—Joseph Simonds, born in Woburn Oct. 18, 1652, m. Mary ——, and moved to Lexington. What was the date of this marriage, and the name and parentage of his wife ?

Was William Simonds, of Woburn 1644, related to Samuel Simonds of Ipswich ? and if so, how related ?

Daniel Livermore of Watertown married, about 1703, a second wife, Mary, who, after his death, married, Aug. 17, 1724, John Goodenow of Sudbury. What was her name and parentage ?

Daniel Livermore (son of John and Grace, baptized Oct. 7, 1644, while they resided in New Haven) was living at the date of his father's will, 1684, but probably died before 1694. Where did he reside ? whom did he marry ? John Russell married in Charlestown, Nov. 12, 1691, Mary Livermore. Was she the widow of Daniel Livermore ?

Richard Sherman in his will [Geneal. Reg., IX., p. 227] calls **Edmund Angier and John Livermore** his kinsmen. What was the relationship ?

.t **Family**.

'ISHER, died 1656.

...s Leverett and Beauchamp, lands between Muscongus, &c. At the ...barkation, 1633, he was an Alderman of the Borough of Boston. ...office of Ruling Elder of the First Church, Boston, Mass., 17 years.

...., d. 1693; m. Hon. Peno ...t Jarvis, &c. Gr. dau. ...t of Th's Hickling, Esq., ...Michael's, m. Hon. Wm. ...D., son of Col. William, ...Bunker Hill; their son, ...g Prescott, LL. D., the ...wan, d. Th's C. Amory. ..., Hon. Franklin Dexter.

Hannah = Hudson, b. in England, 1621; m. 1639; d. 1643.

Sir John, b. in England, 1616; Capt. in Parliamentary Army, 1644-5; Agent of the Colony to the English Court; Major-General of the Massachusetts Forces; Deputy Governor, &c. Governor of Massachusetts, 1678-9. Knighted by King Charles II. D. 1679, æ. 63.

= Sarah Sedgwick, born 1629; mar. 1647?; died 1784.

...ary, h. 1655; m. ...t, Paul, son Gov. ...hes Dudley; 2d, ...ov. Penn Town... ...nd, Chief Judge ...Supreme Court. D. 1689.

Hannah, b. 1661, m. 1689, Thomas Davis. d. 1732.

Rebecca, b. 1664; mar. 1691, James Lloyd, Esq.: dau. mar. James Oliver, son of Nathaniel and Elizabeth, dau. Capt. Tho's Brattle. Grand-dau. Mary mar. Col. John Wendell, brother of Hon. Jacob W. Died 1738.

Sarah, born 1673; mar. 1718, Hon. Nathaniel Byfield, Judge C. C. Pleas 30 years, Judge of Admiralty, &c. D. 1730.

Thomas, surgeon, b. 1674; d. 1706, æ. 32. 〒 Rebecca Winsor, prob. des. from Walter De Windsor, Gov. Windsor Castle, temp. Wm. Conqueror.

Knight, b. 1705; m. 1725; d. 1753 = Abigail Bottolph. She d. 26 Jan. 1776, æ. 70.

..., wid. of ...ker, m. 69.

Rebecca, b. 1728; m. J. Greene.

Abigail, b. 1732; m. Rev. Sam'l Johnson, D. D. of Conn.

...l Margaret Marshall, ...river. Margaret m. 2, ..., Portsmouth, N. H.

William, b. 1770, 〒 Charlotte Whiting, m. ——, d. 1811. dau. Maj. Eben. Frances, Ebro., Augusta, Jane.

Eliza.

Mary, b. 1774, d. 1854.

...m. ...of ...y, ...h. ...C. ...by

William, b. 1760, m. 1786, d. 1817, in Vt. Mary, b. 1792, mar. 1811, Hon. Horace Everett, M. C.; sons of these, William, M.D., Horace, lawyer, Edward, Leonard. Ella, b. 1796, d. 1845, m. George Woodward, lawyer. Lucretia, b. 1805, d. 1842, m. Jona. Bliss, lawyer.

〒 Lucretia Hallam, of Ct.

Thomas, b. 1765, d. 1833, Sec. of St. Vt. John; Charles, Dart. Col.; William, N. H.; George; Tho's, N. H.; Sarah, and 4 unm. ds.

= Susan Johnson.

Abigail, m. Capt. Brush, U. S. A. Mary, m. Capt. Leonard, U. S. A.

' Mary Ball Maxcy, dau. Milton, Esq., lawyer, Beaufort, and Mary Ball, dau. Maj. Gen. Stephen Ball, Rev. Army, gr. gr. dau. Hon. Wm. Ball, Gov. S. C. 1738. An uncle of Mrs. L. was the celebrated Dr. Maxcy, Pres. Brown, Union, and S. C. Colleges. Another uncle, Hon. Virgil, Maryland, Sol'r. U. S. Treas., and Min. to Court of Belgium.

...arolina Col. 1853, Stud. Theo. Sem. Ep. Ch., Va.; Matilda, Anne Heyward, Mary Ball, Julia Marcelline, Catherine Hamilton, Caroline Pinckney.

THOMAS LEVE[RETT]
m. 1619; d.

The name of LEVERETT is found in the reign of John, [and] Henry III. 1216. It is of great antiquity in Lincolnshire, [and] arms in the Herald's Visitation, 1564. In 1639, the Conne[cticut]

Anne, b. 1618; ⊤ Dr. Isaac Addington.   Jane, Clara and others u[

Hon. Isaac, b. 1644, d. 1714; Ch.
Justice, Hon. Secretary, &c.; mar.
1st, Elizabeth Bowen; 2d, Madam
Elizabeth Wainwright: son-in-law
and nephew Ch. Jas. Addington
Davenport. His step-dau. mar.
Hon. Paul Dudley, Judge, son of
       Gov. Joseph D.

Anne, b. 1646, d. ——; mar.
Sam'l Moseley, a distinguish-
ed Captain in Philip's War.
Grand-dau. Rebecca m. John
Winthrop, LL.D., Prof H. C.
1738–1779. Gr. gr. son, Hon.
Judge James, d. 1821; Hon.
       William, 1875.

Rebec[
Daven[
D., Jud[
Gr. dau[
Gov. Jo[
1st Rev[
gr. d. C[
Benj. F[
    gal

Endicott, ⊤ Sarah Payton, dau.
b. 1640, │ Capt. B. and Mary
m. 1661, │ Greenough. Prob.
d. 1694. │ a dau. of Reginald
         │ De Peyton, Peyton
              Hall.

Elizabeth, b. 1651; m. 1668, Hon. J[
1st, Ag't to English Court, Judge,
Hon. Eliaba, 2d, Judge, &c., m. Jac[
gr. grand-dau. of Gov. Ed. Winslo[
dau. m. Judge Richard Saltonsta[ll]
son of Sir Richard. Gr. gr. gra[
Leverett, Pres. Mass. Senate, and [
              D. 1715.

Hon. John, F. R. S., Judge Sup. Court; Pres. H. C. ⊤ Margaret, dau. Jo[
16 years; b. 1662; m. 1697; d. 1724, æ. 62. │ Gen. Denison, gr.

ISHE

Leverett
barbation,
office of Hu

d. 1692; m.
Justice, &
of Th. H
Michael's,
D., son of
Bunker Hill
g. Prescott
uess, d. T
Hon. Fre

ary, b. 16.
4, Paul, so
hus Dudle
m. Fran
nd, Chief
Supreme
D. 169

T

wid. of
wier, m.
69.

Margar
mr. M
Portsmo

of   V
              I
              M
l,   E
C.   M
by   W

Mary B
Stephen
Mrs. L
ther

aroline C
Mary E

Vol. XII.   OCTOBER, 1858.   No. 4.

HERALDRY IN AMERICA.

It may seem a contradiction of terms to speak of so aristocratic an institution as heraldry as being of interest or value to democratic Americans; but a little reflection will show us how this science will be of vast importance to our genealogists.

Coats-of-arms may be divided into three classes,—first, those belonging to any man's ancestors, and used by them for a long time. This is the most important class, and in most cases the original cause of the adoption of the arms is not to be discovered, and we must trust to the strictness with which this privilege was formerly guarded, for a guarantee that the arms were justly appropriated.

The second class embraces such arms as have been granted by the Herald's College by royal command, as a reward for distinguished services to the state. These instances are comparatively rare, and are very honorable to the recipient.

The third class consists of the coats-of-arms granted by the Herald's College on payment of certain fees, which, though legal, are not of any value at present to the genealogist, and hardly a source of much comfort to the possessor. This class of coat armor has been a comparatively modern institution, though some instances are recorded of a date prior to the settlement of New England.

It is with the first class above enumerated that we have at present to deal. Though some abuses had crept into the system, it is a fair assertion to make that coats-of-arms, used prior to 1625, were generally the rightful property of the users.

If we find, then, any person using a seal with a shield thereon engraved, in New England, during the score of years following the first colonization of Plymouth and Massachusetts, we may fairly conclude his social position in England was among the gentry or yeomanry. Even in times subsequent to the date I have thus fixed, considerable reliance may be placed upon the use of seals, as affording a clue to trace a family. We must consider that the high moral sentiment of our forefathers, their cheerful acknowledgment of the different social distinctions, and even the lack of any conceivable motive for fraud, alike forbid the suspicion that any man here, in the early days of the Colony, would have wished or dared to use a coat-of-arms when he was not entitled to it.

Again, as these seals require a skill in cutting and setting them not possessed by any one here, I believe, before 1700, or perhaps 1750, the

19

appearance of a seal on the documents referring to the second or third generation, should not call for any expression of suspicion of its genuineness. It may well have happened that a Puritan, disregarding and undervaluing the deeds of his gallant and roystering ancestor, did not choose to use a seal which recalled his exploits; or where one had separated from a household of Cavalier relatives, he might have been loth to use an emblem which proclaimed his origin much more strongly than an identity of name. Yet in either case, his children or grand-children might use his seal, carefully transmitted as an heir-loom.

When wealth began to increase in the larger towns, and the seaports became the resort of visitors and officials from England, there no doubt sprang up here a desire on the part of the leading families to rival the heraldic glories of their guests. A man, apparently a herald-painter, appears to have visited New England a little while previous to the Revolution, and to have furnished all applicants with a tricking of their arms. I have not been able to learn his name,* and can only fix the date of his visit by tradition. His paintings—I speak from an inspection of a score or so—have all a palm branch on each side of the shield, and, entwined around the interlaced ends, is a wreath inscribed " By the name of —— " Jones, Brown, or the patronymic of his deluded patron, whatever it might be. In some cases he gave the arms used by an English family of the same name, but at others he boldly drew on his fancy, and depicted " gorgons and chimeras dire." I need hardly say that the only importance these documents have to the genealogist, is the vexatious reliance still placed on them, in some cases, by the present proprietors.

To revert to our first point, having settled what coats-of-arms—whether found as seals, embroidered by gentle fingers two centuries ago, or crowning some mossy tombstone—may be considered as proper evidences in a genealogical investigation, we have to inquire how valuable they will prove as evidence.

When we remember that the number of emigrants hither, whose previous habitation has been discovered, is but a very small proportion of the whole body, we shall recognize the importance of any clue, however faint, which shall aid our searches. On investigation it may be taken as a rule, that any given name found on our annals, with a few obvious exceptions, has not been represented in England by more than two or three distinct families of the required rank. Hence in any large " encyclopedia of heraldry," or any " armoury," we have, as it were, a large directory, whereby our labors may be much lessened. For example, JOHN GIFFARDE, of Lynn in 1683, used a seal bearing three lions in pale. Now these being the arms of the Giffords of ——, I should at once, in tracing his pedigree, turn my attention to that branch of the family, as the first and most important source to be searched.

These seals are by no means of unusual occurrence, and I have been mainly influenced to make these few notes in the hope of calling attention to the subject. Many autograph collectors will find the seal as well as the name on their cherished manuscripts. The early governors used their own coats-of-arms, as province seals on commissions, and similar documents, and several of them, like Bellemont and Hutchinson, are very large and richly emblazoned.

It is by no means a proof of the falsity of a coat-of-arms that it is not recorded in printed works like Burke's or Berry's volumes; there being

* His name is generally understood to have been —— Cole.—*Editor.*

no official record extant, these books can only verify those arms they record, not damn those they ignore.

In a few instances authentic documents are still extant confirming the right to bear these arms. Thus the WINTHROPS have a certificate, dated before 1600, acknowledging these claims. The MINERS of Connecticut have a curious pedigree; and several families have recently been successfully traced by H. G. Somerby, Esq., whose labors are well known to the readers of this magazine.

But I can state without fear of contradiction that any family, whose ancestor used a coat-of-arms, possesses a noble corner-stone to erect its English pedigree upon.

On the other hand, I cannot too strongly express my regret and surprise at the attempts daily made, by many, to assume a property not belonging to them. Many American genealogies, even the pages of this magazine, have been marred by the introduction of a coat-of-arms, to which the user had not a shadow of right.* A man using a coat-of-arms, by that act asserts that his ancestors have been of knightly rank, as contemporary evidence declare, or have so distinguished themselves as to receive from the crown permission to assume similar rank. An Englishman may be pardoned, perhaps, if he obtains by purchase a right to maintain a spurious ancestry—but for an American to take this dubious privilege without purchase, is too absurd to be tolerated.

It is useless to allege that a man has a right to use any badge he may like, to put on his carriage, his plate, or the covers of his books; he cannot hoist the revenue flag on his boat, and he should be equally debarred, by custom and the rules of society, from sailing under a false flag, as the proved descendant of a knightly race.

There is no cause for pride in the accident of one's birth, but it remains a fact; and if a Gradgrind deserts his principles and adopts a badge whereby he drops his honest and obscure parentage for a fictitious and more distinguished one, he should be arraigned by the collective body of genealogists, as trying, for the sake of increasing his own pomp and glory, to destroy the noble work of perpetuating our annals, for which they all labor. W. H. W.

WILL OF JOHN FFORD, OF MORRISTOWN, MORRIS CO., N. J.†

In the Name of god amen the Twenty Day of October One Thousand Seven hundred and Twenty and One I John Fford of Hnno [Hanover] in the County of Buntedon and Province of New Jersey Carpenter being Sick In body but of Sound and Perfect Memory thanks be to god and Calling to Remembrance the uncertain Estate of this Transitory life and that all men must Yeild unto Death when it Shall please god to Call Doe make and declare this my last will & Testimony In manner and forme as following first being Penitent and Sorry for all my Sins [&c.] for Settleing of my Temporell Estate and Such Goods and Chattles and Debts hath pleased god to bestow up me I doe order give and Dispose the Same as followeth that is to Say

------

* The Editors never assumed any responsibility in inserting arms furnished by contributors. The readers of the Register have more than once been cautioned in this matter.—*Editor.*

† This John Ford is probably the son of John of the Fortune, 1621, and grandson of widow Martha his mother.

Imprima I give and bequeath unto my Son Jacob Fford a certain Tract of Land being in the fore mentioned place Two hundred Acres of Land, And given to Joseph Herriman and a Brittain Kitchell In the aboe Said town & County the said Tract of Land wch the said Fford had of Mr Bod [Budd] and Likewise all my Lands Lying at Windem above new Norridge and Likewise my Cender Swamp In Duxbery In Matiutes [Massachusetts] bay and also half my Lands that Lyes at Quenebog up New London River, that falls to me by my father—

Item I give and bequeath unto my Son Samuel Fford all this plantation that on after his Mother decesse or day of Marriage agine Likewise the Other half of my Lands that falls to Me by my father at Quenebog.

Item I give and bequeath unto Experince Fford my daughter Fifty Pounds of Cur^t money of the Province to be p^d out of my movfabble Estate if two thirds of it be thought Sufficient by three Indifferent Persons if not to be paid out of Jacob Ffords Plantation, and Samuel Ffords Plantation Equeall between them, that is Twenty five pounds, each Brother, that is after She hath paid Debts there be anough to Pay fifty Pounds to Experience being Eighteen years of Age.

The next I give and bequeath unto my Well beloved Wife Elizabeth Fford whome I hereby I make one of my Executors all my Movfeable Estate and theof of this Plantation that I live on till Death, but if She Marry then to goe off the Plantⁿ that only to Carry away one third of the moveable that is then Left and the above Legesys are Given to them and their heirs and assigns for ever and Likewise I make and Leave mills to be Sold together wth the Rest of my Moveable Estate to the Paying of my Debts and Likewise I make my well beloved wife Executrex Jointly along wth Josiah Ogden of Nework of this my last will and Testimony

In Witness hereof I have herounto Set
my hand and Seal In the presents of Us   **John fford**

    { John Lindly
    { Jo: Hirriman
    { Eliz^a fford

                      Perth Amboy 17th ffob: 1721,
Then appeared Joseph Harriman one of the Evidences to ye within will Came before me Mich^l Kearney Surrogate Authorised & appointed to take ye Probatts of Wills who did depose on ye Holy Evangelist of almighty god that he saw ye within written Instrument to be his last will & testament & y^t att ye Same time he was of Sound mind & memory to the Best of his Knowledge & Saw ye other two Evidences Sign ye Same. Jurat Cora me Anno et die Supadictu.   Mich^l Kearney P Reg^t

Letters of adm^{on} were Granted by his Excellency Wm Burnet Esq &c unto the Executors w^{thin} mentioned who they having Quallifyed them Selves according to law to the true Execution thereof
Recorded in Liber A. Page 207. Trenton, N. J.   **Mich^l Kearney**

[I have the pleasure to inform those interested, that CORDON L. FORD, Professor of Anatomy in the University of the State of Michigan, at Ann Arbor, is engaged in collecting and writing the History and Genealogy of the Fords of this Continent, particularly of the United States. He will be happy to correspond with those who have an interest in the enterprise, and will receive any contributions of records, wills, histories and traditions concerning the Fords, which any may be pleased or able to make.
        Yours respectfully,   ALFRED VAIL.]

GLEANINGS.—NO. 2.

[By W. H. W.]

8.

Names.

On the Medford records will be found the following curious name, MENESIXO, daughter of Richard and Menesing Penhallow, born June, 1768.

At Lexington it is recorded that JONATHAN and CHERRY STONE had four children, born 1715—1723. The youngest was called Love.

I would make an inquiry, whether the name LOVISA, now sometimes seen, is not clearly a mispronunciation of LOUISA. I can well imagine some rather illiterate man seeing LOVISA (Louisa) on the tombstone of a deceased progenitress, and giving his child the same name, but pronouncing it as the modern pronunciation would require. I have known the name LOVICE given, but though usually pronounced the same, it was an Italian name, and given by a sailor to his child.

I have met the name LUSANNA, but its origin is beyond my ken. ANSTERS, thus pronounced, puzzled me much, until, in a recent genealogy, I found ANSTRUTHERS, a well-known Scottish family's name, was the proper spelling. REVILO would have been a most difficult name to trace to its derivation, had I not learned from the bearer that his father made the name by reversing OLIVER. MEPHIBOSHETH ADAMS was of Lexington in 1734. CIBLE BOWMAN I found, on examination, to be a SIBYL. MILLICENT, a most charming name, as well as EDITH, is sometimes found. ELIOT, as a Christian name, bespeaks the veneration of our ancestors for the " Apostle to the Indians." ELIOT BROWN, ELIOT REED and ELIOT WHITMORE are on our records; the latter, at least, a relative of the famous JOHN. BATHSHUA and AMMI-RUHAMAH must have been puzzles to the abbreviator. Mr. CUTTELLER would no doubt resent our present curtailment of his name to CUTLER. MIRIAM, as a family name, affords grounds for a suspicion of the origin of the race. ABRITTAI PHASSETT was, after all, only the gentle AMITY FASSET; but PHILLEBROWNE maintained the primitive spelling till a recent date. The marriage of MARRETT MUNROE and DELIVERANCE PARKER must have afforded the small wits of the day a rare chance for puns.

KETTLE was a name at Medford a century ago; LE BOSQUET, a French neutral, gave his name to a house long standing there. I have the name written by an inhabitant LEMMET, as being the modern method of spelling. GOLDEN MOORE was an early settler on the Mystic. ALLEN NEWHALL had LOVE for his wife. I have had letters from a VENUS, and know a TAMERLANE VITRUVIUS.

Almost any of our larger genealogies will give much stranger names than those I have noted.

9.

[From the original, in the possession of C. H. Morss.]

Leeds, Februare ye 21st 1661–2.

Mr. Wille Hubard,

Reverend Sr. After my servis presented to you, your deare Mother, and ye rest of yr family, these may satisfie you I reced. your letter, with

2 from your Bro. Mr. Ezek. and one from Elder Whippl, all which I must crave leave to anser in this; and according to your dissires for ye ending of strife, have taken oath, as you may see by ye inclosed, which I took before one of y⁰ masters in Chancere extraordinare, which cost me some payns & mony; but am glad I had an opportunitie to doe any servis for any of ye children of him who is with ye Lord, & I in my hart did-and doe so highly honor. It was a mersi to mee y⁴ ye substance of my oath I am see cleare in, for I well remember when I went about y⁴ business, I was carfull in this poym, y⁴ Mr. Ezekiel Rogers of Rowlay would expres what he would sertaynly doe for young Mr. Ezek., y⁴ soe his father might know what to trust to in ye making of his will. I know not what to add more on yr business y⁴ may bee of use to you, yn is expresed in yr oath; though I remember hee did expres something hee would doe toward his bringing up at ye Colledg, yet how much, & whether hee took not a liberti to doe as hee pleased him, I am not able punctualy to speak to. I may not trouble you more, but acquaint you y⁴ I & my wife & ye children are all in reasonable health, notwithstanding all y⁰ difficulties God hath been pleased to cary us through; for which wee dissire your help in thanksgiving to ye L⁴ y⁴ wee may never forget y⁰ wonderfull works of y⁰ L⁴. I had in my thoughts given ye sattan Cap Mr Ezek. writteth of, to Elder Whipple, but understand since, Mrs Rogers of Roulay hath taken it from Mrs Rainer; but seeing Mr Rogers refused it in his life time to whome it was sent, by what rule shee now doth it, I know not. I shall ade noo more, but humbly beg communion in your daly prayrs y⁴ y⁰ L⁴ would bee pleased to keepe us & make us faithfull to him (& ye light wee have received) to ye end, & Rest yours to serve,

Matthew Boyes.

10.

Note on the Lawrence and Page Families.

In the recently published Lawrence Genealogy—page 78—it is stated that Abel Lawrence (family No. 112) m. Abigail, daughter of Daniel Page of Groton. I am well assured, however, that the lady was the daughter of Samuel and Elizabeth Page of Medford, and was born Feb. 11, 1758, which date exactly tallies with her recorded age at her decease.

Samuel Page of Carolina m. Susanna Lawrence, May 20, 1719, at Medford,—perhaps the father of the foregoing. Abel Lawrence was great-grandson of John Lawrence of Groton, whose sister married a Samuel Page, probably about 1700. This connection, in three generations, between these two families, is certainly remarkable, unless the three Samuel Pages were in one line of descent.

11.

In the 11th volume of this work, page 315, I gave copies of some English wills relative to the Perkinses; and I now continue the series, tending to strengthen the tradition relative to the birthplace of the emigrant hither.

John Perkins of Minsterworth, will dated Aug. 7, 1614; wife Joan, daughter Dorothy.

Thomas Perkyns of Harthury, will proved April 12, 1602; wife *Felix*, son James.

Elizabeth Perkins of Hanbury, will proved Sept. 11, 1594; son-in-law
Richard Jeffries.

Easlington lies six miles south of Minsterworth, at which former place
were—

George Perkins, 1623, who had wife Joan, sons Walter and George,
and daughter Elizabeth, and mentions Roger, son of John Perkins,
deceased.

James Perkins of same place, 1630, and

Roger Perkins, 1633.

12.

[From the original in my possession.]

Loueing brother,

I have paid your bill Charged upon me of 100£ to Mrs. Banke, but
she was not at London but left her hand to an aquittance upon the bak-
side of the bill & a kinseman of hers rescived it & set downe for part of
payment for the farme at Marblehead, but (knew) not how much the
farm was sould for; but he said that she will pass your accounts & that
will be as well as that which you wrote to me aboute. I have alsoe taken
care that your bill for 40£ is paid. We are all in good health, thankes
be to God for it, but we pay great taxes by reason of the warrs with the
Dutch; how the successes are you will heere by the seamen better than
I can tell you. Good brother, remember my love to my sister, my brother
John & sister, my brother Davenport & my sister, & the rest of our
friends.

In hast I rest

Your loving brother   Robert Hathorne.

From Bray this 1 of Aprill, 1653.

Endorsed—" To your very Loueing Freind Wm Hathorne," and directed " ffor Mr. Tinker at Mr. William Willsheer's house, Ironmonger, at
the corner of pissing ally in Bredstreet, in London.

To his loueing brother Mr. William Hathorne at Salem in New England, deliver this."

13.

I have been much puzzled to trace the pedigree of the General who is
mentioned below. I have but little doubt that he was an Englishman, but
the pertinacity of some rumors to the contrary make me inquire if any
one can decide the point.

Gen. Edward Whitmore, July 17, 1747, seems to have received a
commission as lieutenant-colonel, 36th foot. 1759, he was colonel of the
22d foot, Lord Rollo being lieutenant-colonel, and —— Way, major.
1761, the same officers were in command, the regiment being at both
dates in America. At the siege of Louisborg, June 2, 1758, he arrived
from Halifax, and on the 8th, with the right wing, effected a landing.
July 27, he received a notice of the surrender of the garrison, and remained as governor of the town. In this capacity he issued a proclama-
tion, Nov. 22, 1758, dated at Boston, announcing that Louisborg would
be a free port for all fresh provisions. In February, 1761, he was
drowned in Plymouth harbor, as noted in Drake's History of Boston. His
property, delivered here, consisted of about £2,700 in specie and mov-

ables. A negro servant Jack is mentioned, as also his steward, James
Gray, and six other servants. He was buried from Hannah Cordis's
house, and among the expenses of his funeral are these items: Paid
Thomas Williston for himself and ten porters to attend the funeral; fourteen mourning rings; eight escutcheons; mourning badges for the Cadet
company.

In Mr. S. G. Drake's library there is an incomplete file of the Boston
Evening Post, which fortunately contains an account of Gov. W.'s funeral.
The first paper is dated Monday, Dec. 14, 1761, and says: "Yesterday
arrived here Capt. Church, in 13 Days from Louisburg, and informs us,
that his Excellency Brigadier General Whitmore, Governor of that Place,
and Colonel of the 22d Regiment of Foot, embark'd on board his Vessel
in order to proceed hither, but that by contrary Winds they were obliged
to put into Plymouth last Friday, when between 11 and 12 o'Clock at
Night, his Excellency occasionally going upon Deck, he by some Accident fell overboard, and was unfortunately drowned, no Body being upon
Deck to give him any assistance; his Body was taken up the next Morning near the Gurnet and is bro't up by Capt. Church, in order for a decent
Interment. The Jury of Inquest who sat upon his Excellency's Body
yesterday, bro't in their Verdict, Accidental Death."

The next paper, dated Dec. 21, 1761, gives the following account of
his funeral:—

"On Wednesday last the Corps of Major-General Whitmore was interred in the King's Chapel with all the Honors which this town could
give. The Procession went from the Town House to the King's Chapel
in the following Manner:

A Party of the Troop of Horse-Guards,
The Company of Cadets,
The Officers of the Regiment of Militia,
The officiating Ministers,
The Corps,
(The Pall supported by six regular Officers,)
The Chief Mourners,
The Governor and Lieutenant Governor,
The Council,
The Judges,
Justices,
Ministers,
The principal Gentlemen of the Town,
A great Number of Coaches & Chariots closed the Procession.

"During the whole Procession, Minute Guns were fired to the amount
of 70, being the Number of Years of the General's Age. The Corps
was placed in the middle of the King's Chapel, whilst Part of the Funeral
Service was performed, and was from thence carried into the Vaults below and there interred. Whilst the last service was performing the
Cadets fired three Vollies."

LAWRENCE WATERS of Watertown, about 1630, afterwards of Lancaster and Charlestown. Information wanted respecting him and his
descendants. Address E. S. Waters, 87 Commercial Street, Boston.

WILLIAMS FAMILY.

[By D. W. Hoyt.]

The writer is descended from HENRY WILLIAMS, who married Deborah Davis in Haverhill, Dec. 5, 1726, and settled at once in Amesbury, West Parish, where he had eight children, and died in 1750 or 1751. The object of the present article is to ascertain the ancestry of this Henry Williams. Below will be found all the information which the writer has been able to gather respecting the earliest Williams families of that region. Any additional items will be thankfully received, and may be sent to the editor of the Register.

(1) JOHN[1] WILLIAMS moved from Newbury to Haverhill about 1643, and resided in Haverhill till his death, Feb. 10, 1673–4. His widow, Jane, died Nov. 21, 1680. In his will, dated Dec. 9, 1670, proved 1673–4, he mentions his children John, Joseph, Mary and Lydia, and his daughter Sarah's child, Sarah Eyers. The births of Mary and Lydia were recorded at Newbury, Lydia and Joseph at Haverhill.

Children of (1) John[1] and Jane Williams.

(2) I. SARAH,[2] b. ——; m. John Ayer (or Eyers), Jr., at Haverhill, May 5, 1646. [It is possible that she may have been the child of a previous wife, as she must have been ten or fifteen years older than Mary.]

(3) II. JOHN,[2] b. ——; m. 1st, Rebecca Colby, Sept. 9, 1661(?); and 2d, Widow Esther Bond, May 5, 1675. Wife Rebecca d. June 10, 1672. He d. April 30, 1698, his widow surviving him. He and his brother Joseph took the oath of allegiance and fidelity at Haverhill, Nov. 28, 1677. He resided in Haverhill, and undoubtedly died there. [It will be seen that the date given in Coffin's History of Newbury is incorrect. It was John, Sen., who d. in 1674.]

(4) III. MARY,[2] b. Sept. 20, 1641; probably m. Daniel Bradley, at Haverhill, May 21, 1662.

(5) IV. LYDIA,[2] b. March 15 or 16, 1642–3 [15 on Newbury and 16 on Haverhill and Old Norfolk records.] Her name was Lydia *Williams* in 1677; hence she was probably unmarried at that time.

(6) V. JOSEPH,[2] b. April 18, 1647; m. Mary Fuller " of Bastable," Nov. 18, 1674 (15). He lived in Haverhill. The last trace we find of him there, however, is the record of the birth of a child in 1683.

Children of (3) John[2] and Rebecca Williams.

(7) I. SARAH,[3] b. June 27, 1662; m. Joseph Bond, at Haverhill, Nov. 26, 1679.

(8) II. MARY,[3] b. Nov. 24, 1663. A Mary Williams m. Thomas Silver, Dec. 28, 1681, by the Haverhill records, but Jan. 4, 1681–2 by the Newbury records.

(9) III. A DAUGHTER,[3] b. May, 1666. A *Rebecca* Williams m. Samuel Marble, at Haverhill, Oct. 14, 1686.

(10) IV. A DAUGHTER,[3] b. Aug. 1, 1668; d. same month.

(11) V. MERCY,[3] b. Dec. 4, 1669.

(12) VI. SUSANNA,[3] b. April 11, 1672.

Children of (6) *Joseph⁵ and Mary Williams.*

(13)　　I. SARAH,⁶ b. Nov. 17, 1675.
(14)　　II. MARY,⁶ b. Nov. 29, 1677.
(15)　　III. JOHN,⁶ b. Feb. 17, 1679.
(16)　　IV. HANNAH,⁶ b. Sept. 30, 1683.

A marriage is recorded at Newbury between Daniel Jaques and Mary Williams, March 20, 1692-3.

The following entries are also taken from the Newbury records; but we are unable to say whether Thomas and Richard were brothers, or whether they were at all connected with the families given above.

Thomas Williams m. Mary Lowle, dau. of Serj. Benj. Lowle of Newbury, Jan. 15, 1695-6. Wife Mary d. Dec. 31, 1711. A Thomas Williams, probably the same one, m. Ruth Woodman, Dec. 30, 1713.

Children of Thomas and Mary Williams.

　I. MARY, b. July 2, 1697.
　II. HENRY, b. Sept. 27, 1699. [Is this the one who m. Deborah Davis, in 1726, and settled in Amesbury?]
　III. HANNAH, b. May 4, 1701.
　IV. ABIGAIL, b. June 4, 1703.
　V. SARAH, b. Dec. 27, 1705.
　VI. JUDITH, b. Dec. 7, 1707.
　VII. BENJAMIN, b. May, 1706 (?).
　VIII. THOMAS, b. June 24, 1710.

Richard Williams m. Ruth Rogers, June 11, 1703.

Children of Richard and Ruth Williams.

　I. RICHARD, b. April 6, 1704.　　　V. ISAAC, b. Nov. 15, 1711.
　II. JOHN, b. April 29, 1706.　　　VI. DANIEL, b. Aug. 9, 1715.
　III. THOMAS, b. Aug. 13, 1708.　　VII. RUTH, b. Aug. 13, 1716.
　IV. THOMAS, b. Aug. 9, 1709.

It would appear that the last two families could not have been descended from (1) John¹ of Newbury and Haverhill; for the only male descendant of the third generation was (15) John,⁶ unless (6) Joseph⁵ had a son born later than 1683. Both Thomas and Richard were probably born prior to 1683.

WILL OF HUMPHREY GILBERT.

[From the Probate Office, Salem, Mass., (not in the " regular files.") Communicated by Mr. E. S. WATERS.]

HUMPHREY GILBERT of Ipswich Mass⁸ makes his will " Ye 14ᵗʰ of ye 12 mo 1657," and gives property to his son John, to his four daughters, to his daughters Abigail and Hester, unto his dear wife Elizabeth, &c.

Administration was granted to Elizabeth Gilbert, widow of the above, ye 30ᵗʰ of March 1658.

On the margin of the paper is written, " In case my son shall die in his nonage, his portion is to be equally divided among my daughters."

The Inventory of said Humphrey was taken ye 10ᵗʰ of ye 6ᵗʰ mo, 1658.

ORIGINAL LETTER OF THE REV. JONATHAN PARSONS.

[Communicated by Samuel H. Parsons, Esq., of Middletown, Ct.]

Newbury, Jan'y 8, 1749–50.

Very Dear & Hon^{ed} Sir,

The News of your being ship'd and gone for England was quite unexpected & very surprising to me, (tho I heard three or four months ago you talk'd of such an undertaking) Because I had enquired of Justice Griswold who was at my House not long since, and he told me that he thought there was nothing at all in it. I wish God may give you a prosperous voyage & Favour in ye sight of our Rightful & Gracious Sovreign King George, in all matters that you shall sprend before him agreeable to Righteousness: and I have no Jealousie that you will ask for any things in your own or others behalf but what you think so. As soon as I thought of writing I long'd to hear of ye particular circumstances of your Family & friends, that I might write to you of them, tho' you so lately took your leave of them, but I could hear nothing in particular tho Capt. Sheldon of Lyme wrote me a Letter ye 28th of Dec^r, wherein he signifies y^t it is a General time of Health in those parts. What affairs you are entrusted with to take up your time & employ your great abilities I know not, but I can't think you would so embarrass yourself with business as to take you quite off from speaking a word in ye Dear Cause of Liberty of Conscience, if a fair opportunity presented, you have often espoused in Connecticut Assemblies, as well as more privately, with arguments y^t can never be answered any other way than by a Majority of Hands. And if need be, I persuade myself y^t you will not be silent upon y^t Head, now you are on ye other side of ye water.

With these Hopes, Hon^{ed} Sir, I am encouraged & beg leave to lay before you some few hints of ye Circumstances of a considerable Congregation of Presbyterians in Newbury with whom I am settled as their Pastor by ye Concurrence of ye Presbytery of Boston. They are a People constantly harrassed by ye Parishes wherein they Dwell on account of Taxes towards the support of those ministers in ye Independent Churches on whose ministry they cannot attend; and can't get any relief from ye General Court of this Province, tho they have frequently sought for ye same, they seem'd very loath to expose the Conduct of the Province in such an affair, & therefore waited with long Patience & went often with prayers to ye Assembly. But since they find no Intreaties will prevail, they have, after seeking to ye Father of Light for Direction, Unanimously agreed that Duty to God, themselves & their fellow sufferers obliged them to prefer an Humble Address to our gracious Sovreign imploring ye Interposition of his Wisdom & Authority & to leave the Event to God.

I am sure you'l allow me to speak a word or two about ye People, since it is on such an occasion; and I have had more than four years opportunity to observe them; They appear upon this long acquaintance, to be a kind, well Disposed, peaceable people in General; and a great number of them are in a Judgment of Charity, solid & excellent Christians. Some of them are esteemed ye most capable men for Publick Business of any in this Great Town, and even their adversaries thro' necessity are glad to make use of them in ye most Difficult Affairs of a Temporall nature which they meet with. And as to their Religion, they are not among ye number of those wild, frekish People y^t are scattered about in some parts of ye Country, but seem to be as careful to avoid an Apish sort of Religion, as any Congregation that I know. Their withdrawal from ye former places of Publick Worship was more than seven years ago, & was then & is still look'd upon Warrantable by some of ye most substantial ministers in Town & Country, as I could easily make appear were it needful. And as to their Temporal Circumstances, some of them are, I suppose, as wealthy as any in Newbury, except some of ye Church of England. Others are Honest, Industrious People; but some are poor, & particularly we have many Poor Widows, left so by ye Death of their Husbands in Cape Breton Expedition. Perhaps we have more Poor Widows than there is in several of ye other Congregations in Town put together; for the People tell me it appears by ye List that more went from our Congregation upon that Expedition than from all ye Congregations besides, altho there are seven Worshipping Assemblies in all besides our Church.

These things In General, I think represent ye Disposition, Conduct, & Temporal Circumstances of ye People—And these people are drem up in Bear-Skins & worried by their fellow creatures, their money is taken from them, some have their goods sold for a song; their bodies drag'd thro' ye Streets & imprison'd with a " *Lie you there till you have paid ye uttermost farthing.*" I dont remember to have met with any instances, in ye History of New England equal to what I have seen of this nature with my Eyes, except ye strange treatment of ye Quakers; And it all arises from no other cause than ye Lusts of Men; unless the Conscientious Scruples of our people, (all things considered) refusing to help their neighbors support those ministers on whose ministry they never attend, may be called a cause. Tis enough to move an heart of Stone to see one's neighbors, but especially to see sober, honest & pious friends, Drig'd about upon ye ground, thrown into Carts or upon Sleds & hall'd to Prison by fellow Protestants who have no better claim to Liberty of Conscience than their oppressed Brethren. If I understand our charter, the Usage that I have seen & ye Language that at such seasons are not fit to be named among a professing People. My Heart dreads the doleful consequences that must follow such things unless God in Mercy prevent. And can you, Honored Sir, hear a sketch of these things & not exert yourself in favour of ye oppressed to ye utmost of your power, if God should give you an opportunity? I am sure you cannot. I know your Attachment to Liberty too well, to think you would not do every thing that appear'd proper to be done by you, upon all seasonable opportunities & before all men. I have still a grateful remembrance of your indefatigable efforts with the Court in Connecticut for the Liberty of the People, & Remember ye Thanks which ye Government gave you for ye same. Had some gentlemen laid by all prejudice, a great deal of ye Confusions that have arisen about Religion had never been known: Will you, Dear Sir, Nay can you forget ye miserable State that your Mother Country is coming into thro oppression, merely from violences used for conscientious scruples in matters of Religion? Now you have crossed the Ocean and are at an higher Board than any here, only look back upon us, & think how many, directly against Charter Privileges, are Rending their fellow servants to pieces, because they dont see with their eyes; Have you the Bowels of a Father & ye abilities of a Master? Surely ye one will be burned within you, & ye other you will make use, for ye Relief of Distressed Children! I am persuaded that our gracious Sovereign ye King

has not any subjects more Dutiful, nor more strictly attached to ye House
of *Hanover* than those that are trampled upon in the manner that I have
related ; and if you should exert yourself in some proper way for their
help, I think it will be a clear Evidence of your approving the Happy
Establishment in that Illustrious Family ; And besides there is Reason to
hope that you will do more service for God & your Country by using
your Interest and Influence for the redress of this Evil, while you are
waiting His Majesty's Pleasure, than you can possibly do in a neglect.
I believe you think that Abundance of that wildness which has prevailed in
C——t and spread from thence, has been very much owing to ye Strange
proceedings of some Courts with ye People that were called New Lights ;
and there is Danger in this Province not only on ye one hand, of an Increase of ye like Evils, but on ye other of ye most open & growing contempt of all Religion by Multitudes, unless the Lord should help us
respecting ye article of Liberty & ye King's most Excellent Majesty
should be most graciously pleased to discharge us from supporting a
Ministry which we. think is not safe & which we can't in Conscience
attend upon.   Therefore I beseech you once more, Honrd Sir, for God's
Sake, for Religion's Sake, & for the sake of y^r Peace and Happiness of
the People that you would (as need may call for it) kindly interpose &
help us in these matters ; Our Committee have mentioned you to Mr.
Parbridge who is Agent for us before the King in Council ; & probably
he will show you their Letter, if you should have an Inclination to see it.

I wrote to Dr *Avery* in ye Fall of the year, & if he should think worth
while to take notice of us, you will be able to let him know who I am,
and what you apprehend of me, if you think proper ; I ask no favor but y^e
naked Truth, and that you will speak if you say any thing.   Herewith I
send you a true copy of the Recommendation which Mr Beckwirth drew
up, & both ye ministers of Lyme sign'd it just as I was taking my Leave
of those parts & expected to go & Preach at Newbury where I am since
settled.   You'l see that y^r Recommendation refers to a Council which
gave me my Liberation.   Perhaps you may see some occasion to Improve
it, & if not it may lie with other waste paper.

That you may be continued for a Blessing to ye World—may be
abundantly succeeded at ye Court of Great Britain—find much favour in
ye sight of our Gracious King & be Returned safely to your Native Country for a Greater Blessing than ever, is the Prayer of Hon^d Sir your most
obedient Son & Servant,   Jonathan Parsons.
    P. S.   Salute Dr. Avery for me and all other Friends.
Yrs ut supra.
Excuse my using a Clerk to write over my Letter from my short hand ;
The want of Time obliged me to do it.
    To Elisha Williams, Esq., London, England.
    (Answered by Mr. Williams, August 11, 1750.)

    (Note.)—" Elisha Williams, Esq.," (to whom the preceding letter was
addressed,) was the son of the Rev. William Williams of Hatfield.   He
was born August 24, 1694, graduated at Harvard College, 1711 ; studied
Divinity with his father, and was ordained as a minister in Newington, in
Wethersfield, Conn., October 22, 1722.   After his marriage with Eunice
Chester of Wethersfield, he studied law and was frequently elected a
member of the Legislature from Wethersfield.   In 1726 he was installed
Rector of Yale College, the duties of which he faithfully discharged until
1739, when ill health obliged him to resign.   He returned to Wethers-
field and was elected to the Legislature, and appointed Judge of the

Superior Court.   Afterwards he was appointed Chaplain of the Regiment
sent by the State of Connecticut to Cape Breton, and was subsequently
appointed to the command of a regiment of one thousand men in an
intended expedition against Canada. *In December, 1749, he went to
England to receive the wages due to himself and his regiment.* While
there his wife died, and before his return he married Miss Elizabeth
Scott, daughter of the Rev. Thomas Scott, of Norwich, England. He
returned home in April, 1752, and died 24th, 1755, as will appear by the
following inscription in the burial ground at Wethersfield :—

"The Honb'le Col'l Elisha Williams, shin'd in excelling Gifts of
Nature, Learning, and Grace, in Benevolence universal. Firm in Friendship, in Conversation pleasant and Instructive. In Religion Sincere, un-
affected, cheerful ; Truly Humble, of conjugal & Parental Affection, and
Humanity. A Wise, Great & Good Man. 5 Years he was an Hon'r to
the Sacred Ministry, in Newington. 13 years Yale College flourished
under his Pious, Learned, & Faitbful Instruction and happy Govern't ;
the Glory of ye College & Ornament of his Country. .He often filled &
adorned several Civil & Military Characters. Heaven claimed what was
Immortal that Glad obeyed, & dross'd here the Dust to Rest till Jesus
comes. Obiit 25th July 1755, Ætatis 61 yrs."

Trumbull, in his History of Connecticut, Vol. II., p. 303, says of Mr. Williams : " He was well furnished with academical literature, was a thorough
Calvinist, and is characterized as one of the best of men." Dr. Doddridge,
in a letter to a friend, writes thus : " I look upon Col. Williams to be one
of the most valuable men upon earth ; he has joined to an ardent sense of
religion, solid learning, consummate prudence, great candor, and sweet-
ness of temper."

He published a Sermon on Divine Grace, 1727. A Sermon on the
death of Thomas Ruggles, 1728 ; and a Pamphlet of 66 pages, entitled
" The Essential Rights and Liberties of Protestants."

The Society, of which the Rev. Jonathan Parsons was the first Pastor,
had its origin in the time of the great excitement produced by the labors
of Edwards, Whitefield and others, one of whom was the Rev. Joseph
Adams, who preached to the new Society, consisting at first of only 12
families, until by the advice and commendation of Whitefield, Mr. Parsons
was called from Lyme, Conn. (where he had been settled as a Minister
from March, 1731, till October, 1745,) to take charge of the new Society.
In November of the same year he came to Newbury, and took the Charge
of the Congregation in March, 1746, &c. In this Church, which from
small beginnings arose to be one of the most numerous on the Continent,
Mr. Parsons labored with great diligence and success until his death in
1776, when he was buried by the side of his friend Whitefield, beneath
the pulpit which he had for so many years occupied.

For a more particular account of the establishment and origin of the
First Presbyterian Church in Newburyport, Mass., see

"Cushing's History of Newburyport, p. 53."

"Coffin's History of Newbury."

"Historical Account of the First Presbyterian Church by the Rev.
Samuel P. Williams, who was installed Feb. 18, 1821."

" Rev. Mr. Searle' Funeral Sermon on the death of Mr. Parsons."

" Rev. Jonathan Greenleaf's Memoir of Mr. Parsons, and Rev. Mr.
Sprague's Biographical Sketches of the Presbyterian Clergymen of the
United States." See, also, Vol. I., p. 272, of N. E. Gen. Register.

S. H. P.

MODE OF PROCEEDING IN THE SETTLEMENT OF ESTATES,

In the early period of Rhode Island's History, from the Records and Files in the office at Warwick.

[Copied for the Register by the Hon. G. A. Brayton.]

Warwick the 14*th of May* 1656

Mr James Greene Walter Tod and Henry Reddocke being desired to scan and value the estate of Robert Potter lately deceased have to the best of our understandings brought in a true inventory of cattels and moveable goods and moneys and we find that it amounts to forty and two pounds and ten shillings besides his housing and lands which we leeve to the consideration of the Counsell to determine as they shall find cause

Also John Potter the sone of Robert Potter late deceased is to be maintained in apparel for four years out of the estate above mentioned.

We also find that the said Robert Potter lately deceased is engaged in New England as appeareth to us to be in debt the sum of Twenty and nyne pounds and twelve shillings besides other uncertaine debts which are not yet brought in

Moreover we find him to be engaged to the wife of Captaine Lawton for twenty pounds borrowed of Capt Lawton in his life time in the year 1646 which is not yet paid with the use annexed for ten years time which likewise we leave to the consideration of the counsell.

June the 11*th*

Ordered by the Town Counsell Whereas Mr Robert Potter of Warwick lately deceased died engaged and this   Counsell fynding not estate to discharge the debts without selling house and land.

Therefore the Town Counsell do further order Mr Houlden and Mr Holliman to make sale of the aforesaid housing and land and to give in a just account unto the rest of the Town Counsell further to dispose of it

Ordered by the Town Counsel that the visible houschold goods contained in the inventory with the cattel and hogs is given by the Counsel as a legacy unto Sara Potter the wife of the late deceased Robert Potter to dispose of as she shall think fit.

Whereas Sara Potter the wife of Robert Potter lately deceased intestate hath without order from the Counsel seazed upon the house and turned out a tenent set in by them as also without their order sould and desposed of goods and receaved some debts whereupon they conceave she is engaged for administrator

The Town Counsell having formerly disposed of the estate of Robert Cole lately deceased and having allotted out the portions of the children ordered that the lands and meadows together with the pasturage on the South side of Patuxet River and the North lyne bound of Warwick bound is allotted out for security of Nathaniel Cole Robert Cole and Sara Cole their portions amounting to the sum of six score pounds

Further ordered that the Mill of Warwick being a part of the estate of

the late deceased Robert Cole is alloted out for security of Daniel Cole
his portion being fiftie pounds.

Randall Houlden Dep
Ezekiel Hollyman Ass
John Weckes
Henry Reddocke
Stukely Westcote
Richard Carder

Whereas it is true that this Collony of Rhode Island and Providence
plantations : out of their great care of the well orderings of all things in
every respective town therein for the good of the whole bodie polliticke
have not only formerly inacted but now of late renewed and confirmed
the same aize, his magesties Royal Charter or Letters Patents appeared
amongst us viz that every Respective town Counsell to observe the state
of things within their perticular precincts and act and perform in all things
for the well orderings and accomplishing of the affairs of the Town in all
such matters as may not entreach upon any publick or general office or
officer but may with conveniency prevent a more publick trouble and
further needless charge.

And Whereas the said Town Counsell is ordered in particular and in a
special manner to have care of the well orderings and execution of the
will and testament of the deceased.

As also that if any shall die intestate that then the Counsell of that
respective town shall with all conveniency take into consideration that
parties estate so dying and draw up a true inventory of the estate and
according to the family kindred or friends of the party so deceased dispose bequeath and distribute the whole estate and draw up a writing
thereof and commit it to the records of that respective town where the
partie deceased was an inhabitant which writing shall stand and bee au-
thentick for the will of the dead.

And Whereas in the Town of Warwick Ruffus Barton an inhabitant
thereof died without making any Will or testament in the year 1648, at
which time the Town Counsel consisted of Ezekiel Hollyman Samuel
Gorton John Greene John Wickes Randal Houlden and John Warren who
according to the order of the Collony and trust comited unto them did
forthwith take an inventory of the estate of the said Ruffus Barton and
did orderly bequeath distribute and dispose of the whole estate and by
joint consent drew upp a writinge of maner and form thereof comiting it
to the records of the aforesayd town of Warwick as the last will and
Testament of the above named Ruffus Barton.

And Whereas the heir of the lands belonging to the said Ruffus Barton
in his lifetime hath made his complaint now in the time of nonage unto
those who were appointed overseers of the execution of the will guardians
and feoffees in trust for the disposing of the children of the sayed diseased and their estates during the time of their orphansie and nonage
namely John Smith Sam: Gorton and Randall Houlden and the sayed
heir finding himself much greeved for violence already don unto him and
insufferable wrong threatened for the future upon his complaint, the feoffees in trust having recours to the records for his relief they find that
the records are Imboismled either through negligence or willfulness so as
the will of the diseased will not be found.

Whereupon the Counsell of the town of Warwick now in beeing are constrained according to their engaged and trust comitted unto them to renew the writing and will of the above named Ruffus Barton as neere as it was before as can possibly be that of the Counsell now in being, being the same that were of the Counsell in the year of the deceased partie.

Which last will and Testament is as follows

We do by these presents allow give appoint and bequeath unto the three children of the deceased Ruffus Barton the whole and entire sum of four score and ten pounds of lawful money of England to be payd in maner and form as followeth   That is to say to Benjamin Barton the sum of thirtie pounds to be payd unto him when he shall come to the full age of one and twentie years.

To Elizabeth Barton thirtie pounds when she shall come to the age of eighteen years or upon the day of her marriage in case she marry before that time.

To ffebie Barton the sum of thirtie pounds when she shall come to the age of eighteen years or upon the day of her marriage in case she marry before that time.

And for the house out houses lands priveledges cituate and being in and about the town of Warwick and parts adjacent the late right of the deceased Ruffus Barton we do appoint and consigne unto Benjamin Barton son and heir of the sayd deceased Ruffus Barton as his right and always provided that Margret Barton widow and late wife of the sayd Ruffus Barton shall injoy one third part of housing lands and appurtenances thereto belonging during the tyme of her widowhood   As also to enjoy the use of the whole estates for the present for the profit education and well bringe up of the above mayd children.

And to prevent any imbesseleing of the estates ill usage of the children or negligence in the imployment of the estate for the benefit of the children we do appoynt and ordain three men as gardians and feoffies in trust namely John Smith Samuel Gorton and Randle Houlden that in case they shall perceive any want of diligence, neglect of the children or ill usage of them and the estate it shall be lawful for the sayd feoffies or any two of them to call for and possess themselves of any or of all the children together with their estates apointed as abovesayd and shall dispose of it and of them as they in their wisdom shall see meete and convenient according to the intent and trust comited unto them.

And the said feoffees shall take bond of Margrett Barton widow late wife of Ruffus Barton for the due performance of all intents and purposes as above sayd

As also that the feoffies in trust shall take care that the above mayd heir Benjamin Barton be possessed of his inheritance at the time of his coming to the full age of one and twentie years

Signed by ye order and apointment of the Counsell of the Towne of Warwick the 20th of March 1666

Edmund Calverly
Clerk of ye Counsell

The Counsell being met againe on the 27th of Sept 1659 about ordering concerning the estate of Mr Ezekiel Holliman having finished a will do in the first place order that it be kept upon record and that those whom it may concern may have coppies thereof paying for it   wee likewise appoint that John Greene doe declare unto Mrs Mary Holliman that the counsell have so perfected matters that they expect her to come before them to hear what is done if shee bee of ability to morrow morning being the 28th day of the instant

Ordered by the Counsell that the charge of the meeting of the Counsell being twenty four shillings sixpence for expense of writing and the house of meeting et cetera be equally payd out of the estate.

At a meeting of the Counsell the 5th of October ordered by the Counsell that two of the Counsell namely Mr John Wickes and John Greene do forthwith go unto Mrs Mary Holliman and publish the will unto her and demand of her whether she will accept to be executrix according to the tenure of the sayd will made by the Counsell for Ezekiel Holliman aforesaid or refuse to bear the sayd will then the Counsell will take it for granted that she refuseth to be executrix and accordingly wait for a speedy answer having already long wayted to the spoyling of some of the estate. The return of the answer is that Mary Holliman abovesayd accepteth to be executrix which answer is sent in by Thomas Ralph.

See original will.

Wee the towne Counsell of Warwick being assembled the 15th of February 1695 at the house of Capt Peter Greene upon the application by petition presented unto us by Samuel Stafford and Abraham Lockwood in behalf of the widow Deborah Westcot concerning a controversie raised concerning the estate of Mr Stukely Westcot late of Warwick deceased which estate the abovesaid widow hath been peaceably possessed on several years past, and to make the matter more plainly appeare before the Counsell have produced the last will and testament of the said Stukely Westcot deceased as being proved by three positive testimonies taken before Major John Greene Deputy Governor the first of Novembr 1695 Whereupon the present Town Counsell saw cause to peruse what had bin done by the former Counsell in the year 1677 January the eleventh and upon examination of the matter do find that the Counsell then through a misunderstanding being ignorant of the law of England that aproves of a will so made and witnessed thereto although a person be disabled to signe and seal thereunto shall be effectual and also wee being better informed that the town Counsell have not power to dispose of lands in case a person had died intestate But the Counsell taking the matter into their serious consideration concerning the written will bearing date January 12th 1677 and attested before the Deputy Governor John Greene the first of Novembr 1695 by three witnesses We cannot but declare our opinions that it is a sufficient probation thereof

John Greene Dep Govr [L S]
Benjamin Smith   [L S]
Benjamin Barton   [L S]
Thomas Greene   [L S]
Peter Greene   [L S]
Randall Holden   [L S]

LONGEVITY.—The recent statement of remarkable longevity in the family of the Almys, in Rhode Island—the average age of six of the family being more than 80 years—has called out a statement in regard to the longevity of the children of William Clark of Townsend, Mass. He had twelve children, one of whom died at the age of 16. Of the other eleven, five are now living at ages ranging from 80 to 79 years. The united ages of those who have died and of those who are living is 926 years, and the average for the eleven is 84 years and nearly 8 months.—May 8, 1845.

INSCRIPTIONS IN THE OLD CEMETERY IN STONEHAM, MS.

[Copied for the Register, by Rev. JOHN A. VINTON of South Boston.]

Erected in memory of Mr. Daniel Gould, who died March 14, 1797, Etat 73.

In memory of Mrs Mary Gould, wife of Mr. Daniel Gould, who died of the small pox, June 3, 1793, in the 52d year of her age.

In memory of Mr. Ebenezer Gould, who died Aug. 8, 1790, in 55th year of his age.

Here lyes the Body of Mrs. Ruth Gould, Wife to Mr. Daniel Gould 3d, who Departed this Life August the 22d, 1758, Aged 27 years & 13 Days.

In memory of Lieut. Daniel Gould, who died March 8, 1788, aged 100 years.

Here lyes ye Body of Mrs Susanna Gould, Wife to Lieut. Daniel Gould, who died March 29, 1757, in the 67 year of her age.

Joseph Gould, son of Daniel & Susanna Gould, Died Sept. ye 25, 1730, aged 1 year, 7mo. 22 Dr.

All the foregoing are enclosed by an Iron Railing, or fence.

In memory of Miss Mary Gould, Daur of Mr David & Mrs Dorcas Gould, who died Janry 21, 1791, aged 18.

Here lyes ye Body of Mrs Dorcas Gould, Wife to Mr Daniel Gould, who died June 5, 1730, in ye 74 yr of her age.

Here lyes Buried the Body of Mr David Gould, Who departed this life April ye 3d, 1760, in ye 69 Year of His Age.

Here Lyes ye Body of Mrs Elizabeth Gould, Wife to Mr David Gould, who Died April ye 18th, 1753, in yr 64th Year of Her Age.

In memory of Mrs Elizabeth, wife of Mr Jacob Gould, who died Aug. 6, 1775, Act. 44.

In memory of Mr Abraham Gould, who Deceased Sept. 4, 1776, in the 84th year of his age.

Here lyes ye Body of Mrs Mary Gould, Wife of Mr Abraham Gould, who departed this life August the 5th, 1764, Aged About 65 years.

In memory of Caleb Richardson, son of Mr Caleb and Mrs. Sarah Richardson, who died April 28, 1772, Aged 10 Months and 2 days.

Here lies Buried the Body of Mr Reuben Richardson, who departed this life Decemr 22d, 1776, in ye 73d Year of His Age.

Sacred to the Memory of Mrs. Abigail Cleaveland, wife of the Rev. John Cleaveland, who died June 3d, 1793, Aged 41 Years, 11 Months, & 10 Days.

Mrs. Abigail Oliver, who here sleeps in death, was the wife of Capt. James Oliver, and Daur of Col. Joseph and Mrs. Abigail Bryant, who died July 3, 1791, Aged 35 Years, 1 month, & 9 days.

Joseph Bryant Oliver, son to Capt. James & Mrs Abigail Oliver, Grandson to Col. Joseph & Mrs Abigail Bryant, died Nov. 25th, 1790, aged 6 months & 18 days.

In memory of Mrs Lucy Osgood, wife of Mr John Fisk Osgood of Boston, who departed this Life, March the 5th, 1776, Aged 31 Years.

Mrs Lydia Nichols, 1776.

Here lyes ye Body of John Hadley, son of Mr Anthony & Mrs Abigail Hadley, who Died Sept. 18, 1746, Aged 1 Year, 4 Mon. & 8 Dr.

Here lyes ye Body of Anna Holdin, Wife to Samuel Holdin, who Died June yr 18th, 1731, Aged 72 Years.

Here Lyes Buried y⁰ Body of Ensig⁰ Timothy Baldwin, who Departed this life Decem⁰ y⁰ 3ᵈ A. D. 1750, Aged 61 Years & 13 Da⁰.

In Memory of Miss Mary Vinton, Dauᵗ of Mʳ Thomas & Mᵐ Mary Vinton, who died Feb⁰ʸ 16ᵗʰ, 1791, Aet. 17 Years, 4 Months, 18 days.

Here lyes Buried the Body of Mʳ Thomas Vinton, Who dparted this life, March 22ᵈ, 1763, in y⁰ 46ᵗʰ Year of His Age.

Here lyes y⁰ body of Mⁿ Hannah Knight, Wife to Mʳ Daniel Knight, who Departed this Life May y⁰ 14ᵗʰ, 1763, in y⁰ 25ᵗʰ Year of Her Age.

In memory of Mrs. Abigail Gould, the wife of Des⁰ Daniel Gould, who Died Jan⁰ʸ, 1771, in the 65 year of her agn.

Erected in memory of Des⁰ Daniel Gould, who departed this Life, March 7ᵗʰ, 1761, in the 79ᵗʰ year of his age.

Here lyes Buried y⁰ Body of Mᵐ Sarah Gould, Wife to Des⁰ Daniel Gould, who departed this life Dece⁰ 4⁰ 1745, in y⁰ 64ᵗʰ Year of her Age. Also their Grandson John Briant, Diᵈ Dec⁰ 5, 1745, Ae. 3 m⁰.

Here lyes y⁰ Body of Daniel Goold, Son of Deacon Daniel & Mrs. Sarah Goold, who Died Octob⁰ 25ᵗʰ 1734, in y⁰ 26ᵗʰ Year of his Age.

Sarah Briant, Dauʳ of Mʳ Joseph & Mᵐ Sarah Briant, Died July 16ᵗʰ 1741, Aged 5 Years & 11 Months.

The above, after Mⁿ Knight, all lie in a row. (Mⁿ Briant was Dau. of Dea. Daniel & Sarah Gould?

Here Lyes Buried y⁰ Body of Mⁿ Ruth Hay, Widow of Mr. Peter Hay, who Departed this Life July 10⁰ Anno Dom⁰ 1748, in y⁰ 87ᵗʰ Year of Her Age.

Here lyes Buried y⁰ Body of Mʳ John Hay, who Died March y⁰ 4ᵗʰ 1730, in y⁰ 31ˢᵗ Year of his Age.

Here lyes Buried the Body of Mr. Peter Hay, who Departed this Life, April 1ˢᵗ Anno Dom. 1748, in y⁰ 91ˢᵗ Year of His Age.

Here lyes Buried y⁰ Body of Mⁿ Sarah Hay, Wife to Mʳ Peter Hay, who Died Mar⁰ y⁰ 3ᵈ 1729, in y⁰ 69ᵗʰ year of her Age.

Mehetable Huy, Dauʳ of Mʳ James Hay, Junʳ & Mrs. Ann his Wife, Died Aug⁰ 17ᵗʰ 1741, Aged 2 Years, 7 Months, & 25 Days.

Ann Hay, Daughʳ of Mʳ James Hay, Junʳ & Mⁿ Ann, his Wife, Died Aug⁰ 19ᵗʰ 1741, Aged 4 Years, 2 months, & 23 Days.

Mary Hay, Daughʳ of Mʳ James Hay, Junʳ & Mⁿ Ann his Wife, Died Sept. 1ˢᵗ 1741, Aged 9 Months.

Thomas, son of Thomas Armstrong of Ireland, Died June 5, 1753, in his 13 year.

Here lyes y⁰ Body of Mʳ James Hill, who Died July y⁰ 17ᵗʰ 1745, in y⁰ 43ᵈ Year of his Age.

Here lyes y⁰ Body of Mⁿ Ruth Parker, Wife to Mʳ Ebenezer Parker, who Died June 26. 1749, in y⁰ 64ᵗʰ Year of her Age.

Here lyes Buried y⁰ Body of Elder Samuel Sprague, Who Departed this Life May y⁰ 7ᵗʰ A. D. 1753, in y⁰ 65ᵗʰ Year of his Age.

Here lyes y⁰ Body of Mrs. Joanna Sprague, Wife to Mʳ Samuel Sprague, who Died June 17ᵗʰ 1739, Aged 43 Years & 3 Months.

In Memory of Mⁿ Lucy Bucknam, wife of Dea. Edward Bucknam, of Stoneham, who died 30 Oct. 1799, in the 65 year of her age.

In Memory of Mrs. Sarah Bucknam, the wife of Dea⁰ Edward Bucknam, who departed this Life, June 19. 1780, in the 50 year of her age.

Here lyes y⁰ Body of William Bucknam, Son of Mʳ Edward Bucknam, Junʳ & Mⁿ Sarah his Wife, who Died Oct. 23. 1750, Aged Years, 3 mon⁰ & 8 D⁰.

Here Lyes Buried y' Body of Lieu' Timothy Wright, Who Dec'd Feb'y y' 10th 1728, in y' 49th year of His Age.

Here lyes y' Body of M'' Mary Wright, Wife to Ensign Timothy Wright, who Died Oct' 27th 1755, in y' 46 Year of her Age.

In memory of Lieut. Daniel Bryant, who Departed this Life March 9. 1779, in the 47th year of his age.

In memory of Polly Bryant, Dau. of M' Elias & M'' Mary Bryant, who died April 3, 1788, Aged 5 weeks.

In memory of Jerusha Bryant, Dau. of M' Elias & M'' Mary Bryant, who died Dec. 23, 1782, Aged 1 day.

Erected in memory of Cap' Peter Hay, who died March 7, 1790, Aged 85 years.

Here lyes y' Body of M'' Abigail Hay, Daur of M' Peter & M'' Dorcas Hay, who departed this life Nov'r y' 7. 1767, in y' 28th year of her age.

In memory of M' John Cutler, son of M' Jacob and M'' Elizabeth Cutler, departed this life June the 4th 1792, in the 21st year of his age.

Here lies Buried the Body of M' Peter Hay, Jun'r, who departed this life Sep' the 12th 1764, aged 58 years.

In memory of M' James Hay, who departed this Life, May 19, 1781, aged 67 years.

In memory of Mrs. Anna Eaton, who died Nov'r 9, 1779, aged 81 years.

Here lyes Buried the Body of M' Phineas Sweetser, who departed this Life Sep' y' 21th 1764, in y' 46 year of his age.

In memory of M'' Anna Bucknam, wife to M' John Bucknam, who died Feb'y 18th 1789, Aged 55 years, 2 months, and 13 days.

Here lyes y' Body of M'' Rebecca Bucknam, wife of M' Edward Bucknam, who departed this life July the 20th 1772, aged 77 years.

Here lyes Buried the Body of M' Edward Bucknam, who departed this Life May the 14th 1773, aged 82 years.

Erected in memory of Miss Polly Crooker, daughter of Cap' Peleg Crooker, who died Sept. 16, 1793, in the 21st year of her age.

In memory of Mrs. Lydia Green, widow of Ens'' Jonathan Green, who died Aug. 29, 1775, aged 80 years & 5 months.

Rebekah Green, daughter of M' Jonathan & Mrs. Rebekah Green, died Octo'r the 8th 1750, aged 1 day.

Here Lyes Buried y' Body of Ensign Jonathan Green, who departed this life July 21st Anno Dom. 1744, aged 64 years, 5 months, & 19 days.

Here Lyes Buried y' Body of Mrs. Sarah Green, wife to M' Jonathan Green, Who Departed this life Feb'y 26. 1745, Aged 26 years, 7 months, & 18 D'.

Erected in memory of Capt. Jonathan Green, who died August 25, 1795, Aged 75 years, 9 months, & 1 day. It is with regret we here part with a loving friend, and valuable member of society, one who in his domestic station was lov'd & Reverenced, & in his more public life gained the general applause. One who serv'd the Town in the most important offices for many years, even to the close of life, to the universal satisfaction of those who appointed him. The adjacent Towns have reason likewise to join with Us in Lamenting the loss of so useful a Man.

In memory of Mrs. Rebekah Green, wife of Capt. Jonathan Green, who died July 20. 1786, in the 63d year of her age.

Here lyes an infant of M' Jonathan & Mrs. Rebekah Green, still-born, Nov'r 9. 1751.

Here lyes an infant son of Mr Jonathan & Mrs. Rebekah Green, born & died Octr 16. 1753.

Jonathan Green, son of Mr. Jonathan Green Junr & Mrs Dorcas, his wife, died Nov. 9. 1775, aged 4 days.

Erected in memory of Mr Jesse Green, who died Jan. 31. 1799, Aet. 33.

The preceding, after Polly Crooker, all lie in a row together, parallel and next to the street.

Here lyes buried the Body of Mr Daniel Green, who departed this life Octr 26, 1745, Aged 23 Years, 9 months, & 4 D^s.

Here lyes the Body of Mrs Ruth Green, wife of Deac^{on} Joseph Green, who departed this life November the 3^d 1770, Aged 63 years.

In memory of Mrs. Mary Wright, wife of Mr. Timothy Wright, who departed this Life June the 20th 1787, aged 78 years.

Here lyes Buried ye Body of Mrs. Judeth Lynde, wife of Capt. John Lynde, who died Feby 4. A. D. 1735, Aged about 63 years.

Here lyes ye Body of Mrs. Esther Green, Widow of Mr. Henry Green, who Died Feby 26. 1817, Aged 98 years.

Here lyes Buried ye Body of Elder Daniel Green, who Departed this life August ye 15th 1769, in ye 79 year of his age.

Here lyes ye Body of Mrs. Sarah Brown, Widow of Mr. Abiel Brown, who departed this life, May 6. 1769, in ye 51st year of her age.

In memory of Mrs. Isabel Hay, the wife of Capt. Peter Hay, who departed this life March 15, 1786, aged 80 years.

In memory of Mr. Nathan Simonds, who died July 30, 1795, aged 28.

Here lies Buried the Body of Mr. John Green, who departed this life, Jan. 30. 1774, aged 74 years.

Here lies the Body of Jerusha Green, dau^{tr} of Mr. John & Mrs. Jerusha Green, who departed this Life Sept. ye 6. 1775, in ye 15 Year of her age.

Here lyes Buried the Body of ye Rev^d Mr. James Osgood, First Pastor of ye Church of Chrst in Stoneham, Who Departed this life March 2^d A. D. 1745, Aged 40 Years & 7 months.

In memory of Mrs Mary Gould, the wife of Capt. Abraham Gould, who died of the Small Pox, May 26th 1793, in the 53^d Year of her age.

In memory of Mrs Moley Gould, the Consort of Capt. Abraham Gould, who Deceas'd Jan. 6. 1787, in the 45 year of her age.

Here lyes ye Body of Mrs Mary Gould, Wife of Mr Abraham Gould, who departed this life April ye 9th 1771, in ye 40th Year of Her Age.

In memory of Mrs Anna Geary, consort of Capt David Geary, who died June 5. 1790, Aet. 32 Years, 11 Months, & 2 days.

In memory of Jonas Richardson, son of Mr Charles & Mrs Anna Richardson, who died March 24, 1796, aged 4.

In memory of Mrs Ruth Ingols, consort of Capt Samuel Ingols, who died May 25. 1790, Aged 34 Years & 6 months.

DIED, Jan. 1st, 1741, Lt. Gen. Kirke, Col. of a regiment of foot.—*Gent. Mag.* London.

Jan. 13th, 1741, Mr. Wm. Montague, an eminent Virginia merchant, and one of the Common Council.—*Ibid.*

Jan. 19th, 1741, the relict of Sir Josiah Child.

RECORDS OF MARRIAGES, BAPTISMS AND DEATHS,

Copied from the Diary of the Rev. Benjamin Fessenden, who was ordained at Sandwich, Mass., Sept. 12, 1722.

[Copied for the Register by J. G. Locke, Esq. of Boston.]

MARRIAGES.

James Clark of Plymouth & Meribah Tupper of Sandwich, md. Sep 20. 1722.

John Freeman & Mariah Bourn of Sand. md. Jany 3, 1722–3.

Jonathan Nye and Deborah Blackwell m. Feb. 7, 1722–3.

Cornelius Clark of Rochester and —— Toby of Sand. md. May 23 1723.

John Chipman & Hannah Fessenden md Sep 26 1723.

Isaac Jennings & Hannah Nye both of Sand. m. Oct 31 1723.

Nathaniel Ewer of Barnstable and Mary Stewart of Sand. m. Nov 8 1723.

Samuel Barlow & Susannah Barlow both of Sand. m. Nov 15 1723.

Samuel Barrow of Plympton & —— Tobey of Sandwich md. Nov 21 1723.

Shubael Smith & Mary Chipman both of Sand. md. Sep 6. 1725.

Elisha Perry of Sand. & Anna Saunders of Plymouth md. Sep 20. 1725.

Gamaliell Stewart and Alice Gibbs both of Sand. md. Sep 23. 1725.

Zepheniah Swift & Lydia Chipman both of Sand. md. Sep 30. 1725.

Isaac Nye & Sarah Freeman both of Sand. md. Feb 7. 1725–6.

Abner Perry & Joannah Gibbs both of Sand. md. May 12 1726.

Simeon Dillingham & Elizabeth Bourn both of Sand. md. May 26 1726.

Joseph Nye & Mehitable Bourn both of Sand. md. July 3. 1726.

John Freeman & Mary Perry both of Sand. m. Augt. 4. 1726.

Nathan Tobey & Thankful Foster both of Sand. md. Sep 25. 1726.

Samuel Tupper and Hannah Fish both of Sand. md. Oct 14 1726.

John Gibbs and Sarah Cushman both of Sand. md. Dec 6 1726.

Zachous Tobey & Sarah Pope both of Sand. md. Jany 1. 1726–7.

William Parlow of Rochester & Orfith Wing of Sand. md. Mh 14. 1726–7.

Nathaniel Ha . . . . of Falmouth & Keturah Swift of Sandwich m. Sep 14. 1727.

BAPTISMS.

Tupper, Thomas son of Eldad Sep 22. 1722.

Bates, Lydia dau. of Daniel & Abigail Sep 22 1722.

Ellis, Benjamin son of Josiah & Sarah Sep 22 1722.

Tobey, Mercy dau. of Ebeneser & Mercy Sep 22. 1722.

Tupper, Benjamin son of Eldad Oct. 8. 1722.

Smith, John son of William Nov 11. 1722.

Ellis, Elizabeth dau. of Matthias & Thankful Dec 2 1722.

Gibbs, Barnabas son of Barnabas Feb. 2 1722–3.

Saunders, —— son of Temperance Mh 3 1722–3.

Bassett, Abigail dau. of William Mh 10. 1722–3.

Pope, Elisha son of Seth July 28. 1723.

Swift, Joannah dau. of Josiah Aug 25 1723.

Tupper, Mordecai, Samuel & Elizabeth chil. of Samuel, [probably Aug. 25, 1723.]
Forrine, Isaac son of —— Oct 27 1723.
Blackwell, Hannah dau. of Samuel & Mary Oct 27 1723.
Bourn, Joseph Nov 17 1723.
Saunders, Jabez son of Temperance Dec 5. 1723.
Bassett, Joshua, son of Nathan Dec 22 1723.
Garret, Andrew, son of Richard Dec 29 1723.

DEATHS.

Pope, Elisha d. Augt. 1723.
Wyat, Ruth d. Aug 12. 1728.
Saunders, Infant of John d. Aug 12. 1728.
Perry, Ezra, Jany 3. 1729–30.
Fish, John Senior d. Mh 8 1729–30, aged 76.
Perry, John, Senior d. Oct 31 1732, aged 78.
Tobey, Remember wf. of Jonathan d. Nov 3 1732, a 58.
Handy, Wid. Hannah d. Nov 9 1732, aged 89.
Tobey, Martha wf. of Eleazer d. Dec 6. 1732.
Blackwell, Mary d. Mh 29 1731.
Nye, Mary wfe. of Timothy d. June 1 1734.

WILL OF JOHN PAYBODY.

[A true copy, by B. PULSIFER, Jr., from Plymouth Colony Records, Vol. 1 of Wills, page 41.]

The last Will and Testament of John Paybody In and upon the Sixteenth of July in the year of our Lord 1649, I John Paybody of Daybrook in the Collonie of New Plymouth Planter being in perfect health and sound in memory God be blessed for it doe ordain and make this my last Will and Testament In manner and forme as followeth ;

Imprimis I bequeath my soule to God that gave it hoping to be saved by the Morritt of Christ my blessed Saviour and Redeemer as for my Worldly goods as followeth

Item I give and bequeath unto Thomas my eldest soone one shilling
Item I give and bequeath unto Francis Paybody my second son one shilling
Item I give unto William Paybody my youngest son one shilling
Item I give and bequeath unto Annis Rouse my Daughter one shilling
Item I give and bequeath unto John Rouse the son of John Rouse my lands att Carswell in Marshfield after my wifes decease.
Item I give unto John Paybody the son of William my lott of land att the new plantation
Item. I give and bequeath all the rest of my goods that are knowne to be mine leaving a Dead unto my wife Isaball Paybody whom I make my sole Executrix of this my last Will and Testament
Memorandum All these legaises before sett down are to be payed by William Paybody my youngest son when they shall be demanded.

John Paybody

John ffernesyde.
Boston New England the 27th April 1667.
Mr. John ffernesyed swore to the above.

HARVEY FAMILY.

[From the North Carolina University Magazine for March, 1856. Communicated by
Prof. F. M. Hubbard.]

GENEALOGICAL TABLES.—Among the earliest enactments of the Proprietary Government to be found in Swaim's Revisal (the Yellow Jacket) ch. xxxviii, p. 69, is the Act to appoint Public Registers, &c. The 15th section makes it the duty of the register of every precinct, when there is no clerk of the church in that precinct, " to register all births, marriages and burials, and imposes a penalty of one shilling per month, on every master or mistress of a family, for each month's neglect in supplying the register with the necessary information to enable him to comply with the law upon the subject."

To what extent the law was obeyed by the clerks of the churches and the register of the precinct we have not at present the means of ascertaining. No such register has ever fallen into our hands.

Barren and unmeaning as such lists of names might seem to be at the first glance, they would not be without value in the dearth of materials which exists for the elucidation of the annals of the Proprietary Government, and gentlemen who have possession of such records would perform an acceptable service by transmitting them to the President of the Historical Society of North Carolina.

The only genealogical table of any family in this State, we have ever seen in print, is the subjoined. We give it a place in our pages, not merely to insure (to the extent of our own immortality) its preservation, but for the purpose of attracting attention to this department of historical literature.*

THE GENEALOGY OF THE HARVEY FAMILY IN AMERICA.

John Harvey was Secretary to Governor Jenkins; he settled on Albemarle Sound, the place is now called Harvey's Neck, in Perquimmons County. John Harvey married Elizabeth, the widow of Governor Jenkins; they had one son, Thomas; he married Elizabeth Cole, daughter of Col. Cole; they had four sons, whose names were Thomas, John, Miles and Benjamin. Thomas, their first son, died without marrying; John, the second son, married Mary Bonner of Beaufort; their family consisted of eight children, Thomas, John, Miles, James, Henry, Edward, Martha and Joseph. Thomas, first son of John Harvey and Mary Bonner, married Mary Blount, daughter of Charles Worth Blount and Mary his wife. Their descendants were as follows:—Sarah, who married John Skinner, had two sons; John Harvey, married Lavinia Skinner, had three children; Charles Worth Harvey, married Ann Wyne Gregory, had one son; Mary Harvey, married James Granbery, had three children; Margaret Harvey never married; Thomas Harvel Harvey, married Elizabeth P. Long, they had one daughter; Elizabeth Blount Harvey died young; Martha Blount Harvey never married; Dr. Edmond Blount Harvey married first Martha P. Barnes, had two daughters—second, Mary Ann Clayton, had four children; Richard Henry and Joseph Edward,

---

* A Genealogy without dates is scarcely worth putting in type at all ; but we insert this because it is so uncommon to get anything of the kind from the quarter whence this comes.

twin sons of Thomas and Mary Harvey, died young, and Ann Blount, their last child, also died young.

The grand-children of Thomas Harvey (second son of John Harvey and Elizabeth Cole his wife,) and Mary Blount his wife. Sarah Skinner's children were Thomas Harvey Skinner and John Harvey Skinner, both died young. John Harvey and Lavinia had three children, Sarah Elizabeth, Mary Frances and James Henry. Sarah married Joseph Harvey Skinner, had one son named John Harvey; James Henry married Ann C. Crary, from New York, had no child. Charles W. Harvey and Ann had one son, James Gregory, who married Ann Wolford and had nine children. Mary Granbery had three children, Mary Harvey, Charles Harvey and Margaret Harvey, all died young. Thomas H. Harvey and Elizabeth had one daughter, Mary Elizabeth, who married William G. Duckett, and had three children, Thomas Harvey (who died young), Sarah Elizabeth and Martha Harvey. Dr. Edmond B. Harvey and Martha his first wife, had two daughters, Margaret Elizabeth, who married Joseph A. Riddick, and had two children, Margaret Harvey and Joseph. Mary Blount Harvey, second daughter of Dr. Edmund B. Harvey, married James Pritchett. Dr. Edmond B. Harvey and his second wife, Mary, had four children, Elizabeth Ann, Martha Blount, Thomas Edmond, and Joshua Skinner.

John, grandson of Thomas Harvey and Elizabeth Cole, married Sarah Blount, daughter of Charles Worth Blount, had one child, Anne, who married John Skinner, had William, Harriet, Joseph Harvey, John Adams and Henry. Harriet married Thomas Singleton, had four children, Anna, Spires, William and Harriet.

Joseph H. Skinner first married Sarah E. Harvey, daughter of John and Lavinia Harvey; they had one son, as has been mentioned before. His second wife was Sarah Creecy, daughter of William and Sarah Creecy; they had six children, Harriet (who married Rev. William E. Snowdon, has four children, Josephine, Thomas, Elizabeth and John), Mary Elizabeth, Joshua, John, Carolina and Henry. John Adams Skinner, son of John and Anne Skinner, married Elizabeth Roberts, had no child. Henry married Mary Creecy, had four children, Anna, Elizabeth, Joseph and William. Miles Harvey, third son of John and Mary Harvey, married Mary Skinner, had four children, James, Miles, Mary and Martha Ann; only Martha married, Charles W. Blount, had two children, Sarah and James. Sarah married Col. Toms, and had one son, Henry Toms; he married Miss Linch. James, fourth son of John and Mary Harvey, married Ann Blount, and had no child. Joseph, fifth son of John and Mary, married Elizabeth Baker, daughter of General Lawrence Baker, had fourteen children, Lawrence Baker, Ann Jones, Anna, Mary Eliza, Mary Priscilla, Maria, Emma, Joseph Henry, William Edward, John, Elizabeth Baker, James Turner, Martha Baker and Agatha. Ann Jones married Devorix, had three children; Mary P. married Brace; Emma married Joseph Gordon, had three children, Emma Susan, William Baker and Julianna. Miles Harvey, third son of Thomas and Elizabeth Harvey, first married Elizabeth Baker, had three children, Mary, Millie and Augustus. Mary married John Gray Blount, had Thomas Harvey, John Gray, William Augustus, Polly Ann, Olivia and Patsy Baker. William A. first married Miss Haywood, had three children, John Gray, William Augustus and Ann, who married Mr. Branch. Polly Ann married Mr. Rodman, had two daughters, Mary Martha and Mary Olivia, and one son,

William.   Mary Olivia married Mr. Myres; Millie married Abner Neal, had two sons, Christopher and Abner.   Abner married a widow, and had one daughter, named Margaret; she married and had a daughter.   Augustus married a widow, had one daughter, named Eliza; she married Duncan McNair, and had many children, Sarah, Susan, Pauline, Duncan and Augustus Harvey, (twin brothers,) and Robert.   Sarah married Mr. Hines, left one child; Susan married Mr. Tannerhill, has four children; Duncan married Elizabeth Cheshire, has two children.

Col. Miles Harvey's second marriage, to Elizabeth Jones—they had six children, Albridgton, Elizabeth, Agatha, Lucy, Robert and Miles.   Albridgton married Mrs. Sarah Skillings—they had three children, Mary Ann, Sarah Ann and Albridgton.   Mary married Richard Wyan, had three children, Albridgton, Richard and Sarah Elizabeth; Richard W. married Susan Thompson, has one child.   Elizabeth, second child of Miles' second wife, married Matthias Colbert, no children.   Agatha married Tulbert Godwin, no children.   Lucy married Gen. Reddin Blount, and had five children, Louisa, Mary, Caroline, Wiley and Reddin.   Louisa married Mr. Worthington, had two daughters, Caroline and Louisa.   Mary married John Myers, and had many children.   Caroline married Mr. Runyan, and had one child, Lucy.   Wiley and Reddin married.   Miles married and had three children, Mary, Tully and Julia.   Benjamin, fourth son of Thomas and Elizabeth, married Julianna Baker, and had five children, Benjamin and Thomas (twins), William, Robert and Martha—two youngest died.   Benjamin married Kesiah Mallory, had one son, named William Mallory Harvey; he married Anna Norfleet Baker, they had many children, Margaret Ann, William Benjamin, Richard Marmaduke, John Mallory, Ann Baker, Julianna and Carolina.   Col. Thomas, son of Benjamin and Julianna, married Agatha Jones, and had two sons, George Washington and John; by second marriage, to Rachel Hardy, had two sons, Benjamin and Thomas.   Thomas married Emma Creecy, had four children to live, Agnes, Sarah, Rachel and Emma.   Benjamin married Judith Creecy, had two children, Julianna Baker and Thomas; he married Mary Ann Banks.   William, son of Benjamin and Julianna, married the widow Riddick, had two sons, Benjamin and George Augustus; he married Elizabeth Gordon, had three sons, Jacob John, George and James.   John married Mary Ann Gordon, daughter of Joseph and Elizabeth Gordon, have some children.

* * *

MALDEN DOCUMENT.

[The following document was transcribed from the original in possession of the Hon. James D. Green of Cambridge.   See Vol. VII. pp. 271, 300; Vol. VIII. 105.]

I John Hale of Beverly in ye County of Essex in Ne: Engl: minister of y⁰ Gospel aged 59 yeares breing desired to give some light in a case depending (as I am informed) between y⁰ posterity of John Lewis of Malden deceased & in possession of part of y⁰ land he once enjoyed in Malden above said=I do hereby testify; That about y⁰ yeare of or Lord 1657 John Lewis of Malden in y⁰ county of Meddlesex in Ne: Engl: Planter did as I was informed & understood it sel unto Paul Willson now of Charlestown husbandman the s⁰ Lewis his house & land lying near Malden meeting house a little before his y⁰ sd Lewis dyed. which I had y⁰ more occasion to be acquainted with by reason y⁰ s⁰ Lewis in his life

& his widdow after his decease had frequent recourse to my father for advice & help in their weighty affaires.—Allso I find in ye account between my father deacon Rob Hale & Paul Willson y^t s^d Willson is made debt^r as followeth—More I paid Mr Adams for him by Mr Russel in wheat at four shil pr bushel ye 2.4.57. 40s. more I discounted for his contributions 40^s. 2.4.57.   £4-00-00

This was to pay a debt of John Lewis. more paid sister Lewis for him 1 y^d & ½ cotton   0-5-2

This amount I know to be my father's hand writing, as fully as I can know anothers hand y^t I see not y^e writing of myselfe; I beeing well acquainted wth my fathers hand.

Allso I fynd a note from Mr. Adams wherein he saith I fynd y^t John Lewis is creditor by so much paid me by Robt Hale=It by Robt Hale on Mr. Russels acc^o 2-00-00—2.4.57. It. by Robt Hale on Church acc^o 2-00-00.

Sam Adams.

Chelmsford y^e 18.7.1672

This I believe to be written wth Mr. Adams own hand I being acquainted with it. These things I signifie under my hand. y^e 5^t July, 1695 & am ready to testify this upon oath

John Hale.

LETTER OF JOHN HANCOCK.

[Communicated by J. Gardner White.]

" To   To the care of Mr Hancock
   Mrs Hancock   Paymaster, Mr Bant or any
    at her House near the Common   Gentleman in Boston.
(franked) John Hancock   Boston

My Dear Dolly   Tavern Called Log Goal in
Pray write me often   New Jersey 270 Miles from Boston
& long Letters   Sunday 12 °Clock June 14th 1778

I wrote you this morn^g from Sussex Court house, have just got here & stoping an Express bound to Boston for a moment, gives me oppor^y to let you know I am safe thus far. My Horse comes on better than I expected; tomorrow I shall cross Delaware River. I Beg you to take care of your Health beyond every other Consideration; how is Johnny? Take special Care of him. Tell my good Friend Mrs Brackett I depend on her Care of our Son, & she may Depend I will Take Care of her, she must not leave you till I Return; I really Love her for her Attention to you & me. My Love to your Sister Katy, Mrs Boyles, Mr Bant, Mrs Bowes, my Brother & Sister, Dr Cooper & to every Friend I have. I long much to have my faithfull Harry with me, Ned is no way Suitable for Travelling; but as I am determin'd not to tarry long, shall do the best I can. The Express waits, can only Add my most ardent wishes for your health & every Good & am with the utmost Love & affection

Yours for ever

Do always mention the   John Hancock
Receipt of my Letters
with their Dates.
   To Mrs Hancock.

OLD PEOPLE.

[Communicated by WILLIAM WILLIS.]

By the census of 1850, there were found in Maine 13 persons over 100 years of age; of whom 9 were males and 4 females. This was one to every 44,755 of the population of the State. In New Hampshire and Vermont, the proportion was much larger, being in the former State 11 in a population of 317,156, or one to 28,860; in the latter 8 in a population of 313,402, or one to every 39,175. In the United States I am astonished to find that the proportion of centenarians is much larger than in any of the New England States, being as one to 24,845 among the whites; one to 1,267 free colored, and one to 2,249 of slaves. The aggregates in the United States are 787 whites over 100 years, 343 free colored, and 1,425 slaves.

I have not the means of determining the number of that age of persons now in Maine, and can speak only of two, viz: Father Sawyer, now residing in Bangor, who was born in Hebron, in Conn., Oct. 1755, and consequently is 102½ years old; the other is Mrs. Wilson, who is now living with her son, Col. John M. Wilson, in Oxford county. I have requested Col. Wilson to furnish me an account of his mother, which I think is interesting enough for an article in the newspaper. I therefore offer it you for publication.

Wilson's Mills, Oxford Co., Me., March 17, 1858.

WM. WILLIS, ESQ.:

Dear Sir,—In compliance with your request, I send you the following facts and incidents in relation to the life of my mother, as she has given them mostly from her present recollection.

She was born in Scarborough, County of Cumberland, on the 28th of February, 1756, and is the daughter of Samuel March and Anna Libbey, who kept what was called the March Tavern, in that town. Her father was a native of Kittery, and by trade a shoemaker. He was the representative of the town of Scarborough to the Massachusetts Assembly, at the time of its removal for safety from Cambridge to Salem, and was by that Assembly commissioned as lieutenant-colonel, with orders to raise a regiment for eight months' service; which, on returning home, he accomplished in his own vicinity in about six weeks, the place of rendezvous being at his tavern.

He was ordered the next year to join the north-western army, and served two years, when he became disabled by sickness. He was previously a lieutenant in the French war.

Her mother was the daughter of John Libbey, one of the first inhabitants of Scarborough.

My mother was the fourth of fourteen children—six sons and eight daughters. She is now the only survivor of the family. Three of her brothers served in the army of the Revolution. Her brother, Col. James March of Gorham, who died about thirty years since, served in Portland, then Falmouth, as musician, at the age of fourteen years. Another brother was lost in a private armed vessel from Portland in the war of 1812. Three of her sisters were of the first inhabitants of the town of Limington, whom she often visited by following a spotted line through the woods on horseback, before there was any road above Standish Corner.

Remaining at home until past forty years of age, the chief care of the house—which was much frequented by travellers—devolved upon her during the absence of her father, and the feeble health of her mother. She has a distinct recollection of many incidents of the Revolution, particularly of the destruction of the American fleet at Bagaduce, the retreat from that place through the then wilderness, and the burning of Falmouth. The men returning from Bagaduce received supplies provided by Government at their house. The man who was sent on shore by Capt. Mowatt to set fire to the first parish meetinghouse in Portland, was brought to their house a prisoner on his way to Boston. He was made prisoner by Solomon Brigdon and Major Libbey, who were guarding the meetinghouse. She thinks that if the Committee of Safety had followed the advice of Capt. Thompson, who had made a prisoner of Capt. Mowatt when he was on shore (on the neck then so called) on a gunning excursion, the town would not have been destroyed.

On receiving the threat from Mowatt's lieutenant, that he would open his fire upon the town unless the captain was liberated at a certain hour, Capt. Thompson, who had an impediment in his speech, answered verbally, F-f-fire away! f-f-fire away! every gun you fire I will c-c-cut off a joint!

A British ship, loaded chiefly with fish for the British army at Boston, went ashore in a snow storm on Blue Point, was broken up on the beach, and the fish drifted high upon the shore. The old gentleman who first discovered the wreck, supplied himself liberally, and then informed his neighbors. This was a seasonable relief to the inhabitants, who were at that time in great destitution.

A few incidents will show the privations of those days. My mother, on losing her metal thimble, was obliged to supply its place with a leather one. She had a set of pins which she used for dressing on Sundays and special occasions. They were carefully laid away at other times and thorns used instead of them. A neighbor having obtained a small quantity of coffee, invited her friends to a treat. Coffee-pots being out of the question, an earthern jug was substituted in this case. The coffee was excellent.

In 1797, she became the second wife of my father, Nathaniel Wilson, who had been an officer of the Revolutionary army, serving in a volunteer company raised in Portland, then Falmouth, and commanded by Captain Partridge. He was at the time a major in the Massachusetts militia, and resided in what is now the town of Westbrook. My father having died in 1818, at the age of seventy-eight years, my mother was left to my care, and she has resided with me until this time, for the last twenty-five years in Township No. 5, R. 2, in the County of Oxford, thus being subjected again to privations similar to those of her early life. She is free from disease, cheerful and contented, sensible of gradual decay, waiting patiently for her final change, and relies upon the faith and hope of the Gospel of our Lord and Saviour.

Very respectfully, your obedient servant,

JOHN M. WILSON.

PAINE FAMILY REGISTER.—Mr. Lemuel C. Paine of Albany has published No. 7 of his very interesting collections concerning the Paines. His industry and perseverance deserve good encouragement.

WILL OF MOSES TYLER.

I, Moses Tyler of Andover, in the County of Essex and Province of the Massachusetts Bay in New England, husbandman, being at present of sound mind and memory, but considering my mortality, have thought meet to make this my last will and testament. And first of all, I commit my soul into the hands of God, who gave it, and my body I commit to the earth in hope of a blessed resurrection at the last day, through the merits of my Lord and Saviour, Jesus Christ;—and, as for my worldly estate, which God hath given me, I give and dispose of the same in manner following. As for my sons, Moses, John, Ebenezer, Job, Jonathan, James and Joshua, I have formerly given them their full portions out of my estate according to my ability. Also, I give to my six sons, first mentioned, ten pounds apiece, and to my son, Jo-hua, the last mentioned, twenty pounds, all which sums are to be paid by my executor in the space of eight years after my decease, and he shall be obliged to pay but ten pounds a year, and shall pay the younger before the elder.

(Item.) I give to my son Jacob all my homestead in Andover and my dwelling house, with all my other buildings, that are upon said homestead, and all my meadows, in Andover, and all my stock of cattle and sheep and swine and household goods, and other moveables. Excepting so much of my household goods, which my second wife brought to me, as shall be left at my decease, which shall be equally divided between my son Jacob and his three sisters, Martha, Katharine and Sarah, and the children of his sisters, Joanna and Abigail deceased; the children of each sister to have one share and my son Jacob shall have the choice of the beds and furniture thereof that was his mothers; and if my son Jacob shall die without issue, lawfully begotten, then the lands, which I have given him in this my will, shall be equally divided among my other sons. And I do hereby constitute, make and ordain my son Jacob the sole executor of this my last will and testament, and if there is any part of my real or personal estate, that I have not disposed (of) in this my last will and testament, I give it to my said executor, and I do hereby revoke and disannul all and every other will and testament by me made. Ratifying and confirming this and no other to be my last will and testament. In witness whereof I have hereunto set my hand and seal this ninth day of April, Anno Domini, 1725, and in the eleventh year of the reign of our Sovereign Lord, George of England, Scotland, France and Ireland, King, &c.

Moses Tyler and a Seal.

Signed, sealed and delivered by the said Moses Tyler to be his last will and testament in presence of us the subscribers.

> John Barnard
> Daniel Colbe
> Sarah Barnard.

Henry Gilbert.—Information of Henry Gilbert and his descendants is desired by E. S. Waters, 67 Commercial street, Boston. Gilbert was of Brookfield, 1672.

LONG-LOST PRE-REVOLUTIONARY BRITISH SONG,

THE WATERY GOD.—Tune, "Ganges."

1

The wat'ry God, great Neptune, lay
In dalliance soft and amorous play,
　　On Amphitrite's breast;
When uproar rear'd her horrid head,
The trident shook, the Nereids fled,
　　And all their fears confest.

2

Loud thunder shook the vast domain,
The watery world was wrapt in flame,
　　The god amazed, spoke!
Go forth, ye winds, and make it known,
Who dares to invade my coral throne,
　　And fill my realms with smoke.

3

The winds, obsequious at his nod,
Sprang quickly up t' obey their god,
　　And saw two fleets a-weigh:
The one, victorious Hawke, was thine;
The other, Conflans' wretched line,
　　In terror and dismay.

4

Then down descend and tell their chief,
That France was ruin'd past relief,
　　And Hawke triumphant rode;
Hawke! cried the chief, pray who is he,
That dares usurp my power at sea,
　　And thus insult a god?

5

The winds reply'd, in distant lands
There lives a king, whom Hawke commands;
　　Who spurns all foreign force;
And when his floating castles sail
From sea to sea, from pole to pole,
　　Great Hawke directs their course.

6

And when his winged bullets fly,
To punish fraud or perfidy,
　　Or scourge a guilty land,
Then gallant Hawke, serenely great,
Though death and horror round him wait,
　　Performs the dread command.

7

Neptune with wonder heard the story
Of George's rule and *Britain's* glory,
　　Which time can ne'er subdue;
Boscawen's deeds and Saunders' fame,
Join'd to great Wolf's immortal name,
　　And cried, can this be true!

8

A king! he needs must be a god,
Who holds such heroes at his nod,
　　To conquer earth and sea;
I give my trident and my crown,
A tribute due to such renown;
　　Great George shall rule for me.

GENEALOGY OF THE McKINSTRY FAMILY, WITH A PRE-LIMINARY ESSAY ON THE SCOTCH-IRISH IMMIGRATIONS TO AMERICA.

(By Hon. WILLIAM WILLIS, of Portland, Me.)

[Continued from page 257.]

1. JOHN McKINSTRY, the first of the name who came to this country, was born in Brode Parish, in the county of Antrim, Ireland, in 1677. He was of Scotch descent, and was the son of Rodger McKinstry and Mary Wilson, who lived in the neighborhood of Edinburgh, until compelled by the persecutions under Charles II., about 1669, to seek security and repose with their Presbyterian brethren in the province of Ulster, and the county of Antrim. Their son John was educated at the University of Edinburgh, from which he graduated Master of Arts in 1712. It may gratify the curious to see the Diploma which that University then granted to its graduates, which we annex in the original language :—

"Ne quem forte habeat cujus scire interest, Nos Universitatis—Jacobi Regis Edinensis Professores Testamur hunc Juvenem Johannem Mc-Kinstrie Hibernum, Post quam Philosophiæ & Humanioribus Literis ea Morum Integritate et Modestia (quæ Ingenuum decebat Adolescentem) apud. Nos vacasset, eaque præstitisset, omnia quæ Disciplinæ Ratio et Academiæ consuetudo præscripserat; Tandem concessu Senatus Academici Magistrum in Artibus Liberalibus Riti Renunciatum, Cunctaque consecutum Privelegia quæ Bonarum Artium Magistris uspiam concedi solent: Cujus Rei quo major esset fides, Sigillum Inclyti Senatores Edinensis Athenæi Curatores et Patroni Nos Chirographa Apposuimus IV. Kal. Martii MDCCXII. Datum Edinburgi.

> JOH. GOODALL,   L. S. P.
> ROBERTUS HENDERSON B & Acad. ab Archivi.
> GULIEL. HAMILTON, N. S. P.
> GULIELMUS LAW,   P. P.
> GULIELMUS SCOT,   P. P.
> ROBERTUS STOUAOL,   P. P.
> COL: DRUMOND,   P. P.
> JA: GREGORY,   Math. P."

Translation.—"Be it known to all whom it may concern, that we, the Professors of the University of Edinboro' of King James, testify, that this youth, John McKinstry of Ireland, after having completed the study of philosophy and human literature with the integrity and modesty of manners which is becoming an ingenuous youth, has graduated with us, and is entitled to all the privileges which the course of discipline and the custom of this Academy is accustomed to confer. And now, with the consent of the Faculty and teachers of this College, he is declared a Master in the liberal Arts, and entitled to all the privileges which are wont to be conceded to the Masters of the Good Arts. Of which fact, that there may be greater faith, we, the distinguished Governors, Teachers and Patrons of the University of Edinburgh, have placed our signatures, this 4th Calends of March, 1712."

How he disposed of himself for the next six years we have no information; he certainly qualified himself for the ministry, and undoubtedly received Presbyterian ordination. He joined the company of emigrants from the north of Ireland in the summer of 1718, and arrived in Boston,

August 4, 1718. He followed the fortunes of that portion of the immigrants which went to Worcester County. He had not long been there before his services were sought by the people of Sutton, a new town near Worcester, the settlement of which had just commenced. At a meeting of the inhabitants, Nov. 25, 1719, it was voted that Mr. McKinstry should preach three months, and have fifteen pounds for the service. In the following March, the town voted to settle Mr. McKinstry, and to pay him £60 a year salary. In pursuance of this and other votes, he was duly settled according to Congregational usage on the 9th of November, 1720. The people were generally Congregationalists, while the pastor, born and educated in rigid Presbyterianism, could not, in his new position, lay aside his attachments to the religious usages of his life. Difficulties therefore arose soon after his settlement, on these opposite views of church government, which produced continued uneasiness in the parish, and led to a separation in September, 1728. Mr. McKinstry concluded to join his brethren of the same denomination in New York. On his way thither, his wife's health failing, he rested at East Windsor in Connecticut. The parish in the eastern precinct of the town, afterwards called Ellington, having no preacher, he was requested to supply the pulpit. This circumstance resulted in a suspension of his journey southward, and a settlement over that parish, as its first pastor, in 1733. He continued in this situation sixteen years, and remained in the town until his death, which took place on Sunday, January 20, 1754, at the age of 77 years. He preached on the Sunday previous to his death. Mr. McKinstry is said to have been a gentleman of good abilities, of popular talents, and unwavering integrity, a quality belonging to the family. His wife died Oct. 25, 1762, aged 81.

Soon after his settlement in Sutton, he married Elizabeth Fairfield, of Wenham, Mass., probably a daughter of William Fairfield, who represented his town in the General Court twenty-seven years, in nine of which he was Speaker of the House. By her he had seven children, viz.:— John, b. Dec. 31, 1723; Mary, b. Jan. 24, 1726; Alexander, b. May 16, 1729; William, b. Oct. 8, 1732; Paul, b. Sept. 18, 1734; Elizabeth, b. May 27, 1736; Abigail, b. March 26, 1739: all at Ellington but the first two.

Elizabeth and Abigail died unmarried, the latter in Ellington, in April, 1814. Elizabeth was killed by a negro servant of her brother William, June 4, 1763, while she was visiting him in Taunton. The negro was fond of Elizabeth, but had been made to believe that he could obtain his freedom by killing some one of the family. He therefore took an opportunity, when his victim's back was towards him, and struck her a fatal blow on the back of her head with a flat-iron. Much excitement was produced in that quiet village and throughout the county by this sad event; and a great crowd attended upon his trial and execution, which soon after followed.

The other five children were married and left issue, as we proceed to describe :—

II. JOHN, eldest son of Rev. John of Ellington, born in Sutton, December 31, 1723; was graduated at Yale College in 1746; was a classmate and chum of Ezra Stiles, afterwards the distinguished President of the College. Students at that time were placed on the catalogue according to the rank of their parents; McKinstry was placed fourth in a class of twelve; he survived all his classmates by fifteen years, and died Nov. 9, 1813, at the age of 90. He was ordained the first pastor of the 2nd Church in Springfield, now Chicopee, Mass., in 1752; the church was formed in September of the same year. He continued the active pastor of the Church and Society until 1789, when he was released from preaching, but discharged other duties of the pastorate until his death. His salary for the first ten years was £45 lawful money; this was raised to £62 and fire wood, and " a load of pine knots yearly to study by." After being relieved from preaching, his salary was reduced to £18. In 1760, he married Eunice Smith of Suffield, Conn, who died Sept. 20, 1820. They had seven children, viz.: JOHN ALEXANDER, b. 1760; EUNICE THEODOSIA, b. 1762; ELIZABETH LUCY, b. 1765; ARCHIBALD, b. 1767; ROGER AUGUSTUS, b. 1769; PERSEUS, b. 1772; CANDACE, b. 1774. The latter, and only survivor, is living unmarried in Chicopee (1858.) The other children died without issue, except Roger Augustus, and Perseus, at Chicopee, as follows, viz :—

JOHN ALEXANDER,[2] April, 1840.   EUNICE T.,[2] Feb. 1844.
ELIZABETH L.,[2] May 19, 1826.
ARCHIBALD,[2] Sept. 11, 1800.   He was a physician.

III. ROGER AUGUSTUS, son of John[2] of Chicopee, was a tanner and currier, first in Ashfield, then in Plainfield, Mass. About 1825, he moved to Geneva, in Ohio, where he died in 1843. His wife was Chloe Elmer of Ashfield, by whom he had six children, viz :

IV. [3] AUGUSTUS, unmarried.
IV. [3] ORIN, married Marcia Cook, and died without issue, Oct. 1847.
IV. [3] EUNICE, mar. Nahum Daniels, and d. without issue, soon after.
IV. [3] LUCINA, married the same Daniels, and is living with two children. Her husband was drowned at Erie, Penn., in 1842.
IV. [3] ARCHIBALD, lives in Geneva, Ohio. He married Mary Silver Thorn, and has children.
IV. [3] LYMAN, died young, without issue.

III. PERSEUS, sixth child of the Rev. John[2] of Chicopee, b. 1772; died August 23, 1829; was a tanner, first in Plainfield, then a farmer in Chicopee. He married Grace Williams, Oct. 24, 1803, and had eleven children, as follows, viz :

IV. [3] ELIZA, b. Sept. 25. 1804; living unmarried on the homestead in Chicopee, in 1857.
IV. [3] EMILY, b. August 8, 1806; married Titus Chapin, a farmer in Chicopee, and died in 1842, leaving five children, viz : Titus,[4] Roxana,[4] Emily,[4] Lucy,[4] and Eleonora.[4]
IV. [3] THEODOSIA, b. Aug. 23, 1807; married Whitman Chapin, a farmer, in Chicopee, and had two children, viz : Moses Whitman,[4] and Edward.[4] Moses Whitman married Augusta Chapin of West Springfield, and has children. Theodosia is living, a widow, (1857) in Chicopee.
IV. [3] WILLIAM, b. June 8, 1809; died Feb. 24, 1845. He was a farmer in Chicopee; m. Mary J. Frink and had two children, viz: Laura Jane[4] and Arthur.[4] The widow lives in western New York with her daughter; the son lives in Fredonia, N. Y.
IV. [3] JOHN ALEXANDER, b. April 9, 1811; he graduated at Amherst Col. in 1839; studied his profession at the East Windsor Seminary; settled as a Cong. minister in Torrington, Ct., in 1842; dismissed and settled at Harwinton, Ct., in 1857. In 1843, he m. Mary E. Morton, of Hatfield, Mass., and has two children, viz: John Morton,[4] b. 1845, and William Alexander,[4] b. 1849.
IV. [3] WILLARD, b. April 9, 1813, and died an infant.

IV.   [7] WILLARD, b. May 9, 1815, publisher of the Fredonia Censor, in Chautauque Co., N. Y.; married in 1843 Maria A. Durlin, and has three children, (1857) viz: Louis,[1] Willard,[2] and Anna.[3]

IV.   [8] MARY, b. Nov. 2, 1817: married John Frick of South Hampton, Mass., and has five children.

IV.   [9] ALFRED, b. May 17, 1821; d. 1823.

IV. [10] ALFRED LYMAN, b. April 20, 1823; m. Jane Granger, and has one son, Alfred.[1]   He lives on the old homestead at Chicopee.

IV. [11] ARCHIBALD WINTHROP, b. March 19, 1828; lives at Fredonia, N. Y., and is associated with his brother Willard in the publication of the "Fredonia Censor."   Sept. 3, 1857, he married Helen E., daughter of N. D. Putnam of Fredonia.

II.   MARY, the second child of Rev. John[1] of Ellington, b. Jan. 24, 1726; married Daniel Ellsworth of Ellington, and had children.   DANIEL,[1] b. 1753, d. Nov. 27, 1755; MINDWELL,[2] b. 1760, and d. without issue, Feb. 7, 1764; ALICE,[3] d. unmarried May 7, 1786, aged 21; ELIZABETH,[4] died June 21, 1786, aged 22; JERUSHA,[5] b. 1768, married William Morgan, and died April 29, 1820.   They had four children, William,[1] and Mary,[2] who died in childhood, and two other daughters.

II.   ALEXANDER, the third child of Rev. John[1] of Ellington, b. May 16, 1728, and died there Nov. 9, 1759.   He m. Sarah Lee of Litchfield, Ct., and had three children, of whom EZEKIEL alone survived infancy.

III.   EZEKIEL, the only son of Alexander McKinstry,[1] who came to maturity, was born in Ellington, Aug. 17, 1753, and continued to reside there, a farmer, until his death, Nov. 25, 1803.   He married Rosina Chapman, June 26, 1776.   His widow, born Feb. 10, 1758, died April 24, 1839, aged 81.   They had twelve children, viz:

IV.   [1] Sarah, b. Nov. 8, 1777; m. —— Ross, and d. Sept. 18, 1829.

IV.   [2] Elizabeth, b. July 16, 1779; d. March, 1794.

IV.   [3] Anna, b. March 5, 1781; d. Dec. 6, 1798.

IV.   [4] Rosina, b. Jan. 25, 1783; m. —— Dunton, a tailor, who died in Rome, N. Y.   She had two daus., also dead; she d. Sept. 1838.

IV.   [5] Alexander, b. April 9, 1785; he established himself in Augusta, Georgia, as a merchant, where he married Elizabeth, daughter of Jesse Thompson of that neighburhood, by whom he had one son, Alexander, living in Mobile, Ala., 1857, a judge of the municipal court of that city; and one daughter, Ann, unmarried.   Alexander,[5] died at Charleston, S. C., Nov. 6, 1823, aged 39.   His widow married Dr. Henry Sullivan Lee, of Boston, son of Dr. Samuel Parsons Lee, of New York.   They have had eight children, five sons and three daughters.

IV.   [6] JOHN, b. June 16, 1787; d. at Ellington, April 25, 1839, leaving a widow and one son, Alexander,[1] living on the old homestead.

IV.   [7] FANNY, b. April 6, 1789; d. unmarried Jan. 27, 1809.

IV.   [8] OLIVER, b. July 14, 1791; was a physician in Monson, Mass., where he died in March, 1852, the last survivor of Ezekiel's children.   He left a family in that town.

IV.   [9] LEE, b. March 8, 1793; d. May 20, 1808.

IV. [10] ELIZABETH, b. May 26, 1795.   She married —— Pease, a merchant, in Hartford, Conn., and d. July 26, 1831.

IV. [11] Jerusha, b. Jan. 8, 1798; d. Sept. 13, 1810.

IV. [12] Anna, b. Aug. 16, 1800; married —— Johnson, a lawyer, in Rome, N. Y., where she died Jan. 28, 1837.

II. WILLIAM, the third son and fourth child of John of Ellington, was born Oct. 8, 1732. He was a physician, and settled in Taunton, Mass. On Nov. 27, 1760, he married Priscilla, daughter of the Rev. Nathaniel Leonard, pastor of the 1st Church in Plymouth, Mass., and Priscilla, daughter of Dr. Nathaniel Rogers and Sarah Appleton of Ipswich. By her he had ten children, viz: ¹ WILLIAM, b. Nov. 13, 1762; he graduated at Oxford University, Eng.; became Rector of East Grinstead and Lingfield, near London; was tutor to children of several noblemen, whom he accompanied in their travels on the continent. He was a good scholar and a polished gentleman, and died on a visit to this country, unmarried, in August, 1823. ² PRISCILLA, b. Aug. 25, 1765; married John Hazen of New Brunswick, and had a large family. ³ SARAH, b. Aug. 14, 1767; married Major Caleb Stark, son of Gen. John Stark, and had a numerous family. ⁴ JOHN, b. March 6, 1769, a merchant in Boston several years; died unmarried Oct. 29, 1825. ⁵ MARY and ⁶ THOMAS, twins, b. Aug. 17, 1770. Thomas d. unmarried in 1796. Mary, married Benjamin Willis of Haverhill, Portland and Boston, Jan. 9, 1791, and had eight children. ⁷ ELIZABETH, b. Oct. 26, 1772; married to Samuel Sparhawk of Portsmouth and Concord, N. H., Secretary of that State, in 1803, by whom she had several children. ⁸ DAVID, b. 1775, and d. unmarried in New York, a merchant, in March, 1802.

They had two other children, viz: William, born and died Nov. 13, 1761; and John, who died Dec. 21, 1768, in the fifth year of his age. All in Taunton.

Dr. McKinstry had a successful business in Taunton, in 1774, although he had a feeble constitution and a consumptive habit. The Rev. Mr. Emery, in his " Ministry of Taunton," says of Dr. McKinstry, " He was a person of highly respectable personal and professional character." At that time a Capt. Gilbert, suspected of tory principles, was seized and so roughly handled by the " sons of liberty," that it became necessary to have a surgeon to dress his wounds. He protested against having a rebel doctor, but was willing that Dr. McKinstry should attend him. This suggestion excited suspicions against this amiable and popular physician. He became the subject of offensive remark, and was exposed to insult and injury. Being in feeble health and of a sensitive nature, which could not bear hard usage nor a suspected position, he thought it advisable to retire for a time to Boston. His family, which was left in Taunton, was now subject to increased annoyance. His wife, a finely educated and high spirited woman, of elegant manners, was compelled, by a large collection of females, to march around the liberty pole. She was niece of the Hon. George Leonard of Norton, and cousin of Daniel Leonard, a refugee, and afterwards chief justice of Bermuda.

This last act of insult decided the question with the family, who, not being able to enjoy repose upon their native soil, were forced to become loyalists in self defence, and they immediately joined the husband and father in Boston. So high was Dr. McKinstry's reputation in his profession, that he received from Gen. Gage the appointment of surgeon general of the hospitals in Boston.

It so happened that on the memorable 17th of June, 1775, a dinner party took place at Dr. McKinstry's house, for which invitations had been given out the day before. The dinner proved to be a solemn and silent one, and was partaken standing. Several officers were present who had been detailed to proceed with detachments of the British army to dislodge the rebels from Bunker Hill. They hastily dined and proceeded to join their corps; among them was Major John Small, a friend of the family, whose name is identified with that momentous battle. Dr. McKinstry's house stood on Hanover Street, near where the Shawmut House now is, and the children went to the top of the house to witness the cannonade. Sarah, one of them, little dreamed that, in after-years, she would become the wife of a gallant stripling of 16, who was then fighting in the opposing ranks, by the side of his veteran father, the renowned John Stark. Twelve years after, she was wedded to that gallant soldier, Caleb Stark. Another daughter, Mary, might also have been a distant witness to the flight from the flames of Charlestown of her future husband, Benjamin Willis, a native of that devoted town, who, with his mother, was compelled to make a hasty retreat, without a backward look to their perishing property.

When Boston was evacuated, Dr. McKinstry and his family went on board the fleet, which lay ten days in Nantasket Roads waiting orders. During that time, viz., March 21, 1776, Dr. McKinstry died of consumption, on board the Dutton hospital ship, and his remains lie buried on George's Island, in that harbor.

The surviving members of the family were taken in the fleet to Halifax, and were on board the same ship with lady Howe, wife of the Admiral, where they were treated with that sympathy and kindness their unhappy condition required. The fleet took away about one thousand refugees. The family remained in Halifax, with the exception of William, the eldest son, until 1778, when they returned to the States, making Newport, R. I., their place of residence, during its occupation by the British. After its evacuation, they proceeded to Haverhill, in Mass., where a sister of Mrs. McKinstry, the wife of John White, Esq., lived; and she died there, May 26, 1786, honored and loved.

The four sons of Dr. McKinstry died unmarried, and consequently the name in this branch is extinct.

Rev. WILLIAM,[*] died at Concord, N. H., August 28, 1823, aged 61.

JOHN,[*] died in Ohio, Oct. 29, 1825, aged 56.

THOMAS,[*] died at sea, 1796, aged 26, the vessel never heard from.

DAVID,[*] died in New York, in March, 1802, of consumption, aged 27.

III. The Rev. WILLIAM McKINSTRY,[*] son of Dr. William,[*] entered the naval service of Great Britain at the commencement of the revolution. In an engagement with an American privateer, in 1776, he lost his right hand and was shot overboard. He contrived to keep himself above water until the battle was over, when he was relieved from his critical situation. This changed the current of his life, and instead of becoming a naval officer, he became an episcopal clergyman, a cultivated scholar, and a gentleman of refined manners. He happened to be on the continent, and at a hotel in Munich, when Gen. Moreau arrived at the same hotel, in a most unpretending style, to take charge of the French army in that neighborhood. In a few days after was fought the celebrated battle of Hohenlinden, and Mr. McKinstry, with the poet Thomas Campbell, had the good fortune to be near the scene of the combat; a cannon ball struck near the spot where they were standing, which rather discomposed the nerves of the poet. Mr. McKinstry had seen the article before. Campbell's immortal poem commemorates this most bloody passage of arms.

We will dispose of this branch of the family by a brief notice of descendants in the female line, all of whom married and left children.

(To be Continued.)

CHURCH RECORDS OF FARMINGTON, CONN.

[Copied by the late Hon. NATHANIEL GOODWIN of Hartford.   Communicated by
DANIEL GOODWIN, Esq.]

[Continued from page 150.]

Sarah Cole, daughter of John Cole, grandson to Deacon Hart, baptized August 27, 1693.

Daniel Andrews, son of Benjamin Andrews, baptized September 10, 1693.

Elizabeth Blackleath, daughter of John Blackleach, baptized October 8, 1693.

Samuel Lamb, son of Samuel Lamb, baptized October 15, 1693.

Elizabeth Gridley, daughter of Thomas Gridley, baptized October 29, 1693.

John Hooker, son of John Hooker, baptized November 19, 1693.

Sarah Porter, daughter of Samuel Porter, baptized November 19, 1693.

Sarah Root, daughter of Stephen Root, baptized December 17, 1693.

Sarah Smith, daughter of Jonathan Smith, baptized December 24, 1693.

Elizabeth Newell, daughter of Thomas Newell, baptized December 31, 1693.

Joseph North and Rebecca North, twins, children of Thomas North, baptized December 31, 1693.

Mary Root, daughter of Joseph Root, baptized January 28, 1693.

Hannah Wadsworth, daughter of Samuel Wadsworth, baptized February 11, 1693.

Samuel Smith, son of Samuel Smith, baptized March 4, 1693.

Samuel Lee, son of John Lee, baptized April 1, 1694.

Abigail Porter, daughter of Thomas Porter, (which Thomas is son of Robert,) baptized July 8, 1694.

Sarah Gridley, daughter of Samuel Gridley, baptized July 8, 1694.

John Cowles, son of Samuel Cowles, baptized August 26, 1694.

Phebe Lewis, daughter of William Lewis, baptized October 7, 1694.

John Lewis, son of James Lewis, baptized October 14, 1694.

Samuel Orton, son of John Orton, and Anna Orvis, daughter of Samuel Orvis, baptized November 11, 1694.

Ruth Smith, daughter of Joseph Smith, baptized December 9, 1694.

Dorcas Norton, daughter of John Norton, baptized January 20, 1694.

Ebenezer Woodruff, son of Samuel Woodruff, baptized February 3, 1694.

Mary Barnes, daughter of Joseph Barnes, baptized February 17, 1694.

Rachel Smith, daughter of Ephraim Smith, baptized February 17, 1694.

William Hooker, son of Samuel Hooker, baptized February 24, 1694.

John Hooker, son of John Hooker, baptized March 10, 1694.

Nathaniel Hart, son of John Hart, baptized April 14, 1695.

John Bird, son of Thomas Bird, baptized April 21, 1695.

Elizabeth Barnes, daughter of Thomas Barnes, baptized July 21, 1695.

Anna Hart, daughter of Stephen Hart, baptized August 18, 1695.

Sarah Wadsworth, daughter of Samuel Wadsworth, baptized October 20, 1695.

Thomas Hart, son of Thomas Hart, baptized November 3, 1695.

Samuel Andrews, son of Benjamin Andrews, baptized November 24, 1695.

Abigail Smith, daughter of Jonathan Smith, baptized December 29, 1695.

John Blackleach, son of John Blakleach, baptized January 26, 1695.

Lydia North, daughter of Thomas North, baptized March 1, 169⅚.

John Cole, son of John Cole, grandson to Deacon Hart, baptized March 15, 169⅚.

Martha Porter, daughter of Samuel Porter, baptized July 5, 1696.

Samuel Root, son of John Root, baptized August 16, 1696.

Thomas Standley, son of Thomas Standley, baptized November 1, 1696.

Daniel Woodruff, son of Samuel Woodruff, baptized November 8, 1696.

Joseph Bird, son of Thomas Bird, baptized December 27, 1696.

Thomas Lewis, son of James Lewis, baptized January 3, 169⅚.

Martha Smith, daughter of Samuel Smith, baptized January 24, 169⅚.

Mary Root, daughter of Caleb Root, baptized April 4, 1697.

Mary Coales, daughter of Isaac Coales, baptized May 2, 1697.

Robert Porter, son of Thomas Porter, baptized May 16, 1697.

Jonathan Lewis, son of William Lewis, baptized June 6, 1697.

Hezekiah Lee, son of John Lee, baptized June 6, 1697.

Sarah Langdon, Joseph Langdon, John Langdon, and Samuel Langdon, children of Joseph Langdon, baptized June 6, 1697.

[Samuel Hooker died November 5, 1697.]

January 6, 1668. It was voted by the church assembled at Deacon Hart's, that with respect to the Sacrament, each brother of the Church should send into the Deacon's a peck of wheat, or the worth of a shilling in current pay, for the defraying of the next Sacrament, as also, for the clearing off that little which according to the Deacon's report, was yet due for the Sacrament already past, as also, that for the future, every brother of the Church should for each Sacrament allow 6*d*,—except such of the brethren whose wives come not to the Supper, because not members of the Church; and to them it was permitted to put in 3d or sixpence, whichever they pleased, for each Sacrament.

June 15, 1673. The Church at Farmington assembled at Deacon Hart's, to attend the admission of James Bird. After the examination of his knowledge, and a brief narration given by the said James, of his experience,—the mind of the Church was taken. About 8 brethren voted for his admission, three against it. The major part by much, chose to suspend acting either way; but the major part of the active brethren voting his admission. Both those brethren which voted against him, as also those who neutralized, did agree that they reported it most regular that he should be accepted.

Whereupon, the Pastor told the said James, that the Church did expect of those that joined, and consequently of him, that he should promise to submit to the government of Christ in his house, walk with his brethren; and fear, and keep all the commandments of God, as far as Christ should enable.

To which the said James returned,—that as some time of old [so be in the present case] as the Lord liveth, I will not close with you thus; and so departed the house; and as he was going forth, added—I desire you to take care of my wife.

Upon which the Pastor concluded the meeting with prayer, and the assembly departed.

So that the said James, seeing so many of the brethren to hesitate and rescind, refused to close and unite with the Church; but to stand a non-member, as he was.

October 3, 1675. Capt. Lewis and Left Steele having twice forsaken the assembly, and turned away from the Church, when celebrating the Lord's Supper, and Mr. Wrotham once,—the Pastor commended it to the consideration of the Church, what was duty in the case.

The same day it was voted, that in case a member in full communion shall turn away from the Supper, and the Church in the celebration of it, that such a member be accountable, or shall be held bound, when called on, to give the reason of his so doing.

From this vote none dissented by voting the negative, (to my observation,) except Capt. Lewis.

At the same meeting the Pastor declared his judgment concerning such as turn away unnecessarily from the Lord's Supper,—namely, that he judged them to sin dangerously,—

1st. Because they brake the second command, which requireth us to wait on Christ with constancy and perseverance in all the duties of his worship, as be given opportunity. Now one part of instituted worship is the celebration of the Lord's Supper.

2d. Because they brake the Covenant with Christ and with the Church; for in our Covenant, we have promised to walk with Christ and one with another, in seeking and keeping all his commands,—one of which is, "Do this in remembrance of me."

3d. It is very dangerous, since thereby such are guilty of despising the body and blood of Christ, (1 Cor. chap. 11.) As he that eateth and drinketh unworthily because he despiseth, is guilty; so he that turneth away unnecessarily is guilty for the same reason.

4th. Under the law, he that unnecessarily forsook the Passover,

was to be cut off from his people. So in new Testament times, he that unnecessarily forsakes the Supper which is come in room of the passover, exposeth himself to great danger.

To the 2d part,—whoever, brethren, forsaketh that part of the worship of God,—turning away from the Supper and the Church in the celebration thereof, were accountable for their so doing, i. e. were bound or obliged in case the reason of their so doing was not obvious and apparent, when called to render it.

Here the Pastor desired that if any were of that mind, that brethren were unaccountable, they would express themselves, and give the reason of their apprehension. [He was however moved and should give his reason, but it does not mind me to preoccupy or prejudice the liberty of any. To this purpose spake the Pastor.]

No brother seconding, he declared his apprehension concerning the duty of brethren in the case forenamed, that they were [reasonable,] and obliged to render the reason of their forsaking the Church and house of God, in case that the reasons were not obvious and apparent. The reasons the Pastor gave were two.

1st. I first take from the 1st of Corinthians, 10th chapter, 32d verse, "Give no offence." Now, if brethren openly forsake the Church of which they are members, and with which they are bound in [siding] to walk in conscience and the worship of God;—the reason of their so doing not being apparent, an account, or rendering the reasons of their so doing, is necessary to their inoffensive walk.

2d. The second reason, taken from 1st Corinthians, 14th chapter, 33d verse,—"God is not the author of confusion;"—but that was, if withdrawing and rendering no reason, when called on, very unaccountable;—

did, of its own nature, tend to confusion, and to lay prostrate the worship of God among us. If brethren may from time to time do so, then 10, 20 may do so, and thus the worship of God may be laid desolate, with us, and no way of healing left;—for the reason not being known, and so the   or case not being understood, could not be remedied.

On October 28, 1675. The Church had further consideration of the matter, and because of an exception put in by Lieut. Steele against a particular account, it was considered and debated whether a general account would reach the end intended in getting an account, now as the general account may be fraught with enough offence, and render hearing impossible.

Whereupon, the Church came to this vote: which was their mind,—that those that turned away from the Supper and the   of the Church, therein,—and the grounds of their so doing, not being apparent, were obliged to give such an account as should evince or evidence that their withdrawing was necessary, or they under necessity to turn away.

To this none dissented; only Capt. Lewis propounded, whether it were not   the Church should forbear bringing to an issue of that case at this time,—because more of the brethren were not at the meeting, or to that purpose.

The Church having considered the desires of their brethren, William, Thomas, John and Benjamin Judd,—as, also, John Standley, Jun., touching their removal from us to Mattabuck, agreed as followeth:—

1. In general. That considering the divers difficulty and inconveniences which attend the place toward which they are looking, and how hazardable it may be, (for aught that appeareth,) that the house and ordinances of Christ may not, (of a large time at least,) be settled among them,—the Church doth advise the brethren, to be wary of engaging far, until some comfortable hopes appear of being suited for the inward man, in the great things forementioned.

2. Particularly. To our brother William Judd,—that it having pleased God to deal so bountifully with him, that not many of the brethren with us have so large accommodations as himself, yet see not his call to remove on the account of straightness for outward subsistence,—and therefore counsel him,—if it may be with satisfaction to his spirit,—to continue his abode with us,—hoping God will bless him in so doing.

3. To the rest. Though we know not how much they will be bettered as to land, all things considered, by their removal,—especially John and Benjamin Judd, and therefore cannot much encourage,—yet, if the bent of their spirits be strong for going, and the advice aforegiven, touching the worship of God, be taken,—we shall not trouble,—but say,—the will of the Lord be done.

(To be Continued.)

———— •◦━◦• ————

REMARKABLE CIRCUMSTANCE.—At the public commemoration of the death of Henry Clay, by funeral obsequies, in the city of Sacramento, California, on the 12th of August, the pall-bearers, who represented every State in the Union, were severally natives of the States they represented.—The *Union* doubts if, with the single exception of San Francisco, there is any other State in the world which contains within its limits native-born citizens of every State in the Union.—*Newspaper*, 16 *Sept.* 1852.

BIRTHS, MARRIAGES, AND DEATHS,

Contained in the volume lettered "Original Distribution of the Town of Hartford (Ct.) among the Settlers, 1639."

[Transcribed by LUCIUS M. BOLTWOOD of Amherst, Cor. Mem. of H. and G. Soc.]

[Continued from page 198.]

Mr Paulus Schrick was married to Mrs. Mary Ambeek widdow the late wife of Mr. Johannes Ambeek deceased, December 30, 1658.

Thomas Gilberd y⁵ son of John Gilberd was born y⁵ 4th of Sept. 1658.

Amy Gilberd, daughter of John Gilbert was born y⁵ 3 of Aprill 1660.

Joseph Gilbert son of John Gilbert was born y⁵ 3ᵈ of Aprill 1666.

PAGE 10.

Anna Allyn daughter of Jnᵒ Allyn was borne the 18th of Agust 54.

Mary Allyn daughter of Jnᵒ Allyn was borne y⁵ 3ᵈ of Aprill 1657.

Margrett Allyn daughter of Jnᵒ Allyn was borne y⁵ 29th of July 1660.

Rebecca Allyn, a daughter of John Allyn was borne the 2ᵈ of March 1664.

Martha Allyn daughter of John Allyn was borne the 27 July 1667.

Elizabeth Allyn daughter of John Allyn was borne the 1ˢᵗ Decembʳ 1669.

Jonath Arnold son of Jonath Arnold and Hannah his wife was born 11 July 1710.

Andrew Belcher son of Mr. Andrew Belcher and Sarah his wife was born the 12 March 167½.

Abigail Butler daughter of Tho Butler and his wife Abigail was born Octobʳ 24th 1692.

Isaac Butler born Nov. 27 1693.

Deborah was born Sept 29 1695.

Amy was born Aprill 27 1698.

Danˡˡ Butler born Oct. 25 1700.

died Dec 28, 1700.

Sibill was born March 6 170½.

Daniell was born Ocʳ 11 1704.

Martha Bartlett daughter of Johojada Bartlett was born July 29, 1674.

John Biddoll son of John Biddoll of Hartford was born Septʳ 1: 1679.

His daughter Hana was born August 31, 1680.

His daughter Sarah was born August 19, 1681.

His son Thomas was born 27 December 1682.

His son Jonath was born 5 March 1684.

James Bidwell son of James Bidwell and Ruth his wife was born July 26, 1716.

Sarah Bull, daughter of Joseph and Sarah Bull was born July 11, 1672.

Joseph Bull, son of Joseph and Sarah Bull was borne August 9, 1675.

Daniel Bull son of Joseph and Sarah Bull was born November 9th 1677.

Caleb Bull son of Joseph and Sarah Bull was born February the 1ˢᵗ 1679.

Susnnah Bull daughter of Captⁿ Joneth Bull and Sarah his wife was born 26 of December 1685.

Sarah their daughter was born August 25 87.

Sibbell their daughter was born Aprill 13, 1690.

Ruth their daughter was born 21 Aprill 1692.

Abigall their daughter was born 24 July 1694.

Jonathan their son was born 14 July 1696, about one of the clock in the morning.

Moses Bull their son was born May 18, 1699.

Ebenezer Bull was born Aug¹ 27, 1701.

Abigail Burchard daughter of Sam¹¹ Birchard was born 24ᵗʰ July 1704.

Tho Bidwell's child was born May 29ᵗʰ 1710, and dyed few hours after its birth.

Barthsheba Barret daughter of Jonathan and Rebekah Barret was born Janʳ the 1ˢᵗ 1716.

Dorothy Barret was born Feb 14ᵗʰ 1717.

Sarah Blanchard the daughter of William Blanchard and Sarah his wife was born Octoʳ 29ᵗʰ 1719.

Esther Bull daughter of Thomas Bull and Thankfull his wife was born Aprill 15ᵗʰ 1721.

Samuel Bull was born Febʳ 26ᵗʰ 1723.

Amos Bull was born March 16ᵗʰ 1725.

Thankfull Bull was born October — 1729.

Susanah was born Febry 20ᵗʰ 1734½.

Jorusha was born June 20 1734.

Page 11.

Hannah Camp the daughter of John Camp was borne Nouember 24, 1672.

John Campe his son was born 13 Feb. 1675.

Sarah Camp his daughter was born 17 Feb. 1677.

Joseph Camp his son was born Jan. 30, 1679.

Mary Camp his daughter born June the 30 1682.

James Camp his son was borne June the 23ᵈ 1686.

Sam¹¹ Camp was born the 29 of January, 1690.

Abigail Camp was born July 31, 1699.

Mary Cadwell daughter of Thom. Cadwell was born January 8, 1659.

Edward his son was born Noumber the 1ˢᵗ 1660.

Thomas his son was born December the 5, 1662.

Edm. his son was born July 14, 1664.

Mathew his son was born Octobʳ 5, 1668.

Abigail Cadwell his daughter was born Nov. 26, 1670.

Elizabeth Cadwell his daughter was born Dece 1ˢᵗ 1672.

Samuel was born Aprill the 30ᵗʰ 1675.

Hana Cadwell was born August 22, 1677.

Mehitable was born the 12 January, 1679.

Edward Cadwell son of Edward Cadwell and his wife Eliz was born Sept [24?] 1681.

William was born 24 August 1684.

Elizabeth was born Dec. 5, 1687.

Rachell was born Aprill 3, 1689.

Aaron Cook son of Aron Cook was born May 12, 1686 and dyed Aprill 5 89.

Aaron Cook was born 23 Septʳ 1689.

Martha Cook was born the 2ᵈ of June 1693.

John Cook was born 23 Dec. 1696.

Moses Cook was born Oct. 7, 1700.

Elizᵃ Cook was born Sept. 4, 1703 Died 23 Sept. 1703.

Mary Cook was born June 2ᵈ 1706.

Nathᶦ Cole son Nathᶦ Cole and Lidiah his wife was born Nov. 6ᵗʰ 1692.

Mary Catling daughter of John Catling was born July 10, 1666.
Sam^ll Catling was born Nov. 4th 1672.
John was born 27 day Aprill 1676.
Thomas was born [27 ?] August 1678.
Benjamin Catling born 1 Feb. 1680.
John Catling son of Sam^ll Catling and his wife Eliz^t was born Oct. 20th
1703.
Tho Catling was born Feby 17th 1705–6.
Sam^ll Catling was born 27th March 170–.
Isaac Catlin was born Nov. 11th 1712.
Abijah Catlin was born April 6th 1715.
Mary Catlin was born March 26th 1717.
Eben^r Catlin was born July 25, 1724.
Hannah Clark, daughter of Dea^n Clark was born May 10th 1694.
Mary Clark was born in March ye 8th 1695.
Joseph Clark was born July 22, 1698–9.
Mary Clark was born
Isaac Clark was born July 25, 1710.
Jacob Demmon son of Jacob Demmon was born March [24 ?] 1696.
Lidiah Day daughter of John Day was born 11th of Aprill 1698.
Mary was born Augt 14th 1699.
John Day was born 6th June 1701.
Abigail daughter of Daniel Miles and Eliz^t his was born Feby 10th
1718–19.
Mary was born Feby 8th 1720–1.
Daniel Miles was born August 20th 1722.

Page 12.

David Ensigne son of David Ensigne was borne the 26 day of Nou^r
1664.
James Ensign son of David Ensigne was born the 8 of July 1666.
Thomas Ensigne son of David Ensigne was born the 7th of Decemb^r
1668.
Sarah Ensign daughter of David Ensigne was born 22 January 1671.
Mary Ensigne daughter of David Ensigne was born the 26th January
1674.
Sarah Easton daughter of Jn^r Easton was born July 18th 1670.
Mary was born Decemb^r 26, 1672.   Mehittabell Jany 17, 1683.
Sarra was born Nov. 15, 1675.   Abigail was born March 16, 1687.
John was born Jan^r 10, 1678.   John was born Octob^r 22, 1689.
Mary was born Octob^r 1, 1681.
Esther Cadwell daughter of Nath Cadwell and Esther his wife was
born Jany 24, 1722–3.
Matthew Cadwell was married to Abigail Beckly daughter of John
Beckly March 25, 1695.
Matthew Cadwell was born June 11, 1696.
Abigail was born May 6, 1700.
John was born Novemb^r 30th 1703.
Abell was born Novemb^r 27th 1703.
John Cole son of Nath and Eliz^t Cole was born Feb. 15th 1707–8.
Elizabeth was born March 18, 1709–10.
Zerviah Clark daughter of Josia and Elizabeth Clark was born Decem
27th 1703. Dyed Feb. 5th following.
Zervia the 2^d born Jany 3, 1704–5.   Barzilai was born August 17th 1706.

Sylvanus was born April 14th 1710. Dyed the [19th ?] following.

Mary Edwards daughter of John and Christian Edwards was born August 20th 1721.

Sarah Case daughter of Richard Case and Sarah his wife was born Octob'r 1st 1703.

Joseph was born Decem 27th 1705.   Elizabeth was born Sept 1, 1710.

Jonathan Edwards son of Rich'd Edwards was born Jan'r 20, 1692–3, and dyed y'e 24th March following.

John Edwards born 27 Feb. 1693–4.

Hanna Edwards born 3 Jan'r 1695–6.

Richard Edwards born June 5, 1698.

Dani'll Edwards born Aprill 11, 1701.

Sam'll Edwards born Novem. 1, 1702.

Rich'd Edwards dyed 20th May 1713.

Timothy Webster son of Stephen and Mary Webster was **born** Octo. 20th 1723.

Sam'll Cadwell was married to Mary Clark March 16th 1707–8.

Joseph Cook was married to Rachel Spencer Octo 24th 1705.

John Camp was married to Rebeckah Galpin June 27th 1711.

Benjamin Colton was married to Ruth Taylor Decemb'r 3d 1718.

Sam'll Catlin had a daughter born Sept. 17, 1719, and dyed the 27th of the same month.

Thomas Cadwell son of Thomas Cadwell Jun'r and Hannah his wife was born Decemb'r 29th 1719.

Abigail was born Jan'ry 5th 1722–3.

Matthew was born July 10, 1725.

Hannah was born August 16th 1729.

Page 13.

Benjamin Graham son of Benj'a Graham was **born Dec. 1, 1685,** and dyed Jan'ry 13, 1685.

George Graham son of Benj'a Graham was born Aprill [29 or 31] 1687.

John Graham born Decem 29th 1689, being Benj'a Graham his son.

Benj'a Graham, son of Benjamin Graham was born March 7, 1693–4.

Sam'll Graham son of Benj'a Graham was born March 6, 1696.

Elisha was born Feb. 24, 1699.

Isaac was born July 3, 1702.

Jonathan Gilbert son of Sam'll Gilbert his wife **Mary was born June** 29th 1685.

Sam'l was born Feb. 5th 1687.   John was born Aprill 12, 1692.

Nath'l was born Sept 26, 1690.   Mary was born Dec. 2d 1696.

Ozias Goodwin son of Ozias Goodwin and Martha his wife was born June 6th 1724.

Nath'l Goodwin son of Nath'l Goodwin was born July 1665.

Sarrah Goodwin was born Aprill 1668.

John Goodwin was baptized May 19, 1672.

Sam'll Goodwin was born Aug. 22, 1682.

Eliz'a Goodwin was born October 14, 1691.

Ozias Goodwin was born June 26, 1689.

Hester Gilbert daught'r of Eben'r Gilbert was born Nov. 13, 1694.

Thomas Gilbert son of Eben'r Gilbert was born Sept. 30, 1699.

Tim'o Kellogg son of Jacob Kellogg and Mary his wife was born Nov. 25th 1723.

Eliz'a Kellogg was born Aug. 8th 1727.

Lydia Kellogg was born July 22d 1729.

Thomas Huxly son of Thomas Huxly was borne the 7th of Aprill 1668.

Watts Hubbard the son of Sam" Hubbard & his wife Sarrah was born the 1st day of March 1686.

Abigail was born Aprill 1647 Died Aprill 1687.

Mary Hubbard born Feb. 1688.

John Hubbard born Aug. 1691.

Sarrah Hubbard born Nov. 10, 1696.

Hanna Hubbard daught of John Hubbard and Agnes his wife was born Dec. 25th 1716.

Abigail Hubbard was born Jan. 29, 1718–9.

John Hubbard was born Aprill 25, 1721.

Zebulon Chappell the son of Sam" Chappell and Hannah his wife was born Decem' 19th 1724.

Lydia was born October 3d 1724.

Hannah was born March 29th 1729.

Nath Goodwin son of Nath Goodwin and his wife Lois was born Feb. 20, 1691.

Thomas was born May 3, 1692.

Lois was born Sept 10th 1694.

Vuis [Eunice] was born March 17, 1697.

Timothy the son of Nath Goodwin and his wife Sarah was born Jan' 14, 1700.

Thankfull was born Aprill 29, 1703.

Daniel Goodwin was born Jan' 15th 170 [torn].

Sam" Gross son of Josiah Gross and Susannah his wife was born Jan'' 24th 1719–20.

Susannah Gross was born June 20, 1722.

PAGE 14.

Hannah Benton, daughter of Caleb Benton was born July 27th 1720.

Caleb Benton was born Jan'' 28, 1721–22.

Mehetabell Bushnell daughter of Wm and Mehetabell born Feb. 28th 1726–7.

Sarah Bushnell was born Jan' 31, 1728–9.

Mary Bushnell was born Octob. 27, 1730.

Elizabeth Bushnell was born Feb'' 24th 1732–3.

Nath'' Bracy son of Stephen Bracy was born Octob' 30, 1711.

Sarah Bracy was born July 4, 1713.

Samuel Bracy was born Septem'' 4th 1716.

Abigail Bracy was born June 19th 1718.

Benjamin Bracy was born Feb'' 5th 1719.

Ruth Bracy was born September 19th 1722.

Irenee Olmstead daughter of Stephen Olmstead and Sarah his wife was born Aprill 18, 1724.

Richard Lord was married to Ruth Wyllys December 31st 1724.

Eliz'' Lord daughter of Richard and Ruth was born October 9th 1725.

Abigail Hopkins daughter of Thomas and Mary Hopkins was born March 11th 1718.

Sarah was born Octo' 29, 1719.   Moses was born Jan'' 1, 1726–7.

Stephen was born May 8th 1722.   Aaron was born July 14, 1729.

Thomas was born August 29, 1725.

John Kellogg was married to Sarah Olmstead Jan'' the third 1718–19.

Sarah Kellogg daughter of John Kellogg and Sarah his wife was born October 30th 1719.

Mr Elisha Lord was married to Mrs. Mary Haynes May 4ᵗʰ 1723.

John Haynes Lord son of sᵈ Elisha and Mary was born Janʸ 13ᵗ 1724-5.

Susannah & Abigail twin daughters of William Bushnel and his wife Mehetabel was born May 12ᵗʰ 1735.

Rᵈ Lord died Nov. 5ᵗ 1685, being 49 years of age.

Mary Lord alias Hooker died May 17ᵗ Sabath day being 58 years and two months old 1702.

Mr. Richard Lord dyed January 23ᵗ 1711-12 being 42 years of age.

Mr Elisha Lord dyed Aprill 16, 1725.

Pagе 15.

Richard Lord yᵉ son of Richᵈ and Mary Lord was born Feb. 1, 1669.

Abigail Lord the daughtʳ of Richᵈ and Abigail Lord was borne ye 15ᵗʰ of March 1694. Died May 22, 94.

Richard Lord was born ye 16 day of August 1695.

Abigail Lord was born Janʸ 19ᵗ in ye year 1697-8 Dyed Aprill 19ᵗ 98.

Jerusha Lord was born Feb. 25, 169⅓ on Fryday night about 11 clock.

Richard Lord died Dec. 16, 1699 Saturday night.

Elisha Lord was born March 15ᵗ Satterday night 170⅔.

Mary Lord was born Feb. 20, on Sunday afternoon 170⅜.

Richard Lord yᵉ 2ᵈ was born Feb. 18, 170⅘ Sabeth night.

Elizabeth Lord was born August 3ᵈ 1707.

Epaphras Lord was born Decembʳ 26ᵗʰ 1709.

Ichabod Lord was born March 16, 1712.

Esther Wells, dafter of Samˡˡ Wells & Esther his wife was born Octo. 22, 1723.

Samˡˡ Wells was born Octobr. 5, 1725.

Ruth Wells was born Decembʳ 17, 1727, }
Ann Wells was born Decembʳ 17, 1727 } twins.

John was born July 29, 1730.

Jonathan was born Febry 20ᵗ 1732-3.

Hannah Wells born April 26th day 1736.

Rebecca born December 16, 1743.

Samˡˡ and John Weston sons of Samˡˡ Weston and Anne his wife was born June yᵉ 2ᵈ 1729.

Elisha Wells was married to Lydia Deming of Wethersfield April 4ᵗʰ 1757.

Elisha Wells son of said Elisha & Lydia was born Sept. 27, 1758.

Lemuel Wells their son was born July 30ᵗ, 1763.

Sarah Merrills the daughter of John Merrills was born Septʳ 19, 1664.

Nathaniel Merrills son of John Merrils was born January 15, 1666.

John Merrills son of John Merrills was born April 7, 1669.

Abram Merrills son of John Merrills was born Decembʳ 21, 1670.

Daniel Merrills son of John Merrills was born June 15, 1673.

Wolterton Merrills born June 28, 1675.

Susannah Merrills born May 20, 1677.

Abell Merrills son of John Merrills born January 25, 1679.

Isack Merills son of John Merills born March 11, 168⅓.

Jacob Merrills son of John was born March 27, 1686.

Joseph Long son of Thomas Long of Hartford was born January 22, 1667-8.

GENEALOGICAL MEMOIR OF THE FAMILY OF REV. NATHANIEL ROGERS, OF IPSWICH, MASS., 1636.

[Continued from Vol. V., p. 320.]

[By Augustus D. Rogers, of Salem, Mass. (158)?.]

(155.) Mr. Foster was an intimate friend of Gen. Washington, whose miniature likeness on ivory, a gift from him, is in possession of one of Mr. F.'s descendants.

A fair estimate of Mr. Foster's character, and an interesting incident connected with some of his neighbors and constituency, may be found in a letter written to a friend in New York, 1846, by the late Hon. Daniel Webster:—

"Of a hot day (says Mr. W.) in July—it must have been one of the last years of Washington's administration—I was making hay, with my father, just where I now see a remaining elm tree, about the middle of the afternoon. The Hon. Abiel Foster, M. C., who lived in Canterbury, six miles off, called at the house, and came into the field to see my father. He was a worthy man, college learned, and had been a minister, but was not a person of any considerable natural powers. My father was his friend and supporter. He talked awhile in the field and went on his way. When he was gone, my father called me to him and we sat down beneath the elm, on a hay cock. He said, ' My son, that is a worthy man—he is a member of Congress—he goes to Philadelphia and gets six dollars a day, while I toil here. It is because he had an education, which I never had. If I had had an early education I should have been in Philadelphia in his place—I came near it as it was, but I missed it, and now I must work here.' ' My dear father,' said I, ' you shall not work ; brother and I will work for you and wear our hands out, and you shall rest :' and I remember to have cried, and I cry now at the recollection. ' My child,' said he, ' it is of no importance to me—I now live but for my children— I could not give your older brother the advantages of knowledge, but I can do something for you. Exert yourself ; improve your opportunities— learn—learn—and, when I am gone, you will not need to go through the hardships which I have undergone, and which have made me an old man before my time.' The next May he took me to Exeter, to the Phillips Academy, and placed me under the tuition of its excellent preceptor, Dr. Benjamin Abbott, still living."

Mary Rogers, the wife of Mr. Foster, died March 12, 1813.

(156) VII. Elizabeth Rogers m. " Mr. John Harris of Ipswich," (a son of John Harris and Anne Franklin, sister of Dr. Benjamin Franklin the philosopher ?) She died Sep. 17, 1771, æ. 25.

(157) VIII. Lucy Rogers m. Capt. Jonathan Foster of Andover, Mass., brother of Hon. Abiel F. (155).

Sarah Rogers (72) and John Watson, Esq., of Plymouth, Mass., had children—

(158)	I. John, m. Elizabeth Reynolds in 1743 ; he died in Jan. 1758, his wife having previously deceased. They left three orphan children—one of them was John Watson, Esq., 2d President of the Pilgrim Society.

(159)	II. Col. George, m. 1st, Abigail, dau. of Hon. Col. Richard Saltonstall, Judge of Sup. Court of Mass. She died soon after,

29

without children. 2d, he m. Elizabeth, dau. of Hon. Peter
Oliver of Middleborough, Judge of Sup. Court of Mass.
3d, he m. Phebe Scott. Col. Watson died at the advanced
age of 83, Dec. 13, 1800, and was said "to have possessed almost every virtue that can dignify the human
character." His children were three daughters,—1. Mary,
m. Elisha Hutchinson, Esq. (son of Gov. H.) who died in
England before his father; 2. Sarah, who was living in
Boston in 1832, m. Martin Brimmer, Esq.; 3. Elizabeth,
m. Hon. Thomas Russell, a merchant of Boston, and, after
his decease, she m. Sir Grenville Temple, and died at
Rome, about 1806, leaving three children.

Margaret (73) and Rev. Robert Ward of Wenham, Mass., had

(160)   1. Margaret, " a minor under 14 years of age in Aug. 1733."

Priscilla (75) and Rev. Nathaniel Leonard of Plymouth, Mass., had

(161)   I. Anna, b. Nov. 23, 1725, d. Feb. 12, 1725–6.
(162)   II. Sarah, b. Oct. 29, 1726 ; m. Joseph Le Barron, by whom
           was a dau. Sarah, b. at Plymouth, Feb. 2, 1747 or 9, m.
           Wm. Hazen of Haverhill, Mass.; they had 16 children,
           the eldest m. Ward Chipman, Chief Justice of New Bruns-
           wick. Mrs. Le Barron's 2d husband was John White of
           Haverhill. She d. Feb. 1802.
(163)   III. Anna, b. July 17, 1728.
(164)   IV. Mary, b. July 8, 1729, or 7, d. Sept. 26, 1729, or 7.
(165)   V. Nathaniel, b. Oct. 30, 1730, of Plymouth.
(166)   VI. Priscilla, b. April 18, 1732, m. Dr. McKinstry of Taunton,
           Mass. A son was Rev. Wm. of the English church ; an-
           other son was John, partner of Major Caleb Stark of Bos-
           ton, (son of Major Gen. S.), who m. his sister.
(167)   VII. Daniel, b. Jan. 9, 1733, d. Jan. 18, 1733.
(168)   VIII. Mary, b. April 2, 1735, d. Jan. 26, 1735–6.
(169)   IX. Elizabeth, b. July 3, 1736 ; m. —— Duncan of Hav'hill, Ms.
(170)   X. Ephraim, b. Sept. 6, 1737, d. Nov. 6, 1737.
(171)   XI. Mary, b. Sept. 11, 1738, d. Jan. 1, 1739.
(172)   XII. Rev. Abiel, D.D., of Woodstock, Ct., was a chaplain in the
           Revolutionary army under Gen. Washington.
(173)   XIII. Margaret, b. Nov. 21, 1741.
(174)   XIV. Col. George, b. Nov. 28, 1742, lived at Norton, Mass., a
           manufacturer; he espoused the loyal side in the Revolu-
           tion, was Col. of a regiment, laid Nantucket under contri-
           bution, and attacked Fall River, where he was gallantly
           repulsed by Col. Joo Durfee. He eventually retired to
           Nova Scotia, (then including New Brunswick,) where he
           became a provincial councillor, and renewed his fortune,
           which had been confiscated, and died wealthy and respect-
           ed in the community in which he lived. He m. Sarah(?)
           Thacher of Boston, a dau. of Rev. Oxenbridge T. His
           eldest son George was a lawyer—Richard, a Col. of the
           104th Reg. of the British army, and Sheriff of the District
           of Niagara ; another son was Henry. A dau. m. Lt. Gen.
           Powell, of the British army ; Caroline m. R. M. Jarvis, Esq.
           in 1805 ; and his dau. Maria m. Lt. Gustavus R. H. M.
           Rochfort of the B. Navy in 1814.

(175) XV. Thomas, b. April 26, 1744.
(176) XVI. Phebe, b. Nov. 29, 1746, d. May 28, 1747.

Rev. Daniel (77) of Littleton, Mass., and Mary Whiting, had

(177)   I. Jeremiah Dummer, Esq., grad. Har. Col. 1762; m. at Boston, Dec. 25, 1769, to Bathsheba Thacher of Boston, (dau. of Rev. Oxenbridge T. of Milton, and sister of Rev. Peter T. of Brattle St. Church, Boston) by Rev. John Lathrop, Dec. 25, 1765. He commenced the practice of law at Littleton; " in 1774, he was one of the barristers and attorneys who were addressers of Hutchinson; he took refuge in Boston, and, after the battle of Breed's Hill, was appointed commissary to the royal troops that continued to occupy Charlestown, and lived in a house which stood on the present site of the Unitarian meeting-house in that town. At the evacuation of Boston in 1776, he accompanied the royal army to Halifax, and d. in that city in 1784." Their children were,

1. ———, m. David Ellis, Esq., of Boston. A son is Rev. George E. Ellis, D. D. of Charlestown, and a Professor in Harv. Univ.; another the Rev. Rufus Ellis of Boston.
2. ———, m. Dr. Wm. Spooner of Boston.
3. Margaret, m. Jonathan Chapman, Esq. of Boston. A son was Hon. Jonathan C., Mayor of Boston.
4. John, } d. young.
5. Samuel, }
6. Samuel, a merchant of Boston, d. 1832; he was a child at the time of his father's decease at Halifax, whence he returned to Boston, where, with his sisters, he was educated by his father's sisters.
7. Jeremiah Dummer, was educated by an uncle; he went to England, where he resided and was a classical teacher—(among his pupils was Lord Byron;) he d. at Nottingham, England, 1832. While on a visit to his friends in this country in 1824, he received from Har. Univ. the degree of A. M.

(178)   II. Daniel.
(179)   III. Eliza, m. Abel Willard, Esq., (son of Col. Samuel W. of Lancaster, Mass.); he graduated at Har. Col. 1752. " In 1774 he was one of the barristers and attorneys who were addressers of Hutchinson; in 1776 he accompanied the royal army to Halifax; in 1778 was proscribed and banished, and died in England in 1781; his widow died at Boston in 1815."

(180)   IV. Sarah m. Samuel Parkman, Esq., a merchant of Boston. Their children were—

1. Samuel.
2. Rev. Francis, D. D., a distinguished divine of Boston; d. Nov. 11, 1852.
3. Daniel, m. ———, dau. of Thomas Macdonough, British Consul at Boston.
4. John, d. at Brighton.
5. Eliza W., m. Hon. Robert G. Shaw of Boston. She d. April 14, 1853.

  6. ———, m. Edward Tuckerman, Esq. of Boston.
  7. Dr. George, m. a dau. of Thomas Macdonough, British
   Consul at B.; d. Nov. 23, 1849.
(181) V. ———, m. Rev. Jonathan Newhall, of Stowe, Mass.

Patience (79) and Capt. Joshua Freeman of Plymouth, Mass., and
*   Portland, Me., had*

(182) I. Joshua, b. 1730, d. Nov. 11, 1796, in his 66th year; m. Lois,
  youngest dau. of Moses Pearson of Portland; she d. Mar.
  21, 1815, æ. 90. Their children were Sarah, Mary, Daniel, Lois, Eunice, Joshua, Moses, Samuel, Pearson, Jeremiah, Thomas, the last surviving son, who, in 1847, lived
  at Portland, and Dummer.
(183) II. George, b. in 1739, was living in Standish within a few
  years, 1849.

Hon. Nathaniel (81) of Portsmouth, N. H., and Dorothy, dau. of
*   Hon. Henry Sherburne, had*

(184) I. Hon. Nathaniel, of Exeter, N. H., an only son, b. Nov. 24,
  1745, nine days after his father's death; was grad. at Har. C.
  When the troubles preceding the Revolution arose, having
  espoused the loyal side, he was consequently stigmatized as
  a tory, and, with others, committed to prison for opinion's
  sake in 1777. After the Revolution, he was consistently
  obedient to legitimate authority. Soon after the adoption of
  the State constitution, becoming a member of the legislature,
  he continued a senator or councillor until appointed by Pres.
  Washington Marshal of the State of N. Hampshire; he was
  appointed by Pres. Adams and held the office of Supervisor
  of the revenue of the State, until it was abolished by the
  administration of Pres. Jefferson. He was afterwards Judge
  of probate for the county of Rockingham. His wife was
  Elizabeth, dau. of Anthony and Abigail Carpenter of Boston,
  where he was mar. by the Rev. Robert Sanderson, Feb. 28,
  1768; he d. 1823, æ. 83. Their children were—
  1. Elizabeth, m. Henry Burleigh.
  2. Olive Plaisted, m. Henry Tilton.
  3. Nathaniel, m. Elizabeth Gelleneau.
  4. Mary Anne, m. John Shute.
  5. Caroline Matilda.
  6. George Augustus, Esq., of N. Y. city, m. Sarah Warner
   Sherburne.
  7. Dorothy, m. Edward Jennings Long.
  8. Sarah, m. Offin B. Palmer.
  9. Caroline, m. 1. Jotham Fairfield, Esq.; 2. Caleb Jewett,
   Esq.; 3, ——— McLowder.
  10. John, m. Frances Gilman; 2. Anne Gilman; 3. Martha
   Cram.
  11. Helen, m. Hon. Timothy Boutwell.
  12. Richard Woodhull, m. 1. Mary Howard; 2. Sarah English;
   3. Rachel Kinsley.

George (84) and Lydia, sister of Gov. Hutchinson, had

(185) I. Nathaniel, b. about 1736; he was appointed Secretary of New
  Hampshire, but died before entering on the duties of the

office, previous to Aug. 24, 1770. He was probably a merchant and left a considerable estate, (and valuable library), on which Gov. Hutchinson administered. His wife was Elizabeth ———. In 1761, he was a fellow passenger to England with Mr. Mascarene, (who m. a dau. of Pres. Holyoke of H. C.) the only son of Maj. Gen. M. of Nova Scotia. He made a tour of England, Ireland and Scotland, and also travelled in Holland and France. When in England, he visited, among many of note, Mr. Hollis, the benefactor of Har. Col., and with Mr. Mascarene went to Court, " where they had admission to the drawing-room, and a very full view of their majesties," &c.

(186)   II. Sarah, b. about 1738 ; lived in the family of Gov. Hutchinson, and died unmarried previous to Oct. 1776. Rev. William Welsted, her uncle, was guardian during her minority, and Abigail Marchant of Boston, sister of Gov. H., administratrix of her estate. A fine copy by Copley, of the portrait of John Rogers the martyr, was in possession of this family, and afterwards of Rev. Dr. Eliot of Boston, and is now at the Rooms of the Mass. Historical Society.

Elizabeth (85) and Rev. John Taylor of Milton, N. H., had

(187)   I. ———, m. Nicholas Gilman, State treasurer of N. H. ; she was mother of the late Gov. John Taylor Gilman of N. H., Hon. Nicholas Gilman, U. S. Senator, and Nathaniel Gilman, State treasurer.

Mary (86) and Matthew Livermore of Portsmouth, N. H., had

(188)   I. ———, a daughter, m. ——— Greenwood.

Hon. Daniel (88) of Portsmouth, N. H., and Mehitable Ringe, had

(189)   I. Sarah, d. unm.
(190)   II. Ann, m. Jacob Treadwell, Esq., of Portsmouth. Their children were Ann, m. Rev. John Eliot, D. D. of Boston, minister of the North Church, son of Rev. Andrew E., D. D., of same church, and Eliz. Langdon—their children were Andrew, John, Ann, George, Eliz. Langdon, and Mary.
(191)   III. John,
(192)   IV. Daniel,   } d. in childhood.
(193)   V. John,
(194)   VI. Thomas,
(195)   VII. Thomas Ringe of Nottingham, N. H., grad. H. C. 1774 ; m. widow Clarke.
(196) VIII. Daniel Ringe, Esq., of Portsmouth, N. H. ; m. Hannah, dau. of Dr. A. R. Cutter. Their children were,
          1. Hannah, m. Lemuel Draper, merchant of Portsmouth.
          2. Charles, d. in infancy.
          3. Anne Ringe, m. Wm. Stocker, merchant of Boston.
          4. Caroline Elizabeth.
          5. Elizabeth Cutter, d. unm.
          6. Nathaniel Cutter, d. unm.
          7. Charlotte Mary, m. Dr. Robert L. Thorne, U. S. Navy.
          8. Charles Cutter, d. unm.
          9. Wm. Cutter,   do.
          10. Mary Cutter.

> 11. Daniel Ringe, m. Eliz. Haven, dau. of John Haven, Esq.
>   of Portsmouth.
> 12. Ammi Ruhammi Cutter, d. in childhood.

(197) IX. Nathaniel Ringe, d. unm.
(198) X. Mark, m. Susannah Gardiner. A dau. was Mehitable Ringe,
     m. Jacob Wendell, Esq. of Portsmouth, merchant, 1816.
(199) XI. William, d. unm.

 Martha (97) and Matthew Perkins of Ipswich, had

(200) I. Hannah, baptized "20 . 10 mo. 1713."

 Nathaniel (103) of Boston, and Elizabeth Porter, had

(201) I. Nathaniel, b. at Boston, Feb. 6, 1717.(?)

 Dr. Theophilus (104) of Norwich, Ct., and Elizabeth Hyde, had

(202) I. Lois, b. July 22, 1721 ; m. Zebulon Lathrop, Sept. 4, 1740 :
     their children were, 1. Lois ; 2. Zebulon ; 3. Uriah.
(203) II. Ezekiel, b. Oct. 2, 1723, d. Nov. 11, 1745.
(204) III. Anne, b. Aug. 26, 1726 ; m. Phineas Hyde, April 5, 1744 ;
     d. July 29, 1766. Their children were, 1. Ezekiel Rogers ;
     2. Phineas ; 3. Anne ; 4. Elizabeth.
(205) IV. Elizabeth, b. April 17, 1729 ; m. Ezra Selden, May 6, 1751 ;
     she d. June 20, 1765. Their children were, 1. Ezra ; 2.
     Theophilus Rogers ; 3. Gurdon ; 4. Elizabeth ; 5. Abigail ;
     6. Calvin ; 7. Samuel Rogers ; 8. Elizabeth.
(206) V. Dr. Theophilus, an eminent physician of Norwich, Conn., b.
     Aug. 4, 1731 ; m. Penelope Jarvis, March 25, 1754 ; he
     d. Sept. 24, 1801. Their children were,
     1. John, b. May 27, 1755.
     2. Elizabeth, b. Aug. 24, 1757 ; m. Dr. Elihu Marvin, Dec.
      25, 1780 ; d. Dec. 30, 1808. Their children were,
      Sarah Rogers, m. George W. Mott ; Elizabeth ; Penelope
      Jarvis, m. John S. Pearson ; Susannah ; Catherine Ma-
      ther, m. Rev. Luther F. Dimmick of Newburyport ;
      Theophilus Rogers, Esq., of Boston, printer and pub-
      lisher, m. Julia A. C. Coggeshall, April 13, 1832,
     3. Sarah, b. Jan. 3, 1761 ; m. Benjamin Snow, Oct. 26, 1784 ;
      d. April 8, 1788.
     4. Anna, b. Feb. 10, 1770, d. in infancy.
      (To be Continued.)

Mr. Drake,—Should not the name Roger Darly. (p. 78, vol. 7 of the
Register,) be Roger Darby? Roger Darby and Lucretia his wife, of
Topsham, Co. Devon, Eng., arrived at Boston in 1671 ; their dau. Experience was b. in Ipswich, 1671 ; their son Richard was b. there in 1679,
and their dau. Lucretia at Salem, Aug. 17, 1681. But I believe the name
of Darly has not been found in the Ipswich records.   E. S. W.

From the Probate Records, Salem.

Letters of Administration granted to Elizabeth Dean, on estate of her
deceased husband Thomas Dean, late of Salem, July 13th, 1705.

Letters of Admn to Thomas Dean of Salem, eldest son of Elias D., relict of George Dean, late of Salem, dec'd, Dated yr 29th day of Nov. 1705.

Priscilla Hillard, Admn of estate of David Hillard, July 9th, 1703.
          E. S. W.

ABSTRACTS FROM THE EARLIEST WILLS ON RECORD IN
THE COUNTY OF SUFFOLK, MASS.

[Prepared by Mr. WILLIAM B. TRASK, of Dorchester.]

[Continued from page 275.]

JOHN RUGGLES.—24. 12ᵐ 1657. I, *John Rugles*, of Roxbury, senio', being an this time in health, yett being old, not knowing yᵉ day of my death, doe make this my last will. Vnto my wife, *Margery*, one Cow, which she shall Chuse out of all my Cows, & yᵉ best pai' of sheetes vnto herselfe, to dispose of as she please, yᵉ sheats she brought with her to me, I Meane yᵉ best pair. Vnto my wife, £4 p' yeare, to bee paid by mine executo' in wheat, 30ˢ. in Indian 30ˢ, in barly or Mault 20ˢ, to be pd quart'rly, if she desire it, in any sort of grain, as is expressed—to bee paid att yᵉ now dwelling house of yᵉ sᵈ Ruggles. My will is, yᵗ my wife shall have yᵗ bed wᵗʰ yᵉ furniture about it wᶜʰ we vsually ly vpon, wᵗʰ two pair of sheats, wᶜʰ my wife shall Chuse, these two pair to bee here as long as she shall live in this wourld. Vnto my wife, fo' yᵉ time of her Widdow Hood, all yᵉ old end of my house wherein I now dwell, provided my son have lib'ty to bake in yᵉ. ovens, togethe' wᵗʰ halfe yᵉ brass.& pewte', old bodgsheads, tubbs, setts, Chaires, stooles, Chests & such like things, to bee vsed wᵗʰin dores, together wᵗʰ Convenient out housing fo' hay & Cattle things fo' two Cattle, & liberty fo' hoggs. in season, & fo' foules to kp within yᵉ hen house, allwayes provided, yᵗ damage may bee prevented as much as may bee, togethe' wᵗʰ half yᵉ orchard & spott of Meadow my heire shall divide at, & she shall chuse wᵗʰ part to have, it being by my heir puts into two parts; also, an Acre & a halfe in bare Marsh, lying next *Robt. Gamlin*, also halfe an acre of salt marsh lying neal *Tho: Warman*, in gravily point, also twenty rod of mudy on hills to sow flax in, if she desire it, & to have it in yᵉ most convenient place for yᵉ benifit of them both; also my son to Cut out & bring whom my wife five load of wood, every year, & to lay it in yᵉ most convenient place we now lay wood in, & this to be done every yeare in season most fit for hir Comfort, yᵉ sᵈ Loads of Wood to bee sufficient loads wᵗʰ two good Oxen & a good Horse; also, my son shall Mow, Make, & bring home all he' hay, every yeare in season, yᵗ grows on he' land, & my son shall keepe all houses in Repair, excepting fire. Also, I give vnto my wife, during yᵉ time of her Widdowhood, pasto' for one Cow in my [underbrush ground?] at home. All my houses, lands Cattle, monie, not before expressed, vnto my son, *Jnᵒ Rugles*, whom I make my sole executor. My sᵈ son to ente' vpon emediately afto' my decease, to him & his heires fo' ev', vpon these Conditions. 1: yᵗ my son shall make good my Will in paying all my debts, leagesies, funerall expenses, & vnto my Wife wt I have injoyned him to doe for her, but if my sᵈ son shall not, or will not, in season p'forme according as is forme'ly expressed, then I impowe' my wife, wᵗʰ Advice of my ov'seers, to ente' vpon my part of my lands, from time to time to sell & pay my wife what shall bee due to her, wᵗʰ all cost, charge & trouble about yᵉ same. My will is, yᵗ my servant, *Samuell Pery*, shall serve out his time according to his Indenture with my sone, *John Ruggles*. I hereby Injure my sᵈ son, to p'forme my part of his indenture vnto my sᵈ servant, hoping my sᵈ son will vse him well vnto yᵉ satisfaction of my ov'seers, but if he shall neglect to doo, I give powe' vnto my overseers to place him elce where, so as he may be well used, but if my son keep him out his time, then my will is, y^t my son shall Add vnto my s^d servant, beside w^t I am Ingaged vnto in his Indenture, £3, in Country pay, my meaning is, to make ye 40^s expressed in ye Indenture, £5. [Of] ye five load of Wood I Appointed my son to bring my Wife yearely, she shall haue liberty to sell one fifth to her own Charge, two or three more yearly at my wood lott, Answorth hill. I desire my friends, *Isack Heath*, ye Ruling Eld^r of ye Church of Christ att Roxbury & my Broth^r in law, *Edw. Bridge, Thomas Weld & William Parke*, to bee overseers of this my will [If any difference arise between his son & wife, to be settled by the overseers.] To my wife, one hogg & one pigg, what flax shall bee vpon ye ground or in ye house or clossib vntill ought att my desease, my will is, my wife shall have one halfe & my son ye othe^r: thus have I finished my will this 26: 4mo: 58.

John Ruggles.

Witnesse *William Parke, Edward Bridge*
who deposed, 30 Jan. 1663.

[Then follows the deposition of *Edward Bridge*; testifying that his brother manifested to him, the said *Bridge*, the intention to add to his will concerning his wife, Margery, that she should be comfortably maintained out of his estate, &c. This, he thought, should be added to the will.

William Parke deposed, that in the year 1658, *Margery*, wife of *John Ruggles*, was " in good health & as active & lively as could be expected to her yeares & ability; but since, she had been disabled by the palsy." For this reason, her late husband told Mr. Parke that he would add to his wife in his will so much as would make her comfortable for life. Mr. P. also was in favor of adding this instrument to the will, and proposed that security be given, by the son, to make it good unto his mother-in-law. 30 Jan. 1663.]

Inventory of the Estate of John Ruggles Senior taken 16th Octr 1663 by *Thomas Weld, Edw: Denison*. Sum £343.1^s. Mentions 24 Acres of Land in ye first division, £68; 14 Acres in three divisions, £14; 9 Acres next Dedham, £1,10^s; 3 acres fresh meadow, £20; 2½ acres salt meadow, £12. *John Ruggles Junior*, deposed, 30th Jan. 1663.

Mordecai Nichols.—1st March 1663. Power of Administration to the estate of the late *Mordecay Nichols*, deceased, is Granted to *Alice*, his wife, in behalfe of hirself & Children, she bringing in a true Inventory, to the next Court, &c.

Inventory of the estate taken 25th of April 1664, by *Wm Bartholmew, Roger Clapps*. Amt. £524. 07^s. 03^d. *Alice Nicolls* deposed, 29th April 1664.

[3 Feb. 1664. The Court being informed that since the Inventory of the estate of said Nichols was produced, by losses and debts, the estate had depreciated " to the value of two hundred pounds & odd : And the widow being readye to dispose of herselfe, the Court Judged it meete to order that the House & Land mentioned in the Inuentorye at £150, shall bee secured" to *John Nicolls*, his son, as a part of his portion, and that his mother *Alice*, the widow, pay unto her said son, £50 more, at the age of 14 years. The house and land to be improved for his use till he come to age—the mother to have the use of the son's portion till that time; " to

Choose his Guardian for his Education, & in the Meanetime His Mother & *Cap' Clap* are appointed his Guardians"—the mother to have all the rest of the estate as her portion—" in case the Child Dye, before he attains his age, y° Mother to have y° whole."]

ALICE SMITH.—*Isack Cullimore, Alex. Adames, Edward Budd* and *Sarah Martin* were desired by *Joseph Bayles* to take a view of such things as were in the chest of *Alis Smith,* late deceased. The above individuals made an appraisement 14th Oct. 1663. Amt. £29. 19° 8d. *John Boulton,* scribb. 9th Oct'. 1663.

14th Oct. 1663. *Joseph Bayley* desired the persons before mentioned, with *Martha Beamsts,* to prise other goods amounting to £8. 4. 6.; afterward, a few more items were added.

Power of Administration to the Estate of the late widdow *Alice Smith* was Graunted to *Joseph Bayly,* her kinsman, and to *Samuel & Abraham Smith,* two of her sonnes, in behalfe of the Rest of the children, of s° *Alice Smith.*—16 : 8 : 1663. *Joseph Bayly* deposed.

ROBERT POND.—[*Mary Pond* relict & Administratrix to the Estate of the late *Robert Pond,* of Milton, deceased, bound herself in the sum of £100 together wth the house & 40 acres of land to it belonging, for the payment of £65 due from the estate. Dated 20th of May, 1663. In p'sence of *Sam: Torrey, Robt. Voue.*]

Inventory of the estate taken 24th of Dec'. 1662, by *John Gill, James Humphry, William Pond.* Sum total £95. 17. 3. *Mary Pond,* relict of *Robert,* deposed 13th of May 63.

JAMES HARROD.—[*John Turell,* of Boston, marriner, & *Daniel Turell,* of said Boston, blacksmith, bound in the sum of £100 to administer on the estate of the late *James Harrod,* sonne of *W°* *Harrod,* of Byddiford, in the County of Devon, in old England, they being appointed to administer on said estate. Witnessed by *Thomas Edsell, Thomas Batt,* 28th of April 1663.]

Power of Administration to the estate of the late *James Harrod,* Deceased, is graunted to *John Turel,* of Boston, marriner, in behalfe of the father of the late *James Harrod,* of Biddiforde, or such others to whom it belongs, he giuing securitye, &c. 26th of Aprill 1664.

Inuentorye of the Estate of said Harrod, left by him in the possession of Jn° Turrell at his deposition, out of this Countreye. Amt. £50. 0°. 7½d. Mentions bill upon *John Conage.* The Inuentorye ueiwed & called p' *John Sunderland & Daniell Turrell,* 23d of April 1664. *John Turell* deposed same day.

THOMAS EMONS.—20 : 11mo: 1660. I, *Thomas Emons,* of Boston, in New England, Cordwainer, being sicke, make my last will. [Debts to be paid.] I giue unto my sonne, *Obadia,* sonne *Samuel,* daughter *Hanna Crab,* & daughter *Elizabeth Hinckman, & p'* peice, to be paid them by my Executrix within a Considerable time after my Decease (Declaring herby that my Children Before named, haue had of my Estate, before the Day of y° Date hereof their parts proportionall with other of my Children heerafter named.) Unto my sonne *Benjamin,* £20, to be paid by my executrix, at or before the end of Fiue yeares after my Decease, by the ualue therof in good paye. Unto my Gran-sonne *Thomas Emons,* sonne of Obadiah, 40° to be paid to him or to his use within three yeares after my Decease. Unto my Gransonne *Samuell Crass*, 40°, to bee paid [as before.] Unto my Kinswoman *Martha Winsor*, 40°, to bee paid her on the Day of her Marriage or at her age of 21, which of them shall first happen. Unto my wife, *Martha*, my two Houses in Boston, that is to say, the House I now Dwell in, & my house now in the tenure of *John Andrews*, Cooper; the said Houses & Land to haue & to dispose of as shee shall think good. Unto my wife all the moueable goods within my now Dwelling house. My Wife Martha I make executrix of this my last will.   Thomas Emons.

In the presence of us, *John Bateman*, *William Pearse*.

[There is a memorandum in regard to the "Raze" made in the will by order of the legatee, signed by *Richard Staines* and *William Pearse*, 11th of May 1664.]

17th June 1664. Richard Staines & William Pearse deposed. Present, Ric⁴ Bellingham Deputy Gouern'; M' Tho Danforth, M' Edward Rawson, Recorder.

Inventory of the Estate of Thomas Emons deceased 11ᵗʰ of May, apprized by *William English*, *Edmund Jacson*. Aml. £440. 5'. Debts due the deceased to the am', of £66. 06. 04.—from yᵉ deceased, £45. 10. 09.

17 June 1664, *Martha Emmons* deposed to this inventory of the estate of her late husband. ______

Jᴏʜɴ Hɪʟʟ.—Will of *John Hill*, of Dorchester, made 11th of April 1660. I giue unto my Eldest sonne, *John Hill*, that Estate of myne now in his hands, & for a remembrance I giue him 5'. For the Rest of my Estate, house, Land & moouables I giue unto my wife, *Francis*, During her Life, for her Maintenance & for yᵉ Bringing up of my Children, and at her Death my will is that my whole Estate bee giuen unto my nine youngest Children, or to so many of them as shall be then aliue, alway prouided there be respect had to my sonne, *Samuell*, who hath been helpfull unto mee in my Infirme Dayes. I giue my wife power to dispose of any parte of my estate as shee shall Judge meet, with the Aduise of my Louing Freinds *Tho: Tileston* & *John Minott*. My dau. *Mary*, hauing had her portion according to my abilitye alreadye, I Doe for a Remembrance giue her 5'. And being confident of the Faithfulnes and Care of my beloued Wife I make her my Executrix of this my Last will.

Signed in the presence of   John X Hill.
Thomas Tileston, *Timothy Tilston*, *John Minott*, who deposed 30ᵗʰ. 4ᵗʰ. 1664.

Inventory of the estate taken 9ᵗʰ of June 1664, by *Thomas Tileston*, *Jno. Mynott*. Aml. £281. 1'. *Francis Hill* deposed to this Inventory of the estate of her Late husband, June 30, 1664.

______

Tʜᴏᴍᴀs Mᴜɴᴛ.—Inventory of yᵉ Goods & chattells of Thomas Munt, deceased, prized by *James Johnson*, *Robert Sanderson*, *Edward Raynsford*, 6ᵗʰ of July 1664. Aml. £214. 07½. Mentions "one peece of land lying between *Robert Sanderson* and *John Brackett*;" "one peece of Land lying by *Peter Warren*."

8ᵗʰ July 1664. Power of Administration to this Estate granted to *Elinor* his late wife in behalf of herselfe and her 3 daughters.

Elinor Munt deposed to the inventory of said estate, on the same day.

(To be Continued.)

EARLY RECORDS OF BOSTON.

[Continued from page 110.]

BRANTRY MARRIAGES.

Samuell Deering & Mary Ray marryed 15 : 9 : 51 by Mr Tho : Flynt.

Humphrey Greggs & Grizell Jewell marryed 9 : 1 mo : 55 by Mr Bellingham.

Wm Savill & Sarah Gamit were married 9 : 6 mo : 55 by Major Atharton.

Christo Webb & Hannah Scott were married 18 : 11 : 55 by Capt Torrey.

James Puffer & Mary Swalden was marryed 14 : 12 : 55 by Capt Torrey.

Sam Tomson & Sarah Shepp'd was marryed 25 : 2 : 56 by Mr Browne of Watertowne.

Tho : Barret & Francis Woolderson was marryed 14 : 7 : 55 by Major Atharton.

Nath[n Minot ?] & Hannah Sh[   ] was marryed 25 : 10 : 56 by Wm Allice of Brantrey.

Robt [Aldridge and Margaret   ?] marryed 25 : 10 : 56 by Wm Aice [Allice.]

John Pray & Johannah Downam was marryed 7 : 3 mo : 57 by Wm Allice.

Martine Saund's & Elizaboth Bancroft was marryed 23 : 3 : 54 by Capt Gookin.

Dauid Walsbee & Ruth Ball was marryed 24 : 7 : 56 by Major Willard.

Sam Deering & Mary New Come was marryed 10 : 9 : 57 by Mr Endecott Govr.

John Saund's & Mary Mungy was marryed the 9 : 8 mo : 50 by Mr Hibbins.

Richd Thayre & Dorothy Pray was marryed 24 : 10 : 51 by Mr Tho : Flynt.

Robt Twells & Martha Brackett was marryed 23 : 9 : 55 by Mr Bellingham.

Martine Saund's & Lyddia Hardira was marryed 1 : 2 mo : 51 by Mr Dudley.

Hen : Neale & Hannah Pray was marryed 14 : 12 : 55 by Capt Torrey.

Jno Harbour & Jaell Thayre was marryed 17 : 1 : 54 by Capt Torrey.

James Mycall & Mary Farr was marryed 11 : 10 mo by Major Atharton.

Sydrack Thayre & Mary Barret was marryed 1 mo : 11th 1654 by Capt Torrey.

John Bamm & Ruth Auldin was marryed 13 : 12 mo : 57 by Mr Jno Auldine of Duxbery.

BRANTREY DEATHES.

Tho : Copeland yc sonne of Lawrence Copeland & of Lyddia his wife dyed 11 : 4 : 52.

Tho Smith servant to Tho : Gatline was drowned 7 : 4 mo : 54.

Andrew Rounsimon a Scott servant to Gregory Belchere dyed 31 : 8 : 57.

Bethyah Deering ye wife of Sam Deering dyed 11 : 3 mo : 57.

Mary Deering ye wife of Sam Deering dyed 1 : 5mo : 57.

Jn° Parmenter sonne of Rob' Parmenter & of Leah his wife dyed 4 : 9 : 53.

Hannah Walsbee y° wife of David Walsbee dyed 2 : 12 mo : 55.

Judeth Saund'a y° Daughter of Martine Saund'a & of Rachell his wife dyed 5 : 7 : 57.

Rachell Saund'a y° wife of Martine Saund'a dyed 15 : 7 : 51.

Hannah Brackett y° Daughter of Peter Brackett & of Priscilla his wife dyed 15 : 4 : 57.

Margaret Flynt y° Daughter of M' Hen : Flynt & of Margery his wife dyed 29 : 6 : 48.

David Flynt y° sonne of M' Hen : Flynt & of Margery his wife dyed 21 : 1 : 52.

Cotton & John Flynt sonns of M' Henry Flynt & of Margery his wife dyed 20 : 9 : 56.

Moses Paine sonne of Moses Paine & of Elizabeth his wife dyed 10 : 6 mo : 57.

Edmond Quinsey y° sonne of Edmond Quinsey & Johanna his wife dyed 11 : 9 mo : 57.

Jn° George sonne of Peter George & of Mary his wife dyed 2 : 9 mo : 53.

Jn° Addams sonne of Joseph Addams & Abigail his wife dyed 27 : 11 : 56.

Joseph Saund's sonne of Martine Saund's & of Lydia his wife dyed 19 : 3 : 57.

Josiah Allice sonne of W™ Allice & of Mary his wife dyed 15 : 8 : 51.

Hannah Harbour y° Daughter of Jn° Harbour & Jael his wife dyed 30 : 2 : 57.

Jane Niles y° wife of John Niles dyed 15 : 3 : 54.

William Ames dyed 11 : 1 : 53.

Tho : French y° sonne of Jn° French & of Grace his wife dyed 28 : 8 : 56.

Rachell Thayre y° Daughter of Sidracke Thayre & of Mary his wife dyed 23 : 9 : 56.

Mary y° wife of Sidracke Thayre 2 : 2 : 57.

Mary Fackson y° Daughter of Rich° Fackson & of Elizabeth his wife dyed 14 : 7 : 57.

Peter Shooter dyed 15 : 5 : 54.

Rich° Hardier dyed 27 : 10 : 57.

Tho Downam sonne of Jn° Downam & of Dorothy his wife dyed 9 : 8 mo : 44.

Mary Chapman y° Daughter of Rich° Chapman & of Mary his wife dyed 15 : 5 : 57.

Sarah Tomson y° Daughter [of Samuell] Tomson & of Sarah his wife dyed 10 : 9 : 57.

John Saund's sonne [of John Saunders & of Mary his wife dyed ?] 2. 11[?] 57.

Hannah y° wiffe of W™ [   ]

Sarah Deering y° Daughter of Sam' Deering & of Mary his wife dyed 4 : 7 mo : 57.

Miriam Aldridge y° Daughter of George Aldridge & of Katherin his wife dyed 10 : 1 : 51.

Samuell Speere sonne of George Speere & and of Mary his wife dyed 5 : 4 mo : 54.

From Braintree By me John Mills, 249 p'sons, chosen clark of y° Writts for y° same Towne.

This page Containing y° Births Deaths & Marriages in Brantrey w°h I reed this first of Aprill 1658 from y° clerke of y° writs there.

Joseph Adams & Abigail Baxter was marryed 26 : 9 : 50.

Stephen Paine & Hannah Basse was marryed 15 : 9 : 51.

Joseph Arnoll y° sonne of Joseph Arnol & Rebeccah his wife borne 16 : 1 : 49.

Jn° Holl sonne of Edw⁴ Holl & Hester his wife was borne 23 : 11 : 50.

Josiah Allis son of W° Allis & of Mary his wife borne 20 : 8 : 51.

Samuel Walsbee sonne of David Walsbee & of Hannah his wife borne 9 : 2 : 51.

James Yorke sonne of James Yorke & of Johanna his wife borne 14 : 4 : 48.

Ruth Curtis y° Daughter of Diadatis Curtis & and of Rebecca his wife borne 8 : 11 : 47.

Joseph Arnoll y° sonne of Joseph Arnoll & of Rebecca his wife borne 18 : 8 : 52.

Daniell Owen y° sonne of W° Owen & of Elizabeth his wife borne 1 : 6 : 51.

BURRYALLS.

Daniell Owen y° sonne of William Owen was buryed 14 : 8 : 51.

Josiah Allis sonne of W° Allis was Buryed 3 : 8.

Henry Adams y° daughter of Joseph Adams & of Abigail his wife borne 13 : 9 : 52.

This is a true Copie of the sev'rall Birthes Deathes & Marriages y¹ haue beene in Brantrey since I came to be Clarke of y° writts y¹ haue beene brought in to me   16 June 1653   Rich⁴ Bracken.

WEYMOUTH BIRTHES.

Feare not sonne of Jn° & Hester King 29 : 4 : 55.
William sonne of Ephraim Hunt   [55.]
John son of Sam & Eliz. Packer 20 : 5 mo : 55.
Joseph sonne of Richd & Sarah Nubery 4 : 6 : 55.
John the sonne of John & Sarah Whitmarsh 23 : 6 : 55.
Eward sonne of Edw & Anne Bate 10 : 10 mo : 55.
Jonas sonne to Jonas & Martha Humpherys 24 : 11 : 55.
Sam : son of Hugh & Abigail Roe 14 : 11 : 55.
Ebenezer sonne of Walter Cooke 30 : 3 mo : 56.
Sam : son of Andrew Ford 13 : 5 : 56.
Richard, son of Richard & Rebecca Garay 18 : 11 : 56.
John son of James & Alice Ludden 13 : 11 : 56.
Enoch sonne of Ephraim & Ebbet Hunt 29 : [ ] 57.
William son of William Hollbrooke 23 : 4 : 57.
Ephraim son of John & Mary Osborne 11 : 6 : 57.
Sam° son of William & Mary Pitty 12 : 6 : 57.
Walter son of Walter Cooke 10 : 7 : 57.
Tho son of William & Eliz Chard 29 : 7 : 57.
Sarah daughter of Giles & An Leach 13 : 9 : 57.
Martha Daughter of Rich⁴ Nubery 6 : 9 : 57.
Lydia the Daughter of James Preist 12 : 12 : 57.

Angell son of Cap* Torrey borne 10 : 4 : 57.
          son to Richd : & Mary Phillips 7 : 10 : 57.

WEYMOUTH MARRIAGES.

Nathaniell Greenwood of Boston & Mary Allen daughter of Samuell Allen of Brantrey marryed by Capt Torrey 24 : 11 : 55.

William Chard & Eliz^e Daughter of Micaeth Prat John Prat sonne to Micaeth & Mary daughter of Ensigne Whitman. Thomas son to Ensigne Whitman and Abigall Daughter of Nicholas Biron marryed by Capt William Torrey 27 : 9 : 56.

Giles Leach and Anne Noaks servant to Deacon Besse of Brantry were marryed 20 : 11 : 56.

Joseph Greene & Eliz^e Daughter of Ensigne Whitman marryed p' Cap* Torrey 3 mo : 57.

John Vineing & Marye Daughter of William Read were marryed by Cap* Torrey 11 : 3 mo : 57.

Jeremy Fitch of Boston & Sarah Chobocke marryed by Cap* Torrey 6 : 8 : 57.

Joseph Joanes of Hingham & Patience Little Daughter of Thomas Little of Cambridge marryed by Capt [   ] 11 : 9 : 57.

WEYMOUTH DEATHES.

Mary Daughter of William Read 16 : 2 : 55.
Mary wife of Stephen French deceased 6 : 2 : 55.
Mrs Pins deceased 15 : 2 : 55.
Grace wife to Wm Chard deceased 23 : 11 : 56.
James Spooke deceased 1 : 5 : 55.
Esther Daughter of Hugh & Abigail Roe 11 : 5 : 55.
Sia French son of Stephen French 31 : 11 : 56.
Eliz^e Daughter of John & Jane Louell 21 : 11 : 56.

This paper Containing the Birthes Marriages & Deathes in Weymouth from 29 : 4 : 55 & 5 : [12] 57. I Receiued from ye Clarke of ye writts y^t this 1st Aprill 1658.

BRANTREY BIRTHES.

Jo^e sonne of Jno Pray & of Johanna his wife was borne 11 : 1 : 58.

Mary ye Daughter of Thomas Barrett & of Francis his wife borne 17 : 2 : 58.

Jonathan ye sonne of Fardenando Thayre & of Huldah his wife borne [   ]

Elizaboth ye Daughter of Francis Nucome & Rachell his wife borne 28 : 6 : 58.

Ruth ye Daughter of Edmond Quinsy & Johanna his wife was borne 29 : 8 : 58.

John ye sonne of Jno Basse & of Ruth his wife was borne 26 : 9 : 58.

Martha ye Daughter of Rob* Twells & of Martha his wife borne 19 : 10 : 58.

Hannah ye Daughter of Robert Parowenter & of Sarah his wife borne 17 : 11 : 58.

John sonne of Jno Belcher & of Sarah his wife was borne 11 : 1 : 58.

Susana ye Daughter of Jno Francis & of Rose his wife was borne 4 : 12 : 58.

[*To be Continued.*]

EXTRACT OF A LETTER FROM GEN. HENRY BURBECK,

*Dated New London, March 8th, 1848, addressed to Col. Samuel Swett,
of this city.*

[Notice of the death of Gen. Burbeck will be found in the Register, Vol. III., p. 101.
He died in New London, Oct. 2d, 1848, æ. 94.—Ed.]

You express a wish to know something concerning my father's history. He was from the humble walks of life, by trade a carver. If you wish to see a specimen of his work, call at the King's Chapel, (opposite the Tremont House); the Corinthian capitals of the pillars, &c., were all done under his direction. There was a vacancy happened at "Old Castle William," of the second officer, or gunner, (then so called,) about 1760, which he applied for and obtained. Being very diffident and of a retiring habit, but fond of reading and study, by close application he made himself a proficient in mathematics and teacher in gunnery. He next applied himself to artillery and its different branches, and having obtained Muller's works, he made great proficiency in artillery, in short a complete master in every branch of his apparatus; also in pyrotechnics in which he was very competent in his day. He prepared the fire-works for the celebration of the Stamp Act, which was considered a great work at that period; wheels, rockets, &c., never were better.

He received an appointment, (or rather, made an agreement,) with his friend, Dr. Warren, in 1774, who was " Chairman of the Committee of Safety," that in case hostilities commenced with Great Britain he should join the American standard; and it was further stipulated that he should receive for life the same pay and emoluments he then received, provided we obtained and established our Independence. The contract was always fulfilled by the State, and he received the pay to his death. I cannot inform you of the date of the agreement, but I presume it was in the fall of 1774. There was a third person, who I generally supposed was Col. Gridley, (but secrets could be and were kept at that day;) this is only a supposition of mine. My father was to superintend the laboratory and artillery and see that everything was prepared for service. I can say without fear of contradiction that then there was no man more capable in this country. My father came up from Castle William in his own canoe to receive his quarterly payment, which happened on the day of the battle of Lexington; he did not return. The next day the cockswain of the boat, (a sergeant,) came to the house, by order of Col. Leslie, to bring him down, but he had gone out. My father soon met with Mr. Harry Williams, who lived on Noddle's Island, (now East Boston,) who asked him if he wished to leave the town; he answered, Yes, but he knew of no way or means to accomplish it, as all communication was stopped both by land and water. Williams had free access to cross to the ships and Boston as he supplied them with milk, vegetables, &c. To make the story short, Harry Williams told him if he would disguise himself and come down to where his boat landed, about one o'clock at noon, (at which time all the mechanics, &c., were at dinner and not so likely to be observed,) and row his bow-oar over to the Island, he would run the risk and land him safe. He did so and crossed to the Island for Chelsea, from thence to Cambridge, and hired a carpenter's shop on the northeast side of Cambridge Common to prepare ammunition. My father was appointed ordnance storekeeper when the British took possession of old

"Castle William," in the fall of 1770; before that, it was a State garrison and supported as such by the State. The Lieutenant Governor was always the captain, and the pay was considered a part of his emoluments. After the peace of 1783, Old Castle William went back to the State, and my father commanded until his death, which took place in 1785.

At the close of 1775, Col. Gridley, from infirmity and age, declined accepting the command of the Massachusetts regiment of artillery. My father being the lieutenant colonel it was right and of course offered to him; but being nearly sixty years of age and nothing of a military man about him, (rather a quaker in manner and appearance,) declined and recommended Knox in the strongest terms, and the latter being known to the State was readily accepted with, and a happy choice it was to the regiment, State and country; he was an officer highly appreciated by Washington, for his talents and soldier-like conduct during the whole of the Revolutionary war. When the army marched from Cambridge, in 1776, my father thought he was bound by his contract made with the State if they required his services to remain; he resigned and remained with the State. Gen Washington was much disappointed and disapproved of his conduct.

* * *

AN EXTRACT FROM A SERMON

Delivered at Leominster, June 6, 1814, at the Funeral of the Reverend Francis Gardner, who died June 2, 1814, in the seventy-ninth year of his age and fifty-second year of his ministry. By Nathaniel Thayer, Minister of Lancaster.

[Communicated by W. Greenough White.]

The Reverend Francis Gardner was born at Stow, February 29, 1736. He was son of a minister of that town, still remembered for the soundness of his understanding; for fidelity in his sacred office; and for exemplary piety. In 1755, the deceased received a degree at the University in Cambridge, and always retained a profound respect for that ancient seminary of learning and piety. Having spent some years in study, with a view to the work of the ministry, he gave the evidence which is desirable that he was qualified for being "an able minister of the New Testament." On December 22, 1762, he was ordained as a minister in this town. It was a time* when a series of perplexing difficulties had produced much excitement, and when the wisdom of the serpent and the harmlessness of the dove were peculiarly needed in a spiritual guide. Ample testimony is preserved of the diligence, circumspection, independence and firmness which marked his conduct, and how he walked amongst the parties who had been in controversy "as a nurse cherisheth her children." He possessed a talent for colloquial intercourse which rendered him highly estimable in private life. This enabled him with ease and familiarity to impart useful instructions and counsels. He left with each person who heard him an impression of the advantage which the Christian cause derives from "the priest's lips keeping knowledge."

As an adviser in cases of controversy he was happily free from precipitancy and prejudice. He had a single eye to the investigation of truth, to the dispensing of justice, and to the promoting of "pure and undefiled religion." In forming and preaching his religious principles I have always considered him, in some respects, a model for all ministers and Christians.

---

* See Half-Century Sermon preached by Rev. Mr. Gardner, Dec. 17, 1812.

ANCIENT MARRIAGE CONTRACT.

[Copied from the original by Dr. Ebenezer Alden.]

A covenant of marriage being purposed and intended between John French and Eleanor Veazie of Braintree in New England, made and concluded this eighth day of July, Anno Domini one thousand six hundred and eighty-three, doe witness that the said John French doth preëngage unto the said Eleanor Veazie not to meddle with or take into his hand any part of her estate wherein she is invested by her former husband William Veazie or any otherwise, nor any wise weakening her right or claim to the same. The said John French doth hereby engage and covenant to pay to the said Eleanor Veazie after my decease four pounds per annum, annually, to be paid each year immediately insuing after the said John French's decease, by his lawful Administrators, Executors or Assigns, at her dwelling house, the specie of which payment shall be paid in cord word, porke, beefe, malt or corne proportionably of each at price current. And that shee the said Eleanor Veazie shall have, hold, possess and enjoy the new end of the dwelling house, in which the said French now dwelleth with the cellar appertaining, during the time of her widowhood. But the four pound annuity to bee and continue to her and her heirs or assigns during the terme of her natural life. To the true performance whereof the said John French doth hereunto set hand this eighth day of July Anno Domini one thousand six hundred eighty three. Before signing. And she shall have apples what she pleases for spending and a place for a garden plot.

    Signed and concluded on
        before us   John French.
Samuel Tompson.
Ben. Tompson.

[In connection with the above was found the following memorandum :—]

To the Hon[d] Will[m] Stoughton Esq[r] Judge of the probate of Wills & Testaments & granting Administrations &c. The Humble request of John French & Dependance French Administrat[rs] to the estate of John French late of Braintree dec[d] their father.

Humbly sheweth praying that your hon[r] will please to apoint Christopher Webb John Baxter Sen[r] Joseph Peneman Sen[r] Samuell peniman & Nathaniell Wales or any three of them to divide s[d] estate & sett out to each person concerned their part & proportion that so the estat may be preserued which otherwise will be ruined & come to nothing husing & fences decaying & running out of repayre which if euery one knew theire part would be preuented. The persons concerned in s[d] estate are John French the eldest son Dependance French, Thomas French, Samuell French, William French the orphan of William French dec[d] Two daughters, viz. Temperance Bowditch wife of Jn[o] Bowditch, Elizabeth Wheelock of Mendon ; children of Mary Lamb dec[d] are Mary Poole, Aliis Thayer by her first husband Poole & John Lamb Samuell Lamb Margarett Lamb, Mary Lamb, Grace Lamb, Hannah Lamb, which if your hon[r] shall please to grant will greatly oblige your humble seruants.

EPITAPHS IN THE OLD BURYING-GROUND IN NORTH DENNIS, MASS.

[Copied by MARCUS SEARS CROWELL.]

<table>
<tr><td>

Here lies the body
of the
Rev Josiah Dennis
Pastor of East Church
in Yarmouth,
who died Aug 31 1763
in the 69th year of his age
and 37th of his ministry.

</td><td>

Here Lyes Buried ye Body
Of Mrs Bathsheba
Dennis Wife to y^e
Revd Mr Josiah Dennis
Who Departed This Life
Nov ye 20th 1745 in y^e
45th Year Of Her Age.

</td></tr>
</table>

Here lies the body of
Mrs Phebe Dennis
Wife to the Rev^d
Mr Josiah Dennis,
Who departed this life,
Oct the 2^d 1775
in the 63rd year
of her age.

Rev Nathan Stone Pastor of the east church in Yarmouth, now Dennis departed this life April 26, 1804 in the 67th year of his age, and 40th of his ministry, Endeared to his family and friends in life and lamented by all at his death.

Of temper humble, mild and kind,
To hospitality inclined
This world's vain wealth he ne'er could prize,
But laid up treasure in the skies.

Mrs Mary Stone consort of the Rev Nathan Stone departed this life the 28th of April 1790, in the 49th year of her age, endeared to her family and friends in life and lamented by all at her death.

We Abner, Elisha and Zenas Howes with filial affection place this stone over the moral remains of Elisha Howes our parent, who was born April 2, 1754 and died May 3, 1831. For the information of his descendants we add, he was the son of Stephen Howes, a son of Amos, the son of Joseph, the son of Thomas Howes, our English Ancestor, who came to this country A. D. 1637.

EPITAPH OF REV. ELIPHALET ADAMS.

'Communicated by Mr. J. H. BADFIELD of New York.]

Here lies the remains
of
the Rev^d Mr. Eliphalet
Adams, who rested from his
Labours Oct 4th A. D. 1753
in the 77th yeare of his Age.

So just the skies
Philander's life so pain'd
His hart so pure
that, or succeeding scenes
Have palms to give
or ne'er had he been born.
Heb. 6, 10.

GOV. THOMAS DUDLEY'S LIBRARY.

" In the Study

It Steph Szegedinj (¹) comunes Loci 6ˢ & yᵉ generall Hystory of Netherlands (²) 15ˢ	000j 0j 00
It yᵉ Turkish Hystory 12ᵈ & Jurij Tremelij Truust Dible Snic 13ˢ 4ᵈ	000j 05 04
It Livius 6–8ᵗ Camdni Annale Regnante Eliza 4ˢ Diction : Lat 6ˢ : 8ᵈ	0000 17 04
It Comentaryes of yᵉ warrs in France (³) & Buchananij Scot Hystory	0000 05 06
It an abstract of Pennall Statutes, yᵉ Vision of Pierc Plowman (⁴)	0000 0j j0
It Apology of yᵉ Prince of Orange, & Cottons bloody Tenet washed	0000 02 00
It Cottons Holynes of Ch— members & a Coment on yᵉ Comandem⁴	0000 0j 06
It Rogers Sermons an exposition of yᵉ 9ᵗʰ & 10ᵗʰ of P'uerbs Byfield doct of Xᵗ	0000 02 00
It Caluine on yᵉ Comandem⁴ & another Coment on yᵉ Comendem⁴ & Baynes (⁵) Lettᵉ	0000 0j 08
It yᵉ Swedish Intellegencer & Mantuanij Ducolica & Alpha Table	0000 01 10
It Jacob (⁶) of yᵉ Church & yᵉ Regiment of health & a Reply to defeñc doña	0000 02 02
It Survey of booke of Comon Prayer, Clarkes ill newes mᵗ Decrings workes	0000 02 04
It yᵉ booke of Lawes Demonstr Causarū bellij in Germania Cordenus	0000 02 10
It Nortoni Resp ad Apoll Mercurius G'allo belg Amesij Cas : Conac	0000 02 06
It Cottons Keyes & Vyalls & de Jure Magistr in Subdites	0000 01 09
It Mathews Reply to Rutherford, Hildershams humiliation for Sinne	0000 00 10
It of Baptisme & yᵉ doctr : of Superiority & Bezd confess Xtiana	0000 01 08
It 8 French books seuerall pamphlets new bookes & smalle writings (⁷)	[no price mentioned.]

Suff. Wills & Inventories, Liber 2, page 133.   D. D.

(1) Stephen Szegedinus was the author of a treatise in favor of the Trinity, written against Servetus, and published in 1573, and another edition in 1599.

(2) There was a book entitled " A General History of the Netherlands with the Genealogy and Memorable Acts of the Earls of Holland, Zeland and West Friesland; from Thierry of Aquitaine, the first Earl successively under Philip III., King of Spain, continued unto the year 1608, in 18 books, chiefly taken from John Francis Petit; Lond. 1608, fol.   By Edward Grimstone."

(3) Commentaries, containing the whole and perfect discourse of the Civil Wars of France under the reigns of Henry II., Francis II., and Charles IX., with an addition, &c. Translated out of Latin into English by Thomas Timme, minister. London, 1573, 1574. 4to.

(4) Piers Plowman, with a Preface, (by Robt. Langland, a poet and disciple of Wickliffe, who flourished about the beginning of the 14th century,) by R. Cowley the printer of the book at London in 1550. Another edition, 4to, was printed at London in 1561, and another same date, also one in 1593;

(5) Defence of the Christian Churches and Ministry of England, against Fr. John-

on and others. Middlebury, printed by Rich. Schilders, 1595, 1599. 4to. By Henry Jacob. This man was the founder of the First Independent or Congregational Church in England. He was a native of Kent, and died in Virginia about 1624.

(6). Paul Baynes was an English Divine of considerable eminence at Cambridge, Eng., a native of London. He died 1617. Letters published 1637, &c.

(7). Rev. Ezekiel Rogers composed a Latin Epitaph on Gov. Dudley, in which he declares the Governor to have been a "prodigal in books." The small writings comprised, perhaps, some of his manuscript poems.

QUERIES.—What is known of the second book mentioned in the second item of the Inventory? What of Norton's book? and of the last four English books mentioned? It is unknown to me whether any of these identical volumes and papers are yet preserved.

LETTER OF GENERAL WASHINGTON.

Copied from the original in possession of the Minnesota Historical Society, April 21, 1858.

[Communicated by Mr. WM. H. KELLY.]

Dear Sir

A person of the Name of Patterson (an Inhabitant of Wilmington) can give you a particular Account of the Situation Strength &c. of the Enemy at that place; from whence you may judge of the practicability of attempting something by way of Surprize (if your numbers are adequate) upon the Garrison. After having made every necessary enquiry proper for an Enterprize of this kind let me know the result by an Officer, and whether the undertaking is feasible, with or without, a little aid from hence.

Your Enquiries into these matters should be made with much Circumspection, to avoid giving Alarm—And your Manœuvres should be towards the Enemy, and retrograde occasionally, to lull them into security, unless your own strength is sufficient to effect the work, in that case the rapidity of the attempt may perhaps contribute to the Success of it.

You will readily perceive that nothing herein is positive, but altogether discretionary; to be undertaken or not as Circumstances & Information shall warrant. If a Successful Blow could be aimed at Wilmington, very happy consequences would result from it, besides possessing ourselves of the wounded which now are there, for the purpose of exchanging for such Prisoners of ours as are in the Enemy's hands—but in the midst of this, it is not to be forgotten, that one great Object of your Expedition is to deprive the Enemy of Supplies from Chester County, & to interrupt their Convoys from Chester Town, Wilmington &c, whilst our Defences upon the River obliges them to have recourse to a transportation of Necessaries by land from their Shipping—Watch the communication between Philad. & the Enemy's Shipping, well, & let me hear from you frequently, especially on the Subject of the proposed Expedition—Patterson can point out others to you (Inhabitants of Wilmington) who he thinks would give every Aid in their power; but then, danger may attend the Communication of the Scheme to too many—If an Idea was thrown out that the Corps you command was the Eastern Shore Militia returning, it might possibly remove a Suspicion of the real design, if it should be found practicable to make an attempt upon the Enemy at Wilmington with your troops alone.　　I am Dear Sir

Your mo. Obed. Servant,

G. Washington.

Head Quarters at Frederick
　Wampoole's Octr 9th 1777

Brig. Genl. Potter.

BOOK NOTICES.

A History of East Boston; with Biographical Sketches of its Early Proprietors, and an Appendix. By WILLIAM H. SUMNER, A. M. Boston: 1858. 8vo. pp. 801.

Persons who have only seen the outside of General Sumner's book, have exclaimed, at least some of them, "What in the world can there be about East Boston to require so large a volume." It is true that East Boston was of but small account, comparatively speaking, until a very recent period. But let any one open this work anywhere, and read but a few lines, and he will see that he is not in a barren path; and it will be safe to say that there has not appeared a local history of late with a greater proportion of original matter.

During most of the time General Sumner has been engaged upon his work, he has labored under the disadvantage of ill-health, and has been obliged to employ several persons to aid him on different parts of it. This may account for a seeming inequality in those parts. But, in the collection of his materials, he has been very fortunate in being able to avail himself of the labors of that industrious and scrupulously accurate antiquary, Mr. William B. Trask of Dorchester. He was also assisted by the quick and ready hand of Mr. Samuel Burnham; and in carrying the work through the press he had the valuable and efficient assistance of his friend and neighbor, the Rev. Mr. A. H. Quint.

Notwithstanding the author has been suffering from increasing infirmities during the several years which he has been employed upon his history, his clear and judicious mind is traced throughout the work. As much as we have studied the history of Boston, and the sources of its materials, we confess we were surprised to find so much entirely new to us. General Sumner had preserved, with great care, all the papers relating to Noddle's Island which had fallen in his way by accident, or which his business transactions had produced. By the most careful comparison of these materials, he has been able to lay before us numerous new items of great interest and importance, and, at the same time, to correct many errors long ago committed by historical writers, and perpetuated by later ones.

Important Boston families, hitherto almost unknown, except by name, now occupy a prominence in the history of the metropolis which hitherto they had not enjoyed, but to which they were eminently entitled. There are the Mavericks, the Shrimptons, the Yeamanses, the Hyslops, Williamses, Monforts, Temples, &c., &c. The first white occupant of Noddle's Island was Mr. Samuel Maverick, son of Mr. John Maverick, an early minister of Dorchester. This gentleman was a man of much consequence in the first years of the Colony. Concerning him and his family General Sumner has published much that is new, and set his character and standing in their proper light. He was most unjustly abused and vilified in his time, and it is surprising that there are some, in our time, who pretend to investigate, and yet revive the old cry of "bad man" against him, without any of the motives which influenced his early slanderers.

A fine feature of General Sumner's book is its numerous illustrations—nearly all of which are now for the first time published. Facing the title-page is an admirable likeness of the author. We next have a plan of the island in 1801; portraits of Samuel Shrimpton, Elizabeth Shrimpton, Simeon Stoddard, David Stoddard, John Yeamans, Shute Shrimpton Yeamans, Governor Sumner, Mrs. Elizabeth Sumner, Henry Howell Williams, and General Gage. These are all from paintings in the author's possession. Then there are fine views of the Sturtevant House, Church of the Holy Cross, and Map of East Boston in 1858. There are also many facsimiles of autographs and other engravings. The work has a most excellent INDEX.

An Historical Account of American Coinage. By JOHN H. HICKCOX, Member of the Albany Institute. With Plates. Albany, N. Y.: 1858. 8vo. pp. 151.

We have here an exceedingly beautiful specimen of a book in all respects—paper, type, plates and so forth. When our readers are told that it is from the press of Mr. Munsell, they will doubtless say, "We had a right to expect this."

A work on the coinage of this country was very much wanted. It fills a place in our libraries hitherto vacant. Mr. Hickcox says, in his preface, "The design of this work is, to give an account of the legally authorised coinage of the United States of

America, during the periods of their colonial history and their existence as a united republic. Nothing as comprehensive has heretofore been attempted, nor is there any separate publication on either our colonial or federal coinage. The materials have been collated by consulting early periodical, congressional and legislative documents and other works, and through an extensive correspondence with gentlemen in other States."

Our limits will not allow of any extended analysis of Mr. Hickcox's work. But we heartily recommend it as a manual of great value in a department where it will stand almost alone. We are surprised that but an edition of two hundred is printed.

Records of the Colony of New Plymouth in New England. Printed by order of the Legislature of the Commonwealth of Massachusetts. Vols. 1—6. [Bound in four.] Boston: Printed by William White. 1855–6.

[The following notice of the Plymouth Colony Records has been handed us, but as it is not such a notice as we had intended to write for the Register, we submit it with a few words of prefatory remarks. Our correspondent, as will be seen, expresses himself a little ironically, and seems disposed to treat the subject rather too lightly; while we hold that a work which has cost the State above two hundred thousand dollars? is not a very light matter, and deserves, at least, serious consideration. In another volume we have incidentally spoken of the Massachusetts Colony Records, and intended to speak directly of the whole, when they should be finished. That time has arrived, so far as respects our present purpose.

In the first place, we have the Massachusetts Colonial Records, in six volumes, though, in the most bungling manner, called, or divided and lettered, as five. For this perplexing sort of a division we are wholly unable to account. Was it to make the number of printed volumes correspond to the original manuscript volumes of records? If so, nothing could be more absurd. By the same rule, we might have had twenty volumes where we have but five, or even but one volume, if our records had happened to be in one large volume. Some people have the remarkable faculty of failing in all practical undertakings. The form in which these records are printed is about as objectionable. They are neither quarto nor folio, but a sort of betwixt and between form—ill suited as books of reference. And then the paper! Who ever heard of printing books for use on such paper! It is no more suited to the work than bonnet board is for a child's spelling-book. Now all this work together—making six volumes read as five, putting them into such a form, printing them on such paper—shows the manager of the matter to have been utterly unworthy of any such trust. It is perfectly obvious that that vain and ambitious individual cared for nothing but a hobby by which he could make a dazzling and ostentatious display out of the money of the Commonwealth, on which he could ride into political position. But, fortunately for him as well as the people, in this expectation he signally failed, as every unscrupulous demagogue should fail.

One of the most astonishing follies of the publication of our colonial records is, that the work should have been stereotyped! This was unnecessary in every view which can be taken of the matter. A fair edition would have supplied all wants for at least fifty years. Suppose, at the end of fifty years, an edition to be wanted—calculate the interest on the cost of this job, and see what the figures are! On the score of economy it was exceeding bad policy to stereotype these records. They should never be republished as they now are; hence the stereotype plates are of no value, or only of the value of type metal. That they never ought to be used can be made clearly manifest; for, if ever the records are republished, they should be edited. Indeed, they never ought to have been issued without being edited. This elicits the remark that it is a pity any one should attempt to impose on his readers by endeavoring to make them think a work is edited when there is no editing about it; unless reading the proofs, writing a page or so of preface, explanatory of abbreviations, (which never had ought to have been used,) and displaying his name and titles in the title-page.

We have said the work should have been edited. By editing, we mean its text should have been elucidated by notes founded upon original papers, and the original papers themselves should have been brought in whenever practicable. This was the only way to make them fully useful. Why was this not done? There has been more than enough money lavished in this job to have secured proper editing. But, instead of editing the records, the manager of the job had other work on hand. It would have required a close application to the old documents in the State archives, (and there are enough of them there,) and required his undivided attention to them. Had this been done by a competent person, we should have—not a meagre legislative record—but a record which may be compared to a beautiful river, with golden sands at the bottom. We know there are thousands of old papers which ought to be used in this work. They are generally, or at least very often, of far greater value than the mere record.

We have said the manager had other work on hand than bringing to light gems of this kind. He had log-rolled himself into a fat job, and now he used nearly all his time to log-roll into another and more important one. His failure we have stated. No personal remarks are intended in this notice, but so much was necessary to be stated that the readers of the *Register* may understand what the State of Massachusetts has published and what it *might* or *ought to have* published.

An expense to the State of some *two hundred thousand* dollars for the publication of its records, we repeat, is not a trifling matter. In proper hands, that sum would give us the records as they should, and must, at some day, appear. The work of printing must be done over again before it will be what is wanted. About *twelve thousand five hundred dollars* was taken by the manager of this job for alleged services performed upon it during some four years. This was not all. He laid his hands upon some eighty copies of the work for his own use. These copies, or the most of them, probably, he gave away! What did he do this for? To whom did he give them? We shall not take upon us to say he gave them to secure the votes of some, and to stop the mouths of others who he feared would or might expose him. But we have our opinion, and it is a pretty fixed one, so far as regards this matter.

We believe, that by law, this *editor* was entitled to but one copy of the published records. Now, if he took more than that, he committed a crime for which he ought to suffer. For a much less one hundreds now lay, deprived of liberty, in this Commonwealth. So *equally* are our laws administered!

We have been particular in speaking of these records, because they are a part of the corner-stone of the history of all New England; and when unskilful hands are employed upon such a piece of masonry, it is the duty of a New England man to protest against such quackery—for a greater piece of literary quackery than this practised upon our Colonial records, we have not met with.

Perhaps it may be said that the authorities under whom this quackery was practised deserve a rebuke, also. They undoubtedly do, and they got it at the ballot-box sometime ago. Thanks to the returning common sense of the people, the demagogues have been "scourged from the temple." A new order of things exists. The work of superintending the publication of the records is in other hands. A gentleman now fills the office of superintendent on a salary of *eleven hundred dollars*—the same gentleman on whom the former manager depended for all difficult labor in the department of the records. But we candidly confess that it is our opinion that Mr. Palaifer (the present conductor) is too poorly paid for his labor, making the old proverb true, namely, that "one extreme usually follows another."

Let it not be supposed, by these remarks, that we have met with any disappointment respecting the matter of these records. We had no "axe to grind" there. We never applied for, or even wished for any finger in that pie. No political scramble ever tempted us, and we never had any ambition for office or its spoils. But we claim to know something of the duties of those who meddle with our ancient records, and if they do not perform those duties as we think they ought, they must expect our displeasure. We speak with confidence, because we know we speak the mind of every honest man in the community who takes any interest in our early history. We hope not to have further occasion to refer to this subject. If we do, we shall feel compelled to exercise less forbearance than on this occasion. Robberies committed against the State are more nefarious than when committed against single individuals—because, in the one case they generally go unpunished, while in the other they are pretty sure to get their reward.

Finally, we have no sympathy with robbers of any sort, and very little with those who hold fellowship with them. A continuation of fellowship with individuals of that class is to countenance rascality, and thereby lower the standard of public morals.]

Six large and beautifully printed volumes, edited by Nathaniel B. Shurtleff, M. D. (asking the editor's pardon for stopping, we must make a little digression.) It seems that, on the 26th of March, 1855, Ephraim M. Wright, Secretary of the Commonwealth, appointed Dr. N. B. Shurtleff to prepare for the press these Records, and superintend the printing of the same to their completion.

Let us see. Dr. Shurtleff has edited these records, not exactly by copying the originals for publication, or bestowing upon us the fruits of his historical studies in the form of illustrative notes,—as the more foolish editors of the New York or Rhode Island records have done,—but it seems by superintending the printing and by putting his name on the title-page.

Well, now we recollect that Dr. S. not only conducted the Massachusetts Records through the press, but continued his fostering care to the bound volumes. We have an indistinct idea that a committee of the legislature was somewhat confounded last spring by finding that the editor had preserved a number of copies from harm by depositing them where he thought proper. Nay, they seem to have censured this excessive zeal, and to have thought it unnecessary for him to send copies to England. Well, committees will judge harshly of the best intentions, but the books have gone and ——.

Dr. Shurtleff is a Fellow of the Society of Antiquaries of London. We forgot that we left off the enumeration of his titles. It is a capital thing to have the right man in the right place—and our records were supposed to have had the care of one of our most distinguished antiquaries. Editors are commonly supposed to be hard-worked and ill-paid members of society; but this can only mean poor devils of newspaper editors—for our editor is a member of the Massachusetts Historical Society, of the American Academy of Arts and Sciences, of the American Antiquarian Society, and—we really do not know what else, though that formidable etc. on the title-page leaves room for much conjecture. Let us see, he also has superintended the registration returns, is a member of the City Library commission,—(didn't some one suggest his name as a willing candidate for the superintendency of the library?) Why, altogether, this editing must be easy work, for he will take charge of any other little matter that offers, and still do all that is expected.

Well, merit creates envy. We believe that the learned doctor no longer devotes his energies to the public records. We have heard that a Mr. Pulsifer, who copied the old records for all these works, has become the sole editor. We have heard that the pittance paid for this important labor was thought to be too little to offer the doctor (and too much to pay for the work.)

Well—jesting apart—we think these volumes will convince the reader that it was a mistake for the secretary to choose the late editor. That it was a mistake for Dr. Shurtleff to allow the style of publication he used to be chosen for the books, as it made them cost about three times as much as was necessary, and brought a "retrenchment" legislature at once on his head. That it was a mistake for him to ignore his humble copyist. That it was a mistake for him to take the title of editor when he did not make a single note, and thus came uncomfortable comparisons and investigations; and, finally, that it will be a mistake if we waste any more shot on such small game. *s.*

Reminiscences of John Bromfield. [Not published.] Salem: Printed at the Gazette Office. 1858. 8vo. pp. 210.

Having acquired this volume by the natural and lawful course of purchase, we feel authorized to make some extracts from it for the enlightenment of our friends.

John Bromfield, we learn, April 11, 1779, the son of John and Ann (Roberts) Bromfield. This John was the son of Edward, the son of Hon. Edward Bromfield. This latter gentleman "was the third son of Henry Bromfield, Esq., the son of Arthur Bromfield, Esq., and was born at Haywood House, the seat of the family, near New Forest, in Hampshire, in England, on January 10, 1648. . . . . He came to this country in 1675." It is curious to learn from it that "he turned the pasture behind his house (situated in what is now Bromfield Street) into a very shady grove, and in the midst he built an oratory; where, even in his most flourishing circumstances and heights of business, he would retire several times a day, that he might turn his eyes from beholding vanity," &c.

The descendants of this upright merchant continued the fame of the family, and we will now see if the subject of this memoir is to be regarded as a degenerate scion.

Of the private worth of the subject of this memoir, no one who peruses it can remain unconvinced. The fondness with which his memory has been cherished by his friends proves his possession of most amiable qualities. The number and extent of his benefactions to the public, as provided in his will, and the humane purposes to which his generosity was directed, prove not only the bounty, but also the kind and sympathizing feelings which must have inspired him. *l.*

The History of Minnesota; from the Earliest French Explorations to the present time. By EDWARD DUFFIELD NEILL, Secretary of the Minnesota Historical Society. "Nec falsa dicere, nec vera reticere." Philadelphia: J. P. Lippincott & Co. 1858.

"A country which boasts but nine years of civilization . . . . of our present social condition, which counts but nine years of . . . . "

apparently a barren field for the historian. And if this were all there would be little to record, little but a repetition of the marvels of Western growth, which have grown almost monotonous, from the uniformity of the conditions on which they repose. But this is simply the crust of our history, and underneath it lie strata, reaching away down to the beds of extinct fossils, and rich with glittering mines of historic wealth. No part of America more abounds in gallant adventures than the Northwest. Its very distance from the Atlantic settlements, and the mystery that enshrouded it, has deepened into the colors of romance, the incidents of its early explorations. There was something sublime in the risks which those intrepid explorers ran in penetrating the vast wildernesses of the Continent, and in threading its vast rivers that led, they knew not whither, through strange and barbarous tribes, to their sources, thousands of miles away from their homes. Very few connected histories still remain, but hundreds of fragmentary allusions to them are buried in obsolete tomes and documents, which have followed the national origin of their writers, to the libraries of France or to the Escurial, or to the archives of Canada, or of the early American Colonies.

"Mr. Neill has performed an immense labor in collating from sources so widely apart and so inaccessible to the common reader, so much that is new and valuable. If the resources of previous writers had simplified some of his work, by amassing a large portion of his materials, still much more remained for him to do—and that he has done it well, is paying but a poor compliment to the elaborate conciseness of narration, and severe but graphic chasteness of diction, in which he has woven together the materials gathered with such labor and care."—*St. Paul Advertiser.*

Descendants of Richard Gardner, of Woburn, of the name of Gardner. Boston : printed for private circulation. 1858.

We trust that we commit no deadly breach of confidence, in attributing this neat pamphlet of 14 pages to W. W. Greenough, Esq., of this city.

We presume, though not expressly stated in the book, that this contains but a single branch of the somewhat extended Gardner Family. This branch includes Rev. John Gardner of Stow, Ex-Governor Henry J. Gardner, Rev. Francis Gardner of Leominster, and Francis Gardner of this city, well known to the younger part of our scholars as the worthy successor of Master Lovell.

It is always an encouraging sign to chronicle the breaking the first ground in the history of a family, and though we cannot desire a better genealogy of the Gardners than this one, we trust that the author may be stimulated to perform for the remaining branches, the pious task of preserving their records, already so acceptably achieved for one.

A Short Poem, containing a Descant on the Universal Plan. Also, Lines on the Happy End of the Righteous, and Prosperity and Death of the Rich Man....By John Peck. *Fourth Edition....with a Preface. Boston : 1858. 18mo. pp. 52.*

To say the least of this curious production, it treats Universalism in a humorous and interesting manner, and in the same strain of argument in which Universalists employ against their opponents. The first verse is a fair sample of the whole :

> " What if the author is no bard, but writes a dog'rel song ;
> What if the metre how and then refuse, while he doth creep along ?"

We give a few specimens of the arguments which he attributes to Universalists :

> " Huzza ! brave boys—loud be our joys, your sins shall be forgiven ;
> O ! skip and sing, our God and King will bring us all to heaven.
> Repent we may, reform and pray ; if not, all will be well ;
> For do our worst we cannot be cursed, nor can we get to Hell.
> Some think the just alone reach Heaven ; but all who curse and swear,
> And lie and steal, get drunk and kill, find sure admittance there.
> So all the filthy fornication, when God bids Lot retire,
> Went in a trice to Paradise, on rapid wings of fire."

The Prince Society—for Mutual Publication. (A Circular.)

This Society was organized on the 25th of May of the present year. It took the name of Prince from the Rev. Thomas Prince, one of the most careful and devoted historians and antiquaries that New England has ever produced. It is well known that there are numerous treatises upon our early colonial history, both printed and manuscript, of great value to the general historian, which are entirely inaccessible to the public; and it is equally well known, that *Historical Societies* fail to bring out their works, except at long intervals, and then they encumber them with matter foreign to them.

Any person becomes a member of the Society, by signifying his acceptance to the Secretary, or any member of the Council, and agreeing to purchase the works issued by the Society. By which acceptance he will be bound to take and pay for such works. Any person can withdraw from the Society at any time, having paid for all issues, inclusive of any which may be in press at the time of notice of withdrawal.

No member is called upon for a subscription until a volume is issued, and the price fixed by the Council. Should a volume be issued the present year, its cost cannot exceed three dollars. The number of volumes to be issued in any one year is to be decided by the Council also.

Officers of the Society for the present year:—S. G. Drake, *President ;* Thomas Waterman, Frederic Kidder and Jeremiah Colburn, *Vice Presidents ;* J. W. Dean, *Corresponding Secretary ;* W. H. Whitmore, *Recording Secretary ;* J. W. Parker, *Treasurer.* These constitute the Council.

Genealogical Dictionary of the First Settlers of New England. By JAMES SAVAGE.

Proposals have been issued by Little, Brown & Co., for this long expected work of Mr. Savage. In these Proposals it is stated that the work will consist of four volumes, octavo, of about 500 pages each, at ten dollars the set, in cloth binding. Two volumes will be issued in 1859, if sufficient encouragement be given.

The Publishers have issued also a specimen of the work; but we hope it is not a sample—if it is, the work will be wofully disfigured by unnecessary abbreviations—unnecessary, inasmuch as no space is to be gained by their use, or none worth taking into consideration. Therefore, we cannot think the specimen altered is to be followed in the printing.

☞ Orders for the work are taken at the office of the Register.

PETITION OF JOHN SMITH.

To the Honored Generall Court of Magistrates And Deputies Assembled at Boston, These Humbly presented.

Honoured in the Lord, Whereas your pore Petitioner, John Smith, Inhabitant in Charletowne, Having Ignorantly thorough mistake Transgressed against an order of Court, And being sentenced by the Court at Charltowne to pay a fine of five pounds, I humbly Request of this Honoured Court Remission of the same, having vnwittingly offended, for I having by hard labour earned a littell money of one of my naybours Hee would pay mee nothing but strong watters, whereoff I had no need, But desired vsefuller pay for my families occasions, But not obtaining other, I must take it, And a stranger comeing to mee bought ten shillings worth of it off mee, and he had it of mee as it cost mee, Now I humbly entreat this Honoured Court To bee pleased to pass by my Transgression, and to forgive mee my fault, my purpos and promise Beeing to bee more watchfull in tyme to come ; soo trusting in your Gentelnes I Cease to be troublesome vntoo you, humbly praying the Lord to prosper you all in your Souls and Bodies Heer, And to Bless you with all happiness in the world to Come.

[May 21 1656.]

Soe desires your Pore Petitioner,
John Smith.

Fine remitted to Ten Shillings.——Consented to by the Magistrates,—
Daniel Gookin, Joseph Hills, John Wiswall.

MARRIAGES AND DEATHS.

MARRIAGES.

BELCHER, John H., Esq., of Rhode Island, at Nantucket, 17 June, to Miss Helen M. Pinkham of Nantucket. By the Rev. C. D. Bradlee of Cambridge.

CROSLEY, Henry A., of New York, 25 July, at New York, to Ellen H. Tapley of South Danvers, Ms. By Rev. D. M. Graham.

CUSHMAN, Hon. Henry W. of Bernardston, to Miss Annie Williams, dau. of the late Thomas Ferryplace, Esq., of Salem, at Salem, June 2d, by the Rev. Mr. Clapp.

DEANE, William Roscoe, of Lacon, Ill., at Wells River, Vt., 14 July, to Miss Mary Ellen, dau. of Hon. Abel Underwood of Wells.

DEFRIES, Geo. W., Esq., at Nantucket, 17 June, to Miss Amelia Colburn, both of Nantucket. By the Rev. C. D. Bradlee of Cambridge.

RICHARDSON, Mr. Henry L., of Boston, at Longwood, 25 March, to Miss Fanny Mitchell, dau. of Henry Lincoln, Esq., of Longwood.

SEARS, Mr. Kayven Winthrop, of Boston, at Salem, 10 June, to Miss Mary C., dau. of Geo. Peabody, Esq., of Salem.

WHITMORE, Mr. Andrew E., of Worcester, at Somerville, 11 June, to Miss Ann Maria Langley of Somerville.

WHITMORE, Mr. Charles John, Boston, 6 June, to Miss Sarah Olcott Murdock, dau. of the late Geo. Blake, Jr., Esq., all of Boston.

WHITMORE, Mr. James, of Waldo, Me., at Belfast, 18 July, to Miss Mary Higgins of Belfast.

WHITMORE, Dr. Stephen, of Gardiner, Me., at Topsham, Me., 1 June, to Miss Ann Maria, dau. of Major J. Haskell of Topsham.

WHITMORE, Mr. William D., at Gardner, Grundy Co., Ill., (formerly of Boston,) March, to Miss Sarah Amelia Pomeroy, of Gardner.

DEATHS.

ABBOT, Mrs. Alice, Whitefield, N. H., 1 Aug., æ. 84.

ALDEN, Mrs. Mary, West Randolph, 3 June, æ. 51.

ATWATER, Rev. Jeremiah, New Haven, 29 July, æ. 84; a grad. of Yale, 1793; President of Middlebury College, Vermont, and Dickinson College, Pennsylvania.

BAKER, Mrs. Alice, Charlestown, 23 June, æ. 76.

BANCROFT, Mrs. Mary, East Granville, 4 July, æ. 76; wife of Mr. David W. Bancroft.

BANCROFT, Aaron, Esq., Boston, 27 May, æ. 82.

BARNARD, Mr. Samuel, Watertown, 14 June, at the house of Mr. D. A. Talbot, æ. 89; formerly of Salem.

BASSETT, Mr. Samuel, South Danvers, July, æ. 89 years, 4 months.

BARTLETT, Mrs. Hannah, at Medford, 21 June, æ. 81; widow of Mr. Zacheus Bartlett of Plymouth.

BENJAMIN, Mrs. Achsa, Montague, 21 May, æ. 86.

BLAKE, Mrs. Elizabeth, Boston, 15 June, æ. 74.

BOND, Miss Joanna, Waltham, 3 June, æ. 60.

BOWEN, Mrs. Mary R., Philadelphia, 30 July, æ. 86; widow of Daniel Bowen, Esq., formerly proprietor of the Columbian Museum, Boston. See Vol. X., p. 192.

BURNHAM, Mr. Seth, Essex, 13 May, æ. 87.

BURROUGHS, Mrs. Susan P., Gilmanton, N. H., 19 May, æ. 81.

CALEF, Mr. James, Auburn, N. H., 1 Aug., æ. 68 years, 3 months, 11 days.

CAPEN, Mr. Benjamin, Stoughton, July, æ. 85.

CHAMBERLAIN, Mrs. Sally R., Lebanon, Me., 7 June, æ. 90 yrs. 6 months.

CHAPIN, Rev. Alonzo B., D. D., of South Glastonbury, Ct., at Hartford, 9 July, æ. 60.

CHAPIN, Mrs. Susannah, Enfield, Ct., 29 June, æ. 80; and on the following day died her husband, Mr. Timothy Chapin, æ. 86.

CHAPMAN, Mrs. Margaret, Boston, 3 July, æ. 80; wid. of Mr. Jonathan Chapman.

CLAPP, Charles, Esq., Bath, Me., 4 June, æ. 84.

CLARK, Mrs. Deborah, Easthampton, 19 June, æ. 78; wid. of Mr. Luther Clark.

CLARK, Mr. Samuel, Bernardston, 29 July, æ. 80.

COLE, Mr. Edward, Middleboro', 16 July, æ. 87.

CORLISS, Mr. Ephraim, Haverhill, 5 July, æ. 75.

COVERLY, Mr. Edward, Boston, 13 June, æ. 70.

CROSWELL, Dr. Andrew, Mercer, Me., 4 June, æ. 80; a native of Plymouth, where he was b. 9 April, 1776; H. C., 1798.

CURTIS, Miss Azubah, Worcester, 20 July, æ. 83½ years.

CUTTER, Mr. John, South Malden, 8 June, æ. 75 yrs. 2 mos., formerly of Boston.

DEANE, Ezra, M. D., Cambridge, 6 Aug., æ. 76 yrs. 6 months, formerly practising physician at Biddeford, Me., and father of Mr. Charles Deane of Cambridge, of the firm of Richardson, Deane & Co. of Boston.

DEXTER, Miss Rebecca Parker, Malden, 24 May, æ. 70.

DOLE, Miss Polly, Newbury, 18 June, æ. 78 years, 5 months.

DUDLEY, Mrs. Mary, Roxbury, 24 May, æ. 70 yrs. 9 mo., wid. of the late Thomas Dudley.

EATON, Mr. Zenas, Dorchester, 14 June, æ. 76 years, 5 months.

EDWARDS, Mr. Julius, Northampton, 14 June, æ. 72.

ELLERY, Mrs. Judith, Gloucester, 5 July, æ. 77; wife of Mr. Benjamin Ellery.

FALES, Mrs. Hannah S., New Bedford, 12 June, in her 78th year, widow of James Fales.

FAIRFIELD, Mr. Stephen, Saco, Me., 12 June, æ. 86.

FISKE, Mrs. Dolly, Weston, 24 May, æ. 84 yrs. 2 mos. 10 days, wid. of the late Ebenezer Fiske.

FORBES, Jehiel, Esq., New Haven, 17 July, in his 90th year.

FOSTER, Samuel, Esq., South Scituate, 14 July, æ. 60.

FOSTER, Mr. William, Salem, 14 June, æ. 84.

FRANKLIN, Mrs. Sarah, widow, Roxbury, 26 July, æ. 87 yrs. 8 mos.; formerly of Guilford, Vt.

FREELAND, Mrs. Ann, Boston, 31 July, æ. 77 years, 7 months, 12 days.

FRISON, Capt. Samuel, Braintree, 12 June, æ. 67.

GAGE, James, Esq., M'Henry, Ill., 24 Jan., æ. 88 years; son of James and Sarah (Lamson) Gage, and was born in Amherst, N. H., 5 August, 1767. His mother (the first white child born in that town) was dau. of Samuel Lamson, born 21 Sept. 1739.

Mr. Gage was one of the first settlers in Litchfield, Herkimer Co., N. Y., to which place he went as early as 1791-2. Here he resided until 1845. His was the first death in a family of six brothers and sisters, whose united ages amount to over 508 years. Their grand-father was Thos. Gage, who lived in Pelham, N. H., and died at Fort William Henry, 8 Oct., 1756, in the French war. His paternal ancestor was John Gage, freeman, 1633, settled in Ipswich, in March of the same year.　　　　J. L. O.

GAMMONS, Mr. William, North Fairhaven, 4 Aug. æ. 81.

GARDNER, Henry, M. D., Boston, 19 June, æ. 79; his principal residence was Dorchester. He was father of Henry J. Gardner, of the firm of Gardner, Wolcott & Co. of Boston, bankers.

GARDNER, Mrs. Polly, Swanzey, 26 July, æ. 75; one of the Troy Indians.

GIFFORD, Mr. Joseph, Fairhaven, 14 June, in his 83rd year.

GOODWIN, Mrs. Ann, Lancaster, 2 Aug., æ. 93.

GRAY, Mr. Ellery, Fall River, 16 July, in his 86th year.

GREENE, Rev. Zachariah, Hempstead, L. I., N. Y., 22 June, in his 99th year. Mrs. Benj. F. Thompson, widow of the historian of Long Island, is his daughter, at whose residence he died. He was a soldier of the Revolution, having joined the army at Roxbury, Mass. in 1776. After the evacuation of Boston, he marched with the army to New York, and there heard the Declaration of Independence read for the first time in that city. Was in the battles of Throgg's Point and White Plains, and in 1777 was wounded, as was his brother who was with him, at Whitemarsh, near Philadelphia. His wound disabled him from farther service in the army, and he became a soldier of the Cross. He was a native of Hanover, N. H., where he was born, Jan. 11th, 1760, A. M. D. C., 1800.

GREENLEAF, Miss Nancy M., Newburyport, 1 June, æ. 77.

GREELY, Eliphalet, Portland, 1 Aug., 1853, æ. 71 yrs. and 3 mos. He was born in North Yarmouth, 1 May, 1784. His christian name was the same as his father's; and his mother was Sarah Prince, a descendant of the Rev. John Prince, rector of East Stratford [Shefford] in Berkshire, Eng., whose son, the elder John Prince of Hull, Mass., came to New England in 1633. Mr. Greely was descended from Elder Wm. Brewster. His grandfather, Philip Greely, was killed by the Indians at North Yarmouth, 9 Aug., 1746; and was son of Jonathan, b. 9 June, 1711, great-grandson of Andrew Greely of Haverhill, Ms., who died in Salisbury, Ms.; in 1697. Mr. Greely early commenced a seafaring life, and being well educated, and possessing a stern integrity, soon rose to the head of his profession, and eventually an eminent merchant. He acquired a large estate, filled important offices, as President of the Casco Bank, Mayor of Portland, &c., &c. He was married to a Miss Loring of North Yarmouth, but had no children.　　　　W.

GRISWOLD, Mrs. Louisa, at Buckland, 28 July, æ. 80; widow of Mr. Joseph Griswold, and mother of the Hon. Whiting Griswold of Greenfield.

GUNNISON, Mrs. Experience, Boston, 23 May, æ. 80; formerly of Newburyport.

GWIN, Mrs. Mary, Brunswick Place, Mississippi, 22 June, æ. 84; mother of the Hon. William M. Gwin, United States Senator from California. She died at the residence of her son, A. M. Gwin, Esq.

HANSON, Mrs. Rebecca, Windham, Me., 22 July, æ. 83, wid. of Timothy Hanson.

HARDING, Mrs. Ruth, at Mason, N. H., 21 July, æ. 93, widow of Capt. John Harding, of Harrington, R. I.

HAWKS, Mrs. Elizabeth, Enfield, 8 June, æ. 74.

HEALEY, Daniel, Esq., Boston, 26 May, æ. 71; for many years well known as an auctioneer.

HERSEY, Mr. Martin, Hingham, 3 June, æ. 77; formerly of Boston.

HICKS, Mr. Hezekiah, Rehoboth, 2 June, æ. 83.

HOBBS, Mrs. Abigail, Wells, Me., 21 July, æ. 90; widow of Mr. Thomas Hobbs.

HUSBAND, Mrs. Alice, Oldtown, Me., 14 June, æ. 88.

BEAMAN, Mrs. Ellen, Boston, 17 June, æ. 78.

HUMPHRIES, Mr. Edward, Roxbury, 20 July, æ. 82 years, 9 months, 20 days.

HUNTINGTON, Rev. Daniel, New London, Ct., 20 May, æ. 70; formerly pastor of the Congregational Church at North Bridgewater.

HUTCHINSON, Mrs. Sarah, Dorchester, 27 July, æ. 74.

JACKSON, Mrs. Elizabeth Willing, Philadelphia, Pa., 5 Aug., æ. 90 years, widow of Major William Jackson of the Revolution, and private Secretary to General Washington.

JOHNSON, Mrs. Charlotte, New Bedford, 5 June, æ. 70.

JOHNSON, Joseph, Hill, N. H., 4 May, æ. 83.

JORDAN, Mrs. Mary, Charlestown, 1 June, æ. 71 years, 9 months, 5 days; widow of Mr. Christopher Jordan.

JOSSELYN, Cyrus, Esq., Roxbury, 15 June, æ. 68.

KELLOGG, Mrs. Susannah, Amherst, 7 June, æ. 74; wid. of Mr. Wm. Kellogg.

KIDDER, Miss Ann, Boston, 12 July, æ. 57; sister of Frederic Kidder, Esq.

KNOWLTON, Mr. Thomas,[*] Willington, Ct., 14 April, æ. 93 yrs. 9 mos., having been born at Ashford, in the same State, 15 July, 1765. He descended from William Knowlton of West Boxford, Ma., who emigrated early in life to Connecticut, where he died a few years subsequently, leaving, besides a widow, three sons and four daughters.

His third son, Col. Thomas[*] Knowlton,[*] after serving six successive annual campaigns in the war ending in the con-

---

[*] The writer of this sketch, in a communication to the Hon. Mr. Hollister, which was published in his *History of Connecticut*, 1st edition, Vol. II. page 561, was in error in stating that Col. Knowlton was born at Ashford, Ct. Subsequent investigations make it evident that he was born at West Boxford, Ma., where he was baptized 12 Nov. 1745.

---

quest of Canada by England in 1760, in which he attained to the rank of lieutenant; and, after assisting in the reduction of Havana in 1762, became a distinguished officer in the war of the Revolution, and was finally slain in battle, at Harlem Heights, 16 Sept. 1776.

The subject of this brief notice was the second son of the latter (Col. K.), and, like the father, was a devoted patriot. Though young, he was not slow to espouse the cause of the Colonies against the mother country, and served, toward the close of that contest, for a period of about eighteen months. His post of duty was at New London, where he was at one time in command of the garrison. — a. w. of F. O.

LAMSON, Mrs. Fanny, Hamilton, 25 Feb., æ. 80; widow of Mr. Obadiah Lamson.

LARKIN, Mrs. Leah Moulton, Natick, 6 June, æ. 83; formerly of Portsmouth, N. H.

LAWRENCE, Mrs. Susan R., Boston, 7 Aug., æ. 71.

LINDSAY, Mrs. Lucy, Lynn, 19 June, æ. 68; widow of Rev. John L.

LITTLEFIELD, Mrs. Rebecca, Kennebunkport, Me., 10 June, æ. 86.

LOCKE, Mrs. Margaret, Charlestown, 25 June, æ. 70; wid. of Mr. Jonathan L.

LONGFELLOW, Mrs. Susanna, Winthrop, Me., 17 July, æ. 86; widow of David Longfellow, and dau. of the late John Adams of Newbury.

LORD, Rev. John, Portland, Me., 2 Aug., æ. 67.

LORING, Ellis Gray, Esq., Boston, 24 May, æ. 52; a well known and highly respected citizen of Boston, and a liberal and consistent supporter of the anti-slavery cause.

LYMAN, Dr. Eliphalet, Lancaster, N. H., 19 July, æ. 77.

McCOBB, Mrs. Hannah, 6 June, æ. 77; widow of Gen. Denny McCobb.

McLELLAN, Hon. John, Woodstock, Vt., 1 Aug., æ. 92.

McCULLOCH, Geo. P., Esq., Morristown, N. J., 8 June, æ. 80; a distinguished citizen of that State. He was born in Bombay, his father being a Scotch officer in the East India service.

MARSDEN, Rev. George, Manchester, Eng., 16 May, in his 86th year; of the Wesleyan church—well known in the U. S.

MARSH, Mr. Edmund, Quincy, 2 June, æ. 70.

MAXIM, Mr. Silas, Paris, Me., 21 May, æ. 92; one of the first settlers of the town.

MAYO, Mrs. Sarah, Waltham, 9 June, æ. 90; wife of Mr. Charles Mayo.

MILLIKIN, Mrs. Hannah, Newtonville, 10 June, æ. 75; widow of the late Capt. Nathaniel Doak of Boston. She was formerly of Ellsworth, Me.

MOORE, Mrs. Hannah, Montgomery, 6 June, æ. 86; widow of Mr. Guy Moore.

MORSE, Mr. Samuel F., Boston, 10 July, æ. 57.

MUNROE, Mrs. Esther, Boston, 27 July, æ. 75; widow of Capt. Reuben M. of Worcester.

NASH, Mrs. Experience, Williamsburgh, 23 May, æ. 80; widow of Mr. Elisha Nash.

NEWELL, Mrs. Priscilla, Enfield, 2 June, æ. 74.

NEWHALL, Isaac, Esq., Lynn, 6 July, æ. 75; for many years a merchant of Salem.

NOBLE, Mrs. Sophia, Chelsea, Vt., 10 July, æ. 66 yrs. 10 mos.; widow of the Rev. Calvin Noble of C.

NORTH, Dr. Erasmus D., Westfield, 17 June, æ. 51; born in New London, grad. Univ. of N. C. 1826; instructor of elocution at Yale in 1831, resigned in 1834; has since resided at Westfield. He prepared an edition of Percival's Poems for the press.

OSBORNE, Mr. William, South Danvers, 29 May, æ. 88.

OTIS, Mr. Wm. Foster of Boston, at Versailles, France, 29 May, æ. 56.

PARKER, Isaac, Esq., Boston, 27 May, æ. 70; an estimable citizen and substantial merchant. The immediate cause of his death was the effects of injuries received the Saturday previous, by being thrown from his carriage in Washington Street. He was President of the Traders' Bank, and a member of the N. E. Hist. and Gen. Society.

PARKER, Mrs. Milly L., at Dorchester, 16 June, at the residence of Thomas Groom, Esq., æ. 83 yrs. 6 mos.; widow of Major Nathan Parker.

POOR, Mrs. Martha, Boston, 4 July, æ. 75; widow of Henry Poor, formerly of Newburyport.

POPE, Rev. Augustus R., Somerville, 24 May, æ. 39; pastor of the Unitarian church in that town.

PRENTICE, Mr. Joseph, Grafton, 28 July, æ. 86.

PRESCOTT, Dea. Abraham, Concord, N. H., 1 May, æ. 68 yrs. 9 mos. and 26 days. He was the fifth generation from James Prescott, who settled in Hampton, N. H. about 1665, being the son of Abraham, son of Abraham, son of John, who was son of the first James, as above. He was born in Deerfield, N. H., 5 July, 1789; married Sally, dau. of James Freeman of Deerfield, 5 July, 1816, who died 30 Oct. 1836. He m. 2d, Mrs. Abigail C. Brackett of Rochester, N. Y. in May, 1843. Deacon Prescott was one of the original members of the First Baptist church in Deerfield, which was organized some thirty-three years since, and was one of its deacons several years previous to his removal to Concord, which was in Dec. 1833. In 1840 he was elected a deacon of the First Baptist church in Concord, which office he filled with satisfaction and uniform approval until his death.   w. p.

PRESCOTT, Miss Sarah, Boston, 18 June, of paralysis, æ. 86; dau. of the Hon. James P., Sen. of Groton, and niece of Col. Wm. P. of Bunker-Hill memory.

POTTER, Mrs. Nancy, Monson, 9 June, æ. 89; widow of Mr. Job Potter.

RICHARDSON, Mr. Charles, S. Reading, 18 July, æ. 79.

RIPLEY, Rev. Lincoln, Waterford, Me., 14 July, æ. 96 yrs. 10 mos.; formerly pastor of the Congregational church in that town.

RISING, Mr. Abraham, Southwick, 25 June, æ. 99 yrs. 5 mos.

ROCKWOOD, Rev. Elisha, D. D., Swansey, N. H., 18 June, æ. 80; formerly of Westboro', Ms.

ROGERS, Mrs. Ann, Somerville, 6 Aug., æ. 80; at the residence of her son-in-law, Charles Foster, Winter Hill.

ROGERS, Mrs. Martha, Bath, Me., 9 July, æ. 86½ years; widow of Mr. William Rogers of Topsham.

ROGERS, Nathaniel L., Esq., Salem, 31 July, æ. 73.

RUSSELL, Capt. Henry, Brooklyn, L. I., 24 May, æ. 73; eldest son of the late Hon. Benj. Russell of Boston.

SARGENT, Sarah Maria, Somerville, 9 June, æ. 7 yrs. 7 mos. 3 ds.; youngest child of Aaron and S. Maria Sargent.

SAWTELL, Mr. Eleazer, Fitchburg, 20 June, æ. 88.

SAWYER, Mr. Jacob, West Newbury, 1 Aug. æ. 74.

SCAMMON, Hon. John F., Saco, Me., 25 May, æ. 72. He had held public office for a long period—was a member of the first legislature of Maine; collector of customs in Saco from 1829 to 1841; member of Congress from 1845 to 1847; assessor in 1855.

SEARLE, Mr. Ira, Southampton, 7 June, æ. 87; the oldest man in the town.

SEAVEY, Mrs. Sally, Chichester, N. H., 15 May, æ. 85.

SIMONDS, Mr. William, Lexington, 23 July, æ. 64.

SKINNER, Col. Solomon, Bucksport, Me., 5 June, æ. 74.

SMITH, Mr. Jedediah, Springfield, 20 June, æ. 71.

SMITH, Miss Thankful, Salem, 30 May, æ. 77.

SOULE, Mrs. Lucy L., Boston, 20 July, æ. 67; wife of Mr. Richard S.

SPINNEY, Mr. Thomas, Lynn, 28 May, æ. 75.

STEVENS, Mr. Luther, of Boston, at Mount Vernon, N. H., 13 Aug., æ. 79 years, wanting 20 days. He had been gradually failing for about three months. His father, Calvin Stevens, was a soldier of the Revolution, and his grandfather, when a lad, was taken by the Indians at Rutland, the residence of the family, and carried off to Canada. Mr. Stevens was a kind-hearted and benevolent man, and his loss will be heavily felt by his numerous friends. Few persons were better known in Boston for the last forty years. He was a copper and steel plate printer, and publisher.

STODDARD, Mrs. Hannah, Pittsfield, 5 July, ae. 81; widow of Mr. Joseph S.

STOWE, Mrs. Susan, Boston, 12 June, of cancer, ae. 53.

STUBBS, William, Yarmouth, 2 Aug., ae. 85; formerly of Lee.

SWAIN, Mrs. Eunice, Nantucket, 24 May, ae. 71; wife of Mr. Alexander Swain.

SWETT, Mrs. Sarah, Marblehead, 8 July, ae. 72 yrs. 10 mos.; wid. of Mr. Samuel Swett.

TENNY, Mr. Geer, Enfield, Ct., 25 May, ae. 83.

THACHER, Mr. George M'Donogh, Boston, 2 June, ae. 49 years. He was son of Peter O. Thacher, Judge of the Municipal Court of Boston for many years, and the seventh in descent from Thomas Thacher of Duxbury, the emigrant ancestor.

THAYER, Mr. Asa, Plainfield, 11 June, ae. 79.

THOMAS, Mrs. Nancy, Gloucester, 25 June, ae. 78 yrs. 2 mos.

THORNDIKE, Hon. Albert, Beverly, 14 June, ae. 58.

TOWLE, Mrs. Hannah, Concord, N. H., 27 May, ae. 91; wife of Dea. Jonathan T.

TOWNSEND, Henry Watts, New York, 11 June, ae. 20; only son of Henry B. Townsend, formerly of Boston.

TUPPER, Mrs. Beulah, Palmer, 30 July, ae. 79; wife of Jeptha T.

TYSON, Job R., Esq. of Philadelphia, at his country residence, Woodlawn Hall, Montgomery Co., Pa., 27 June, ae. 54. He was a lawyer of good attainments, and had done much for the history of his State. He was a corresponding member of the N. E. Hist., &c. Soc.

UPHAM, Dea. Joshua, Salem, 20 July, ae. 73 yrs. 7 mos.

VINCENT, Mr. John, Salem, 23 May, ae. 90 yrs. 5 mos.

VOSE, Mr. John, Boston, 8 Aug., ae. 80.

WADSWORTH, Mrs. ——, Brookline, N. H., 7 July, ae. 88; wid. of Rev. Samuel Wadsworth, the first minister of the town.

WADE, Col. John, Woburn, 9 July, ae. 78; a worthy and prominent inhabitant of that town. He was born 3 April, 1780, and Woburn is greatly indebted to him for his untiring devotedness to its best interests. He had been a State senator, and had held other important offices. He was interred at Mount Auburn.

WARD, Rev. S. D., Agawam, 19 June, ae. 57.

WELCH, Miss Deborah, Boston, 19 July, ae. 91 yrs. 6 mos.

WELSH, Mrs. Abigail, Westfield, 26 May, ae. 82.

WHITING, Anna DeWitt, New York, 11 May, ae. 6 yrs. 8 mos. 9 days; fourth dau. of Wm. H. and Mary J. W. She was buried at Hudson, Columbia Co., N. Y.

WHITMORE, Mrs. Elizabeth B., Salem, 11 July, ae. 73; wife of Mr. Stephen W.

WILCOX, Mrs. Matilda, Westport, 19 June, ae. 84; widow of Samuel W.

WILDER, Mrs. Mary, Boston, 15 June, ae. 75; wife of Thomas W., Esq., and sister of the late Rev. Dr. Leonard Woods of Andover.

WILDER, Miss Sarah Jane, Dorchester, 28 July, ae. 16; dau. of Hon. Marshall P. Wilder.

WINSLOW, Mrs. Anne, Ware, 26 June, ae. 76; widow of Mr. Ezra Winslow.

WISWALL, Mr. Geo. R., Plymouth, 5 May, ae. 62 yrs. 6 mos.; formerly of Provincetown.

WOODMAN, Mr. James M., Havana, 6 June, of yellow fever, ae. 50; formerly of Newburyport.

WORTH, Mrs. Betsey, Edgartown, 6 June, ae. 67.

WRIGHT, Rev. Luther, Woburn, 21 June, ae. 88, having been born (at Acton) 18 April, 1770; was son of Samuel and Rachel (——) Wright; H. C. 1796. Ord. at Medway, 13 June, 1798; m. Miss Anna, dau. of Rev. Josiah Bridge of East Sudbury. Remained at Medway 17 years. In 1817, settled as pastor in Barrington, R. I., where he remained 44 years.

We insert with pleasure the following notice, as Mr. Hawley has been for some years a member of the Historic-Genealogical Society, and a subscriber to this Journal from its commencement. Mr. H. has, as we learn, made great progress with the families named except the *Strong*, which he is just commencing; an immediate response to his notice is therefore very desirable. ED.

Hawley—Strong—Sill—Selden.—Any person interested in, or who is willing to aid in the collection of a COMPLETE HISTORIO-GENEALOGICAL ACCOUNT of either of the above named families, is respectfully requested to address the subscriber, at *Buffalo, New York*, who will furnish circulars and blanks showing what is desired.
ELIAS S. HAWLEY, *Buffalo*, N. Y.

N. ENGLAND HISTORICAL AND GENEALOGICAL SOCIETY.
Resident Members.

[Continued from Vol. XII., page 192.]

1858.

William P. Apthorp, Boston.
William T. Smithett, do.
Amos Baker, do.
Charles B. Sherman, do.
Edmund T. Eastman, do.
Josiah W. Hubbard, do.
J. Gardner White, do.
George E. Henshaw, Cambridgeport.
Samuel D. Bell, Manchester, N. H.
Josiah K. Waite, Fall River.
Charles D. Cleaveland, Boston.
Edward R. Moore, do.
William G. Wise, Lowell.
John S. Tyler, Boston.
John F. Dunning, Boston.
Jonathan Peirce, do.
Henry F. Johnson, Southborough.
J. B. Mansfield, Boston.
George Noyes, do.
Lorin A. Tolman, do.
David A. Boynton, do.
William Bates, do.
Josiah A. Stearns, do.
Thomas Gaffield, do.
Frederick W. Chapenne, Ellington, Ct.
Nathan Allen, Lowell.
Aaron E. Fisher, Roxbury.
Samuel A. Green, Boston.
Edgar K. Whitaker, Needham.

Present number of Resident Members, 287.

Corresponding Members.

[Continued from Vol. XI., page 287.]

1857.

S. Austin Allibone, Philadelphia, Pa.
Joel Munsell, Albany, N. Y.
S. B. Sleek, Newark, Del.
Eli French, New York, N. Y.
Henry M. Smith, do.
S. Alofsen, Jersey City, N. J.
Reuben H. Walworth, Saratoga Spr., N. Y.
John L. Blake, Orange, N. J.
Henry D. Paine, Albany, N. Y.
John A. McAllister, Philadelphia, Pa.

1858.

William Darlington, West Chester, Pa.
A. Fuller Crane, Baltimore, Md.
Samuel Osgood, New York, N. Y.
Frederick De Peyster, do.
Griffith J. McRee, Wilmington, N. C.
Henry T. Tuckerman, New York, N. Y.
William Meade, Millwood, Va.
Thomas De Witt, New York, N. Y.
Edward Peacock, Bottesford Manor, Eng.
William J. Davis, New York, N. Y.
Francis W. Brinley, Perth Amboy, N. J.
David McKenney, Pittsburgh, Pa.
Edward Robinson, New York, N. Y.
A. W. Putnam, Nashville, Tenn.
Joseph B. Varnum, Jr., New York, N. Y.
*Elam Smalley, Troy, N. Y. [*1858
William Dudley, Madison, Wis.
John D. Bruns, Charleston, S. C.
Henry S. Clarke, Philadelphia, Pa.
Francis B. Fogg, Nashville, Tenn.
Robert Townsend, Albany, N. Y.
Luther Bradish, New York, N. Y.
John B. Morton, do.
Henry C. Bowen, do.
William H. Tuthill, Tipton, Iowa.
William H. Kelley, St. Paul, Min.
Frederick P. Tracy, San Francisco, Cal.
Francis A. Fahens, do.

Present number of Corresponding Members, 269.

Tabular Statement of Increase of Members,
From the formation of the Society to Aug. 16, 1858.

Year.	Member-ship.	No. of Members, Jan. 1. each year.	Admitted	Whole number.	Died	Ceased to be mem.	Changed membership.	Total Loss.	No. of Members Dec. 31
1844	Hon.	0	5	5	0	0	0	0	5
1845	Res.	5	37	42	0	0	0	0	42
	Hon.	0	5	5	0	0	0	0	5
	Cor.	0	40	40	0	0	0	0	40
	Total,	5	82	87	0	0	0	0	87
1846	Res.	42	21	63	0	2	0	2	61
	Hon.	5	8	13	0	0	0	0	13
	Cor.	40	27	67	1	0	0	1	66
	Total,	87	56	143	1	2	0	3	140

Year	Membership.	No. of Members, Jan. 1.	Admitted each year.	Whole number.	Died	Ceased to be members.	Changed membership	Total Loss.	No. of Members, Dec. 31.
1847	Res.	61	32	93	0	2	1	3	90
	Hon.	13	33	46	4	0	0	4	42
	Cor.	66	84	150	2	0	3	5	145
	Total,	140	149	289	6	2	4	12	277
1848	Res.	90	14	104	1	3	0	4	100
	Hon.	42	2	44	2	0	0	2	42
	Cor.	145	16	161	1	0	0	1	160
	Total,	277	32	309	4	3	0	7	302
1849	Res.	100	2	102	2	7	0	9	93
	Hon.	42	0	42	2	0	0	2	40
	Cor.	160	2	162	1	0	0	1	161
	Total,	302	4	306	5	7	0	12	294
1850	Res.	83	29	115	2	5	0	7	108
	Hon.	40	3	43	2	0	0	2	41
	Cor.	161	10	171	3	0	1	4	167
	Total,	294	35	329	7	5	1	13	316
1851	Res.	108	22	130	4	6	0	10	120
	Hon.	41	0	41	2	0	0	2	39
	Cor.	167	10	177	2	0	0	2	175
	Total,	316	32	348	8	6	0	14	334
1852	Res.	120	21	141	1	8	0	9	132
	Hon.	39	1	40	4	0	0	4	36
	Cor.	175	9	184	3	0	0	3	181
	Total,	334	31	365	8	8	0	16	349
1853	Res.	132	40	172	4	9	0	13	159
	Hon.	36	1	37	5	0	1	6	31
	Cor.	181	4	185	4	0	0	4	181
	Total,	349	45	394	13	9	1	23	371
1854	Res.	159	12	171	2	9	0	12	159
	Hon.	31	4	35	2	0	0	2	33
	Cor.	181	10	191	10	0	1	11	180
	Total,	371	26	397	15	9	1	25	372
1855	Res.	159	40	199	5	8	1	14	185
	Hon.	33	5	38	2	0	0	3	35
	Cor.	180	60	240	8	0	3	11	229
	Total,	372	105	477	16	8	4	28	449
1856	Res.	185	30	215	2	5	0	7	208
	Hon.	35	1	36	3	0	0	3	33
	Cor.	229	10	239	5	0	1	6	233
	Total,	449	41	490	10	5	1	16	474
1857	Life,	0	1	1	0	0	0	0	1
	Res.	206	43	251	2	3	1	6	245
	Hon.	33	0	33	0	0	0	0	33
	Cor.	233	16	249	3	0	0	3	246
	Total,	474	60	534	5	3	1	9	525
1858	Life,	1	3	4	0	0	0	0	4
	Res.	245	48	293	2	1	3	6	287
	Hon.	33	0	33	0	0	0	0	33
	Cor.	246	28	274	4	0	1	5	269
	Total,	525	79	604	6	1	4	11	593
1843 to 58	Total,	5	777	782	104	68	17	189	593

There have been 768 persons connected with the Society as members since its formation; of these 16 have held two different memberships, and 9 three memberships, making a total of 782 entries of members.

STEELE FAMILY GENEALOGY.

Mr. Daniel Steele Durrie, Librarian of the State Historical Society of Wisconsin, has issued proposals for a Steele Genealogy. His address is Madison, Wis.

EXTRACTS FROM PROBATE RECORDS, SALEM.

[Communicated by Edward Stanley Waters.]

Gamaliel Hodges of Salem made his will Aug. 23d, 1765, and gave property to "his wife Sarah Hodges," his dau. "Austice Hodges," his children, Joseph, Gamaliel, John, Mary the wife of Richard Derby, Hannah Ives (m. 1st, an Ives, 2d, an Archer), Ruth, the wife of Edward Allen, and his "grandson, David Ropes."

Elizabeth Beadle, Nath¹ Beadle, and John Buttolph, were Adm⁰⁰ of est. of Thomas Beadle late of Salem, Mariner, dec⁴, husband of sd Eliz⁰ June 24ᵗʰ 1700. His Inventory taken July 16ᵗʰ 1700.

Thomas Bray Sen', who "dyed y⁰ last of November, in y⁰ year 1691," left a widow Mary, a son John, (?) eldest son, a son Nathaniel, son Thomas Bray, dau. Mary, youngest daus. Hanna Bray and Hester Bray; mentions land which Edmund Clarke sold. Will dated Nov' 2ⁿᵈ 1672. The last not in the regular files, perhaps.

Letters of Adm⁰ on est. of James Gillingham, late of Salem, dec⁴, granted to Rebecca his widow, and Benj⁰ eldest son, Sept. 10ᵗʰ 1719. Sd Gillingham left also other children, Rebecca, Hannah, Martha (m. Capt. Thos. Deane), Deborah, Mary, Will⁰, Jonathan, and David.

County Records.

<table>
<tr><td>John, son of John Gilbert b. July 14 1678.
Mary, dau. of " " b. Jan 10 1682
W⁰ Reimer m. Eliz⁰ Gilbert Sep' 24, 1656.
Humphrey Gilbert died Feb 13ᵗʰ 1657.
John Gilbert m. Eliz⁰ Killam Sep' 27, 1677
Nath¹ Deane mar. Deliverance Haselton Dec 12ᵗʰ 1673</td><td>} Ipswich.</td></tr>
<tr><td>David Beadle to Rebecca Gillingham Dec 6ᵗʰ 1716.
Benj⁰ Ives to Anna Derby Jan 2ⁿᵈ 1718.
Clifford Crowninshield to Martha Hillard May 15 1721.
Samuel Gray to Eliz⁰ Ward Mch 22, 1721.
Joshua Hicks to Martha Derby Oct 22, 1719.
Edm Bishop to Eliz⁰ Cash March 9ᵗʰ 169]</td><td>} Salem.</td></tr>
</table>

Major John Gilman to Mrs Eliz⁰ Hale Dec 29, 1720.　Beverly

John Dean, Senior d Sept 29 1684.
Philemon Dean m Mary Thompson Oct 7. 1685 } Ipswich.

Nath¹, son of Daniel and Deliverance Dean, b. Mch 26 1684.　Andover.

W⁰ Waters to Eliz⁰ Latimer Aug 1ˢᵗ 1686.　Marblehead.

Payments.—*Amherst*, E. Tuckerman, L. M. Boltwood; *Baton Rouge, La.*, E. Vose; *Boston*, J. H. Wolcott, S. L. Wheeler, T. R. Marvin, N. W. Coffin, E. Everett, J. R. Kimball, G. G. Smith, M. G. Cobb, M. R. Wilds, H. A. Whitney, D. C. Colesworthy, L. Child; *Cambridge*, E. Washburn, J. Sparks; *Danvers*, S. P. Fowler; *East Middleboro'*, Z. Eddy; *Franklin, O.*, A. B. Smith, A. Woodward; *Hopkinton, N. H.*, D. H. Sanborn; *Ithaca, N. Y.*, E. Cornell; *Lynn*, A. S. Moore, E. W. Mudge; *Mineral Point, Wis.*, C. Woodman; *McConnelsville, O.*, E. Hayward; *Manchester*, T. V. Gentlee, D. Crafts; *Middletown, Ct.*, J. Johnston; *Norwich, Ct.*, J. L. Devotion, W. Williams; *Natick*, O. H. Bacon; *New York*, W. S. Hoyt, H. T. Wright; *New Bedford*, C. Taber & Co., H. Leonard, H. C. Leonard; *Portsmouth, N. H.*, J. Wendell, C. Burroughs; *Providence, R. I.*, S. T. Olney; *Philadelphia*, B. T. Tredick; *Stonington, Ct.*, R. A. Wheeler; *Suffield, Ct.*, H. A. Sykes; *Washington, D. C.*, R. Mayo, R. Dawes; *Woburn*, A. S. Wood; *W. Bridgewater*, C. Reed; *Yarmouth*, A. Otis.

There are a few persons who take the Register, but neglect to remit for it. Such are desired to take notice, that, though the amount of their subscription is to them a small matter, it is not so with him who must promptly pay the printer. If any of this class do not receive the work hereafter, they may consider it not sent to them because they are in arrears.

INDEX OF NAMES.

Index of Names.

ERRATA.

Vol. VI., page 257, the marriage of Daniel Johnson should be 1700. In note to page 256, read 1745 instead of 1744. Page 260, house on Washington Street should be No. 154, now 164. Page 261, line 11, the marriage of C. H. Johnson to Mary Johnson should be 1823, not 1822. Same place, line 17, Elizabeth married John H. Bowen, not J. H. Brown. Page 265, erase the word "inherit" in second line.

Vol. X., page 191, line 1, for Josiah read Isaiah. Page 218, line 1, for John³ read John⁴, and for Dea. Thomas read Elisha³.

Vol. XI., page 72, line 2, read Craster—on line 8. Page 273, line 11 of first, for 1656 read 1626. Page 275, line 2, for 21st read 21st. Page 277, line 11 of first of second article, for Marcus read Marcus; line 9, same article for Rebecca read Mary. Page 329 wherever Trumbull occurs, read Trumbull; line 11 of first, read Abbie Kennecott Trumbull. Page 335, 5th line of first, for Wrentham read Windsor. General Index, page iv., reference to Lee Family Bible Record should be 339.

Vol. XII., page 115, &c. The author of the article on General Warren requests us to say that he has been informed that the paragraphs in that communication relating to an interview between General Warren and Dr. Jeffries are erroneous.—Editor. Page 154, article Patterson, Mr. Chester, for aged 73 read 80.